CHIVALRY
Nigel Clayton

CiP data:
Chivalry, 1st ed. ISBN 978 0 6489 863 7 9
1. Templars - Fiction. 2. Islam - Relations - Christianity - History - Fiction. 3. Istanbul (Turkey) - History - Siege, 1453 - Fiction. 4. Turkey - History - Mehmet II, 1451-1481 - Fiction. 5. Byzantine Empire - Civilization - Fiction. I. Title.
A823.4

BISAC
FIC002000 FICTION / Action & Adventure
FIC042030 FICTION / Christian / Historical
FIC014020 FICTION / Historical / Medieval

Other titles by this author:

The Long Road to Rwanda
The Templar: and the Temple of Káros [Part 2]
The Templar: and the Cross of Christ [Part 3]
Amazon [Part 4 of The Templar series]
Underworld
Templar, Assassination, Trial & Torture
Underworld
Dreamtime - An Aboriginal Odyssey

Epic poems by this author:

Afghan - Song of the Desert
Orcinus Orca - Song of the Ocean
Hollandia Nova - Song of the Coast
Kibeho - An Epic Poem
Song of the Templar
Songs of Australia - A Poetic Trilogy [Hardcover]

BOOK ONE
The Templar: and the City of God

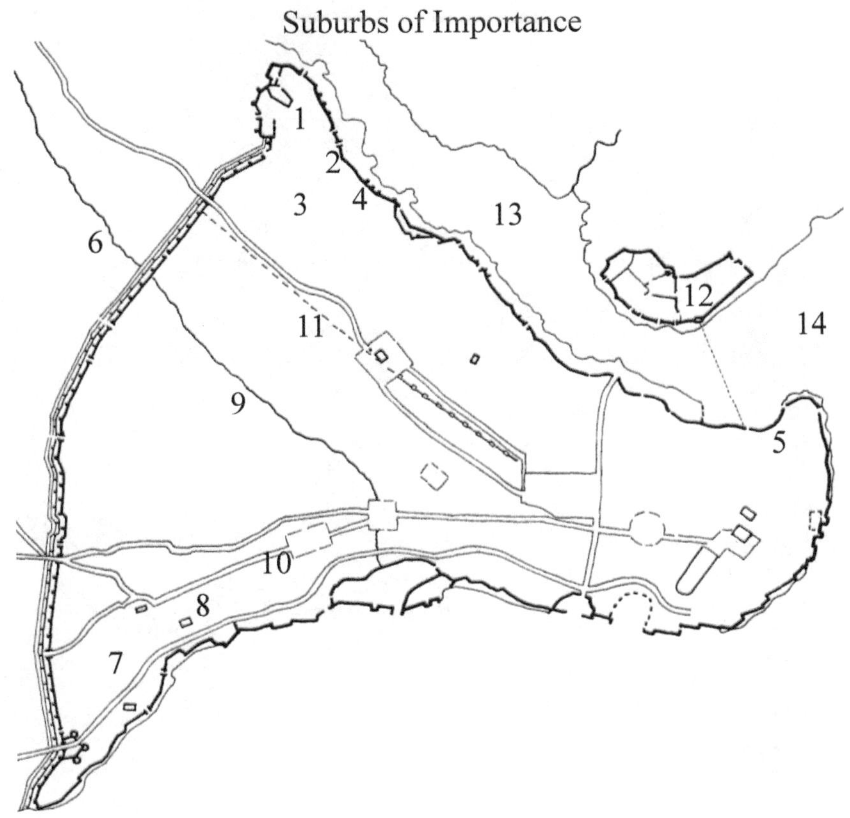

1. Blachernae
2. Phanar
3. Petra
4. Petrion
5. Acropolis
6. mesotechion
7. studion
8. psamathia
9. River Lycus
10. Triumphal Way
11. Middle (Mese) Street
12. Pera
13. Golden Horn
14. Bosphorus

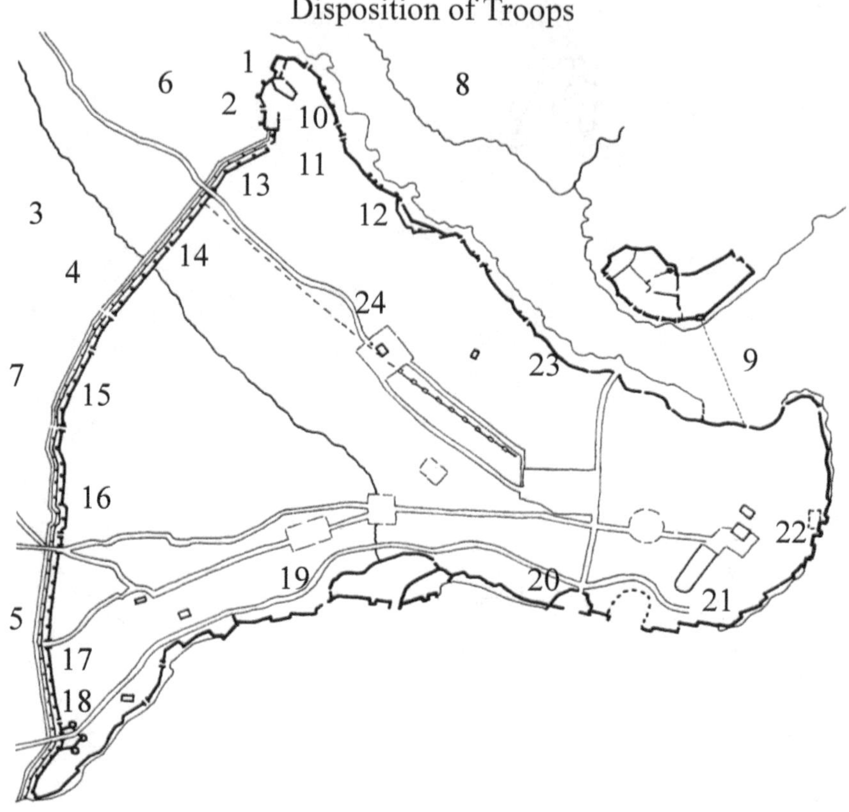

Disposition of Troops

1. Karadja Pasha
2. European Divisions
3. Sultan
4. Janissaries
5. Ishak and Anatolian Div
6. Bashi-Bazouks
7. Bashi-Bazouks
8. Zaganos Pasha
9. Alviso Diedo
10. Minotto
11. Bocchiardi
12. Lucas Notaras

13. Giustiniani
14. Emperor
15. Theophilus
16. Filippo Contarini
17. Manuel and Genoese
18. Jacobi and Demetrius
19. Greek Monks
20. Orphan and Turls
21 Pere Julia and Catalans
22. Cardinal Isidore
23. Gabrielle Trevisano
24. Nicephorus

Churches and Harbours

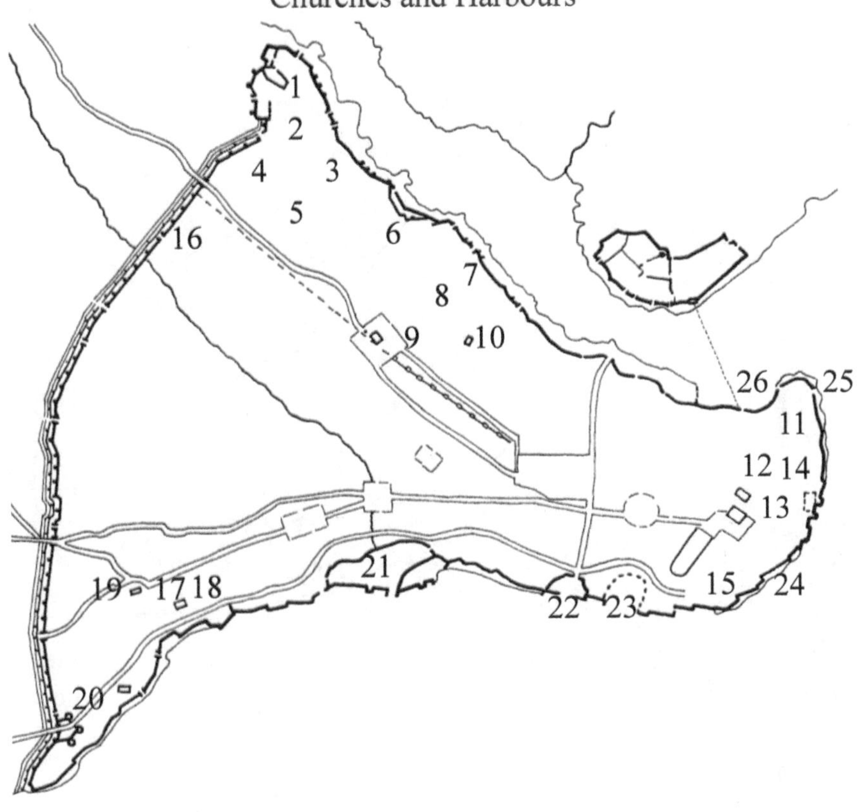

1. St Mary in Blachernae
2. Imperial Palace
3. St Mary Pammacaristos
4. St Saviour of the Chora
5. St John in Petra
6. St John in Trulo
7. St Theodosia
8. Christ Pantepoptes
9. Holy Apostles
10. Christ Pantocrator
11. St George Mangana
12. St Irene
13. Holy Wisdom/St Sophia
14. St Mary Hodegetria
15. Nea Basilica
16. St George
17. St Mary Peribleptos
18. St George of the Cypresses
19. St Andrew in Krisei
20. St John In Studion
21. Harbour of Eleutherius
22. Harbour of Contosalion
23. Harbour of Julian
24. Boucolean Harbour
25. Seraglio Point
26. Prosphorianus Harbour

Gates and Posterns

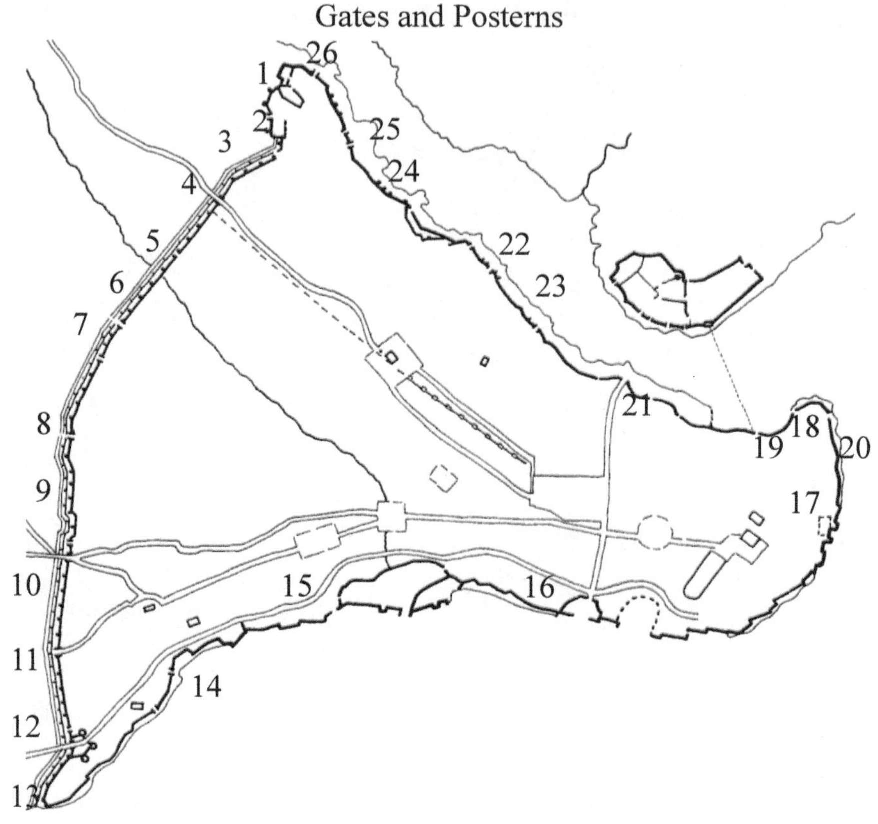

1. Blachernae
2. Caligaria
3. Kerkoportaa/Xylokerkon
4. Charisius
5. St Romanus/5th Military
6. St Romanus-Civil
7. 4th Military Gate
8. Rhegium
9. 3rd Military Gate
10. Pegea
11. 2nd Military Gate
12. Golden Gate
13. Postern
14. Psamathia
15. St Aemilianus
16. Contoscalion
17. Gate of the Lighthouse
18. Eugenius
19. Horaia
20. St Barbara
21. DrungariiPerama/Cornibus
22. Theodosia
23. Eis Pegas (Porta Putei)
24. Petrion
25. Phanar
26. Xyloporta Gate

PROLOGUE

NOTE

This Book was originally planned as an historical-fiction, to end where it ended, however, since writing it there have been three additions made to Stephen's adventure. You can follow these by reading the following, each of which is written as a fantasy-adventure more than anything else:

The Templar: and the Temple of Káros - Part Two
The Templar: and the Cross of Christ - Part Three
Amazon [where the adventure ends] - Part Four

PRELUDE TO WAR

The Sultan's men: what fools they must have been to insist that the city of Constantinople was so unbelievably fortified that not even God himself could enter without the appropriate authority: or so it seemed. What must it have been like for such thoughts to inhibit one's mind? Such a heavily burdened religious faith it must have been. They must have been strange to say the least, the sheer audacity of those to believe in such tripe and the sacrilegious stand they took in their belief's defence. But that is the way it was, for this 'was' none other than the City of God, and although God may need no authority, all others would be scrutinized, and believably or not, regardless of religious belief, even if Christian. No assault upon the city's inhabitants could secure victory, nor a surrender obtained by siege alone, for supplies could be brought in by sea. And what of the Sultan's weapons? Nothing but cheap replicas from a bygone era; catapults, battering rams, bows and arrows: nothing but a falsehood really. Musketry was well known, but keeping the powder dry enough for use with the firearms was a master's art. And further still, never before in the history of man was there any such weapon as the one that did face the north-western exposure of the city at that moment in time, 1453. Such a magnificent piece of engineering this monster cannon was, in this, the lead up to the city's final demise; not to mention a further 14 batteries pounding at the emplacements – over 130 cannon of smaller calibre all told; although the smaller of the cannon did little against the masonry of the walls when compared to the monster.

It was Urban, a Hungarian engineer who had been approached by the Sultan months before; and Urban did advise the Sultan that he would be able to construct a massive cannon capable of breaching the land wall of Constantinople. Mehmet was pleased with this to say the least, and once the beast was constructed Mehmet ordered another built, but the second was to be twice the size of the first. At 26 feet and 8 inches in length, capable of firing a ball a mile in distance, the monster did prove to be very destructive. The cannon's main downfall was the time it took to prepare each shot, whereby it was restricted to firing up to only seven times in a single day. This was one of the many cannons that were to subdue the citizens of Constantinople.

The Sultan had ordered the immediate building of triremes, biremes, fustae, galleys of all description, and parandaria; and by the hour of his need he had accumulated 6, 10, 15, 75, and 20 respectively. The Sultan's land forces were also numerous; the minimum number calculated as constituting 80,000 regulars, 20,000 Bashi-bazouks, and 12,000 Janissaries (Christians converted to Muslim, recruited as youngsters).

The last of Mehmet's land forces were in place by 5th April, 1453.

April 22nd, 1453, a Sunday of all days for the besieged of Constantinople, and on this day of worship the hearts of all within the safety of the walls faltered to some degree. Mehmet II had done the unthinkable, something even the most imaginative of minds would be unable to consider. Mehmet was ferrying many seafaring vessels by land and into the northernmost portion of the Golden Horn. Vessel upon cradle, cradle upon platform, wooden platform upon roller; pulled by oxen and men. Men and women alike, standing upon the walls and towers of Constantinople, their children, if any, standing close by their side, bore witness at some time or another of this historical event. Ten miles was the distance covered by the boats, ten miles of dry land crossed, rollers anointed with the fat of oxen and sheep to aid in the move, sails also unfurled to catch what wind they could. This was nothing but a calamity of infamous magnitude. The siege had already been running for 50 days and all of Constantinople's inhabitants were weary to the core. Breaks in the walls were being repaired relentlessly, and as if that wasn't disheartening enough even young children were used on the front line to help with repairs. Women folk, their children, the men, monks, and even nuns; none saw relief from the constant barrage of cannon, nor the demand for details of workers, to be sent off for forage of rock and soil was considered a normal day's duty. Barrels had to be filled, for the breaks upon the great tripled wall needed to be repaired, and even temporary as such efforts may be, repair the defences they must. But now this; all night and half the day they came, vessels of all description invading the Golden Horn by way of land.

Mixed emotions were sallied from the factors presented, some points for the defence, and some going against. And so sure they all were in their thinking, even if pretentiously optimistic (as even the Pope himself did believe), that a rescue would be planned for; but a rescue was not to occur, even endeavoured – until it was too late and the fall of the great city had already taken place. But long before the attitudes of the Pope and others like him were known, a courageous group of volunteers, dressed to appear like Turks, took to the waters of the Golden Horn and sailed towards the west in the hope of organizing a rescue. And courageous they all were, for to be caught would have meant certain death after torture, by uncompassionate execution, or impalement. On the 3rd May, 1453 they sailed, the chain between Constantinople and Pera removed momentarily at midnight for their rendezvous with the unknown, and hoisted high above the sails that latched onto the north wind flapped a Turkish flag, for they were in disguise. Across the open waters of the Marmora and unhindered into the Aegean Sea they sailed.

It may be surprising to assume that such a vessel, even disguised as it was, could go unchallenged amongst the waves, making its way on its voyage of urgency. Although it is true to say that in the past, over the years, the Sultan relied so greatly on Christian ships, for the ferrying of his troops and supplies from coast to coast, between Asia to Europe: how was it that such a vessel could sail by without a second glance? Due to flag and familiarity, of course; and by this we know that familiarity is not always a friend. But plans for a siege must incorporate all means, and if Constantinople was to fall, through siege along the land walls, then the waters surrounding the city must fall from Byzantine hands and into the grasp of the Turks. And so the Turks had let down their guard, even if momentarily.

And here, before we continue, a short note of distinction must be brought to bear upon the Templar knight, for gross behaviour before the year 1124 led to a church council in Troyes where the Council Fathers scrutinized the Templar's past with stabbing fingers. The defending of the widows, poor, churches and orphans were the duties laid down, not to plunder and kill. Now the Order was to put things right or be disbanded. They were to lead life by canonical law, to give their souls to their chosen way of life. Chastity must be adhered to and as a symbol of this a white habit should be worn. Without chastity eternal rest would not come. Black and brown habits could also be worn, though their symbolism slightly askew, for married men would desire to serve as others did and a requirement for squires also existed.

Measures would be entertained to ensure chastity remained binding, for Templars when they slept would do so dressed in breeches, shirt, belt and shoes, and a light should be maintained within the sleeping quarters to curve promiscuous behaviour.

Hair was to remain short, meat could be eaten but only three times in a single week, and eat in silence they must. A strict diet was adhered to, fasting days incurred, and laughter banned. More than 600 clauses would one day be seen in the Templar statutes, but in the year 1124 only 73 existed, all approved and accepted, even the cutting of cheese was mentioned – all to be adhered to, for it was a written law. Such discipline, such fortitude, such could only lead to one thing: fighters of loyalty and service to the heights never seen before in the history of man. And by the middle of the twelfth century rule 337 came into play: a Templar could only be, if descended from the son of a knight, or be the son of a knight himself, and this is almighty important, for in the year 1453 the Templars are no more. History knows that they no longer exist upon this world.

PART ONE
Wednesday 23rd May

THE APPROACH

It was that very same vessel that the onlookers of the city now saw, the brigantine, as it made its hazardous way back towards the city it had left most temporarily some three weeks before. For those that watched in anticipation it was thought to be the scouting vessel of an armada to come. It was eventually the belief of all those in the city to be a mass rescue, and had the whole of Constantinople talking as it made its approach, for good news always travelled fast: bad news faster. But on board the ship they had a different perspective, and with good reason.

"Get the rope, man, tie it fast; they come full speed from behind and with the help of Allah it seems."

"Speak those words again good sir and I shall run you through with the sword I carry at my side."

"Why…." A ship's mate, name unbeknown to John, turned to face the big man, but he immediately stumbled when he saw whom spoke the words he heard so true. There to his front was John, a knight of the Hospital, dressed in full regalia; dressed in black with a more-than-distinctive white cross displayed both front and back of the man of religion.

The shipmate would not forget the look of scorn upon John's face, not so long as he lived. "The Infidel… he gains ground. Look yonder; you can see for yourself."

"Aye man, and more come ahead the wind to our West," spoke another, pointing off into the distance, upon waters where the waves were graceful.

And from somewhere else: "To cut us off."

John drew his sword from its sheath then and tempted every man there. "Words of cowardice from a crew of courage I say. The only cutting here today will be with the sword of God, and with God by my side I shall see no devilish Turk gain neither loose nor sure footing upon the boards of this kind vessel." He put his sword away as he continued, staring blankly at those standing around. Everyone seemed transfixed that moment, looking upon John as some augmented giant pillar of knowledge, being both bold and brave. "And kind she is I say." He continued, stirring the silence abruptly. "But this however is no time for speeches; just tack the breath of God, use the sails as He has commanded, and kindly so if you please, for to tack without panic will see you delivered to the harbour of Constantinople in one piece. Do what you know best and in the safe hands of a virgin tonight you will find yourself right." There was a ferocious outburst of exclamation then, orders began flying in all directions, men jumped to the aid of others and the brigantine was steered well towards Constantinople. John looked then to the top of the mast, where a flag flew. "And someone be so kind as to hoist the emperor's own, and get that damn Turkish cloth out of sight, once and for all." And within minutes the Imperial Eagle and Lion of Saint Mark were flying high above.

John turned then to scurry below deck in order to peruse the verses of God and to convey an urgency to the captain himself, but instead came face to face with a solidly built young man of beautiful features. "To look like a squire is bad enough, but to get under-foot of my engagements is tempting fury, boy!"

"I'm sorry, but I must get to my chest."

"Chest; your chest is it? What urgency lies in the dark confines of a chest that doesn't currently loan itself to the starboard and aft of this good vessel? You do not see the calamity of our predicament, I trust?"

"Something… something…."

"Some words with you, boy. I watch you closely and don't trust eyes that pry through fish netting at groups of men as they play cards, and take a drink of the little rum that can be found below deck in the hold. I have noted well, as others have here, that you hide well below deck, wrapped in your blankets and void of responsibility; a leper you were thought to be. You were on board after me no doubt, and have seen no daylight, or so it would seem, other than what you have seen today. May I advise that if you don't help with the rigging, this moment cometh, then I will see to it that your arse does gather speed and is jettison overboard, therefore departing before me. Now get to work, boy!" John continued on past the young strapping lad as a few laughs were heard to rise from amongst the crew.

Stephen quickly looked around, forgetting the words of embarrassment spoken to him by the Hospitaller Knight. Work may be the need of the moment, he thought, but to his chest he should go. To be delivered to Constantinople was his pledge to God, but currently dressed as he was, as a pauper of sorts, was not appropriate at all. And then a voice came to his ear, soft in tone: "Don't worry lad. Help with the rigging and you'll have time enough for your chest. Come, give me a hand."

"I went to great lengths to be here today… I assure you now that I am no leper."

"Aye, I'm sure as sure can be that you speak the truth, but time is not on our side at present. To loan a hand would be accepted now more than ever," and a short smile caressed his lips, "even if it be from a squire," he smirked.

"Stephen is my name."

The sailor's eyes then turned in on themselves, clenched teeth could be seen showing between his lips. "And repeating myself, kind squire, is not to my liking, now lend a hand or go join the fish in the Marmora."

With that Stephen well understood the predicament. All aboard, except for himself, understood the situation as it must surely be. He now understood that they were all very much on a sword's edge and to get the sail right, and the rigging secured, was as important as prayer and the air they breathed. It hadn't appeared to him that there was much to be in a panic about. He then took a few steps over to join the sailor of many years, and grasped the rope above the hands of the gent now at his side and helped to pull, in unison, the great cloth that wavered above, as tight as they could.

"The wind will see us clear before time, but tack and tack again we must. And you may call me Franco."

"Indeed I shall, and I thank you for your kind words of before."

"You mean in defence of the words from John? To be kind is of minor conscience, for with the devil I play, aaarrgh… when not at work… aaaarrghh… with damn sails or sword."

THE CHEST

They pulled and pulled the ropes, hitched them securely, employed every ounce of knowledge they had, until the sail was firm, and steadily they distanced the Infidel as they tempted to catch each good wind that came their way. Only then, as they sailed at good speed towards the next tack, was some time allowed to watch the Turks to the Starboard and the walls of Constantinople to their north.

Stephen mused to continue the conversation long considered by the sailor to be dead fish in the water. "A sword, you; for a sailor you were taken."

"Sailors bear arms too," He stood erect, a little shorter than Stephen but no less the man. "How else would we be expected to defend against the boarding of pirates and…" he turned to look momentarily over his shoulder, "…these damn Turks." He exhaled heavily, catching his breath. "I'd say we catch every bit of wind that the Infidel misses, plus more some; favour is ours this day, squire. We now have a lead of some twenty good boat lengths or more." And to the City he stared. The features of the city stood out as nothing more than dark silhouettes upon a skyline marred by cloud. The citizens had taken to the walls, to watch the chase: the brigantine from the throng. They all appeared as nothing more than tiny scratches of ink on paper left by a quill. "To those souls I take off my hat. They would have endured so much to date. The vessels that give chase this moment indicate the siege is still holding strong against us, and look beyond the city wall along the shore, the billows; so much smoke – more than I've seen in a lifetime I say. My sword did see some fighting before we departed Constantinople, and I'll wager all I have that plenty more blood will encase my sword before this siege is lifted – or be complete."

Sadness then came over him, deep as can be, scratching into his face, just momentarily. "Did you leave your family behind, Franco?" asked Stephen."

His spirit then lifted slightly. "No, squire, not me; but many of the other twelve that journeyed with me have – or did." His sadness then hit again, a forlorn look fell upon his knowing face, for the city would have surely undergone a shattering transformation over the past three weeks; but unbeknown to Franco the walls still held firm. "But tell me, Stephen," he turned to face the pretty man, a smirk falling upon his face, the announcing of his true name befitting the thoughts that transgressed his mind. "What have you in this chest of yours that you hold so dear? All I know is what I overheard some days back, and that was that although small, your package was heavy. You hold little concern for us, Stephen, for we are men of much experience, but you, coming aboard dressed in near rags, and requesting passage to Constantinople…. You were told of the siege, you were warned as to the severity of the situation, but yet you still insisted."

"Aye, I almost forgot, my chest. Much excitement we have had. And I do pray that I shall have time to answer your questions when time permits."

"Time permits now, lad. Make time from what time you have, for later you may be dead." Stephen stood, straight as though in shock, leaving his leaned posture upon the side of the boat, along with his thoughts and dreams, for a future of heroism and great feats. "To my chest I must attend, for what lies within will answer many questions."

Franco grabbed the boy by the arm, a stare of friendship met. "To your chest you must go, but allow me to ask a question, squire," huh, squire… for the boy was acting… strange. "You joined this vessel not moments after John the Hospitaller, but you know not of him; and where did you think this vessel was going if not into oblivion? I know you were told of the siege in brief, but oblivion is just what I mean, and in its largest form. You will not believe it when you see the true size of the enemy fortified in front of the land-side walls of Constantinople."

"It was by chance that I took post when I did, for I was in search of any other that might wish to bring me here. But it is hard to find a ship, of any description, willing to sail this way, little beside the fact that no man, sailor or otherwise, has the courage enough to journey here. I spoke to your captain formerly before we set sail. As for John, we have only two things in common and no knowledge of one-another."

"And these two things, Stephen, what might they be?"

"We are both aboard this good boat and we share a similar heritage. But to my chest I must attend." Stephen turned to move but stood fast, turning once more to Franco before departing. "And when you see me next; you would be kind enough not to mock me, I hope."

And as he strode away to the hold Franco said: "I know you not enough to mock, but if you return dressed as a barmaid, speak to you I shall not."

Stephen disappeared down the steps, to attend to his chest, a chest of secrets, which had been delivered to him from a church in Portugal.

Stephen traversed the steps into the hold, a deep and narrow approach into the dark that required sure-footedness. A few lanterns came into view, each giving off a tiny circle of light that diminished as it extended outwards from its point-of-origin, the conjoined concentric circles fading and then finally blending in with the darkness around. Pallets were scattered willy-nilly, blankets askew the floor of the hold. A few supplies could be seen

at one end, supplies gathered from ports-of-call, places where the search for the great Armada of rescue had taken the initial crew of twelve. A barrel stood steady, upright, between several wooden chairs. It acted well as a tabletop for drinking and the playing of cards; and just beyond, his sleeping quarters and chest.

He approached his chest slowly, the voices from high above muffled by the slapping of the sea against the hull of the brigantine and the stamping of feet.

He must hurry; time was short. He bent and revealed a key on a chain from around his neck and inserted this into the lock. It turned with ease, an antiquity; its surface looked like new, as though forged yesterday. He lifted the lid of the hinged chest, a musty odour arising to his nostrils, and there in the wavering light he saw the cloth of his ancestry true. He lifted this from the confines of his possession and commenced to dress.

He first placed on his hose and undershirt, followed by a well-fit quilted vest, both sleeveless and snug around the collar. Leather greaves were then strapped on to his lower legs and over these shin guards that reached to his knees. Lower cannons of the vambrace were attached, covering each forearm, made of leather and held in place by three straps. Over this he placed the body armour of chain mail with hood, and a breastplate to protect his chest. Mail sabatons covered his feet. Over this he placed the tunic of white that he cherished so, a red cross adorning the front and rear of the vestment. A steel bassinet almost completed the outfit, though one more garment remained in the bottom of the chest. He pulled a surcoat from within, careful as could be. He stood and looked it over, similar to a habit or robe, the surcoat fit well over that in which he was now dressed, and was also adorned, front and back, with a red cross.

He stood there then, and looked upon the chest. A sword therein, and alongside this a dagger, that was all that remained. He reached in and drew the sword from its sheath, a scabbard of wood. It had a medium to long blade, a double-edged weapon, wide at the shoulder and tapered to a fine point. It was well made for both thrusting at the body and shearing off limbs, the portion closest to the crossguard was blunt, forming an edge for index finger in order that control over the point of the weapon could be maintained. A thick broadsword belt sat ready to be laced to the chain mail, covered with jewels that added lustre to the beautifully manufactured leather. The dagger simply complimented the sword, and one was rarely seen without the other.

Stephen closed then the empty chest, no intention of taking the chest with him once in harbour, for what he wore was his only burden, and once ashore and within the walls of Constantinople, his life would be in God's hands.

His metamorphosis was now complete.

A KNIGHT REVEALED

The sun had started to set as the boat drew nearer the dying city, and Stephen had only now begun his journey to manhood, taking one step at a time as he climbed his way up to the deck, the stairway to a new life.

John the Hospitaller was ironic enough to see the transformation, and as Stephen emerged from the hold below, more upon more of the handful of volunteers turned to stare open-mouthed at what they saw. Stephen was wearing what appeared to be none other than the white habit of a Templar knight… a surcoat.

None around said anything, and why should they? None had taken the time to acquaint themselves with the now transformed lad into a man, the pauper into a relic of courage, a squire into a knight; none knew of his past, ambitions, secrets, spirit, or accomplishments. But if a knight he be, then pleased they were, for the protection of the city depended upon courage, but if courage this man lacked than the white habit he should be refused.

John, as was expected from his temperament, knowledge and position, was first to speak: "What do you know of religion and honour, squire."

And with that spoken, as quick as a flash, Stephen drew his sword and held its tip firm at the point of John's chin. "My name is Stephen, and what do you know of me?" He looked around at his audience; "I shall be mocked no more." He then stabbed a look, eyeball to eyeball with the Hospitaller. "I claim rights to this good cloth under rule 337, and take not kindly to threats of swims in the ocean."

John stood steady, and the seconds fell. A small smile then commenced to grow upon the face of the Hospitaller. "A knight. Well; it's to be believed. To all those men around, I declare before you now, that only a knight would tempt to provoke my good nature by drawing a sword against my good humour. But lucky, I must say you are, that there is no one here to bring justice upon you and your scorn, for a

Templar is not welcome in many a land I've seen. If you were to be seen in such a dress 140 years past, roasted well your feet would have been. I've seen many men with scars upon their body, but nothing near what those poor devils, the Templars, would have suffered in France, all of those damn-dark years ago." With those words spoken Stephan began to lower his sword, and within an instant had it back in its sheath of wood. It was then that John turned his back on the Templar and spoke two words as he moved away to view the city as it came ever closer: "Sir squire." All those around remained open mouthed but slowly dispersed to lower some sail and to tack a little more. The wind was dying and the night had almost pulled its curtain of darkness upon the world, torches upon the walls of the city clearly seen and ships behind the chain at the Golden Horn recognized for what they were, Venetian. It wouldn't be long now and they would be safely behind the boom, amongst friends and comrades in arms.

THE ARRIVAL

Little was spoken between the men. Each and every one knew where his responsibilities lie. The brigantine had to be safely secured and the hold cleared of all its imported merchandise, along with any weapons of war that could be better put to use on the walls of the city. The vessel would not be put to sea again until the outcome of the siege had been decided, at which time they would be making good their escape – laden with refugees – or putting their good faith into repairs and cleaning whilst toasting victory; though for the moment it was unnecessary to be weighted by concern for either circumstance.

Their boat, now safely moored at the Prosphorianus harbour, had the few supplies remaining carried ashore by a workforce of women and children, some nearby sailors giving aid, the supplies quickly snapped up and purchased via the purse of the emperor: by one of his many in league. This had been common practice for many weeks, for all supplies were divided up as fairly as possible amongst all within the confines of the city walls. It was fair to say that soldiers needed to be fed in order that they performed well, but many of those within the city were Greek, and had families: for a Greek to remain on the wall, his mind needed the assurance that his family was being looked too, or he would leave the defence of the walls to others in order to search for food and supplies for his family. The defence must come first, and so the emperor acted accordingly.

Stephen stood just paces from the moorings when John strolled up and stopped beside him, two knights, one beside the other. "I know my way around this city blindfolded and tend my duties as a good knight should. My many religious friends of Rhodes believe duties lay elsewhere, but I have debts to pay and honour to uphold. I'm best to see the emperor right now, to be handed me a position suiting my skills, somewhere on the wall and close to the combat. As for yourself, if you are truly a knight and not a squire or jester, then may I suggest you familiarize yourself with your surroundings and find a post most suited to your skills," and for the first time in his short speech looked Stephen in the eye. "Whatever those skills may be."

"You believe not of my right to wear the surcoat or bear the arms affiliated with it."

"Not your right, just your good honour. I know well that the great Pope Clement V suppressed the Order of Templar; if I recall, in the year of our Lord, 1312."

"The effect of history on my being cannot hinder my actions. I have rights to this surcoat. But if we are to part on such poor terms, so be it, but to be rid of me in the direction best suited to my desire: please advise."

And with those words spoken the captain of the vessel drew alongside. "Ah, Captain; please kind sir, generate enough advice for this young man to take so that he may find his way to hell."

"John, the only advice I can give is this;" and what followed was not to the Hospitaller's liking. "Come with us Stephen. I've heard the men talking and not enough is known of you to either draw any conclusions or assume. I'm sure that the emperor would be most pleased to receive such a humble sack of bones and flesh for him to employ against the infidel's scimitar. I was ordered to return with news or an armada, but two knights are just as good." He walked off for both knights to follow in silence, and as they walked the work around them increased, the harbour a flurry of activity. It would appear that sleep and the working hour were a luxury, and not commonplace.

They made their way through a guarded entrance, the Gate of Eugenius, and commenced the climb towards the old imperial palace. The Church of St Irene was passed and commented on, Stephen's eyes bewildered by what must have once been a most beautiful building, but this was nothing compared with the Church of the Holy Wisdom (St Sophia). But now, at almost two-thirds of a mile from their mooring, the old imperial palace came to view. It was utterly catching to the eye – but it was only the beauty on the surface of Constantinople that Stephen saw, not the hunger, not the foreboding future nor anxieties, not the short fall in quest for military arms and powder. He saw what he wished to see, for he was living his dream this very moment. But then, suddenly, Stephen was shaken to reality, for explosions from the direction of the front wall broke the silence of the night. The noise was thunderous, it echoed, it was unbelievably ferocious. He stopped in his tracks but the others continued; the sheer size of the battery must be staggering, to say the least. The others seemed to ignore the cannonade, and continued; Stephen quickly realized how he had faltered… a knight as he wished to be, stopped in his tracks by the sound of cannonade. Would he freeze in battle? He then shook his mind clear and maintained focus on his task; it was the emperor they'd come to see this night. And the cannonade continued sporadically, echoing throughout the city.

The emperor's palace was itself only a short distance from the main wall, the Imperial Palace in Blachernae. He certainly did not entertain himself too often by crowning himself in what luxury could be found as soldiers manned their posts, on the contrary, the emperor was a brave soul and fought well beside his brothers in arms and religion. As the Greek kings of old used to fight side-by-side their men in battle, he too took part in the dirtiest of conflicts. The two knights continued. And it was now that Stephen started to see his surroundings as they truly were.

The Old Imperial Palace had been neglected beyond repair, as were most of the buildings and structures around the immediate area; this included the Hippodrome some distance from where they were. But the Saint Sophia Cathedral was in fact inspiring to say the least, drawing special attention and monetary upkeep in the order of maintaining its beauty. The cathedral was also one of the only buildings around to still have a roof as most roofs had been sold to help maintain the cities defence and basic needs in regards to the upkeep of the triple wall over the centuries. Only two other churches were later found to have been maintained equally well, these were the Nea Basilica and the Church of the Mother of God.

Stephen now saw the decay of the city's people, embellishments, and structures, both great and small, with more clarity, some portions worse than others. The city itself was once known for its fields and gardens of piercing beauty, and houses of a decorative bond that linked them to the mortar of the triple wall itself; churches they passed, one after the other, monasteries too. Keeps were here, shops there, and yonder the Church of the Holy Apostles. And it had struck him that the harbour too looked less like he'd anticipated when he first arrived, and he understood more, the closer they stepped towards the north. Everything was in ruin, poorly maintained, and burnt to the ground, in particular the church known as Valayerna, so badly ruined and scarred from fire that nothing would restore it. This was the legacy left by the Latins during the sacking of the city in 1204. And such a legacy it was. No restoration could be obtained from anywhere. The more the Turks took in the form of land from the Byzantine Empire, the less tax there was available to maintain their society, standards, and gardens of beauty. Outside the walls of the city, without the appropriate protection, property and ownership was lost; no province remained unaffected.

And the palace itself, Stephen would soon find, boasted no gold goblets or grand artefacts; there was nothing to be seen, most was pawned in order to pay the merchants, and for the upkeep of necessity. Food was scarce, in particular due to siege, even with the open sea and its abundance of fishes to aid the city in its time of need. Many of the people had left over the preceding years, but those that remained were clothed in what appeared to be rags, not a happy soul to be seen anywhere, all wandering around extremely weary from work on the triple wall and other defences.

Lack of money also decree that only a small number of men could be maintained to defend, most of whom could not be adequately fed, and few taxes from merchants could ever be pooled. The Genoese and Venetians in particular were both exempt from paying taxes to the city due to services provided in the past by their governments, the emperor of the time promising to waive all tax, for that was the only means of payment for services rendered.

But if this great city did lack everything that had come to pass the gaze of Stephen, it did prosper in another field, that of its art, literature and science. For the years leading to the siege, even with the obvious discomfort offered by a city tempting the very ravages of war, many scholars of all descriptions flowed through the learning centres of Constantinople. Could it be that this city under siege could spark a European Renaissance?

But regardless of its culture, background, or people, Constantinople was still the city protected by God. But protection itself didn't keep the people from straying. 50,000 souls existed in Constantinople, where three hundred years before there was one million. At one stage in its life there existed 13 suburbs, each seemingly separated by orchards and fields. Now… to be aghast at the openness in some parts would be an understatement, where some districts within the walls seemed to be nothing but an ill-manicured countryside.

Many houses and shops were evidently lived in and business conducted from such along the main road between the Old Imperial Palace and the Gate of Charisius; The Church of the Holy Apostles, although used and a rather dominating feature, was also in poor repair. The more heavily populated areas were those of Blachernae and Acropolis, and between these two points, along the wall of the Golden Horn. The Imperial Palace was closest to the wall near the Kerkoporta Postern.

Pera lay across the far side of the Golden Horn, and was strictly a Genoese colony, the Venetians however maintained and lived in a well-catered for, and rather successful quarter, down at the harbour named Prosphorianus. Here, alongside the Venetians, could also be found the Catalans, Jews, and other Western traders who maintained a living in this dying city. Further towards the Sea of Marmora one travelled the more sparse life was, little existed here. The Studion quarter was maintained well; the University, Church of Saint John, and the library within the monastery, all were cared for. Stephen was starting to take pity now, not for the people under siege, but for the wasted grounds which at one time in their past would have been so beautiful and put to good use. Such a waste it was.

THE EMPEROR

The Imperial Palace finally came to view where several men stood guard. The emperor had taken time out from the wall when he had heard, via messenger, that the brigantine dispatched on such an urgent errand, as it was some weeks before, had entered port; and so anxious he was to hear of good news. And the cannonade continued sporadically, echoing throughout the city.

So to debrief the captain entertained, with the news spearheading a devastating blow to the heart of the emperor, and as the news grew the truth that the emperor knew he must face finally slapped him in the face. The news was simple; no Venetian fleet was coming with aid, not a single vessel was to be spotted anywhere in the Aegean Sea. Such a demoralizing blow to all positive thinking that was. And slowly, in the build-up of silence, tears welled upon the emperor's eyes, and he thanked the brave sailor for all he had done and for his very performance. But suddenly the captain's lips parted, further news, something, if only minor which may cheer his lord's frame of mind, to hold back the flood of tears which had been held back for so long. A Templar and Hospitaller knight were awaiting orders. The emperor was quick to stand when he heard of the two knights that had boarded the brigantine and cordially excused the captain so bold for delivering such a precious commodity to him. The Emperor Constantine stood, Phrantzes alongside him, though Phrantzes himself departed with the captain as the knights entered.

Both knights then paid compliments and were seated opposite the emperor, separated by nothing except his rank and their stature of obvious achievement. To Be seated? All were equal to this emperor, who led by good example.

The emperor's frame of mind was quickly changed. "I am most pleased to meet the acquaintance of two fine knights of courage as you surely are, for no man would come to Constantinople unless he was seeking a hard battle against such insurmountable odds. But we will prevail."

"Ours is but to aid as you see fit, my lord." Said John.

To Stephen the emperor did then look, and with a smile maintained upon his lips did question: "A Templar. Do not my eyes deceive? With history I am widely tutored, accomplished, and familiar. For you to be in my presence is a wonder in itself."

"My history, my lord, is one that even I have trouble contemplating, let alone comprehend."

"History is for men like George Phrantzes, but alas, he has important matters to attend. Such tutors are hard to come by; a true friend he is." A silent domination was quickly prevented, for the emperor could not believe the arrival of the two knights, and further questioning followed. "But what should bring a Templar to this part of the world?"

"I seek the approval of God, and do to serve Him as best I can."

The emperor nodded approvingly. "And to you John. I understand well the politics of Rhodes. A personal vendetta perhaps?"

"My lord sees me as I am. My services as a Knight of the Hospital I do declare to provide." The emperor doubted whether such explanation was true, for within each man was hidden secrets and agendas of a personal nature.

"My wish would be to extend this conversion into the late hours of the morning, alas, pressing engagements don't allow me such a privilege."

"I believe I speak for both," commenced John, "when I say that we understand fully and request that we be delivered, at your convenience, to a station more suited to our Orders. And if I may be so bold as to say, my lord, as soon as possible, so that you may presume your endless appraisals and governing of such a siege that must be stretching you and your council to the limit."

"Your understanding and foresight is indeed a gift, and as such, I am sure, will aid you and your companion in good stead." The emperor did then stand, and the knights followed his action. "I shall be honoured to show you personally to the wall, a portion that will do well to have your attention delivered to it. Although few Christians have yet been killed in this conflict, many have been wounded, and weaknesses have been appearing along the lands-side of the defences." And as quick as they were in meeting, equally did they find themselves mounting a segment of the wall most in need of being strengthened.

And so here this day a prophecy began to unfold, part there-of was that the last emperor to be known in Constantinople would be of similar name to that of its founder – Constantine.

THE WALL

The two knights soon found themselves upon the segment of wall to the right of the Gate of Charisius. Here the wall of the quarter known as Blachernae could be seen running off towards the North where it turned to its right and fell out of sight as it dropped off towards the waters of the Golden Horn. With the cloud cover overhead, the moon at its fullest shed little light, but the torches of the Sultans camp lit the ground like the stars in the sky. John had expected such but Stephen took charge to hold back this unbelievable wonder, for to show surprise at the numbers would show doubt upon his abilities, though he was sure, and as confident, that no doubt existed.

"Marlon, Marlon; here kind man. Reinforcements of the kind even you'd take to heart." Marlon turned to see the Emperor Constantine and was quick to release himself of conversation with one of the men under his charge. The emperor turned to the knights: "John, Stephen; this man who approaches is a good soldier. He is under command of The Bocchiardi Brothers, Antonio, Paolo, and Troilo. The brothers have equipped their company through their own expense. They have all been here since well before the siege commenced to turn as ugly as it has. Ah, Marlon, please acknowledge these kind gentleman, knights both as you can see."

They shook hands feverishly. "A knight of St John, direct from Rhodes I must presume."

"I take no pride in the fact that the Aegean lords, and knights Hospitaller as a whole, refuse to attend this great battle, but for them a coalition must first be formed."

"I understand. And a Templar knight; surely my eyes are pulling tricks."

"I am Stephen."

And although John knew not of Stephens accomplishments, knew that his age would reflect his experiences, for one as young as himself would unlikely have killed a man. "He is yet to have bloodied his sword whilst in my acquaintance," said John, sidestepping his thoughts, and following a stern look from Stephen, added, "but sure to get his fill here."

"Any man, experienced or not, is welcome to fight under the Bocchiardi brothers."

"And where are your lords at present?" asked the emperor.

"I believe Troilo is at the other end of our responsibility, the other two are searching for supplies, quills I believe for the shaft of arrows."

"Good luck to them both. Supplies won't be easy to find," remarked the emperor. And the cannonade continued sporadically, echoing throughout the city. "Yes, my lord." The moon then came from hiding, showing itself in the night sky, cloud moving off towards the west.

"And I must be on my way back to see if Giovanni has killed any more of those damn infidels."

"Yes, my lord, good night to you."

"Good night to you." The knights said in unison.

"I look forward to seeing you both again, and to hear of your splendid behaviour," he said on departing with a wry smile in a courteous manner left to remind the knights that although they were appreciated they had not yet earned the respect of those in the defence.

The indication of such, picked up so very slightly by John, was a hidden indictment of unnecessary proportion, but he realized that such trait in voice was the same as he had bestowed upon Stephen. This hit John hard and he immediately felt a guilt he had not felt since he'd relinquished all of his rights in civilian life, for the one he now relished as a Hospitaller Knight. He had been charged with the care for his elderly mother, but passed the burden onto his brother. What did John know of Stephen or his past? What right did he have to silently accuse the Templar of the highest deceit?

Marlon lifted his chin from his chest, the emperor disappearing from view. "Sir John…."

"A knight I may be, but please refrain from all politeness whilst we are here; brothers of the same flesh we are."

"I could not agree more."

"So I hear that there is a Giovanni here, I must presume the emperor refers to Giovanni Giustiniani Longo of the house Doria?"

"Could there be another? They protect the most vulnerable, the Mesoteichion. It's constantly under barrage and threat of mining. He brought 700 men with him, and 300 spears recruited from Chios and Rhodes."

"Mining?" questioned Stephen, happy for the opportunity to partake in the conversation.

"Look; I've finished here, little needs to be done at present at our post. Half of the men are resting. What say we take to some refreshment, though little that will be. There's a small tavern not far from here that still has a quantity of not-so-fine ale from Athens. Please, follow me."

Both knights followed, John by Marlon's side, and Stephen just behind. "I'm glad to hear of these numbers: three hundred you say? It was fortunate for Giovanni that he could manage to recruit so many from Chios and Rhodes. I'd not heard till now that any such recruitment had taken place."

"It's of little consequence. All political views aside, any help offered is appreciated. Your views as a knight of the Hospital are obviously different than others, and for that we can only be thankful. You'll find that the only discomfort felt here amongst the allies defending the wall, is that between the Venetians and Genoese. A poor history loans for weak companionship. It's hard for us to fight in such close quarters. But the Venetians – such a cowardly lot they are. I despise them all."

"I find it hard to believe that men should wear such dirtied words when proof sits before our eyes that heroes be they all." Stephen said, who then bore the stern look of Marlon. The Hospitaller was more intrigued than not, and showed such by the way he held his eyes and forehead. Stephen continued: "If we are to presume that every man is here, by his own accord, then brave they must be." And the cannonade continued sporadically, echoing throughout the city.

"The numbers they have here are far less than could be, and I am sure I need not mention those that turned their tails and fled not so long ago. But I shall give way to your insight, no one country can be deemed unfit, from the scrutiny placed upon a handful.... Ah, here we are, a den as good as any from what I remember of an ale house."

Each ducked in through the doorway.

A DEN OF FRIENDS

The scene inside was masqueraded by darkness; but time is sometimes an ally, and as each pupil adjusted to the little light given off by candles around the walls, clarity did soon avail itself and each saw their surroundings. Shadows caressed the walls, expanding outwards, perspective to the light given, each of the dark patches forming features and shapes, a picture being drawn upon the once dark interior. Like lost infants wandering into mysterious lands they stepped cautiously, but now the security of sight aided each as the group headed towards the bar. A crackled and old voice could be barely heard to greet the three men as they approached.

"Marlon, I'd recognize you even with shit in my eye."

"Ah ha ha ha; thank you wench." And unsure as to whom it was, he wished not to display a lack of courtesy, nor appear dim-witted amongst new friends. "I see old age hasn't tamed your tongue any more than I hear the warts on your nose have changed your nature." She was most assuredly a whore. "Still at your tricks with the young."

"Indeed, Marlon," the woman's hunched form disappeared behind the bar momentarily as she bent to put several tankards away. "By serving man on my back is as good as your loaning of sword and war hammer... ha ha ha... to the defence of this city," and she began to cough and splatter as phlegm entered her windpipe.

"Take care of that, woman; and I doubt you not. It has been a few seasons since I saw you last, I'm sure," he replied as he finally recalled who she was. "Please good knights, sit yonder, the corner seat allows us good visual of all that enters. Although not a man of law or crime, I do take to watching my back at all times," said Marlon.

"A fine idea," agreed John, wondering if his hatred towards the Venetians had purchased more enemies than he could handle, and as he peered around to survey the establishment he noticed but only one other in the tavern. He and Stephen moved over to the table.

And the cannonade continued sporadically, echoing throughout the city. "My fine lady," said Marlon as he leant towards the hag. "Some fine ale for me and my guests in order to appease our thirst and a good coin shall fall down your blouse, and possibly more still, before the day gives light, if you shall be so lucky."

The promise of horizontal pleasure brought a smile to her cracked lips. "You are a cruel, brave man to be tempting me with your kind words; or are you simply teasing an old woman that has not a tooth in her head?"

"A man grows lonely in times of war, my dear." Marlon smiled and the woman let out a shrieking bout of laughter followed by another disturbing cough. "And a coin for your trouble, my fair lady." He slammed the coin down hard on the bench top. "Whatever you have hidden in your darkest of basements would do my fine companions well."

"Knights both I take, but the one in white: what manner of cloth is that? Means nothing to me."

Marlon leant against the bar and whispered into her ear: "A knight from heaven," and winked at the hag.

"Ahh, be off with you."

Marlon joined the table and became so taken with the conversation that he didn't recognize the wench approach and deliver three fine ales, in three wooden tumblers: each very-much watered down. Stephen continued with his domination of the conversation….

And his points of view were taken well by Marlon, and John said little; seemingly bemused. But who was God and what did He stand for? Against the Muslim He must have been mighty superior, but any Turk would have captured the reverse thought. So a comparison must be drawn. Stephen was a learned young man and knew well of his adversary. So a comparison it was, between Jesus, the Son of God, and the prophet Mohammed, the founder of the Muslim faith. The Muslim faith: - a vision in AD 610 that enthralled all in the country.

God had his son, Jesus, Allah his prophet, Mohammed, but what differences were apparent; what was one against the other? If one thing was known… if the Latins could create such destruction for the Christians of Constantinople, imagine what the Muslims would be capable of, and the following thoughts flashed through Stephen's mind, and this he shared with his friends at the table.

Jesus was generous enough to give favoured prayer to the poorest of the poor, but Mohammed only gave honour to those that fought wars. Jesus was a loving man and cared to ensure that a non-violent life was led by all, and Mohammed would sway all judgements with the sword.

Jesus insisted on each and every man to love and hold but one wife, Mohammed encouraged each man to take up to four wives and a league of concubines. Jesus asked those around to follow in his wisdom and to embrace the cross, to banish suffering; Mohammed gave freely of all that plundered and offered slaves where possible to serve the strong. But most impressive of all Stephen saw that Jesus looked poorly upon men who sought separation from a wife, but Mohammed allowed men to end a marriage by simply allowing his voice to be heard.

Stephen could go on. To honour life, to take it in his arms and hug it dear; to lead a life of good and greatness; this is what he was searching for. But how could he best serve this notion?

Christians had more than not, always been dealt a blow by a Muslim majority, though a Christian majority would allow Muslims to worship their God. Maybe time would change the way a Muslim looked at a Christian. Six hundred years before a hermit by name Peter of Capitolias was stoned to death for preaching openly, and five hundred years ago 50 Christians were stoned to death for the same act of worship. But no act was more greatly sickening than that of a Muslim chief in Salerno whom took a different nun each night and bled her of her virginity by his penetration, this done upon a communion table and at the altar of the church in which they served.

How should he serve his personal quest; to honour God in the only way he knew, to serve and protect with the sword and worship?

"Well, your time here will be taken to the heart young Stephen, a quest is a quest and honour shall be upheld. Deep down we all have strong reasons for being here this day. Wouldn't you agree, John?"

"This taste of ale has quenched my thirst but not my mind. To see a man fight and defend his words with action is what stands with me. I admit most secretly to you that harsh words I have spoken, but I will give Stephen his chance," and a salute with the eyebrows and slight nod gave Stephen the confidence he needed to follow in what he knew his forefathers' steps to be.

"I am most pleased by your kind words, John. I realize now from all that took place in the few days of sailing from Rhodes that you are the most looked up to figure. From what I see and hear I can only imagine that the Colossus has escaped from the Muslim melting pots and raised itself from its grave in the harbour before being turned into a great Hospitaller knight. But alas, I can't say that, as too many kind words may spoil what little friendship we currently have." The other two at the table smiled.

"Friendship between knights comes and goes with the tide," said John, and with that placed down his tumbler. "And time it is for rest, for the sun will be upon us soon enough."

"You part with our thoughts comrade," said Marlon, "and I shall see you when the sun comes up."

"I shall lay on the wall tonight, gather my bearings first thing, and arrange appropriate quarters for my prayer and solitude later. Good night to you both."

Stephen remained silent, John departed, and Marlon but smiled, "'tis great to see such a fine man put his sword to the defence of something so true," said Marlon.

"I agree wholeheartedly," concurred Stephen.

Marlon was slightly in disagreement with what he had heard

Stephen speak earlier, but wished to say nothing in front of John. The Hospitaller was of such a form that he did intimidate without even knowing it; but to Stephen, he was but a knight of Rhodes. "Your comparisons, Stephen; Jesus and Mohammed. If I am to believe that Mohammed sits at the head of the religion, then too, I am fixed in opinion that God should be the comparison when drawing up an argument between the two religions."

"Your disagreement points to the beliefs you hold, that are different than John's and mine."

"I just think that God should be the comparison. Jesus is too favourable to humankind, where God is more vengeful. God seems to me to be more like Mohammed than He is like his son, Jesus."

This provoked Stephen, but he held his temper well. "To believe in God as you state, in regards to my points in argument, would make you Jewish and not Christian."

"I am Christian, fighting a Latin cause in an Orthodox city. But to be Jewish is of no consequence. We have Jews here; we also have Turks who are fighting for our cause, they are stationed on the Marmora, fighting under Prince Orphan."

Stephen then announced: "I guess we fight then for different reasons, for although I fight in the service of God, it is with Jesus that my faith resides."

"It matters little in any case. We are all aware of the situation here, and fight for whatever cause we fight, be it for religion, credence of a personal nature, or nationality. John too is most aware of the situation here; having found himself within this great city in the past does help with the stability of reason. And yourself, Stephen; you have not been to Constantinople before?"

Stephen was unsettled. "I've journeyed far and wide, a Vagabond if you will, even if considered young. My being here is no accident, but to fall into place like a finger to a glove is but coincidental. I knew before reaching Rome of the forthcoming demise of Constantinople, and knew… felt it my duty to attend."

"A duty such as this must have a beginning. What is it you hold so sacred that makes my mind quiver with excitement?"

"If I were to tell a story, you would find it as unbelievable as… anything you could possibly believe."

"A story that holds so much promise must be heard," and with that Marlon leant forward on his forearms.

Stephen had the floor once again.

ANCESTRY

The history of the knight was largely important and aided in the coming of the Templar hundreds of years before. Such devotion was not given easily, but certainly by choice. To become a vassal of any lord, prince or noble, of any description, gave self-proclaimed high status, high reward, and self-satisfaction. Even though a knight would receive a benefice, sometimes by way of money or by land, such contracts were far from written in blood. Knights were known to shift allegiance between those that they worked and their enemy, especially if the obligations for salary were not met. A contract of vows also brought with it a limit of 40 days' worth of military service – the law quite often on the side of the knight. Family men took knights as vassals, knights took lesser knights, and the lesser knights served whole heatedly, and in more cases than not, held no possessions to speak of except a horse, a sword, and a shield.

Before the founding of the Templar Order on Christmas Day in 1119, Count Hugh of Champagne had toured the Holy Land, in 1104, and with several knights at his side returned to Europe in 1108, and after a short and unhappy spell in Europe returned again in 1114. With the Count came another of similar name, for the second time, Hugh of Payne, a Vassal and relative of the former. It was Hugh of Payne who remained behind in the Holy Land when the Count returned again to Europe. It was then that Hugh of Payne and a knight known as Godfrey – along with seven others – that the proposed Order came under scrutiny and was formed before the Patriarch at the Church of the Holy Sepulchre. These men took their vows seriously; the wholehearted protection of pilgrims journeying to the Holy Land, to provide support wherever required; but chastity and obedience were to be observed in accord with any other priest. They were housed in the Temple of Solomon and soon became known as The Knights of the Temple – The Templars.

In 1125 Hugh of Champagne, seemingly disgusted with the happenings of 1124 and the reports of gross behaviour, returned once and for all to serve with his relative of Payne, leaving behind a son he disclaimed as his, and a wife who was as unfaithful as a lap cat. But Hugh of Champagne did one thing more before returning to Jerusalem as he did; he begot a son through a woman of many talents. She gave birth to a boy; this boy a son, the son a daughter, till one day, far from the backwoods of Troyes came a lad named Stephen, who held dear to his heart a chest of many secrets.

"My God, great heavens above; you are the ancestry of the Counts loins!"

"I am."

Marlon stood and thumped the tabletop hard with a clenched fist. "My God, man. You are truly a great knight, even if your sword is not yet baptised. You may or may not have spilt blood in battle, but with the blood that flows through your veins… I am lost for words."

"Please, Marlon. Can we keep this quiet; I do not wish this

knowledge to pass your lips? I, myself, do not look favourably upon all aspects of my history, but to a duty I believe I have been sworn, and that duty I shall perform during the defence of Constantinople." Marlon stretched out his arm and slapped Stephen hard on his upper arm. "You are a good knight and.... Antonio! I am sorry good Stephen, but my commander has just passed. I must speak with him in earnest."

Stephen turned and saw a shadow move away from the doorway. "Please, go. I shall find shelter soon enough."

"Shelter here Stephen, and I shall see you before I search for John." And with that Marlon was gone, through the entrance of the tavern and on the heels of his commander. And the cannonade continued sporadically, echoing throughout the city.

PART TWO
Thursday 24th May

THE HOSPITAL

Stephen looked around the little tavern. Such a dingy place, its reputation most definitely in doubt. The hag was talking with a man, whose crossbow lay upon the bench top, hand clenched tight around a chunk of stale bread, laughing loudly at something she had obviously said. He must have entered unnoticed at some stage during Stephen's conversation with Marlon.

The hag turned her head momentarily to look in his direction, something the man at the bar had indicated, for his eyes had spoken more than his voice could clarify. She turned quickly again to the man and grabbed at his hands with a laugh, a chuckle of excitement. Stephen wondered if she rather desired him at that instant, a knight to keep her warm in bed. He must have seemed like quite a prize, a knight so clean, so lavishly dressed; enough to coax any fair maiden to mischief. The man then grumbled and tore with great exaggeration at his bread from which the hag received great excitement and leaned forward, whispering something dirty in his ear no doubt, for the man with the crossbow kissed her hungrily.

Stephen shook himself to reality, a near fantasy with a witch of a woman only just avoided. He was not here for the pleasures of female flesh, but for the doings of war. And battle he would see soon enough.

He stood then and stepped quickly towards the entrance, all seemingly quiet and serene, the night air refreshing.

And then the cannonade did disturb the peace once more as it echoed sporadically throughout the city.

So much for the quiet. And then something else, something…. He strained his ears. Something then caught his attention. He could hear faint mumbling, screams from not so far away. It seemed strange that such noise should come from where the wall was not. It came from a man; not child or female.

He strode down the cobbled road, passing homes and businesses as he walked, many abandoned and naked, the screams growing louder and murmurs of suffering coming to ear. The noise of terror was coming from towards the inner part of the city, away from the action of the defence.

He continued down the cobbled way, reflections of moonlight catching upon the wet of the stone underfoot. A little rain must have fallen whilst he sat in conversation, a little rain to dampen the efforts of the enemy at the foss, though he was sure their enthusiasm would not diminish, for greed was a buttress of support at times of discomfort.

He arrived then at a junction and looked to his left. The scream came again, quite muffled, as though a pillow were being held to his mouth, or of a man resting, delusional.

A door then opened about 50 feet away, and there he saw her for the first time in his life. A most extraordinarily beautiful young creature with tousled hair held tight under a bonnet-like headdress or veil, an unbelievable picture of beauty, enough to entice any man. Several frays of hair appeared from beneath the bonnet of white. But what was such a damsel doing up at this time of night?

She wore an apron of white that was covered in blood, and held in hand a bucket and sponge. She placed the bucket down and squeezed tight the sponge, the red-saturated water falling to the roadside and gutter. She then deposited the bucket's contents across the cobbles with one swift movement before turning and re-entering through the door. Stephen looked around, as though entering into mischief, as though he was about to undertake something quite unlawful. He could see quite clearly now the cross atop the church of St Saviour of the Chora not so far off to his right rear. He had travelled only a short distance.

He stepped delicately at first towards the entrance and increased his pace; there was something about this woman that intrigued him, though he knew and understood one thing only, and that was of her beauty; anything other he did not know. His brain had frozen, all common sense relinquished of its responsibility, for his body was acting on its own, without the spoken authority or choice. He was being swayed by a whim. He now moved forward in a rush before coming to a stop just in front of the door. Then, for the first time a thought came to mind. Was it a question of attraction, or perhaps it was his subconscious simply intrigued by a woman caked in blood and up at such an hour.

He entered through the partly open door and the single room dwelling came to view. It appeared from the front to be a bread kitchen of sorts, though the interior had been ransacked clean of everything except bench tops and a few litters that leant against one wall, all of which were smeared in blood.

The screaming had stopped but murmurs erupted soft and loud from the lips of men as though they were all suffering a child's nightmare. He'd walked into a makeshift hospital. Seven patients on top of benches, two nurses, and… "John."

The Hospitaller looked around, his habit removed and sleeveless quilted vest revealed; his forearms and hands were caked in the blood of a man with his leg half sawn off. "Give a hand, Stephen, and quickly, before this man wakes," Stephen jumped at the words. "Take over from Maria, grab both legs at the ankle and hold tight; thank you, Maria." Maria gave a shy smile before turning to her other patients and chores. She was dressed in a similar manner as to her female accomplice, though quite a bit younger in appearance.

Stephen took position and held on tight as John continued to saw through the bone, just above the knee. "He shall probably die by first light, but my prayers will aid where my skills as a surgeon fall short." Stephen noticed almost immediately that the man was bound tight to the bench, three leather straps wrapping him securely around his chest, waste and upper thigh.

"A master surgeon?"

"I am a knight of the hospital, my sword is my cross, and my other skills are wide and fair."

Stephen continued with the pressure as John cut, looking around and seeing again the beauty of the girl he'd spotted outside, the one that had drawn him most powerfully into the den of misery. And as his mind drifted into a dream, so his concentration lapsed.

"Hold tight, squire!" John yelled forgetful of Stephen's rank, "This man kicks like a mule, even when unconscious." Both nurses gave a quick stare, understanding fully the importance of the task.

Stephen was embarrassed by the name-calling but quick to steady himself to the responsibility and within minutes the leg came away from the bleeding stump. "Clover," the nurse of Stephen's dreams was already at John's side, handing bandages over. "You interpret well, lass. Is this all we have?"

"Yes, John."

John dumped the leg into a bucket and Maria rushed the remains away. John soaked up some blood, ensured the tourniquet was secure, and stepped back, allowing Clover to clean the stump and prepare for the sealing of the wound. She smiled as she motioned to squeeze past the young knight, in the confines of the room, Stephen smiling clumsily in return. "That will not be enough cloth, Clover."

"We have no substitute and none in store. We shall have to beg for more tomorrow."

"We will need it soon. I think some white sheet is to be had aboard the brigantine in which I arrived."

"I shall see to it at first light," Clover said. "Meanwhile would you be so kind as to take up my dress from behind, tear the tail into strips."

"But you are filthy, Clover… you have no clothes… shouldn't you try and change; find something…."

"The wounded must come first," Clover interrupted.

"I…" began Stephen. "My surcoat; it's relatively clean, just put on this evening. I am sure it will do the trick. Please feel free to tear it into quarters… my tunic too."

"I won't argue, Stephen, the cloth is needed." John came closer to assist Clover. "Quick, take your surcoat off before you change your mind."

"That is unlikely, for this man's need is greater than mine." Whilst his beautiful Clover smiled he took his belt and sword off, slipped the surcoat up and over his head, then removed his tunic, and stood there in nothing more than his mail over a quilted vest. Stephen then did as he was commanded, and handed the surcoat and tunic over, to hold the much-needed Templar uniform out for Clover to recycle. Stephen then took to helping hold the open wound closed by applying pressure to the recently exposed stump of bone and flesh, hands pressing in ever-firmly and just below the highest tourniquet as John sealed, as best he could, the open amputation.

His Clover? Did his thoughts make an error? Did his thoughts mimic his desires and feelings of heart? The answer came to him in a flash; yes she was, she was a dream come true, she was his destiny – but what of God and his promise to serve.

And the wound was soon sealed sufficiently for the final applications of cloth to be applied.

As Clover started to apply the surcoat strips, John spoke to Stephen, finished with the task at hand. "I am sorry. I know the surcoat is worth more than gold to you. It must have been hard to come by such a handsome fabric," but Stephen wasn't listening. "But all is now in order here, and I shall retire to sleep upon the wall and return later." John took to a basin to wash his hands before taking hold of his own tunic. He slipped it over his head, and turned then to a corner of the room where his sword had been placed. The next thing Stephen knew was that he was holding tight the wounded man's leg and Clover was tearing the last of his surcoat into strips and applying this to the packaged wound as tight as could possibly be permitted. She bandaged firmly and slowly, the seeping of red from wound appeared to have stopped, or at least slowed dramatically, the pressure of the tourniquet released a little more each time another layer of bandage was applied.

So much was passing through his young mind. It was so hard to concentrate on what he was doing; the task at hand being almost complete was also far from thought. And then, before he knew it, the job had been accomplished. Clover stood back from the basin of red water which now looked like wine, and gave a slight exhale of assurance, that the wound was sealed for healing to commence. Stephen smiled and looked into her eyes and Clovers met with his. She had been unaware until that time that Stephen was staring strong, and he was oblivious of any idea that he was doing so. She saw him then, as he really was, a young man, not much older than she. How helpful he had been. A knight to the rescue. Someone to be relied upon when the need was strong.

Stephen was half in trance, and without thinking asked what must have been a stupid question, for the only persons to come to Constantinople voluntarily were mercenary, paid for with the emperor's purse, and other soldiers of fortune. "Are you from here?"

"I am from near Petrion. I have lived here my entire life; from what I understand."

"Greek?" It was a statement rather than a question.

"I am Hellene, not Roman or Greek; I am a mould of the two; I also believe strongly in my religion."

Stephen's eyebrows slumped slightly, he was in mid conversation but his daydreaming had taken control. She was orthodox, not Latin, that he understood. He'd been daydreaming of this beautiful creature, of things that may come, but more-than-likely not. "Yes, Hellene, of course," he stumbled.

Although this was colloquially fashioned a Greek city by many, it still retained a Roman heritage. By terms of affection the people within were known as Hellenes, or the Hellas. This by no means was favoured, nor openly accepted by all that regarded this a Roman city, and belonging to that of the Roman Empire. Hellene was initially intended to indicate a person of Christian background, being Byzantine or vowed to the Christian cause – though unmistakably not Latin. But a pagan, or Greek, was not notably known as Hellas for some time. But mainly due to the now current size of the Empire, Hellenes they all were and the community as such accepted this knowingly.

"And you, Stephen; I know you are from afar; your accent; a mix of English and French it would seem."

"You must have travelled far yourself, to interpret and note such differences within a voice."

"I was brought up in Constantinople and have ventured no further afield than where the Turks are camped at this moment. You forget we are a city of many religions and cultures, many colonies combined by influence more than anything else. I do admit that most are committed to their belief in Jesus and the scriptures, but Jews live here too, and Muslims. I have spoken with so many and heard stories from all around Europe, the Mediterranean, and the Middle East. I would know an accent if it was yelled to me from under a ringing church bell and as far as the wall is from us at this moment."

"I believe you would," and he smiled.

The smile intrigued Clover and she looked around consciously at the sleeping wounded, and single nurse that remained. "Stephen, if you don't mind, may we take this conversation outside; I don't wish to disturb the patients any more than is necessary?" for she was falling for this man without even knowing it.

"Of course not." And with that they stepped outside.

CLOVER

On stepping into the night, Stephen was half brought back to reality, for the first thing he heard was the cannonade as it continued relentlessly.

"The man with the leg that John took off so magnificently; how did he come off his injuries?"

"He was tortured by the emperor." It came so matter-of-fact that Clover seemed unconcerned over the details of such an event, though knew enough of the predicament as it stood.

Stephen stopped where he stood, "Tortured, but why in God's name!"

"He's a miner." And Clover told the story as best that she knew: the talk of the city flourished through every tavern and home, every business and church, from every public place, monument and park. Every group about, regardless of age, religion, or nationality, was talking of the siege and what must be done to aid the emperor in defying the infidels. Keeping the Turks out was the order of every day; keep them out at all expense. But what can't be seen is hard to parry.

It was in the Christian's favour that the Sultan had inexperienced men in regards to mining, though some professionals were gathered from the silver mines of Nova Brodo in Serbia; an indication in itself as to the lengths the Sultan had gone to secure the services of such knowledgeable men. To these individuals, groups and teams, a task was set, to breach the walls of Constantinople via mining. Zaganos Pasha was handed the responsibility and surveyed his troops before giving orders for a mine to be started near the Charisius gate. This task, although initially favourable due to the soft soil, was soon considered too hard due to the required digging under the foss. The attempt was soon laid to rest and a new mine commenced, the target wall this time around being the Blachernae, near the Caligaria gate.

"It was a week before your arrival Stephen, that the knowledge of this mine was passed to all in the defence of this great city, for the noise of the digging could be heard underfoot. Such a strange noise could only mean one thing: mining was taking place." Clover continued with her story: A report had reached Lucas Notaras, and he in particular took to advising, in person, Johannes Grant.

Grant was a learned man with much experience, and took to counter mining immediately. He succeeded in burying the Turk miners by entering in behind the head of the mine and burning the supports thereof. "I can imagine the scene within must have been horrific. Imagine all of those men, being suffocated and buried alive. Some said that you could hear the muffled screams coming from beneath, that those caught and buried alive took quite some time to die."

"Such an event must surely be accepted with thanks. I can imagine the carnage if they were to be successful and the gates of the wall were opened from within. Constantinople would have been swamped by the enemy."

"I agree fully, Stephen, but death, by such means, must have been a dreadful thing. But Mehmet did not give in there." Further mining was ordered by the Sultan where upon Notaras gathered his Greek troops, and under the advice of Grant commenced an evil upon their counterparts by further choking the enemy to death by fire and smoke, and drowning them via the cisterns normally directed to the foss.

"It was then that a great fortune fell before the defenders of Constantinople, for a mine was encountered on the day of your arrival, very early in the morning. Several miners were captured, including an officer of some established rank. He was quickly taken to torture as were all of the others, and information was revealed to Grant and Notaras, but the emperor had spared the captured by roasting only one foot over an open coal fire. I heard that the officer put up a great resistance, but eventually, and before many inquisitors, all of the mines under current construction were revealed." Clover took a breath before continuing. "It will not be a surprise to learn if from this day forth the Sultan gives up all thought of penetrating Constantinople via tunnel."

"So the man is the enemy." Stephen said bitterly.

"He is." Clover sounded somewhat angry at Stephen's tone. "Unless I misunderstand you, it would appear that you are trying to tell me that he should have been executed after revealing such accurate information to the emperor?"

"But he is the enemy. He has brought fear and misery to this great city."

"It is a great city to me, Stephen, for this is my home, but what do you know other than what you have been taught by word of mouth?"

"No more than you would know of this Europe which you have never seen."

"That is indeed most cruel of you, to insult my word and intelligence. I think you have much to learn about me, for I have welcomed you Stephen, and you attack me with unkind words. I am sorry that you feel the way you do and turn to sarcasm as a means of defence from a poor woman as myself."

Stephen fell to one knee, "Please forgive me, Clover, for I meant you no ill will." Clover commenced a giggle and then a controlled laughter, "Oh, Stephen. So young and foolish... like me. Get up, before someone sees you. Besides, the cobbled way is cold and wet, and I do not want my escort to fall ill with fever. It is not many-a-maiden can appreciate a knight as her…." She blushed; "as her confidant."

Stephen stood with a smile, the metal of his mail chinking. "Your confidant I am much pleased to be, and you are right, Clover, and I am terribly wrong. My brother was a teacher you know…."

"You have a brother?"

"Did have. He died terribly. I know little of the story except that it was one of mistaken identity."

"That's terrible; I'm sorry. I suppose you miss him very much. Were you very close as children?" asked Clover, genuinely interested in Stephen's past and family.

"He was from my Mother's second marriage. She was extremely lucky to be offered such an agreement considering that she had me at the time, and at 12 years in youth. But I guess the man of average wealth that she married was also fortunate. Although his son was 15 and under heavy loads of study and assessment for future employment as a teacher of science, and almost out of home, was disfigured in ways which would turn the eyes of any possible bride."

"Poor man."

"Much is poor in this world of ours, Clover. Wherever I look I see nothing but sadness and hurt."

"Is that why you decided to become a Templar, to help those in need?"

"You don't just become a Templar, you are born to it."

"The birth was a well delivered one." Stephen had a look of surprise upon his face; such compliments. "Oh yes, I know a little of history. Constantinople is not as much of a city now, as compared to what it was many years ago, but it is still the largest learning centre for all things both old and new. Many things have changed since the Turk did become encamped on our doorstep. Our gates are barred as opposed to open, and our freedom… to all – except for access to knowledge – has been denied."

"The siege will be thwarted, you will see."

"I hope you are right, Stephen, but we all know what we are up against. I think too that we shall all live long lives, but it will come at a terrible cost. We are but less than 50,000 women, children, old men and monks, in a city defended by less than 7,000 soldiers and mercenaries. The enemy…."

"Yes, the enemy are well above 100,000 but poorly armed and not suited well for battle."

"Their position is well defended, they out-number us, and the cannon are numerous."

"Their disposition is well suited for siege, but when the time comes for an assault to be conducted, then you shall see the wonders of the men on the wall take shape." Both were then silent for several seconds as each contemplated life as it was. The present was so overcast with doubt and delusion.

"So tell, Stephen, the reason why a white habit should reach out a call to you so strong that you would wish to throw life to the wind and live a life of one so restricted by religious law?" "When I became a Templar it was for a few reasons. Due to my Mother's impure second marriage I am to suppose I will also be the end of the line."

"You may marry, Stephen."

"I am not so sure. The Templar habit is one of many rules… as you may well know."

"Why did you become a Templar?"

"I owed it to my ancestry to serve. Sometimes I think it is for adventure, maybe a journey into the unknown."

"So adventurous. Maybe with age you can settle down. You don't have to serve as a Templar all your life."

"That is quite true, Clover." Stephen had stopped suddenly, a thought coming to mind. He looked Clover in the eyes, so beautiful and pure, waiting, he could tell, for a knight in white to carry her away in the sacrament of holy matrimony. "You are right, Clover. My time is here and now. The Templar is no more. I shall be the last of the line and this siege upon us now will be put down; that I swear. When the last battle has been pitched I shall swear allegiance to life itself."

Clover seemed so happy by what she was hearing, a smile caressing her expression to jubilation.

Stephen took Clover's hands in his. "I will go now to the duty which awaits me. Will you do me the honour in allowing me to return?"

"Wait Stephen, please. To go so soon would be unforgivable." And the cannonade could be heard, echoing through the city. "The church bells will toll when the attack comes, and it is least expected when the foss remains the obstacle it is."

"You know well of the defence, Clover."

"I see the stockade almost every day."

"Too dangerous it is. What need of you is there to visit such a hazardous place as the stockade of the Mesoteichion?"

"I help with the digging, the preparation and gathering of soil for the barrels." Stephen came to a stop then, Clover too, half turning to gaze at him in the light that was given off by the moon so high above; and romantic it was. Stephen felt great concern for her then, and saw a worrying glance fall over him as he saw the facial features of Clover reach out and touch his soul. "You endanger yourself for no good reason." So soft in voice he was just then, and his hands lifted to hold hers in endearment.

"Is not the defence and protection of this great city reason enough?"

"Not if it means placing your life in danger." And they stood there, hand in hand, looking deep into each other's eyes, as though nothing mattered at that moment except the feelings that were growing, matter of fact, in each of them, for the other.

"I must do my duty," said Clover.

"I shall do it for both of us. I shall work harder than ever before. Your skills are better needed in the hospital."

And Clover could not argue with that, though at present there were few needing surgery or poultice for tending of wounds. She smiled.

"Such a beautiful look you have, Clover."

She blushed. "You too, Stephen, are very handsome." She turned away then, bashful or embarrassed of her show of emotion.

Stephen grabbed her ever so gently and turned her to him. He cared not if she found him abrupt or rude, charismatic or chivalrous; he took her in his arms, drawing her close, and kissed her like a soft breeze kisses the petal of a rose. Her eyes closed then, her lips opening to his, embracing him as he embraced her. Stephen drew back slightly, Clover's eyes still closed, and then they slowly opened. He searched within them, looking from one to the other as though trapped in a trance that would not let go.

"I am sorry, Clover." His hands dropped to his sides. "I wished not to offend you."

"Offend me you did not," she said in reply and held him again, pulling him softly towards her, embracing him as he had embraced her. "For I feel the same for you as you do I," for she was a woman of the world. To live as she had lived: she had no choice but to learn by life's gifts and misdemeanours. She knew what Stephen felt, and he did too, and surprised he was that he could feel so emotional; so much, so easily.

"My feelings for you are strong, Stephen." She turned away again.

"I understand not, how such an attraction can arise so quickly." Clover turned again, to look him ever deeper in the eyes.

"My feelings too have shocked me. Could it be that we were meant to meet?"

"Such talk…." Clover could hardly believe what was unfolding between them and sounded a little pessimistic.

"Surely this is a sign of our bond for one-another," said Stephen, optimistically, and as the conversation continued, they convinced each other that what they felt was justified.

"Love is kindling and growing within," said Clover.

"Love is a furnace, a smithy's cauldron of molten steel, for I feel the heat and warmth of your touch growing within me this very moment."

They smiled and looked again, deep into each other's eyes. The silence was comforting and with the comfort a familiarity that was only felt amongst couples of entrusting year's acquaintance, was spawned that morning.

"I must go now my love, to play my part upon the defence of the city, for my station must not remain vacant all night."

"Shall I see you during the light of day?"

"I shall seek you out."

"I shall be in the makeshift hospital, Stephen, and I shall be awaiting your return with a great anxiousness."

And with that they parted, arms outstretched and fingers slowly moving over one-another till parting they did. To the wall, Stephen turned and ran with exuberance, to stand guard and maintain watch throughout the remainder of the night as best he could. But tiredness did catch up with him and on the wall he slept till he woke to stand his post several hours later, before retiring to another station, ignoring the strong and rustic music of the cannonade, which did continue for the better part of the morning, til morning's first light.

THE KITCHEN

Something to satisfy his hunger was needed, for as he woke – trying hard to rub the tiredness from his eyes – the pangs of hunger did attack with full ferocity.

He recalled quite clearly the morning he had spent with Clover under the accompaniment of the moon. This brought a smile to his face. And the return to the wall after seeing Clover, to look out upon the enemy camp, as huge as it was, was a stab in the heart. He had then maintained watch for some time before retiring for an hour or two at a rest point located behind the dangers upon the wall.

He had noticed a smithy not far from the point where he was resting and headed towards him now. It was only a short distance, barely enough to have his mind wake completely, but his thoughts on Clover, during the night before, came to mind as clear as a picture seen on any bright-spring day.

As he approached the smithy he noticed several others engaged in conversation, swords being attended to by the sword smith, the huge man in apron hammering down hard upon metal and anvil.

"Good morning to you kind sir," greeted Stephen.

The smithy looked up and continued hammering, a short lasting smile not breaking his rhythm, and the conversation between the men in wait for swords continued undisturbed. "I seek a morsel to appease my hunger. Could you aid me in my forage?"

"There is a kitchen not far, a shelter erected on the far side of those stables." Stephen looked over to the empty shell where horses would have once been kept. "Thank you." And to the kitchen he attended in great stride, his sword scabbard slapping against his thigh as he walked, and the talk between the men awaiting their swords not missing a beat.

His move around the stable brought him upon a street of cobblestone, dark and still shaded well by the rising sun. A short distance down the road was an open hamlet where steam poured upwards, escaping through the thatched roof. Few men were gathered in wait for a meal and others still could be seen walking away, having already seen to their hunger. The scene within came into view as he approached, ladles and pots and pans atop tables, and within the shelter, to the rear, some tables and chairs where men gathered with their eating knives to stab at what little nourishment was provided them, and spoons to swoop at the soup.

It was obvious even at this point that those present were Venetian, for a Greek would have been seeing to the sustenance of his family, and a Genoese would not eat with the former unless a knife was held at his neck. Stephen also took great pride in his eyes: for Venetian and Genoese armour, when supplied for by the wearer, and not the emperor, was as good an indication as to their nationality than anything else.

A bristly looking cook, heavy around the waist, stood over a pot in an open fire that was surrounded by a temporary arrangement of brickwork. The smell was enough to melt his tongue, hot soup with garlic and stale bread it would seem, with seed of aniseed upon bannock and beans.

And the cannonade continued sporadically, echoing throughout the city. Stephen retrieved a wooden bowl and took some bread from the same table, the cook looking him over. Unfamiliar he was, but speak to Stephen he did not. Stephen simply smiled and sat, placing the bowl upon the makeshift table and drawing his dagger from within its sheath. He used this at his leisure to pick at the little meat and potato within the bowl before draining the liquid by lifting it to his lips and soaking up the remains with the bread as best he could. He then used his open palm to wipe what dribbled from his mouth as his eyes fell upon the cook, whom with his eyes indicated the same tabletop from which Stephen had retrieved the bowl. He followed the cook's gaze and saw a familiar item resting there next to the bread. A wooden spoon, for the drinking of soup, was staring him in the face. The cook then let out a short hearty laugh, scaring the wits out of those eating his fare, which subsided quickly before his facial demeanour regained its look of solemnity. Stephen then shook the embarrassment away and took the bowl with him, stood, sheathed his dagger, and quickly placed his bowl in a cleaning pot of water. As he left he looked over his shoulder to see a small bird perched on a post of the hamlet, hopping with a single shift of its wings to the place he had been sitting, and commenced to clean, quite ceremoniously, away what crumbs could be found. Stephen then thought; at least some creature will get his fill this day.

On making his way back to the wall he heard a noise, unfamiliar it was, though it sounded in close comparison to that of two large tree trunks rubbing together in a strong wind. He investigated.

THE WALL II

As Stephen turned a bend in the road a machine in the open came to view, with its crew of men working hard to set things in motion. It was one of the few Trebuchets that Constantinople possessed, a great weapon employed in the targeting of men in mass, or areas densely built, but scarcely worth their weight when employed against men in pits and single structures like siege towers – if in range. Such a task was for an artisan or engineer of infinite knowledge and a mind so calculable that they were a wonder.

The Trebuchet could throw a stone of weight in excess of that compared to two men, and sling it to around 300 paces. The one Stephen was looking at had stopped him in his tracks. He'd not seen it the night before, too much playing upon his mind to take in everything, not to mention the men of the machine being at rest during the dark of the night. Its monstrous throwing beam was 36 feet long, mounted on an axle, and as thick as a man. One end was three times longer than the other, the shorter of the two weighed down, weights in a box equivalent to that of up to 100 men.

Stephen watched on undisturbed, utterly taken by the men at work as they wound most strenuously the windlass taut, the longer of the beams ever so slowly being bent into place, the box of weights being drawn up from the ground.

Stephen's mind was suddenly jolted back to the task at hand. At best it could take another half an hour for the trebuchet to be ready for firing, a rock nearby waiting to be loaded; but it was to the wall in which he had been stationed, and he had neglected it for far too long.

On reaching the top of the inner wall Stephen could see John contemplating, looking out over the crenel, the merlons either side showing the wear and tear of its years; both weathered and battered well, scars from years of seeming abuse. The walls all around, for matter of fact, seemed to carry a story and appeared ready to crumble to the earth on command from the emperor himself. He approached the unaware Hospitaller.

"Morning to you, John. Sleep I hope you proved to gain, as you so deserve."

"Little at that, but enough to allow me clear thinking this day," said the giant. And slowly he turned with news of the day as Stephen climbed the last remaining steps to be at his side, himself glancing out to the field in front of the triple-wall defence.

He could see clearly now, the Turks dug in, to the far limits of his sight, along the stretch of the wall and some distance out. It was a ditch deep enough to offer those inside protection from the arrows of crossbow and bow. The ditch for its entire length was supported by rampart and upon the rampart a wooden palisade, although there were gaps in the wall, here and there; this was all offering further protection to the infidel, though the palisade was crudely built and not strong. Stephen studied even more closely now and could see the sally ports that adorned the wall, ports from which arrows could be launched. Tents littered the scene to the rear of this entrenchment, thousands of them, but one in particular stood out amongst the rest. John pointed to it now. “The Sultan is there in his tent of red and gold, a quarter of a mile out and not close enough to be hit by any of the missile weapons found in Constantinople.”

“Not even cannon? I’ve seen many lying around on the inside of the defences, covering the main entrances to parry off any intrusion. Surely they could be employed; I’m sure I saw cannon balls piled close by.”

“It’s not a matter of availability, nor even the question of powder. Powder is to be had, though limited I must admit. The emperor has decreed, through experience past and through undeniable advice, that placing any of the cannon upon any segment of the wall could send such reverberation, through the very essence of that protecting us, that it could well fall down around our ankles.”

Stephen nodded. “I see the Sultan has set himself up nicely, square to the Mesoteichion.”

“And behind are his Janissaries. You will notice to the rear of the Sultan, and to either side, men and tents in their thousands. Those house the Bashi-bazouks. My guess is that when the time is right he will employ those scoundrels first, to weaken the walls, he’ll have the Janissaries to their rear to ward off their cowardice as it arrives with defeat. The Janissaries are his elite and protect the King Turk well.”

“You believe we have a chance.”

The Hospitaller snapped back his reply before lowering his tone, “And why would any man be here to be defeated; to die? I’m here to live and carry out my duty. I’m sorry, Stephen. When you fight you must fight without fear. You must fight from the heart, for what you believe to be right. If I had a wife, and she was behind this very wall on which I stand, I would fight even if leg-less and with my right arm amputated.” John paused for a few seconds to look back over the field and turned to Stephen again, looking him square in the face. “Every man, woman, and child, in this great city today, and tomorrow, is my wife. Don’t you forget that, Stephen.”

“I shan’t, John; I will remember, I promise and I am sorry; I meant not to imply you doubt.”

“Look around, what do you see?”

He did as commanded. “Nothing, except the obvious.”

“And what is obvious?”

“The Turks, the cannon they fire continuously, the crumbling wall, the men….”

“The men. How many men do you see?”

“Too many to count at a glance,” for Stephen was looking out upon the field of enemy.

“How many are close; where is the closest?”

Stephen looked again, this time to those of the defence. The obvious had been denied him for he was distracted by the size of the opposing force.

"Holy Mother… The closest man is 100 feet away."

"We are on the innermost wall, before you is the Parateichon and in front of that the centre wall, but many refer to the centre wall as the front most section. The foremost wall, to the front of the Peribolos, but behind the foss, is of little consequence during this siege, not worth the effort in manning." Stephen perused the scene to his side, behind, and in front. The enemy had his task cut out for him, but so few men mounted on the wall did little for the defence. The offence started for the enemy at the foss, which was a deep ditch capable of being flooded and was 60 feet in width. This would have to be filled in with soil, bodies of the dead, and other materials, in order for any siege machinery to be brought forward. On the defence side of the ditch was a small wall that ran the landside from the Blachernae to the Sea of Marmora, as did the other two; all three being known simply as the 'triple wall'. This low set crenelated work of stone was designed for a fighting man to stand his ground without the aid of rampart; open ground directly behind this was called the Peribolos and could easily be withdrawn across to the safety of the centre wall. The Peribolos itself was 50 feet in width along its entire length. Then rose the centre most wall to 25 feet in height, towers along this placed at intervals that average approximately 170 feet apart. At 50 feet behind this wall was the inner wall, the ground between being known as the Parateichion. The Parateichion was 20 feet above the ground plain when viewed from the Peribolos to the grounds of the city level. The inner wall was 40 feet in height and spaced as per the other with towers. These towers were built to cover the interstices to the towers of the wall to its front. "For every man here that be armed to defend, and counting all that which is exposed to the Turk, we are one man for every 18 feet of wall. We are moving Stephen to the front most wall of another quarter. I have spoken with Antonio Bocchiardi and he favours our defending the right hand most part of the triple wall, where the single begins."

And the cannonade continued sporadically, echoing throughout the city. "The Imperial Palace."

"Indeed; or there-about. The Venetian Bailey Minotto stands there, he defends the Blachernae quarter. Another stands between the Gate of the Caligaria and the furthest right hand side of the triple wall; his name is Teodoro Caristo. Minotto and he have been busy of late ensuring that the moat stays clear, to ward off any easy assault across the foss and Peribolos. We will be between them and the Bocchiardi Brothers, near the Gate of Xylokerkon, added to the buffer between Minotto's forces and Giustiniani's. We will be assigned a station with a small band of mercenary that exists there."

"Would the move have anything to do with the Genoese belief that the Venetians are untrustworthy and more cowardly than not?"

"Such a belief that passes your lips now must never part again. No Venetian, no matter how deserving, must hear anything of what has just passed here between us. The emperor, and other strong men like him, have been fighting hard to keep the peace between the Genoese and the Venetians. We can better help, as suggested, nearer Blachernae, to act as a buffer between these two nationalities of men."

"I understand."

And as they turned to station themselves a great crashing thump was heard; the Trebuchet had slung its shot up into the air, the rock departing its housing in the leather sling. It sailed ever upwards at great speed, up and out towards its target. The great rock seemed to slow as it reached its highest point, before commencing its journey down, increasing its speed with every passing second. The rock hit the ground just feet short of the ditch, but managed to crumble slightly a small portion of the hole, embedding itself below the surface. The engineer atop the inner wall turned from his observation and yelled with his hands cupped, a message to his comrades. "A hit." The men of the catapult screamed with jubilation, jumping up and down. "Ready another shot, a quarter turn on the winch more will be needed for another kill. Tallow the beast."

John spoke without looking at Stephen, "Sometimes a little lie goes a long way." And as they moved Stephen's thoughts sped through his mind: the Genoese and Venetians, the men available to defend the wall… and those unwilling to fight for the freedom so deserved.

DISPOSITION

An important thing it was, a Templar's past, and history is taught to all that enter such an Order, but no more so than religion. It is interesting to note that a Casanova of sorts could be directly responsible, in some ways, for the role that the Templar played. Back in 392 Augustine became Bishop of Hippo, but only just 5 short years before was actually baptised. It was the very rules [influence] that had been established by this man that the Templars took to heart.

But many joined the Order for the Crusades for lust of war more so than religion, even excommunicated knights were known to serve. For the murder of Thomas Becket, an Archbishop, saw several knights serve a sentence of 14 years with the Templars. It was also true to suggest that others joined to forget their past lives, to shed their memories and hurt of a lost love. But for Stephen, his quest was for personal reasons more than anything. His ancestral background had written his way, and his path was now sealed; but what of his promise to Clover? He had made a most definite decision to stay, no matter what the cost, and now with his thoughts on Clover; he was more determined than ever to stay, a Templar till the siege was lifted, or worse, until Constantinople had been defeated… and then after that, he would be a man and live a family life.

Stephen tried hard to understand the situation as it stood, heeding well to all he had heard and learnt.

It was clear that Constantinople had lost control of the Golden Horn, attempts to win her back were futile. Stephen could see where the Turks had moored their vessels, afloat the waters a little to the north. It had happened on April 22nd, a little more than a month ago. Both sea-faring vessels and canons of the Sultan's naval and land forces had good control here to maintain a constant bombardment of artillery against the walls of the Blachernae quarter. All of the Christian ships were safely pooled at the boom with eager eyes always looking out towards the south for any ships that might be sailing towards them, to offer salvation.

Vessels amongst this pool of veterans maintained watch also upon the Turks; any making for a move of attack against the wall between the Church of St Mary in Blachernae, and the Plataea Gate, would see a swarm of activity where many a variety of men and boat would be put to duty. Indeed, the Venetian and Greek seamen took pride in their favours and being guard to the walls of the Golden Horn was not a pest of any kind.

It was during these weeks leading to the arrival of the soon-to-be talked-about-knights that the conditions within the walls had deteriorated so badly that the situation had to be taken control of by the emperor himself. There was no food, grain was low, and pigs, sheep and cows were almost non-existent. Gardens and fields produced nothing, fish could not be sought, nothing was coming in from outside. A special committee of sorts was ordered, collectibles were gathered, coin included, resources gathered and purchased, and everything was shared as evenly as possible to the people in most need. Soldiers now originally forced from their posts to help seek food for their families now took to a more vigilant stance against the Turk, but little, if any, hand-to-hand had taken place for some time now. The siege was working well against the minds of the people en masse and submission must surely rise sooner rather than later – but still they held on. It was clear to Stephen that the lack of attack upon the walls was due to the efforts put into mining during the previous weeks, mining that had now drawn to a close. It was therefore easy to see that something was brewing in Mehmet's pot of war.

It was aid from Venice that was waited upon, but no help was to come. The emperor had sent his messengers and a fleet was arranged via promise, but delays were called upon, for various orders for a variety of scenarios had to be considered, before such a venture as rescue or salvation could be attempted. This fact may have been part to blame for the hatred the Genoese had for the Venetians and vice versa. It took the emperor himself to intervene, but the resentment still lingered. There was the resentment and blame – for example – of the fiasco that fell upon the Genoese due to a bungled attempt of arson against some Turkish vessels on the 28th April; it was a task undertaken by the Venetians, but it was the Genoese inability to keep a secret where the blame should have rested. Agents in Pera were the suspected villains and two postponements didn't help. With two Venetian galleys, and three small fustae – these following a Genoese and Venetian transport – the Turkish fleet was to be burnt to the decks and sunk.

The Venetians lost a galley and a fustae, and ninety sailors fighting for the honour of Christendom had lost their life.

But such relations between the two powers were strained from the start. It was in 1291 when the Venetians and Genoese went to war, which was confined mainly to the Mediterranean, Andronicus II the emperor of the times favouring the Genoese and having all Venetians in Constantinople murdered – how times heal wounds.

And now, although Venice was willing to send aid to Constantinople, delay after delay saw to it that no help arrived. But help could be secured from some other quarter, surely; but nay. Hungary was low in forces, and Russia was too far; Moldavia was in a conflict between two of its Princes, where Wallacia and Serbia were vassals of Mehmet. Albania disliked the Venetians, Morea couldn't manoeuvre due to opposing forces, the lords of Aegean were in no position to send aid, nor were the knights of St John at Rhodes – whereby John had already expressed his sincere apologies to the emperor himself. Although a small contingency from Rhodes soldiering under Giovanni Giustiniani Longo was present, the knights were not willing. All of these circumstances reminded Stephen as to the history of how the Hospitaller Knights had won Rhodes. He recalled how Rhodes was taken, seized from the Roman Empire, a weakness at the time on the part of the Byzantine Emperor. This brought King Philip IV of France in 1305 to consider a manipulation of the political scene of the time to force the capture, from the emperor of Constantinople. To do so he needed to bring both Orders, the Templar and the Hospitaller, together, to fight as one. The only difference between the two in any regard was the fact that the Templar was primarily a military force, the first uniformed in history, and the Hospitaller were learnt more towards charity work. It was James of Molay, the Templar Grand Master, who had persuaded the Pope, Clement V, via memorandum, to keep the Orders separate.

Strange as it may seem that men could volunteer their lives by standing to a task surely known to fail. The Venetian colony would remain and so too would the ships currently in the harbour. As for the

Genoese, those at Constantinople would stay to the last, for it was enough that their country would not send aid, others had flocked as though to a banner. Names such as Maurizio Cattaneo, Geronimo and Leonardo di Langasco, Paolo, Antonio, and Troilo Bocchiardi (along with a good company of soldiers paid for from their own purse). Giovanni Giustiniani Longo also attended to what he saw as his duty as a good Christian, bringing with him 400 soldiers from Genoa and a further 300 from Chios and Rhodes. It was Giovanni who was entrusted to the defence of the triple wall, where it was most prone, and now faced the troops of Mehmet and his batteries of massed cannon. Giovanni even persuaded the Venetians and Genoese to be more tolerant of each other. Men, women and children also came from across the Golden Horn, departing Pera for fear that they too would feel the brunt of Mehmet if indeed he did succeed in taking Constantinople. There was the Catalan Company under Péré Julia, Don Francisco de Toledo from Castile, and even a Scottish traveller known as Johannes Grant whereby hearsay did well, many believing him to be German. So much courage and so little cowardice, but yellow bellies men did have, as seen when 700 Italians fled with 7 boats under the command of Pietro Davanzo.

But could cowardice have been a good thing, for at present, against the numbers surrounding them, they were no more than 7,000 men. There were 2,000 visitors who had taken up arms against the infidel, including monks, and approximately 4,983 Greeks. These gallant men had in the vicinity of 14 miles of wall – in total – to defend.

It was well known by now that the advisers of the emperor had tried to persuade him away from Constantinople, to rally aid wherever he could find it. Stories lingered that the advisers understood that there was a greater need for his protection, that aid from abroad would only come from a person to person request from the emperor himself, others said it was a disguise in order that the advisers may make their escape from Constantinople. Nevertheless, Constantine refused to submit to a retreat, along with surrender to the Sultan. He would remain with his beloved city and defend the walls as every other man would.

One thing, although not truly clear, was to aid the defence. On the 21st May the last Muslim move against the boom was made. The bells rang out throughout the city on this day, and men took their posts and sailors manned their stations. The enemy vessels sailed up and down the boom, drums and trumpets sounding the advance, a great musical tidal wave as they drew closer and closer. But no attack came, instead they drew back to their points of departure – and that was the last the boom saw of any direct Turkish threat by sea.

THE MERCENARY

The Hospitaller pointed. "There Stephen, that is our new station. The Gate of Xylokerkon."

"A little quiet, if I may add the obvious. Doesn't look to be able to withstand much of an assault." And as Stephen spoke those words more cannonade was heard.

"The people here are strong, my friend," and that was the first that Stephen felt as though he was indeed to accomplish something in this adventure, "and won't give up easily; though they do tire so." John paused then. "Where were you prior to the break of day?"

"I was in the company of Clover. Why do you ask?"

"What sleep did you have?"

"Very little."

And they continued to close the distance on the Gate of Xylokerkon.

"Well sleep you must have. The defence is thin during the Sultan's weakening of the wall, but by night all semblance of citizens is fixated to mending the walls that during the day take such a battering. It is the Mesoteichion that is mainly at risk, and the stockade needs constant attention. But the enemy does forage in other places in order to find a weakness. It is then, Stephen, by night, when the wall needs to be defended. And don't worry, the church bells will ring loud enough to shock anyone to a wide-eyed reality when the time comes for a major assault, for the night hides many foes. No matter what preoccupies the minds of those at watch, their actions of mind will allow the bells to toll when the time is right. Many things do loan to weakening a man's attention to the task at hand, and women are but one of those things." Stephen knew full well what John was referring too.

"You seem to have learnt much during my short absence," was Stephen's teasing reply. "To acquaint oneself with his surroundings is to aid in the parry of attack." John felt he may be assailing Stephen's good intention to aid in Constantinople's defence, so decided to give the young man a little leash and embarrassed him instead. "But then again, I am getting too long in the tooth for falling in love." And before a reply could be received he pointed to an abandoned shelter. "That roofless hut, probably an old storage shed or smith's workshop from years past; I do not recall seeing it during my past journeys. After our introduction upon the wall you should grab some shelter from the day's sun, along with a warm blanket from any number of sources should you think you need it, and I shall wake you if needs be."

"And what of you?"

"I shall sleep behind the merlons. But now, we seek the defenders of the gate; the left most responsibility to that of Teodoro Caristo."

And up the steps they proceeded to a figure of a man in his late 60's, dressed in a chest plate and a German helmet, his crossbow held tight in his two hands and a double-edged sword encased in a leather scabbard resting against his right thigh.

"Good morning to you kind sir," announced John, but his greeting went without reply, just a short cold stare. Both knights continued their approach up the steps. "I said good day." Again no reply, not the slightest move other than the cold dark eyes that moved within their darkened slits, to fall upon the front, looking down upon the foss and beyond.

"How strange."

"Stranger things have I seen, young Stephen." The gap was closed, the steps left behind, and then beside the man they stood. "We are looking for your commander, is he about?" The man turned his head abruptly and his mouth fell open. "Ooo. Ooo." His left hand released his hold on the crossbow and pointed to within his mouth. "Ooo." The man opened wide, showing his mouth to John and then Stephen. He had no tongue.

Stephen stared though half in disgust, John, notable for his charitable work, and not a stranger of such atrocities, continued with his questioning. "Can you point to the whereabouts of Teodoro Caristo, or better still, the Venetian Bailey Minotto; we are here to defend the wall at the request of Antonio Bocchiardi."

The man shrugged his shoulders, looking neither interested nor for the requested individuals.

"There must be someone stationed nearby, even a second in command would do us well in our efforts to find our post." The ignorance continued. John looked around then, saw nothing in particular, a few men here and there but no one of great importance stood out. "A second in command; where may I find the next in command of this post?"

The old man pointed, "Ooo."

Both knights looked in the direction indicated. "Thank you. Let us go Stephen and see what we can do." The man pointed out was just 40 feet away and had what at first looked like a staff in his right hand, but as the gap was closed, the staff came to be recognized as a longbow of all things. The yew stave must have been a good 6 feet long and unstrung, the beeswax coated linen string kept in safe storage in a poach awaiting to be strung upon the stave when the time for killing was near. The man was well protected with armour; helmet, breastplates, plackart and greaves; a fauld of four lames with a tasset attached was also present. The remainder of the man was covered in mail, except for his hands that remained bare and at the ready for the stringing of the stave.

And as the two knights approached, the man turned to face them and directed his speech to John. "Well be, a Hospitaller Knight, and with a pup as a bodyguard. What say you, good knight? With protection like that you need not one, but two swords to defend yourself."

"And where may I ask, does the jesting come: from deep within perhaps?" John pulled his sword from his sheath. "For I shall cut you open to find what ails your tongue and infests your most ugly exterior; and well before you have time to quiver and piss in your shoes, let alone string your weapon."

The bowman turned full on then, placing his stave gently to rest upon the inside of a merlon and raised both hands. "Ha ha ha ha ha, what is this, my friend? Please, kind words with a little sarcasm is all. I meant nothing more than to say that a fine looking gent as yourself need not of any protection, truly a worthy knight… both of you are worthy."

John sheathed his weapon and the hands of the bowman were lowered, Stephen then was quick to take offence and drew his ancient sword, for to allow John to act in his defence was a sign of cowardice.

"Hah. A sword like that belongs in a smithy's melting pot."

"And you deny that such a sword could spill your guts, to pool at your ankles."

"I believe any man with the courage to carry such a sword… has courage, but his brains nowhere else but in his big toe."

Stephen then took to putting into action what he had been practicing for so many years. He understood full well the way in which men think. He was being insulted directly and in the presence of a Knight of the Hospital. To accept the criticism would be to accept sarcasm and chastisement for the remainder of all time. On the other hand, he couldn't kill a defender of the wall. This bowman was dealing out what he felt he could get away with, to prove his manhood by tempting all those he spoke to. What were Stephen's choices: to take a defence against his strong words, or be known as a coward for the remainder of all time? All of this sarcasm in order to raise a response, without the need for the spilling of blood. Stephen swung his sword, slicing the left cheek of the man with the stave, just missing the mail which covered his head but not his face, one more scar to accompany the many, the sword continuing around to just miss the head of John – who didn't so much as flinch.

The bowman let out a small protesting scream and aided the cut by placing his left hand ever so quickly to it. "My God, what have you done?" He promptly pulled his dagger from its hide, attached to his enamelled-clasped belt, with his right hand.

John then interceded, drawing his sword once again, holding its point against the man's throat. "I grow tired of your actions against my good friend, Stephen the Templar. You have but seconds to plead your case or be dead."

"A Templar, of course. My mistake, I beseech you both. I am but a miserable mercenary, paid little what the emperor has in his purse as an up-front payment. These past few days have seen little action, but the cannon fire continues. I grow tired and uneasy. My harsh words are but the sleepless nights and days that we all have suffered. Please forgive me."

"Your true colours have been witnessed." Swords and daggers were then sheathed. "Let us all hope that in the hour of need you rise above your display of cowardice this day. Have you any command over this group? If not, where is the commander?"

"We mercenaries have none of any real importance. We travel as friends and oppose those who pay the least; but in these times payment has come via different means. We have been promised much additional wealth once the siege has been lifted, and that will be soon now."

"How so?"

"You have not heard? The fleet. It is arriving within the next few days. 20,000 men with arms are coming to our rescue."

"When was such news provided to you?"

"Prior to our arrival. The Sultan's offer of wages was good, but the emperors great."

"Who told you such a story? Is he here this minute."

"He sleeps yonder; the one with the axe," the bowman pointed with his right hand, still holding his cheek with his left.

"Good, we shall speak with him; and any thought you may have of stringing your stave and seeking vengeance, remember this. I have 300 friends from Chios and Rhodes who would love to seek you out." And they left the man to sulk.

THE PILLAR ALFRED

Once out of earshot, Stephen prompted John: "You have no friends here."

"I know that, but I am sure that the bowman has heard of the 300 spears on the Mesoteichion."

"And what of the 20,000 men?"

"A fabrication, I am most sure of that."

They came to stand over the sleeping form of a man in his 50's. "Shall we wake him?"

"No, Stephen, we'll sit and wait; and sleep ourselves."

"No need." Came the deep voice as the eyes opened on the once sleeping form.

"We were to seek the man with the courage to hold together this small force of well-paid mercenary, but instead we have been directed to your company in search of rumours that a fleet with 20,000—"

"Rumours indeed they are, but by the time such is known by my men, we shall have been victorious in our defence, or defeated by an inferior force."

"Inferior you say; such optimism; such promises as saviours arriving on the morning's wind will soon be uncovered as they really are, nothing more than stories in the mind of a madman."

The Axeman stood and thrust his clenched right fist up to meet his chest, bowing his head slightly. "I am pleased to meet with you; John, the Hospitaller; and you; Stephen, the Templar."

"And how may I ask, do you know of us?"

"I too have heard stories afloat the wind." The Axeman picked up his fearsome looking battle-axe and looked both knights in the eye. "Please, this way. My name is Alfred," and with a smirk hidden by the back of his head, Alfred did commence with the tour, down the steps of the ramp, and continued with the introduction. "My men call me, The Pillar Alfred."

"Your men?" prompted Stephen.

"Aye," Alfred acknowledged with a slight turn of the head, "though none here would advise of such. All of my men like to think of themselves as leader, or equal."

"And of your promises?" Asked John.

"All will be forgotten once the last battle has been thought. These men need stories to keep them in check, or none would be standing here this very moment. The man with the stave, he is English, though has spent more time abroad than one can imagine, fighting for others of course. The many scars he carries are the gratitude of many for his 'kind' words. He joined our crew just six months ago, and has been wagering a personality war with all he meets."

"Does the stave carrier have a name?" continued John."

"Paul;" and with that he stopped, turned, and with a whisper added, "the Puller." And the cannonade continued sporadically.

John saw the light of the pun and laughed with Alfred, though Stephen stood silent, having missed the swift humour and remained patient, waiting mindful of further orientation. The laughter quickly subsided. "But truly, he is a good marksman and can hit his targets well. We have men willing to rush the field of slaughter at night to fetch his arrows for reuse, for he is worth his weight in gold. Mind you, none such words would be offered to Paul himself, not by anyone."

"He thinks himself as second in command."

"I am sure he does. However, the one with the crossbow was being convenient, not accurate."

"And of the others in your company?"

"We have many, but only one worth mentioning, and his secret should remain just that."

"It can't be much of a secret if we are to be told, and by such a tone that you possess, it sounds just so."

"Well put, Stephen, but yourself and John here are knights both; are you not?"

"We are," rushed Stephen."

"Then such a secret can be revealed, but silence maintained; if you catch my meaning."

"We do," said John, eager to learn of those he was to fight alongside.

"The one with the crossbow you questioned—"

"You saw this?"

"Aye, John. You wonder why I said nothing?"

"To study our actions."

"You are indeed wise. Yes, I overheard a conversation of two knights arriving upon the breath of God. But the one with no tongue; he is Lars; deep within Germany he has come; been with me for nearly two years now. Getting long in the tooth, and quite senile. He is a knight of the order Teutonic – or was."

Both knights seemed speechless, then John smiled. "Another story no doubt."

"Good knight John, a story indeed, if I were such a knight, but to praise another for holding such service would be beyond good reason."

Stephen would be first to admit of the little he knew in respect to the Teutonic Knight, but what he did know gave status to the man with no tongue.

In 1196 the Germans took to founding their own Order. These were to cater for the special needs of the wounded, as for the Hospitaller, or knights of St John, but characterized a persona to that more suited to the Templar Knight. They came to wear the same white habit but clearly marked with a black cross as opposed to a red one. The affiliates were christened the Order of Teutonic Knights.

A close tie was formed between the Orders, in particular the Hospitaller and Templar – although fighting between the two was also evident. Templar would often rally to the flag of the Hospital, and at one time, during a withdrawal from Jerusalem, The Templar insisted they wait for those of the Hospital before fleeing as ordered.

It was not so much the fault of the Templar, but those that led them and gave orders in respect to Christians of a Latin background. The Templar in 1242 set upon to siege a Hospitaller hospital compound, not only this but those within the confines of that besieged were not granted food for the sick, nor ability to remove the dead as requested. The Templar in the same year also saw to it that Teutonic Knights were ejected from certain premises as directed by higher authorities.

In contradiction, October 17, 1244, saw all three Orders fight side by side, more than 600 in number; only 33 Templar, 26 Hospitaller, and a few Teutonic Knights survived to tell the tale of the lost battle at Herbiya in Egypt.

But one thing was known, that in 1410 the Teutonic Knights were defeated at Tannenberg, 400 lost. The Order went into decline after that, but remnants lived on for some time after. So here, to be fighting alongside Stephen was a Teutonic Knight, old as he may be, to fight for a cause that he knew best served the Lord his God.

THE RALLY POINT

The Teutonic was still on Stephen's mind: "And here we are." Stephen immediately recognized a roofed shelter hidden beyond the structure originally indicated to Stephen, by John, as the place where he should gather rest. It was just beyond the Kerkoporta Postern. "This is our rally point. From here any number of decisive actions can be forged."

"You mean a formed withdrawal?"

"All manner of scenarios must be considered. Yes, a formed withdrawal if the need arises can be conducted from this point. And quite safely I may add, through the suburbs along the North-Eastern wall."

"At least that's one point we can both agree on, Alfred; only an assault from the land-side can be facilitated and victorious," agreed John.

"A withdrawal, victorious in withdrawal," said Stephen.

"Life cannot be denied a straight-thinking mind. You would not lay down your sword in the pitch of battle, to be stabbed in the heart. Nor should a man stand his ground when the battle is lost. Anyone of sound mind will do what he can to preserve life, especially his own." John was momentarily concerned for Stephen, but quickly pulled himself into check. "It may be the only sensible thing, but you may do as you choose, Stephen. Once this siege is fought, whether we are victorious or subdued… our service will be required elsewhere."

"Listen to John, he speaks of experience."

"Are you saying I am without such and should henceforth have my lips clasped," and then he again recalled his fondness of Clover; he may well decide to withdraw if the need arose, but his life he would lie down in order to protect her innocence.

"Every man must decide for himself, and although a mercenary I am, I do have standards; one of those standards is withdrawal under means." Alfred turned to sympathy, placing his open hand upon Stephen's shoulder. "A knight you are, decisions you'll make, but under my command this will be our rally point."

And Stephen could see that his immaturity had risen, even if momentarily. Orientation then proceeded; a tour of Blachernae, its gates, and keepers, all was touched upon. The conduct of sorties upon enemy siege engines and talk of battles so far won were also something Stephen received excitement from: to know that he would soon be baptised in true battle.

It was well into the morning by the time the three had returned to the rally point, and The Pillar prepared to depart for the wall, with a few final words: "I have a few simple tasks to perform this day. You may as well both get some sleep, for nightfall may see some action, even if minor."

"Our many thanks to you, Alfred," said John. "We look forward to fighting at your side."

"The honour shall be mine," and he bowed slightly.

John and Stephen then sat after a few seconds of silence before both looking up and through the thatch of the roofing of the rally point, a bird having gained their attention. "A little protection from the rain, not much. I think some sleep would be a good idea, Stephen, I myself will need some rest prior to returning to the hospital."

"You are returning tonight?"

"This evening is more like. I wish to ensure all is well with the patients, although both nurses are doing a tremendous job. Most of the procedure here consists of applying herbs and ointments. Medicines are kept for the more serious injuries, though such a commodity is hard to come by. Good medicine is hard to find. Blankets and sheets for bandage need to be sought. Much preparation for the weeks ahead needs to be planned for. I also need to check on any news of the siege."

"I am sure news will travel your way, John. I have not heard of much here that has not passed your ear. But it is the stories of heroism that I like to hear, where the Turk has been pushed back from near victory. Do you know of the story of St Romanus being captured by the Turks? All this talk of battle has intrigued me."

John thought for a quick second and wondered what Stephen had heard of the siege prior to his arrival, for he himself had heard a lot during times of small talk with the nurses. But the St Romanus Gate was a story to be told, one to be listened to, and needed a man of knowledge and skill at storytelling to capture the essence of the battle as it was.

"I do."

"Can you tell me?"

"Yes, Stephen, I can." And before John had finished with the tale, Stephen was asleep. John got to his feet then, and with a smile placed a nearby blanket over the knight's sleeping form, knowing full well that he'd not seen good sleep for several days and nights.

FOR CREED

John had one thing on his mind at present, the sheets from the Brigantine that he'd promised Clover, so on he marched to ensure his promise was upheld.

Along the way, silent thought dominated John's mind, seeing the churches of Constantinople, those in poor repair, and others that were well maintained via the purse of the rich and bold, brought clarity to the view of decades past. He recalled well the times when he was a boy and playing joyfully within the streets he knew so well. Good times to put a smile on his crusty face, to lighten the look of such a dominant expression as the one he so often carried. He had seen a lot of death in war and even more so in the hospitals he had worked. He had killed as many men as he had provided aid. Many a man was grateful for his skill as a surgeon, for without his aid many would have died. To give life and to take it away, that was the way in which he led his existence. So lucky he was in war that God himself must have been at his side on many occasions, to aid him, to defeat his opponent, so he might mend another with cutting-knife, cloth, and good healing hands. He then thought of God and the Order of the Hospital, of the siege and possible aid from the west. Religion was the key to salvation, always was, and always would be.

God was not beyond knowledge, but he was beyond understanding. How could philosophy itself determine any answer, query, or problem raised, by any such thought of a divine materialist nature, if understanding was beyond reach? A visit of the emperor to the Pope in 1369 did nothing to unite the churches of the east and the west. Byzantine belief was split in conscious thought and practice over a religion that had the same base, benefits, and values as those of Western Europe.

But help against the Turk, from the west, could surely be secured, and openly promised, if a union between the Latin Church, and what was the Greek Church, could be sanctified. But it was the monks and others of the clergy of lesser importance who opposed such a move as to accept Latin beliefs, and no concession was going to be given by the Latin Church.

Theological beliefs: The Greek Church in the Procession of the Holy Ghost and of conflict surrounding the word Filioque contained within the Roman Creed. Should the bread be leavened or unleavened – to accept a Latin belief after suffering under the hands, for so long, of those of a Latin Creed, would this be acceptable? And what of the west, their use of unleavened bread was disrespectful to the Holy Ghost to say the least? And of the west's refusal to admit Epiklesis, which through the eyes of a Greek meant unsanctified bread and wine.

A further meeting was pressed for in 1439 at Florence. The Latins won time and again in debate, under advisement from the Pope of course. The Greeks were also not unified in what was spoken and were more diffuse. The Emperor John VIII persuaded his bishops that the proceedings were appropriate and all that which unfolded should be accepted, so all but one of Constantinople signed a paper submitting to the Latin usage. It was now seen that the Holy Ghost proceeding from the son was the same as proceeding through the son. On return to Constantinople the emperor found it hard to implement what had been signed as the people displayed much anger. The union would not be carried. The people and the emperor knew full well that their safety net would now be cast aside and that no further council would be entered into. Their beloved Creed would remain, it seemed to them best to be met by the sword of the Sultan than the Creed of the Latin Church. John VIII died on 31 October 1448, in pain from the hurt he'd caused his people over the initially forced union that had been brushed aside like a rat carrying the plague.

The Pope in 1451 decree that if union wasn't met then measures would be enacted upon them, either directly or indirectly. It wasn't until 12 December 1452 that union was forced upon the community.

Union was proclaimed and would now remain. But this was of little concern to the population, for from that day forth they would only preach in Churches where their Creed was upheld. It was also well believed by many at the time that if the population had witnessed the arrival of ships and soldiers from the west, in order to help defend the walls of Constantinople against the infidel Turk, then the Creed could have been accepted then and there.

No aid came.

MARIA

John was suddenly shocked, although gently enough, back to reality as he continued on his way via the suburbs along the shores of the Golden Horn. It was here that Maria shouted out, loud enough it seemed.

"Yes, Maria. What is it?"

"I was on an errand for Clover, begging for herbs and searching out other medicines. She has emphasized an urgency for more bandages."

"I am on my may now in fact, to salvage what I can from the brigantine. Will you join me?"

"Thank you, I think I shall."

John led the way. "How did you fair with your task?"

"A little tonic, but nothing much. I fear that the worse is to come. What will happen to the injured when all is gone?"

"Pray as I do. Besides, I think we will have few casualties. The fighting spirit within the men is so great that I see not how Mehmet will capture this great city." John himself did not wholly believe this, but to put the burden of fear upon the shoulders of a fledgling life was not his deed this day.

"With you here, John, I believe what you say to be true."

"It's men like Stephen too who help greatly at times of strife. He will prove most efficient when the time arrives, you can wager your last hen on that."

"He seems very fond of Clover."

"Yes." John appeared temporarily angered. "Love in times of battle can be as dangerous as a double edged sword. I believe his devotion to the Temple will give him strength to fight when fighting is needed, and the good sense to love when the Turk is at rest."

"Have you known Stephen long?"

"Not long. A few days and some passing of words aboard ship is all. But I grow to know his character as though born in the same house."

"He strives to be a good knight."

"No, he strives to please his ancestry."

"But you seem so content with your work, as though born to it. I wouldn't think for a minute that you were displeased with the Order that you serve."

"I follow God through passion, I wear this habit through pride, but my soul belongs to the sword. I believe Stephen is similar at heart, but his passion has had little time to mature, my young Maria. I initially followed the wishes of my father but grew to love all aspects of my role, in different ways. I am married to the Hospital and nothing will change that now. But I feel that Stephen's passion will grow into something more; especially if he continues to see Clover." Maria smiled at those words. "However, we each have our own affairs, to worry about the health of others more in need than ourselves is what has been bestow us, and Stephen has his own goals in life, I am sure of that. Believe me; Stephen is strong enough of character to do well here. He won't cower in battle; I know this from experience. But love at such a young age will strangle his urge to remain a knight and sword bearer. Ah, here we are." The gate to the Harbour was open and many men could be seen resting on ships and upon the pier.

The wall here, along the Golden Horn, was single, as too was the wall along the Marmora, the Marmora wall however, jutted straight out of the sea, where along the Golden Horn there existed a foreshore enriched with warehouses.

"The sheets will be aboard the brigantine. Come, Maria, let us see what we can find."

A SIGN FROM ABOVE

Stephen awoke suddenly amongst the clamour and fear, people and children of all ages running around helplessly in the growing dark. He shook himself to full consciousness and realized that he was at the rally point, a blanket having been thrown around him in the early afternoon, after a lengthy orientation. The last thing he recalled was the story of the tower of St Romanus, near the civil gate of the same name, being captured momentarily by the Turk. It was a wooden turret on rollers, so large as to be inconceivable, with its three layers of hide and internally fixed stairs linking platforms that had been to blame. Loopholes within the hide allowed protection for the sorties, as time and time again men would embark to fill the foss prior to the tower closing the gap on the wall. It was then that a ladder of immense proportion was lowered from the top most portion, allowing men brandishing, shield, armour, and scimitar, to capture the tower. It was the night itself however that was to also be the saviour, for as night fell the soldiers and other labourers of Constantinople, under the emperor and Giustiniani, took back the tower, the emperor himself remaining onsite, all the night through. The dark hours were fed with non-breaking activity, and by daybreak they had emptied the foss, restored the tower to its former self, and reduced the threatening siege tower of assault to a ruin of ashes.

Stephen was now witness to the reverse, for as the night had aided those of Constantinople in their fight to take back St Romanus, the day was now the devil in disguise. Something so unbelievable was taking place that it could never be conceived as being true, nor of this mortal world. It was history in the making, history itself being forged from the past, to take its part in the present.

It was long since known, and remembered by all, that the city would be well defended against any siege or assault unless the signs of evil fell upon them as prophesied in the past. They had already suffered a few omens of the approaching evil, those were in the form of minor earthquakes and torrential rain. But what was to follow would only assure their feelings that Mehmet was the Anti-Christ and that their demise and departure from this world would not be far off. Amazingly enough all of those in the city kept their spirits high and maintained a denial throughout the siege in the hope that help would soon arrive from the sea in the form of a fleet of galleys; but now: It was now quite dark, and getting darker, for high above the moon was in full and a transformation was taking place. An eclipse was in the making, and for many hours the men, women, and children of Constantinople stood in sheer terror as darkness prevailed and the blood moon watched down upon them.

A LONG EVENING

There seemed to be much panic amongst the streets of the city, but nothing could be seen, for night had set in long ago and Stephen's view behind was blocked by the height of the inner wall. Such an omen it was... that had occurred. It had people talking for many hours. Screams and dogs barking were but few of the sounds that reached his ear. Some of the more optimistic citizens and leaders beckoned all to throw aside any fear they felt, for the defence must hold, and in order for that to be they must set about repairing the damage done to the stockade and other places along the wall.

It was a slightly different story for the men of the defence, standing upon the wall in the cold of the night. Many Greeks had departed for their homes, and where this had occurred, the walls were manned quite sparsely. As for the mercenary, each and every one stood his ground in preparation for an assault. Whatever was going through the Turks minds right now was an unknown factor, an incalculable factor, and a factor that could change the course of the siege.

He looked around from side-to-side. The Pillar was standing erect, right palm over the hilt of his sword. Lars, the Teutonic Knight was asleep, his crossbow laid at his side as he himself sat with his back against the wall. Then to the Puller he stared. He had strung his yew and looking out into the dark of the night, searching for sound and movement, looking for a target that would not waste his patience. Any target, which did appear, would have been scrutinized well, for a wasted arrow was not the way the archer worked. His talent for seeking the most opportune target was well known, as too was his mouth that let loose at a moment's whim.

On occasion Stephen could see the stars through the blanket of cloud high above, as the night's shroud did shift in the wind above

Constantinople. Peaceful it did seem to him, and strange that such a feeling should be felt. Here he was, set upon by siege, standing guard against an army that was more than 20 times the size of the defence. How could such a feeling of peace exist? Calm was the feeling that inhibited him that moment. All thought of the siege was not really there in his mind at all. He too felt proud to be here, proud to be serving Christ as he knew he should. He had come a long way to be here, covered many miles by land and nautical miles by sea.

He was making history, but no one would know his name.

And the cannonade did continue sporadically.

PART THREE
Friday 25th May

CLOVER II

A cannon ball then hit near where Stephen was standing, but it only dented the wall every-so slightly, a small piece of mortar and rock crumbling away. The reality of the strike hit the defence with no more clarity than any of the previous, but it did bring about a notion of safety.

Stephen felt a strong urge then to seek out Clover, to hold her tight, to protect her from harm. But why should he feel so strongly? Was John right? Was he in love? It mattered little; he would seek her out in any case.

He took the time to look around in order that the situation could be accessed fully. As things stood he'd finished his watch, not only that, but it appeared that every soul upon the wall was now wide-awake and quite frozen in place due to the cannonade that continued. The eclipse was also still firmly implanted within the minds of those maintaining watch – though Lars, for some unsusceptible reason, was still asleep. Each and every man, woman and child, who bore witness and testimony to the shrouding of the moon, presumed the three hours of darkness to be nothing other than an evil apparition. As for the Turks, Mehmet was sure to be at council with his commanders and astrologers this very minute.

The Turk was quiet and the wall stood-too, which was good enough for the Templar Knight.

Stephen departed his post without providing notification of his departure and scurried down from the summit of his position, through a gate of the inner wall and to the city level. He wasn't exactly sure where Clover would be but had to take a chance upon the makeshift hospital where he'd seen her the night before. In particular with all that was happening, she was sure to be fully awake, and keeping her mind and hands busy.

Through the street and assembled throng he hurried, as though to the rescue of a damsel in distress. The more he saw and heard the more he worried. Each crowd he passed seemed to be quarrelling over the eclipse and its meaning: not the usual, not as though over nothing, haggling on the true price of a garment, but words of a religious virtue for extricating the true religious belief of what it was they saw. The words amounted to nothing in a real sense, just a loud jumble of tones as though a pack of a hundred wild geese had just landed and were squabbling over a piece of freshly baked bread.

He hurried past the tavern and down the street before turning into the lane where he knew the hospital to be. It was only now that he decided to slow his approach before coming to a complete stop, to gather his composure. He was breathing heavily and by now had completely forgotten the eclipse of earlier, only wanting to see that Clover was safe from all harm.

He commenced a controlled approach to the front door and could hear a few whispers from within, prayers to God and the Virgin Mary, phrase upon phrase of religious pose. He stood then in the open doorway and could see both Maria and Clover with rosary in their palm.

Stephen knelt down, there in the doorway, left hand on knee and right palm onto the back of his hand. His kneeling gave wake to a creaking door as his shoulder did scrape against it and Clover opened her eyes, which were followed seconds later by a wide smile and uplifted head. She stood slowly and pocketed her rosary, herself and Stephen unaware of Maria who by now had done the same with her rosary and had turned to see to the only remaining patient on tabletop.

"Stephen, what a lovely surprise."

"I felt I should… I thought I would take some time from the wall. All is quiet at present and nothing needs to be attended to."

Clover then rushed Stephen and they held each other momentarily, Stephen feeling a little bashful, seeing Maria smile before she continued with her work.

They looked at each other, eye to eye and eye to lips. The eyes did all the talking that needed to be done, and for some minutes Maria wondered if something might be wrong, for she was several years Clover's junior, and did not understand love fully.

"You look less tired than the morning before, Stephen. I hope you have settled in alright and that you have good sleeping quarters when needed."

"We have a dwelling where sleep can be accommodated, but the wall is also quite comfortable."

"I don't believe that for a moment. Maybe through sheer exhaustion, but other than that the brickwork and masonry must be quite cold."

"But some thoughts do bring warmth to the heart."

Clover cocked her head to one side. "Oh, and what thoughts are they, may I ask?" Stephen felt she knew full well what he was referring to, but didn't want to say too much in the confines of a room so inappropriate as a makeshift hospital. His hands lifted slowly as did Clovers, until they held hands, both as willing as the other, "Shall we walk?"

"With a knight as an escort, how can I refuse?"

"You can't." They turned then, still hand in hand, Clover on Stephen's right side. "But let me get my shawl first."

"I see you only have one patient today."

"He shall be gone by morning, nothing to worry about."

"And the Turk with one leg."

"Taken away by two of the emperor's own guard. I don't know where to." They were now clear of the doorway and the light of the moon gave aid to what romance could be found in the air. It brought a smile to each of them, and then the cloud that was thick and swirling above shrouded the moon but once again.

Stephen jolted to a stop and turned Clover to him. "Clover, the dark of the moon, the talk of the city. How are you tonight? Do you feel safe and content within? Are you scared?"

"I feel safe now. I'd forgotten about the moon until just then."

"But your prayers. I assumed they were due to the moon."

"They were, but your presence seems to have alleviated any worry I had about the evil shroud of darkness that covered the light of the moon."

Stephen stroked Clover's upper arm then, though she seemed not to notice, as she was falling ever further in love with this man of such handsome features. Her entire being this very moment was fused to Stephen, every thought.

"Tell me of you family, Clover. I forgot to ask of them the other night." They continued to walk their way through the city. "I don't have any true relations to speak of. An old man and woman, whom I consider to be my parents, did find me outside of the church Nea Basilica. They bought me up soon after I was born. They christened me and provided for my Christian life in Constantinople. I am forever in their debt."

"Is there anything I can do for them? I would love to help if it is within my power to do so."

"I'm sorry to say that they both passed away some years ago now. My adopted father died when he was 64 years of age and my mother two-days later, from a broken heart. It was such a terrible time. I can only be thankful I suppose that the tragedy occurred at an age where I was able to fend for myself. With aid from the church and the city's people I developed a plan and moulded my life to suit."

"Are they buried nearby?"

"At Nea Basilica. It's a good mile from here."

"Are you tired?"

"No."

"Then I am all yours, Clover. I would love to see the resting-place of those that brought you up, for you have turned out so beautiful, in so many ways. I am in debt to them for the work they have done in helping mould such a fine woman as yourself, a mould that would have been broken soon after your birth, for you exceed the beauty of all imagination."

And with a smile and batting eyes, Clover pulled Stephen off in the direction that would get them to their destination with the quickest of ease.

And the cannonade continued sporadically, echoing throughout the city.

They headed towards a point two-thirds of the way towards the Church of the Holy Apostles from the Charisius Gate. The Street that ran along the ridge was well maintained and would have been bustling with activity by day, as the street was well endowed with shops and houses of private residence. The walk along the street brought the Church of the Holy Apostles into better view with each passing step, the great building dominating all that around, but unfortunately in very poor condition and quite neglected. Nea Basilica of Basil I, having been built by Basil 500 years earlier, was still some way off and before reaching the well-maintained church, the Forum of Theodosius, Forum of Constantine, and the Hippodrome would have to be passed.

As they passed the Church of the Holy Apostles, several guards of one of the two detachments of reserve could be clearly seen on the centre ridge. Stephen knew that one such reserve was stationed immediately behind the land walls and close to the Imperial Palace – this being under command of Lucas Notaras and in control of several mobile cannon; the reserve on the ridge was under command of Nicephorus Palaeologus.

Such a fine looking church was the Holy Apostles that many dreaded its sacking in the wake of a successful Turkish Campaign, its treasures currently intact. The Sultan, however, had already passed orders unto his soldiers declaring the church to be untouched and maintained for his soon to be, Christian subjects, on the understanding that the Church of the Holy Wisdom could be taken intact and converted into a mosque. Mehmet had even arranged for a special detachment of soldiers to deploy immediately to this Cathedral under such stressed orders that paved the way for its security, he had even planned for the Patriarch Gennadius to be its over-seer, if the man could be taken alive.

THE CEMETERY

On reaching the Nea Basilica, Clover took Stephen by the hand and led him to the site of those she knew as her parents. Although the cannonade could still be heard in the distance it was reasonably quiet and poetically peaceful here in the church grounds. The numerous headstones came in all manner of shape and size; many of those at rest here being of a common background and of little money or importance. The grounds appeared to be well kept, well-manicured, a few trees here and there, and an owl could be heard, hidden well by distance and dark.

They soon came upon the headstones so important to Clover, and Stephen could see right away the personal care she had provided to the site. As her parents died within days of each other it was convenient, and morally judged, that both should be buried within the same grave. The headstones also wore an inscription, but Stephen could not quite see what it read.

The church itself was quite beautiful and appealing to the eye and situated to the higher ground, the graves more towards the sloping landscape that lead down towards the wall near the sea. The view itself was quite breathtaking, and was in itself well worth the trek by foot to come and see.

"They were very sad days, after they died. I must have cried for a week or more." A forced smile caressed her lips and tears began to well in her eyes. "I can picture them now, as though they are still here with me."

"You must have suffered much burden during your mourning." Stephen wrapped his right arm around Clover's thin waistline, feeling quite easily the warmth of her body and could smell the sweet scent of her flesh.

"I did… but life must go on."

"Did your parents pick this church out or…."

"No," interrupted Clover. "I decided it was best. The most beautifully adorned little church around, quite quaint and overlooking the Boucoleon Harbour, and sea of Marmora."

"I think you chose wisely."

"The view is spectacular, particularly during the summer months when you can see far and wide, right across the Bosphorus, and as clear as the hand in front of your face. The view across the waters of the Marmora is also quite relaxing. Such a nice place to be at times of trouble and when mourning the loss of a loved one… or two."

"What does the inscription say?"

"It says: 'tell all that pass, that Greek we be, for all time hence, till parting of the sea'."

"Who wrote that?"

"I am not sure. My mother must have found it in a book at the library and had it written on a piece of parchment. I found it after her death. She was always in the library; she read well. I didn't think much of it at the time, but I seemed to be important, so I decided to have it chiseled into the headstone. I must suppose that they are saying, with regret for the Latins of this world, that orthodox they are for all time, for the only person able to put back the ocean is God himself, and it is His own creed, His own making, a power which only He holds; and God will not change what is His own."

"It sounds similar to something else I have read."

"And what is that, Stephen?"

"I am not sure, but something to do with the Spartans, of that I am sure."

"Well, they are as Greek as one can be."

"There is no doubt about that," agreed Stephen.

They stood there then, for some time in silence, a fresh salty breeze being whipped up from the surface of the waves below. "It is getting quite cold now." She said. And after a while Clover simply turned away, still holding tight to Stephen's hand and they both walked off towards the entrance of Nea Basilica. Here they cowered under the arch of the entrance and pulled each other close for added warmth. There was comfort in that, like no other comfort Stephen had felt before. He was sure he could stand there for ever and a day.

"This feels so good, Stephen. I feel so safe and secure. Even if the wall was to fall this very minute I think I would remain here under your protection."

"I wish I could be as confident." And he was very pleased to hear that she felt the same way that he had felt.

"Do you think we are right? Do you really think the siege will be thwarted and that we can both live long lives?" they looked into each other's eyes with great tenseness being portrayed.

"To live long lives I believe. But for now it is getting late and we must be getting back. You have rest to gain before a new day brings more casualties, and I have a wall to protect." They kissed then, for a long time prior to heading back to Petra, both contented with the feelings they shared, the love that they felt, the security given off by such a romantic affair as the one they had discovered.

On reaching the junction where Clover was to depart, Stephen jumped to one last opportunity to please his newfound love. "Clover. Do you yet have sheets for bandaging; I can fetch those from the Brigantine if you would like?"

"John has already done that for me, thank you, Stephen."

"John? Why are you asking John?"

Stephen's tone was somewhat sour and Clover wasn't sure she liked the sound of the words as they fell from his lips.

"John is a master at healing and a great religious man from what I can tell, and I am a good judge of character, Stephen; John has even spoken highly of you."

Stephen understood his mistake and fell to one knee for the second time in less than so many days, holding onto Clover's right hand. His words had come out completely wrong and he was deeply misunderstood. "Please, Clover, so much in a single life has been burdened, so much in one day. Please forgive me, for I meant you no harm. The words I spoke were meant to offer a tone of surprise, nothing more. You are so fair a lady as one would wish to burn in the blazes of hell for. I only meant to say that I am at your service for any errand you wish performed."

Clover smiled. "Well," and then sternly, "no one asked you to burn in hell."

"Shall I be forgiven?"

"You shall. Now be up-standing Stephen, before someone sees you." And they both laughed as smiles leapt from their hearts and to their lips, not only for what had happened, but also for the fact that no one had been seen by either of them since before they had arrived, hand in hand, at the Nea Basilica.

"And how was John when you saw him?"

"It was Maria. She ran into John on his way to the brigantine I believe. He gave her escort to the ship's hold and collected all that could be spared." She smiled again and let out a little chuckle. "I believe he ransacked the vessel well, leaving little behind."

"The brigantine will be of little use anyway," said Stephen, "for its task is done, and all aboard did come back to Constantinople to stand and fight the infidel we now face. Not one man among them; well, maybe one… but all other members of the crew did wish to return by their own accord."

"One from so many is of little consequence, Stephen, in particular when two of them are knights both bold and brave."

Stephen was silenced by the comment, and then he spoke. "I have yet to face a true fight. The only fighting I have done in the past is with chickens, pigs, and rats the size of small cannon balls… and built as strong."

Clover grabbed around his waist and pulled him close. "It matters not of your past, but of your commitment here, now. You will not desert your post, nor fight badly when the time arrives. You will see yourself hold back the tide of the Turk when he attacks, and want to jump the wall after them when they break and run from the heavy losses they will receive. You will be surprised, my knight, what you will accomplish. You shall see me on the wall beside you and dare not allow a single scimitar wielding scum of the earth gain foothold upon the rampart. You will swing your sword as though born to it. The sword will be an extension of your arm, to pivot by way of your wrist. It will dance through the air around you and parry all that comes near, and stab at those scrambling up ladders to meet with your fury. The blood you spill will be too much in the end, my love. You will be sickened by the work you did achieve, but thankful for your life and of the Turk's death. And when the fighting is done I shall still be there, standing at your side, ready and willing to give aid where best I can. And whether that aid is but to place a cup of water upon your cracked lips, or to remove the point of an arrow from your limbs, the task will be done with true affection. You will not waiver in battle, Stephen, for you have come here at your own expense, a volunteer, and offer the true mark of a man who shall become a knight. Your armour will rust with the sweat your body gives out, and at the end of it all you will be able to face any man of this world and say to him that no other knight deserves to bed with me, than you; yourself."

Stephen was stunned by the words, so many, so much praise. And the prize of the day was the woman of his dreams, for if he was not mistaken, Clover had just promised herself to him. "I shall make you keep your promise, my dear Clover, but as an honest woman, and not a cheap trick of the likes I have seen in the den of night."

The silence slowly grew then and they looked into one another's eyes, as though for the first time, becoming lost in place and time, nothing seemed more important at that moment than the two of them.

"I feel as though I have known you most of my life, dear Clover. And even if you should choose to chastise me this moment for my words, I must say this to you now. Time is short, I feel, in this world of ours. Little help is coming our way. I have spent days on the sea coming here, and others have spent the weeks before that looking for relief in the form of supplies of men and food. We are to defend the wall as we are, no aid to come. And though the task looks grim, I stand by my word and say to you once more, we will be victorious." Stephen's right hand stroke lovingly the side of Clover's cheek, but blemish she did not, for some uncontrollable reason she felt the same as this Knight of the Temple. "Although we have only been together for the shortest time, I am completely begotten by you, in every form, and this night I have grown so fond of you. My fighting shall be done, but to you my life will go."

"Morning." Said Clover clumsily and with dazed eyes, not sure of what she spoke or even that she had said anything at all."

"Hmmm." Stephen prodded.

"Hmmm." Clover came back, unsure of what she had said that needed repeating. "Oh, morning."

"It is morning, Stephen, look, the birds are commencing to wake and the sun is beginning to show itself."

Stephen looked once again into Clover's eyes, as deeply as the first. "The most beautiful morning I have seen in my life." He shook himself to mind. "I must leave you now my dear, for I'm needed on the defences."

"And you, my love, I shall see you soon." And yes, she had spoken those words, and although she was not sure if they sounded right in this much early introduction, or even if she'd used them earlier on, she certainly believed them to be true and fitting. But something other than that, the words seemed so natural.

Stephen took off, quickly striding out as though to meet the enemy head-on and in person, taking one final look and letting loose with a wave and a smile. His Clover waved back, standing there, watching him go, and once he was out of sight she did return to the hospital.

ISMAIL

Mehmet's plan of assaulting the frontal wall had now been reinforced. By his taking and maintaining control of the Golden Horn, meant sure victory, or so his advisors had agreed. He had provided himself with a means to easily and readily move troops across the natural obstacle via a man made bridge, he also had another portage ability: boats provided to him. Mehmet now also held the advantage of targeting any part of the Blachernae wall along the Horn with cannon resting upon floating platforms, thus allowing troops the much needed 'cover by fire', if necessary. It wasn't so much as allowing his troops to gain ground whilst keeping the heads of the enemy upon the wall down, as much as it was to tie up the much needed manpower of the emperor. The emperor needed as many hands as possible on the frontal wall. To target the Blachernae on all sides, and to assault premeditatedly from land and the Horn, would force the emperor to employ his reserve immediately. It was a tactic of the day, to have a reserve in defence, to block up any weak spots or holes as they appeared, to keep the enemy at bay. The Sultan wasn't sure how much reserve the emperor held, but it couldn't be many. To attack, or feint attacks, in as many places as once, was going to be the requirement of the day when the time arrived. But the Blachernae was important. It would allow his land forces quick and easy access into the city. And if need be he could change his mind and move the cannon to help target the Mesoteichion instead.

The act of neutrality that Pera was currently playing had allowed the Sultan to do as he pleased, and although currently neutral, Pera still gave aid to Constantinople in regards to the boom being connected to the wall at Pera. Before the Golden Horn was taken into the Sultan's hand, spies from Pera were free to relay to the emperor information on the disposition of Turk troops. Now the avenue to which information was received was cut due to Mehmet having taken the northern portion of the Golden Horn for himself. Mehmet was in a grand position to keep watch on all movement within the area, in particular any vessel, of any size, moving to and fro Pera and the city. Mehmet had also taken the advantage of planting his own spies in Pera.

The Genoese fighting in Constantinople were not pleased with the path Pera had chosen for itself, but those citizens still acting under a flag of neutrality could not see why they should jeopardize their own safety for those residing in Constantinople. The Genoese in general disliked the Greeks and the Venetians; the latter returned the feelings. The only real guarantee that Pera held in regards to safety from an assault from the Sultan was the threat that a Genoese fleet may be sent to their aid, hence the Sultan losing possible control of the Golden Horn and his sea blockade jeopardized. It was clearly seen therefore, by many, that if the city of Constantinople were to fall, Pera would follow. Mehmet had to wait patiently before making any planned move against Pera, henceforth, war with Genoa. It was also clear that some of the Genoese in Constantinople also had family and friends in Pera.

Mehmet's position was fragile, though strong. Something had to be done, so he devised his plan, and planned it well. Meanwhile he would try and persuade the emperor to give up the defence, by one means or another.

A messenger named Ismail, a young noble whose father was known well by Mehmet as a traitor amongst the Greeks, was to be employed. For services rendered Mehmet had appointed his father vassal prince of Sinope. The Sultan in person, sent to the emperor this man named Ismail, to offer one final chance for peace. Negotiations were still possible. The Emperor Constantine recalled well, after council with his aids, that Ismail had many friends within Constantinople.

Ismail pleaded his case from below the battlements, saying that the Sultan required that the emperor loan his kind ear to what was at offer.

Teodoro Caristo looked down upon Ismail. "My lord, the emperor has been sent for. He shall be here soon. But tell me, whilst you wait there upon your horse, what beckons that your call of duty should lie with the Sultan?"

"He has much to offer and it is the way to secure my passage into heaven."

"Everyone speaks of God and heaven. Why, like the Latins, should you believe yours is the path, the righteous way?"

Ismail answered immediately. "If you were to take the time and learn of your adversaries, you too would throw aside your pitiful belief in the Bible and take up the Koran. It is the way; there is only one God."

"Yes, and if he were here this day he would strike you down from upon your horse." But before the Turk could answer the spite the emperor did appear upon the wall. He held onto Teodoro's arm lightly, "It is alright my friend. I shall speak."

And Ismail opened the conversation.

"Lord Constantine." Ismail paid his compliment to the emperor. "My esteemed Lord Mehmet does grant you a good morning. He would further wish to discuss with you options for the lifting of this siege."

"And I could do the same, and provide him the option to leave now and save embarrassment."

"We know your heart is strong. No one doubts that. To task I have been sent, and that task is to request that you appear for an audience with the Sultan in his tent."

"I see little need for discussion, but you shall have your audience." Constantine knew what was to come about in regards to the meeting with Ismail and thought well on the subject as he made his way to the wall, so before they even set eyes upon each other the emperor had drawn up a set of plans within his mind. If he did send an ambassador of any great importance, the chances were that he would be killed, possibly tortured. But a small chance did exist that Mehmet was genuine in his quest for a peaceful resolution. He would send someone in his stead. He turned to a soldier at his side. "Do you know of the Templar?"

"No, my lord."

"And you."

"Yes, my lord. He no longer wears a habit of white, but I know him by sight."

"Fetch him now." The emperor turned again to Ismail. "I shall send a messenger with you. Your Lord Mehmet can speak with him."

"I understand fully and shall wait upon my charger at the gate of Xylokerkon; if that be to your approval."

"It does."

Within a short span of time Stephen approached the emperor at the base of the wall near where the exchange of words with Ismail had taken place.

"Good day to you, my lord."

"And you too, Stephen." The emperor smiled, putting Stephen at ease. "I have a request which requires your urgent attention. I need a messenger for the Sultan, an exchange of words if you will, in his tent in front of this city. Are you willing?"

"My lord. I am at your disposal." And Clover came to mind as quickly as a flash.

"Good," and the emperor ushered him aside, "A quiet word with you. I have an urgent need of an ambassador, but certain death awaits all of those familiar to Mehmet. Are you sure you are up to the task?"

"I am, my lord."

"Mehmet will set upon the negotiating table a request for payment in order that the siege be lifted. Whatever he lay down you must convey to me, including his mood and the mood of those around him."

"I understand."

"Then go now and convey."

Stephen made his way out from the gate upon a warhorse handed him by the emperor's page and said nothing to Ismail until he brought himself up alongside.

He was a fine looking man and dressed well. He sat upon a fine saddle and a fine horse. "Your name, sir; what shall you be called?"

"Call me Ismail."

"I am Stephen."

They slowly rode off towards the encampment. "Do you hold title, Stephen?"

"No, sir."

"Do you hold office with the emperor?"

The cannonade continued sporadically at the furthest point from where they rode, but this subsided, for the sultan had commanded a temporary halt to their firing for the coming meeting. "I do not."

"Then may I ask what manner of envoy the Emperor Constantine has entrusted this most important meeting?"

Stephen was little more than an inexperienced guard of two days service, he thought: little more than a lap dog. "I am a professional at arms and serve the Lord Constantine as I serve my Master in Heaven; with the honour and sacrifice He so demands from me."

"You are a prized conversationalist." Said Ismail sarcastically. "But to serve is of little consequence if such is done with provocation and reprimand."

"And would you dare question Lord Mehmet if he were to command you to the field of battle, to fight alongside his Janissaries?" The look Stephen did receive, from Ismail then was proof that he had won the first round. Although Stephen was inexperienced, Ismail was truly no more than a lap dog of royal status.

The remainder of the ride to the Sultan's tent was carried out in silence. Stephen decided then to take the opportunity to also gain as much information as to the true disposition of the Turkish Army.

MEHMET

The troops on the ground to the front of the Blachernae wall were those under Karadja Pasha, the European Divisions. Their dress was mixed, as were their flags, pennants and standards flapping in the breeze, all of an assorted hue, and the weapons and armour were as varied in consistency as were the uniforms worn by each of the hostile forces.

Stephen rode to the right and slightly rear of Ismail. On reaching the trench and palisade they moved through an area that remained unsealed in the defences before changing direction. Ismail now commenced to weave his way through the tents and soldiers at arms, along stretches of hardened ground, which now resembled an unsealed road, and towards the tent of which housed the Sultan himself. Several monstrous cannons could be seen not far from the tent, so huge that Stephen could not believe his eyes. It was no wonder the wall of the Mesoteichion was collapsing.

As they made ground on the fixture so easily seen from afar, Stephen realized just how marvellously the Sultan wished to live. The tent was rather grand, and monstrous men stood either side of the entrance, very intimidating. The tent of red and gold was as robust as any other in the area, though did have the added beauty of hand-woven designs along the line of the main entrance and in other places. The width of the tent tapered as it grew taller, coming to a point, which did fly the Sultan's colours.

Two slaves came running out of the tent as Ismail and Stephen approached, grabbing the bridle of each, steadying the horses as the expected visitors dismounted. "Please, Stephen, be patient with the Sultan. His command of your tongue is good, but sometimes he will think before he speaks. Please remove your sword and dagger; the servants will tend to them for you." Stephen removed his weapons. "Be so kind as to follow me." Ismail led the way into the confines of the large tent. They skirted around a hanging silk and came into the main area.

The Sultan could be seen there, seated upon a throne of modest worth, helping himself to the fruit being offered on a tray of gold. He acknowledged Ismail and bid he approach with his hand before waving off the servant. "It is so fine to see you, Ismail." The Sultan said as he stood and stepped from the platform on which the throne was set. His speech was foreign to Stephen: "An envoy from the emperor, I see, has taken the opportunity to attend this meeting. So good of you to attend; historic it may prove to be."

Stephen understood none of what Mehmet had said. He looked the Sultan up and down but careful not to insult with the body language he displayed. Mehmet had what appeared to be a red turban upon his head, which was more like a silk wrapped around the top of his head to keep his hair in place; a feather could be seen affixed on top of that. He was very young in appearance and appeared to be of fewer years than what he was known to possess. His beard was thin, especially at the chin, but immaculately kept; no hair inhibited his upper lip. The most outstanding feature of him was his nose, very large and seemingly low-set. Stephen felt that he displayed a comical look, though he was known to be very dangerous. Of little maturity he was sure to display, and it would be a wonder that sovereigns, kings, and princes, of other lands, could take such a man as ever being serious. Stephen was sure to remember however the one thing he did possess, one of the largest military forces known to exist, along with what was considered to be the best troops known – the Janissaries.

"My Lord Constantine sends his regards," lied Stephen, presuming a compliment had been given, for when the Sultan had spoken in his foreign tongue it was with his eyes upon Stephen.

"Opponents in battle we may be, but gentlemen all the same." Mehmet returned, Stephen now understanding well due to Mehmet's change of tongue, for the conversation now turned to the reason he was here. "Can I offer you something to eat; some fruit perhaps, from Sarakhan, beef from Menteshe, or vegetables from Rodosto? Many lands entertain us with gifts and commodities, it is for us to ensure they are enjoyed."

"I must decline your humble offerings, Lord Mehmet, for I would be doing a disservice to my fellow man if I were to accept." Stephen fell short of advising the Sultan first hand in regards to the lack of food that there was within the walls of Constantinople, but the Sultan was sure to know this in any case.

"Yes, indeed. Our business is the siege, and foremost is a desire for both armies to see an end to the slaughter. I am sure your emperor would relish the opportunity to once again trade freely within the Mediterranean."

"Trade is all important, but more so is to guarantee the safety of the inhabitants of Constantinople."

The Sultan was silent for a short term, Ismail moving around to stand nearer his lord. "Which brings me to the question of tribute. You refuse to sup with me, maybe you will barter?"

"I must confess to what little I know of such making-of-agreements. I shall return any message you so have back to my emperor, and return again with his answer."

"And if the answer wasn't to my liking I could have your head on a spit."

"Such will be to your entertainment, my lord. I am but an unimportant messenger in this exchange of words. Little can one man do on a wall against your soldiers so skilled at arms, in particular whilst being torn apart by your great cannon."

The sultan laughed out loud, pleased at the man to his front laying down his courage: or was he being quick in revealing his cowardice… and the sultan was disappointed that no challenge of any kind was to be met. "You will return to your emperor and convey the following. An annual payment of one hundred thousand gold bezants must be paid to me in order for the siege to be lifted." But little did Mehmet think that such a tribute could be raised. "I also offer a second option; for all of the inhabitants of Constantinople to abandon their city. They may take all of their possessions with them. I give you my word that none will be harmed."

Stephen was a little surprised by the words that reached his ears. "With your permission I shall return to my emperor and pass on your generous proposals."

Again Mehmet let out a bout of rumbling laughter. "I like this man, Ismail, so polite and agreeable. Go young man; tend your errand like a good errand runner should. I await your reply. Ismail will escort you so that you may go unmolested amongst my men."

"I thank you for your concern," and Stephen departed with a bow. Once outside the slaves hurried in with his weapons and horse, it was then that Ismail appeared at his side. Ismail took his horse and spoke to Stephen. "I shall return with you and retrieve word."

"There is no need. To the palisade is as far as you need to go. I am quite capable of finding my way back to the Sultan's tent."

"I shall return with you to the wall and await your return, or a cowardly reply."

Unknowingly to those of Constantinople, the cause behind the Sultans sudden change in heart was the fact that his army was at a stalemate, had been that way since the commencement of the siege some 7 weeks before. They had not won any major conflict through the army or navy, help from the west could arrive at any time, and the Hungarians could quite readily cross the Danube causing him to lift the siege and engage 'them' in battle. There was also the question of morale amongst his men. Mehmet had little time left and had to act immediately, with or without the spilling of blood.

On reaching the defence Ismail was ushered aside by friends within the wall and brought to conversation. Ismail did spend much of this time trying aesthetically to convince the men to surrender, that they should save themselves despite their religious beliefs. Meanwhile, Stephen was taken aside by the emperor who took the conditions of surrender, not so lightly, before consoling with a council on the all-possible undertakings likely to please the Sultan. Stephen waited outside of the palace as the council retreated to within, on their most important errand in regards to finding a solution to their predicament, which would bring relief to the grief of all within the city.

Some argued that to pleasure the Sultan was not the aim of the council, not to give in to the evil of a man with little more than a nose for trouble, which some found humorous, for big it was. A suggestion was made that the tribute could be promised. The time gained would do well to serve them in their time of need, and by the time the Sultan had realized that the payment was not forthcoming, an armada would be approaching to save their souls. Others within the council knew that the Sultan would not adhere to any time limit. If the tribute wasn't paid immediately then the siege would continue and the likelihood of a battle was very promising. The emperor put forward the final word and a decision was made; though all knew that such an answer would not be pleasing to the Sultan. The answer could do one of two things. If Mehmet was so sure of victory, he would attack, if he were insecure he would tempt further proposal.

The emperor came out from the main entrance to the palace and saw the Templar waiting there. "Stephen."

"Yes, my lord."

"The council and I have reached a decision, but it is for you to decide if Ismail should return with or without you."

"Without me no reply can be conveyed."

"Most likely such a reply will be in the form of the cannon, which have only recently grown silent due to these futile talks, but will commence again soon enough. But it does give us more time, even if only a little, to repair the wall." The emperor stood silent before continuing. "Convey to the Sultan the following..."

And again Stephen stood in front of the Sultan, one final time, to deliver the answer, or alternative, to the man upon the throne.

"I see you have returned with news. I hope it is good, for all our sakes," said Mehmet with wonder in his eyes.

"My Lord Constantine does hope that you will consider his gracious offering as an all possible agreement."

"And what is that?"

"My lord does offer you everything that he owns. He is willing to pass onto you everything that he possesses; but… my Lord Constantine will give all of his wealth to you, but he will not give to you the city as this belongs to the people."

It was to Mehmet's understanding therefore that the emperor was not able to gather one hundred thousand bezants. But how large was his possession; what did he own that was not Constantinople? It was therefore quite clear that what he, Mehmet, was doing to Constantine, was also being done to him. The emperor was asking him to give way to an ultimatum that was just not going to take place. Mehmet's eyes shot wide open. "Your emperor does not own anything other than Constantinople. The city is all that he possesses. Is this some kind of trickery?"

"No, my lord. I am only a messenger which brings both good and bad tidings, but knows not the difference between the two."

"You shall return to Constantine and tell him this. He has but three choices from this point on. He shall surrender the city forthwith, along with everything in it; die by the sword, or convert to Islam." And the features of the face, as young as it were, was not pretty at that moment.

"I shall do as you have requested."

And so Stephen returned, unmolested in any way.

The emperor was displeased that such pitiful negotiations had taken place. There was no way in which either he or Mehmet were going to accept anything that the other offered. It bought time for the defence and that was all. The siege for the time would continue. As for morale within the city, something would be done. Ismail was dismissed to return to the Sultan.

Negotiations were over and the cannonade recommenced as before along the entirety of the sieged wall; relentless in its pursuit of obliteration.

THE PARADE

By late morning all within the city had heard of the brigantine's return, and although the arrival of two knights brought about bouts of conversation, it did little for morale. All within Constantinople now knew what the emperor had done, and that no help was forthcoming;

even The Pillar Alfred had trouble calming his mercenary. Panic was starting to take hold upon the citizens of all faiths, young and old, fragile and strong. None could ignore the signs so far received, those given by the grace of God, and those handed down by the Captain of the brigantine. The moon had commenced its cycle of waning, and the three hours of darkness the night before was a phenomenon unable to be perceived by any, as anything else but evil, and yet there was more, for the symbol of the city was the moon itself. Such a treasured object she was, warding off all danger during the weeks preceding, for all knew that Constantinople would never be seized whilst the moon was waxing in the heavens, but that was not the case at present.

It came later in the morning, when Stephen was standing upon the wall with John, that word of a parade had reached his ears. A great calamity had to be avoided so a precession was organized. Through the streets they slowly marched with a great statue carried upon a litter. It was a symbol of their Christian religion, a relic of the past, the Mother of God.

"Come all, see the Holy Mother."

"Gather around, children, see for yourselves."

"God bless you all."

"Oh my, a sight to see, even if in heaven."

"The Holy Mother will be watching us today."

"Sacred be all that is touched by this parade today, and long life to all."

As the icon of the holiest of relics was carried around, men were granted permission to leave the wall unattended where they could be spared.

"John, Come see the Mother of God," urged Stephen.

"I have seen Her much these past decades. You must make the most of your stay here. You go, join in on the parade."

"Are you sure you will not attend?"

"A force, even small in size, must remain upon the wall. Besides, I heard of your humble act as messenger; such an act deserves a well-deserved reward."

"I did as the emperor requested. I would not have volunteered."

"Few men would have, Stephen. But nevertheless, attend you did. And what did you think of the Sultan?"

"Strong in his conviction, immature in stance; quick in thought and powerful of mind; careless in speech. To be of such noble status should require great experience and understanding, surely."

"Blood is blood. With few else to take the reins in his predecessors' steps, he had but a few options. But I ask you now, who would not wish such power?"

"I for one would not want the responsibility."

"Responsibility belongs to those of peace, like the Emperor

Constantine; those who would invite war at every turn hold no responsibility, either for himself, or his people. The Sultan does little else but think of himself. His own greed will be his undoing. Time will tell Stephen. If the siege is thwarted then he will be doing himself ill service, as his army will suffer greatly, being cheated of strength in number. Even if he is victorious, he will still suffer the losses. If Europe was to attack when he is on his knees, then the Turk will be no more. But the honourable, those that care more for their people, they will take longer to consider a move against the Sultan."

"Politics of war; too much for me, John. I prefer the simple life."

"Then all you need to do is prove it, young Stephen, by taking to the streets this moment and join in on the parade. Waste no more time upon the wall this day, for it will hold whilst the Holy Mother is paraded."

With that Stephen simply smiled, turned and departed.

And the cannonade continued sporadically, echoing throughout the city.

Dressed in his mail with sword and dagger in sheath, Stephen departed the rampart where the mercenary maintained a watchful eye on all to their front. Nothing but the pendants upon poles and pikes of the Turk army could be seen to be making the slightest move at the moment, although the cannon continued sporadically with more than normal lapses given to the silence so seldom experienced. Overhead was a slightly different picture however, for cloud cover started to build with a cold breeze fast approaching.

Stephen made his way without haste towards the voices of celebration. It was quite clear where the Holy Mother was at this moment and Stephen's only concern was whether or not he should seek out Clover in order for her to join in on the parade. He then thought better of it, for if she wasn't already at the parade, she would be sleeping or tending the wounded.

He increased his pace but refrained from running, soon finding himself turning a corner in a road and coming face to face with the crowd as the main attraction made its way through the winding labyrinth of Constantinople.

Stephen was absolutely overjoyed to be confronted by such sheer happiness, the exuberance of the crowd, the great optimism that flowed from each and every one that was present. And on the litter the relic continued, paving the way for the following crowd, through streets so narrow and squares so large.

He wanted so much to fight his way through the crowd so thick, to get a hand to the litter, to touch, even if momentarily, the object of so much affection. His happiness could not be any more than it was, surely, so he would hang back and let the citizens enjoy their day to remember, for their needs were greater than his. Then the urge for the former hit him hard and he pushed slowly forward until he was just arm's length from that which gave all around so much joy.

Then a voice familiar to him penetrated all those around to be delivered as clear as day to his ear. Stephen turned ever so slightly, averting his eyes from the statue to one of the bearers, and saw who it was that had attracted him by voice.

"Franco," Yelled Stephen.

The sailor turned his head away to the rear of the litter and back again, his right shoulder bearing no weight but joy, for he was at that moment helping to carry the relic. "Ha, if it not be, Stephen of Europe. Come, held with carrying the Mother of God and feel the warmth of her blessed love."

"I shall." And with smiles caressing both, the litter continued its journey, both Franco and Stephen supporting the litter from the rear as it continued on its way.

Then suddenly a mishap occurred.

The icon suddenly shifted and the litter began to shallow at one side. Men rushed in to prevent the idol from toppling, but Franco and Stephen saw little of the front end of the idol, just the fear and panic displayed upon the faces of those watching the parade from either side. The move forward came to a stop and the stability of the idol upon litter became very hard to control.

The cries for assistance then came to ear: "Please God, give me strength."

"Let not the Mother fall."

"Quickly men, rally aid."

"Hold onto the Holy icon, quickly man."

"She's slipping; it's too heavy."

"God, give me strength!"

"Push, Push damn you!"

More men still gathered and all hands finally put stability back into the statue, bearers being changed with care in order for them to rest, not just from exertion, but also from the panic that had enveloped them all. Then suddenly, as though from nowhere, a wind started to penetrate the bodies of all within the procession. Men bent over from carrying the idol suddenly stood erect; bystanders once given relief of the heart due to the instability of the icon were now panicked once again, everyone looking around in fear for some explanation or encouragement. Then suddenly and without warning, to accompany the wind came a torrential downpour that no one could recall ever experiencing before. The streets became flooded, like a river in places, buildings and cobbled roads; hardened soil and street guttering; all aided the natural disaster of mind and spirit. Like a tidal wave the crowd dispersed in the wake of a coming calamity, like the waters that recede from a beach before a giant wave comes crashing down upon them. The hail stung at their hands, faces, and backs. All celebrating the procession then felt a heavy sadness, for the procession was most disappointedly cancelled. People ran for shelter, children were nearly washed away in the storm, and a miserable afternoon was about to be suffered by all of those remaining on the wall.

Stephen was dumb-founded, as though slapped in the face. One moment carrying the Mother of God, the next a bystander, having been relieved from his most temporary post. Franco had also disappeared into the crowd, obviously hurrying for shelter. The fall to the front of the litter, the collapse, was it his fault? Was he so tall that he had toppled the relic himself? No, impossible. He now followed the few that remained until the relic had been redeposited into the Church of St Mary before returning back to his post, all expression on the faces of those that accompanied the Mother displaying bitter disappointment.

JOHN

He stressed the point: “And it was terrible, John.” Yelled Stephen. “People running in all directions; here and there, like hunted rabbits.”

“A bad omen this is, Stephen, a bad omen indeed. Something terrible is looming close by, and sleep tonight I will not. Prayer, Stephen, that’s the answer to our current misery. Pray we must in order to endure the devil’s work.”

“The devil sided with Mehmet will give his army much strength.”

“Prayer will sap the strength from their bones.” John unnecessarily wiped the rain droplets from his face, which appeared again seconds later. The stinging upon his face was unrelenting, only turning his back on the downpour brought temporary relief. “This weather is not going to yield, but I think I may. I think we shall seek shelter, Stephen. We will see The Pillar and advise of our retreat to a warmer station. We can relieve our comrades a little later. Besides, these mercenaries are paid to stand their posts, as I am prone to pray.”

They found Alfred at the half-sheltered post of the rally point, a little material added to give relief from the elements of nature.

It was quite hard to hear in the downpour, but when close, conversation could be carried out, all could be conveyed, as was proven when John had called out several times to Alfred on approach to the shelter: Alfred could hear not a single word.

John got close enough and tapped Alfred on the shoulder. “We are going to retreat to a warmer station, and shall return to allow our comrades the same comfort later this afternoon. Our strength and health must be maintained, for the audience with the Sultan this morning did not go well, and he may attack at any time.”

Alfred agreed heartedly by nodding his head, wrapped in a blanket and seemingly quite miserable; John then departed for the nearest church and Stephen to the tavern for some warmth. Stephen would attend to the emptiness in his stomach by seeking out the sustenance of some broth, and if it could be found he would pass on the word to those he was to relieve later.

As for John, he commenced his miserable retreat to a warmer station, where psalm and prayer could be taken into effect for the relief of anxieties he was currently feeling. The nearest church to his knowledge was the Church of St Mary Pammacaristos. After giving praise to the Lord he would search for some nourishment before again returning to the wall.

As he rounded a corner he bumped into a man wearing a seafaring uniform, thereby dislodging a package from within his grasp, which the man bent to retrieve immediately: "My esteemed apologies dear sir, for…." John could see the man appeared unsettled by the encounter. "In my hurry I seem to have failed in concentration. An accident I am sure you are willing to forgive."

"My belongings are now saturated. By what do you think you display by such careless action? Nothing but impossible irritation." The frown upon the man was pure indication as to his unsettled state.

"Please, I meant not to ruin that which you carry." John was sincerely regretful of the incident. "My name is John."

"And mine is Rodrigo, Don Rodrigo. I suggest that you try to remember that much when you are running about the city unleashed."

"Sir, I do not take lightly to your poor attitude."

"Not pleased ah? You are more stupid than a mule." It was then that the habit of the Hospitaller came to be noticed, Don's previous anger hiding the fact from view. He brushed himself down as though flushing out invisible creases upon clothing he had not, quite obviously, changed for more than a month.

"You need not forgive me for my transgression, but accept my apology you must." Both men eyeballed each other, John ready to defend himself should the predicament turn ugly, and Rodrigo changing his tone slightly."

"Accept your apology I shall, but to forgive your stupidity I shall not."

"Don Rodrigo is it? Shall I tell you, good sir, that you tempt my fury like none other has done these past few weeks? Your ignorance shall be your undoing. I have good mind to teach you a lesson in swordsmanship."

"Man of the hospital you may boast to be, but proof you have yet to unveil."

John wielded his sword then, removed from its wooden casing as quick as Rodrigo would care to contemplate; as smooth as a dancer on the move; as silent as a mouse scurrying across a room. "I shall teach you of my experiences. I offer you the chance now to prepare yourself; you miserable piece of filth. For vermin such as yourself belong in the dung heap of a camel's stable."

Don Rodrigo realized then that the predicament was not in his favour. He was used to fighting from the deck of a ship, stabbing his sword downward upon any enemy wishing to board his vessel. To be confronted by someone more skilled than himself was not to his liking. There was too much in favour of the knight to his front, and not enough for himself.

Don looked from side to side briefly. They were quite alone, no witnesses. His cowardliness would not be seen by anyone. "Forgive me my attitude, please. I have not had a pleasant day, and I have urgent business I must attend."

John sheathed his sword slowly. Today was not the day for conflict against another of the defence. "You are forgiven. I shall not delay you any further. The weather is against us both. Please have a good day, if that is possible with the misery we have to contend." John lowered his head slightly in acceptance and Don Rodrigo took off, looking behind him as he stepped past the knight, weighing up the Hospitaller for all he was worth, and happy that he had not discovered just how good a swordsman the knight really was.

A STORY TOLD

Stephen was drinking his ale, seated in the same seat as he was before, when the man to his side told a story, how it came about that on Easter Sunday, of all days, a disruption was felt within the city. It was spring and the flowers were in bloom, displaying many exquisite colours, along with the blossoms upon the fruit trees. News came fast and furious, for Turkish scouts could be seen, and on the morning of 2nd April the first of many detachments of Mehmet's army set themselves up to the front of the land wall in preparation for the siege which was to follow. And amongst the upheaval a melody could be heard. Nightingales were nesting, as too were the storks, the smaller of the quarry amongst trees, the latter upon the rooftops; but the drum of horse and oxen were ever present as they made their approach to congregate in front of the city.

Three things now occurred that gave clear message to all of Constantinople:- All gates to the city were closed and secured strong; all bridges across the moat were destroyed; and the boom across the mouth of the Golden Horn was secured: from the Tower of Eugenius to the sea wall of Pera. The boom was a massive link of chain, made buoyant by use of empty wooden barrels; this protected the wall of the Golden Horn from a direct assault from the waters of the Horn itself by denying the Turks ready access from the Bosphorus.

The security measures were not questioned, it was welcomed, for within 4 days the entire Turk army was in place, and within 5 the cordon was closed in, a firm hold on their very freedom being forged.

The first real horrors of the siege were then realized. The Turks assaulted two small castles, one at Therapia and the other at Studius. The first held out for several days, but the latter just hours. Altogether the Sultan had taken himself 76 prisoners and these he paraded in front of the triple walled defence of Constantinople, showing all watching what was in store for them if they did not surrender; all 76 were impaled. The emperor, on behalf of the city, turned down his offer of mercy with surrender. No surrender was going to take place, and the citizens would stand with complete resolution beside their emperor.

Then commenced the firing of their cannon, including the monster creation of Urban's – which due to the mud created by the April rains, and other servicing problems, could only be fired approximately seven times in a single day. So it was here on the Lycus Valley that the outer wall was dealt blow after solid blow. Such was the destruction that the wall was completely destroyed, but men, women, and children kept to their maintenance, and the rubble and ongoing repairs created a stockade, a stockade that was forever being replenished. Barrels were employed, filled to the top with earth, planks laid here and there, holding together the very ground which trembled at every shot fired – the barrels themselves also displayed the character of any crenellation, providing just protection for those firing arrows from behind cover.

The constant work did the job and kept the hordes at bay, the stockade was strong and very much important to the defence. It must be defended at all costs.

Mehmet soon came to the decision to send in the troops just after sunset. On the 18th April, at the weakest part of the wall, came a rush of men bearing arms. Archers, javelin throwers, and others more heavily armed; the Janissary Guard came on a wind, battle cries drowning out drums and clanging symbols. Hooks affixed lances attempted to pull down any loosened merlon, torches set fire to planks and barrels, but these were quickly put out by buckets of water being poured upon the dancing flames. The soldiers came on strong, but none of their weapons, with the diminished strength of the attackers, could penetrate the heavy armour worn by the defenders. After four hours of fighting the Turks had lost 200 men where the Christians lost not a single soul. God had surely, this day, looked upon the defenders with favour. If no mortal mistake was made then Constantinople would surely win the day, week, and month, till such a time that this siege would be lifted, the enemy in front of their wall made to turn with their tails between their legs like they were withdrawing this very moment. Cheer upon cheer went up from the ranks, but it was too soon to be rejoicing too drunkenly. As a commander of troops, Giustiniani had done his job well, the people's hearts and thanks going out to him in their thousands. To have this man on their side, and at such a time, was as though God was fighting from within the skin that bound his body strong.

Such a tale, such honour and bravery, unbelievable it was. This siege would be remembered in history as a victory, even if Constantinople was lost.

THE TEMPLAR

But such a pretty picture, of such a pretty tale, did not cloud Stephen's mind. It seemed to Stephen that this current siege was as disastrous to the people of Constantinople as Philip, the King of France, was to the Order of the Templar.

Yes, the King of France, Philip, had considered the merging of the Hospital and Templar, in order that he may command and lay great influence upon the Mediterranean. Two Orders to operate under the one name, a single banner. But he pondered still at the arrogance of others to assume the role of organizing the merging of 15,000 knights and 5,000 foot soldiers to crusade against the Holy Land; such a hatred he did have for James of Molay. The last thing the king needed was a strong and united Order. Dubois, a propagandist at the time, advised King Philip quite openly in 1307 that it might be as well to destroy the Order of the Templar once and for all. To eliminate the Templars might be the only way to control them and their assets. Philip would await his opportunity with great patience.

It was not long after that three expelled knights laid accusation against the Templar, jealousy in such a case being a curse of gigantic proportion. The King of France then promptly ordered the arrest of all of those enlisted within the Order, for they had committed crimes that were too horrible to hear, absolutely disgraceful, and intolerably inhuman.

Within 24 hours 15,000 knights throughout the country had been arrested and the order of the day was torture. The torture brought about the results required, as many of the Templar were in fact not battle-hardened veterans, but farmers, carpenters, and the like. Having the soles of one's feet basted in fat and slowly cooked was enough to make the quietest of men speak out. In one report, 134 of 138 Templars arrested, soon admitted the crimes they were accused of, and although not every man was tortured, those that were suffered a great deal, 34 to the degree where they would never see the light of day again due to death. Death in some cases was a godsend, for some had their feet so badly burnt that their bones charred and fell off. In the year 1310, the month of May, accusations and findings continued with the burning at the stake of 54 Templars, a further four followed some days later. Of the Templars that admitted to the crimes branded them, a large majority were set free; of those not willing to ascend the allegations, they were tortured, imprisoned for life, or burnt at the stake.

In the year 1312, on the 3rd April, Pope Clement, in front of King Philip of France, announced that the Templars were to be abolished.

Stephen, now seated in the corner, at the table by himself, shed silent tears for all that had come to pass over the Templar.

Stephen did then return to the wall, to relieve a comrade, but the thoughts that inhibited his mind were those of the Templars' history. For many hours he stood there upon the wall, being drenched to the bone, the rain unrelenting in its savagery. But the time did soon arrive, just before midnight, when he was given the opportunity to relieve himself, warm his body and dry his clothes, and to take leave from the pressing duty for something, as tasteless as it may be, to eat.

He then returned forthwith to the bar that he was becoming so familiar with, the hag with a tale to tell ever present with a large tumbler of refreshment being placed upon the bar, standing ready as he made his approach. One large piece of stale bread and cheese he did secure to push back the tide on the rumbles created by his gut before a little slumber he did achieve upon the surface of the table at which he sat. The storm outside continued, and with the noise a dream did enter his mind of a loving wife and children at play – and the wife looked very familiar.

PART FOUR
Saturday 26th May

DON RODRIGO

It was early in the morning when Stephen was woken from his deep sleep, by a voice erupting from a man in command – unmistakably a sailor. A further two accompanied him, neither of whom he'd seen before, though one of which gazed at Stephen with a knowing eye, stumbling momentarily over his words before joining back in on the conversion.

All three sailors continued over to the bar and soon had ales in front of them, a rather sober look of disheartenment appearing on them all.

"Nothing but …."

"But what? I command you to speak, Gonzalo. Speak your piece on this phenomenon; oh, but stranger than that. Something is amiss here – surely," said Don Rodrigo. "Nothing but an apparition that will dissipate with the rising of the day's sun, the Lord will see to that."

"Maybe He has no power over such," said the third.

"To speak such words is treason, Arias, and treason put to the Lord is like a lamb put to the slaughter."

"Treason is for captains on board a ship, a weapon of word, phrase, or written command, which sees to it that all under such command remain on a disciplined leash," defended Arias. "Treason in some places will be dealt with regardless of the footing beneath your feet, be it on sea or soil, but to the Lord in Heaven, treason is treason. I for one believe in the Lord's words, no matter what their meaning." Gonzalo needed no proof or miracle to prove why his strong belief in his faith would never whither. Constantinople was the City of God. Ever since the city's founding, artefacts of Christ could be found within its very walls. The blood of Christ may not have been shed here, but it certainly ended up here, even if in its smallest quantity, carried upon artefact as a stain.

"You both talk gibberish. I would wager that when the sun rises that the fog will still be shrouding the city."

"A fog!" gasped Stephen aloud.

All three turned to the interruption. "Who are you boy?" questioned Don Rodrigo. "I was about to make a fortune from these two brainless eunuchs and then you disrupt my play." And the cannonade continued sporadically, echoing throughout the city. "He is the one they refer to as The Templar." Voiced one.

"And how would such knowledge befall you Gonzalo?"

"He is right," said Stephen as he stepped out towards the three, taking time to look out through a small window and into the night, seeing the fog first hand. "I am Stephen, a knight of the Temple."

"A knight of the Temple. You look not old enough to be out of the crib," laughed Don Rodrigo.

Stephen contained his temper as best he could. "To spill your blood for such an insult would be criminal. But alas, not only do I not know your name, but we need every sword we can muster for the defence of the walls."

Don Rodrigo lifted himself from his leant poster, straightening to a height more significant than Stephen's, but only just. "Such words of defence. Grand to meet a soldier so brave," Rodrigo said with sarcasm, and then. "My name is Don Rodrigo," Spoken as though Stephen should have heard of the name.

"At least that's an improvement; soldier is better than boy, wouldn't you agree?" and Stephen's gaze met those of Gonzalo and Arias.

Don Rodrigo was tormented by the stance of the young man to his front and the way in which he looked over his two companions, as though they themselves would party their words with the knights to form an alliance against his.

"If the spilling of blood must be sported then yes, I agree, the wall is the place. But to back down from a fight is not my way."

"The Hospitaller," said Gonzalo.

"The what?"

"Hospitaller; John be his name. Go against this Templar and you go against him." Don Rodrigo was suddenly reminded of his encounter with the Hospitaller.

"And you Arias. Whom do you side with?"

"I side with no one. I have not insulted, nor praised, this wearer of mail."

"The choice is yours, Don Rodrigo." Stephen placed his hand on his sword's hilt.

Don Rodrigo was silent for a second and then looked both his comrades in the eye for a voiced opinion. "I shall retreat till the siege has lifted, after which I shall run you through on first sight."

"I look forward to the meeting, Don Rodrigo."

Rodrigo said not a word but left with a scoff from deep within his throat, "To my station I must attend". The other two sailors said little for a short time, fidgeting slightly but remaining composed.

"It would seem that the lad has frightened poor Rodrigo away."

"Seems true enough," replied Gonzalo and then directed his speech to Stephen. "How would you feel to fill yourself with brew in the accompaniment of sailors?" Stephen looked into both men's eyes before answering. "My mind must not be dulled further if fighting is to be done; and it would appear that further bad omens such as a lingering fog will only make matters worse in the scheme of things to come. But to turn down such an invitation as that of a friendly meet is not my way. A tumbler will not pass my lips this day, but I don't see why words should not be permitted to fall from my tongue." And with that he sat alongside the sailors, taking the place made vacant by Don Rodrigo.

WHY WE FIGHT

Gonzalo made the announcement: "If worse is to come, it shall only be for the peasants, for sailors and soldiers have swords to sway better judgement. A crowd at unrest can always be subjugated by force."

"The peasants, as you call them, are those that we are here to defend. On one hand you announce your faith in the Lord and on the other you curse the right for a common man to fear for his family."

"A man shall fear where he has no faith. If he has no faith then why should I fight? I am here to defend the good word of the Lord. It did seem to me that you were here for the same reason, but now I am unsure. My companion on the other hand has different views, to which I am appalled."

"And what views are they?" asked Stephen.

"Coin, good knight. Coin is all I answer to; a good ransom is what I like. It is fair to say that my chances of living are few, but to chance the making of a fortune is what I seek. But; well… I may do some fighting to help quench my thirst for adventure." And with that the two burst out laughing. "There is nothing quite like the flow of Turkish blood."

"Please, forgive us. Much fighting have we seen already."

"On the walls?" asked Stephen.

"Fighting on the walls is for the faithful," spat Arias.

"The sea." Stephen nodded to himself.

"Where else is there if not the land? We can tell you stories that will make your head spin. The valour of sailors upon the Horn is nothing to be boasted, but to be praised from now until eternity."

Stephen took the opportunity to learn more. "Sleep I've had tonight, a tale would not go astray."

"So be it. Your name again, good knight?" asked Gonzalo.

"Stephen."

"Stephen. It was on the nineteenth day of…."

"Twentieth day."

"Are you sure?"

"The twentieth."

And to the background noise of the cannonade he continued with his tale.

GREEK FIRE

All around him were silent. "It was that day in April when we, including your nemesis, Don Rodrigo, fell upon the waters of Marmora. The wind was strong that day and the walls of

Constantinople soon came to view...."

Mehmet himself was quick to act as the vessels approached the city, three Genoese galleys and a large imperial transport. The galleys were laden heavily with supplies, provided for by the Pope himself, provisions and weapons enough to help in such tight times. The imperial transport was also used to import goods; she held corn, barley, oil, wine and vegetables; all purchased by the emperor's purse in Sicily.

Mehmet was pleased that his watchmen had completed their task well by bringing the alarm to his attention as early as they had; now it was for his admiral to act quickly in order to ensure the vessels did not make the boom. Baltoghlu was his name and his life was at stake; failing here he would be forbidden to return to Mehmet's council alive. The ships must be captured or sunk at all cost.

It took three whole hours for the entire Turkish fleet to be at sail, and a southerly wind made for poor progress. But many vessels were dependent on oars, and here it was seen that thousands of men were hard at work dipping their instruments of seamanship in and out of the salty sea.

It was like a grand show of man versus man, Christian against the Turk. Literally thousands of citizens within the Christian city, and men in their hundreds taking relief from the wall, crowded ever thickly on the slopes near the Acropolis and Hippodrome. Women and children were breathless as the scene unfolded, women on their knees at prayer, and others still giving silent cheer as they held their hands together in tight enthusiasm. The Turks too, where available, took to watching the battle unfold, and Mehmet, along with his staff, stood beyond the walls of Pera, eager for victory to be delivered.

"And the air was filled with the sound of trumpets, symbols and drums." And amongst the sound of music also came the thump, thump, thump, of the drums of coxswains, the sound of oarlocks, all manner of vessels moving in for the attack.

The amount of girth between Christian vessels and city walls was almost too close to bear, but the boom was their sanctuary and so continue they must. Compared with the Sultan's armada and its distance from the supplies being run into Constantinople, it was a surprise to many that no sailor attempted to desert and make a break for the defence of the city by jumping overboard whilst time was still on their side. But all of the sailors upon the decks of the four ships remained loyal to himself and his cause. No man here was arriving on the wind to desert his post in the hour of his need. All on board knew of his likely demise should he venture to Constantinople, but still they pushed on as did Mehmet's Navy, and the distance currently between the two forces was going to allow for a long day to be had by all, for once they did meet there would be a fight like none other seen before upon the waters of the Bosphorus. The scene unfolding in front of the citizens of Constantinople was in comparison to four elephants of war being met head on by a herd of stampeding warthogs. It was early in the afternoon that the vessels from both sides clashed. Oars of the Sultan's navy snapped like thin pieces of wood between thumb and finger, a rain of javelin were flung down from upon the decks of the Christian ships, and a few arquebus could be heard to penetrate the shrieks of war that were thrown up from the clamour of melee between seafaring vessels.

Baltoghlu's voice could be heard against the wind, an order for the good captains of the Christian ships to lower their sails immediately; this they did not do and continue on their way they did, though heavily impeded. But luck remained with the Christians, for the wind continued in their favour and on they sailed, the Sultan's triremes, biremes, fustae, and parandaria, all finding it hard to tackle the larger vessels, their ability to manoeuvre being impeded ten-fold by the wind and increasing waves from waters and close proximity of city wall. It was therefore here that the strategy became apparent; by sailing so close to the wall, the Christians were in fact denying the Turks the ability to assault from all sides simultaneously.

For an entire hour the battle was waged, the Turks trying time and again to gain footing upon the vessels so tall. But the Christians held on, clinging to crownests and ropes, at the port, bow and stern. Weapons from the ships supplies were employed, rocks were gathered, javelin was taken into hand, these rain down upon the enemy like the slashing of rain that stings at the face of a new born baby. Christian arrows were used well against the sailors of their foe, some with armour, though most without. Barrels were also brought up from the hold of the imperial transport, barrels containing a lethal substance – Greek fire. The flammable liquid was poured copiously upon the enemy from high above, not a drop wasted, the crew and vessels of the enemy burning well. Many men could be seen jumping into the waters of the Bosphorus in an effort to put out the flames which burnt their hands, chest, arms, heads and hair.

Suddenly an outcry could be heard from upon the slope of the city, for the wind suddenly died to nothing, the sails showing little sign of assistance from God himself, like dead birds hanging from the branches of a tree, they hung without song. It was now that a phenomenon took place. A particular current that was well known took play and the four vessels drift uncontrollably past the boom and towards the Sultan himself. The sailors at Stephen's left and right could recall quite clearly how close the wall was; practically within touching distance. Baltoghlu then made a decisive decision to ease on the assault, to pull back enough and engage the Christian ships from a distance. From upon barges and other vessels he commenced to engage the ships with cannon fire and fire-bearing lances, though the cannon themselves did little, due to problems with elevation. As for the fire-lances, the Christian crews quickly put out any blaze that ignited upon their decks.

Baltoghlu was growing incessantly tired of making little headway in his quest to board the enemy ships. His attempt at wearing them down in spirit and in regards to arms was proving to be impossible. The order must be given, and so it came to pass. He personally commenced the new attempt to storm the Christians by ramming his trireme into the poop of the imperial transport, the less endowed of the Christian ships when considering munitions and manpower.

High above, from the slopes of the city where the crowd grew larger still, confusion reigned, for the battle was a melee of such close proximity, one such Christian ship being surrounded by more than 70 enemy vessels, whereby almost half were parandaria filled to the brink with enemy foot soldiers.

The Turkish ships were persistent, and where one would be disabled permanently from battle, as Greek fire was poured upon them from the Christian deck of the imperial transport, another would take its place. Man after man would endeavour to board, to have his hands cut off at the wrist or just below the elbow, and heads were being removed with the single swoop of axe or sword in the hands of a determined Greek. The galleys being manned by Genoese sailors were also kept busy as parandaria clashed against the side of the vessels, the enemy putting much effort into trying to board them.

Phlatanelas commanded the imperial transport well, a genius he was, but weapons were running low. To hold out for much longer was doubtful, to defend for long was impossible. And suddenly, as though a signal had been passed to the Genoese captains aboard the accompanying three ships, all converged around the imperial transport. The four ships were then lashed together by rope and chain, to work as one, to either live a victory or die as heroes, one and all. Cheers could be heard from within the city walls, great shouts of enthusiasm being passed to the men defending their ships so gallantly. And the Turks too took to encouraging their sailors, Mehmet himself being drawn into the waters to shout curse and encouragement, his horse up to its belly in water. The battle was being watched by so many and was lasting so long. It was now late afternoon and the Turk kept coming, more men replacing the fallen, more ships to take the place of those disabled. The Christians were going to lose, their power was diminishing, and they were going to be drowned from this world.

But then, as though by miracle, a wind lashed up from the north in the face of the setting sun. The sails gathered the wind and the ships made their aggressive move towards the boom as the light of the day commenced to say it's goodnight. The Turks could see little and organization was hard to come by. Then out of the night came the sound of trumpets calling, a Christian rescue was being mounted.

So loud was the call from trumpet that shudders were felt down the spines of many Turks, each believing this to be a major assault upon them, but nothing could be further from the truth. The boom was opened and the four ships – three Genoese and the imperial transport – were escorted to safety within the Golden Horn.

And the anger in Mehmet grew as he called Admiral Baltoghlu to a meeting. Carrying a wound to the eye, the disheartened sailor approached to be advised that a punishment befitting his failure was to be carried out on his person. He was to be beheaded. On hearing of the punishment several high-ranking sailors spoke out in his defence and gave praise where praise was deserved, and instead of death Baltoghlu was removed from his official holdings. He was to walk the earth as a recluse, to remain the rest of his life a poor and broken man.

"I tell you," continued Gonzalo, "if we killed a hundred, we killed ten thousand, and not a single Christian lost to the battle at hand, although I must admit, a dozen or so died sometime after due to injury."

"And the day after this."

"You speak of what, Arias?"

"The collapse of the Bactatinian on the Lycus Valley," replied Arias.

TO COUNSEL

Arias now looked to Stephen. "A tower so huge. It was brought down by the concentrated cannonade of batteries assigned the task, but the Sultan failed to assault the breach. Such an assault would have been successful, but we managed to sew the breach by our usual means. It was the day after the great sea battle, on the twenty-first. Fortunate we were, that the Sultan was not available to give orders to his troops."

"A city at siege and not a commander in sight," Stephen thought out loud.

"It is said that he was preparing further action, for it was the following day that the Sultan's armada crossed the land by cradle," added Arias.

"Yes indeed," nodded Gonzalo, then turning his head and quite obviously referring to the fog: "Two miracles of great fortune in as many days that was; and now we have the reverse. It seems that much evil is coming our way. So many bad omens in the past few days that few can deny that our hope has but many holes which need attending."

With those words, Arias smiled, "I told you so."

And Gonzalo turned with a spat of venom: "But I do hold much hope that the good Lord will aid us all, even those that hold contempt against him."

Stephen was invigorated with the stories, and as the cursing continued between the two sailors he thought of the heroics involved and spoke out loud. "Heroes all, I have no doubt. Such fighting, such comradeship."

"You sound anew to this life of slaying, young Templar, how be your sword; a virgin or veteran?"

Stephen knew of his sword's history, and although he himself had not spilled blood, his sword had. "As veteran as they come, Arias. More men's blood has caked this steel as you have bedded women."

And Gonzalo laughed out loud, "Then your sword is as virgin as they come."

"Enough of your lies, Gonzalo. For I have bed more women than you. A man of religion you are; women are for me as the Lord's word is to you," condemned Arias.

"Do not loan the Lord's name out to such comparison, Arias, for the day will come when you too shall see the true light of the day." Gonzalo was then quick to control his composure and added: "One more story to bid our farewell."

"You mean one more story to change the subject."

"Another story for you, Stephen; Arias may leave or listen, it is for him to decide," and as Gonzalo talked, the rising dawn saw the thickening fog shroud the city.

INTERLUDE

Being 21 years of age meant much for having no experiences in regards to battle, but Mehmet was prudent and with this his commanders found security, so on the Friday, after the meeting with Stephen, he did call for a meeting to be held. But the council didn't start off too well.

Mehmet didn't like advice unless such was warranted and he'd be damned if he would allow Halil of his inner council sway what he believed was his better judgement. Words rose from the pasha's throat to rumble words of defeat and stories that a fleet from the west was on its way to Constantinople. But others were quick to put a thorn in his side and most rallied around Mehmet saying how bold he'd been and how sure they were that he'd done the right thing in regards to the commencement of the siege. But most assuredly they were after caution in action.

Some believed that Zaganos was the instigator of what was to follow, and the other commanders simply followed suit, inspiring Mehmet. So here he stood with his fist buried in his hand. What Mehmet was hearing from his council was pure delight: Action was needed and needed immediately.

Mehmet did turn to Zaganos and gave orders for him to go amongst the troops to seek word from them:

"Go amongst the men, Zaganos, ride all afternoon if you must, but get an answer. What do the men of my great army wish?" And the wish from all was for an immediate assault to take place against the Christians cowering behind the walls of Constantinople; the word was strong to press forth with an immediate attack.

So the decision was easy. The citizens of the city had already been given three choices; surrender, conversion to Islam, or death by the scimitar. The first two choices had been waived quite abruptly. An attack would henceforth follow.

Christians from within the Sultan's camp did then send messages to the defenders of Constantinople of the impending assault via notes attached to arrows, Christians who would soon be slashing away at other Christians for the glory of gold and ransom.

THE HORN

It was the day after the move by cradle, of the Sultan's boats into the Golden Horn, that a plan was devised to impede a blow to Mehmet's arsenal, however, proposals made by Captain Giacomo Coco of Trebizond were delayed until 24th April in order to prepare the Venetian ships. Word got out and due primarily to the rising anger felt by many Genoese a further postponement was made. To the Genoese it was a disgrace that they should be kept from the planned assault against the masses of Turk trireme, bireme, fustae and parandaria, as they felt strongly about loaning a helping hand; after all, why should the glory of such a strike go to the Venetians alone?

So the strike was planned for pre-dawn on Saturday 28th, but unbeknown to the assault force, a Genoese of Pera, who received wages from the Sultan, advised his employer via messenger of the impending strike to come. It was quite understandable that amongst the citizens of Pera there were many spies. Some believed that it was wise to advise the Sultan of any pending attack, that the Christians may mean to deliver upon his vessels of the Horn, or upon siege machinery in front of the wall, in order that they may receive special compensations. It was also quite clear to many in Pera that the current neutrality between themselves and the Turk would not last long once the city of Constantinople had fallen. Their individual safety was therefore their soul concern.

A Venetian and Genoese transport, along with two Venetian galleys, approached the Turkish fleet. In command were Trevisano and his deputy Zaccaria, under them, forty men of oars to each vessel. This advance of ships was followed by three fustae, to which each was full to capacity with 72 souls.

As the vessels approached a light could be seen to flare up from within the walls of Pera, high above and easily viewable for some distance. Coco, as for the others, put it off as nothing of importance, for all was quiet except the splashing of water upon the sides of the boats that they commanded. It was now that impatience was getting the better of Coco, who gained ground on the slower ships, and soon found himself urging the fustae on silently. Suddenly cannon upon the shore opened fire. The Turk had been lying in wait, informed well by their spy in Pera. Coco was the first to die that day.

The bales of wool protecting each side of the larger ships did well against the torment of the cannons, softening the blow of each ball as it hit and the sailors aboard took to pales in order to extinguish the fires that ignited everything around. Such exhausting work made for little time to aid the sailors of the smaller vessels scramble aboard the larger ships.

The cannon fire could be directed most skilfully by the light provided by smouldering fires and flares, and as each shot reverberated through the night air more smaller vessels were sunk, those on board forced to swim ashore as best they could due to lack of aid from the larger ships. The galleys too were targeted well, more so the vessel under command of Trevisano that took on so much water that she had to be abandoned.

It was now that the light of day crept up over the horizon, and as the rays of the morning sun commenced its dance across the waters of the Golden Horn, so did the Turk fleet within the Horn which now set out to attack.

The fighting continued for an hour and half whereupon both forces retreated to their stations.

The Christians counted their losses; one galley and fustae, along with 50 sailors lost in the heat of battle, whereby only one of the enemy ships was delivered to its grave. To add further to the Christian misery of the morning's activity 40 sailors who had swum ashore to the Turkish lines were summarily executed in full sight of all those upon the walls of the city. The emperor took the news with great anger and had his men escort 260 Turk prisoners to positions on the wall where they were beheaded without second thought: This was eye for an eye.

THE FOG

The cannonade continued sporadically, echoing throughout the city, as into this morning fog Stephen did walk with mind fast at thought in regards to battle and the part that he was going to play in the near future; would he live or die? He recalled when he first decided to attend the defence of Constantinople. He minded little for sacrificing his blood and bone, for Jesus had given Himself for the torment of others, in the hope that salvation may be brought to bear on those more deserving. Now, since his meeting with Clover, he had received a second thought, a new breath of air into his lungs so wondrous that the feeling was unbelievable. Such thoughts however were kept buried deep most of the time, for he was primarily here to fight, not to flirt.

And as he walked the path he knew so well, from alehouse to wall, he couldn't help but think of his beloved. What was she doing this morning? He wanted to see her, but neglect the wall he'd done too easily over the past few days. Today he must pay more heed to his sworn duty.

Onwards he trod, through the mist so thick, voices in the backdrop of misty white reaching his ears with teasing mystery. Here he was, in the month of May, a veil of bad omen shrouding the city and the country around. Such a phenomenon was unheard of in these parts, especially at this time of year which was normally set aside for the roses that came of blossom amongst the many gardens and hedgerows.

Before he reached the wall he heard a shout from somewhere behind: - "the Spirit that is all divine, is departing us this day. Don't you see; the fog? The fog is concealing His withdrawal from the city He once loved so much."

Stephen did his best then to try and ignore the voices and goings on around him, for the wall must be attended to.

On reaching his post he could hear the faint voices of several of the mercenaries. The quiet on the wall was more so now than ever before, and even with the fog so thick, the batteries played their part as the cannon fire continued relentlessly, and was the only thing that pierced the silence to any great extent.

Would the Turk attempt to approach unseen under the cover that nature was providing, or would they too be weary of the omen's message?

His first instinct was to search out John, but something inside of him advised against it. He was a man unto his own and he should not need to seek the support of others to carry him through the torment of the siege. He'd already met with embarrassment when the sailor Don Rodrigo was advised that John be sided with Stephen, hence the sailor backing down with second thought far from mind. He did feel inadequate, being saved from a fight due primarily to a man that wasn't even present at the time of crisis. Don Rodrigo had backed down through sheer panic. And as his mind lingered a voice was heard, for the figure of a man stepped up beside him.

"Did you hear of John?" asked the commander of the mercenary.

"No. What is the word?"

"In order that he be able-bodied to do his work he has joined with one of the reserves. He will be called upon to defend the wall, I have no doubt of that, but meanwhile he shall be well employed as a man of medicine."

Stephen looked at the mercenary and then out towards an enemy that couldn't be seen, though was most certainly present. "I shall probably not see him again," he said with such a straight face and monotonous tone.

"You don't sound too disappointed in being torn from your friend."

"A friend he is, but we are all here to defend the women and children of this great city."

"To defend one's brother in arms is also sacred, not to take recognition away from the glorious religion we shield with our souls."

"Do you think the Turk will attack soon?"

"No, not yet." The commander then paused for a second or two and turning to walk back to his post said: "You will know soon enough when their intention nears."

THE STOCKADE

The bombardment against the walls was relentless and by far increased in its volume over the past twenty-four hours. It was therefore quite obvious to all that an intended assault against the city would take place sooner rather than later, and this notion had already been confirmed by the arrows shot over the walls from Christians within the Turkish camp. Notes attached advised all within of the conclusions drawn from the council meeting on Friday.

It seemed more than coincidental how the cannonade was increased just a day prior to a decision being made in regards to the assault. It was to the amusement of many to suggest that Mehmet had somehow intimidated, and instigated, the very foundation of all thought in the minds of his council and warriors, in order for an immediate assault to be carried out, but how was such plotted?

The stockade of the Mesoteichion was now targeted with more cannon than before. The damage wrought was horrific, but the damage was reinforced and built upon, barrels filled with earth and planks for the containment of the fill. Segments of the old wall were not wasted, and the defence stood strong. With great courage and will power, the citizens and soldiers, of all ages and ranks, put to mending what the Turk did destroy.

All within the defence could hear quite easily the difference in the volume of fire being targeted against the portion of wall on the Mesoteichion, known widely by now as the 'stockade', when compared with other areas. Even from where he stood, Stephen could hear the hundreds of volunteers, both soldier and citizen alike, ferrying materials up to the wall in order that it be reinforced and built strong. Between the inner and middle wall they worked feverishly, the continuous move of soil from within the ditch – being formed by the digging – ferried to the engineers. Volunteers still came now, the weary being replaced by fresh workers, along Middle Street, turning left at the Gate of Charisius, and continuing down towards the Gate of St Romanus. From his current distance and visual, in particular with regards to the fog, nothing much could be seen by Stephen, not even the faces of those closest to the wall, behind him, could be made out.

His sweet Clover. Would she be working on the wall, would she have devoted herself to replenishing the defence; or would she be at the hospital, tending the wounded? There was more than one hospital in the area, quite a few larger ones existed further from the wall. Clover's station was but a small pen in comparison to some of the others. It was logical to Stephen therefore that Clover would be helping out with the refortification of the stockade, putting her life in danger at this very moment. If he were a man, which he believed whole heartedly, should he be more concerned with the defence, or a pretty woman. But this woman was the one he loved, felt so deeply for, someone so beautiful that it was beyond comprehension. As Stephen saw it, the defence was more at stake at the Mesoteichion. Where he currently defended was standing fine. There was no pending assault of foot soldiers from what he could tell.

He would remove himself from the wall temporarily. He'd been standing guard since first light in any case and deserved a rest.

CLOVER III

Instead of the Mesoteichion, Stephen attended his intuition and visited the hospital; there he found his beloved curled up upon a bench with a blanket wrapped tight around her fragile form. She appeared quite exhausted, the idea emphasized by the amount of noise coming from the cobbled street, to which the outside lane adjoined; it was enough to wake the dead, but still she slept.

He approached stealthily and looked over the sleeping form, so beautiful and peaceful, enough for one to forget the siege for a moment. Stephen then noticed, quite easily, that her face had a few minor scratch marks upon it. Four fingers of one hand were also in view; the other concealed by the blanket. Her fingernails were clogged with dirt, a bruise to the back of the hand, with a large graze down one finger. It was quite evident that she had in fact been working on the defence as most Christian women had.

Such a delight it was for this man of mail to see his woman out of harm's way, even if temporary that may be. He couldn't bring himself to wake her and felt guilty for the thought having even entered his mind. She'd done so much more than he had, but his turn would come.

He looked around himself then and returned quickly to the door, closing it quietly before placing himself at its foot to aid in being alerted to anyone trying to enter. Here he slept, but for a short span only, for Clover woke soon enough, refreshed from her mornings work on the defences.

"Stephen. What are you doing here?"

Stephen was woken immediately on hearing his name mentioned in such a loving way. He was quick to his feet and wiped the remaining tiredness from his eyes before smiling. "Clover. I couldn't help but search you out. I was worried about you, in particular when I heard so many people heading towards the Mesoteichion." And before the sentence was finished he'd closed the gap between himself and Clover, the palms of his hand rubbing lovingly up and down her upper arms as she sat upon the bench. "Your hand, Clover, so bruised and withered," he then tenderly touched her cheek, "and your face. You've done too much labour this day, my love. I hope the rest you just gained has seen you recover, even if slightly."

"Yes, Stephen. I think the sleep I've had has done me well, but to return to duty I must."

"Your duty upon the wall should be suspended for the time. Your skills as a nurse are in much more need; if not right now then certainly later. What if you aren't rested enough when the men need you most? Your tender fingers, the hands that support them, and the arms that command the mechanical respect for working such gifts. You must refrain from approaching too close to the wall, my love. You are needed elsewhere, and you know I speak the truth."

"You are right, Stephen. I have forgotten my teachings, my skills as a nurse; and even if minor they must take precedence." And with that said Stephen did smile as he had never smiled before. "And you, you have taken leave from the wall?"

"I felt an urge so great, it welled inside me like a cup being filled by the carafe of a thirst crazed giant. The urge was so strong that it couldn't be ignored. I had to see you at all costs. My leave from the wall is only temporary, but I have sworn to be available at the time of counting. When needed most, my flesh and bone will be upon the wall."

"I think that time comes soon, Stephen. The cannonade has been increased; I fear the worst."

Stephen grabbed out at Clover then and brought her to her feet, hugging hard, almost to breaking point, his lady, and she too returned the gesture, holding onto her man as though there was no tomorrow. Here they remained, not a word spoken, until Clover pushed away.

"I am worried for you, Stephen. I don't doubt your courage or good nature, but I know of your inexperience. You have followed the Lord's word all of your life, and now you have sworn to give your body to Him, to serve whole-heartedly."

"No, my love, I am sworn to serve you," and they were drawn together again, lips touching lips, as each embraced the other in what was a final commitment for their show of unanimous affection. "I swear this day that no Turk will endanger your life, for if the wall does give way to those in front, I shall save no time in rallying at your side with sword in hand."

"Stephen, I have some bread, olives, and cheese; honey pastry has even fallen my way."

"You've planned a feast fit for a king."

"A feast fit for Constantine, but none will pass his lips. I intended to save it for tomorrow, a picnic for the two of us, but.... Let's go now, my pet, feast whilst this evil fog shields the day. Let us eat to our future and see to it that all days, from this one forth, are nothing but improvements on which to build." And together they left the makeshift hospital and headed to the one place they knew would be vacant, the cemetery in which Clovers adopted parents did rest in eternal peace.

"Clover, the view has changed since last we were here."

"Indeed. I should think that no vessel sails the Marmora this day, for fear of falling into enemy hands."

"Just think; what a miracle it would be if a fleet of Christians, using the fog as a shield, was to enter the Golden Horn with supplies of men and sustenance."

Clover looked into Stephen's eyes as they sat. "Let us forget the siege exists. This moment in time sees us in the dawn of a final winter's day, where migrating birds fill the skies and men of war exist as sentries standing their posts, and nothing more."

"I believe that very thing." And the cannonade continued, though slightly muffled by distance.

The bread was broken, still fairly fresh, and eaten slowly along with the olives, the flavours and smells savoured for what they were. "Even my mother would have trouble preparing a meal as good as this. I hope you did not spend too much in acquiring such fine morsels."

"A requisite which is undeniably worth what I did indeed spend. If I had authority over this city I could not have achieved better."

"And the bread," motioned Stephen.

"Just a few days old, though it tastes like one."

"The fog has moistened it delightfully."

"So even the most evil of omens has some good in them."

And they continued to eat, their eyes locked to the other, all around forgotten, their predicament put aside; no siege existed at that moment.

Clover drew the honey pastry wrapped in cloth from the basket. "I wish I had time to warm it for you, Stephen."

"No need, for the love in my heart will warm the pastry well enough. By the time it reaches my stomach it will be a burning furnace, as hot as the flames from a dragon's mouth." Clover laughed playfully as she chewed and swallowed, their silence one of comfort, their looks for one another sheer bliss; hours seemed like minutes, and as they lay there, their arms wrapped around each other, the man and woman fell into a deep sleep.

When they woke it was just after dusk.

"Stephen, are you awake?"

"I have been resting, thinking of things to come. What shall become of us, do you think?"

"I am sure you have already made your mind up in regards to that." Concluded Clover, as they gathered their things together in silence and commenced a return to the tasks that awaited them both.

THE LIGHT

All day the city remained under the blanket of fog, men, women, and children, going about their business as best they could, though scared to the heart for the omen that persisted. And as the sun sank, the fog remained, diminished slightly, but was lifting unnoticeably and slowly. Then, within the hour, the fog was gone.

The fog was an omen too soon after the previous sign, but all was not over yet, for high above and looking out over the city was the dome of the Church of the Holy Wisdom. Like a beacon or lighthouse a strange light danced around the upper most portion of this building, an unexplained phenomenon that set the hearts racing within all that experienced the sight. Vessels upon the waters of the Marmora, tall ships in the Golden Horn, Soldiers upon the walls and even Turks of the Sultan's entourage of forces; all could see the spectacle. Every person giving witness to this brought forward his or her ideas on its presence, good or bad. The majority of Christians saw the omen as something heinous, though in a religious sense, whereby the soldiers within the Turk camp were advised in time by the old and wise of the Sultan's council that the light was a grand spectacle granted them by Allah himself.

Clover stopped momentarily and looked behind, a feeling of despair falling over her. Looking up at the light that seemed to have no logical explanation and gave little comfort to the happenings of the previous days. A cold shiver suddenly enveloped her from head to toe. She let out a little gasp.

"What is it my love?" questioned Stephen, wondering as to why Clover had suddenly halted. He noticed then her jaw, ajar slightly and eyes tinted in what could only be explained as a display of fear.

Stephen was more worried now and shook her gently. "Clover, what is it?"

She said slowly: "The light." She lifted her hand and pointed her finger with grace, "The light upon the church, dancing around the dome of…." She broke down in fear and shook, tears commencing to well and flow from her eyes. "I don't think I can take much more."

Stephen let the basket fall from his grasp and fell to his knees where he could more readily comfort his lady.

The Church was a good mile behind, and from such a distance the knight in mail could see quite clearly that no fire was present. It was as though fairies had come to play as the site, to give their own praise to the Lord in the only way they knew.

"It will be alright, Clover. Trust me. Look at the light. It dances, prances, and plays. No evil could possibly be emitted from such a gracious flow of mystery. The light speaks of celebration, of praise for the City of God. No fear should be read into this phenomenon. Please Clover, stand now and you will feel no fear. Look at the light for what it is, a beautiful reminder of the Lord's existence."

And Clover did just that, taking heed to what her man had spoken, and indeed it did appear so. The light was nothing to fear. It was majestic, if nothing else. "You are right, Stephen, it is rather pretty."

Her shaking had subsided quite quickly and a smile appeared to light up her face, aided by the presence of the moon so high above. Again they held each other tight and looked deep into one another's eyes. "So fragile you are."

"And protection I need."

"Protection I can give, and love too. I am a man of my bond and I give such to you this very moment in time."

Clover was pleased to hear such words. "You are a man to be trusted even without the accompaniment of such a bond." And the dancing light was forgotten.

"But such a bond will be given, my love, my bond that I shall be by your side always, even when upon the wall slaying heathen Turk."

Clover placed two fingers upon his lips. "Such words of hate are not warranted tonight, Stephen. Words of hate shall not spoil this day."

He took a short breath in acknowledgement, for they had both been drawn to each other quite strongly over the past few days. "The bond I give today shall last a lifetime, longer still, for life in heaven is eternal."

"Such a long life with you will be a gift like no other."

"I pledge my soul to you, my skin and bone. My life is yours"

"And mine, yours."

"No harm will befall you, Clover, not whilst I am here. And when we depart this city it will be together, to be wed at first opportunity."

Clover kissed him then, more feverishly, a pounding of the heart accompanying their hold on each other. Their hands fell and rose, caressing small of back and nape of neck, their love grew now, even more than before, and that indeed did not seem possible, for their love was already overflowing from all pores.

Their lips drew apart and Clover opened her eyes. "Let us not wait, Stephen. Let us wed here, in the City of God. Let He be witness to our love and bond, let the city of Constantinople be a place to be remembered." Her hands fell to his torso. "I do fear the worst for my home and I see no way of returning in the future. This is where our love has blossomed, let this be the place where it is set forever, to never be swayed or judged."

Stephen smiled as each word passed her lips, his eyes wandering from Clovers, left and to right, and left again. "To wed here is a decision most pleasing to us both. I would feel honoured to have God present as we take vows. Our marriage to one another will never be forgotten, dear Clover, for it is too strong not to be recognized."

And the cannonade continued sporadically, echoing throughout the city. "Let us retire for the night and seek counsel on this tomorrow."

"Retire we must but to separate quarters. The wall must be manned when possible. I know my work is not neglected, for the wall I defend is of little consequence, but I must still return."

"If a duty you need to perform, then to duty you must go."

"I shall see you at first light, my love, and a new life shall be born for us both." A final kiss brought the curtain to fall upon their rendezvous, and outstretched arms they both did have, each moving back from one another but in plain view. And as they parted he did slowly turn, each of them to head towards where their individual responsibility lay. As they parted, a great pain suddenly fell upon Stephen, for he didn't wish to leave Clover's side. The pull was so great that he stopped and turned, to see Clover walking off towards the direction of the Church of Christ Pantepoptes. Then, as though aware of her companion's burden, she did turn to see him standing there.

They raced towards each other that moment, Clover dropping the basket she did just retrieve. No words were necessary that moment, they just held each other tight. "There is one other thought that has come to mind," said Stephen. "And that is John."

"John? What of John?"

"He can wed us this very night. He is stationed nearby with the reserve. He will not be hard to find at this time of night. If we are lucky, he would have just eaten."

JOINED AS ONE

Luck indeed was with them both. Nicephorus Palaeologus, a keen man of arms who took great measures to ensure the readiness of his small force, commanded the reserve stationed at the Church of the Holy Apostles. It was he who advised Stephen with a smile, that John could be found in one of the small monastery buildings attached to the triple church of the Pantocrator.

As the couple approached they witnessed a soldier being carried away from the front of the building, bandaged well around the torso and in deep sleep. On entering they found to their surprise that John had summoned Maria to his side and both at present were scrubbing hard the bench on which they had just completed their work.

"Maria," shouted Clover, and rushed to hug her friend. Stephen smiled too.

"So what brings a knight of the Temple to this part of the city?" asked John.

Stephen wasted no words. "We wish to wed. We were of hope that you could conduct the ceremony."

"It would normally be against my better judgement," said John. "Actually," a second thought coming to mind, "an old friend, a lay philosopher of some years back. George Scholarius acquired a monastic name back in 1445, Gennadius. He is a scholar of these parts and quite against the union of the Latin and Greek Church in many ways; do you know of him?"

"No."

"A great traveller of the Western World he is indeed. I think such a union between man and woman would do his health well at this time in siege. Come Stephen, wed you shall be, but I shall not perform the ceremony, for all honour would be lost me if I were not to bear proper witness."

Both John and Stephen knocked politely on the great oak door of George's cell, who was busy looking over papers, and on hearing of the proposed ceremony was quick to smile that monkish grin. And with a small ceremony, in the sight of God, John and Maria as witnesses, both Clover and Stephen were wed, conducted at the hands of George Gennadius.

A room in which the couple could retire was offered by John, but refused, for Clover had a room not far from the Church of St John in Trullo and a walk is what was needed right now. They both wished to look upon this day as something very special.

TO STAND HIS GROUND

A little later on in the evening, though not witnessed by Stephen or Clover, more lights were seen, far afield and beyond the camp of those in league to destroy the Christians forever. People gathered to view the lights, campfires in the distance? The Army of John Hunyadi, has he come to the rescue? Let it be recalled how in 1444, the great Hungarian John Hunyadi and Vladislav, did attempt a crusade against the Turk, but such was crushed in the battle of Varna. But alas, the lights were nothing of the sort. Scouts from the Sultan's camp were even sent to scrounge the area for proof of what was witnessed from a distance, but nothing was uncovered. The light's source was a complete mystery and only God could explain their existence.

And news of the lights travelled fast.

Outside of the emperor's palace, where council was fervent, the bustle of work and flight of arrows into the night continued unabated. The Turks were putting into place their well thought out strategy, and all through the night, encouraged by the music of many a band, they filled in the foss with whatever they could find. The bodies of their dead were piled in, as one after another bore the fatal brunt of a crossbow dart or arrow from bow.

A new attempt was then made, an appeal to the emperor for him to board a ship and make well an escape from the besieged city. The emperor then spoke out loud at his ministers, in particular Lucas Notaras, voicing once again his intention to stay and fight amongst his people, even if he was to die by the blade of a scimitar. Constantine was a brave soul and came from a large family.

Born unto his parents, Manuel II and his Empress Helena, he was one of six boys and fourth oldest, only Demetrius and Thomas being younger than he, and in respective order. His parent's first eldest was to be emperor, Emperor John VIII, who died in October 1448 in Mistra, after living a life whereby he kept a promise, to his father, to keep up negotiations in regards to unification between the Latin and Greek Church. He was, however, to keep short of making any commitment which might serve to destabilize the well-being of the citizens of Constantinople, or make promise of anything else that may prove impossible to carry out to the fullest.

Theodore; being second eldest, had died of the plague in July 1448, his only daughter being married to king John II of Cyprus in 1438; Despot of Morea in the year 1407. It was to his discredit that the Turks destroyed the Hexamilion, a fortification of which Theodore did raise, which passed from Corinth to Isthmus. Constantine re-established the fortification in 1446, however, the Turks once again demolished the wall after pounding the structure with his artillery for two weeks. Once Theodore's brothers, Constantine and Thomas, both lucky to escape with their lives, had fled the scene, the Sultan of the times saw to it that the wall was destroyed once and for all, down to its very foundation.

Andronicus; the third eldest son died in march 1428, and was rather thought of as insignificant, other than the fact that he'd seen to the selling of Thessalonica, in 1423, to the Venetians.

Constantine was fourth in line and born in 1404. He saw much conflict in 1427, standing side-by-side with his brother John, and by early the following year was wed to Princess Magdalena, and received lands of the Peloponnese as a dowry where he'd been fighting hard against the Franks. It was a sad end to a short marriage when, Theodora, his rechristened wife, died in 1430. He had no heirs.

Again he wed, to Catherine, in the year of our Lord, 1441. This marriage, as for the first, did not last long, for she died after just a year.

He was further disheartened in 1450, when Helena, his mother, died on the 23rd day of March; but before that day much did happen. The fifth eldest son was Demetrius, a great believer in the Greek religion and not softened by Latin beliefs, as per his brother John, who treated with tenterhooks the Latin Church. It will be remembered here however, that such a tender treatment of the situation and conflict between both religions, be persevered with for the people and their stability in life, and nothing more. Demetrius did show his true character when in 1442 he moved to take control of Constantinople for himself, with aid from a large Turkish force, but Constantine who arrived with reinforcements put down the manoeuvre. Demetrius was given Selymbria, on his brother Theodore's death, a rather soft treatment for such guilty actions. On hearing of John's death in 1448, Demetrius again hurried to Constantinople, this time to claim the throne for himself. His ploy was to gather support from those that supported the Greek church and no other. His dislike of the Latin Church went unabated. Unfortunately for Demetrius, the crown power of sovereignty went to their mother, Helena, who, understanding the ways of the world, the city, and her children, did ensure that Constantine was made emperor. The crowning of such a position was conducted in Mistra on 16th January, 1449, after Manuel Palaeologus and Alexius Philanthropenus ported the crown over much land and sea. It was in this same year that Demetrius took control of Mistra and its southernmost portion in Morea, whereby Thomas took Patras into his palm along with the north; Thomas was the youngest and ever fond of Constantine.

Constantine contemplated his life; he was thankful that the scum Albanian mercenaries were not present on the walls of Constantinople as they were at the Hexamilion fortification; their lack of courage was disheartening at best. Now 49, tall and with shoulders square, a commanding look of authority and able to yield much loyalty and devotion from his council and the citizens of Constantinople, he swore unto himself to stay in Constantinople till the bitter end if need be. Such a great administrator he was, and loved by all.

PART FIVE
Sunday 27th May

A COWARD TRUE

The Sunday morning started as with many of the past, with an opening of thunderous fire from the batteries dominating the high ground to the cities northwest. The cannonade didn't slow, the pounding rhythm ceaseless in its torment and damage. It was the stockade that took the brunt of the fire, a concentration so fierce that a section of the repaired wall was brought down temporarily by several shots fired by Urban's monster. On the third shot fired, a fragment of wood did pierce Giustiniani, whereby the great man was forced to remove himself for treatment. His personal supervision of the refortification of the stockade would be sorely missed. And the news of Giustiniani's wound did spread amongst the man as wild as a fire out of control.

The word on a lot of lips at the moment was of a pending assault. What if the position was attacked during Giustiniani's absence?

The emperor himself made provisions readily available for subordinates upon the wall to continue with the work on the fortification of the Mesoteichion. To push the work harder during their commander's absence was a must if the torment of a victorious Muslim assault was to be swept from their minds, and furthermore, a busy mind was sheltered from fear. The people en masse must not be given the opportunity to dwell upon the situation as a negative, for negative thought did loan to defeat as easily in battle as it did in the political world, or a lion dying of hunger due to giving up on the chase of the game. Negative thought was nothing more than a danger if not averted and such thought was pure poison. The news of the injury to Giustiniani even reached Stephen's ear, who appeared quite refreshed and relaxed, amusingly at peace with himself – at least to the mercenary around. The love in his heart was medicine enough.

The Pillar Alfred stood beside the young knight as they looked out amongst the field of tents and moving figures, and Stephen said: "The Turk gathers well the material he needs to thwart our defences. Never a dull moment amongst the throng. Forever gaining material and readying weapons."

"Indeed he does. But does material exist enough to thwart our courage?"

"A good rest you must have had, Stephen. You have the men talking."

"For the time I've been absent?"

"No man; for the company you keep. It's rumoured that a fair maiden has cast a spell upon your very soul; that you've been seized by an angel and can't escape."

"Escape is not my plan."

"With a maiden as fair as the one rumoured to have leashed you, a plan of escape would be exactly what I'd be seeking, not from her clutches, but from the Sultan's choking, grasp," said the Pillar.

The two men looked at each other then. "Is that the suggestion normally given by a man who has spent so many years at war for others?"

"No, Stephen, just the advice of a man who is growing old and tired of fighting their battles." Alfred was most serious that minute in time.

"It is possible that I already have a plan of escape."

"I hope for your sake you do."

"And what meaning is there behind such words? You believe us beaten, no doubt."

There was then a lapse in the conversation and the Basilica gave out another enormous 'boom'. A change of tone then came about. "Paul the Puller has been seen talking of you."

"And what does the Puller have to say which should be whispered behind one's back?"

"I fight for myself Stephen, unless paid good coin; and when I say good, I mean outlandish. The company I keep changes like the seasons – sure, some do stay, though never long. Part by death or by choice, those in the ranks normally change seasonally. But mark my words here and now, Stephen. I am not a defeatist, but the wall will fall and the battle will be lost, that I am most sure of. When the tide of Turk starts to gain a foothold within this great city, many men will turn and run. But some have other business, Paul is one such man. Watch your back, Stephen. The Puller rarely misses a shot, even if out of anger or urgency. Guard your back well, for you have enemies within these walls as well as out. You have unknowingly angered a coward and that wounded man shall seek out his vengeance even in the face of death. His feelings of vengeance towards you will protect his nerve from fear of death, even with the Turk knocking at the yew stave he carries."

"Thank you for the warning, Alfred. Such information in my ear is like gold in my purse."

"Ah, such warnings matter little with one as bold as yourself, I'm sure. Besides, tomorrow will probably see me telling you of our pending victory. Anyway, you have more at stake. You have to watch the maiden, before she hooks you, Stephen."

"Like a fish, ah?"

"Aye, like a fish, yes."

"Then would you do me the honour of removing this damn harpoon?"

Alfred stood agape at the riddle; then: "You have been hooked."

"I was wed shortly after the dancing lights of the Holy Wisdom dissipated."

Alfred slapped him hard on the back. "Well, man, you truly need to consider yourself carefully now. More power of mind has a woman than the entire army you see to your front. You may shiver at the thought of being captured alive by the Turk, but a wife can move mountains if she so desires. I trust you spent a good night aloft, perhaps without sleep these past 12 hours. But what of your vows; the Temple? Your ancestors will be turning in their graves this day."

"I have thought long and hard. Although I have rights to the habit, and have a history of ancestry that depicts my future, I can't help to acknowledge that abolishment means exactly that. I have a life to live. I shall see this siege through as promised, but will not shy from the opportunity to rally when my wife needs me most."

"I know of what you speak, and it does worry me so. Many men here today have family to consider, most of whom are shackled to wageless employment. Consider a break in the wall if you can, a dribble of Turk gaining foothold within the walls of this great city, even if momentarily. All it takes is for a few poorly footed souls to reflect on their wives and children, then; we all be damned. A break in the defences will soon see the floodgates open, a pouring of scimitar like you've never seen before. The streets will flow red with the blood of these good city folk. No one will be spared. I know you will not falter too early, Stephen, but a man must tend to his flock as eagerly as he attends his post on the wall, no matter how large that flock may be."

"And you would blame me not for withdrawing."

"I too will withdraw when the time is right, but remain to keep these mercenaries in check I must; I may yet get my chance at capturing a good fortune in ransom. Besides, if I am to presume that this band of mercenaries belongs to me, then I am to assume the responsibilities for their actions. You are here because you have followed your heart, I am here because I have followed my greed. You will not be cursed for withdrawing, but Paul the Puller may be of another opinion." And with that both men looked to Paul some thirty feet away, to see his expressionless stare turn away from where they stood, to his front, to take in the great Turk army as they continued their preparation for battle. "He seeks to harm you, Stephen, I am sure of that."

"I shall be wary at each corner I turn, for an arrow in the back is not the death I desire."

"Death should not be desired in any form, young Templar, especially when delivered by such a coward."

"If a coward he be… then why have him in your small band?"

"A coward he be with sword in hand, which is why he carries the mightiest bow known to Europe. It is of English origin, as I believe I have mentioned. He kills at the greatest distance possible, and little hand-to-hand has he ever seen. The armour he wears also tells the tale, for it is hard to find armour like that; it is truly of the best-manufactured talent that Europe could spare. Where he lacks armour, he has mail. Only his hands, neck and face dare bare themselves to the wind, the rest of his flesh hides behind a protection of chain male and plate. It is wise to know of your adversary, and now I hope, you know a little of his good and bad."

"He is not exactly hard to read, now that you mention it; the yellow streak he carries is quite nauseating."

"Well put, Stephen, but please don't throw caution to the wind so easily."

"Good advice, advice that will be heeded."

"Well, Stephen, let me leave you now, I have some errands I wish to perform." And with a nod from each the Pillar departed.

TO ESCAPE

Stephen now stood in silent contemplation, all around blocked from his senses, even the cannonade going unnoticed. So much had happened over the past few days, mostly good; and a smile formed upon his mouth. His thinking of Clover and the future they had together was clouding his mind. What were they to do once the siege was over with? So many scenarios offered themselves to his situation. The siege could be lifted, that was not out of the question. If help did arrive from the land as thought the previous night, then all would go well for the besieged.

What were the strange lights from far inland? Campfires they seemed to be. Was it possible that an army had approached, but turned its tail when the scouts returned with the true numbers of Mehmet's army revealed? Was it an army of scouts, or merchants travelling from town to town? What would he and Clover do in such circumstance, if the siege was lifted? They could live their lives in loving seclusion amongst the populace of Constantinople. Then again, they deserved the chance at a new life, far away from the dangers of another possible siege being placed against them. So depart the city they should.

What of the reverse, what if the siege was to remain? What lay in store for them then? If the siege was successful, and the city gates were thrown open to waves of Turkish soldiers, then many inhabitants would die, male and female, regardless of age. Stephen had never witnessed a massacre first hand, neither had he seen the after-effects, but heard stories he did, and the stories themselves were sickening enough. But that was the way of the world and all its nationalities, of all religions, succumbed to the ways of misery like thirsty cattle to water. If the siege was a success then Stephen must withdraw at the most opportune moment, keeping clear of the Puller's bow as he fled.

A meeting place was required, somewhere safe for he and Clover to meet. He would see her later in the day and organize such a place. She would be his saviour, and he, hers. She would know the best route to the harbour, the least treacherous of streets and alleys to take.

The ships on the harbour then came to thought. They no doubt, with captains aboard, would have a plan of evacuation, even if such orders had not been revealed to the remainder of the city inhabitants. No sailor, no matter how insane, would remain behind the shelter of a chain when the city was burning and its people were being slain. The chain between Constantinople and Pera would be flung aside at the first sign of defeat being imminent. So he and Clover must act with much haste.

The harbour in which he had arrived was fair enough an object of interest at such times as a withdrawal. Then again, if it had come to his mind so quickly then others would have thought of the same. The Church of St Irene, just below the Church of the Holy Wisdom. From here it was downhill to the Sea of Marmora. The Gate of the Lighthouse, from there they could make for any passing ship. But could Clover swim? He swam well enough, but would have to strip off his mail prior to entering the sea. And what of the weather conditions that day. Would an all-out assault occur on Monday, Tuesday, or Wednesday, perhaps even later? A small boat would have to be secured and hidden close by. Such a boat could be sheltered out of sight of those defending the wall. Cardinal Isidore and his 200 men were responsible for the protection of that part of the wall within the defence. Such a man as he would surely have a way of escape secured, perhaps even a galleon put aside for such an ambitious affair.

Then the Turks: They would have three days of looting as laid down. It therefore stood to reason that Middle Street would succumb to heavy traffic, Turks searching for treasure, gold, and ransoms. He would have to ensure they kept clear of the Church of the Holy Apostles and St Sophia. Stephen would talk to Clover in the evening. A plan would have to be drawn.

Stephen then shook his mind to reality as further cannon fire hit its target. The Turk Army to his front was a determined force. There was going to be no letting up of the siege. They would attack until victorious, or defeated through sheer exhaustion to numbers and spirit.

THE ENEMY

To his front he could clearly make out the masses on the ground, each grouped as ordered by the Sultan. From the gate of Charisius to the Golden Horn was Karadja Pasha with his regular European troops, several land guns also fell under his control and were set up to target the single land wall between the Horn and the point where it met up with the triple Theodosian wall.

From the point where Karadja's responsibility finished, the

Janissaries began. Across the Lycus valley and facing as square as possible to the Mesoteichion, the very best of Mehmet's troops. This strong arsenal was accompanied by Urban's monster. It was quite clear that any assault upon the city would commence here, not just for the amount of action already seen by this quarter, but also to the fact that the Sultan had his tent pitched just behind this force of soldiers.

It seemed to Stephen that the southernmost length of the wall was to be least worried about. Out of his current view, little could be seen, but he knew that the Anatolian Divisions stood strong here and under the command of two, Ishak Pasha and Mahmud Pasha. Mehmet trusted Ishak little, and although Mahmud was half-Greek he was trusted without question by the Sultan and an important counsellor to him.

To the rear of the Sultan, spread out both to his left and right, were the Bashi-bazouks, a large force but of little merit, cannon fodder to be fed to the Christians iron pointed arrows and swords. As it had been mentioned to Stephen before, these troops were most definitely to be the first unleashed in any assault upon the city.

The only other forces he had heard about, apart from the Sultan's navy, were the troops held in reserve between the pontoon bridge – across the Golden Horn – and the shore of the Bosphorus, placed more so to ensure that Pera remained neutral and in check.

So what did this all mean to Stephen? The Bashi-bazouks were the least of their torment, irregulars, with little armour and poorly disciplined, but feared like the devil, for they had a liking for rape, looting, and the slaughter of all to whom stood in their way.

The Anatolian troops were well trained and well-armed with armour of a better quality than those of the irregular force. They were also well disciplined, as much so as the Janissaries. The Janissaries were the shock troops of Mehmet's force. Disciplined, well trained, unafraid of death, well-armed, and well protected with the best armour available to the Sultan and his purse. These troops were extremely fanatical and would stand-down for little less than a direct order.

The more he looked out upon the sea of men, the more he contemplated their size; immense and ugly. They were a force indeed to be contended with, no doubt of that. And upon the sea a colour did emerge more so than any other. The uniform of the elite troops stood out quite uniquely, blue dress and large white felt hats.

So this is what confronted him now, a great ditch spread for the length of the triple wall, backed by a palisade. Tents galore, and for all uses; cooks and blacksmiths going about their business; cannons here and there being prepared with ball and powder, supplies nearby maintained with a tender touch and protected from both wind and rain. Wherever soldiers could be seen, flags and banners flew, all colours and sizes being tossed by the breeze, nowhere amongst the throng were they absent. The activity to his front was ceaseless, and everywhere a spear, here and there, the entire scene was like a forest of miniature but branchless trees.

How was it possible for the small force of Constantinople, spread out as they were, to defend against such outrageous odds?

MEHMET'S PROMISE

It was now growing dark, and hunger was hitting Stephen hard, the small morsel he'd had in the morning was soon digested. The pounding of the guns during the day did much damage to the wall, in particular across the Lycus Valley, damage that would have to be repaired by night. He had heard some good news however, and that was that Giustiniani had returned to his post. Many a man was eased by his return.

And unbeknown to those on the wall, a bearded figure with a well-proportioned nose exited his tent. The Sultan now took great pride in viewing his troops from atop his horse, riding through the tents and ranks, around campfires and crowds, along the line of artillery and the ditch backed by rampart and upon the rampart its wooden palisade. Everywhere he turned, wherever he rode, the throngs would grow and cheer him on as he passed on the news that the assault would soon take place, the final attack that would see the end to the Christian inhabitants of Constantinople – a city protected by the Infidel's untrue god.

Mehmet and his entourage were passing on the rules of such a victory to come, how they all would be permitted three days in order to pillage what they could from all within the walls surrounding Constantinople. Rape as you please was the word, grab what ransom you can; the gold, the works of art; all was for the sacking. But kill and plunder you must, for it was a written custom that such should be carried out. And the cries of sheer joy from the lips of all could be heard from within the city itself. And then the chanting started, but dissipated slowly, the same verse over and over: 'there is no God but God, and Mohammed is His Prophet'. And more news still was delivered to all ears, for it was the promise of the young Sultan himself; all treasures, no matter what their worth, would be shared amongst all within the army, this he swore unto God and His Prophet. He swore this by the soul of his father and his children, though little mention of his mother came to lip, for she was little more than a slave-girl who went by the name Huma Hatun. Such a promise appeared to some, to be a contradiction by terms, for they'd already been provided the authority, by customary law, of the right to sack the city. What one soldier took for himself was not going to be easily removed and divided amongst the masses.

CONFIDANT

Retire Stephen did, soon after dusk, where he met with Clover in the half abolished home of her adopted parents, now dead. He opened and strode through the door as though born to it, straight into the arms of his petite and loving wife of less than a day.

"I am glad to see you made it through another day, Stephen. The cannonade always scares me so."

"Little damage did our wall receive this day," he lied.

"I heard that the Mesoteichion was in extremely bad repair and that work tonight will need a miracle to mend that which is smashed."

"It is not that bad, Clover, really."

"A miracle is what we may receive in any case." Clover could feel Stephen's pretence. "We are to go to church tonight Stephen, most of the city citizens will be there, though not all to the same house of God. We did receive a special invite from John. It will be a small service."

"That does sound appropriate enough," agreed Stephen.

"I think we will work on the wall too, tonight, for they will need all the hands they can spare, whether you agree to it or not."

Stephen could understand well that Clover was concerned for the place where she was born. "And what of your day, my pet?"

"I spent the afternoon moving all of the supplies possible from the makeshift hospital to another that John has founded. It is nearer the Church of the Holy Apostles, though off the main street."

"I think that John has logic in his choosing just a site. I think he believes that the Holy Apostles will not be sacked, and as such, a special guard of the Sultan's entourage will be dispatched to secure the site. A hospital nearby will surely be aided by such strength of disciplined guard."

"You do not know the Turk as others do, Stephen. Believe me. When the time is right, the Sultan, and all those in his force, will sack and plunder all they can, and none of the living will stand in their way."

"Not much standing can a man on a bench accomplish when lying senseless from his wounds."

"The arm of a Turk will wield a scimitar and such will be brought down upon the neck of all within this city, whether incapacitated, old, or newborn."

Stephen placed his side arms down and began to remove that which he wore, for embers were burning well the logs of the fireplace, rendering the dwelling quite warm. The chain mail took a little while to remove, first the leather greaves and then the remainder. Clover aiding where she could, the truer form of himself, his muscular build, his strength of shoulders, all beginning to show through the quilted vest which he wore beneath and did sit body tight.

"I smell something fit for a king. A smell long since missed by the nostrils of my nose."

"Bannock with beans and assorted meats."

"Quite a price it must have been."

"Many are spending big where possible, but ration still remains. I had a quantity of jewels that—"

"No, Clover. You didn't sell anything of ancestral importance did you?"

"I have nothing, just a few small items which meant nothing to me, really. We cannot take them with us, Stephen. I am sure of mind that evacuation will be required."

"I am sure of that too and must speak with you of preparation."

"And what did you have in mind?"

Stephen paused as he sat and Clover turned with the meal in a bowl, a little steam rising from the morsel. "Hmm, smells good."

"Your idea, Stephen."

"I must ask you a question, and a definite answer I must have; can you swim?"

"Swim? Surely you jest?"

"Jest is not a commodity or characteristic I am currently acquainted with."

"Who can swim? Very few of these parts: that I know." She said, and then answering her own question she stated; "You are thinking of swimming to the safety of a passing ship. No one will await you, Stephen. Any sea-faring vessel which makes it past the boom would not wait for you, not the emperor himself."

"What about a boat; a small one, to be concealed near the shores of the Marmora."

"Out of the question, Stephen. Nothing of the sort will ever be purchased, even if available."

"A plan of escape must be had, Clover. By the time a retreat from the wall has been achieved, and a run for the Prosphorianus Harbour secured, all ships would have begun their run."

"Have you tried talking with John?"

"Such is not an idea I would consider. He is here to stay. You need not know him to see that, just look into his eyes. You will see that withdrawal is not his plan, though he makes it known that such would be a good idea. He advises that the northern suburbs would make for an advantageous route."

"He could be right, but I know little of tactics, especially those undertaken by the Muslim army currently sitting to our front."

"They will be searching for ransom." Stephen paused then. "This meal you have prepared Clover is extremely appetizing."

She smiled and shied. "I can do better Stephen, but thank you."

"Meals like this come by but once in a full moon."

"Yes, and ours is waning."

"I agree. The fight for Constantinople will soon be over. I shall speak with John."

MEN-AT-ARMS

And the night's activity proceeded as it had the day before, with much music accompanying the work being carried out on the foss. Many torches were lighting the way for the work as usual, and whilst the Turks filled the foss the Christian churches were filled with frightened civilians, for all knew well of the pending doom and few had given worship this Sunday as yet.

As Clover and Stephen approached the small out-of-the-way church, John could be seen to be conversing with a few men-at-arms. John did notice them quite readily and waved them over, the three men-at-arms looking over to see who it was that could so easily place a smile upon the face of the Hospitaller.

"Stephen, Clover; please meet these men of grandeur." All three smiled at such an introduction, it was no wonder John was so likeable – hard when the time was needed, but fair and friendly when required. And John said something to the htree, but it could not be heard.

The introductions were passed all round. The three men-at-arms were from Spain; Vicent de Chinchilla, Ruy de Teva, and Diego de Villarubia.

"And what do you praise, would three men-at-arms from Spain be doing in Constantinople, hmmm? I ask you Stephen, such splendid character, is it not?"

"It is indeed grand to see that men have come so far to join in the struggle against the infidel Turk." And with that said the three smiles evaporated as quickly as they had come. "I am sorry, Stephen, I should explain. These three men are only passing through, old friends from an acquaintance long since passed, but never-the-less unafraid to attend Constantinople in order to reacquaint themselves with those that they know. They were of Christian faith, a Latin belief, but have joined the many in taking to heart that of the Muslim belief."

Stephen's jaw dropped, as did Clovers, but Stephen was quick to recover. He bowed slightly for forgiveness. "My apologies dear sirs."

"No apology is needed." Said Vicent, waving the insult away. "We don't share the militaristic views of our comrades in faith, any more than the Christians of Mehmet's great army believe that your head should remain in place upon your shoulders."

"Yes, another concept I find hard to comprehend," agreed Stephen.

A surprising statement from John did rise: "Religion is a tiresome companion at times."

"Here, here," said the three in unison.

"May I be so rude as to ask your reason for being here this day?"

asked Stephen.

"Today is as the day before, and the week before that," said Ruy de Teva. "We were on our way to give praise to Allah when we were momentarily put to rest by the siege. Our travel plans were soon changed and our only wish was then for a way in which the Sultan could be convinced for all to live in peace."

"You have spoken with the Sultan?"

"Not in so many words, young knight," said Ruy, who had been advised by John, as he approached, of his status. "We have been able to establish communication, but little negotiation has been founded. Due to the now message received from the Christians in the Sultan's Army, we have decided that to move on, and avoid any further hostility and blood shed, is the better of the options we have. We are currently seeking a small vessel to ferry us across the Horn."

Stephen knew better than to pry, he was aware that Muslims, Christians, and Jews, had been living in relative peace in Spain for quite some time, hundreds of years. Vicent did notice however, the frown upon Clover's forehead. "All men were created equal. Regardless of one's religion, one should be treated as one's brother. Conflict in this world will not cease until all religion has been accepted as an equally true faith."

"If all religion was an equally true faith, then how does one choose which faith is the one to follow?" questioned Clover.

"Each religion has its idiosyncrasies, and it is these which have been tailored to suit an individual's existence," explained Ruy.

"With such an explanation it would be fitting to say that a new religion could be construe from Islam, or Christian alike, to form another belief, and another God," said Clover.

"Paganism is not unheard of. There are many religions I have encountered in my time, some more heathen than others." Ruy looked over Clover and Stephen. "Your friend John is a hard but fair man. Such a religious man is he that no swaying of his belief would ever be seen, never to yield to another, but always compassionate with those that have compassion."

"I have been acquainted with John little more than a few days. I find that most of what you speak is true, but for him to make such a bond of friendship with one of another religion is hard to believe."

"You recall when you were wed, Stephen, the monk so eager to see the vows sown into blessing."

"I do, John; George Gennadius."

"He is so against the union of Latin and Greek that he has become a great power in the fight to prevent the churches from combining, but both religions are almost of the same meat." John could see that an explanation would not do. It was hard to draw upon evidence for necessity when such was hard to be drawn.

The third man-at-arms then spoke, Diego de Villarubia. "My conversion from Christian to Muslim was for many reasons, one of which was the squabble between Latin and Greek. They are schismatic like many here in Constantinople, though being a Muslim, and with the beliefs we hold, we too see that we are guilty of such a crime. The Latin and Greek do argue so; 'they don't venerate the holy images', 'they use unleavened bread'. Christians of a Latin faith have said without question that the Son is not of the same seed as the Father, and quite argumentatively because the Father is presumably to have existed since the beginning of time itself. But the Father created the Son as he so desired such an element be placed upon the earth. So it is clear to me that the Son is more of an adoptive creed in relationship with God. In this view, how can the Son be of the same flesh as the Father? It should be easy to see therefore that Jesus was not of the flesh of God, and in comparison, could be considered as an illusion. What the apostles did see was exactly that, an illusion of pure appearance. Jesus, Son of God, may have died on the cross, but if He was not of the same flesh as you and I, how can it be said in mass that this bread is my body? Communion should be sworn therefore without bread. The Latins of the West think that the Holy Spirit proceeds from the Father and from the Son. The Holy Spirit for those of the Greek faith advises that the Holy Spirit proceeds from the Father. Such an argumentative state is the belief that the religion becomes an illusion. It is such illusions that have become a part of other religions, though not in the same context. But one last thought if I may; it is said that the religion of Buddha is Illusion. So who is right and who is wrong?"

"And such a debate could take all evening my friend," advised John, for his main concern were the church bells that had started to ring so solemnly.

"John, it was good to see an old friend again." And each of the three men said their farewells prior to departing.

"Where will they go?" asked Stephen once they were out of earshot.

"Once they have been evacuated to Pera, they will head for the heart of Islam." They commenced the move into the Church of Christ Pantepoptes. "I find it hard to believe you are friends with men of such views."

"Those men did save my life through brave actions given without greed. Friends they will always be, but their views on religion are always treated as unclean. I do however owe them the opportunity to speak as they wish and would not go against my vow of thanks. They too understand that views on religion should, if at all possible, remain unspoken whilst we are of one another's company. Please, let us proceed inside with the others." And it was true enough, for not far from them a small crowd of followers had grown, unnoticed by the Clover and Stephen, all ready for the service that was to follow.

FAREWELL

The church service went well, 43 people in all having attended, and soon after the completion of the service all 43 congregated outside for small talk and conversation on the battle to come.

"John. I must ask you something."

"Please, Stephen, proceed."

"I am glad that Clover and I can talk with your ear in private. We would be obliged if you could attend some supper with us. I also wish to talk of the fall of the city that is in sight of us all."

"We shouldn't throw caution to the wind, I grant you that, but you could be a little optimistic."

"Our optimism means little if we can't live our lives in safety."

"I grant you that, too. What is it I can do for you?"

"We need to consider a boat for escape when the time arrives."

"Help you I cannot. Without asking for passage myself, no captain will wait around. It would be pointless. What if you were guaranteed a position for a voyage from here and the unfortunate was to happen to you and Clover, would a captain be expected to wait around indefinitely when the tide turns? I tell you this Stephen, if the wall falls you should stay clear of the high ground. By way of the suburbs along the Golden Horn should you travel. Each gate you pass, if open, should be considered an opportunity. From the wall to the harbour in which we first landed, each open gate must be scrutinized with the eye. On seeing a ship anchored, putting out sail, or readying for voyage, it should be approached with haste. Be aware though. Many innocents will gather strength in retreat, and the meekest of meek would see you dead in order to gain safe passage from Constantinople. And don't stop to open a gate obscuring your view, for it would have surely been bolted from the outside and gain entry you will not. Don't waste the time you have."

"Then there is nothing you can do to ease our pain and torment."

"Pain enough there is for all of us and to help you further I cannot."

"And you, John, what will happen to you?"

"If the wall falls then I will surely die, for I am not agile enough to make an escape, but still fierce enough to hold back the tide in order to gain you time in withdrawal."

"Then you will have surely done more than any mortal man could ever do in helping us in our cause."

John then thrust his hand out and said his final words to Stephen. "I wish you and Clover well in your lives together, for the next time I see you I will no doubt be in heaven." And not a further word was spoken as John stepped off and wandered peacefully back to the reserve upon the high ground, on which the Church of the Holy Apostles did stand.

John had quite discretely declined the offer to attend supper with Clover and Stephen, whom themselves did depart for home, and soon after some dry bread and beans, hurried over to the Mesoteichion to commence with the repair work on the wall.

CLOSE CALL

There was already a line of workers ferrying materials forward for the repair work to be carried out on the Mesoteichion. The sacks of soil, rubble, planks, barrels, posts, rocks and an assortment of other fill, was being carried either directly to the more needed areas upon the wall or, in some cases, deposited nearby where it was picked up by others. These 'others' had been given specific areas of responsibility, which included soldiers from other parts of the wall (where they could be spared) and a few from the detachments of reserves.

Stephen did note, but saw little point in saying anything to Clover, that the sound of the cannonade hitting segments of the wall had become somewhat terrifying. The walls literally reverberated as each ball from cannon hit an area already weakened from the past weeks of torrential preparatory. It was easy for Stephen to see why the emperor did refuse to place a cannon of his own upon the walls for the targeting of objectives within the Sultan's camp, for such action would have seen a further demise of the structure. But cannon within the city did exist, and these small and cumbersome machines of war were currently held within the ranks of the reserve closest to the wall, which, under command of Megadux, was stationed near the Church of St John in Petra.

It was seen that the civilians of the city were at work as close to the danger as were the soldiers posted upon the wall. It was inevitable but quite necessary. If the Turk were to succeed in breaching the foss with a footway or road carrying the masses with hooks, ladders, and assailing ropes, then the city would be lost. It was up to all to prevent a single Turk from entering any portion of that which protected them. With each Turk that entered there existed the opportunity for the defence to collapse. The longer it took each Turk to cross the foss to the wall, the longer the defence had in neutralizing the threat. Even now, as civilians and soldiers alike came under the maiming effect of cannon and death by crossbow, bow, and arquebus, the misery was subdued, for the fear of being captured was by far more overwhelming.

Stephen gave advice to Clover that was not received well. It was his understanding that, now wed, responsibility for her safety was not hers alone. What if she was to die, and her argument, what of him? What if she was with a child already? She had placed herself in mortal danger so many times in the past, but now thinking of Stephen and not herself, realized where such emotions were coming from. She obliged

Stephen's request with appreciation, for his feelings for her were very strong. Clover decided to provide aid further back from the defence by taking up responsibility of ferrying materials to the rear of the wall, from there Stephen helped immensely.

The moving of materials and sacks of soil to the rampart via steps was done so via human chain, where being large of brawn was a gift. Empty barrels sweating of wine and ale were few and far between, and planks from nearby housing, ransacked for their good, were a commodity much sought and obtained. It was the soil that tempted fury, for the grains of dirt on sweat got into every crack, crevice, and crease, in regards to skin and armour alike. Stephen maintained a good rhythm, whatever was passed to him stayed within his grasp for the shortest time, the man a few steps above him looking the worse for wear each time he turned to face the knight, for Stephen's fervour in work was unprecedented.

After several hours of tormenting those on the steps with his speed and fury, Stephen did take time to refresh himself with water whilst maintaining a watch for his beloved, and on seeing her momentarily he did retire to the wall for a spell in order to maintain security along with several others whom had taken time to rest. Before he had taken ten paces atop the rampart an arrow did strike the stone to his direct front, ricocheting to strike his mail at chest height with enough force to push him sideways.

He was quick to balance himself, and although momentarily paralysed by the event was relatively quick to recover. Remaining sure-footed, and ensuring that his mail was intact, he turned to an open-mouthed monk and said: "Praise be to God," whereby the monk took to forming a cross upon his person, head to chest and shoulder to shoulder.

"The Lord has eyes for you, my son. May you remain a favourite of His for all time." A chink in his mail was of little consequence, but with such a harrowing first experience as this he was sure to maintain a visual on all enemy movement to his front from now on. He was thankful for the archers at his side, at numerous intervals upon the wall, for a constant barrage they did lay to slow the Sultan's Army from filling in the foss, though hard it was against the covers of hide that assisted the infidel below.

"Look out there, my son. Do you see the pavis from which the blow was delivered?"

"I do."

"I have seen our archers awaiting the chance to neutralize the heathen, though smart he is, and quick with his fingers. Such fingers on a chain and resting upon my chest would do well to remind others of the infidel's patience. That pavis has been standing for most of the night, and he who commands the crossbow is a brilliant marksman.

Such pity that great praise should be given to one with such a misled soul. Tormented in hell he will be when the time is right. Kneel, my son." Stephen did just that, the monk making another sign. "Blessed and protected you now be… but a watchful eye never hurt any. May God bestow upon you great favour; may you be his sacred vessel." With that said the monk continued along the rampart, giving praise and prayer where he felt the urge.

Flabbergasted by such speech his mouth opened to ask a question but was shocked back to reality when another arrow was shot between the merlons, striking him in the left arm, throwing him to the stone rampart. His fingers went to aid the stricken area, his fingers coming away blood free. Another chink in his mail, another reminder of the hazards of siege, and a cry did suddenly erupt, immense pleasure escaping the lips of one of the archers, for the crossbowman behind the pavis was just then silenced forever.

REST

Stephen did then remain on the wall until the hour approached midnight. Then, as suddenly as the arrows had appeared in the night, silence did dominate the area, for all work was abruptly ceased, the fifes, trumpets, and lutes, pipes and drums, all noise dropped away as quickly as it had started.

The cannonade had also stopped, it was no longer echoing throughout the city. The silence was deadly and a sleepless night was had by most.

A rest day had been ordered by the Sultan, for his warriors to prepare for the assault to come. The soldiers upon the walls still remained alert and looked out upon the sea of torches, as one by one they were extinguished and the army at siege retired to their tents for the commencement of their rest.

But even as the soldiers retired, the mind of the young Sultan did continue to turn. He had played his cards well and organized as best he could the siege that currently stood in place. From his younger years he had learned well from predecessors and learnt well of the minds of his enemy. He was cruel and bloodthirsty and knew the limits of his Generals; he also spoke five other languages outside that of Turkish. Although cruel at birth and heart, Mehmet II was also a man of clemency. A learned man he was, of the arts and of science. He had in his possession the fortifications of Rumeli-Hisar and Anatoli-Hisar. Cannon fired from emplacements here put the narrowest point of the Bosphorus in his complete control; the supply of corn and other necessities, in particular from the Black Sea, was now completely under his control. Any trading vessel, of any foreign nationality, could be easily boarded or sunk by the Turk navy. Even the Despot of Morea was prevented from providing aid to Constantinople, for the Sultan had invaded that island of Greek nationality, cutting off the deliverance of aid – a strategic preliminary. It was even established by Constantinople's senior minister, Lucas Notaras – also Admiral of the Fleet – that the fall of the city was inevitable, and that such a Turkish victory was better than having to see the city under the control of the Latin Church; such views were quite widespread.

But for all that Mehmet II was worth, his predecessor was a bird of a different feather. The relationship between Mohammed I and Manuel, years prior to the 1422 siege of Constantinople, was quite strong and full of bright greeting, even exquisite dishes were exchanged between the two on one occasion. Friendly, cordial, and understanding of each other's needs, peace had reigned for some time. It was with deep regret that Manual retired from state affairs, John VIII, his son, taking stage, with Murad II taking to the throne in place of Mohammed I. If it wasn't for John's support of a Turkish rival, and an ill-fated attempt to overthrow Murad II, then the city of Constantinople may have foregone the agonies of 1422, even if they were the victor. But victory cannot be measured by such achievements, for the remainder of the empire, that which was to be found outside of the walls, did suffer immensely. Though let us not forget the Mongol, for if it wasn't for the battle of Angora in 1402 then Constantinople would not be standing in defiance in 1453, for the forces of the Turk army had been much damaged by Timur's ferocity.

One ingenious move however did save some spoils of Byzantine worth, for Andronicus, the Despot in 1423, was quick to sell Thessalonica to the Venetians on seeing that a Turk siege was forthcoming. It was with further regret, this time on part of the Venetians, that the Turk did still take Thessalonica for themselves. It was no wonder that those of a Latin belief now stood side by side with their Brothers, even if of the Greek church. Battles and wars did make for strange bedfellows.

PART SIX
Monday 28th May

MEHMET'S TOUR

The day of rest for the Turks was an unnerving one for Mehmet who did spend the entire day inspecting his great army and armada. One of his first tasks took him to the Double Columns, where Hamza Bey was giving some orders to his men of the sea, though change to such was expected after the Sultan's visit, though the basics of the assault to come was quite rudimentary. He was quite unnerved by the expected meeting with Mehmet, for the Sultan's frame of mind could change at a whim and no manner of time allotted in preparing for such a meeting would be enough. Never before had he been handed orders directly from the Sultan himself. His current post was one of surprise and did come about due to the misfortune of his predecessor.

Hamza did breakfast well after a short stroll amongst some of his navy, ensuring all would be in inspection order, just in case the Sultan decided on a brief review of his men of the sea. He knew, as others did, of Mehmet's liking for small boys, his appetite for such quite disgusting to Hamza, though would be tolerated, for not to do so could lose him his head – literally. It would be important to him this day – even though giving to all as a day of rest – that the sailors under his command, both direct and indirectly, did not parade about in a drunken stupor, raping women slaves. The last thing Hamza wished to do was to upset the one that had made the final decision in his being crowned Admiral. Hard to fathom that was, the new Admiral of a naval force, such a distinguished position in a force so worldly renowned as one of the best in the world – if only they had the formula for creating Greek Fire, then all that sailed the Mediterranean would fall before them.

Mehmet did approach as expected, upon a horse of white and with an entourage of guards, who were as large as any man could be, agile as antelope, and as flexible and as strong as the sinew of any limb. Mehmet's mind was a flurry of thought: His entire navy, as readily disposable, was to be spread along the boom and Marmora coast to assault where possible the single wall that mused to grow up and out from the depths of the sea itself. The object of the move was designed quite primarily to ensure that the walls of the defence remained manned in order to prevent the main land-wall being reinforced. If at all possible Admiral Bey was to assault with ladders in order to gain footing within the city and open a gate. It must be emphasized.

Hamza Bey stood fast as the Sultan approached, many thoughts on the coming assault also plaguing his mind. All he could do was wish that the Sultan would not be displeased with any effort he should make, regardless of its success.

"Good morning to you, Admiral Bey. Rest I hope you did get plenty of, after the cannons were ordered to cease their firing, along with the rest of my army."

"Yes, my lord. My thanks for your asking."

Mehmet dismounted, as did a servant boy from the rear, who raced up with such speed that he was but a blur to the eye. The boy took the reins of the horse into his command and Mehmet approached the entrance of Hamza's tent, the admiral bowing in greeting, to reflect his respect.

Both men wandered inside where several servant girls were ready to please the Sultan with fruit as fresh as the morning breeze. "I have eaten well this morning and wish to get to details for the assault to come," and he sat upon the cushioned ground.

Hamza waved off the servant girls and sat opposite his supreme commander, the man whom so many feared, the one in control of a force so mighty that it would offer fear to choke the heart of any nation, if opposed.

"Time is short and the deeds of the day endlessly in need of my attention." Mehmet took a deep breath. "I wish to start with congratulating you on your promotion one last time, for such a rank is the grandest one that can be received," and with the congratulation came a foreboding fear, that the Sultan was relying on Hamza, to the greatest of degree, in regards to the coming assault.

Hamza felt sick in the stomach. "Thank you, my lord."

"The disposition of your forces is what has plagued me so, but such is at your disposal. I wish today to only give a little advice to my urgent need, and this not only for the good of the army, but for the good of our lands if we are to become a nation as grand as I believe we can be." He pushed a tray of fruit to one side. "The vessels that you dispatch to assault the boom must be full of men ready with swords, but not endowed too strong to upset the balance of fighting hand-to-hand. Much damage the navy did receive, not so long ago under the command of Baltoghlu; this must not occur again. The men must be ready with tools for the cutting of the boom to be carried out and with the quickest of ease. Create as much noise as one can muster, distract those of the Horn in order that the Blachernae can be assaulted with as little resistance as possible. Keep the men of the defence busy, that is the basic order of the day."

Hamza Bey nodded anxiously as each point was delivered.

"And those of the Marmora. They should be packed to the hilt, to the brim I tell you. Ladders must be carried for the scaling of the seaward wall. Scaling ropes, archers; employ your pavis well. Many men will be needed in order to gain footing within the grounds of Constantinople and it all starts with the harassment you can muster along the seaward walls, my friend.

"Most of the fighting men with experience would have been stationed at the landward wall in order to counter our attack. For those idle enough to be warm in bed, a warning for them to attend their posts would have been delivered as in the past, with the ringing of the church bells within the city.

"Footing you must gain, distract the defence as best you can, and at all costs, you must keep all of the defence as occupied as possible in order to give relief to those fighting along the Lycus Valley. But take heed, my friend, take heed. If you are able bodied enough in brawn and brain to penetrate the wall, you must, at all cost, deliver to me an open gate within the walls obstructing my Janissaries and other divisions. I have seen too many battles to know what goes through a man's mind. They will be after the booty of this great city, so it is paramount that once penetration has been established that you take full command and responsibility to the tasks laid down upon you. Only once the army itself has entered the city, shall your men be granted the three days of looting.

"Do you accept such responsibilities, 'Admiral' Bey?" Mehmet emphasized his rank and for good reason.

"I do," answered Hamza, chest puffing out as though exhilarated.

"Good, for to disappoint me will be unfortunate for you, as I will not settle for another failure as I did with Baltoghlu, even with such good reports having reached my ears." The meeting continued for a short time after, little idle talk being entertained, for the Sultan had too much on his mind at present.

On departing, Hamza Bey did give praise to Mehmet, the opportunity of a lifetime had been provided to him, but dire consequences would prevail if he failed to do as he was ordered, for failure was not an option in the eyes of the Sultan. It was an obvious point that escape would be the fervour of many in Constantinople if the walls were to be penetrated with any great success. It was also understood that some would take flight through the sheer volume of fear and apprehension provided by the force of the siege picking up their stakes and charging ahead, charging the walls in such large numbers. Even the strongest of the strong would be forced to question his strength of character. It was this idea of escape that tormented the Admiral's mind this moment, for any attempt at escape must be subdued and prevented at all costs whilst still feigning assaults along the entirety of the sea wall and boom. The Sultan would want as many captives as possible in order to fund future enterprises.

Mehmet had next allowed for a scheduled call to be performed upon the magistrates of Pera, emphasizing to them, as he does so well, the effect that coercion with those of Constantinople would have upon the community of their Genoese as a whole. It was quite strictly forbidden for any one of Pera to give aid of any description to those of the great city, and those listening to Mehmet's detailed speech would not even contemplate what punishment, for such intervention, could be mustered. A bow and a smile acknowledged the wishes of the Sultan, followed shortly after by an invitation for a midday meal, which Mehmet was quick to wave away as he had much more that he needed to attend to. Mehmet mounted himself upon his charger and then returned to his tent whereupon he indulged himself in some of his more favourite foods. As he ate his mind continued to play out the scenes of war as he saw them; as he jaw moved up and down he considered all that must be considered. His reflections on all that had come to pass, and all that which was soon to be, made him very happy and warm inside. He felt more content this minute than he had for a long time. Constantine would soon be his and capitulation would be a word he wanted to ensure was put into place. Each and every circumstance that unfolded before him would have to be considered as each presented itself. Some citizens of Constantinople would be tortured, others freed to stations already assigned to them, in accordance with Mehmet's wishes; some would be ransomed and others employed as slaves; and his Janissaries would need replenishing. Yes indeed, much had been planned for, but much still was to be considered, for behind the great battle ahead would be revealed many things his mechanical mind had not yet given hindsight to.

When the refreshment was finished he climbed upon his horse again and paraded himself around for all of his army to see, witnessing first-hand the jubilation of news on the coming assault being received so well. Addressing the men face to face, as individuals, and in their groups, he felt more at ease now than he did at any time in his past. He could feel the victory which would be delivered him on the morrow, see the blood of the Christians flooding the streets of Constantinople, the churches turned into mosques and free men into slaves. Again his mind considered his fortunes to come. Quite a bounty awaiting him with regard to the women and children, each of whom would be sold as slaves or employed well within his empire – those that did not succumb to the scimitar. Many a ransom was also to be had in regards to educated men, monks, and others of the cloth. Mehmet could only smile that grin so seldom seen.

For hours he rode around the encampment before returning to his tent to give his orders to subordinates and ministers alike, a speech that was uplifting and informative. "The prize will be what you plunder, the spoils of the land yours. Much ransom and riches are for the taking. It is our honour that Constantinople should fall to us on the morrow, for it is written in the scriptures, both far and wide, that Constantinople should be but controlled by those of a true faith. For so long it has been a duty to be performed, and such duty shall be ours for the undertaking, we shall be those responsible for installing the true faith upon its rightful throne. Those cowering behind the walls are holding on by such a fine thread, that the cutting of such will need nothing more than the flick of a finger, for they tire so and are short on supplies. Their weapons are but few and supply of arrows and javelin near depletion, impregnable the city is not. We have already seen how the Christian behaves, how those that call themselves Italian board their ships and flee on a notion, and how those that defend, fight between themselves. The morrow will bring great jubilation to our people, for Constantinople will yield, even if out of sheer weariness, for our land forces will attack, wave upon wave, until such a time that victory is secured. The irregulars must not waver, the assault must be pressed on, gaining courage from you, their commanders and officers alike, and discipline shall hold within all ranks. Go now, and eat well, for your next meal will be within the walls of Constantinople. And remember this above all things, God is God; there is but one and Mohammed is God's apostle," and after a short minute, to allow for the encouragement of all to subside, he added: "Go now and make final preparations for battle; commanders are to remain."

Orders were then laid down to his chief commanders. Zaganos was to dispatch a small force to the Admiral, to reinforce the numbers for an assault along the wall of the Golden Horn. As for the remainder of his force, they were to concentrate their prowess upon their objective, the wall of Blachernae. Karadja Pasha and his European Divisions would concentrate upon the triple wall between Blachernae and the Gate of Charisius. The Asiatic troops under Ishak and Mahmud were to concentrate on the wall between the Sea of Marmora and the Civil Gate of St Romanus – the 3rd Military Gate being a prime objective. Halil Chandarli was to accompany Mehmet, his once tutelage, (whom would succumb to the death penalty in August, handed down by Mehmet himself for an interference of his plans to have put siege to Constantinople in 1446). Saruja was also to accompany Mehmet and together they would direct the main assault upon the wall on the Lycus Valley.

IN GOOD COMPANY

For most of the morning, Stephen did rest upon the walls of Constantinople, for two pleasures; the pleasure of rest and for the safekeeping of mind-sake, whereby he would keep from his new wife the news of the near-death experience he had received twice over. But a new vigour had taken hold of his heart and mind once more, and after an afternoon of working on the wall he did feel much more comfortable with the thought of confronting Clover with two chinks in his mail.

He entered the room with an air of confidence, a smile big enough to encompass his beloved, enough to envelop her with the fullest of feelings in order that she may not see the troubled scars upon his mail.

She hugged him close, a smile in return, and as she held him close, her lips did part in speech; "And what of the chinks upon your mail, my once betrothed?"

"Work on the wall has taken its toll on both body and dress," and they released their holds on each other.

"If I knew not better I would say such marks could only be that as delivered from a solid blow."

"I cannot lie," and Stephen grasped the shoulders of Clover. "Shot twice I was by a pavis archer."

"Thieves of the night. They do cower." She turned her back to Stephen and he placed a comforting hand upon her.

"He thieves well, my love. Several lives he did take, more still, I'm sure; but no more." He released his hold on Clover, turned to the table of two chairs and sat. "The thief is now decaying as many others do this night, within the foss, cannon fodder no more. Struck hard he was, so I am told, through the throat, by The Puller himself, would you believe; though such I did not witness."

Clover had her back to Stephen as he shared his story, all news of the wall comforting, except the death of those who were loved so much, for the pavis holders along the walls length had taken many lives this past few days – and who on the wall went without love? Even the mercenary had mothers to love and hold.

Clover then turned to reveal a folded mass of white cradled in her arms. She smiled again. "And what is this you hold before me?"

"You gave something up that you cherished so much and I have chosen to return it." Stephen took the garment and let it fall to hang between fingers. He gasped as he saw immediately a red cross appear upon the fabric. "I have made you a white habit to replace your surcoat, and although it can't replace the history of the other, it will give you some…." Stephen had thrown the habit to the table and held Clover so tight to his body that she marveled at his muscles under her fingertips as he tensed and kissed. And there they stayed, standing as one, hearts beating as one. Never had anyone given Stephen such a gift worthy of higher praise than he could bestow or pledge.

Stephen was dressed again in full uniform as he had brought with him and he smiled at Clover as he pulled the habit on over his head. He brushed away imaginary creases and tied the garb around his middle, stretching out the fabric so that the red cross became a beacon upon which his very ancestry would be proud to see him display.

Again the two looked upon one another. "This day I shall always remember," said Stephen. "These past few have given so much to me that I feel that my life cannot get any better; but I know within me that our love will grow… and that seems impossible at the moment."

"It is what I believe also. I believe that our love will grow with each passing day and will never fade," confirmed Clover.

"It shall be as we say, mark my words, Clover. Our life will be our covenant and by our covenant we shall allow our love to blossom."

"So agreeable we are that it seems impossible."

"Two of a kind."

"What plans have you for tonight, Stephen?"

"Not many. I will do as I need to upon the wall." Clover turned as he spoke those words, so he added without conviction: "Keeping my head low of course. But my mail will see me through the night."

"Yes," said Clover with eyelids pushed down by the frown that now appeared upon her forehead. "I'm sure it will."

Stephen changed the subject matter, and quite convincingly. "I must admit I grow tired of saying this to you, my love, but I smell something that is so appetizing that I see not that you will have enough to satisfy my hunger."

"If I had a big enough kitchen I could do you no end of favours in regards to your big eyes and empty stomach."

"I shall get you such, as soon as the siege has been crushed."

Clover allowed the silence to linger a little and then added something for Stephen to contemplate during his long hours upon the wall. "And what shall you do in order to pay for this kitchen. What line of work shall rule our lives… or do we live off the land; some farm property perhaps."

Stephen had no answer. He was a stranger to the idea of doing anything other than fulfilling his dream. What would become of them?

THE PAST

It was Christmas Day in the year 1400 when Manuel II Palaeologus found himself in the company of the King of England, the then Henry IV. He had made his way here for a single purpose, to rally aid against the Turks. But other than relish praise and comfort upon the emperor of the Greeks and Romans, as did other great heads of Europe, such as the Italians and the French, not much more could be done. The Emperor Manuel II in centuries past, had lost all herald between Byzantine and Italy to the Norman invasion, and the upland of Anatolia to the Turks. Constantinople was nothing but an island surrounded by an aggressive sea. Manuel was indebted to Crusaders and mercenaries alike – though 1204 did blemish the Crusader-Byzantine relationship. And too, the Genoese who had been rewarded Galata [now Pera] for ousting the Venetians from the walled city of Constantinople, did take from the emperor, not land, but much trade; and still the plague commencing 1347. Manuel appeared as a pauper to most in Europe; but what riches could be secured from lands so far from home?

The city of Constantinople was once home, in the 12th century, to over a million inhabitants, now there existed little more than 50,000 and the number was in strong decline. War and plague had taken its toll, and the city of intellect was suffering greatly.

1348 was the year of the Black Death, where terror came to fill the eyes of all those of a Christian background; though the Death did not discriminate. It saw to it that three quarters and more, of the population of Constantinople, were knocking on death's door, before it departed the streets of the city. It was the years following the Genoese victory of the lands opposite the great city, where Galata, fell into duties of annual income exceeding 200,000 gold coins (more than 6 times that received by Constantinople) and much bloodshed – but what else is news if blood wasn't to be spilt. From the ports of the Black Sea came much wealth, and Galata was the only port-of-call before Constantinople; so much did she take from the City of God.

It was the Venetian-Genoese war that saw Genoa escalate in its prowess. The shipping lane of the Bosphorus was taxed heavily by the Genoese held land; such a strategic point of commercial worth, it was. And what was the Byzantine fleet to do about such treachery? Nothing – for its Greek fleet was smashed to smithereens during a storm of a ferocity deeper than that bestowed by Mehmet.

The plague passed many lands, port-to-port, ship-to-ship, and trade-to-trade. The islands of the Aegean Sea were infected, as too, was the coast of the Mediterranean. No man of medicine or science could stand in its way. The Genoese did then spread the disease further afield, Italy, Spain, France, England, Germany, Norway, the Baltic Sea, Poland, and by 1353, in a matter of five short years, the whole of Russia. One day a man would be standing with his closest of friends, the next morning a corps.

It appeared that Pera was as dangerous to Constantinople, now in 1453, as it was when known as Galata.

The university of Constantinople, however, did stand strong and proud, a heritage of historical importance, both past, present, and future. The re-founding of the university towards the latter part of the 13th century saw much work of the literal sense and funds go into the building. The era of Palaeologan demanded much merit for the intellectual and artistic advances that it brought into the kingdom. Much philosophy passed lips, arguments on Plato, Aristotle, and theology – and as God was beyond the realms of all human knowledge, the solving of problems spoken went unsolved.

And the city did sparkle with the new bound life, where gold did deposit joy upon the citizens of a free land – but free for how long? Life was abound with fruits and blossoms, but the political situation was rife with terror and shame. The beauty of the churches, the mosaics, the art; it mused to leave all Italian work to gather dust, for

Constantinople was bursting at the seams with renaissance. But such splendour does come at its price, as it was seen just prior to the outbreak of the plague in '48, and the productive life did falter. It was also the time when the jewels of the coronation of John VI were found to have been made of glass; decades to produce such mystique, and moments to destroy.

ATTENDANCE REQUESTED

On attending church: The emperor did request that John attend with his friend the Templar, but too many deeds did the emperor attend that he could not recall Stephen's name, and knowing full well of his meaning, John did dispatch a messenger from the reserve, to Stephen immediately.

Stephen continued to eat the last portions of the meal, Clover had prepared, and although full of vigour did seemingly put his eating knife down and slump rearward as though exhausted. "The day has seen many views being voiced, no shortage is the thought that the Turk is preparing to withdraw," said Clover.

"Nothing could be further from the truth, my love. I have seen in front of the walls this day, and no withdrawal has commenced. I have seen much bickering upon the wall, and behind, between Greek, Venetian, and Genoese. Although they show high spirit in the optimistic view that such words of yours are true, the adverse is portrayed by their petty bickering. Further is the evidence delivered by arrow, announcing that the attack is to commence quite soon."

"What is the word of the day? Is the defence strong; are they scared?"

"This afternoon I drew witness to Greek and Genoese hatred of Venice grow, for the Venetians of the workshops have been requested to construct shields and mantles for the defence of the city. Minotto did order some Greeks to carry such to storage, but such orders were strained when wages were asked."

"You understand such asking?"

"I understand the asking, but not the refusal to aid in the defence which is strained as it is."

"Those of this city share a common plight," said Clover, "but the Greeks have more to lose than just their life and home. The Venetians have their families tucked safely away in another land, those of Genoese have families in Pera. Those true Greek who have taken to defend the city have their families within these very walls. They scrounge for food, from day-to-day."

"But the emperor has taken to commandeering all that imported, purchasing with his own purse all food, from all avenues that present itself, a purchase of all that is edible."

"It is not enough, Stephen. The Greeks need money for sustenance, for their families. The black market is here and there, some Greeks seek shelter for their families aboard ship; others simple security of passage from this place if the walls should fall. All Greek women caught in the city will be raped and killed, or sold into slavery, as too, their children. The elder will be executed."

"But great excitement I did hear today as I helped repair the defences. The bells were tolling and voices amassed as they turned out a chorus of song."

"I was there, Stephen. I saw the emperor join in and call his commanders to his side, to whom he gave a great speech."

"And what did he say, Clover?"

"He addressed the community as a whole, advising that each had a duty to perform, for we were to put witness to an assault to come, one that would never be forgotten in any of the centuries to come. We had a duty to fulfil and that we should be willing and ready to die for faith, country, sovereign and friend, that we should give our life, God willing, to protect our families, and the history of such a noble place in which we live, as Constantinople. He drew on a comparison of Imperial tradition and the Sultan's evil ways; how Mehmet would set to seat a false prophet upon the seat of Christ. He said that whether we chose leavened or unleavened bread should not draw any cause for concern, for our goal was one of the same. He drew on the history of Roman and Greek warriors past; men like Achilles of Troy, The Spartans of Thermopylae, and many others. He finished his speech with praise to the Lord, that He would allow us to be victorious. He then went inside and dispersed further speech, where each of the commanders embraced one another."

"Such embracing can be deciphered." And Stephen looked into Clover's eyes. "They expect defeat. They can each and every one feel the massacre to come, as though here already."

A knock on the door gave disturbance to their flow of conversation, and a look of surprise, or astonishment, fell upon Clover's face. "Who would call upon this house among others?"

"If a beggar… give them all we have."

A soldier in uniform and fully armoured stood panting. "Dear lady," he bowed. "I have a message from John, an urgent request for Stephen and his bride to attend communion this evening with the emperor himself."

"I am the bride, and acknowledge such a request. Will John be meeting us there?" Rain had drenched the man entirely, cold he was, and he stammered a little. "The Hospitaller John advises that matters of war need to be deliberated. He shall not attend this day, but does request your timely attendance for the emperor's itinerary in time of war allows for little deliberation."

Clover turned to meet Stephen's eyes as he came to stand beside her. "We will attend. And thank you for your time."

"Something for your appetite, perhaps?" asked Clover.

"No, but I thank you. I shall be on my way immediately." And with that he departed.

"Thank you, kind sir," said Clover. She turned to Stephen then. "Let us not concern ourselves with too much pessimism. Let us join others in praise. Let us go to church as so many others are to do this evening. Let us join them at the Church of the Holy Wisdom."

As they readied themselves they could not only feel a breeze commencing to build but also hear the wind as it hit the roof and rattled the door.

"It seems to be getting dark," said Stephen as he pulled his head in from his vantage at the window.

"It is almost sunset," replied Clover.

"No; it's most surely a mass of cloud."

"It matters little. We will be inside the church and won't have to worry about bad weather."

"A storm will see to it that our walk back is not a pleasant one," added Stephen.

"And will hinder the Turk at the foss." Clover turned then, having stopped what she was doing and with a smile said, "Do you wish to go or stay?"

"Go."

"Then let us continue, for time is short and we have a fair distance to travel," and she continued with what she was doing. Clover seemed to ponder something then for she stopped again and half-turned to Stephen. He was pulling on his habit, the one she had made him. Stephen didn't notice her watching. She saw his body, as well built as he was, fill the emptiness of the cloth she'd sewn together with such love. She felt very warm inside that moment. She was quick to bring herself back to normality as Stephen's head protruded from the neck of the garment. "You look well worth a king's ransom, my love," and suddenly panic struck her. "Ransom; should you wear the habit during battle, Stephen? What if you are taken ransom and sold into slavery."

"Better to be a slave than dead," he said but quickly noticed that Clover was being serious. He went to her and held her tight. "Which will not happen. I will die of combat before being taken a slave, and I shall only die if you are already dead, for my ambition will be to protect the wall and then the woman I love. Nothing will come between us, Clover, and once this horrid siege is over with, we shall live a life of love and always be within reach of the other."

"If you wear the habit you shall be targeted by many hungry men."

"I shall wear the habit nevertheless and if I be targeted for wearing such then many men will die trying to rip it from my back, for this garment of gold was made with the love of one that cannot die. If I alone were to stand the wall amidst one hundred thousand of the enemy, they still would not have the power enough to rip from me this garb that I wear."

TO BE A KNIGHT

Shortly after sunset the sky became a mass of black clouds, a curtain of darkness drawing over the scene to the front of the triple wall. It was as though orchestrated, for at that moment the Turks sprang into action. The cloud above opened up and a heavy rain did drench the earth, as thousands upon thousands of the enemy stormed forward. The enemy had one purpose in life at this moment, and that was to complete the filling in of the foss, in order for the machines of war to be brought forward. What could be done to counter such a threat – nothing? Only one thing could be done – to await the assault to commence. And all evening the rain did fall, neither drowning any idea the citizens of Constantinople had for mass; nor hindering the end of the work being carried out by the enemy.

And the congregation saw a mass of citizens and soldiers attend, with as few as possible seeing to the defence of the walls. There was now a union of the two, both Latin and Orthodox, birds of a feather, the two coming together as one. Each and every one held each other close on this day's ending. Cardinal, bishops, and priests, two religious beliefs embracing one-another, the altar of the church to serve two brothers. Confession and communion were to be served to both creeds, with little care about the differences each held in regards to their religious belief.

Stephen saw clearly the emperor arrive, his commanders spearing off to attend other family and friends, to be seated amongst those of familiar approach and forethought. And the secretary Phrantzes could be seen, the last to depart the emperor's side, to meet for further record on the inside of the church.

The emperor waved a hand at Clover's attempt at curtsy and Stephen's paying of compliment. "Please, not tonight. Tonight we are as one. I'm extremely glad you could attend and feel the sorrow for both of us at John's absence, but the life of a man does not rest whilst we serve God at the altar. John's deeds must be done as they are called to his attention, for the wounded cannot wait."

"Thank you, my lord. We too received a messenger from John and we are most honoured to be your guest for this evening's communion."

"Not at all. We shall be seated amongst others, so I must most humbly apologize beforehand if I seem transfixed, separated, or ignorant," and with that, Constantine smiled.

"Not at all, my lord."

"We shall be seated as appropriate, your forefathers, I hope, shall take this as an honour to be bestowed upon them, from me."

"The honour shall be ours," insisted Stephen.

"And there is one matter more that I wish to attend." With that he turned to an anonymous guard who stood some distance off and waved him over. "And this man shall bear witness, for news has reached my ears that you have not yet received the benevolence as appropriate for one as honourable as youself."

Stephen knew the emperor was referring to his title.

The emperor looked upon Stephen with a softness seldom seen or sensed and drew his sword with the words, 'kneel before me', escaping his lips.

Stephen knelt, Clover looking on in astonishment, for no one could have foreseen such an event that was about to unfold. And Stephen knelt there, head bowed, dressed in his habit of white and red.

And with the touching of sword on shoulder the emperor did declare, "By this token I dub you knight. Arise, Sir Stephen. Be you a good and true knight until your life's end." Stephen was speechless. "Your service rendered to date has been exemplary. I know such service will continue."

"Service to you, my lord, has been a pleasure… and will continue to be so."

"I notice your form of dress has changed slightly."

"A handmade garment, my lord."

"I think it looks better than the other you wore." With that said the emperor smiled and they entered and sat without further word, Clover taking hold of Stephen's arm as though strangling a chicken for dinner.

THE SERVICE

There was much clatter of word and heart-felt comradeship within the old church; old faces meeting new, and acquaintances long since lost, renewed; as though the siege had been lifted already, or in the least, forgotten. But nothing could be further from the truth, for all were fully aware of the army filling in the foss, but the rain beating down upon the roof of the building was a pleasant change to the cannon fire they had become accustomed to.

The crowd not yet seated, swelled amongst those of prime position, taking comfort as best they could, or simply standing where they would not be in the way of the procession of priests as they entered, watched on. For there was rumour that the service was going to be one of grandeur, so grand that it would not be forgotten; not even in death.

And indeed it was.

The clergy of sorts paraded themselves in full dress, in full light of the people who looked on in silence, families stood or sat together in clusters as though an invisible force held them, friend standing close to friend, neighbour to neighbour. The flame of thousands of candles gave an heir of peace and tranquillity, the flickering of each promoting the beauty bestow, by them, the images of mosaics seated in each of the windows of the church. A fragrance could be smelt within the church, a sense of calm being experienced by all. The mosaic of the Saints and Christ Himself, images, idols, and tapestries of a history's blend, all gave to the service of a lifetime. The very atmosphere breathed praise to the Lord their God, The Christ, Jesus, and Mary, to the Apostles and more. The atmosphere here this night was heaven and could not be taken from the mind or heart of the people.

The deliberation of ceremony was exactly that, and care was taken when offering the flesh and blood of Christ to each that offered their open mouths to the authority. The people filed down several lines, in silent prayer, which was continued once they returned to their seat or position. The ceremony then continued for a short time until the emperor was called upon to give a short sermon.

The emperor also gave a short speech at the conclusion of the ceremony for many reasons, for the most part it was a farewell to his people. But for most, what was passed was already felt or known. It was evident to many that they were fighting a dying cause, that the Sultan had under his command many guns, cavalry, and infantry, all of which out-numbered Constantinople to more than twenty to one. But what they, the Christians, did lack in number, they did have superiority in defence and in the power of God. The emperor's thoughts were let out, his feelings on the three conditions of war: to want victory, to be ashamed of dishonour, and to obey one's leaders. And all of the above must be adhered to, for if the Turk succeeded in storming Constantinople, there would be three days of pillage to follow. "I beg all of you, to abide by your chiefs, according to his military position, and if all are carried out as fitting then God will surely aid in our defence. With God's aid, His punishment will be lifted. So let us give praise this night and beg Him for his forgiveness. I know within my heart that if we follow His commands that the siege will be beaten, but heed Him not and we shall be damned."

The emperor handed the congregation over to the church authority as the service was concluded and families moved away to attend their needs. Some would try to rest, others sleep; some would go to work on the stockade, others to home where they would pray a little more; but in individuals where religion was felt the strongest, they would attend churches closest to their homes.

The service would not be soon forgotten. Such sorrows will hardly be felt again, not in a lifetime; such tears would never again touch another cheek.

THE LAST NIGHT

On conclusion of the service the emperor did call a council, the final prior to what was considered to be the coming of the final assault, and although he had said much on this day, a few things needed to be reiterated for the sake of Christianity.

Another speech was given to all of the attendance. His commanders saw greatness in his words. He was so compelling, so sincere, and was honestly concerned for the well-being of all within Constantinople, regardless of their religious belief. Constantine knew well, as others did, of Orphan and his Turks, who were stationed to defend the sea wall. He spoke of the Genoese who were giving up all possible safe sanctuary within the walls of Pera, of those Italians who did indeed stay behind to help defend their religion and the common good of all those that believed in such, regardless of how they took their bread. Jews and Venetians; mercenary and unpaid foreigner; all were fighting for the same cause, and such cause should be praised.

And the time finally arrived, the time to say goodbye was here and now. It was evident that the emperor had finished with any idea of spending further time at council, for the ministers and commanders alike were dismissed and returned to their duties. The emperor bid them farewell and praised them with good fortune as a soldier will do when the devil comes knocking at the door. Each forgave the emperor as he had requested, with words of encouragement, and all refused to accept that any unkindness had been done to them to begin with.

The emperor then visited the cathedral alone and gave praise to God, relishing the moment so dear that the time spent passed quickly. He returned in the stormy weather then to his Palace and released the servants of the house before taking comfort in the company of his secretary, Phrantzes. Together they rode the length of the inner wall in the downpour, ensuring that all gates were in fact sealed.

They both stopped and mounted a tower near the Gate of the Caligaria in Blachernae, taking in the scene around over the next hour or two. They could see the lights from the decks of ships in the Golden Horn as the rain continued, and in front heard the enemy bringing up siege equipment, and saw down the length of the wall towards the Mesoteichion. The assault would be upon them soon, and as to whether or not they survived was in the hands of God. And Phrantzes took to pointing out that man sometimes did ill against God's bidding, and that the walls were only sound so long as the hearts of men did not whither. The emperor embraced him then and released him of his duties – they would never set eyes upon each other again.

The emperor stood there a few minutes longer, alone, contemplating. The enemy was hard at work, filling in the foss as needed for the machines of war to approach closer to the walls. The rain continued, and he then retired to his station upon the wall.

PART SEVEN
Tuesday 29th May

THE BELLS TOLL

It had been stressed many times in the coming weeks, to all soldiers alike, that the most vulnerable portion of the wall was that of the Lycus Valley. On the 14th May the Golden Horn had been secured for the Turk to have his way with free and easy passage to and from the landmasses separating his great army with Constantinople. This also meant that the batteries of the Valley of the Springs could more readily abandon their position to take up a more favourable post for the bombardment of the Blachernae wall. Several days later the batteries were combined to do their worst against the defence of the Mesoteichion. It was here that the Sultan had moved the last of his guns on the 17th May.

The last hours before the major assault against Christendom commenced was spent well in preparation, troops and cannon, amongst siege machinery, being brought forward to the edge of the foss; all according to the envisaged plans of Mehmet. Upon the waters of the Marmora his sea-faring galleys and vessels sway, very nearly smashing into the others stationed either side. Here they floated, ready with scaling ladders, soldiers, and sailors alike, awaiting the command to attack. Constantinople was indeed under great threat and was about to be assaulted from all possible angles.

Now the stress of the weakness, a weakness reinforced over the many weeks past, was about to be revealed as it was considered. Since the beginning of April the city had been held at bay, and now the time had come for the Sultan, "Barbaro" – the dog-Turk – to put into effect the final play of the siege. Siege machinery was in mass: ladders, siege towers and more; cannon galore and arquebus. Balls of stone fired from cannons of bronze, unrelenting, and unmistakably deadly. And a grand assault was to take place under covering fire on three fronts; the stockade of the Mesoteichion was the weakest link.

Some of the soldiers were in position to counter the assault, many others were still with wives and family, but would ready themselves and arrive at the wall in time enough to join the slaughter to come. And fair warning was given, for at half past one on the Tuesday morning the attack was ordered along the entire triple wall.

And the gun sounded the signal for the assault to commence.

The bands played aloud; trumpets, drums and fifes. Clarity from the walls was not the best, but the cries from the Turkish ranks unmistakable. Every Christian citizen and soldier; every Turk, every religious bound man, woman and child, gave to a wavering of the soul, shaking in their boots, shoes and sandals; everyone in the city at that moment heard the cry of war as it was carried throughout the city with great volume.

The church bells then tried effortlessly to drown out the yells of battle as thousands upon thousands of Ishak Pasha's Anatolian troops sprinted for the wall. Every bell tower, church tower, steeple and timberworks that housed a bell was rung in earnest. Dozens upon dozens, each spread the warning for all soldiers and military men to take to his post, if not already stationed.

The Church of the Holy Wisdom, some three miles from the wall, did toll relentlessly as its worshippers continued with their prayers. They were soon to be joined by a monstrous crowd of citizens seeking shelter, holding to hope that the Lord himself, holding fast to the sword of perdition, would assail the intruder and protect the innocent.

Nuns and womenfolk alike reported to their posts as well, between the second and third wall, ready with spade and bucket, barrels in their plenty, ready for the filling. They had periodically stockpiled materials here for the strengthening of the defences; beams, rocks, and planks. As the defences fell, so the breeches would be filled. The women feared for death no more than a man, but feared for their family, their children and old folk too, and those crippled of the ability to defend themselves. And too-young-in-youth teenagers were to be thrown amongst the throng to thwart any idea the Turk had of entering the city uninvited – and uninvited he would always be. But one Turk was always welcome, the Turkish Prince Orphan, who was at this moment defending the wall, between the Harbour of Eleutherius and the Harbour of Contoscalion, with his detachment of Turks, to do their best in holding back the Sultan's armada of sailor who held their own greed for a purse full of ransom.

Stephen was shocked to full-sureness by the warning and looked into Clover's eyes for one long time. "I must go, and now. Time is short, my love." He was standing and placing his habit on; as for the most part he was already prepared and ready to join the fight.

Clover grabbed him by the arm. "No," she cried. "Don't go. Don't leave me." Stephen looked her in the eye again. "I have been without family or love for so long to give it up now."

"And what if the wall should stand and the city is successful in its plight to survive? What should happen to us then?"

"We can leave this place."

"I must fight. And you know that Clover. You would want that in the years to come, a memory that we served, to comfort you in old age."

"And if the Turks do enter and pillage for three days."

"We will prevail, Clover. We will make good our escape; but not before time." He turned to go then, grabbing his basinet as he prepared to depart.

"Stephen," said Clover softly. "Your sword," and handed it to him.

They hugged one another close for a few seconds and Stephen pulled away. “You remember the plan of evacuation, Clover?” Asked Stephen as he adjusted his sword.

“I do and won’t forget. I shall be waiting here with eyes and ears open, and as soon as the city is entered I shall be at the ready.”

Silence dominated their senses and they kissed one final time before Stephen stepped out onto the cobbled surface and turned to look Clover in the eye. He then departed to serve as he had promised; Stephen turned and ran off towards the wall and Clover watched as he disappeared into the night.

STEPHEN’S BAPTISM

The assault, when it came, was fast and furious. The assault upon the wall of the Golden Horn was undertaken by the sailors stationed there; there was Zaganos trying his hand at the Blachernae Quarter, keeping up a constant harassment of the forces so stationed, with Karadja further up on the high ground, up against the Bocchiardi Brothers. From the Gate of the Charisius to the Golden Horn, the Bocchiardi Brothers, Teodora Caristos, Minotto, and the Langasco Brothers, with Archbishop Leonard, were kept under constant assault by the aforementioned and the European Divisions. Success here was not the soul ambition of Mehmet, but constant harassment was. And this was not the only portion of the defence that came under a barrage of enticement. Hamza Bey was feinting against the Greek Monks and Orphan and his attachment of Turks, Hamza Bey experiencing much trouble in gaining a foothold upon the shore, for few scaling ladders were at his disposal and he had few detachments of men of any great value engaging in hand-to-hand combat.

The southernmost portion of the triple wall: Manuel, Demetrius and Jacobi Contarini were stationed at this portion of the wall where it met the sea, to their right was Filippo Contarini and the troops under his command. At the Pegea Gate was stationed Theophilus Palaeologus, the emperor's kinsman, and then on the emperors left, but further down on the sloping ground towards the Lycus River, was Cattaneo. All but Cattaneo, to any great degree, came under constant attack by Ishak Pasha and some of his Anatolian troops.

To the disappointment of Ishak, his best fighters, easily recognized by the breastplates they wore, and other distinguishable marks of uniform, were saved for a follow-up assault after the Sultan’s initial weakening of the defences of the Mesoteichon, which was achieved via the irregulars.

The irregulars did swarm upon the defence in such large numbers that they impeded upon each other. There was little to no room to swing a scimitar or mace, little room for error when firing a crossbow at short range, no room for lack of judgement when throwing javelins or thrusting spears. Here and there a few arquebus and numerous slings, the promise of booty ever pushing them forward.

The soldiers upon the defence that stood their place did well, for all held back the tide, and the attempts of breach were repulsed. But danger did still linger. But still more reinforcements were welcomed as latecomers came upon the hoarding, the wall walk of the second wall where the fighting was to be done, the innermost gates, of the innermost wall, being secured so that retreat was not possible, as the last of the soldiers took to their stations.

Stephen gained footing upon his responsibility to see the mercenary hard at work, only a few soldiers missing from their post, but spaces filled quickly. No pause for breath could be taken, no time to look down the left or right of the wall to see if the defence was holding. Stephen found himself fighting against Karadja and the European Divisions, and the irregulars, those troops thought earlier to be the first into the fray, they were stretched between the forces of the Sultans both north and south, thousands upon thousands, shoulder-to-shoulder and as deep as can be, between the Gate of Rhegium to the Gate of Charisius. The unclean of the unclean they were, dregs of society, fighters for gold and ransom, mercenary to the highest bidder, Hungarians, Germans, Slavs, Italians and Greeks, the same Greeks whom not so long ago were firing messages attached to arrows to warn Constantinople of the impending attack.

The Turk made their charge en masse, no prudence permitted, for the Sultan had his military police positioned to the rear of the assault, and behind them his Janissaries, ready to cut down those cowardly enough to retreat and get past the positioned police. And as ground was made towards the foss the Bashi-bazouks did continue to encourage the rush with screams from their bowels so loud as to wake the devil himself.

The musketry of the defence was in good position for downing many at a time, even with a single shot, piercing the enemy army with ease – as it had done in the past. But alas, the rain had done its work well in most cases; and as though God was shaking a finger at the defenders, warning 'thou should have listened when thou were told', each of the pouches of powder, even if producing dry, did not last dry for long. But some of the defence did indeed heed the warnings well and kept their power and matchlocks hidden from the foul weather until the raining subsided to practically nothing. Here at least, when a weapon was fired in unison with others, many of the enemy could be slain with much ease. The powder though did not last long in any case.

Stephen had pulled his sword and held it vertical in front of his body clad in armour and chain mail. There was much to his task and he had several feet of exaggerated length of which he was held responsible. He had never killed a man before. This thought and many others on death and killing came to pass his mind, but the reality of the situation was far too strong, and soon drained his mind of all that existed on the parameters of life and existence. Several of the enemy were clambering up a scaling ladder to his right so he stepped to his side. Their faces bore snarling mouths and gnarled teeth of black and brown. Stephen took a deep unnerving breath and exhaled, nervousness enveloping his entire body, but this lasted but the for the shortest of seconds, for as the hands of the enemy came to within reach Stephen did thrust out strong, his sword disappearing into the chest of the man on the ladder, his snarling withering to that of horror as he slowly looked down to the metal sticking in his body. His grasp upon the ladder faltered and he fell backwards, only the stronghold that Stephen maintained on his ancient weapon preventing it from falling with the corpse. The body fell from the sword, blood encasing the iron. And as the sword pulled clear, and the body of the enemy fell away from view, another appeared to his front in as quick as a flash, scaling the defence to take on the Knight of the Temple.

Stephen would later be amazed by the way in which he fought if he'd given to any contemplation, for as the sword came under his command it continued its move rearward, continuing out around to the left of his body where it commenced a gathering of speed. Again the look upon the face of the enemy changed to horror as out from Stephen's right the sword came out of its swing, horizontal to the ground, having continued its ballet, connecting with and cutting at the flesh of the enemy's neck. The slicing continued as the swing lost nothing of its momentum, the cutting of sinew and blood vessels the result. All were severed and the head fell away from the neck, to fall upon the bodies below which had now commenced to grow, for along the entire wall's frontage the enemy was being cut down with what seemed to be the greatest of ease, but still they came. Thousands upon thousands of Bashi-bazouks were flooding towards the wall for their chance to enter the city.

Stephen glanced quickly to his left and right to gauge how the fight was going, for the last thing he needed was an enemy planting a scimitar into his side, or decapitating him as he had done to the man on the scaling ladder.

All appeared well, Alfred, Paul and Lars holding their station against the hordes, and beyond them was of little concern, for it was too much to take in. his responsibility was being filled and that's all that mattered at this point. The adrenaline was pumping, the temples of his head throbbing, his heart beating at a tremendous rate, and as though by instinct he lifted his sword up and slashed downwards upon the head of another that was clambering the side of the defence. His sword buried itself deep, but was pulled out with ease, for the enemy head was split in two.

It was then that the cries of the enemy seemed to increase, fervour so great being voiced over the bands that played and the cannons that roared. The attack on the Blachernae had been increased.

Anchors were being flung up from below, ropes attached for ease in climbing; more scaling ladders appeared, enemies were standing on the shoulders of their comrades, whatever means was available to them was being utilized. And to Stephen's great relief two soldiers of unknown address, or familiarity, appeared to either side of him, to aid in the felling of the Bashi-bazouks. It was good company, that did arrive none too late, for if aid was needed, it was at this moment.

For twenty minutes the attack came on strong. The mercenary and few reserves that had arrived held back the tide. There was no time to tally the kills, no time to wipe the sweat forming at the brow. No time to speak, none to praise the Lord; none to think of loved ones, nor the health of comrades in arms. The only thoughts were those given to survival and to the fight.

Lars had taken to the sword as a partner of battle, for the crossbow could not be employed at such close quarters, where no time was given between one man falling and another taking his place. The Pillar Alfred was covered from head to toe in caked blood, and as the blood dried it did restrict his movement slightly; it was as if a thin skin of leather had formed over his dress. The Puller was also holding his ground, though only due to aid provided by the reserves, otherwise he would have fled the fight long ago; there was no using his longbow at present.

The fighting continued, the dead continued to mount at the foot of the wall and time passed quickly, and as the time passed, the attack seemed to subside. The Bashi-bazouks were being ordered to concentrate their attack on the area around the stockade. The reserves that had served Stephen and the others so well fell back to other quarters as ordered by messenger, and pavis holders appeared to the front of the mercenary.

Paul the Puller took to his bow once again and Lars picked up his crossbow, the others of the defence did what they could to hold back the few enemy that harassed them continuously, but it wasn't easy with the aid the enemy were receiving, from the marksman with crossbow, hiding behind pavis.

The attacks along the line of defence, from Golden Horn to the Bosphorus, from the sea itself and the boats near the pontoon bridge, all pushed on the assault, preventing the re-positioning of soldiers on the line to help those most in need: the soldiers defending the Lycus Valley.

The weakest point in the defence: It was as expected the St Romanus gate, and as expected as it could have been, for the emperor had stationed himself in that very location. To the right of this was also no exception, being defended well by Giustiniani. Here the Greeks and Italians were by far better trained than the irregulars, better trained, better armed, and better protected with armour and a strong defensive position. Here, between the 5th Military Gate and The Gate of Charisius, was distributed the hand-held weapons of fire-and-boom – the Culverines and Arquebus. Arrows fired always found a target, rocks of enormous size thrown upon the enemy brought more than one to his knees. The work was tiring, the work was hazardous, but defending the city was their soul task. The soldiers and citizens of Constantinople would not quit.

The irregulars fighting were far from the talents of the Christians. Clambering over the bodies of their comrades they fought, fixing ladders where possible, all trying to attain the unlikely – the glory of being the first into the city beyond the wall.

THE SECOND WAVE

It was three thirty in the morning, the fighting had been going on now for a full two hours. The Bashi-bazouks had made no headway and were summarily removed from the pitch of the assault. The Christian defence had been little dented, but tired they were and holes in their line, both of flesh and wall, had to be filled.

The citizens of the city started to come forward, to fix what could be fixed. The moon was waning but gave off a bit of light, but the cloud cover was still thick and aided the citizens little. Even during the assault, when flares had been fired high above, it was hard to see the action far afield. The call at the time was that the repulse of the enemy had taken its toll on the forces of the Sultan and that nothing further would be ventured this day in regards to a full-on assault.

As the defences were still being attended they were all shocked back to the reality of Mehmet's dream, for at that moment the night air was filled again with the cries of battle, trumpets, fifes, and drums. Church bells again filled the city with its warning. It was then that the artillery recommenced its work on the fortifications, all batteries firing as one. The precision of the second phase of the attack on the city was well orchestrated. The best of the Anatolian regiments swung down from the slopes of the Lycus Valley, down from the West in front of the Gate of St Romanus – the 5th Military Gate. They then came full on, in nearly as straight a line as could be expected and hit the wall hard as the artillery slowed slightly in its deliverance of shot. The sea wall also came under the harassment of sailors, and the Blachernae and Studion kept busy with pockets of enemy to their front, all as the Anatolian commenced to do their worst upon the defenders of the stockade. The ground was wet, restricting movement, it was mushy underfoot, an obstacle in itself. But the Anatolian guard cared little. And once over the foss the footing again became unstable, brought on by rubble and the corpses of men. Bodies were everywhere, eight deep in places, and the massacre continued. The Anatolian were by far more experienced and disciplined than their counterparts, but they died just as well as a Bashi-bazouk. The armour was well suited for the push forward, and the weapons they carried handled well. The Annotations now experienced what the Bashi-bazouks had before them. The fray was restricted by space, by the closeness of comrades. There was little room to fight, the fight they were asking for, a fight so recently granted them by Mehmet. Their determination, courage and ferocity; their actions as a group, as a regiment, as though a single entity; their staying together and belief in what they were, it only aided in their downfall.

The pavis holders, to Stephen's front, did appear to have withdrawn, and in their place a storm of enemy dashed for the opportunity to assault the men on the wall due to their lack in number. It had been considered that all reserves would have most definitely been employed to the area of the stockade, but nothing could have been more misread of the defence.

As soon as the wave assault came out of the night a signal was sent to Lucas Notaras, who acted with great speed, and his men sprang to the call with inspired agility. A dozen men of the depleted reserve were soon standing by their comrades in arms, filling the gaps that presented themselves amongst the mercenary. A detachment of Bashi-bazouks, some men under Karadja Pasha, and remnants of the European Division, all now assailed the Blachernae.

Stephen, as for the others, had already seen two hours of fighting with only a few minutes rest and now the onslaught was about to begin again. As strong as he was he couldn't believe how sore his muscles had become. He had pushed them to the limit, his sword made to dance through the air as though born to it. So smooth was his actions that anyone witnessing his courageous fight for survival would have decided then and there that it was due to many decades of fighting and practice. Yet nothing could be further from the truth. He had spent much of his young life working on a farm; which would have accounted for his stamina and build. He had known many good men in his younger years, men whose names would never be repeated, for they were nothing to history or the community as a whole. Great men they were, but great to Stephen and none other. They had helped instil the confidence he now displayed and the good will that he felt in regards to helping those less fortunate then himself, namely the citizens of Constantinople.

Again he fought as before, killing men one after the other. A thrust to the heart would see one man fall, with another he would decapitate his head, and yet another to which he would hack down upon the man's wrist, cutting his hand away from the forearm with much ease. Metal clashed against scimitar, but most of all, his sword cut at the flesh and bone of the enemy. His long-bladed sword was well made for the shearing off of limbs. The blood upon his weapon massed and dripped, the double-handed grip taken good control of and always under his command. The sweat from his brow had long since stopped and if it wasn't for the cool of the night then he would have collapsed a long time ago from heat exhaustion.

The defence for the time was being held with the majestic grace of swordsmanship being displayed by all upon the wall. Compared with the strength of the enemy, the defence had a lot to be desired; yet the Christians had lost few lives, where the Turk had lost thousands.

A HOLE IN THE DEFENCE

The closeness of rank and comradeship saw to it that the Anatolian Guard were dealt a heavy blow, regardless of their actions. Their valour and wickedness was faltering. They were straining. Their losses were growing by the minute.

The men on the wall were tiring ever so. Many couldn't see that they could hold for much longer, but they did. The sun would be upon them within one and half-hours or better and with it a little reprieve, for they would have clarity of the battlefield up and down the entire wall, being able to see at a glance in order to determine where reinforcements were required. But before such could take place the greatest cannon in Mehmet's collection of bronze did hit the stockade so hard that it almost demolished all hope and enthusiasm in a heartbeat. The stockade collapsed.

No less than three hundred Anatolian warriors then attacked the hole in the defence, all believing in his own mind that the Turkish army would be within the walls of Constantinople in the time it takes a mercenary to rape a woman. Through the dust and smoke they rushed, clambering over the rubble, gaining precious feet towards the opening that the great cannon had achieved. Over the bodies of the slain they trod, lifting one another upon the shoulder of the man in front, clinging to whatever they could in order to achieve a strong hold, clambering as quickly as possible over the rubble.

The emperor saw the move and counter-attacked, Christians from all around closed in on the Turks, sword clashing with scimitar, slash against parry, parry against thrust, thrust against any open opportunity to bring a bloodied body all that much closer to death. Inch-by-inch and then foot-by-foot, the Anatolians were pushed back towards the foss and forced to retreat to the safety of their banners, many of their comrades lying dead amongst the fallen rubble and corpses surrounding the stockade.

Here was the fiercest fighting of the entire siege, here the fighting continued relentlessly, without break, without remorse. The stockade was looked upon as a prize to Mehmet, it was the weakest point of the entire wall. The Blachernae Quarter was second only to St Romanus, for the fighting there, where Stephen lashed out with his sword and courage, was one the fiercest many men had known in the history of warfare.

The feints elsewhere did well to prevent reinforcements, other than those provided for by Lucas Notaras and Nicephorus Palaeologus, coming to the aid of the stockade. Other points along the wall would not be arriving to give support to those at the Lycus Valley, nor to the northernmost tip of the defence. But the preventative measure did little in aiding the Turk gain a permanent hold on the ground to the inner grounds of Constantinople. All breeches achieved to date were quickly sewn up and the damage repaired. All could see well that the Imperial Eagle and Lion of Saint Mark were flying high above the towers, and whilst the flag of the city flew, all was safe and in Christian hands.

THE POSTERN

A hurried move was made to reorganize the line, and resources were brought up from behind the second wall, a long ditch having appeared through the weeks of excavation, where the soil was taken for the much needed repair of the stockade and other breeches similarly affected. Whatever the citizens or soldiers would decide upon, would have to be decided and acted upon quickly. And after just a few quick repairs, and barely enough time for men on the wall to water themselves, Mehmet gave the order for his Janissaries to attack. Indeed, he had saved the best till last and they did not disappoint as they screamed forward.

Mangle, ballistae, and cannon; javelins, arrows and ball from hand held weapons; all were let loose. The Janissaries followed up behind this barrage of hand weapons, pushed ever forward on a wind that carried the sound of music. The well-orchestrated barrage of cannonade also continued, the music taking up the tempo during lapses in the batteries fire.

Within the wall it was a different story. The church bells rang and rang loud; and prayer, prayer was delivered as it was over the past twelve hours; delivered from the hearts and souls, the rubbing and kissing of rosaries continuing now more than ever.

Weary, so weary, yet fight they must. Over four hours of defending the city and yet still more fighting to come. The Janissaries were the key to Mehmet's quest. If they succeeded, where all else had failed, Constantinople was doomed; if the defence should succeed, Mehmet would be forced to lift the siege. Every Christian and Turk fighting for the defence of the city knew the odds they were up against, and it had come to this. The best-trained regiment known, they came upon the defence in tight formation and in perfect line – slower than the Bashi-bazouks and Annotations, but by far more deadly.

They fell, man after man, and as one fell another took his place, the line unbroken. And although Mehmet could not be heard over the noise of the battle in progress, he could be seen as he spurred his Favourites on from the Turk side of the foss.

The Janissaries would soon be engaging in hand-to-hand, a melee so thick that a swarm of flies over a week old carcass was nothing in comparison. The defences were being torn apart, fingernails lost through sheer effort of adrenaline, ladders being flung against the stockade, wave upon wave of finely-equipped, scimitar-wielding soldiers, grabbing for his taste of the battle being fought.

So fierce was the onslaught, on both sides, that the Christian reserve had been called upon to fill the gaps some time ago, and no other men were left to aid in keeping back the rising tide of Janissary troops. But under the emperor and Giustiniani the Christians did what no one else could do; they held the enemy in check.

The emperor sent out a messenger for his cousin Theophilus Palaeologus to attend his aid this moment with a detachment of men as large as he thought could be spared from the fight against Ishak Pasha and his rabble. His cousin answered by availing himself and several dozen others.

The melee against the Janissary had been heavy now for one hour and the sun was expected to appear at any moment. The Janissaries were wavering and all looked well. The stockade was holding. The Blachernae Quarter too was doing well against the constant barrage of a few guns, the European divisions, and Zaganos.

There was a small door here, at the Blachernae, hidden well from view by a tower near where the single wall became three, which aided the defence. Sorties were passing in and out of the city through the Kerkoporta Postern. The enemy was harassed from time-to-time via the use of this sally port. Some siege equipment had been destroyed and enemy cut down from enfilade fire, culverine and arquebus being used to their fullest potential, though through sheer numbers within the assault, any firing angle would have proved worthwhile.

It was through sheer panic that the last sortie through the door had forgotten to bar it on their return, and a single Turk, now passing the area concerned, could see a dark patch of suspicious value. He was quick to investigate and quicker still to draw the attention of his comrades in arms.

A group of foreigners and Turks fighting for the Sultan, approximately fifty strong, soon found themselves inside the courtyard of the Blachernae Quarter, searching frantically for the best way to seal their good fortune.

The sudden flux of men through the postern did affect the amount of enemy scaling the wall to Stephen's front and with the fall in numbers came the opportunity to immediately access the situation. He looked left and right to see all in order and then a voice could be heard calling out a warning. Someone's attention below had been drawn to the enemy entering the manicured grounds of the palace, several dozen Turks making for a rush across an open area.

Several of the defence were close enough and available to meet the enemy in hand-to-hand, but the numbers that had gained access, through the sheer lack of concentration in regards to sealing the postern, was by far superior in volume.

Stephen was quick to adjust to the new threat and within the shortest time had made his way down the inner stairway to meet the scimitar wielding foot soldiers head on. Two men approached him, teeth bared. The closest held his scimitar high behind his strong arm in preparation to swing; Stephen ducked as the scimitar began its swing and thrust up and out with his relic of iron. The sword pierced the stomach of the Turk, his bowls punctured and spine severed. The body fell like a sack of potatoes dropped to the deck of a pier from a ship. The Templar pulled the weapon out of the scabbard of flesh and met the second threat by blocking the fall of the scimitar as an effort was made by the Turk to slice his head in two.

Still on one knee he gathered his strength and courage, and on blocking immediately rolled out to his right, at the same time slicing outwards from the left. The Turk just stood there momentarily and looked down, his guts spilling out to the grass of the courtyard, and then collapsed as per the first of his brethren in arms.

Stephen stood and parried a third, thrust out and punctured the enemy's lung, he too, being drawn to the bright light of death. Six others could then be seen coming his way, time enough to weigh up the new threat and to feel the pangs of fear as they began to well inside his temple of tissue. He had time to give praise to the Lord, a quick prayer for his courage to see him through, and for Clover's safety. A few more seconds and they would be upon him.

Then a voice suddenly gave him strength: "Squandering all the fun is not the way of the Order, Squire; you must share your lot with all that accompany you."

Stephen knew the voice without turning, for there was no time. "John!" And his courage then soared. "I think I am man enough to provide you with work in the hospital to last a lifetime."

"That is what I fear, young Templar, for these scum must meet their maker, not be wounded to stab us in the back as we work our way towards the postern," and work their way forward they did, for with those words spoken the fight was on. Stephen and John were near the path leading to the inner stairway when several others of the defence joined them, for across on the other side of the courtyard came a small bunch of enemy. A call then went up and the Bocchiardi Brothers took heed, another small band of men being dispatched to aid in the keeping back of the Turkish tide.

An inner stairway leading to the hoarding where the defence stood strong, was soon assailed and under direct threat of the enemy from both behind and from the front, men fighting under Karadja Pasha, who continued to scale the walls and enter through the open postern. Men fighting under the Bocchiardi Brothers then arrived, and tried to seal and bar the postern, the first real fighting within the wall having well commenced, but not yet under control.

The Turks were surrounded and the slaughter continued, when suddenly, from down the line, something terrible did occur.

WOUNDED

Giustiniani was wounded badly, through the breastplate did penetrate a ball from an arquebus, and the wound was now pouring blood, the infection of such spreading fast and wide, up and down the wall to all ears. Panic in the men began to rise, the resistance so well founded was now faltering. Then suddenly from nowhere, becoming a deliberate target, an arrow did pierce Giovanni's shoulder. He fell then to his knees, spittle forming momentarily at the mouth. The emperor was called to the scene, who did try and convince Giustiniani to stay for the strengthening of the hearts of all men of his command, stating that the wound, although severe in appearance, was slight in the current reflection regards the defence of the stockade. Danger was pressing and his presence at this time was very much the requirement in order for the defence to hold.

"I shall retire," was his reply, and he did urge the men around him briefly to continue with the fight, but to pass through the door of the wall to safety was his only concern, for the pain was immense.

Giustiniani's palm touched others on the wall as he was carried away by two men, one under either arm and as delicately as possible, for the wounds were deep and much pain was becoming quickly evident. "Stay men, you must, for the sake of the good Lord." A little blood appeared to the corner of his mouth, a cough was followed by a stammer, and the men either side took the weight of their commander in battle.

The look upon the emperor was most excruciating, for he was just about to see depart his best hope for defending the wall. It was then that a messenger appeared at his side. "My lord. The Bocchiardi Brothers report a catastrophe. The Kerkoporta gate has been breached by many men, and much more now, for the gate was forced open again as we tried to aid it secure, and the Turks – they are streaming through.

The emperor wasted no time at all. He looked behind him to see panic in the eyes of all the men upon the wall as he descended the stairs through the small gate of the tower in which Giustiniani wished to pass. He called out over his shoulder, "Stay, Giovanni, I plead you to stay," and raced off upon his mare of white feet, his cousin left in command to do what he could to save the day.

The Bocchiardi were doing their best to hold the melee in check, but the Turk came on like a ball from a culverine. The defence had been fighting for so long, with so few, that exhaustion was taking its toll. Each and every individual did what he could to deliver, from the pits of hell, every last ounce of energy reserve.

The emperor could see the fight was fast approaching victory for the Sultan. "The gate, seal the gate immediately." He turned his horse once again, for he saw the worthy Templar just then, John at his side, both thick in the fight. They would both hold the ground of the courtyard, this he was sure of. The Bocchiardi Brothers would seal the postern. He had little choice then but to trust in his instincts. The two Orders, fighting side-by-side would not wither. The Templar and Hospitaller would see death before they gave an inch of ground to the Turk. He thought then only of the stockade. That was the danger, for the Janissary was most deadly at the stockade and must remain at bay in order for the defence to hold.

The emperor rode off in haste and as he rode he saw something that could not be believed, and this he shook from his mind as a figment of his imagination. Marlon, one fighting under the Bocchiardi Brothers, a Genoese with a great hatred for the Venetians, was cowering behind the wall.

A MASS GRAVE

The emperor had returned to the stockade with little time lost. The great Giovanni was gone, removed from the battle, and panic could be seen to rise amongst the men, and as suddenly as it was calm a rush for the gate was made by the men defending the stockade. The Genoese were withdrawing en masse, but the Greeks stayed put, held their posts, and fought back as only a Greek can. The gate couldn't be sealed for the rush was too great, and the Janissary on seeing this did make good use of it. The ranks of the defence were thinning greatly; something was amiss. And out of the depths could be heard a Turk yelling out as loud as could be, "The city belongs to us," for it was at that moment that the enemy had taken hold of a tower in the Blachernae Quarter, lowering the flag of the city, and had raised in its place a Turkish flag – a waning moon with a star in its arc. The Templar and Hospitaller had failed him; the enemy had achieved success.

The Janissaries received a flux of strength that instant and were spurred on by valour. A group of thirty pressed forward under the command of the monstrosity of a man – Hassan; a muscle bound giant. He held a round buckler in one hand, his scimitar in the other; he stood upon the open way of a breach, spurring on all on-lookers

To the emperor's valour the Christians can salute, for along with Don Francisco, his cousin Theopilus, and John Dalmata, he did stay and defend the wall. Giustiniani was not to be seen by him again, he had withdrawn; it was over.

Theophilus looked into his cousin's eyes then and drew his sword from scabbard. "My Lord Constantine. I would rather die now than live my life out as a coward," and disappeared into the rush of the enemy. Constantine knew his time was up, the city was about to die, so he too threw away his regalia and let leash with an adrenaline rush of power, thrusts, and parries, hacking at the enemy as they clambered up and along the wall.

Eighteen, including Hassan, were slaughtered in the short venture, a stone from a sling knocking the Turk commander to his knees before he was slain as he looked up with eyes wide. It was here that the emperor was seen, ever pressing forward amongst a group of the enemy, to block the breach with his very soul.

The emperor was then felled in battle, after fighting a fight as any soldier would – not dressed in refinery, but dressed to kill – and after the siege his body would not be found, his body unaccountable. The Sultan would therefore be denied one of his bequests.

The influx of enemy upon the breach was too much, but withdraw the Greeks did not; they were forced back by sheer weight of numbers and soon found themselves in the unfortunate position of fighting from the long ditch dug over the previous weeks, the ditch from which soil was taken to aid in refurbishing the stockade.

Here the Greeks met with death, in a ditch, backed by the inner wall, nowhere to go but forward, but forward was out of the question, for that was where the Janissary stood in their thousands, having stormed over the stockade to stand upon the rubble. The air then became thick with arrows as Janissaries upon the stockade fired down upon the Greeks in the ditch. All were killed within less time than it takes to draw several breaths, and the enemy then continued to pour through the breach.

And the breaches within the wall grew at an alarming rate, Turks rushing into the city unopposed in a majority of the cases; and where such opposition could be found, subjugation soon followed. And yells went up everywhere, "The city is taken."

A FIGHTING WITHDRAWAL

The Bocchiardi fought on for some considerable time and as they continued their fight the sun did break the line of the horizon. The fighting was fierce and the Kerkoporta could not be barred. Stephen had fallen back slightly, but not due to lack of valour.

Paulo Bocchiardi was felled and shortly after an order passed from soldier to soldier, for everyone to conduct a fighting withdrawal towards the Golden Horn where they could be ferried over to Pera or make good an escape into the Marmora.

Stephen could see the Turkish flag flying high above, heard the order given by the Brothers, and could see the mass of Turk in front of him was growing in number. It was time to withdraw. The Venetians under Minotto had been slain to the man, so there was no resistance to be met as the enemy now commenced to clamber over the wall.

Stephen turned to John: "We must withdraw, John, with the others, for the numbers will aid in our survival."

John could see the boy had grown into a man, for he was thinking well of the tactics of battle, and as John lax in concentration an arrow from a crossbow did pierce his right eye, killing him instantly. Stephen just stood there then, shocked beyond the feelings of anything he'd experienced before. The man he had come to love and honour was standing there one minute and the next laying upon the grass of the courtyard with an arrow standing erect from within his head.

Stephen's sword arm fell to his side and the other covered his mouth as vomit spilled from his convulsing gut. He was quickly jolted back to the reality of the situation when an arrow was miraculously deflected from his forearm by the lower cannon of the vambrace that he wore. He then did as any other would, ran for cover, away from harm, for he was obviously in easy visual of one who carried a crossbow.

Stephen could see the panic around him as it commenced to grow and his thoughts of Clover took over his mind. He ran as fast as he could for the Church of St John in Trullo and he saw the irony of the situation. The Hospitaller was dead, gone forever. He had never considered seeing John again, especially in the circumstances that brought their meeting to an end, but Clover was all that mattered now. Men all around him were doing as he, fleeing the wall for family or a quick ship; none even considered what they were doing as cowardly, for to stay on the wall was sheer suicide and only a mad man could consider such an end. He must meet with Clover as planned and do all in his power to ensure she was safely delivered to a way out of Constantinople.

And it didn't take long for the news to reach the eyes and ears of those at the harbour. It also came to pass that many of those in Pera also felt ill of the Sultan's word, and took to evacuating their homes – even if under truce. It was a mass exodus, and few places within the city put up any resistance. But down near the boom, near the Prosphorianus Harbour, at the gate of Horaia, Cretan sailors did barricade themselves in three towers and would not surrender their position.

MASS PANIC

All soldiers and officers alike along the southernmost portion of the triple wall became surrounded soon after the city was breached. They were mostly slaughtered, commanders of high rank taken for ransom where possible. Along the Marmora ships were abandoned, the landwall being rushed in anticipation. Little to no resistance was encountered. Suburbs at the southern-most tip of Constantinople gave into Hamza Bey, surrendered forthwith, allowing their gates to be opened in order for reprieve to be received. Their homes would forego pillage, and the sailors' head inland towards the real booty. The Monks, if not slain, would be ransomed, Orphan and his detachment of Turks had little choice but to fight on – they were soon cut down. The Catalans were slain to the last, those under Cardinal Isidore taking to escape. In the Golden Horn, the Gates of Phanar and Petrion were opened freely, once again a promise to forego pillage was given.

And as the wall along the Golden Horn was taken, those that weren't taken in battle, or who were simply swept aside in the rush for booty, made for the ships and other vessels of the Horn; escape was their only plan.

The screams of victims meeting death, those being raped, and others being put to torture, were coming from Stephen's left, towards the Horn. The defence was collapsing in its entirety. There would be little hope for escape, but a surge of optimism spurred him on as Clover came to sight in front of the Church.

"Stephen!" she cried and tears of hope flowed momentarily from her eyes. "We must hurry!"

"I know, my love," he replied and continued his run.

"No, I mean it." He reached her and held here briefly. "Several Turks have already passed here. Quickly, take off your habit. We will go more unnoticed without it."

"A man in arms, running with a fair maiden, that in itself will draw attention to us."

"Now, Stephen, quickly." A shrieking cry then escaped her lips, "Behind you!" He turned to see a scimitar-yielding Turk running towards him, but on seeing the Templar draw his sword, did quickly change his mind, turned, and ran off in another direction. "They are after gold and anything else they can sell to fill their pockets," voiced

Stephen.

"Which includes ransom."

"Quick, help me off with this," and he took the habit off and let it fall to the ground. They then both turned and hand-in-hand ran towards the Prosphorianus Harbour as fast as their feet would carry them, the place they were to meet if the church was to fail them.

Looting was rife throughout, the lands in front of the wall becoming almost bare of all human semblance, and the sea around was also abandoned, for the sailors knew that to enter the city too late would secure nothing of great worth.

Alviso Diedo let his feelings be known to the authority of Pera. He was Venetian, those of Pera were Genoese. By all aspects of this siege and assault, the Greeks were the ones currently at war. War had not been declared in any form against any Venetian or Genoese. If foreigners of such countries wished to fight and die in Constantinople, then that would be their undoing, and Mehmet cared little for the defenders' creed, religion, or affirmations. It was passed to Alviso that the Sultan would not wish war with Venice and Genoa, but in the same token, it was in the best interest of all Genoese, in particular those that had taken some form of hostility out upon the Turk, to hasten for an escape.

Ships within the harbour were signalled and the boom cut free with the head of an axe. Citizens were swimming out to the vessels and the sailors did wait for the cargo of flesh where practicable, and even once clear of the harbour, the ships did wait for over an hour.

Stephen and Clover turned a road within the suburbs along the Horn, relatively safe at present, for the wall between the Gate of the Drungarii and Seraglio Point had not yet been breached, namely due to friendly ships still at anchor, or making ready their escape.

"Quick, Stephen, this way."

As they turned the corner they came to a stop, a man with bow in hand was to their front. He had heard Stephen's name called and turned on his heel. The speed of his next movement was amazing. In as quick as a bolt of lightning strikes the earth, Paul the Puller had drawn a 36-inch shaft of birch, fletched with goose feathers, ready to release. The front part of the bow was flat, the belly – innermost portion – was rounded. It was tapered at the ends and tipped with horn nocks to aid in the pulling back of the 150 pounds of pull, yard binding attached round the middle to aid in maintaining a firm grip. Great strength indeed was required to bend the yew stave. The arrow had a range of 365 yards, and even at that range the bodkin point could easily pierce armour. He could not aim by looking down the arrow shaft. With the string pulled back next to ear, natural instinct took play in pointing the arrow at the target.

Stephen had no escape.

The Puller was still protected well with armour and mail; helmet, breastplates, plackart and greaves, a fauld of four lames with a tasset attached. The Puller smiled, he now had his chance of revenge against the Templar. Stephen could only wonder as to how long the man could hold onto the drawn bow before having to let loose the arrow; there was a lot of pressure placed upon the fingers of this cowardly archer.

"Paul, we must ready ourselves and escape. The Turk lingers near. Only together can we succeed. Your bow and my sword will aid us well against the enemy both far and near."

"I agree, Stephen, but I cannot trust you. Besides, I like your woman. I have not held one for a long time. Order your woman here to my side and I shall consider your freedom from leash."

"We are wed," announced Clover.

"You shall be a widow if you don't do as I command. Now come to me or I shall kill Stephen this instant."

"You have no control over my wife, Paul. You will not escape with her consenting to you."

"I wish your wife for one reason only, 'Sir Knight', and it is not to tie me down in my escape."

"I shall not come," and Clover stood in front of Stephen as Paul the Puller let loose the last of his arrows.

The flight was quick and smooth, and pierced Clover's chest, deflecting slightly against bone as it exited and hit hard against the mail at Stephen's torso, it ricocheted off; the Puller had flinched at the last moment due to Clover's movement. She slumped heavily within Stephen's arms and agony enveloped Stephen as he had never known before. His eyes filled immediately and he cried out in pain before looking up at the Puller.

Paul too had given to pause, but returned to his old self and grinned at the knight. "You shall be next, Stephen, and it will be a great pleasure to see you fall."

Stephen had put Clover down during this time and pulled his sword, got up and started to run towards the Englishman, closing the gap between them.

Paul grinned weirdly, he had time to respond. His right hand lifted behind and searched for another arrow, but none was available. His grin disappeared and he realized his error. He had no arrows left. He quickly dropped his weapon of choice and pulled his dagger but Stephen was already upon him, blade of sword having effortlessly entered Paul's throat and pulled clear, whereby Stephen just stood and watched as the Puller grasped at his open wound and slowly drowned as he gargled his own blood.

Stephen turned and ran back to Clover, dropping his sword before he dropped to his knees. He lifted Clover to his lap and the tears flowed freely, like they had never flowed before. He lifted his own head then and a loud wail of terror escaped him, a shriek of pain most stirring echoed out towards the far reaches of the city. He sobbed for his beloved but she was well past saving. Her death had been instantaneous. There was no turning back the tide. He shook his mind back to the reality of the situation for this was no time for mourning. He must do what he could, for his one and only. He stood and flung her as delicately as possible over his left shoulder, picked up his sword with his right hand, sheathed it, and recommenced his run towards the harbour.

PILLAGE

The Sultan's troops did as ordered and swung past the Church of the Holy Apostles. But not through discipline was the church to go without sacking, for Mehmet had dispatched guards to the church, to have it surrendered to the Christian population at a later date. The Sultan's plan was for George Scholarius to be Patriarch of Constantinople, and the Church of the Holy Apostles to be the Patriarchal Church.

Citizens of Constantinople fled to the far reaches of the city, hoping for a way to be clear of the slaughter, a terrible massacre, quite easily comparable to the onslaught inflicted upon them back in 1204. From the high ground of Petra, and down past the church of St Mary, blood flowed its worst, a stream of red passing down the street as though water delivered from a storm.

The Sultan's troops stormed the wall, the gates and the breaches. Treasures were to be had, to be held, to be ransomed; for not all treasure was made of gold, for many personages of high rank and worth were spread out through Constantinople. Many slaves were to be had, but many also cut down in their weary form and youth. Women were raped ten times over and then put aside for further enjoyment later – if not beheaded. Nuns lost their virginity upon the altar of their church; little girls were taken for the same enjoyment, others evacuated to be sold as slaves. Young boys and babies would do well amongst the Janissaries, for their numbers would need constant replenishment as the years progressed through this day and age of warfare.

Greek upon Greek fled to the Church of the Holy Wisdom. Here they barred the great doors and listened to gospel as they kneeled and prayed. The doors took moments to break through, for the church was a favourite in the minds of the Sultan's troops for sacking. Here too, in the sight of God, in his very presence, were the people slain and the women insulted as they were anywhere else in the city. Women lay screaming, arms and legs held down, raped over and over. Some gave in freely, to forego the hostility of the snarling Turks, others felt the more brutal side of being violated. Few escaped death within the walls of the church once held so sacred to heart, fewer still could understand what they had done for God to curse them so. And whilst this took place in this church, as well as the other monasteries and churches of minor importance, the library and other well established premises, were robbed of their worth. And what could not be robbed was burnt or defaced, by hammer and nail, faeces, or simply pulled to the ground to be smashed upon dirt or marble floor. For an army that had three days and nights of pillage, they worked quickly, for all were aware that within a few hours there would be little left to pillage.

The library was a target as any other, a majority of its volumes destroyed; Plato, Aristotle, Homer; names too numerous to contemplate. 120,000 volumes were to become unaccounted for. And there, too, were the gospels so many had heard about, as prestigious as a gospel could be, with its fine covering of gold and silver type, so calligraphic as to behold sainthood itself. Their covers of majesty were ripped from the spine to be sold for what gold could be had, the remainder of the volume being discarded, to be burnt in the flames of a fire whilst soldiers sat cooking their main meal of the day.

It was within that studied, of such a place as the libraries of Constantinople, that a renaissance could unknowingly, but all possibly, be born. Italian scholars, students and philosophers, held so dear the very conscious idea of the Hellenic form of knowledge, that Europe in its entirety should be surely grateful. And the man of the future, behind such influence, was to be Barlaam, though history would later argue against this. But it was from the very salvage of books that all of Europe was blessed, and it is those that saved the classical writings from the destructive hands of the Turk during the siege that the coming renaissance should really be thankful. So many volumes, so many authors, all saved for mankind to savour; but too, so many to be lost in the days to come.

So yes, a renaissance could be affiliated with Constantinople, most definitely, and the spark would grow into a flame.

TO SEA

Stephen was close to the harbour now, his run having subsided to a fast walk. He could never consider Clover as heavy, for such a burden she could never be, but the weight and hand-to-hand fighting had all taken its toll. A burial she deserved as good as he could provide, even if that burial was conducted at sea.

He looked up then. The way in front of him looked familiar. He turned one final corner and saw relief in all its glory. The gate to the harbour was open, many people streaming through the entrance. He must hurry if he was to gain a secure passage from Constantinople, but leave Clover he would not do.

The citizens of Constantinople were still trying to gain passage even now, as the gap between ship and harbour commenced to grow. How was he to manage passage for himself and a dead wife? No one was going to give a place to someone that had already passed to the world beyond where they would be forever at peace.

Stephen managed to walk to one corner of a short pier and sat, having placed his Clover down gently. Then a voice came upon his ear: "Squire; here kind sir." Stephen looked up and saw the familiar face of Franco, the sailor of whom he had spent time with. "Quick lad. Swim for it. I shall help you board. We have room for one more."

He looked down upon Clover, her blood soaked front having started to congeal and currently attracting flies. He waved his hand over the corps to disperse them, but it did little to help. He couldn't go without her. He looked to Franco who was some distance off. The Brigantine hadn't yet set sail but was getting ready for the sea, many smaller boats clinging to her side in order to unload their precious cargo of men, women, and children.

He must make a decision and that decision should be to stay with his wife. But she was no more. If indeed heaven did exist, she would be there, looking down upon him, urging him to make good his escape.

Franco called again, this time with some urgency. "Stephen, behind you!" The Templar turned to see his fate. Don Rodrigo was coming full pelt towards him with a sword at the ready. Stephen had been taken by surprise but time did allow him to reach for and draw his own weapon.

His right hand moved across his body for the ancient sword, to allow him to spill more blood; but such spilling of blood was not to be, for Don Rodrigo was flung backwards and brought to a halt.

Stephen couldn't believe his eyes. One minute he was to be skewered by Don Rodrigo, the next his opposition had been put to rest. He looked more closely. An arrow was stuck in his head, having pierced his helmet and entered the brain. The Don was done for. Stephen turned around and searched behind, looking over the area from which the arrow must have come, and there upon the waters of the Horn knelt a single man within the confines of the smallest of boats; it was Lars.

Lars put the crossbow down and started to row towards Stephen, and Stephen wasted no time at all in lowering Clover to the boat before stepping from the harbour, to allow the lands of Rome to be vanquished forever. He had done all that he could, but it had all come to no good. He had a wife for a few days and would have to bury her soon, and two friends to speak of that were still living; Lars of whom he knew little, and Franco of whom he knew less.

The two men rowed towards the brigantine, Stephen saying nothing to Lars, for words were not necessary. All he could do was look down upon his wife as he helped Lars with the rowing. It came to his mind then; he wanted so much to be with his wife and hated the very thought of her being put to rest under the waves of the Marmora. If her final resting-place was to be the sea then he would spend what time he had on this earth sailing its oceans, inlets, and bays. It was the least he could do, for she had saved his life.

On reaching the brigantine, Franco did help them board, saying nothing in protest as they lifted Clover's body to safety, he was a man of the world and knew that many that were brought aboard would have to be delivered to the depths of the ocean over the coming days, for many of them were severely wounded.

Clover was carried below deck and Stephen mourned over her as all above deck commenced to put the brigantine to sea. It wasn't long before the vessel left the Horn behind, for good this time, for the crew would not be returning a second time, as they did the week before.

A steady wind then picked up from the north and the ships at the head of the Bosphorus could wait no longer, taking the advantage immediately, setting sail, their holds filled to the brink and decks riddled with passengers galore.

And as the armada of 7 Genoese ships and 2 warships, 5 Greek galleys and all that remained of the Venetian warships set sail, their escape was seen. The Golden Horn was then quickly corked up and 4 Greek galleys, 2 Genoese galleys, and all of the merchantmen from Venice, were captured.

Clover's burial was indeed a sad occasion. Stephen said little during the ceremony, only offering a little verse from the bible on her being delivered to the waves. The captain of the brigantine that had performed the service did pay respects by placing an open palm momentarily upon Stephen's shoulder. As for the others that anyone could consider close to the Templar, they too went about their business to leave the strapping young man the time he needed to recuperate from his wounded heart. He was in fact afforded all the time he needed, for the wind was in their favour and Constantinople was being sacked; no one was going to be chasing them down, least of all a Turk.

THE CITY FALLEN

Eight hours after the battle had been fought and the grounds safe to enter, did Mehmet, 'the Wretched Mohammed', enter St Sophia, with his ten personal guards, each of a stature equal to and greater than that of Hassan. He gave open prayer then to Allah, for the Church of the Holy Wisdom was now a mosque, and would be transformed to appear as such before too long. It was then that he took up residence in the palace of Blachernae. Once settled the Sultan would have his keen eye open, and mindful, for any pretty boy to pass his way, in order that he could have his lustful way with a male youth – and in this venture he was successful.

As for the Roman Empire, it was no more.

The sacking of the city was quite widespread, amazing was the destruction which could be called to fall upon such a beautiful city. Few areas within the walls went unscathed. Constantinople was a city that was widespread, with many great open areas, farms and orchards; other open spaces, all separating village quarters. It was not surprising then to understand that many avoided devastation. It was to the genius of several of these 'quarters' that surrender was quickly decided, as the walls of Constantinople were being breached, by opening their gates to allow the Turks admittance with their swords sheathed as opposed to falling upon the inhabitant's necks.

The city was now ransacked and completely in the hands of the Turk, that was beyond question, and as the sultan supped on refreshment within the Palace he had so recently acquired, Stephen did stand on board the brigantine, alone, reflecting on the life that he had shared with his beloved Clover.

And as he looked up to the sky above he was certain that he noticed a star in the heavens winking at him, and then he looked down upon the surface of the sea, the final burial place of the only one that could ever steal his heart.

And now begins his many adventures: the story of a legend.

HISTORICAL NOTES

KNIGHTS

First and foremost; the eclipse actually occurred on the 22nd of May, not as mentioned in this book. I did this for one reason only and that is because the heroes of this story didn't arrive onsite until Wednesday the 23rd and I did so much want to mention the blood moon as it was so much a part of the siege.

The Grand Master of the Teutonic Knights, Albert of Brandenburg-Ansbach, did dissolve the Order in 1525, they had been in strong decline since after the Battle of Tannenberg in 1410, when 400 knights were conquered and left laying slain upon the battlefield. Of the 55 survivors a minority continued to follow their path as best as possible, but a majority took wives and settled.

The Knights of the Temple, and of the Hospital, had however made their mark on the European Peninsula, where they were present, and helpful, in driving the Muslims out of Spain. The Temple was renamed the Order of Christ, and resided in Portugal, those of the Hospital remained in Rhodes.

Rhodes was taken by the Turks in 1522, but the Hospital were extended an invitation 5 years later to take the city of Valletta, on the island of Malta, as their new Capital. Under siege by the Turk in 1565 saw 1,250 knights slaughtered during a five-month siege. The last 250, under John Parisot of La Valette, did assist in contributing to the defeat of the Turks upon the sea in 1571, the galleys of the white cross displaying much value during the battle of Lepanto. They were now most commonly renowned as the Knights of Malta, Knights of the Hospital no more.

THE TRIPLE WALL

I have heard: 'Constantinople; so magnificently fortified, that a relative handful of men could hold it against countless attackers.' For many centuries the impassable triple walls of Constantinople did preserve the Byzantine Empire, allowing it to withstand the repeated onslaughts of barbarian, Persian, Arab, and Turk alike. The city was only known to fall to Christians, though at the time she was corrupted by civil strife and those outside its walls aided from within the city. But she always won back. The 15th Century saw this old empire, feeble as it was, enter the new age with little territory from which to draw its soldierly requirement. Cannon purchased, and few in quantity, were unsuited for use on the walls so fragile, but not so for the Turks who took to raising one of the first modern armies. The Ottoman Turks, originally constituted of nomadic light cavalrymen, had now adopted more sedentary ways.

The Turkish Army was largely successful and gradually came to dominate through south eastern Europe and Asia Minor. Turkish success was attributed to the use of light cavalry and of what was considered by many the finest infantry in the world, the Janissary Corps. The Janissaries were recruited through a form of taxation, for according to Islamic law, Muslims were not supposed to fight Muslims. By employing Janissaries (Christian slaves) the religious law could be observed and Muslim enemies of the Sultan forced to pay homage. The eldest son of each Christian family, within the Sultan's empire, had to be yielded for service within his army, to be raised as a Muslim. They were amongst the first infantrymen to be armed quite routinely with handguns, and proved themselves loyal and elite in many battles. The last group of Janissaries were killed off in 1826.

Mohammed II (reigning 1451-1481) secured the services of a gun founder, Urban of Hungary, a Christian. He designed and cast 70 great cannons. The largest was named "Basilica", weighing in excess of 19 tons and firing a ball of 800 pounds. It required 42 days for a team of 60 oxen to drag Basilica 120 miles; despite the barrel being made in two pieces that screwed together, thereby making it easier to move. It took hours to load and had a maximum rate of fire of seven shots a day.

The barrel began to crack after only two day's firing and the piece had to be reinforced. Alongside this was a matched set of eleven bombards, each capable of firing 500-pound balls. These proved to be very useful. The best of the field were fifty, 200-pounders.

Mohammed's guns constituted fourteen separate batteries. On April 1st, these commenced the greatest bombardment known to man. Urban had done his work well; unfortunately he did not live to see their success, for an explosion during the siege did kill him. Safety was still very much a matter of luck.

The defence of Constantinople was heroic, but could not hold against such a mighty army. The first breach was made at the military gate of St Romanus on 11 April. Through efforts that the Spartans would have been proud of, the defenders beat off a storming party and managed to patch the walls. Other breaches followed, each time the enemy being beaten off and the damage repaired.

On Tuesday, 29 May, the structure on both sides of the St Romanus gate, weakened as it was over the time of the siege, did collapse. The Janissaries did enter the city, the defence falling amid great slaughter.

The cannon had written itself into history, and by the middle of the 15th Century the cannon was supreme over masonry.

But most of all, the following needs to be remembered: It was very common for soldiers of both Christian and Muslim faith alike, to fight for whomever would pay them, in a majority of the cases, the most. Even Christians of Spain, such as El Cid, served Muslims at one time or another. Mercenaries were not overly concerned how their employer prayed. So long as his master paid, the soldiers would fight.

CHRISTIAN

Constantine was his name. Man of faith or war, he waged his battles well, and against those of similar lineage. These conflicts came after his proclamation to become emperor of the quarter including Britain and Gaul, for the Empire was split. But the many legions that had rallied to his side soon entrusted and encouraged him to take the seat in his father's place, to subjugate all claimants and unite the Great Roman Empire once again, for the Empire to be ruled by a single voice.

It was the belief in his God who laid hand to aid Constantine in defeating those claiming rights as emperor, defeating Maxentius on the grounds surrounding the Milvian Bridge, the place of his dream, which would shape many things to come. It came to him as a vision, the cross on a shield, and another after that, till all the men of his glorious servitude bore great semblance, 'and with this sign you shall conquer. It was but a vision!' A vision where religious men went into battle with hand clasping swords and minds worshipping the one and only true Lord, Jesus Christ.

Conquer he did and great victory goes by with little boast alone. Now with victory aside the Christian belief grew strong in this pagan of old, and what a great god it must be to uphold that which many from his old belief took burden to protect: - one god to replace the many.

So the pagan life was left to the roaches by many, an infestation of the mind to soon be forgotten. Life was lost as a breath was exhaled, swept by the wind across valleys, fields, and mountains. A fresh new start was now commenced, in a place far in the East known widely as Byzantium; so it was that Byzantium and Greece were now birds of a feather. And as this wind of faith and belief withered and died the birth of something new in the world of Rome was witnessed, the birth of Christianity and the beholding of a man called Constantine. The Empire had come of a new age. But the religion was not like that of its brother, for a difference so small was evident, and this difference would upset the very fabric of all the Roman lands as a whole.

And in time the Great Centre of power in Rome was to behold a new home, and with this new home a name. Although still largely referred to by kings, clerics, and servants, as Byzantium, the site soon bore the name of Constantinople, after its founder; this written in the year of our Lord 324, the same year which saw another rival, Licinius by name, lose all power and influence at Chrysopolis.

From 313 to 333 many changes befell all Christians, these changes occurring both before and after the move of the throne to

Constantinople. Christian prisoners were released from their bonds, possessions being returned post haste, and members of the cloth were given special privileges such as the acceptance of their word upon a bible in testimony and use of the postal service through the most treacherous of lands. Constantine's own mother Helena even took to the new religion of her son and tempted salvation of the birth of Jesus by having churches built over his birth place, site of crucifixion, and last resting place known to all men. A great artifact was miraculously uncovered during these deeds of great worth, a short plank bearing the inscription 'Jesus of Nazareth, King of the Jews'. Helena's heart and mind were now assured their place in heaven.

Such changes gave great relief to those of the Christian faith, like a great weight lifted from the shoulders of their meekest, a mountain moved by the weakest of the weak. Death, torture, and imprisonment for accused crimes against the very fabric of all that dominated a pagan society were forced against Christians, but no more. Scars of malicious wounds would now be caressed by feathered lips. A Christian existence had, after all, been unlawful, and anyone caught preaching such faith was once met by heinous death.

So life in the new city flourished, Constantine himself residing in his newfound fortification, the city expanding to more than three times its previous size. Peasants, merchants, traders, teachers, and great minds, all flocked like birds on a prayer. Citizenship was offered and buildings built. Public baths, Hippodrome, churches of great magnificence and endowed with the most beautiful of windows, adornments and art. Paved streets, imperial palace, and statues were given a place to stand and watch as the people milled and wandered around most happy and content. Great works of art and sculptures were brought in over the years from cities all around to fill Constantinople with a pride not witnessed ever before.

By 381 the city of Constantinople was as bold a city as Rome, and at some time after 387 the Roman Empire was split into two. Constantinople was now truly part of Byzantine, and as for the language, the use of Greek was taken up in place of a discarded Latin.

Since then many tragedies have been faced. In 1184 tens of thousands of a Latin faith residing in Constantinople were met by Greek ferocity. Some were beaten, but many more slaughtered, none escaped unscathed, the old nor the young, either sick or frail, and those in good health; all suffered. Latin churches and homes were burnt without second thought, but times change and tides turn.

A greater sin was the 4th crusades sacking of Constantinople on 12th April 1204. En route to the Holy Land to wreak vengeance upon the Islam faith, they were steered aside. Inadequate funds were the cause, so plunder, pillage and rape was the virtuous answer.

Although the crusaders initially faltered in their attempt to take the walls, held back at the point of spears in the hands of Alexius III's Varangian Guard on 17 July 1203, they did soon succeed. Alexius himself fled the scene whereby the crusaders were quick to throw on the throne Isaac Angelus, in order to gain funds for their continued march against the Infidel's tide of poisonous worship. But Isaac was to become murdered by the Greeks, Alexius V Ducas taking the seat of power which infuriated the rage of the crusaders, whom on 12 April 1204 then attacked Constantinople and stormed up and down the city doing as they pleased. Much consternation was felt as relics and gold were stolen, a land so holy in the foresights of those making such a grand trek was soon forgotten; far too much wealth was at hand now.

So it came to be that Constantinople fed the greed of the crusaders, and the many Christians, who, relying on the aid and protection from the west, stuck hard in the Holy Land, beleaguered and forgotten, were going without much sustenance. And continue the crusaders did not. The great Papal trek had ended at a fruitful site. And so the Pope became pleased at the accomplishments of the crusaders, for now all of Christendom was united, but united is not a permanent work and the Greeks were to soon have their way. Constantinople was returned into the hands of the once forgotten Roman Empire, their schismatic ways taking hold once more.

MUSLIM

And whilst the Christians squabbled, although similar in interests, the enemy lurked close by and seemingly united.

Osman had two children, Ala ed-Din and Orphan – Ala not to be confused with Orphan's minister of the same name. It was here that Ala had insisted that all inherited from their father, Osman, should not be split. Now Orphan wields his wand and commenced to conquer land by submission, taking into his hold the city of Nicaea in 1329, and Nicomedia in 1337, he was the obvious stronger of the two.

Orphan soon became self-proclaimed Sultan and drew up a treaty of sorts with John Cantacuzenus, providing him with 6,000 Turkish troops to aid in his civil war in Thrace, and more still for his fight against the Serbs. But this aid wasn't easily given; it was considered a just gift from the Sultan for the hand in marriage of Theodora, the daughter of John. But such seemingly friendly gestures would turn to favour the giver, for once John had fallen from power in 1355 the Sultan took his army and employed a great political scheme to encourage all Turkish tribesmen to follow the ghazi leaders and settle the land they conquered; and lands fell. Chorlu, Didymoticum, and Adrianople; Eskishehir and Ankara; the whole of Germiyan would be nothing more than a vassal of sorts by 1381.

By the time of the Sultan's death in 1362, Thrace had fallen into his palm, and what a palm. He had conquered true enough, his rule was fair and taxes were lighter than those of the Roman Emperor. Christians were able to keep their religion, but many changed their belief. Churches as well as their way of life were maintained. However, for those that resisted there was slavery and boys of certain age were forced into his army – easier to capitulate than fight for rights.

All victories of the military to date had been secured by the cavalry, quite reasonable really, as no foot troops bearing arms were encouraged to carry a banner within the Sultan's army. But along with the influx of young boys into his service a reorganization was undertaken. Communication and immobilization were factored into the scheme of things. The Christian boys, both slave and volunteer, were taken into service and called Janissaries. In later years they were to form a crack regiment of guards who were forbidden to marry. Piyade and Azabs were infantry, and the infamous Bashi-bazouks were the irregulars whose main source of income within the army came from what could be secured in the form of plunder.

Murad I had taken power after Orphan's death and was on operations in Europe, seizing lands and conquering once-were-heroes. But in 1365, on his return, he was forced to take Thrace back from Byzantium, for the emperor in Constantinople had made play for the lands, and although successful found all hard to control. The Sultan soon established himself a capital for his European borders at Adrianople, whereby all that was left of Rome and its pitiful lands were surrounded completely by the Turk; the only channels of freedom now open to Constantinople was that offered by the sea.

Serbia had fallen by the end of 1389, but alas poor Murad I was not around to see such sweet victory. He had been stabbed in the heart by a Serb promising loyalty and the defensive dispositions of Christian troops. Bayezit, Murad's son, saw to it that King Lazar of Serbia was executed on the spot of his father's assassination, and also saw to it that his brother be strangled to death so that he would inherit all. The whole of the Balkans was now in his control. It was now that Bayezit married Maria, King Lazar's daughter.

In 1370-73 talks of an alliance against the infidel were being held between Venice and Genoa, but these gave way to little and an attempt from King Sigismund of Hungary to send forth a crusade was short lived when it was destroyed at Nicopolis. Constantinople was saved from another attempted siege when a small force of troops, with Marshal Boucicault, were thought to have a larger force following some months behind; this was untrue.

In 1402, when flowers were coming of their bloom and fragrances slowly wafted on the breeze, a message was sent to the now Emperor John VII from the new Sultan Murad II, a message to surrender. The reply was one of courage: 'We are weak but in God we trust, He who can sally and put down the mightiest. Do as you please.' But such rising courage was assisted, a slight push from knowledge attained – for Timur the Tartar was fast approaching.

Timur the Tartar was from the line relating to Jenghiz Khan. He was a pious Muslim by faith but massacred Muslims. He died at age 72 in 1405, but just 3 years before became a saviour of sorts. As he conquered and pillaged he became the monster of Bayezit's mind, for as the latter lay siege upon John VII a messenger was received from Timur ordering that all the lands, belonging to those of the Christian faith of Constantinople, should be returned to them intact.

So Bayezit broke the siege, met Timur the Tartar on 25 July, 1402, at Ankara, and was defeated. Unfortunately for any crusader of the times, no Christian of Europe took this opportunity to topple the Turks once and for all, for such a play was hard to force as hundreds of thousands of the Muslim faith were spread out across Western Europe. More still were flooding the gates, forced from their homelands, due quite primarily to Timur the Tartar's savagery.

Now, here, the year 1405 to 1413, Muslim brother slaying brother, one stab in the back for another; Isa killed by his brother, Suleiman by his troops, and Musa slain by Mehmet; Mehmet, self-proclaimed Sultan in 1413, called a gentleman by many, and such wonders he created. Fortresses and mosques were surely a forte. His death in 1421, was followed the following year by another siege upon Constantinople, but soon lifted by Murad to deal with a rebel presence in Anatolia.

Murad lead a life of war and died in 1451, where both Muslim and Christian alike saw greatness in him. Mehmet II, both 19 and inexperienced, was now Sultan.

BOOK TWO
The Templar: and the Temple of Karos

IMPORTANT NOTE:

Mahon is the name denoting a boat employed by Mehmet's naval forces; the same vessel is referred to as a galleass by those of Constantinople.

Many seafaring vessels within this book are referred to as boat, as opposed to ship, due to my interpretation of the description given in the dictionary.

And now the story continues....

Stephen stood there, stabilised by his grasp upon the rail of the brigantine as it creaked under full sail, roller coasting along the surface of the sea, breaking waves as it gained in its distance from the calamity of that which had devoured the souls of the men aboard. He was still dressed in the mail that he had fought in, less the tunic, a gift from his wife, and he had long since discarded his breastplate and basinet. And even though the dark void of night had been cast over the sky, like the falling of a blindfold over eyes that burn for the satisfaction of sight, the burning of Constantinople did pave the way for the boat's retreat, the entire horizon ablaze with oranges and reds.

The sparkling of the stars in the sky, where the blaze was strongest, had hidden themselves from all possible view, from the dreaded and poignant disaster below, where the Sultan had secured his victory over the Christians; all Greeks, Venetians, Romans, Slavs, Jews, and mercenary alike. Stephen stood there in his grief, the loss of his one and only true love, gone forever. He, the last of the Templar, and a youth on a journey from that of a child to a man…. but his journey had faltered. Within the wake of fervent need to prove and set an example he did leave behind the virtue of his innocence, for it to catch up if it could. Like the wake of a large boat before him, he could see where he had surrendered his youth, as immature as it was, for the splendour of 'cause for action'. His blood had boiled as he fought so strongly, though his mind was leagues behind, gathering the courage to see the fight through… and he knew now that the fight was life itself, not just the battle which had been waged over a few miles of sea and soil.

He had made a vow unto himself, to venture this world both far and wide; to see himself surrendered to the sea like the faeces of an old man left to decompose in the gutter of a city street. He had vowed, in the face of the Lord himself, to do unto himself that which he would not be willing to bring upon someone else. He would die upon the sea, that was his testament to the Lord; no word of living, for his life he did solemnly surrender as being worthless and shattered beyond repair. He thought: God will forever own that which is cast within my blood and bone; never again shall I consider myself a mortal and surrender myself to the whims of man. And he recalled then - for reasons unknown - what the monk at Constantinople did say to him: "Blessed and protected you now be… but a watchful eye never hurt any. May God bestow upon you great favour; may you be his sacred vessel."

Be his sacred vessel.

What did it matter, a simple monk's verse, for Stephen was beyond feeling, he was beyond caring, and he was beyond life. Death was his calling, and should that devil-ghost make calling upon him this night, then he would go without protest and allow his last breath to be strangled from the weakened shell he called a body. No, his life belonged to his religion, and although his love was for Jesus and everything he stood for, God was Jesus' father. And for a second, Stephen did contemplate what he was thinking, of how irrational it may have been: never to give in to the whims of man… never to take part in sexual pleasure again. He was a widower, a man with a wife… who, even though parted of this world, was awaiting him, aloft in heaven. He could not, would not, join with another in wedlock.

He was dead already. He was ashamed and saddened by all that had occurred over the past week. An unknown future lay before him now. But be it unknown, be it of little consequence, for he cared not. And he looked again to the sky where several of the stars had become visible, far from the fires that illuminated the night sky over Constantinople, and he did recall the short life he had shared with the one he called Wife.

His dear Clover; how would she see him now, with the knowledge that he had vowed… to end his mortal existence? Her burial at sea had torn him apart from within. And further contemplation: I cannot call myself a man; I am but an empty shell, a cocoon without maturity, and a pestilence of mankind. I am… who I wasn't before. He had no future, but here he stood,

awaiting the break of another day, another dawning to bring further torment, awaiting his mind to fester and decay.

How long had he been standing there upon the deck? He had no idea. He had no education on the reading of the stars; no one had tutored him on the secrets of sailing across the sea. He could navigate across land no better.

He looked up at the stars; the shimmering of the night sky over Constantinople was almost gone of its fiery brilliance… what was that? He turned his head in the direction of the sound, something to his rear. At such a time that it surely must be, with the sky as dark and cloudless as it was becoming, it must be reasonably late; he couldn't see how it would have been possible for him to have been standing there alone for any great length of time, but he had. Stephen knew too, that as few as two men would be stationed upon the vessel, their saviour, their victorious brigantine, as it sailed towards the southwest. One man would be stationed to the bow, where the forecastle met the bowsprit, and the other at the helm, where a constant eye could be maintained on the square-rigged foremast and lateen-rigged mainsail.

A two-masted vessel she was, designed for sail alone, the ability for power by oar and sweep left well alone, and steered by a stern rudder. Here, at the helm, the boat could be steered, its rounded stern allowing for short rods running beneath the captain's cabin to steer the vessel as desired: this was a merchant boat of private enterprise, a sea-going vessel purposely built to cater for the commercial needs of the captain, a working horse as grand as a carrack and with the manoeuvrability to match.

He tried emphatically to see into the dark shadows of the boat. He could barely make out the man at the helm, behind the broad triangular sailing cloth attached to mainmast, nor the crudely structured cabin to the rear of the boat itself – which was low set and only several feet high, for it was sunken into the decking to allow the man at the helm good visual both front and aft of the brigantine as it moved smoothly across the surface of the sea. A lantern did burn fore and aft, either side of the helm too; and there it was… a figure looming to the rear. Was the man – or woman – drunk? What need was there to be sneaking about the aft of a boat at full sail, and with such quiet aptitude, a boat endeavouring to be as far as possible from calamity and capture. Turk boats would be after those that had cheated death, the Sultan's orders would have seen to that. Sailors and soldiers alike would have been readied for the capture of anyone who tried a retreat by sea… and land. Mehmet would have set aside a purse of overwhelming extravagance in order to persuade the capture of all of those that had once been a member of the community of Constantinople. The chance of a ransom would also have been a player of mind, enticing many a sailor to forego the promised sacking of 'the City of God' for the chance of riches paid from a secured purse, for captives of all creeds.

Stephen moved his head to the left, stepped to the right, lowered his level of sight slightly and sidestepped again. He decided upon closer scrutiny of the object, and moving slowly and silently towards the rear of the boat did attract the attention of the man at the helm, who did reflect on Stephen's manner of approach but said nothing.

Suddenly Stephen saw a figure of dark temptation playing with something as large as a pottery vase, an oversized chalice for wine, a helmet of war. And it sparked to life, a lantern revealed. Stephen pondered on the formality, which was, to be least implied, without warrant. Why should such be lit? And the man at the helm reflected upon Stephen, he being a darkened figure seemingly looking in his direction, being oblivious to the light that had just come to life to his rear. The lantern also looked quite familiar, but he wasn't sure where he'd seen it before.

The figure of the man… the unknown… he gazed out then, towards the rear of the brigantine, far out to sea where the wake did settle to merge as one with the steady rolling of waves around. And far as far can be, out of the reach of any weapon of war, a signal was received in return. A boat was afloat and following astern, a boat that was sailing in darkness, the only light evident being that of a returned signal. The lantern on the brigantine, on which Stephen stood steady, was then suffocated; the light denied another breath, and then the figure ducked for temporary cover and the man at the helm turned to look towards the rear. He saw nothing, brought his attention to bear once more on Stephen and his strange behaviour, before returning his state of thinking to the sail and the steering of the brigantine.

Stephen crept with stealth a little closer towards the rear of the helm and bare witness to a partial clarity of face, a small beard and shallow eyes, teeth rotten and body hunched forward. The boat far off to the rear then lit up with a dozen lanterns, there, in ones and twos, lit to signal further a field before being extinguished, as was the original signal. The sea was dark but once again.

The Templar continued to watch as the figure of the man moved into the smallest amount of light that was cast from the lanterns of the helm and saw for himself a confirmation as to who was responsible for the signal sent. The features of the man burnt themselves upon Stephen's mind, and his mind leapt into action – as slow as it was. The man must have been a spy, planted to aid those that followed. But the very capture of the brigantine must have been anything but a priority, for if it was desired, the spy could surely see to it that those few currently steering the boat went for a swim amongst the fishes. Why was it so important that a signal be given to their location? Were not the lanterns, at their current positions upon the decking, good enough to provide sufficient indication as to their location and direction?

He shook it from his head. Even at best, those that followed – going by the signal – were unlikely to close the gap. He would remember at first light and bring it to the attention of the captain, but for now he must dwell upon the occurrence, to think carefully about what had just happened… for it was entirely possible that a friendly boat was following, providing secretive protection, for a reason that he did not yet know or understand.

He continued to watch as the figure of the man slipped away and he himself decided upon retiring for the night, to lie awake upon his makeshift bed whilst the minutes of the night passed him by.

It was only a short clamber down into the hold, which despite its usual cargo of prized possession, was now filled with sacks of flesh and bone. Women and their children, a few husbands amongst the throng. This was what remained of a great city, a few of the meagre that had been spared their lives, on the pure generosity of sailors aboard this boat. There was little room for passengers to move around in by day, let alone sleep by night. Bodies lay strewn upon the bare boards, beneath hastily erected sleeping platforms and pellets that had been put in place from one end of the hold to the other, each and every space available filled with at least one person. Few belongings existed here, for all of those that had clambered aboard under the protest of others, but approved of the captain, had flung what they carried into the sea at the Prosphorianus Harbour, unless such belongings was a consumable of some description. But what manner of food could anyone have brought aboard? Much it seemed. It was quite apparent that many people did accept their fate as though it was drawn upon the mortar within the walls of Constantinople, long before the collapse occurred. Most people had taken the opportunity to have a plan of escape ready to execute at a moment's notice, regardless of their faith for the soldiers who stood upon the defences of Constantinople. Good fortune it would appear to be.

Stepping delicately and with much caution, Stephen made his way towards the empty bed – three damn planks of wood set side-by-side, his only burden, his soul possession, a gift from a new found friend, the Teutonic Knight, Lars, the man of no tongue, the legend of a shot when it came to the crossbow, the one and only that had saved Stephen's miserable life.

What light there was in the hold was given by the moon as it commenced to reveal itself upon the horizon, sending a measure of illumination through the few open ports and hatch of the decking above, a moon which was continuing to wane, ever present in the evil it had stirred as part prophecy to the downfall of the city of Constantinople, for it was written that the great city would never fall if the moon was waxing.

He saw his sword resting upon the hung bed of wood and swung himself up into the comfort of his nest, where a blanket had been prearranged, bringing his sword up into his grasp, hugging it close as though for comfort or warmth, companionship or love. He had ventured to Constantinople to fulfil a dream, to bloody his sword, to become a man. He now believed that he had failed, for he was to be forever without his beloved Clover, and as he lay there he finally drift into a tormented sleep, a sleep that was filled with dreams, dreams of death and torture, mayhem and blood, turmoil and defeat. And somewhere in the night so cool, where silence was only broken by the movement of the boat rolling through steadily breaking waves, a voice did lay command over Stephen's senses: He who breaches the bounds of my scripture; he shall be delivered unto everlasting contempt. This is a covenant of your Lord.

Stephen awoke as though shaken by the hand of a heavy man. The voice? Is that what woke me? What does it mean? And the words formed in his mind, so deeply that they would not budge, and would be easily recollected for closer scrutiny when he rose with the morning sun.

*
* * *
*

There were two priests aboard the brigantine, two men of the cloth whom Stephen had seen shortly after boarding the brigantine, by the helping hand of Franco and Lars. He dwelt further on the evening's events, of the day before. One of the priests had given a sermon at the ceremony, the captain availing himself to Clover in regards to service, prior to her body being delivered into the sea; for the two priests aboard were not able to be torn from their current business interest. He'd not heard their names mentioned, but recalled their burden, for they were seen to be inseparable from a chest that they guarded, as though it was made of gold. That in itself seemed nothing more than sacrilege: to carry a chest on board when space was needed for a citizen of Constantinople… wait; he too had committed this same sin, though his was worse. He'd carried the body of his beloved aboard the brigantine, knowing full well that she would have to be delivered to her ever-waiting tomb below the waves; in the least, these two priests still had their chest. But who was he to argue with a priest and his business? They were both a mystery unto themselves; they seemed inseparable, except the first priest, who Stephen did see in quiet conversation with the man who gave signal to the rear… the signal!

Stephen made his way above deck, pushing through – as politely as possible – the throngs as they commenced to converge upon an orderly, who had been provided the authority to ration all sustenance that could be found. At such a time as this, where calamity, sorrow, and bewilderment was stagnating, in the least, these people, having been stripped of all belongings, gave willingly to a single man who they did not know, all they had. Two meals a day, whilst afloat; morning and late afternoon. None received more than another, child, woman, or man… even the priests and captain were there the evening before, to assure all that the rules of rationing would not be treated lightly by anyone on board the boat. Heavy punishment, lashes to the back, would be punitive enough for a thief over the coming days, until such time that fresh food and water could be secured from ashore. Men needed food and water in order to fight and sail, women to tend the young and sail when men were fighting, and the children of the voyage because they were in their youth, and no one in their adolescence, or early adult years, could bear to see one so young being tormented in ways that should be spared even an animal. But Stephen pushed on, beyond the queue for food, disfigured as it was, for he would forego his meal on this first morning.

He stepped over to the rail of the boat and looked out towards the south, towards the quarter port of the vessel as it approached the strait between Thrace and Karasi, the Dardanelles, 40 miles of sea where the width of the strait was no more than 5 miles at its widest point and well less than 1 mile at its finest. It was doubtful that the Sultan had a force of any strength desirable enough to cause a concern for those making good their escape. The major concern at present was for the lack of a friendly boat. It had seemed, quite apparently, that the captain of the brigantine had waited until the last moment to set sail into the Marmora, for all other semblance of an ally had disappeared from view.

Stephen looked up towards the nest upon the mast where a crewman could be seen scanning the horizon all around, and upon the nest a pole, vacant of flag and identity. Shortly though the crewman was making his way down from his post, a look of slight anxiety falling upon his face. Even now, as he made his way down from the platform above, he did look out towards the rear of the brigantine from where they had journeyed. The Templar looked too but saw nothing. The night before he had seen someone give a signal to the rear of the boat, and it was his intention to see the master of the vessel; the good captain should be delivered the news post-haste. And as he turned to make for the door of the captain's quarters, the crewman from aloft did push past, infuriating the Templar who thought no good of any other important matter other than his own.

The man pushed on, an odour afloat the sailor seeping into the air as he moved. Stephen was almost brought to convulsion, the man stank like nothing he'd known before: of rotting meat and garlic. And could there be a good reason for this? Stephen did ask himself this question. This man's clothing, which hung in rags from his puny body, was stained with the blood of men, his shirt cut into ribbons by the scimitar of the enemy who now resided in Constantinople. Well then, if the picture should be painted as such, then he was a hero, and whether he stank or not, he was a man of the earth.

The sailor had flung the door out and practically fell down the short run of steps. Stephen followed without invitation, the door ajar invoking within him the urge to make some good of the opportunity that he had been provided.

"Captain, captain… ah captain, there you be," said the sailor.

"What is it, good man? What service can I provide you?" asked Captain Homer, his name indicating somewhat that his forefathers had something to do with the manufacturing of helmets from iron.

Stephen took the words in his ear as he fell down the short descent, thumping upon the floor, bringing blood to his nose and a little dizziness to his head.

The captain was on his feet in a flash, the two priests rushing forward to provide a helping hand, and the sailor stood back to wonder at the clumsiness and ill manner of one that should intrude on his important news.

"Ah, Stephen is your name, I believe," said the captain as he came to his aid, holding out his right hand in support, the cuff of his coat riding up his arm as though too small to fit. "To your feet, good sir, for one as bold as you should not be leagued to the floor like a common wife," the smile upon the captain's mouth announcing to all of those around as to his poor attempt at humour. "But even then, a wife belongs to the confines of a strong bed."

"Where this man should be right now," added one of the priests.

"Please, Stephent," added the second, "a seat for you."

"Thankyou, one and all," said Stephen in return for the kindness, and as explanation was warranted, jumped right to the point. "I saw this good sailor coming to report. I believe I know what news he carries, for I too have something to tell."

"Well, two messages, seemingly of equal importance. Please, men, come sit around the table… my office and quarters."

Stephen got to his feet and was escorted with a delicate touch from one of the priests, the second turning to a chair and seating himself. The sailor stood, deciding that unless directed personally he should remain on his feet. The captain took his position behind the desk, which in itself was larger by one-third as compared to the door of his cabin. Stephen rubbed at his nose and took the offer of an old rag from the second priest, holding this to his sported bleeding.

The captain looked around. "With all due courtesy, I believe we should allow this good sailor to report, as he deems so important." The captain looked the sailor in the eye. "Your name?"

"Peter of Pera."

"I'm sorry. Do you have family in Pera?"

"I left no family behind, but a wretched dog of useless manner, an animal with the ambition of a goat." He was rambling and eyed each man as they were seated around the table. The captain was square to, and facing the entrance of the cabin, the two priests to the captain's left pushed back a bit from the desk, and the knight sat with his back to the door; Peter was between the captain and the knight. "My time spent above the deck has been as luxurious as any other," and each smiled as he said this, "but just before I descended the mast I caught a glimpse of something on the horizon. A boat, Captain; a boat to our stern, and she looks to be carrying the flag of one in league with Mehmet."

The priests and captain looked from one to the other; Stephen lowered the rag from his nose and delivered his news. "I know how it comes to be afloat our rear, following in our wake as though tracking us through the grassy mounds of a swamp."

"Speak, Stephen; you are amongst friends," announced the captain.

"I drew witness to something last night; something which I decided should be slept upon, as all indications pointed to there being no urgency. It is all clear in my mind, and I know who I seek. A man gave a signal to the vessel behind… but why they trace our journey instead of intercept us is beyond me. Further still, it numbs my mind for lack of understanding as to why the man at the helm was not killed where he stood." Stephen's eyes had dropped slightly, to look at the floor, and then as quick as a flash, to bring a start to the hearts and minds of all of those around, he looked up quickly. "They must be following us to some place important, into a trap!"

It was then that the 40-mile strait came to mind. The captain looked at the two priests as they sat knowingly. He could draw on his good ability to see into a man's heart… but what choice did he have anyway; they were all retreating; running scared. "Stephen… Peter; may I introduce to you two men of great calibre. Unfortunately I cannot give you their names, for such an introduction has not been granted me. These two holy men have something of importance, a chest that contains the very fabric of our religion, something that is said to be worth much to the enemies of Christ."

"A chest?" said the sailor, Peter, as though questioning. He knew, that of the five currently sitting around the table, he was least known about. It wasn't, however, a thing of trust, for it was easy to read the script of one's eyes, but Peter also knew, as did the others, that he would be hung by the words of God if he were to feint his good word or promise.

"Yes," the captain confirmed. "What is more is that they have in their possession a letter from the Emperor Constantine. Without revealing the contents of that letter I must advise of the following: the chest that these two good priests carry, must not, under any circumstance, fall into the hands of the enemy. If such was to occur… I can only hope that it will not. The very thought of the contents of the chest falling into the wrong hands… it's just too overpowering to consider."

Stephen listened with concern. He couldn't help but to wonder if this had anything to do with the dream he had the night before; and it came to him again in a flash: He who breaches the bounds of my scripture; he shall be delivered unto everlasting contempt. This is a covenant of your Lord. The Templar again looked to all and said: "I believe in the Lord's word, and because of such belief must hereby accept sole responsibility for the chest and its contents." Stephen had not realized it, but during his short announcement, had stood up.

The priests looked to one another. The first priest said: "You are Stephen, the Templar knight granted knighthood by the esteemed Emperor of Constantinople. We know of you Stephen, and too have sworn allegiance to the Emperor Constantine." He then addressed the knight. "In this knight is our sanctuary. In you Stephen, is the light of our word… our bond with one of the many sovereigns of religion. The chest must not be surrendered to the enemies of Christ. Furthermore, good knight, it must not be surrendered to any other, be he priest, bishop, or pope. This secret we carry must remain such. We took an oath, a bond to protect that which must remain protected."

"I understand," said Stephen and he couldn't be more sober than he was this moment in time: Clover had been forgotten, even if momentarily.

It was then that another voice came to air. "I, Peter, do solemnly swear to act in the good faith that such a mystery deserves. I too will swear an allegiance to Christ's work." All stared at the sailor, so young he appeared, but of great character he must be. He had been in a fight so fierce that none could doubt his words.

Stephen thought of the dream that had come to pass him during the night; but it was no dream. "I had a vision last night… whilst I slept." Everyone was listening with baited breath; a dagger could have cut the silence that moment, it being so thick that all noise from the outside had been as though drowned from existence. "He came to me and said: He who breaches the bounds of my scripture; he shall be delivered unto everlasting contempt. This is a covenant of your Lord."

The second priest fell into his chair, the other simply stood there, his jaw open as though trying to catch a fly, a Venus awaiting its prey. "You are truly the one we have been seeking. The Emperor of Constantinople must have worn the inner sight. So strong he must have been not to have allowed it out into the open. A secret that he took to his death." The priest moved towards Stephen, slowly. "This is why you are a knight, Stephen; not because of your skills as a fighter, or a man empowered with the means to be a good leader, good follower, or good ambassador. You are a knight because the emperor saw you in your true light." The second priest continued to close the gap between them. "You are a knight because you have been chosen by the Lord, Himself." And the priests knew of something more, and that was of a short inscription engraved upon the chest in Aramaic, it read: He shall know his way, upon his quest, travelling far, as bequest, to surrender life, so dear and strong, his way will be painted, with voices strung.

Like a message in a bottle… his way will be strung with the words of the Lord, a map of words which was to provide assistance where required, as though a guardian angel. The priests could now rest a little; their knowledge and quest had now received the support of one led by the words of the Lord. But there was something more, something else that the priests had not revealed, for beneath the chest, inscribed upon its belly, was the following inscription: Only the purest of mind and body will survive the contents of the chest.

The captain broke the short silence. "Stephen; the one you saw last night? Please tell us more."

And without further hesitation, Stephen provided all ears with the notes of the song they wished to hear, of a man who had given signal to the boat behind. A signal given without any authority, or the support of those in command, a signal meant to draw them into captivity or the arms of death. The captain looked to Peter for his need. "We need to bring this man in for questioning."

"Please," interrupted the first, "if I may suggest… the two mercenary."

The captain looked to Peter again. "Do you know of Anthony and Toran?"

"I do, captain."

"Please fetch them so I may give orders for an arrest."

"No need, captain, I know of the man to whom Stephen has described. If it pleases you I shall pass on your orders directly."

"It does… for the longer he remains free, the more fragile our position grows."

*
* * *
*

Peter had departed the group of five, closing the cabin door behind him. The first priest looked the captain in the eye.

"I know what you think, father. They are two good men who fought with Giovanni."

"They are mercenaries and should not be trusted with the secrets of the chest," said the first. "These two mercenary did not abandon the defence of Constantinople until ordered to do so; they were amongst the last to run."

"I would still insist on secrecy," said the first, "for it is against our better interest to have too many ears made wise of the chest and its contents."

The captain added, "I do not even know what contents the chest holds. I pledge my life to Christ and His father; I pledge my good position, granted me by highest station, to provide you with assistance, but still I have no information… other than what you offer."

"We understand your curiosity, captain," said the second. "But you have not been chosen."

"Is it simply curiosity to me; to want to know what it is that I fight for?"

"Nevertheless, the chest will remain secure… at least until the key can be found."

"A key?" asked Stephen.

"Yes, Stephen," replied the first, "a key of wood: cast in wood so that it may be used but a few times, for an overuse of the key would render it useless. A key so perfectly manufactured that even now, after so long, moisture may have rendered it obsolete."

"Why such a restriction?" questioned Stephen.

"To limit its use; to ensure the chest remained sealed; to secret the contents. If the key is broken then so will be our spirit. An overuse of the key will see to it that it will be used no more. The chest will become locked forever."

"In fact," interrupted the second, "the only way to open the chest, without the key, is to defile the very existence of our religion and its beliefs, for it would have to be broken… smashed beyond repair."

"Where is the key?" Stephen looked from the priests to the captain.

The captain fidget slightly, leant forward with his arm extended in a quest to relieve his thirst, grasped the tumbler in his hand and drew it to his lips. He drank and then placed the tumbler down. "It is said to be secure and in good hands."

"Where?"

"Not far." The captain looked to the priest. "The exact location is not known to me, but somewhere on the island of Káros, Southeast of Náxos."

"There is a temple there," explained the first. "A small dwelling protected by some knights from Rhodes. We shall deliver the chest to the location of the key. Once the chest has been secured, its contents can be revealed. We can then decide upon its fate."

*
* * *
*

From an Anatolian port they had originally sailed, aboard a Turkish mahon of little but striking proportion, a galleass of 25 oars to each side, quite capable of running down many of the enemy boats. It was propelled primarily through its use of oars, but did have mast and sail as a secondary means of propulsion. It carried three masts and had a forecastle and aftcastle, and was steered by a stern rudder, of which its wheel was situated to the rear of the cabin. It was 150 feet in length and required the logistic allotment of 100 men to thrust the vessel through the water at top speed: which was maintained through coxswain beating upon a drum. In almost all cases, that could be scrutinized, the crew of rowers were provided for by slaves, convicts and prisoners of war… Alas, so hard it was to get a trusted crew, for most would spend the best part of any day shaking in fear and chained to the oars. But the crew in this case was provided for through ingenuity and greed, for men were fuelled better via the offering of gold and pillage than through terror alone.

The oarsmen were exposed to the open air, for the mahon itself was open, though decked at the bow and the stern, and along the centre of the boat it was well stocked with provisions and arms. But for the attainment of speed the vessel had been lightened by giving up all formality of protection, and the sides of this particular mahon could not be raised in order to offer protection to the crew.

Currently the mahon was running off of the charity provided by the wind, for the power of the oar was not currently required. The Turk in his greed was more after salvage and ransom, than the complete destruction and sinking of an enemy boat: at least until it had been ransacked of all its wealth and its women raped.

Ah yes, a good raping was what lingered upon a soldier's mind, to tear at the under garments of a wench on heat, to smell the sweat of her body as she perspired in terror. Such were the glories promised a soldier in the servitude of Allah, that it was favoured most amongst the crew that were now on the tail of the brigantine ahead. What ransom awaited them? What plunder would there be for them to take for themselves, to hold in their grasp, to clench so dearly, so closely to the heart? Few of the crew, in actual fact, knew the truth. Gold and coin, the wealth of a good ransom… ahhhhh, and the rape of a good woman; yes indeed! Few knew the truth of the trophy, the reason and cause for their being, the circumstances surrounding their chase at sea. Few knew of the chest and its secret, but the orders had been given. What man would surrender the opportunity to sack Constantinople? None! It was absurd! No man in his right mind would forego the three days of pillage, which had been promised him… without good cause. And good cause had been provided. For the sanctity of all minds a story had been hatched. The crew had been told of the gold aboard the boat to their front, of the strategy that was to be played out. Yes indeed – and beyond all thought – they were going to be very rich men before the week was out.

Their commander was known as Abu 'the strangler', for it was said that he suffocated the women he raped: pleasure wasn't for a woman, so therefore, if enjoyment was received by the woman then death she must meet… and what woman wouldn't be satisfied by 'his tormented', the manhood he kept locked away between his legs, awaiting a release from the dark of the trousers that held it at bay; like the leash of a dog, it restrains its venom. He had only now raised himself to the waking of the new day, the second of many to come, he was sure of that. But whether the chase was two days or two hundred he would not quit until his task had been completed.

He traversed the short climb with ease, exit, the cabin now behind him, and looked briefly over the crew: left to right and left again, along the entire length of the mahon's nakedness. Most of the men were sleeping below deck, in its lowest quarters. All was to his satisfaction, all seemed to be in order. He then peered up to look at the platform high above, to the lookout above the deck. Abu recognised the man immediately, it was Ibrahim, one of his best men, a sailor of much experience who was worth twice that at sea as he was on land… and even then he was a most potent soldier.

"Ibrahim," shouted Abu. "Ibrahim!"

He went unanswered, but all around turned to see what the cause of the shouting was, although in reflection, it was not a voiced command or scolding, but carried a note of friendship, of happiness.

Abu cupped his hands together around his lips and shouted again: "Ibrahim!"

Ibrahim looked away from the bow and down to the aftcastle, seeing his commander standing there with his hands cupped around his mouth: Abu with his hands cupped, as though ready to strangle. Ibrahim would tread carefully this morning, he knew of 'the strangler' and his reputation, and this morning Ibrahim had nothing but bad news.

He descended the mast to make his report, to provide news on the situation, direct to the commander, the man Abu, who considered all to be his friend… yes indeed, friends for the feeding of cannon, fodder to be employed as he saw fit. Ibrahim proceeded quickly, the palms on his hands running over the coarse rope of the rigging, the pores of his skin not a stranger to rough treatment, for they had been hardened through many years of hard fighting. He descended his post most professionally… quick and with ease, landing foot strong upon the deck of the mahon, turning erect and with a smile, looking to Abu above him. He scampered along past the oars and up past the coxswain's seat and drum, to stand before Abu, looking him in the eye.

"Ibrahim. Tell me good friend, what did you see aloft that will bring warm salutation to my ears?" Abu lifted both of his arms, clenching Ibrahim's shoulders between his palms (the strangler), a show of affection short lived, and then they dropped to his side. "Speak."

"News on the Christian vessel is good, Abu. They sail directly ahead, for the narrow pass; but…"

"But what?"

"I am sorry, Abu; no good news this morning on those that accompany us. I received a report last night… as you did, that the signal was received from the brigantine and then passed onto the port, starboard and stern, exactly as ordered."

"You have no sighting of our second in command? No sighting of the other four boats which accompany us?"

"No, no sighting at all. You heard yourself, Abu; that signals were received from the other boats… but now… they are gone."

Abu's look of optimism soon passed, and a worried and stern look commenced to develop upon the cold lips of the 'one that strangles'. He turned side-on to Ibrahim and lifted his gaze to take in the ocean around; the few birds that seemed to float upon the breeze, and the sky, as clear as the night had become in the early hours of the morning. Abu had all intention of closing the gap between his small armada and the Christian boat. There would have been no escape for the Christians. Then, as they exit the pass, and into the Aegean Sea, he was to pan his force out into an extended line prior to enveloping the hunted on all sides, it being impossible for the Christians to escape. But now… now he had nothing. And Abu looked up, a change to his facial expression coming of age, for the plan that had died had given rise to a new.

He turned abruptly. "Ibrahim! We shall speed up, close the gap between the enemy and us, and when the time is ripe, before we enter the Aegean, we shall board the brigantine with grappling hooks and planks. We shall have our victory, but before the original pledge. Go now, order for more speed." And his voice rang out loud. "All listen hard to the words I now speak! Get to work as though for Allah himself. More speed is what we need; more speed! Prepare to set oars!" turning to Ibrahim he gave a command. "Fetch me Ahmad Kadir and Mouley Bakar. Have them in my cabin before I have time to pour myself some wine."

"Yes, Abu." Ibrahim set to the ready; scurrying to the task he had been set. The two commanders, of lesser warrant, would be given the invitation immediately – or was that an 'order'?

The captain had poured refreshment for the priests and Stephen, tumblers of wine: this was no sacrament, so healthy portions were provided. All drank but one. The captain looked at Stephen, the Templar sitting there.

"A tumbler of my finest, grown in Constantinople. The taste must be sampled in order to grasp the true character of the grape, for the fragrance alone tells but only half the story."

"If I am to fight for what I believe, if I am to protect the chest as I have so sworn, then a clear head I must keep; above all I must remain vigilant, and in command of all my senses." The priests put their drinking vessels down in unison. None other could give such praise to the Lord than the words that had just been spoken, and no sooner had they both returned their hands to their laps then the commotion outside did reach their ears.

"You are all aware that torture may need to be performed," said the second, as more of a statement than a question; and if it was one thing that the first knew, and that was of the second's love for torture and the truth. All present looked at one another… All now stared in anxious wait, towards the entrance of the cabin as the noise drew closer and grew in ferocity. Muffled sounds were then heard, commands given by one, or both, of the men who escorted the man responsible for the lanterns that night… a hand over the devil's mouth? An order for the traitor to cease with his physical demeanour was then accepted, for little could be heard but a cluttering of feet upon the deck.

The door suddenly swung open and the traitor was unceremoniously pushed into the confines of the small cabin, to fall in front of the counsel that awaited: "In there you slime," said Anthony, his open palm giving an almighty push, the traitor falling to his knees before looking up with pity in his eyes.

The traitor wore a black eye and shrivelled hair, long and to the neck. Dirt covered half his face, blood upon the other, and the look of dismay upon his face began to evaporate. From far beneath his breath, in a cavity of ill-will, he summoned his courage and spat out a ball of slime towards the captain.

"Why you, filth dog…!" exploded the escort.

"Wait!" commanded Stephen, for Anthony held in his left hand the hilt of his short sword, which by demeanour of movement did wish to discipline the traitor. "A blow to the head will do little for us at present."

The captain wiped the slime from the tabletop. "Check his bonds; have him kneel before us."

Anthony did as ordered and Toran turned to the gathered crowd, reaching out to receive the traitor's possessions, before turning again and placing the belongings in front of the captain, for all to see. The captain eyeballed the crowd as each and every sailor, or so it seemed, tried to peer into the darker confines of the cabin.

"Close the door." And his order was carried out. He now looked the prisoner up and down, a traitor as was not denied. Guilty by pride, guilty by acceptance, guilty by witness. Guilty he be and for such a finding… death. "We know of your escapades… of your willingness to do us all harm. We have spotted the galleass which follows." The captain stood as all watched. He paced around, looking down upon the head of the traitor: the traitor, little amused, kept his eyes to the front. "You know, no doubt, that death awaits you." He paused to let the word sink into the head of the man on his knees. "But death can come in many forms. Is it to be quick or slow?" The captain placed his left hand upon the shoulder of the intruder, as though a friend: consoling his victim. "A quick death would be much preferred… by us as much as by you; I am sure."

"Death is my calling, my calling is God, and God is most powerful."

The comforting hand slipped from the shoulder. "Will it be a quick death?" asked the captain.

The traitor in tattered clothing looked up at the captain and allowed a wry smile to caress his lips. "I shall see you in the fiery furnace of hell before submitting to your charity." Stephen knew of torture, had seen its effects in Constantinople. "You should save yourself the torment and trouble," said Stephen, "for we know much already."

"Then why do you see the need for torture?" the traitor's eyes connected with Stephen's. And Stephen thought: this is a most wise man, for he understands he is to be tortured without such words parting our lips; and then again, how else were they to get the information. The captain continued: "Who else of you is amongst us?"

"That shall be my knowing and your demise," replied the guilty.

The captain continued back to his original position and stood there, looking down in disgust, seeing no alternative but torture. "So be it."

*
* * *
*

Ahmad Kadir and Mouley Bakar were commanders little sought, for their prowess in delivering a finished product; for with any task, it was always tarnished with something that had spoilt, and in most cases, due directly to their individual or combined incompetence. So why should men of such little calibre be chosen for the task of netting a great prize, a prize that was in fact beyond the imagination of even the scholars of Mehmet's inner circle.

Ahmed Kadir was expendable, as too was his companion Bakar, and due solely to this expendability was often chosen for errands of great worth and longevity… it was also widely known of his barbaric attitude towards anyone of his current opposition. He was extremely strong in regards to his virtue and greed: for ransom and gold. If a coin was to be had then Ahmed was your man. Courageous not, but what courage does one entertain when commanding over a servitude of scimitar wielding vermin. The sailors he commanded were nothing more than rabble, sloths of a grandeur not usually accepted within the Turkish ranks; but their willingness to kill… to torture their victims, to kill women, children, and babies at a glance – and not feel the worse for it later. Never gamble with your life, but take company of these men and life is what you will be short of. Lustre was rare, sodden cloths and rotting teeth were bountiful. How could such a coward of the high seas, as the one just described, be so able to tend a flock? Two men of particular form, muscle bound giants with wit to spare, educated in many tongues and scorned for their knowledge on all things to do with war. Abdullah and Muhammad, two men whom were but dog's on a leash… Mehmet's dogs of war. Directly to the sultan they answered, and his bidding was for them to command this venomous crew of faeces through one who had tested the tide of his patience. To death Kadir would have been marched, but for favours the sultan owned the sister of another in his league. Rather a delicate, political situation this was. Yes indeed; Abdullah and Muhammad would see to it that command and structure remained set in place.

And then Abu's voice could be heard, mixing with the noise of the wind, an order for more speed and something about 'square the oars'.

It is here, upon the open deck of the mahon, that Abdullah and Muhammad can be seen by Ibrahim as he made his approach, Ahmed Kadir having walked off to relieve himself over the side of the boat at sail. Abdullah was playing 'dice-n-cup' upon a rowing bench, with several members of their band, when Muhammad announced rather poetically that the roller of the die had cheated. It was in fact a false accusation, for the branded cheat had in fact done nothing wrong except have a bad word to say on reflection of their task. Such mutinous talk was unequivocally forbidden, and all of the crew knew it. None of the crew wished to be disciplined by Kadir – though in fact it wasn't a discipline from kadir, as so much from the sultan himself. Abdullah and Muhammad ruled the roost, and their persuasive attitude and command over Kadir worked wonders when so far from the rectitude of a port. Kadir also knew that to receive good praise from the two giant men was to receive good treatment and exercise from Mehmet himself.

Muhammad stood abruptly from the blanket strewn across the bench, thundering loudly his accusations, pointing a finger down upon the head of the man still kneeling, the smile upon the face of the soon-to-be vanquished diminishing as though like a clap of thunder. "You have cheated for the last time. Your dice is crooked, and the other is loaded with lead," and indeed it was, but only because it had been planted by Abdullah.

"No! NO! You are wrong!" And as quick as the words had failed him, the quicker a blade did penetrate his lung from behind, Abdullah delivered the deathblow. No sooner had the accusations been laid and the man was being prepared for an unceremonious displacement into the waters of the Marmora.

Abdullah pulled the blade from the flesh, letting the body slip to the floor. "Syahid; get this filth monger from off of the deck and carry him to the port. For bait he will be used… though God knows, probably bad in taste."

"Yes, Abdullah; immediately." And the body was carried away before it even had the chance to fall completely to the decking, amongst the oars, and ropes and other things found upon a boat.

Abdullah looked at Muhammad. "Such a dislike I had for this man that to waste my words on him would be an insult to Allah."

"My friend," Muhammad said to Abdullah, nodding his head in the direction of the messenger Ibrahim. "I would hazard a guess that we are needed."

"Indeed," agreed Muhammad, and looking to the other three sitting around the blanket upon the bench gave further advice. "I hate cheats; but I dislike those who believe that uttering mutinous words is a mandate for sanctity in heaven on death. Ahmad Kadir has a good head for tactics, and will be worth keeping alive… do you hear?"

"Yes Muhammad," the three said in unison, and picked up the die and blanket, departing without so much as an exhaled exclamation of disagreement.

Muhammad quickly turned with a smile and warm greeting, extending both arms in order to show his affection for Ibrahim, "Ah, my good friend. Allah be praised for treating you with the respect you deserve, for this morning you look wonderfully refreshed."

Both parties released the hug of greeting then and Ibrahim looked Muhammad in the eye. "I seek your commander; Ahmad. More speed has been ordered and oars are to be set. As coxswains it would be in your better interest to make-ready."

"Kadir… ah, indeed a good fellow who not only looks to our health, but also keeps our minds fed with sanity. You look after us far too well." Muhammad was known widely for his sarcasm, even at the best of times. "Our comrade in arms is attending his need right now."

"And what need is that?"

"The need for privacy," and he winked.

"There are no women on board to speak of, so you must be referring to his going for a shit," Ibrahim thought himself rather witty at this, for he smiled.

"Such lovely to hear words of wisdom from a scholar as yourself, Ibrahim." Muhammad pointed, his eye planting the burning look of ridicule into the head of the messenger. "He is over there."

"Thank you; I bid you good day." Ibrahim departed, walking with great stride over the open floor of the decking of the boat as it rolled to-and-fro, towards the place where Kadir could be found, ignoring the laughter as it exploded from the mouth of Muhammad, like the burning vapours of sulphur from the pits of hell, waves of desecration exploding from a volcano.

"Muhammad," said Abdullah, once Ibrahim was out of earshot. "Be careful."

"You think me afraid of that weasel?"

"No, but I call for caution."

"You always call for caution. In actual fact, you call for as much caution as I yearn for the touch of a good woman."

"Ah, yes. I too yearn for the opportunity to have my way with a woman. And we will both get our fill when we board the Christian boat. Not long now, my brother."

"No, not long at all," said Muhammad, looking around to ensure no ears were invading their privacy. "I think we should retire to the hold; our good friend Syahid should be reporting shortly."

*

* * *

*

Several planks had been retrieved from below deck and placed parallel to each other upon the captain's table. The wish was to have the man tortured elsewhere, but with a cargo of old men, women, and children, what could one do? Wasn't it bad enough that torture should have to be exercised?

A small vase of oil sat upon the table between the traitor's legs, and an open pan of burning fuel – wood, coal, and a little fat, positioned just out of reach at the base of his feet. The coals were red hot: and there was a poker there too, its handle sticking out like a big plump, long thumb. The instruments of torture were simple here. A red-hot poker did well in purifying the mind, in relaxing a knotted tongue; and the oil, well enough for roasting the underparts of the feet. But the poker was best, for it created greater levels of fear within a man.

The traitor lay naked.

Both priests stood, one to either side of the traitor as he lay upon the planks, his arms straight, tied at the wrist, and then the ropes were secured to the table legs at that one end. His legs were parted a fist's width apart, a block of wood positioned between them just above the ankles. His feet were also bound, the loop of the rope placing inwards pressure upon the legs, the block secured and unmoving. It took little for the imagination to realise what was about to take place.

With the priests were the two men, Anthony and Toran; they would do well to serve the holy men as required, though the need to now restrain the traitor was little needed, for he would be unable to move.

Stephen was not present and nor was the captain. Stephen was where his bed had been laid; resting as best he could whilst the torture took place. Such actions should not be the will of man to enact upon another, even if such a man was a traitor. The captain was to the other end of the hold, giving a short speech to the cargo of flesh, assuring them as best he could that little fear should be dwelled upon. Stephen could hear well, all that the captain said.

"And what if the galleass should catch us?" asked a frightened soul, a woman of her latter years, a child under either arm. The children were not hers, but had given aid to her in Constantinople, as she now gave comfort to them.

"The men will see to the galleass. But you women must be prepared. You must all help where you can. The children must stay below and out of harm's way. All of the rest must play their part in the fight that is sure to come. Women can help with the sails; they can help with reloading arquebuses…"

"Fire crossbows," yelled a female from somewhere towards the back of the crowd.

"Anything to prevent the Turk from boarding our vessel," continued the captain. "Should we be boarded… that will spell the end of our retreat."

"A retreat!" yelled another. "You speak as though we are to gather our forces and fight again, to simply withdraw to another defensive position."

"We are heading to a place where salvation can be attained. Some of you will know of the island of Káros. A garrison exists there, strong enough to repel those aboard the galleass. The long run to the island will be easier to manage than anywhere else within the Aegean Sea, due to our advantage with wind. I know the wind patterns of the Aegean."

"Why not Lemnos?" someone in the crowd questioned.

"Euboea." The crowd was becoming agitated.

"Chios." Anywhere but Káros, for that was so far away.

"Please, good people." The captain had his hands in the air now, holding at bay the mounting fear. But the truth could not be told to them. "We have to consider much; for one thing, the manoeuvrability of the galleass and this good brigantine; their comparative speeds, the sailors who sail them. The wind will be in our favour for a move to the south. We must venture to a place where we know there exists a garrison of good men. Káros is the answer."

"But what are we to do in Káros? What—"

"And I am the captain!" he was losing patience. "You good people are under the protection of this boat. We sail for your better need. I would not subject you to capture any more than I would subject myself to torture," and he remembered where he had to be, his calling. "You must organise yourselves into groups fitting the task to which you are most capable of rendering service. There are men here that can help you in your choosing. Every able-bodied person must play his or her role in the conflict that could fall upon us soon. When we enter the Dardanelles, we are of limited movement. If we are to succumb to the Turk, then it is likely to be here. It is a long journey. You must all prepare for battle." He then turned to a shuffling sound: Stephen was standing at his side. The captain needed not introduce the Templar, but gave acknowledgement as to his skill, freely: "This man, you all know. He will sort you; he will give you knowledge where it is lacking, and the spirit to continue as we do…" and he looked upon the gathered throng, "but courage you do not need, for you have all the courage one could ask. I know you shall all serve the Lord well, as you have already done."

The captain turned to Stephen before departing, giving a slap of encouragement and a smile to boost morale; signs that the Templar knew were of trust and knowing, and on his expedient departure Stephen did take the floor. "Each of you here has a special gift or talent, even if you know not of such a trait. Each of you must search deep, look into your souls; it is there where you will see the measure of your vocation."

"My father was a fisherman… I helped him several times when the sea was wild," said one woman.

"And I shot a crossbow once," said another.

"I am a master boat builder," came an encouraging word.

"You all have a gift," continued Stephen. "Lars? Lars my good companion; where are you?" a hand was seen to shoot up from the rear. "Lars," and Stephen addressed the crowd, looking over them all as he spoke. "Lars: the beast of the Teutonic." A murmur from the crowd. "That's right! You see him there! Standing firm! He is but beyond doubt the greatest marksman one could ever expect to meet… with the crossbow I say." the crowd looked behind, heads bobbing left and right to catch a glimpse of this man of iron. "I tell you good people, a tale that will astound you. That man there, Lars the Teutonic, has but no tongue," gasps were heard; more shooting glances. "Cut off, I tell you, to prevent from revealing the true defensive strategies of a castle he helped protect against Muslim invaders… that's right, cut off by action of his own hand." The crowd was flabbergasted at such heroism, such courage: but of course it was all a lie, but warranted. "Seek him and teach he shall, and within minutes you will be a master as he." A few people moved on the spot where they stood. "But wait! Of sailing you need but another, someone skilled, someone as good with a rope as Lars is with his crossbow. Most of you know Franco…. Do you not?"

"I do!" shouted one man,

"And me! Over here!" came another.

Their courage was growing, their spirit, their confidence, their very inner strength. These common people were the answer to a prayer.

"Then let it be said and done. If you seek knowledge on sailing, go to Franco; the master Lars awaits your good attendance… and I shall teach the sword."

The crowd was bubbling with excitement and divided themselves as equally as one could expect, between the three men.

A woman came up to stand beside Stephen. "I am a nurse. I know a few good people that can fill my needs."

Stephen looked the woman in the eye and smiled, a tear beginning to form as he recalled his beloved Clover. "Good woman, you choose your own ground and take what supplies you require. Even if the men have to fight naked, you shall have all the cloth you need."

*

* * *

*

Ibrahim skirted around a few barrels fastened to the inner deck, roped and strapped, around the centre mast and other wooden boxes of cargo, before coming face to face with Ahmad Kadir. So nearly did he bump into the man that he picked his arms up to cradle his carelessness, by holding Kadir's forearms and taking a step backwards.

Kadir looked up as he finished putting away his manhood and did his belt up fast. "If I did not know better, Ibrahim, I would say that you meant to reach out for my privates for companionship, rather than my arms for stability."

"Excuse my haste, but Abu wishes to see you in his quarters, immediately."

"Ah… I see… and what good news is it that forces Abu's mind to conjure up a meeting so early at dawn?

"It is to do with the Christian boat."

"Ah, yes… the Christian boat… always the Christians," said Kadir, talking down to the deck before looking up and finishing with what he had to say. "We would do better without the vermin, Ibrahim. The worse for wear I have been since resigning my life to the sea," and the subject changed as abruptly as it had started. "Chastity it is, which can never be broken…"

Ibrahim seemed lost of words.

"Look you…" Kadir scoffed and pointed. "Down there you fool, upon the water, swimming through… no, dashing through the waves."

Both men looked down, over the side of the mahon at full sail, a porpoise swimming alongside, enjoying the chase.

"A fish."

"A porpoise, you uneducated vile of filth. What manner of man are you that cannot tell one creature from another?"

And indeed it was, quite dissimilar to a dolphin, by few characteristics and visual signs. A small toothed whale it was, growing no bigger than 6 feet in length. Its triangular dorsal cut through the waves as it swam, carefree and without concern. "So rare a sight as this may never pass your eyes again, good Ibrahim, even if a life at sea is all you come to know."

"Little concern it is to me. A fish is a fish. If it fills my plate and the hole in my stomach, then fish it is for eating."

Kadir considered the words. "Eat? EAT? You don't eat such creatures. This is majesty of the waves, a feature to test the senses like the… the…. Consider the appeal of your favourite dish; such appeal brings joy to you, to sing out loud."

"My favourite dish is sauce of garlic poured over a steamy hot plate of fish."

Kadir gave the man to his front a stern look and then shook his head. "See it, Ibrahim. Look at the porpoise as it swims. It feeds on fish too... just like you."

"Its oil is to a lamp, like its flesh is to my tongue."

"And what manner of tongue is it that can bring such a majestic life to the dinner plate?" With that spoken Ibrahim pointed, for another sailor, up front and aloft the forecastle, did suddenly thrust down a harpoon that penetrated the porpoise's head. It let out a faint shriek of horror in tribulation, and was quickly reeled in with much joy enveloping the one who had caught it.

"That man, soon to become my best friend, has the tongue... and I have the plate." And with that Ahmad strode off quickly, for he wanted nothing more than to be rid of the defilement and the collar that he wore in regards to his current station.

*
* * *
*

The captain returned to his cabin in time for the commencement of the torture, the scene to his front rather demoralising. He had sailed many seas and an ocean, had sailed into ports right across Europe. There wasn't a language he hadn't heard spoken, all colour of man-flesh having passed his sight at one time or another, but nowhere on this earth had he yet found the stomach for the word 'torture'... and now he was condoning its very use.

The men to his front went about their business, finishing up with their individual tasks. He was surprised to see so few instruments of pain upon the cloth of white, which had been laid upon a chair. There was a knife and a brush, and a smaller container... containing what, he did not know. The traitor was lying quietly, not a word passing his lips. He was looking to the roof and beyond, praying from within, asking Allah for forgiveness if he should be so cowardly as to relinquish the information that he carried – and little that was. He was praying for strength, for salvation, for a quick death, even if such was to be the uninvited.

Toran looked up, standing to the right side of where the traitor lay, beside his head; Anthony was to the right. "We are ready to begin, Captain."

All eyed each other then, for a brief moment. The captain gave a nod, it being received by the priests who stood at the victim's feet.

The first priest took up the brush from the cloth of white and dipped this into the vase of oil that lay between the victim's feet. He withdrew it, and as though painting the bare boards of a boat in dry dock, did paint the feet of the traitor quite thickly.

The first priest put the brush back into the vase, his robe rubbing, seemingly by accident, against the traitor's feet, a vast majority of the oil being removed. The captain saw this and was about to give advice when the priest continued: "I shall tell you now what is about to fall upon you. Your feet will be roasted and the poker we are to employ will scar you from head to foot. We also have a quantity of powder: it will be amusing to see the effect of it as it burns upon your flesh. If you answer our questions now, then you will go to your god unscathed. What is your decision?"

The traitor said nothing; just laid there, his lips murmuring to himself a prayer for salvation. The traitor's mind had readied itself, as best as possible, for the effects that were about to be delivered unto him.

The priests' first assignment was to make the man of guilt talk quickly though bring as little pain as possible to him. Only in this way, with a slow built up of pain, was the victim to be assured that a compromise could be reached. If the priests were to escalate the pain to its highest degree, then the man laid upon the planks could well be pushed, both mentally and physically, beyond reproach. The last thing the priests needed was a gibbering wreck of a man, whose tongue wagged a song of a different tune to the one they were after. But also, how best to ensure that the truth was being spoken. They knew a little of this villain, and thankfully, he did not know what they knew. They would call his bluff, pass on to him false questions with known answers. The traitor too, knew much of the science of torture, understood the formality and torments, false questions and answers, of the questions that would be asked over and over again in order to try and prove that he was lying. But there was something else, something that both priests and the traitor knew, and that was that even if he talked and gave willingly to the questions asked, the priests would still continue with the torture to ensure that they were indeed receiving the truth. The traitor, indeed, knew as much about torture and the proceedings, as did the priests – the priests however, did not know that the traitor knew as much as they. There might well be a compromise, but it would only come after much pain had been delivered.

And so begins the lengthy task of torture.

Mouley Bakar was the other that Ibrahim was seeking, and he was found below deck, where it was customary to keep the convicted and prisoners of war, during times of rest between turns at the oar; he was enjoying the comforts of a late morning. Bakar had no caretakers as such – not like his good friend Kadir – but he did have good reason to command as best he could, the foot soldiers under his command. His one and only son, a youngster of just several years of age, was being held at the point of a blade. Bakar served in order to preserve his son's life; but what was such an impoverished life to one like him? His son was to remain in a cell for the remainder of his life… or until Bakar, himself, had served adequately. And who was to say if he'd served well enough to secure the release of his son, and why was this life so important? One of the soldiers under his direct command was a spy… he'd been given this much information, but he didn't know who it was… the identity of the spy had been kept from him. In order for the release of his son to be secured, this man's life was to be kept intact. Such pressure made him a tough leader, but over cautious. He was crazed with paranoia. As for his son… he cared little for the sack of shit he called family, but his son was the last heir to the family in which he had been married. Yes indeed, on his son's release, Bakar would become a very wealthy man. But Bakar was no fool. What if he was to find his wealth during this very voyage? Did he really need to return to Mehmet for the gift of his son's life, hence the gift of the fortune that he desired? But what of the spy? And what if there was more than one?

Ibrahim approached Mouley Bakar as he washed himself, splashing a little water upon his face, rinsing the look of sleep from the creases that formed his brow, mouth, and cheekbones. A few scars, tiny in comparison to the ones he wore upon his body, stained his right cheek with a blemish of red. But it wasn't so much the scarring that turned women away from the man, but his personality.

Mouley could hear the steps of approach as Ibrahim closed the gap between the two. "And what does our beloved commander have for me this morning, good Ibrahim?" he said, not even tempting to look up.

"He wishes to speak with you in person; on matters of great importance."

"Great importance is it?" Mouley took his shirt, wiped it across his face, and placed it over his head and onto his body. "Every morning our esteemed commander has some important matter that needs my undying attention." He began the task of tucking away his garment and picked up his sheathed scimitar and belt. "Come Ibrahim… surely you know something. Tell me, what is in the air this good morning?"

Calm and sarcastic: nothing new for Mouley. "The brigantine is ahead, we have no other friendly boat in sight, and… well… the remainder must rest with the imagination."

Mouley stopped and looked at Ibrahim. "Do you have the foresight? Can you see for yourself," and continued to finish dressing. "Or do you lack the imagination of that which you speak?"

"I only come to request your attendance; as ordered."

"As ordered… of course. And I thank you most graciously, good Ibrahim, for your task is now complete, and mine just begun. You may run away now and report to our commander that I come panting like a

female dog on heat, evading a male, with its tail between its legs."
And off Ibrahim did run, allowing the sarcasm to drop away.

*
* * *
*

The captain stood back and allowed the priests their prestigious task of communication with the traitor; for the interrogation was about to commence.

"Tell me of the other boats: how many are there?" asked the first priest.

"I can tell you no truth."

The second needed no signal, he commenced quite calmly and with little effort, the build of the fire that had been given birth. He poked the coals with his iron stick, a little flame licking its wrought features. In and out he poked, and it was then that the finest of gasps did escape the traitor's lips. Before now the pan containing the fire had given off nothing more than a little warmth; but now it had well and truly started to build. The radiant heat was spilling outwards and heating up the oil baste upon his feet.

"It is never too late," said the first, "to adhere and repent."

"Repent. Not only do you wish me to sell my friends to their grave, but now you wish me to repent. What shall I repent to, father? Ah… I ask you… to what should I repent?"

"You have joined a brethren of infidels, to bring calamity and disheartenment to our great religion." The traitor scoffed. "You bring upon your very breath the devil's own work of words, voicing his sacrilegious verses and blaspheme openly."

"It is you," said the traitor, "who blaspheme." And with that the red-hot poker was pulled from the coals, as warmed as it was, and was dragged slowly across the stomach of the restrained and guilty victim. His screams were exasperating, to say the least. The captain shied, his arms crossed in front of his body, the two guardsmen held down the shoulders of the traitor, and the two priests' eyes battered not a single shudder.

"Speak now and you can prevent further pain!"

The burning sensation… no… the sheer agony, the uplifting excruciation, the burning torment which penetrated the traitor's body as the poker was drawn across the flesh and returned to the fire: it was too much to bear, surelly. The skin continued to bubble up, the first priest employing his skill well, and the fluid from the wound being contained. The smell of burning flesh hit their nostrils.

The traitor calmed down momentarily, catching his breath, the heat building slowly upon the soles of his feet. And before the traitor could compose himself completely, and without warning, the glowing poker was drawn once again across the body of their victim; and the screams did penetrate well into the confines of the cargo hold, where children cuddled their mothers – mothers who were too old to fight or sail a boat – and men looked up momentarily, as though able to see through the boards of the brigantine that partitioned them from the open air and scene above.

"How many boats follow in our wake?" asked the first priest again.

The traitor was gasping now, in much pain; as much as he had ever encountered in his life – as a free man or as a soldier.

"How many boats? Answer this question and you shall have a drink of water."

"Your water will not be enough to extinguish the flame that burns within me this moment." The first took the iron from the heat and applied it again, this time a little lower, just above the groin, dragging it skilfully across the flesh in order to prevent the skin from rupturing. Screams again filled the air around the confines of the cabin, screams that penetrated the very soul. The captain shook the smell of burning flesh from his head and Anthony entertained a wry smile.

The priests were in for a long day; they both knew this. Answers they needed, but such answers: would they aid them in their defence against those following? It would be true to say that regardless as to the numbers that followed, those aboard the brigantine would have to prepare the best defence they could muster; but what also of other traitors on the boat?

"How many boats follow?" his exasperation was building; he was growing tired, and yet he had just commenced. If the man tied to the table top knew not the answers to the questions being posed, they were going to end up with a dead man, torture being endured all day. If the traitor knew the answers then he could well receive reprieve, even if of minuscule compensation for that which he'd already suffered.

"You have but a few marks upon your body. I am sure you will wear them well… but will it be through pride, judgement, or hatred, that your memories of this day will be rekindled after death?"

The penetrating heat upon the soles of the traitor's feet commenced to build quite effectively. The constant feel of burning underfoot could not be extinguished from his mind. He knew for sure that this day would be his last on earth.

"Does such…" he gasped, "a question… help with your… cause?"

"I am the priest," said the first. "I shall ask the questions. How many boats?" The question went unanswered. The traitor was forgetting himself, losing his mind; all he needed to do was answer a few questions, which were unlikely to help the Christians cause in any case. The first took the iron from the pan; it was now glowing white at the tip, and the priest ensured that the traitor could see this. The priest averted his eye contact with the man on the table and applied the furnace-hot iron to the inside of the traitor's thigh. Screams immediately erupted from deep within him, and continued unabated as the poker was dragged skilfully across the flesh of his leg, down towards the knee, and up again. The poker was withdrawn and the convulsed body of the traitor stopped immediately, relaxed completely, not a taunt muscle existed anywhere. The man's chest heaved up and down, but he was unconscious.

"Toran: some water, quickly!" urged the second. Toran turning for a bucket filled with water. "Let us wake this man whilst the pain is at its worst."

The first priest could see the conviction building within the other; he wouldn't be stopped. Toran grabbed the handle of a ladle and withdrew it, splashing its contents unceremoniously over the head of the traitor. He awoke, gasping… his guts screaming for oxygen and a release from the pain that burned across his body and up the inside of his leg. "How many boats?"

"Five… boats… all manned… manned…." He lost consciousness again.

"Toran," the first indicated for another ladle of water with a signal of his head. The traitor burst out again with further gasping. How many men on board?

"I… I…"

"HOW MANY?"

"One hundred…and… twenty."

There was silence: it lasted but the time it takes a whore to secure her wages within her undergarments. "Who is in command?"

"I… don't know."

The priest was on a winning note, and wished to keep the upper hand. He lashed out convincingly with the iron poker, to the same thigh as before. The screams attained this time around were the worst yet to fill the vacuum of the cabin.

"The Strangler… Abu, the Strangler."

The knowledge was tucked away into the backs of their heads, for further information was required. The second priest then voiced a question, one that he was interested in hearing the answer to. "And of others amongst us that spy as you do: how many are they, and who?"

Ahmad Kadir and Mouley Bakar entered the small cabin, Abu seated to their direct front. He was sipping on some wine, a luxury of office that was not permitted to the men who worked beneath him. It was no surprise to see him sitting back in the lap of luxury – as good a luxury as any could expect, in particular when cast out to sea.

"Ahmad, Mouley, please, come and sit so that we may talk." His display of rank and confidence didn't impress the two men, anymore than the belief in their faith gave them the right to strike out at a woman, with heavy and clenched fist; but still, it was done; and so, with chins up and chests puffed out each took their position in front of the desk with a degree of pride embellished upon them. They stood there, the two, waiting to be spoken to; and then it came. "I have been the recipient of bad news, as is normally the case when commanded by chimpanzees and eunuchs. No one can expect full flavour of choice to overwhelm a palate when one's tongue is wrapped in an iron cloth… and this voyage of ours has been more than a shackle when it comes to orders; but still I follow them as a good commander does." Abu stood, his hands interlocked, placed behind his back. He turned away from the two men then and faced the open porthole at the rear of the cabin, looking out at the wake of their boat at sail. He turned abruptly and faced the two. "Precise orders have been given, but incompetence on the behalf of those that follow, have seen to it, quite clearly, that such cannot be followed, as they are nowhere to be seen."

Ahmad looked to his side and Mouley did the same, looking each other in the eye, temporarily lost in the avalanche of words, before returning their attention to their commander.

"Yes men, I see your look. Understand do you, the orders I have been given? Why, you haven't even seen them, yet as commander I am left with a choice. Specific instructions were gained by me as an advantage to this great voyage of ours," and the two in front could only wonder as to why the word 'great' should be spoken, "and orders followed shortly after." Abu sat, looked left and right upon his desk, and stood again. "Orders to remain linked with others to our port, stern, and starboard, before gaining upon, and then surrounding, a boat full of slaves and ransom. But where are the boats; where is this great armada of support and power that was promised...? gone. Like the wind which casts a thousands clouds to sail the skies into oblivion, to sail until released of its purpose. Are we to be released of our burden? No, I say." Abu was silent long enough to draw a few breaths and looked at them standing, though they were advised to sit; and then he continued. "Please, draw in a chair and seat yourselves." The two men did as requested and in silence. Abu sat too. "The orders I passed onto you are a direct reflection of those I did receive from higher station, and as such would normally remedy precise action to ensure they were fulfilled. However… we can no longer comply, as we are now sailing upon the sea, behind a Christian boat of riches, and not a friend to speak of; and not only this," Abu drew a deep breath, "but a traitor… yes, that is what I said, a traitor. A traitor aboard the Christian boat did give a signal to us last night, at a time when the sands within my timepiece did herald the hour as being late, whilst you were both asleep in your cabins of refuge. I received the signal personally before organising the other signals to be delivered to our boat's stern… and so on." Abu fell silent, he had prompted enough, or so he thought. He awaited a response from the two men, a question that did not come. He continued: "You may ask yourself why such a traitor didn't press for a slowing of the boat to our front, and… I am sure you are intrigued. The boat to our front is heading for a location, which we yet do not know. The boat is to be followed until such a time that the location can be revealed to this; traitor. Ample time was to be provided for him, and then we were to strike. With five boats to our side, we were to board and take all for ourselves, to be washed in the riches found aboard, in both flesh and gold; all that is, except a chest of secrets."

The men's jaws dropped in unison. "A chest…?"Ahmad asked.

"…Of secret's?" finished Mouley.

"Aye. I thought that would grasp your attention. But alas good men; good leaders that you are; for the chest is not of our belonging. It is for the sultan to do with as he sees fit. We have but been granting the sacking of the Christian boat, as though it was a suburb of Constantinople, a floating city where 3 days and nights of pillage will be granted."

"You deem to declare the right to sack and pillage a boat as though it were a city?" asked Mouley.

"I do. Your men will be permitted to do as they please, so long as the chest remains unmolested. The women may be raped at the good humour of your men, and the gold and ransom split equally… or as you see fit."

"This chest must have great value," concluded Mouley. "Good enough perhaps, for me to be granted my freedom and my son's release."

"I have the power to grant just that, but you and your men must fight as though empowered with the vigour of five, for no friendly boat is nearby. The men beneath you must be willing to sacrifice themselves, if the need arises."

"They must be granted special favour, above and beyond the sacking you so openly promise," added Ahmad.

"And so it will be granted, to all the men… once we have returned to safe harbour of course."

"And to our orders, Abu?" questioned Ahmad.

Abu stood, the other two followed in action. "I have ordered more speed, as much that can be mustered. I wish oars to be set, within the time it takes me to piss. We must gain on the Christian boat; now instead of tomorrow, or the day after that. We must strike whilst the manoeuvrability of the Christian boat can gain but little, to no advantage. We will attack whilst sailing down the Dardanelles. It would be in my interest to fight at first light, allowing us good wind for our closing of the distance tonight. Men can do without sleep: all will remain stationed at oars. We must employ 80 men at all times stroking the surface of the sea... 20 at rest should do it; and the marine detachment shall remain on call to duty and must be provided the opportunity to rest, where rest can be granted. The brigantine is weak and manned by old men, women, and children, so nothing more than a handful of marines should fill our need... nevertheless, rest they shall be provided. So go now, and give your orders. Ready yourselves on this eve of fighting to come, for tomorrow you will be given all of the freedoms your hearts so desire. If a friendly boat follows, we will leave it in our wake. The spoils of war will be ours alone. Go now... and if we need to speak again before last light, it will be for me to bring discipline to bear upon your shoulders."

Both of the lesser commanders stood without further word, and bowed to Abu before turning on their heels and departing with purpose.

The door to Abu's cabin burst open and Mouley let out a roar: "Boabdil, Abdar, and Hamed, bring yourselves to me! NOW!"

And from Ahmad: "Abdullah, Muhammad, bring me your ears! Men... good men around... prepare for battle, for by morning's light your scimitars will be caked in Christian blood!"

*
* * *
*

Weapons, ammunition, and other supplies were scarce to say the least, but where good supply the Christians did lack their spirit was overflowing.

Lars had lived many years, more than half his life, with no tongue in his mouth. He had learnt well to deal with the accustomed remarks and cold stares, the manner in which mothers would shield their children from such a monster as he. But for the years of torment that had been felt and rubbed in deep, came a foreboding insight, and he was a natural when it came to reading the minds of others around him. He could read the look on a face as well as he could hear their tone, whisper, or malice. He could read their walk as well as a touch or a slap. He could adjust himself readily to any situation as though born to it.

Lars stood to the front of his small congregation of seven. Two women in their 40's, a man in his 70's, three boys of their mid-to-late teens, and a girl of eight years. It was to the girl he first looked. She was bewildered and calm, looking up to him as though lost to the world of sanity, a lost sheep in search of its flock. She had lost her innocence and was looking for comfort, but here, where Lars did stand, was only one type of comfort... and that was the closeness drawn from a crossbow and its quarrel. What a pitiful creature of beauty, what innocence of life this was, to be wasted upon the defence of the Christian boat, where life would soon prove to be put out to the slaughter. Lars knew as any other, that this girls life depended on her being able to defend, being able to shoot at will, being able to kill without second thought: for if she did not, then she would be raped as any other women aboard this boat, raped repeatedly, until she did die from the loss of blood… and even in a circumstance as this, it is hard to comprehend, but even in death, the Muslim pirates would still be slapping their groin against hers, grabbing what sexual pleasure they could as she lay void of life. Be it for them, they did not care. Be she dead or alive mattered little. The soft touch of her skin would be to their delight, and rape they would, and without repent, regardless of how cold her skin did turn. Yes indeed, they would have their way with this little girl, as though she was a sheep in the fields of slaughter, to be molested as well she deserved, for she was a Christian upon a Christian boat, and as anyone of the Muslim faith would deliver, she would be taught of her faults in life and religion.

Lars offered his helping hand to the girl of eight, a smile upon his face providing support, his delicate touch appealing to her in many ways. His touch was a friendly touch: very warm and open. He was her friend and father, brother and king. To the little girl, Lars was everything, and to see her lightened smile, as she looked up into his eyes, did bring a tear to one of the women who watched from the side.

Lars knelt down beside the little girl and put his arm around her, bringing her in closer, dragging her across with his left arm. And in his right he held the crossbow, balanced perfectly upon his open palm. Lars looked to the weapon and then into the girl's eyes. He held it to her, bringing it closer to her body, to place the stock of the weapon against her shoulder. He meant no harm to her then, but grunted and bore his teeth, for she wouldn't relent to the lesson. Her smile disappeared, and Lars grunted again, more forceful this time, pushing the stock of the weapon into her shoulder. She sobbed gently but did her best to hold back her tears and gave into the instruction being delivered. The moisture that built upon her eye clouded her vision and her face showed the torment that she felt upon body and soul. Lars grunted once more, forcing the stock into her shoulder once more. The girl took it and looked down the groove upon the barrel, seeing first-hand what it looked like to peer down the length of a crossbow. Lars stood up then and grunted once more, indicating another man from behind to come and relieve him, the only other aboard the boat that was a professional when it came to firing the crossbow. Lars relieved himself then, of the lesson at hand, and strode away quickly, to hide his face in a dark corner of the hold, to shed a tear that couldn't be held at bay. The floodgate was open and he would rid himself of this burdened pain, this inner stabbing-of-the-heart that he felt. He would rid himself of this anguish and return afresh, for these people, regardless of age, had to be taught a few lessons on self-preservation: for the last thing Lars would accept, was the repeated raping of a child still of her youth.

*
* * *
*

Franco stood atop the deck; women and children of age, swarmed around him like bees after a honey pot. To work the sail and rigging one had to have strength and courage… no less courage does one need to climb the mast to crow's nest, any less than one needs to fight a janissary. "It is a different courage I tell you. You know yourself, deep within your very hearts, whether or not you can scale the rigging of this brigantine, to place yourself within the confines of that wooden palisade… a wooden box from where you can peruse… at your leisure, mind you, the seas around as you sail upon its waters." And Franco felt the confidence building within and paced the deck like a good tutor does. "Why, what do I see before me? Young Master Andrew. Why, boy, how old do you be?"

"You know that, Mr Franco, sir," answered the boy.

"Tell everyone here, announce it so they may take heed."

"Ten years, I am ten years, this year."

All around smiled at the display of confidence. "Well, ten years and full of pride; ready to pull at the rigging I bet, and you too… yes! You lad! Come here, tell all around your name." "John, my name is John – I am eleven years, this year."

All gave to a round of applause, smiles set freely upon the mouths dirtied during the withdrawal from Constantinople. "Well, I never," exclaimed Franco, now turning to address the crowd, "never in all my years of sailing, did I see such grandeur as that displayed by these two young men here before us today. Great hope they have instilled within me this very moment, the very hope, no… the very knowledge that the fight to come will be won." And the gathering slowed in their applause, for they were but meagre old women and men in need of revitalization, and they all feared the fight. Franco could see… could feel the very fabric of that which held them together, stretched under strain. He drew alongside of, and sat upon a small barrel, open palms placed upon his thighs, elbows held high. He got up again. "We stand alone good citizens. We alone must help ourselves in the fight that draws near. The larger vessel that follows from behind has set extra sail, a galleass from behind which will no doubt catch up to us before we reach the Aegean Sea. It is up to us to ensure that martyrs are made of those that follow. It is as important to them, to be remembered in death, as it is to us, to be benevolent in life. Look to these two young men, both have many years to look forward to, and both are willing to fight for their right to live. But they also fight for you. We fight for each other. But our skill at fighting is not as sound as it is in those that seek victory through the sword. For victory to be savoured we must set upon the tasks that are to be surrendered by those that relinquish their posts during the fight to come. We must all be able to replace the sailors, when the sailors take up arms against the vermin that follow." Franco then indicated the two boys coming of age, referring to them, that the others may follow their example. "Such confidence, such marvellous displays of courage that I ever did see before. We must all learn the ways of this boat like we know our own arms and legs. Each rope is a sinew; each mast is a bone. Your eyes are the lookout, your feet are the sea; the wind is your stride… the manner in which this brigantine was built; that is the essence of you all, the spirit that must surface and be clear for all to see. This boat is our last refuge… we have nowhere else to run. We can no longer retreat."

*

* * *

*

Stephen stood in front of the gathered men: half a dozen in their later years. There also stood amongst these volunteers, ten women, five boys of around nine years of age, and three girls of between six and eight. He first wondered about his approach, a speech that may be appropriate to the situation. He was a man, no doubt, but one so young… could he muster the essence, that which was required to forge these refugees into fighters? What choice did he have?

He stood there in silence, looking over the small congregation, wondering about his ability to teach, and their ability to learn. Old men and women; young boys and girls. The sailors aloft the decking, shifting sail and tying down rope… they had a degree of knowledge on fighting, had to… in order to keep at bay the boarding of pirates.

Old men and women: what were they that he should trouble himself to teach? These people couldn't have the power to inflict damage upon a foe. The galleass that followed was higher out of the water than the brigantine, at forecastle and aftcastle – this was against them. Those that followed were better trained – in actual fact, any training, regardless of how professional, would be better than that about to be taught these poor sacks of flesh.

It was then, as though in a flash of light that the voice came to his ear but once again: Greater love has no man, but he who surrenders life with good cause. You will not see decay when delivered unto the Lord; and there shall be no prejudice comparison between servant and master, for no one is above the Lord. This is a covenant of your Lord. And all of those around Stephen stared in bewilderment, for their teacher seemed to be reflecting on some unknown apparition, his facial features aghast at something mystical, his mouth agape as though in awe of an empowering enlightenment. The people looked to one another, wondering on the sight before them all, of Stephen, as the gaping hole beneath his nose did close, and a smile commenced to develop upon his face.

Stephen looked to the men: "Do you believe in compassion, do you believe in love?" and said it with such a radiant smile that those that listened were compelled to answer. "I… I believe in the love between a man and a woman, the strength that it holds," said one man.

"I shall say that a parent's love for his child is greater," said another, for he knew of parenting and its responsibilities.

Stephen gathered his thoughts in the silence, the sound of the sea voicing its opinion, waves slapping against the hulk of the boat as it cut through the turbulence created by movement of wind upon the surface. "Two have answered; one for marriage and the other for God." Stephen gave pause to his reflection. "Is it not God who bestows his love for us, better still, our love for Jesus and His love for us. God sacrificed so much by giving us His only child, to be slain upon the cross like a common dog. Yes indeed, that is love. The love Jesus held for us all, this also called out, for he gave His life in order that we may be forgiven." Stephen looked at the children, so sweet in their early years, so different when older. "Little girl, so pale and tall, what is your name?"

"I am Catherine, sir," answered the six year old.

Stephen looked behind, took a spear that had been leaning against the side of the boat. He held it out to her. "Do you know what this is, Catherine?"

"A spear…"

A woman gasped and then quickly covered her mouth, shocked to think that Stephen would wish the girl to defend the boat against being boarded.

Stephen stood erect. "The child is right, it is a spear. And now Catherine, another question for you: What would you do with this?"

"Enough!" voiced one of the men, the Templar's gaze distracted. The teacher then scolded the man, but without his voice being heard, for the look within his eye told all around that there was more to his words than question alone, and that his voiced opinion should be heard without drawing false conclusions in reflection to the movement of his body.

Stephen smiled and looked at the girl again. "Do you know its purpose?"

The girl took the spear and held it in her hands. "I can do this!" and thrust the spear out at the rail of the boat, as though into the flesh of a pirate. Stephen stood as further exclamation was received from the gathering, more from surprise than not, for the action of the girl spoke for itself: she was willing to fight.

"To the gentleman who prefers the good love for a child," and Stephen recalled what John the Hospitaller had told him days before, whilst in the defence of Constantinople, "would you accept that this child, although not of your own in blood and virtue, be yours in faith and honour? Do you honour this child? Will you treat this child as your own? Would you protect her with all of your heart?"

"I can accept… No! I cannot accept responsibility for that which is not mine."

"And of the gentleman who preferred the good love of a marriage, the bonding of a man and a woman: did not such a bond see to the deliverance of this child?"

"I cannot say… I know not the parents."

"It is not a direct question, kind sir," continued Stephen. "But rhetoric of belonging. Did not Jesus, and God, believe that all men were of his body, belonged of his flesh. Was it not spoken? Father, forgive them, for they do not know what they are doing."

"What is a belief in religion to do with this child?" voiced the man so fond of love in marriage.

"It is our duty to perform our belief. This child has shown merit. She has told us that she will do what she can to prevent the boarding of the infidel. In return, I should hope, that you will do as much by protecting her from the devil's lust for pillage and rape. Should you not give your life to a good cause, as Jesus did give His? I ask you not, kind sir, to throw down your arms when confronted by the enemy, but to call upon all of your spirit to defend this child's very innocence. If you throw your life down, like common garbage is thrown into the sea, then you will not reap the reward of everlasting life. I am… we all are, asking you to give your life for this girl, as Jesus did give His life for you. This girl is one of yours, and one of mine; we are of the same flock… we are family. It matters not of your wealth or good station in life. Jesus does not prejudice between servant and master, and neither should we. Even if this girl were of darkened skin, she would still be ours to protect. Look inside yourself, sir… all of you, look deep. We are all one and the same, we are all God's creatures. This little girl has already sworn to protect you: will you do the same in return?"

The one so fond of marriage spoke: "And what is it that we must do; for the fire in me can hardly be rekindled, and the youth of those that follow in our wake will deliver the edge of their scimitar in such a way that I stand not a chance of parrying such a blow."

"What is your name, sir?"

"I am Niketas… I was born of Constantinople," said the 40 year old.

"No," said Stephen. "You were born of God, and Jesus is your Lord and Master." Niketas said not a word but accepted the chastisement for what it meant. "And you… yes… the man who would see the bond of his family strengthened through the love for his child."

"I am Rainald," said the man. He then appeared to puff out his chest, ever so slightly. "I am of 51 years… and I am still full of fire."

"To be full of fire is not good enough, for you must ensure the flame is delivered. And Niketas… if you believe you will be struck down by the scimitar, then that is what will happen." Stephen paused for a short second. "You must expel all of your energy within, to fight as you have never fought before. I shall say this to all of you now: if you should collapse to the floor of this deck, then it shall be through sheer exhaustion. You cannot feign courage of strength through training, you cannot prove your worth through strenuous exercise with sword or dagger. But the spirit you display when the fight does come, that is what matters. It is here that we must train ourselves. Yes… I can teach a little on protection; the tactics that we must employ to keep the infidel at bay; but the victory will only be won through the exuberance that you deliver when the time is ripe. When a man comes to you, to fight you alone… what do you do? Niketas?"

Niketas wasn't sure as to the answer, but something within spoke for him. "I must fight like there is no tomorrow… that is the only way to beat the beast."

Stephen smiled, walked up and down in front of the gathered throng. "Is he right? Is he…? No, don't answer," he held his open palm. "For I can see that none of you will know the answer, none of you here can give me the correct response." And the small crowd was dismayed and hurt; they couldn't believe the unkind words that had been flung in their direction… and then the Templar finished with: "For you are all too generous and proud; you are all too merciful. I shall tell you what you should do." He looked Rainald in the eye. "When Niketas is confronted by the devil, you my friend, Rainald; you will come in from the side and push the point of your blade into his body, and as he withers upon the deck, another of you will fall upon him, and dig his heart out with a dagger."

The crowd were silenced… mostly; but one gave way to a dry-reaching, sickened by the explanation. And there, amongst the crowd, was one that stood silent and smiled. Stephen looked at her then and smiled in return and the gathered were silenced. All stared then to the one responsible for domineering over the class: it was the little girl. "If this one, being so pure, can convey to the actions required, then you ALL can follow the example. We do not fight with rules. Rules are for the merciful, for the proud, for the strong. You must all become weak and surrender to the ways of cheating. The only way to win this fight is to be as low and vile as those that fight us. You must surrender your conscious motives, you must not give into charity… you must NOT give mercy. This is your path to victory, and on this path are the actions you must embrace. To win against filth you must become filth.

*
* * *
*

Syahid thought: A chest of secrets. What secrets could lie within the confines of a chest at sea?

He shook the thought from his head and continued listening, stooped as low as he possibly dared to hope, over the lip of the stern of the mahon. He had already – although in a precarious position – been paid off well. Eavesdropping on the commander, Abu, was daring enough… to do so in full light of day was pushing the limit.

Again it thumped within his head: a chest of secrets. He listened more on the conversation being undertaken between Ahmad, Mouley, and Abu.

What? Three days of pillage. 'The strangler' was offering everything. This chest of his must be worth a mighty sum; if only the situation could be manipulated to best suit my needs. Ah, ha. Mouley is going to receive special favour, and… what's that? All of the men will receive special favour… more speed… no sleep… by morning's first light… time to vacate my position, for to be caught will see my head bound to a log and displaced by unfavourable means.

Syahid slipped away quickly and quietly, his listening post above the rear cabin's porthole having served him well… better than even he could appreciate. And he waited for some time before moving on.

He took off soon after, upon a new and urgent need, though careful not to arouse suspicion..

He moved towards the entrance of the hold, a segmented portion below, which had been partitioned and made ready for use by the officers and other official men, and down into the darkness where his eyes would take time to adjust.

Syahid looked left and right as he approached Abdullah and Muhammad, having been running the errand on which they had been sent. Both Abdullah and Muhammadb stepped into the confines of a shadow as they saw him approach, a corner within the hold that hid them well from any prying eye. No one else was around when Syahid came calling, and this was to their liking. Fleeting eyes drift here and there, ears open to all manner of sound, ready to scrutinize anything out of the ordinary.

"Syahid," said Abdullah. "What did you hear?"

"Abu sang well and gave orders to pursue the Christian boat."

"So early," stated Muhammad.

"Abu sees no reason why caution should be displayed, for the others that are with us, are… not with us."

"We know this already," Muhammad was tempered. "Tell us something we do not know."

"Abu has ordered that we should gather speed and capture the

Christian boat. He has also pledged three days of pillage."

"Pillage a boat over three days when it can be done in far less than one; absurd," said Muhammad.

"But something more… something which will be sweet to your ears," continued Syahid.

"Speak the sweetness, before I grow sour," said Abdullah. "Wait!"

A noise of clatter, something dropped down a rung of steps. Someone was entering the hold. The three in hiding slunk back: ensuring the security of the shadow they sought did cover them well.

It was Abdar. He was rummaging through his belongings, muttering away to himself, something that couldn't be heard. And then an exhale of satisfaction came from Abdar and he ascended the hold as quickly as he had arrived.

"What did you hear," reiterated Abdullah, signifying that it was all clear to continue with the information.

"There is a chest…"

"A chest?" asked Muhammad.

"Let the man finish with his report," said Abdullah. "Go ahead Syahid, before someone else comes calling."

"Abu is after a chest, a chest of secrets."

"Secrets," again Muhammad interrupted.

And Abdullah interceded, clearing his voice.

"I am sorry," and Muhammad waved him on.

"A chest of secrets exists, a chest that is for the sultan's eyes only. It is of great worth. Mouley has even been given the promise of freedom from duty and all of the men are to receive special favour… once the task is complete and the chest is secure."

"What worth does a chest hold that the sultan should be intrigued by its very existence? It must be filled with gold and title, jewels from across Europe, and grants of distinction," said Abdullah. His greed was being met, the cavity he held within, for the better consumption of riches, was getting its fill.

"Syahid, nothing of this must pass your lips," said Muhammad. "We have been close friends for so long that I believe trust has developed enough for us to draw parley of distribution… much wealth there must be for the sultan to be entangled in, what appears to be, insurmountable interest." Muhammad touched his finger to his chin. "I believe I can draw also, upon the trust of three under my influence. Boabdil, Abdar, and Hamed."

"Do you really think such is a good idea, Muhammad?" asked Abdullah.

"Indeed I do; with you, Syahid," and he looked him in the eye, "and these other three, we stand to attain much power. What is Mouley to us? He is as expendable as the rats I chase from my blanket each night, and the ones I kill supping on my breakfast each morning. The fool thinks a spy is watching him… such pity I must draw… what a pathetic wretch he is. If the sultan thinks I am to return, to be treated by him, as the dog of a servant, then he needs to think again. But, Ahmad is different. I believe that with a little persuasion that Ahmad will come to our banner. He owes his niece nothing, although in fairness he does owe his life to her existence. What do you say, Syahid, Abdullah; do we pact? Are we in agreement to form a union between us with Boabdil, Abdar, and Hamed… Ahmad will be nothing more than a puppet. Others will be happy to follow, once they know the structure of command."

"No, Muhammad," answered Abdullah. "We must be seen to have control, to maintain coercion and command."

"And which of the two, of you and me, shall be seen to be in command?" replied Muhammad.

Abdullah thought upon this. "You are right. Two in command will not do."

Syahid felt a little left out. He was as good a man as Abdullah and Muhammad. Why should he not be in command, or at least in communion with the conspirators? "I too, agree with this." Both other men looked at Syahid, who in return felt the stabbing of eyes and curses fall upon him. "We are three, not two. Ahmad will do well to command… he is a good tactician. He can serve well. If we are to band together, with just a handful: what is it to us that they know, that Ahmad only commands as a puppet?"

"So it is agreed," concluded Abdullah. "We allow Ahmad to command… due to his ability of strategic importance only, and we… as three… shall be his masters."

"Let us shake on this agreement," said Muhammad, and the three did secure their unwritten contract.

Peter looked upon the table of the captain's quarters, his cabin of refuge, his office and sleeping quarters. He had entered half way through the torture of the traitor, but now it was complete. The priests had the information they had sought, and the captain was satisfied, to a certain degree, that a defence would now benefit from the information gained.

The two mercenaries, Anthony and Toran, had commenced to clean away the tools of torture, the hot iron was put out in the bucket of water, and the ladle affixed its place upon a cornice. The priests said their last prayer and the captain sat in his chair and poured a handsome dosage of wine… that which he had prescribed himself, to ease his nerves. As for the traitor, he lay upon the planks, scars numerous across his body. The stink, as well as the mess, was horrendous… as could be expected, for his feet had been roasted well and his bowels had been released. The traitors left foot had been so mutilated that the sole of his foot had been burnt half off: such is a trait of torture. As for the traitor… he was dead. No chances could be taken on his lying. The truth had to be known, even at the expense of another human being. But he was an infidel, and with such a label came misfortune. He was the devil in worship, a beast of malevolent worth.

Peter had never seen torture before, and now that he had, wished that he had not. The tormented screams of the traitor would live with him forever, the smells of burning flesh reside with his nostrils till his dying day, and the instruments of pain would remain forever inscribed upon his mind.

And then, in the back of his mind, something shook him back to reality, awakening him from his fever-pitched guilt and apprehension.

"Peter, do you hear?" continued the first priest. "Get for me a blanket, enough to wrap this carcass in, for even with the devil he worships, a burial at sea he will be given. For his contribution of information, he will be forgiven; for his devil worship he shall be burdened… in death, like the torture he did submit to, with sheer agony, for he did commit to false worship."

"Yes, Father, I shall see to it," and off he scampered, to the task he had been provided. He exited the cabin door, sped past several men who were standing around talking amongst themselves. He caught a brief glimpse of Stephen to one side, where lecture was being administered, to strengthen minds and obedience, and Franco to the opposite, further towards the bowsprit.

He continued to the hold, where he brushed past another and continued to his place of quarter, where a blanket was secured under his armpit. He then turned to make his way back to the priest but fell upon Lars as he moved, bumping delicately into the idol… this brought the knight to a temporary frustration before he summed up a benign look of disregard.

"Good knight… sir Lars… I am aghast at my carelessness. My esteem apologies, good knight." Peter's cluster of words were well heard by Lars, who stood his ground and shook the ignorance from within, and with the helping hand of the man who had astonished him, brought to head the finishing touches of composure. The Teutonic let out a little huff, but gave no indication that he desired to reprimand the sailor. "I beg your forgiveness."

Little forgiveness there was to offer, for Lars felt little troubled by the occurrence of Peter's action – in particular now that he realised that such a foolish collision was far from being on purpose. The knight looked at Peter, realising that the good soldier was aboard the brigantine well before he, and having such honour, was more than likely more astute as to the provisions of the boat.

Peter could see lustre develop upon the man's eyes and wondered as to the thoughts that lingered and festered upon his soul, it was then that Lars – with a grunt – held up a quarrel within his left hand. Peter looked the missile up and down, and then to the eyes of the knight himself.

"Ah… I see. You want to know if further supplies are at your disposal?"

Lars smiled, "Ooooo," and nodded.

"There is, sir Lars. I saw provision wrapped in canvas, marked with the stamp of a symbol representing an arrow… but… that could have been for a bow; does it matter?" for Peter didn't know the specifications of the crossbow that Lars did carry.

Arrows for one were not arrows for another. Seldom was one made universally, where it could be employed with more than one type of manufacture. Thought Lars: A boy, even if immature and of unfledged wings, must surely know as anyone, that it is best to have arrows made specifically, where they are manufactured with specifics in mind, where they are different from one weapon to any other. Arrow points were just as significant – depending on the task and desired effect. Lars nodded.

"Well, maybe I can show you… yes?" and Peter felt the excitement well inside him. Lars looked at Peter and nodded, amused that the boy seemed to think him illiterate, for his tone and action of words mounted argument that Lars was nothing more than a retarded beggar woman of little disposition.

"Please, sir knight; this way."

Lars followed, his lesson left far behind, and his thoughts now entwined around the boy, Peter. Here Lars was being led along like nothing more than a dog off a leash. "This way, sir knight. That's it. Not far now."

Lars considered the triggers within his companion's head. Even if the knight were of six years of age, he would find it hard to believe that he would be treated in such a way… but this was the law of being misunderstood. It was in fact this very action that brought people to the conclusion that Lars knew nothing of fighting and should be shuffled aside in order to fetch dry powder for arms, water for thirst, and food for celebration. Be he, he thought, the most misunderstood man who did walk the face of the earth. Then he thought further still, of the question in regards to arrows. It was only due – primarily – to Lars' unquestionable perfection of his art that he believed each brand of arrow did harness special powers, which would be reflected when employed in the specific weapon strung for such a missile. Peter on the other hand, was still a boy (by comparison), and had not founded a particular skill… therefore, he would be quite satisfied and apt to employ an inferior arrow with a particular choice of strung apparatus – even if such a weapon gave poor performance due to the poor choice of quarrel or arrow.

They finally arrived at some cargo strapped upon the centre of the forecastle, where indeed, Lars did meet with a little surprise. The canvas packages, resting aside the stack, were unwrapped carefully, and although not of much use to the crossbow that Lars did carry, were of good quality. Not only this but a large quantity of bows was also in existence: the only other type of weapon that coincidentally enough, did suit the skills of the Teutonic. But why were they found here, why were they not employed during the defence of Constaninople?

Lars beamed a smile that fell from ear to ear, and the joy he felt in securing such a find was only heightened by the enthusiastic handshake that Lars gave Peter, and the slap on the back that would have knocked a well-rooted tooth out of the head of many an old woman. Peter smiled too, happy to have been of service.

Abdullah and Muhammad reported to their station, the stern end of the open decked galley. Along the length of the boat, on both sides, sailors had taken their positions, oars had been thrust out and men took their seats upon the benches of work. So old was the mahon that imprints of the men's backsides could actually be seen, scars of indented buttocks, a signature of the boat which read character into the very planks that moulded the mahon and spoke of its spirit. An old relic of war still at sail, that's what she was, a beast… not of burden, but of a sacrilegious trend, for this boat had seen to the misery of many enemy… and for all of its years at sea, had seen as many enemy boats sunk, due primarily to its builders and the double planked bow of superior construction.

Abdullah sat upon the coxswain's throne: and although not a seat of power, was most definitely a seat noted for its distinction. Big men they were, Abdullah and Muhammad, yet never in their days had their palms brushed faces with an oar or a sweep. Muhammad sat comfortably to his left, a pallet of blanket and straw drawn up by Syahid, sitting just to his rear. This bed was the station for the relief, where one would rest and the other would beat upon the drum. They were quite different from the sailors, in all respects. Both Abdullah and Muhammad had worked together for many years, and this year was the first that they had worked on a mahon – or any other boat for that matter – which did not have slaves or prisoners of war manning the oars. This was a fresh idea, from one of the high officials who worked under the sultan. Why beat a slave to death, hence, reducing your power at oar, when condemned men could be provided a promise of reprieve if they did stroke the sea well. There was also the promise of ransom and rape – not bad for a convict. Many convicts erupted into smiles when advised of the possible payment: the opportunity to stroke the bare flesh of a woman, and all they needed to do was to stroke the sea with as much enthusiasm.

As for Syahid, he was their companion, their runner of errands. If Abdullah or Muhammad thirst for water, Syahid would go running; if they hungered, he would fetch an appropriate dish. As coxswains they never went without, for their task was of utmost importance, and Syahid was to see to their every wish. In fact, Syahid relied upon the generosity of Abdullah and Muhammad, as they depended on him for the much-cherished privy information. He was most definitely a spy like no other.

Abu approached the open floor of the deck and looked down upon the men… in their two's, forty men to each side of the mahon, the oars were taken hold of and pushed forward in readiness to receive that illustrious first drum beat. Abu smiled. He was happy this day, even with the poor news of the others in his small armada not being anywhere in sight. There would come a day, he told himself, that he would see to it that precise orders accompanied any task, and if such orders were not obeyed to the letter, then heinous punishment would be the just reward. Promotion: such a cleansing word that offered great gifts of station, where one could enjoy the fruits of one's labours, even if struck to sea for years on end. It was well within his grasp… a promotion to reflect his abilities, and when such a promotion was received he would ensure all orders were carried out as required.

All was at the ready. Coxswains were standing by, as was Syahid. The oars were manned; Ibrahim was standing by to press home any order given him by his commander. Ahmad Kadir stood at the ready, to the side and between the coxswains and rowers. Mouley Bakar was standing upon the forecastle, his marines stationed in pairs around the mahon in readiness to receive orders (such were the delights of discipline and parade, where all would maintain their post until all formality had been concluded, and once they were under full sail and power of oar they could be stood down to maintain a rostered picket). Boabdil, Abdar, and Hamed, stood by Bakar's side – group leaders of good sense and background (many years experience between the three).

Abu glanced one final time towards the bow of the boat, over the forecastle and past the bowsprit, across the great expanse of the Marmora Sea and to the Christian boat, which was not much more than a dot on the horizon. He lifted his right hand, which held a baton, and with open mouth gave vocal order at the same time that the baton came down. The beating of the drum commenced immediately, slow at first in order for rhythm to be built, and within the shortest span of time did arrive at a cadence of a mere 15 strokes to every sixty heartbeats.

*
* * *
*

It was late afternoon on the brigantine, and to the rear of the boat the priests had gathered with Anthony and Toran. It was nothing but the smallest congregation, to put to sea the body of the traitor, who had, after so much pain and torment, given the inquisition the information they desired, although little aid it would bring them.

The two strapping men balanced the foot of the board to rest upon the rear rail, the priests giving final prayer prior to allowing the board to be uplifted, hence delivering its cargo of meat to its final resting place beneath the waves.

The wrapped body bobbed in and out of the water for a few seconds, stabilised, and then sank without further ado, and not a shark in sight. It was then that the group of four looked up and saw the galleass following behind, gaining ground on their brigantine. The oars could be seen quite clearly now, pulling in and out of the Marmora, the sails above billowing in the wind. It was quite inevitable, their capture, the struggle to come. They all doubted that they could win, or for that matter, out run the boat that followed.

Anthony turned his head, he'd heard a sound, and from his peripheral he saw Stephen approach the captain's quarters with Peter in tow. He then looked up to his slight left and right, seeing first-hand the approaching mouth of the Dardanelles, their escape, the only route from Constantinople open to them: mountainous peaks on either side, the mouth of which must have stood at around 18 miles.

"We are entering the Dardanelles now, fathers," announced Anthony.

The first turned and looked for confirmation. "You are too ambitious and optimistic, Anthony. When the strait is but a few miles wide, and only then will we be within the Dardanelles. We will be confined much by restriction in movement. My guess is that we shall be fighting hand-to-hand before first light tomorrow."

"I had heard once," added Toran, "that a boat could gain much speed by posting rowers to the front of their boat, tied fast by a long rope they could pull for more speed."

"It is so typical that such ideas and optimism should proceed one's fear," said the first, looking apologetically at Toran. Here was a man who had fought well and hard during the siege of Constantinople. Such a man as this should not be distressed by the inheritance of an unkind word. He put a palm to his shoulder to comfort the man. "Such harsh words… I am sorry Toran. Regardless of how much additional speed we can muster, we will be caught up with in the end." He removed the comfort of his hand. "Besides, we need to retain our strength for the fight to come. Better to rest and make ready." He looked around at the others, connected with each individual. "Those behind are losing strength, they sap their energy in rowing for speed. We must rest and ensure that we are strong to meet the enemy when they board this boat of ours."

"But the traitor," added Anthony. "He told of over one hundred men, twenty of whom were a detachment of marines."

"Marines won't be rowing," concluded Toran.

The first brought the ceremony to a close: "More the need for rest, for we will have one hell of a fight, once it arrives… and it will come… soon." He walked off with the second priest close behind.

*
* * *
*

Peter and Stephen stepped from the short fall of rungs and positioned themselves to the front of the captain; he had his back turned on them but soon corrected the rudeness of his stance and faced them both with a smile.

"Captain," said Stephen. "I did hear that the interrogation was complete, and went quite satisfactory… for some."

"If I was a bitter man, Stephen, I would say that you are pinning insult to the back of a dead man; but as I know better, all I can say is yes… and as you have already suggested," Homer sat, "better for some than others." And Stephen could tell that the captain, too, was inflicted badly by the torture. "Better things I have to do than watch over the burning of a man. Not so bad, it would have been, if conducted at the stake, and in earnest. But such are the glories of war, that much torment must be inflicted upon both the enemy and us. But to inflict such terrible wounds to the minds of the innocent, is not a measure I take pride in," and he looked down upon the boards of the cabin in which they stood, indicating the cargo of innocent women and children stationed below.

"Which brings me to my immediate quest," prodded Stephen. "For it would seem that each and every one aboard this grand vessel, has the pumping heart of a professional guardsman, but yet… we lack the weapons." Stephen fidgeted on the spot. "Captain Homer, we have no swords and few spears, the quarrel for crossbow will also be short in supply. If the men and women aboard this boat were Spartans then yes, I could expect them to attack the enemy with tooth and nail, to bite and scratch at the eyes of the enemy, to sink their teeth into the groin of those assaulting them, all in order to draw victory from a one-sided fight. But we have nothing. They know well, captain, to take the sword of a fallen comrade, and how to employ a stick sharpened at one end, in order to tease the enemy with its sharpened point, but tease is all they can do. Surely there must be something… something you have forgotten… some hidden supplies?"

Homer looked upon Peter, hearing all that Stephen had said but refused to answer the question directly, for to do so would only be to agree. It was a common misconception that people should think he was aware as to what was carried in the hold; for sure, he was captain, but not a cargo master. With the up evils of Constantinople much had happened. Supplies were unloaded, and supplies were secured – many of which were done without his knowing and only hours before the fall of Constantinople was secured. He was Captain Homer: surely these men, aboard this brigantine, had heard of him, and as to how courageously he did fight upon the wall at Seraglio Point. It was then that a little shame befell him, for the fighting he had taken part in was by no means comparably to that of the Mesoteichion: of course he didn't know what was aboard his boat. "Peter, my good fellow, one sworn to the protection of the chest; I need a runner, a good pair of seafaring legs to run my errands and messages." The captain stood and a look of sheer seriousness fell upon him… he thumped the table. "Do you accept?"

"Yes…"

"GOOD! That's all I need to hear, the confidence of a young man as you. Your confidence is brimming, overflowing I say."

"Captain Homer; supplies are in need," prompted Stephen but once again. Peter looked to Stephen and then back to the captain, Stephen stared Homer down, but only so slightly that no one would have noticed.

"Go Peter. There is no manifest of cargo, no list of provisions that we carry. Go now, Peter, and get me the report that we all wish to hear."

"I shall, captain," replied the youngster. "I shall also make enquiries with the sailor, Franco."

"Good man. Feel free to get others to help you if needed."

With that all said and done, Peter did depart the cabin and pushed past the two priests in a private conference as he went to fulfil his task.

The priests looked at one another, and then to the cabin – something was wrong. And shortly after Peter had disappeared from view the priests crept towards the cabin's entrance.

Peter saw Franco as the group he was lecturing dispersed about, to spend a little more time in familiarity with the boat and its many ropes. Franco sat as though exhausted, letting out a heavy gasp to reflect on his inner feeling.

"Franco," announced Peter as he made his approach. "I have been sent to task by the captain himself, an errand of urgency of which only Stephen can currently concur."

"I would be happy to help where I can, Peter." Franco looked to the rear of the brigantine. "We are short on time, I would guess, so any urgent matter would be best acted upon immediately. What is your urgency?"

"Captain Homer did request a list of provisions."

"Provisions? A list you say? Why, that's absurd, Peter. What time do you have to prepare a list for the good captain, when the damn Turk is clawing at our backs?" Franco contemplated a little. "Do you have a quill and ink? No, don't answer," said Franco, holding up his hand as Peter opened his mouth to reply. "I mean to say: little provision is tucked away, that to find even the most medial of items would be to strain the limitations of our cargo."

"Would you be able to direct me to where my best effort will be rewarded?"

"No, Peter. You will have to look for yourself. Nothing will be found below this deck. Items will be strewn all over. But for food, water is our need… and weapons. Food we can go without, for the fight that comes knocking at our door is but hours away. Weapons dear, Peter, are needed, and they can be anywhere… anywhere I say."

"Well, I thank you for your time"

"Wait!" interrupted Franco. "Let me think a minute." The silence lasted but a second; seemed like an eternity. "By God, I have it," and Franco stood, all around turned and gazed.

"Lecture adjourned," announced Franco. "Come, Peter. I have something. Quickly, follow me."

*
* * *
*

Anthony and Toran sat below deck, upon their pallets of blanket and straw. Anthony was sharpening his short sword, as Toran was his single edged broadsword. Toran looked upon Anthony, and in his usual manner gave into wit. "I see you are short on sword, as you are with sense."

"Toran; if you were a stranger to me, I would show you just how short this sword is."

"As short as the one between your legs," a burst of laughter erupted from the mouth of Toran. "You know what they say, don't you? About the size of a man's sword," and laughed some more.

"I should imagine it is the same that they say about his brains being as thick." Toran came to his senses then, for the comment hurt. He looked over his weapon of choice, holding it vertical, stroking it gently with a stone he held in the palm of his hand. "That's why you carry a broad, is it not?" asked Anthony. "For you don't have the brains to influence control over your swords movements."

"Hey; my sword shears off limbs," Toran hacked at thin air. "What does yours do… scratch the skin, infest the flesh with boils, or bring minor scars to harbour?"

"She cuts well, Toran; as good as your sword." Anthony punched the air, his weapon an extension of the arm. "I stab and maim, slash and cut, parry and… who is that?" he looked to the entrance of the hold, two men scampering down and disappearing into the shadow at the far end. "Hey! You there! Who is that?"

"Peter," came the answer, the young man answering for himself. "And Franco is with me."

"What are you doing down there, boy."

Franco came out of the shadows and looked the two men over. "I take it that you are talking to Peter? Even so, he is a man, for I heard from several, whom I have but just tutored in the setting of sail, that he fought well during the defence of the city."

"Thank you, Franco," said Peter, "But I need no defence against unkind remarks."

"Unkind remarks," barked Anthony. "I was teasing. No need to take offence."

Peter shook the remarks from his head; he knew better. "Franco has come to show me something. Quickly, bring a light."

Anthony clambered over the straw bedding and neared the closest lantern within the hold, turning the flame up to better light the area. He walked over to where Franco and Peter stood, Toran content to sharpen his tool of war. "What are you searching for?"

"A barrel," said Franco.

"A barrel of what?" asked Anthony.

"Greek fire."

"Damn!" Anthony nearly dropped the lantern.

"Careful with that light. Treat it like a woman… better still, give it to me," said Franco. He took the lantern from Anthony who made a protest.

"What for?"

"Because I recall where… ah, ha. Here she is. Just as I thought;" and Franco allowed the light given off from the lantern to bring clarity to that which they looked upon. It was indeed a barrel, with but one marking upon its surface, the mark of skull and crossbones.

*
* * *
*

Stephen was sat opposite the captain, a tumbler of wine withdrawn from Homer's lips as he swallowed with a resounding gulp. The sea was calm, the temperature outside cool, and the mood of the evening stifling. Homer rubbed at his neck and placed his index fingers into the corners of his eyes, giving them a good rub. He exhaled a breath of defeat, of sheer tiredness, and seemed agitated – if not panicked.

"Stephen, we do not have much time. This boat is small and with many vices running around upon its deck."

"Do you talk of evil, or of people?" asked Stephen.

"Both, my boy… sir knight: oh gentle knight; are you free of the devil… are you pure?" Homer was solemn, meant every word, and spoke as though a poet, and with such soft undertones.

"The devil? No… of course the answer is no."

"The devil exists in everyone, Stephen. All people, even the pope himself has the devil inside. Only the purity of our soles may keep his evil doings at bay." Homer lowered his look, his shoulders falling lax, showing defeat.

"I don't…"

"It is a cancer, Stephen. A plague that inhibits everyone."

"But…"

Homer erupted into voice again, looking Stephen in the eye. "I have read the letter that Constantine did give to the priests. In it lays much evil."

"But the letter is one of good; is it not?"

"I shall tell you what I remember, Stephen, before we are disturbed." Homer prepared himself for explanation, digging deep into his memory, deciding carefully, but quickly, on how best to describe the contents of the letter. "I cannot recall the exact reading or the quotations where stresses were pressed on particular subjects – although it is all one and the same. The letter from Constantine did announce quite clearly, and without restraint that the contents of the chest should not fall into the hands of the enemy. Most of those that have read the letter believe this to mean those of Islam; but nothing could be further from the truth. We are, all, the enemy, Stephen. Every single person, regardless of his vocation, is the enemy… or rather, has the devil within." His eyes locked well with Stephen's. "This is the enemy, Templar knight. The enemy is the one we have been fighting since the birth of our great salvation; but who is to believe that the fight must begin within; inside us all is where the fight must commence." Homer stood and paced around. "The enemy is not one you can see, but rather feel. His very existence is as real to me as is that tumbler upon my table." He pointed to the drinking vessel and sat down upon his chairs, elbows resting upon the desktop, and he continued with his lecture on the contents of the letter. "It is fair to say that the contents of the chest will empower those of a Muslim faith, by bringing down the Christian." He sat back and waved a hand into the air, brushing away his verbal text as though a crowd of Christian faithful. "Gone forever those of impurity. A Muslim cannot be affected, for his belief belongs to Allah: he has already been recruited by the devil and his worship. The chest holds the scripture of Jesus, a codex of great worth: within the chest is the secret gospel of Jesus… yes, and the look upon your face right now, Stephen, tells of your knowing. I see you believe every word I say, and why shouldn't you? For it is all true. The contents of the chest are true to religion, hidden through the ages to protect the innocent… those that believe they are pure. Anyone holding a supreme position, as that initially heralded as per the Pope, must be free, so wholly, of all corruptness and evil; but this is not always the case. Any amount of activity deemed as inappropriate will see to it that death befalls that individual. Believing in his heart of his honesty, towards the religion and church he has taken to his bosom to embrace, it will all be scrutinized by Jesus himself. Any form of misleading, any swaying from the scriptures, will result in death. No one individual or group must hold the smallest of unfair practices of body or mind. If released, the energy of the chest will strike down any that are impure, and only those with the spirit deserving of sainthood will walk as though free." Homer took a breath, relaxed himself, and then continued. "Eternal life will be given those that are pure, and in order for the word of the Lord to be passed onto the generations, a chosen few, like messengers to travel the passages of time, to pass on the great giving of Jesus and His father, will continue in life on earth, as it is in heaven. A true spirit will be provided for in life. Death of the body will not come about, unless someone, or something else, inflicts injury upon it. Even then, only a strike at the heart will render the body lifeless, for other than that, if injury is obtained, then the body will shut down until repaired. It is the heart, Stephen, which holds the gates to heaven, the stairway to everlasting life. It is the heart that is pure, but this can easily become infected by the devil of one's mind. The way in which a person thinks will be is undoing. Anyone can become corrupted by body or mind. The heart Stephen, that is what is sacred." He stood again and turned to look to the galleass – it was gaining on them. "The chest must not fall into the wrong hands, for if the power of the chest is realised, then all those around it will be scrutinized equally. Those of another religion, other than that decree by God, will go unmolested, for the bounds and scripture of their religion will be different, and the guidelines for existence different. Their very belief in the religion of the devil will tax them not." He turned to face Stephen again and sat one final time. "Only once baptised, and surrendered to the life of a Christian, will that individual be swayed by the confines of the chest. All of those of impure body and mind will be struck down without delay. If, however, a pure mind and body you keep, as laid down within the scriptures, then you shall reap the reward of eternal life; you will live your life as you deserve, and on death of old age will be given a place in heaven. As for the taking of life," and Homer did stutter a little, slightly confused by what he had read, "this is in fact the surrendering of 'that' existence for the one of 'eternal' existence. All of life will be accepted into the realm of heaven, for once death has come to pass we no longer hold power of mind, and the purity of heart takes form. The chest is nothing more than a test, Stephen. If you pass the test then you receive eternal life in heaven, but the selected few will reap the reward and service the Lord for the remainder of all time." He scoffed at his own explanation and waved it aside. "However, some believe that the contents of the chest, once revealed, will lead to eternal salvation, and that death does not exist for anyone. Of course, the chest must be opened in order for the scripture to be read, but the warning on the chest itself… it must be adhered to. To open the chest in a crowd is dangerous."

Stephen was lost for words. He waited a little, just in case the captain wished to continue, but he was finished with his task for the moment. "If what you tell me is true… then the chest must be hidden away, never to be opened." And Stephen found it hard to believe that Jesus would purposely allow a power to exist that could see to the downfall of His religion. But on the other hand, Jesus was obeying his own scripture, by not preaching prejudicial behaviour – was that correct? "I must also admit that I am wholly confused. Why would Jesus, our saviour, one who did give his life for us, empower the contents of a chest to strike us down like drunken sailors?"

"It is a condition passed down by His father. In order for Jesus to save us from our sins, God did wrought condition. The chest must be opened in order for the scripture to be read," said Homer. "Only then can we be sure."

"And how many times must it be opened? How many times has it been opened already?"

"I cannot answer such questions, and I suspect that the two priests who carry it, will also be unaware of the answer. But I tell you this: I believe in the letter from Constantine, for the bible itself tells of the wrath of God, and of the good of his one and only son."

The door to the cabin burst open and the two priests walked in, careful to close the door behind them. They took their seat in the silence that now dominated the scene. The first looked around the table and spoke with a whisper: "We were outside and heard you talking. Be thankful that no one else was within hearing distance."

"I am surprised you allowed me to finish," said Homer.

"Not only did we arrive late in the discussion, but realised that Stephen is entitled to hear of the letter. Not only this, but to adhere to the scripture of His, I would have to allow you full courtesy and without provocation or rudeness."

"Unless," said Stephen, "we can presume that such rules or

guidelines that you preach, dear Father, are of no real meaning or purpose." All looked at the Templar with stabbing eyes. "I listened well to what I was told. I may speak the truth, as I see it, and still be pure of heart."

The second priest smiled. "Stephen, if there is one thing I have learnt over the past few days, it is this: And there shall be no prejudice comparison between servant and master."

"Well spoken," said the first sarcastically. "Is that to mean that Stephen is as holy as the pope and that the pope is nothing more than a lap cat?"

"Not at all, father," replied Stephen. "But it does mean that he is no more pure than I."

"That in itself is the devil talking," accused the first. "For you should not brand yourself of higher station than the representative of our faith."

"Maybe you are right, father; but knowing of the letter and its contents is as important to me as the chest's existence is to you."

"I apologise, sir knight, and understand. I understand that you believe you are following the scripture as it is written; even if wrong." The first then turned on the captain. "And what is the meaning of this, that you should believe you have the right to recite the words of Constantine?"

"I thought it helpful… in the current climate. You said it yourself that Stephen was entitled."

"So be it," said the first. "It will be the last time in any case." He was then met with stares from Stephen and Homer. "The letter has been destroyed… I… we cannot allow it to fall into the wrong hands, and it would seem we are closer to capture than not," and the look within both priests' eyes gave indication that further was to be said.

Stephen felt as though he saw within the scheme of things, that the priests meant for privacy. He stood up to leave. "I shall be on my—"

"No, Stephen," said the first. "Please stay so that we may talk. There is much we need to discuss in regards to the chest. Please, forgive my rudeness; the good captain is right, all should be revealed to you."

Stephen nodded acceptance and returned to his seat.

The little girl, who had shed a cupful of tears whilst under the instruction of the Teutonic, once again stood to the front of Lars. He was seated upon the deck looking out upon the ocean. There were a few white gulls aloft gliding along on wisps of wind, eyeing the water below for that lustrous feeling of opportunity by finding the catch of the day. He wore a smile that was contagious and slowly it spread to the lips of the girl. She sat beside him and leant her head against his shoulder. She knew what was about to arrive on the galleass that followed, but at this moment felt a little self-assurance within that all would be okay in the end. They sat there for some time, in the silence; but what conversation could you have with a man who had no tongue?

The girl lifted her head and looked at Lars, who in turn returned the gaze. "My name is Lois," she said. She was of Greek origin, most likely born of Constantinople, for no soldier would be docile enough to drag a daughter into the lion's den when hard fighting was known to have been on the horizon.

Lars beamed a smile, so happy to have made a new friend. It did appear that his laying of foundation had won through, and the little girl was no more afraid of him, nor the task to come. And then something shocking did occur, something of which Lars could not comprehend, something that only happened in dreams. Lois looked hard into his eyes and with all seriousness said: "I will kill many men today, Lars; and I will not allow you to be harmed in any way." She hugged the man with all of her strength and rested her head once more upon his strong shoulder, and as eye contact was lost his smile did slowly evaporate, for he had created a beast within this child.

The silence then dominated the surroundings, though Lars' mind was far away. The wind stirred up faint whistling sounds, caused by its current passing over wrought iron and ropes. There was a little cloud in the sky but relatively clear – it was sure to bring on a cold and clear night.

Lars contemplated his past, his time with the Teutonic, the massacre that had taken place during the Battle of Tannenberg in 1410. How lucky he was to have been one of 55 survivors. He considered the death, the blood and the maimed, of how 400 knights were left lying slain upon the battlefield, of how their very dignity had been lost to the enemy. Now it was Lois' turn to meet death face-to-face… if she'd not already done so during the siege of Constantinople. Chances were that she'd been saved from the acts of murder and rape that had taken place, but now it was a different story, she was to become one of the above… murdered or raped, possibly both and in no particular oder. But that was not the end. After rape came death or slavery; slavery, where repeated raping would be the order of the day. She would be better off dead. But she was willing to stand and fight, to see justice rise to the occasion, to put her best foot forward in trying to 'deny' the Turk. It was here, where the Christian forces were to be charged but once again by the devil himself. Here, sometime during the night or early morning, they would once again meet with what they had already met. During the drawing of the curtain in Constantinople a handful of defenders fought against overwhelming odds; those odds were now to be repeated, for the expertise, the very fabric of experience, was all stretched to the limit. At least on the walls of Constantinople they had well-armed, outfitted, and trained men of war, now they had but a handful of experience and a cargo load of old men, women, and children. But now this girl, this little child named Lois. She had rekindled something in Lars. Even though he was an experienced soldier, even though he was tough and felt little fear, there had always been something that he had been without, something that he had lost at the battle of Tannenberg in 1410; and that something was about to resurface.

"Lars, Lars, where are you?" said Peter as he saw the knight and the little girl, sitting there in their embrace. "Lars, are you…"

Lars opened his eyes and drew a finger to his lips. The girl, Lois, was asleep, warmed by the flesh of Lars, as though warmed by the comfort of a mother's bosom. Peter drew closer and knelt beside the knight. "I must ask you to accompany me, Lars. Please come now, for I have something quite urgent to show you, and it cannot wait." Lars locked eyes with the young man and gave a nod. He would be along shortly. Peter laid a hand upon Lars' forearm, "Thankyou, Lars," and was gone as quickly as he had arrived.

Seconds later and he returned, shrugging his shoulders, opened his palm indicating an invitation for Lars to attend, for Peter was expecting the knight to follow as per his request – immediately, and did not understand that the knight meant to attend his urgent need after prying himself gently from the arms of Lois. "Please, Lars. We must go, now."

Stephen wasn't sure exactly what was to be revealed. There was much to the captain's speech that the Templar found disturbing, even though, quite realistically, most of it sounded sane and made sense. But he was delivered a rude awakening, that the idea existed of God's implied conditions; it was simply too much to accept. He had read the Old Testament when he was a young boy and was struck with great awe in regards to the power that God possessed. The New Testament was like the changing of a season, from winter to summer, for the touch of Jesus was so warming and delicate, that the harsh qualities delivered by His father seemed but such a great expanse of difference between the two; or for a single religion to hold so dear.

They all sat and Homer smiled, placing tumblers in front of everyone, including Stephen. "No drink for me, captain, for my wish to remain clear headed is as strong as before." Homer smiled contentedly and commenced to fill the remaining three cups of wood. Stephen looked at the captain and considered him carefully. Homer appeared to recite the contents of Constantine's letter so deliberately, even possibly, so accurately, that Stephen questioned it, as to the true merits of the written work, or that it even existed. The fact that two priests had advised of its existence prior to it being destroyed, gave little proof as to its merit and origin.

"Thankyou, captain," said the first.

And further still: if the Emperor of Constantinople was so knowledgeable in regards to the chest, how was it that such information had leaked out or not even employed to aid in the defence of the great city? Was it in fact as Constantine said, and that was that the scripture – whatever it revealed – had no power over the devil, in particular when prevailing within the very structure of another religion or belief. There was also the hint of a miracle, which was to be delivered a chosen one, or few. The only clues he had yet picked up on were that in order to be protected from the confines of the chest, you had to be pure; you could also go unscathed if not yet baptised. But such traits couldn't be right, for how was a new born child, still of crib, to accept baptism with the purity of heart when understanding of such a religion was not yet… wait! That was it: could it be? An understanding of religion must first be attained before bowing to the codex written by Jesus. What does a small child know except that which it is told? Being forced into religion was like being forced to purity, but purity had to be attained, not forced.

"If this wine is as good as before, I shall be most pleased," said the second.

"It is the same," replied the captain.

Yes indeed: one could not be pure of heart simply because they were being forced. Religion was a structure of learning, a pyramid of steps that lead you to the pinnacle of understanding. Such understanding could not be attained simply because you were exposed to baptism. To first accept baptism, you had to be pure. If baptism was accepted without being pure of heart, then understanding went by the wayside, hence, your ability to mould yourself to the beliefs of the religion you did take to heart, did not actually exist. And then it suddenly struck him… the fact that the devil actually resided within the mind of every man and woman. That was it, surely, the fact that the devil was constantly at play, forcing those of impure heart to accept their chosen belief in God, in order that baptism could be delivered… and on such being accepted, death being embraced.

"There is much being done upon deck; I see Peter running around in great anxiousness," said the first.

"No doubt a boy of heart, but still a man," said the captain.

If the codex of Jesus was as Stephen considered, then many people, if having accepted the word of God through baptism, whilst impure of heart, would be justifiably struck down dead. It was too much to contemplate. It was a test within itself. Only the pure of heart should willingly accept baptism, for to otherwise accept it was to do so under falsehood, and under the very influence of the devil himself.

"But to task we mean to deliberate, and that is the purpose behind our voyage," said the first, putting his tumbler upon the table, the second priest holding his, close to his lap, as though in anxious wait.

Homer sat down and looked around, everyone was seated now.

"I am sure there are many questions that dwell upon your tongue, Stephen, like a fire awaiting to be extinguished, or a great thirst looking for that first mouthful of refreshment," said the first. "So few know of the chest, and yet it is a most prized possession." The priest seemed to wander off, just for a second, as he looked off into the dying night behind the captain, the outline of the galleass standing out quite clearly and just hours away. "Quite astonished I was to hear that Mehmet himself knew of its existence; as though the devil had given the information to him whilst dining in his tent." The priest looked to Stephen and Homer with an apologetic eye. "Understand you both, I should think, as to why it was necessary to destroy the letter?"

Stephen took to answering and in doing so requested further information. "Indeed I do, and quite understandable was your action… but please, can you tell me: what of the chest?"

"Ah, ha; what of the chest indeed, young Templar? What shall be done of the chest and its contents?" The priest's eyelids shot open in emphasis then: "Burn it! No, such a gift cannot be burnt."

"Is this an attempt to ridicule?" asked Stephen.

"Not at all. Please… see it from my point of view. We cannot allow it to fall into the hands of the infidel, any more then we can destroy it. Few options are open to us. We can disguise it as another object; we can open the chest – which would mean defacing it of course – and hiding its contents; or perhaps drop it over the side of the boat."

"To sink and never be found?" asked the captain, a slight chuckle of jest escaping his lips.

"No, of course not. But we could secrete it beneath the boat, where no one is likely to look. But first we would have to ensure the contents would not be damaged; that a clue as to its whereabouts could be left – in case we all die, of course – or that a selected few of us keep such delicate information to themselves."

"And as you have already divulged such information to our ears," concluded Stephen, "we are to be that selected few?"

"Indeed, Stephen, you are," continued the first. "I have deliberated much with my colleague and we have both decided that this is for the best. We would both prefer that it not be necessary, but the galleass, as you can see," he pointed to the boat behind, easily seen through the porthole, "is closing fast."

There was a little silence then as each turned and contemplated the Turk boat, its oars thrashing at the sea, the drumbeat of the coxswain being delivered their ears upon the wind that filled their sails. But much deliberation was still to be met. "So short on time and we are still without the promise you spoke of," all eyes turned to Stephen as he said these words: "that all should be revealed in regards to the chest and the secret it contains."

*
* * *
*

Anthony, Toran and Franco, stood talking in their leisure as Peter and Lars arrived upon the scene. All were in high spirits, or so it seemed, even though, as Lars looked out upon the rear of the brigantine, the top of the mast belonging to the galleass could be seen quite clearly. They had little more than several hours left and it was growing quite dark.

"Lars, here my man," invited Franco. "I have something which should be of use to you, as discussions with Peter have turned quite ripe."

Lois sat herself against the rail of the boat and remained there in silence as Lars and Peter joined the small group.

Those around continued with small bouts of discussion, bringing to air various points on different subjects. Lars was more interested in what Franco had to say, so concentrated on the subject of his necessity.

"Lars, listen," continued Franco. "We have found this," and slapped a hand upon the barrel of Greek fire. Lars' eyes lit up. "Yes, I knew it. You know well what it is, don't you?" and stabbed a finger in Lars' direction.

And indeed he did. He was quite unfamiliar as to how it ignited, but knew exactly the effect that the substance could have if primed and delivered correctly. "We have many bows and arrows, and this huge barrel of Greek fire. I see no reason why we could not defend our boat now against the infidel. With the bows we can engage the enemy at a distance…"

"As they can us," interrupted Peter.

"Yes, yes; as they can us. But look here; Lars has the good ability to teach," Peter frowned at the suggestion as it was uttered. "Please, Peter; a little enthusiasm if you will." He turned his attention again to Lars. "I am sure that with a little coaching, even with the time we have left, that the men and women aboard this boat can be taught enough to engage the enemy."

Lars was not so sure. It took great strength to pull on the tautness of a strung bow. By the time any structured lesson or familiarity could be taught, they would be too tired to deliver, to the best of their abilities, a well-aimed shot. He looked around and waved a finger. Muffled sound then came from deep within his throat as he first pointed to Anthony, and then to Toran; he gave a nod and then looked around the deck, pointed to Niketas and gave another nod, and then to Rainald, where he shook his head.

"Too old and frail?" questioned Peter.

Lars shook his head and holding up his palms, gave indication that he did not know. Lars then slumped forward as though exhausted.

"Ah, you mean to think that he will be too tired to fight…," said Peter, Lars nodding his head as Peter continued, "after any length of training?"

Franco interceded. "Our strength must not be sapped. We must seek those who hold good hunting ability with bow, even those with little to no ability, but brawn and full of vigour, for they may be able to produce a good shot when the time arrives."

"It would seem to me," said Toran, "that regardless of skill or strength, that when the galleass is within range, we will only be able to get away several shots each prior to us all being stuck like a porcupine ourselves."

"But what choice do we have?" asked Anthony, when the group was suddenly sprung upon by an energetic little girl by the name of Catherine.

All turned their attention to her entrance into the fray of words, as each commenced to bustle for the lectern of place and speech, for each held a different view in respects to how the defence should take form, but the voice of Catherine could be heard to build in volume, to rise above the dying voices of each man: "We could built a raft, a small one, and place the Greek fire upon it."

Peter looked to Lars and then Franco; Franco looked to the decking of the boat and then Toran; and the two mercenaries looked to one another, for they recalled the suggestion made of a rowing boat being placed forward in order to gain an advantage by placing rowers into it.

"Yes indeed!" yelled Toran with excitement. "A raft – or boat – could be placed behind, attached by a rope in order to guide it."

Franco looked to Catherine. "Is that what you wished to convey, young child?"

"It is but one of many ideas, but will give us a slight advantage; I have heard people talking. I have heard of its use before… a story told me when in Constantinople."

"It is a grand idea," insisted Peter, punching his fist into an empty palm. "It could indeed work," agreed Anthony, "and give us the advantage."

And a muffled sound of agreement came from the tongueless Teutonic.

*
* * *
*

The messenger landed with a delicate thud, landing flat-footed upon the coxswain's heightened deck, where good visuals could be maintained upon the rowers of the mahon. Abu looked to the messenger, Ibrahim, as he appeared at his side, a message from the stern that another vessel had been seen, somewhere to the rear and slightly to the port, closing slowly.

Abu appeared not to be interested, for he knew that any boat or ship that approached from the rear would be none other than a Turk vessel manned ready for war. "A ship or boat, good Ibrahim, and what is the news on its present course?"

"It would appear to be travelling on a course parallel to us, and too far out to currently consider its sovereignty or status. With all that is to be considered, it is best thought to be one of the vessels of our small and weirdly assembled armada," said Ibrahim by his briefest means.

"Very good, Ibrahim. And so I do agree with such an appraisal, for it could be nothing more," and a smile formed upon the face of Abu as he turned to look at Ibrahim. "It is about time that one of our own finally decided to seek us out and bring about a little common sense. The commander of the vessel has done well in deciding to ensure that speed was of the essence. At least now we can rely on a little help… as though we really require it. I think, Ibrahim, that we should reconsider our situation, for it would appear that the boat behind is gaining upon us, which would mean one thing only: it is the mahon of extra sail, for none other could move so swiftly through the sea. Yes indeed, I believe we need to reconsider our situation and reconsider it carefully." Abu looked out upon the bobbing heads of the rowers, the sweat falling from their foreheads, men gasping for air, breathing heavily under the strain of the oars. They were working hard and gaining a good measure of distance on the enemy, the brigantine, and the Christian's hopeless situation.

Abu recommenced to think through his strategy as the messenger Ibrahim turned his attention to the rowers – for a short span of time – before moving off, back to his station at the aftcastle. It would be dark soon, and in the darkness he would find an ally. Abu turned quickly and strode off towards the rear of the boat, to see for himself the vessel that was approaching fast from behind, and as he looked out over the cresting waves of the Marmora he could see for himself that the vessel was indeed a mahon. As he expected it was the boat that held extra sail and was capable of surrendering rowers for fighting when the need did arise. The best Abu could muster was a top speed and 20 marines; those that followed could slow their advance, though matching his (due to extra sail) and avail themselves to a fighting force of 20 marines and 30 sailors.

How best to tie this to his advantage?

Within minutes he believed, most humbly, that he had the answer.

He would ensure that as he closed with the brigantine that he was between the Christian boat and those that followed, in order to deny the information to the commander of the brigantine; and with lanterns drowned he would pass out to a flank, revealing the mahon behind to those that believed in the false god of heaven. The Christians would think nothing of the apparition, rubbing their eyes for confirmation, to see for themselves that, yes, indeed, the mahon behind had slowed in its pursuit and that the gap between them had widened immensely. Why waste his manpower on the fighting to come; better still, if he was quick, and with good measure, he could manoeuvre himself to a position whereby he and this good commander of the other friendly boat could surround the brigantine and board it without so much as a single loss of life.

Abu smiled to himself, a plan that even Mehmet would be pleased to hear. Yes indeed, he was a man of great calibre.

Now what was the commander's name? Think, Abu; you know him by sight.... Abu considered all of that which had passed over the days before they had set sail. Ha, ah, he had it. Commander Said. Abu spat contempt, ridding himself of disgusting thought, for he remembered now the hatred and contempt he held for the man. Better Said be burnt in hell than receive favour of pillage and ransom.

The first priest looked into Stephen's eyes and became very solemn. "I cannot... we cannot," he corrected, indicating with a nod, the second, "agree full-heartedly with the letter from Constantine. It is so ambiguous, that it would be correct to point a finger in question. The key to the chest has been locked away in the temple of Káros for many centuries, and the chest itself within the protection of the walls of Constantinople for so long, that it would be far beyond doubt that its contents would have been revealed to the emperor, of past or present. The information within the letter must have been derived from other sources. We believe it's from earlier records, all of that recorded by the founder's mother, Helena. Helena did uncover the sacred artefact of Jesus' burial, an inscription upon a short wooden plank that read: Jesus of Nazareth, King of the Jews."

"But that is not all," interrupted the second.

"Indeed not," continued the first, "for she also came into contact with the chest that we carry, and did ensure its safe keeping by bringing it to Constantinople and delivering the key, in person, to the temple of which we now intend to lay visit. It was recorded by a scribe that mystical powers were inherent within the chest. Whether such records advised of the chests aspects, or whether Helena was visited by the

Holy Spirit, we will never be known… it may even be that Constantine, so recently departed, did receive visions from his mother, or Jesus Himself. One thing we are sure of, however, and that is that the key and chest have not been of the same proximity for over eleven hundred years. This being the case, it is impossible for the letter from Constantine to bear any substantial merit." The priest stopped then, his explanation coming to an end, for there was a build-up of anxious calling coming from upon the deck of the brigantine.

All of those within the cabin immediately looked to the porthole to the rear of the boat, but the galleass was still several hours away. It was then that the cabin door was flung open and in poured, Franco, Lars, Toran, Anthony, and Peter; Catherine could be seen standing in the entrance. Peter looked behind. "Come child, don't wait for an invitation, for it was your idea."

The first priest stood tall and faced the interruption with eyebrows turned inwards. "What is the meaning of this?"

"Forgive us, father," pleaded Toran, "For the child has given us an idea."

"Idea: for what?" asked the first.

"For the defence to come," said Toran.

Peter felt that further information should be posted, and did so diligently. "Your check on provisions, captain, is not yet finished, but such a task can wait, for we have found something..."

"Several things in fact," voiced Franco.

"Out with it then, lad," prodded the captain.

"Greek fire, sir, and as much as you please, to sink that damn galleass that follows," answered Peter with much swiftness.

"And the girl?" Questioned Homer.

"The idea is hers, captain," continued Peter, "an idea to thwart all others, for we have also found many bows, with a plenty-full supply of arrows. Lars knows," Peter nodded to the man, "that the weapon can deliver a good flame. We set the Greek fire upon a wooden raft, let it out behind and attached to a rope, and when close enough to the front of the galleass we deliver a payload of arrows, each burning with flames good enough to put a finish to those following."

"It will be dark soon, almost upon us already is the night," said Toran. "It is our only chance to impede the enemy in order for us to make good our escape into the Aegean."

"We may even sink her," concluded Franco.

The priests looked to the captain, the importance of their explanation in regards to the chest well and truly forgotten.

"It may well work," said the first.

"Sounds sweet to the ear," said the second.

"A grand idea," said the captain. "Franco, set upon preparation; take some men and ready a raft. Toran and Anthony, bring forth the Greek fire. Lars, prepare your bowmen; and, uh, bow-women." Homer stood, continuing with orders. "Stephen, get ready your men for battle, and fathers, pick your ground well, for once the Greek fire is ignited there will be little place to hide, for the night will be as bright as the day."

*
* * *
*

They had been waiting half the night, but finally they could hear the galleass, the coxswains drum, the oars thrashing at the sea, and then suddenly, appearing out of the night, a silhouette did appear. Most of the lanterns upon the enemy boat had been extinguished, though surprise was never to be gained, for those of the brigantine had known of their intended capture to come. They were reliant upon the wind alone, where the enemy were able to draw upon sail and the stroking of the sea; the noise was enough to awaken the dead, let alone scare them out of their skins. Certainly, not, no surprise at all, and the enemy would too be aware of the Christians lying in wait.

But they had a little defensive strategy. The brigantine had allowed a single lantern to remain alight, enough to give signal to the galleass that followed, that they were indeed still being gained upon, to lead the hunter into a false sense of security; they also weakened one of their own sails, so that when the need arose they could be granted more speed.

All was quiet upon the deck, men and women ready for a quick fight and easy escape. All they needed to do was cripple the galleass enough to allow them easy passage to the mouth of the Aegean, and the rest would be history. The captain, for one, didn't wish to make an artificial reef of his boat, anymore than he wanted the flesh of his body to be food for the sharks.

Stephen had a few men ready with swords, hiding behind the rail of the brigantine, and in front of the cabin – though little protection that would be from a straight-flying arrow. Niketas and Rainald were to his left and Catherine to his right, spear in hand. There was also Lois, a child with crossbow at the ready, prepared to shoot at any man trying to board their boat, as well as two other girls of similar age, Zoë and Irene, both holding tight to short swords and several quarrels.

Further to the forecastle of the brigantine, ready to move towards the stern, forward into firing position beneath the mainsail, were six men of their latter years, 5 women, several boys and Peter. Toran and Anthony were at the side of the boat, having lowered the raft and its cargo into position – they held tight to the rope, ready to feed this through their palms when the time was right. The captain maintained vigil upon his crew and cargo in order to ensure the defence held strong: he personally was to ensure the brigantine was steered slightly to the port in order to allow the raft easy movement in its short journey to the front of the galleass and hence securing them their victory.

Toran and Anthony had attended their task with great anticipation, having lashed the barrel of Greek fire to the makeshift raft of planks and posts. The lid of the barrel had been damaged slightly in order to allow the combustible to be easily lit, having been spilled enough to cover the wooden raft, soaked well with the contents of mixture. All that was needed was for a single arrow to hit the raft and the night air would be filled with a great calamity of noise, burning flame, and volumes of black smoke.

The two priests had given prayer, but had also taken position within the cabin, to avail themselves a little cover as they set upon delivering a few well aimed crossbow quarrels to the galleass that followed, and it would not be long now before it was upon them. They had also decided against surrendering the chest to station below the waves, for the priests were optimistic and couldn't bear to see the chest ruined or lost forever.

Lars crept forward to a position just behind Stephen with crossbow at the ready, having just seen to the late delivery of Franco, Master Andrew and John, to the two priests below. Other less endowed women and children were spread out upon the deck, ready with spears and swords, prepared to throw these aside to help with the rigging and tacking of the brigantine when the time did arrive, as well as being able to attend to the wounded. Sailors aloft had also taken to the deck, ready with swords for killing and able-handed enough for the setting and shifting of sail.

The orders of the boat's commander could be heard above the beat of the coxswain's drum, the oars churning up the water loaning fear to all, a dragon's breath and heartbeat allowing panic to mount; and the priests eyes bulged with fear as the sail and bow of the galleass came into view, to be plainly seen to be decreasing the gap between the two, both Muslim and Christian drawing closer, the gap between the two closing quickly. The galleass, its bow pulling up out of the water, surging forwards with each stroke of the oars, seemingly preparing to ram the brigantine, and with this thought entering the minds of those that witnessed the galleass gain ground came a sobering thought: in order for the enemy to draw upon so much speed, must mean that very few of the enemy were ready with weapons that could strike at a distance. This was news to be taken to the heart, a cherished moment which would be short lived, for if the Greek fire failed, and the initial flurry of arrows were wasted upon the raft and sea around, then they were in for a hard fight of hand-to-hand – the barrel of combustible upon raft must be a success, for anything else spelt the end of their voyage to safe harbour.

Homer then gave a whispered command for the brigantine to change direction and the raft loaded with Greek fire was allowed to float away towards its target, the coarse rope being fed through the hands of Toran and Anthony. All appeared well, the raft was on target, and the galleass seemed to gain in speed – although the beat of the coxswain's drum didn't change and nor did it miss a single beat.

The time was almost upon them and then suddenly on command, from the hold, did appear several young boys with torches alight, to set flame upon the arrows that were cocked and ready to be released into the cold night air. And as each arrow was ignited into flame, each was released into flight, streaking through the breeze, from point 'A' to point 'B', the shallow trajectories of each shot being visible to anyone looking into the night, where not even the waning moon gave aid, for it was still below the horizon; and with the mystical sight of fire in the air came a muffled scream from the galleass, and the coxswain's drum thundered into a rhythmic sprint, the boat behind surging even further out of the water then it had before.

Shudders of fear shot through the Christian crew and gathering of passengers, seeing first hand that the arrows were falling into the sea around the raft, missing the target completely – and this be a lesson to the Christians, for as they watched, they were neglecting their responsibility, for no more arrows had been strung in readiness to deliver a follow-up of the preparatory.

Peter looked to his side and spat out the command, rushing up and down the line, pushing them forward, and ordering for better fire positions to be taken. The bows had to be employed, a continuous rain of arrows had to be maintained, and the Greek fire had to be ignited. It was then that the true horrors of war commenced to take its toll, for out of the darkness came the whistling of air rushing past shaft, for the infidel had let loose with their own shower of pain and death, arrows appearing out of the night, streaking towards their targets as though lead to them, like rain delivered from a thunderstorm, though alone a horizontal plane, and as the old men and women fell in screams of pain and torment the galleass struck hard against the brigantine. Suddenly a heathen crack could be heard by all around, for something had borne the brunt of the ramming and would take its toll on the seafaring ability of the boat and its refugees... if they should live.

People fell to the deck and quickly stood again, one old woman remaining there on her side, clenching at her leg, for it had been broken below the knee, the bone protruding the flesh of her leg, a dribble of blood seeping to the cold night air. And too, the blood of the dead and dying commenced to flow, seeping into the cracks of the timber, and running here and there towards the rail of the brigantine.

Toran and Anthony held onto the rope as best they could. Their initial target was to be the front end of the galleass, but they could not control the raft any more than the tide of the waters around. The raft drifted slowly but surely, along the port side of the boat of the enemy. It was hard to see as it bobbed up and down with the waves of the sea. It was sure to be a hard target to hit, even with the little illumination about to be given off by the arrows in the air and the few lanterns aboard the brigantine.

Stephen could see well all that was being delivered by the Muslim men aboard the galleass, yet he was in no position to do anything except wait. His hand shot up and pulled the head of Catherine down behind cover, offering his body as protection, as best he could. An arrow then hit hard against Zoë's chest, forcing a last gasp of air out of her lungs, death being delivered unto her as quickly as life had been accepted at birth. Irene then stood in panic, an arrow hitting her square in the face.

Peter turned in horror, looking down upon the deck, his eyes shooting a glance upon the bodies of two boys, two of the three who had put flame to arrow. "Draw your bows! Fire when ready! Don't wait for the command! Boy, BOY; THE FLAME; BOY, GET THE FLAME!"

The child was alone, standing there in shock, his friends dead, with arrows sticking out of their back. He clamped his jaw shut then and pulled himself together, shaking the grief from his mind, setting light to arrows as they were pulled to the ready by the women standing their ground.

A woman of old age saw the calamity, fell to her aching knees, snatched a torch from the clenched fist of one of the dead boys, the other beside him, gasping for air – he was still alive – for the arrow had pierced his lung. He was drowning in his own blood. The woman stood and put flame to more arrows as several of the younger women drew on their bows.

The arrows flew through the air, passing in mid-flight another flurry from the galleass, enemy arrows which were ten times in number compared to those fired by the Christians, Muslims in their dozens standing upon the fore and aftcastle. More women took the brunt of the wall of iron as it struck the Christian defence and the decking, Peter, too, receiving a shot to the head. The last of the boys then whirled around, pivoting on the spot, seeing a lone man of wrinkled flesh standing as crooked as could be, holding tight to a strung bow, awaiting to be lit with flame. The boy went to him, fast upon his feet, and as the flame was delivered to the arrow, the boy fell heavily to the deck, an arrow having pierced his neck, cutting the main artery between head and shoulders.

The arrow was let loose, spent of the bow, reaching its halfway point unobstructed by mast, sail, or body of flesh, and then commenced the final leg of its journey, striking the barrel mid-on. The Greek fire exploded then, a ball of flame leaping into the air, illuminating both boats in their entirety. Men, women, and children dropped their weapons of war to shield their eyes from the burning brightness, and as quickly as all was lit, so it died in the wake of the fire it had born, to become a burning furnace of flame. The front side of the galleass nearest the brigantine was burning feverishly, and amongst the mayhem came the screams of several Turks, heard to mingle with the sounds of war as a command to board the Christian boat with scimitars drawn came to the ears of Stephen and his good friend Lars.

Along the port side of the galleass, oars were being pulled to the boat and those that burnt were flung to the sea. The vessel was turning to meet the flank of the brigantine, the ramming of one vessel against the other having the effect of forcing the two together, like the hinge of a great wooden door helping to draw one plank to another. And for a short second a little joy did leap into Homer's heart, for he could see what had made that heinous sound of cracking wood: the short bowsprit of the galleass had snapped in half and its foremast had buckled – though such a small mast it was, and of little consequence. And as his mouth opened with a smile an infidel's arrow did strike and pierce the back end of his throat – death being instantaneous.

The flame along the side of the galleass commenced to spread. Several Christian sailors saw the closing threat and took action to ensure that extra speed was attained, and by tightening the sail and pulling in unison the ropes around, the brigantine leapt forward as though refreshed after a long race. Several men cheered then, though drowned by the fire that fed off the galleass; but the fight was far from over.

The bow of the enemy boat, although damaged, was still close enough to the brigantine for men to take a run and leap. Half of the contingent of marines made it across, several falling into the sea, its surface burning, coated well by Greek fire. Some had their scimitars at the ready when they made the jump from boat to boat, others sheath their weapon of choice to be revealed once safely upon the Christian deck. It was now that the hand-to-hand commenced to play its role in the fight for survival, a survival that the passengers and crew had been fighting since well before their escape from the Golden Horn of Constantinople.

It was no surprise to see that Stephen was the first to meet the assailants, taking two angry men on, putting in a well planted parry, followed immediately by a downward slash across the infidels' legs. Screams erupted from the Turk, and before any man or woman could blink an eye – or believe what they were being told was witnessed: unless, of course, seen for themselves – Catherine did charge in with her spear, thrusting it hard into the belly of the second. The contortion on the Turks face spoke its own meaning, for his eyes locked with the child. So close he did come to slicing off the face of Stephen that the joy of the soon-to be victory had commenced to grow within him; now all he had was the penetrating point of a spear sticking in his gut, held by the hand of a six year old girl. A snarl then formed upon Catherine's face and she yanked the spear free, immediately crouching down behind the Templar, awaiting the opportunity for her next victory, awaiting for it to appear.

Lars was crouched upon one knee and spent a quarrel. He released his grip to grab another and became startled, faltering for a second to collect the true nature of what was occurring, for Lois had placed into his palm a missile, its point facing forward, ready to be loaded and fired. And Lars did not disappoint, for no sooner had the quarrel been placed within his hand he did fire into the small crowd of marines as they boarded the brigantine.

The quarrel was fast and flat, burying itself deep into the belly of a man as he landed sure footed upon the deck, and as Lars looked up and readied to replenish his crossbow but once again both Anthony and Toran leapt past him, joining in on the melee, not wishing in a hundred years to miss out on the fight.

Niketas and Rainald sat cowering just behind the group now in melee, when they saw how Catherine had delivered her thrusting spear, and to how the two mercenaries had leapt without second thought into the building fray, they lost all conviction for the preservation of their own lives. They looked at one another. How could they sit back like this, hiding from the fight, as though clawing for protection? Was it not bad enough that they both turned down the opportunity to fire the bow, in pretence of favouring to fight with the sword? How many women and children had lost their lives already? Enough was enough, for no man could live with himself under such pressing circumstances. They drew their swords then and stood up with a vastly new conviction having bloomed, good conscious now restored, Rainald immediately being delivered his place in heaven for an arrow pierced his heart. The sheer anger that welled within Niketas could have been likened to the build up of pressure within the depths of the earth itself, prior to the rupture of a volcano, letting loose its destruction of rock and fire. A yell so terrifying came from deep inside of him and with the sword held high he joined in on the fight for survival, for if a six year old had the courage to kill and protect, surely he could do the same.

The clash of sword upon sword, and scream of encourage-ment mixed with the screams of death and terror, was all too much to bear for those few that were hidden within the cabin of the brigantine. The priests knew not how to fight or steer a boat; fire a crossbow, maybe: they knew only of prayer and psalm, of preaching and service, of burial and of how to forgive those that sinned. The two boys with them were not much better off; what did they know of fighting. But if they could have seen the fight that Catherine and Lois did deliver to those that called themselves the righteous and only religion, of how they spent their sweat and good nature to help win the fight, then they would not have been hiding. And as the fighting above them grew in ferocity so did the torment within their hearts… and one final note struck them hard, for they suddenly heard Catherine screaming at the top of her lungs, for she had delivered another thrust with her spear, bringing down another of the marines who had boarded their boat.

Franco looked at the two boys, grabbing them by the shoulders. "The time has arrived men," and the eyes of the children grew wide with hunger on hearing Franco speak that word: men. "The time has arrived. The fight will not come to us; we must go to it. Come! COME I SAY; let us skewer those infidel like there is no tomorrow." And as he drew his sword from within his scabbard of wood, the boys, Andrew and John, picked up the short swords that had been handed them by Lars prior to his earlier departure. Franco looked to the door of the cabin, the corner of his mouth pulling up, anger so fierce being portrayed as the main feature of his face. A scream then erupted and he raced into the night, to find himself a victim, to kill himself a heathen Turk, for no devil-maker deserved to stand upon the deck of a Christian boat, in particular one on which he had sailed for so long. The boys followed suit, yelling, as did Franco, joining in on the fight above them, to partake of the horror that had been dealt them, to do what they could in the name of the Lord.

The melee continued to be as vicious as it was, but no sooner had Franco and the two boys turned out to meet the foe which awaited them, and the sail was pulled taught so well it did harness the wind as expected and commenced to pull the brigantine away from the danger. The gap between galleass and brigantine grew, as did the fire upon the hull of the enemy's boat. The flame licked up the sides, spreading left and right. A little cloth caught alight and this sparked embers that lifted with the heat from the fire as it burned, delivering them to the dry sails above. Within minutes the entire boat of oarsmen had proceeded to douse the fire as best as possible, making easy targets for Lars' crossbow as they dipped their buckets and other paraphernalia into the sea for water to smother and put out the death that currently enveloped them. And Catherine, as sweet and innocent as she was, partook in the killing, drawing up alongside Lars and commenced the shoot quarrel after quarrel into the mass of men as they attempted the impossible.

Few of the enemy were left alive upon the deck of the Christian boat, so few indeed that Andrew was the only one of the three latecomers to have a jab at the stomach of an infidel as the body fell backwards from wounds delivered by Stephen's sword. It was then that shouts for all to take cover were received by all ears, for the enemy knew they had lost the day and were now making a handful more pay the price for the victory won, by letting fly with more arrows, several of which had been soaked in fat and were burning as brightly as the boat left in the wake of their glorious escape. Several more women and old men, along with the child, John, met with death. Franco was the last to die that night, as he, holding onto the brigantine's mainmast, leant out to yell obscenity to the infidel as they slowly sank.

And the boat proceeded into the night, along the narrow straight of the Dardanelles, further and further from the sea that burned with fire, and the last glimpse of the wooden galleass disappeared from view forever as it sank beneath the surface of the waters around.

*

* * *

*

By morning's first light several dozen bodies had been delivered unto the sea, the priests having paid special tribute to the slain, for they had given their lives so that others may go on in life. Old men, and in particular, women, too frail to tend themselves, by all realistic measure, but they had put forward a stiff upper lip to deny the devil his victory.

The sun commenced to bring light to day and with it the four remaining sailors – after the carnage – took to evaluating the true condition of the brigantine, Andrew following in their footsteps, learning all he could in regards to the seamanship that was being displayed before him. He felt a heavy heart for the loss of Franco, but so did others aboard the boat, in particular his drinking mates of sea and ocean. The world they had seen, and a little more too; voyages into the far horizons that had brought them all many adventures and sore heads. Arguments between friends often broke out where women were concerned, a lovely lass her, one there; wherever the tide decided to take them they would leave their heart… and the contents of their purse, for their thirst for women was as strong as it was for wine.

There was an old man below deck, holding onto dear life, and not through careless action, or mortal injury to flesh or bone. His actions of the night before were as heroic as they could be, but his age: too old in flesh for rescuing damsels in distress, let alone a boat full of aging men, women and children. He was seen to fight as the others, where he could… and it was he, who had set light to the Greek fire. He was to be congratulated, to be given a good slap on the back for a job well done, but alas, he was too frail for such a compliment and remained upon his pellet of straw and blanket being attended to by Niketas.

Lars was also resting below deck, worn out from the scuffle, the melee that had come to hand. His palms were red raw from pulling on ropes, stock of his crossbows, and flinging of spears, and his sword bloodied from point to sword hilt. He wore the brunt of several cuts to the face and lower arms, where his chest plate did nothing to protect –

if anything the armour proved to be little more than an inconvenience; he should have known better and have removed the plate prior to engaging in close quarter action with the enemy: for compared to him they were weak in mind and spirit. Yes indeed, he had committed himself, and fought like ten men, so proud were others to be associated with the knight of old. Lois was with him now, and as tired as she was she simply adorned the man who was once a Teutonic. As he slept she bathed his face in a little warm water, a commodity that had been gifted to her by one of the sailors on deck.

Anthony and Toran had committed themselves to other duties, such as tending the women who had survived the fight – there were only four of them now, and one of those had a badly broken leg. They had heard Stephen mention to the injury earlier on, that the leg would most likely have to be removed in order to save her life. Short arguments did arise in regards to this, for all were aware that they were heading for Káros, where there was an abundance of Hospitaller knights, all quite capable of performing their charitable work and surgery upon her leg.

Catherine stood by Stephen, even now. They were both steady as a rock, standing upon the decking of the forecastle, looking out past the bowsprit as it moved gently up and down in respect to the scene of the sea beyond it. The sea was comparatively calm. It was a cloudless day, a light breeze blowing from the rear, and there was no sign of an enemy vessel, until….

"Full to the bow: galleass for sure!" yelled the sailor from the perch of his station upon the mainmast. "She looks to be blockading our escape into the Aegean. I see the mouth of the Dardanelles to my front. The boat is steady in the water, not a sail to be seen."

Stephen – looked to by many to now be in command: without anyone actually committing to such a comment – glanced up to the sailor. "How far?"

"Could be two leagues, possibly three… at the most," spat the sailor as he remained at station. "Nothing from the port or starboard, all clear to the stern."

"How long have you been aloft?"

"Just this minute, Stephen," the sailor was a little confused at the question, looking down to the man he had relieved.

Stephen then looked towards the main cabin of the brigantine, a sailor slipping into it as though trying to go unnoticed, the man who had just left his post and lookout. Stephen's softened look peered down to the face of the child at his side. She was steadfast, no hint of discouragement, no ounce of fear. Catherine was cast of iron, an unbreakable link in the chain that the survivors now formed. He turned on his heel: "I must speak with the priests."

*
* * *
*

Ibrahim attended his orders as good as good can be, slipping quietly into Abu's quarters with not so much as a sound. The only reason Abu knew of his entrance was to the fact that he was facing the door to his cabin. He looked up from the chart sprawled upon the table. "What do you have, Ibrahim?"

"The brigantine is heading this way. No sign of any other boat. At least two leagues out at present, and heading directly towards us. I should think that they are aware of our being here."

"What makes you say that, Ibrahim?"

"A guess, Abu. Nothing more."

"Guesses can be fatal, Ibrahim; very fatal: but naturally they see us." The captain looked down to his chart, pointing a finger. "It is well that we left the brigantine to that dog of a captain, Said, that was following in our wake. I hated the man, to tell the truth." He looked Ibrahim in the eye. "It was due to him that I fell out of favour with the admiral. But things will change soon. The Christians may have gotten away clean… lucky for them – and us – that they had the Greek fire, employed well I must say and easy to see as it burnt the night sky so brightly. I doubt very much that they have anything of substantial value left in their boats hold that will serve them well in any further defence. Only cunning will tell the story, Ibrahim, and I believe we have that right here. Our munitions are as they were when we departed Constantinople; our rations are as they should be and no one thirsts for fresh water. We can stay here; right where we are, for several months and a few days more, if we have to. By then a friend is sure to drop by, prodding that scum of a Christian boat right into my hand. No, they won't wait around. It shan't be long and we will have our catch. They have no choice but to attack in order to make it into open water; if they do that, they've defeated us, but I shan't allow that to happen. Like thieves in the night we stole this victory. Redeployment has worked its miracle. We will have our catch of the day, and soon."

"Ah, good Stephen, sir knight," said the first, as the man of youth and charisma clambered down into the confines of the cabin. "We were just speaking of you, concerned we are in regards to what actions you tend to sally from our little victory."

"Rations we need," added the second.

Stephen turned to Catherine, who followed. "To the entrance, I wish not to be interrupted."

Catherine gave a nod of her head, accepting the order (which came sweet and so softly, as to be a request) and departed. The sailor present sat down next to the first. "I wish to know your names, and if I do not receive them, here and now, I swear to you both that you will be dispatched ashore this very moment, and without your chest of secrets," commanded Stephen, looking down at the sailor who was previously aloft and then both of the seated men of God, their robes stained from weeks of wear, only their hands and heads revealed to the world. They were a poor sight, patches of discoloured cloth sewed into place where the fabric had worn thin, holes having once appeared where the squares of material had been placed. Stephen was particularly drawn to the large stain that was evident at the waist of the first, a thick stain of oil that was easily seen, and not present on the previous day of the voyage, when the knight had last laid eyes upon them.

The first looked to the second, the other did the same. The first spoke: "If I am not mistaken, I should think that you are giving us an ultimatum."

"You may take it as you wish, I care not," Said Stephen, and sat upon a chair. "All I care about now is for the safety of those aboard."

"Then to waste time taking us to shore would—"

"Who said anything about taking you ashore," Stephen faced the first in reply. "I mean only to advise that you shall be dispatched; possibly to even survive this unfortunate predicament in which we find ourselves, and in particular with the enemy not so far away. Does torture ring a bell?"

"The heathen Turk, torture… I would prefer to drown than…"

"STOP THIS, DAMN YOU!" Stephen thumped the tabletop so fiercely with his clenched fist that one of the tumblers of wine upon the table went sprawling, its contents drifting to the edge and depositing the wine upon the robe of the first.

He stood in a huff. "You clumsy fool!"

Stephen drew the sword, quick as quick can be, and its point just inches from the chin of the man in robes.

"Sit," said Stephen calmly, "you damn Turk."

"What is the meaning of this?" stammered the second. "What are you saying? Have you lost your mind?"

"I wish it was as simple as that," continued Stephen. "You see, the good captain Homer did speak to me prior to us having taken station last night; before the fight."

"Ah," was all that the first could register. "And you think that he spoke the truth?"

"I have not yet revealed what it was that Homer was supposedly to have said, yet you seem confident in the knowledge that something indeed was spoken in ill-will." Stephen paused. "Can you explain this?"

"This is absurd!" shouted the second.

"Not at all, father, for I do not speak of the Turk torturing you, but of the torture you did carry out upon the traitor," said Stephen calmly.

"I see not..." started the second, but the first held up his hand.

"It is alright, brother. Please abstain from my defence. The Templar has the right," no longer a friend, it would seem, by the way in which the first did address Stephen. "Please, tell me what you know and you shall be granted the truth."

Stephen had made a little ground, but nervous all the same... and the sailor who sat in silence; he was the one... he was the other traitor.

*

* * *

*

Catherine had been stationed and stood her ground. She had been set to task and was committed to the order given by the Templar. Her stomach then grumbled, hungry for something to eat. She licked her lips – she needed a good drink too.

She saw a few gulls flying through the air, a little cloud here and there. She commenced to daydream then, when one of the others onboard approached her with a smile upon his face. "Good child, what are you doing standing here?" asked Niketas.

"I am on guard... at the request of Stephen," answered Catherine.

"Why, child? What is going on inside that chamber of misery?"

"Misery?"

"It's a torture chamber, child. It is where brave men are tortured for the truth." Catherine could see the devil surfacing in the eyes of the man named Niketas, and she didn't like it.

"You are scaring me. I wish you to stop."

"Ah," said Niketas, bursting into a smile and giving Catherine's head a good rub. "I'm only teasing you, Catherine. But tell me, before I enter, what is being said."

"I do not eavesdrop, not for anybody. It's rude and insulting."

Niketas stood tall, tired of the game. "Come child let me past."

"No, you cannot enter, I have my orders."

"Are you a girl or a soldier? Let me past before I lose my patients with you." He looked down upon Catherine: she was stubborn and intolerable. He then gave plain notice that intimidation and access was his desire. "NOW, CHILD!"

"Captain Homer did advise me that during the act of torturing the traitor, you, father," Stephen indicated the first, "did request that your brother of the cloth did attend to some urgent need. The need is not important, for the good captain was so sickened by the torture, that most of what was said could not be recalled by him. But such is the ploy you performed in ensuring that no other, familiar with the rudiments of torture, were present. It was then that I decided to commence my private investigation and to put together my thoughts."

"Please," said the first, arms now crossed, "continue."

"Toran and Anthony are mercenary, not conversant with methods employed by an inquisition. It was you, father, who suggested the captain employ their services. Not only this but you were also seen to be conversing with the traitor… how should I say: quite secretively. You were quite ready to dispose of your accomplice priest, during the torture, when it suited you best. There was also the lantern that was employed by the traitor to signal the galleass behind. It took me a while to realise, and in all honesty, shrugged from thought… but it is yours, father. I saw it sitting beside your sleeping pallet."

The second priest couldn't believe what he was hearing; he was utterly dumbfounded. The first then ushered the Templar to continue with his speech. "Please, something else perhaps?"

"Oh, yes indeed, father. You were quite aware of your Brother's warming to torture," and Stephen indicated the second. "Giving the traitor a warning – and possibly even indirectly; how else was he to know of the impending pain to come?" Stephen gave way to another pause, as short as his first, looking around briefly to ensure all were attentive. "You had few instruments of torture prepared, indicating to me that you were in fact after a quick end to the traitor's life, as opposed to what should really have been the appropriate measure of a long and hard format of question and answer – I was surprised your brother didn't pick up on this, and nor did he say anything."

"Are you accusing me of being an accomplice to your false accusations?" questioned the second with an air of fright.

"Not at all, father, but please, let me continue. I can also tell you that the stain upon your robe is in fact from the same oil that was present upon the feet of the traitor. You were quite discreet when removing a large quantity in order to relieve the traitor of his torment, by rubbing your robe against his feet. The traitor was even polite enough to call you, father: during torture… absurd. Yes indeed, I have asked questions of Toran and Anthony, enough to convict; but let me finish. From what I can understand, it was shortly after the traitor was questioned in regards to, 'who else amongst us preaches as you do?' that your brother was sent on errand." Stephen let out a little exhale, as though slightly satisfied. "And, of course, you, father," again Stephen indicated the first, "kept your promise and gave the traitor a drink of water; one that had been spiked with poison."

"Are you finished?" asked the first.

"All except one task," and with that said the Templar thrust out with his sword, like a strike of lightning, penetrating the heart of the sailor who sat at the table, the sailor who had clearly seen the enemy waiting but had not reported it. A horrible contortion to the facial features presented itself; the priests were sickened, and the hands of the sailor, having gone to the aid of the injury, fell limp. "For the reason the traitor was able to send a signal to his rear was because the man at the helm at the time was none other than this dead man before me," and withdraw his sword from the scabbard of flesh, blood momentarily squirting out upon the table surface before flooding copiously over the sailors dirtied silk shirt. And then came the sound: NOW, CHILD!

"What…" Stephen stepped back carefully from the table, the body of the sailor slumped over, dead. Niketas pushed the child aside with gusto, Catherine falling to the deck, but soon back upon her feet. The cabin door burst open.

"What, in the name of God, is going on?" asked Stephen, shocked at the intrusion.

"I would like to know the same," and Niketas saw the body of the slain. "My God." He rushed forward.

Stephen looked past Niketas as he rushed past, seeing that Catherine was alright: "I am sorry, Stephen."

"It is alright." Stephen felt for the child. "Please, Catherine, you have done nothing wrong; go and see to your nourishment."

"What has happened here?" Both priests were standing now, as calm as calm can be. "This man is dead," stated Niketas, for he was confused enough to think that the obvious had eluded those present. "What is the meaning of this?"

"He was a traitor, Niketas," explained Stephen. "He was an accomplice to those who have been sent to see to our demise."

"My God… how many others can there be?"

"Just one, Niketas," said Stephen. "Only one other traitor exists amongst us." He looked to the first priest and back again. "And what is your urgent need, Niketas?"

"The old man is dead, but his legacy shall live on."

*
* * *
*

"We know not of your previous vocation, but to the fact that you are born of the devil, we must cast you aside," said Stephen.

The remainder of those aboard the brigantine had gathered around; others that could not be taken from their errands, tasks, or commitments, were elsewhere. The first priest looked up from the makeshift raft, where he had been deposited. He was lucky to still be alive, but as Stephen had said, enough blood had been spilt, and the spilling of more would not make an overall difference. The first priest and those in the galleass that pursued them already knew about the chest, so the priest's death would not achieve anything; the priest was sure to be rescued of his predicament and in some small part might be reprimanded for his failure. The chest was now stored below deck, in safekeeping, to be delivered to the temple in Káros. There were at least two to three galleass behind them and one more up ahead. No other words of farewell were given, no calling of indictment considered. And as the priest pushed away from the brigantine in silence, Stephen turned to the other and addressed him, as he should be addressed, for the first and the second were completely different men, in all respects; their callings, and names, known to all. "Father Norotus. The old man from the night before, the brave soul he keeps; he must be released of his worldly sins and bitterness, given a place in heaven, for his actions did speak louder than words, and the devil he does not possess. He is as pure as they come."

"Indeed, Stephen," agreed Norotus, the priest who now considered that he had a flock, and such a flock must be tended to. He shook Stephen's hand and smiled. "You are in command of us all, we all look to you as our saviour, and I hope in all sincerity, that you have a plan for us to employ. For the Turk sits in our path and it would seem, there is no way out, but straight ahead."

Norotus attended his flock and Stephen considered the idea behind the priests' names being kept secret: it was simply a measure of security, which the first had put into place to ensure his identity remained unchallenged. But now, with structure and commitment being laid, all of those upon the brigantine knew his and her place. As the gathering dispersed, Stephen saw one final act that brought comfort to heart. Niketas was down on his knees, looking Catherine square in the eye, giving his most humble of apologies, for his rude, and unforgivable actions and remarks.

All aboard the brigantine knew of the galleass, sitting in wait as it was; what they didn't know was of the sails tied away neatly, prepared with slip knots to be unfurled with the quickest of ease, oarsmen at rest, marines preparing their weapons for battle, and the commanders lying back in their pallets of blanket. But it was an educated guess that an enemy, in particular, one in full view, would take advantage of every minute that passed them by. The distance between the two vessels was a little over one league, and with the current speed and tacking of sail, the two weren't presumed to clash any time early: but most assuredly before mid afternoon. There wasn't much chance of slowing the advance any further, without actually going backwards, and to go back, into the advancing hand of three enemy boats, was not as favourable as continuing on course for the Aegean, where only one enemy galleass was currently at station.

Stephen had called for a general meeting of all of the survivors, of which there was only fifteen (sixteen including himself); this list of fighters consisted of the following: Lars, Lois, Andrew, Niketas, Catherine, Anthony, Toran, Norotus, three sailors [Fabian, Eben, Jacob] and four women [Lucia, Dorothea, Eve, Drusilla]. The woman, who had approached Stephen the night before, offering her assistance in regards to nursing, had not survived the fight, and little need for such services existed at present in any case – apart from the woman with the broken leg, and that needed more than the gentle touch of a nurse. Introductions amongst the crew and passengers were made and predicament indicated quite strongly. When the time came to fight they would all have to do their part in bringing down the enemy attack: although, as Stephen saw it, attack was the best defence in some cases, their predicament being such a scenario. The wounded and dying would have to fend for themselves until such a time that the brigantine was well clear of the enemy boat – that was surmising that they could in fact escape the Turks' clutches. Once escape had been secured, and a course set and sails full of wind, they would be able to breathe a little easier and attend to anyone with a wound: until such a time, however, it was every man, woman, and child, for themself.

"We shall have to take the fight to the Turk. We will tack for the bow of the galleass, and at the last moment possible, shift to fly past her stern. We will be under heavy fire from arquebus, Culverins, and arrows. I am also aware that we have a sufficient enough supply of bow and arrows for ourselves, but what we have in number, we lack in skill, and rest assured, the enemy will have many more missile weapons than what we have at our disposal. The seaworthiness of the brigantine is what matters most, for without such we will never outrun the enemy, but in the same token, we have to ensure ourselves of our survival in order to escape to safety. We cannot have one without the other. I have therefore devised a plan which is sure to help us in this predicament." Stephen commenced to pace the deck as he spoke, the entire throng listening with bated breath, and their very lives hung in the balance… lives that rested within the hands of this young knight.

Stephen had come to defend Constantinople, and now he was a commander, a man in charge… in control. "We shall cut away a portion of the decking, like the slits of a knights helmet, so that we can lie in wait beneath the deck, ready with bows in hand. I will position you all personally, and we shall rehearse our attack. We shall fire our volleys through the opening within the deck and kill as many Turk as possible, without bringing fire to bear down upon ourselves. Direction of flight can be directed easily enough, but many volleys must be placed into the air in order to allow the good sailors of this boat to steer her away from danger, when the time is right. With the wood we cut away from the deck, we can build a little structure about the helm, to help provide protection and cover for the sailors so stationed. No one must be exposed to the Turks' fire for any more time than is absolutely necessary. Only, and only if the Turk sends marines, or other ravenous dogs aboard our boat, will we meet them in hand-to-hand.

"Lars, Lois, and Andrew; station yourselves within the cabin, cut a hole from which to deliver your quarrels… on either side, for port and starboard could have equal exposure. Everyone else must be prepared to provide sustained volleys with the bows. Once we have steered well away from direct assault upon the galleass, those firing the bows can prepare themselves as required: to either sally a boarding party, or help with the sails and rigging. Catherine will advise as to direction of flight, left and right, up and down; she will watch from a makeshift hole within the boat's side. She will have a spear in her hand, one that she has used so professionally in the past. This she will hold parallel to the hull, holding the point of the spear in the direction of the enemy target. Toran, Anthony, and all other able bodied man, must be prepared to fight with sword in hand, and if you have no sword, and one cannot be found, then find yourself something pointed and sharp that can inflict such heinous injury to the assailant, that such a sight will make even the toughest of billygoats puke. If you wish to see the sun rise tomorrow, you will heed my warnings and prepare yourselves accordingly. If you wish to see another day born, do what has been requested of you," for Stephen wasn't quite ready for the feelings associated with giving-an-order. Far too many times had he seen commanders ignored, or spoken of poorly behind their backs. He wanted those around him to appreciate his command and structure; he wished all of those around to be comfortable with his presence, as he was with theirs. "Master Andrew?"

"Yes sir," came the solid reply, Andrew growing ten inches taller with the call to recognition.

The Templar addressed the small crowd then: "Stephen will be fine, Andrew: for all of you here, I am no more deserving of authoritative obedience than anyone else. I am at your service, more than you are at mine. I do immensely appreciate your admiration, but we are all friends here," he looked to Andrew once again. "I think we need to attend to the woman with the broken leg, but when time to fight arrives, she must be made comfortable and left to tend to herself. I, and Father Norotus, shall see to her injury soon," and to the crowd. "If any one here needs to speak then the time is now, for the fight will be upon us soon."

"Aye," said the sailor Fabian, known by few, for he was contentedly busied with sailing the brigantine. He held up a cloth, some fabric, and a myriad of colours. "I have something, found in the captain's chest below… I was not intent to steal…" and his stance sank miserably, "but a little wine to wet my throat. But I found something, Stephen." The sailor held it up for all to see, as it unfurled and flowed to the deck of the boat beneath their feet. It was the flag known by all that watched, the Imperial Eagle and Lion of Saint Mark.

A smile formed upon the Templar, as too with others around. "Hoist it immediately," said Stephen, "for we have been without a flag for far too long." A few tears welled here and there, others looked up proud, some even slapped the back of the person beside them. They still had a sovereign identity and their hearts were as proud today as ever before.

*
* * *
*

"Abu, Abu!" Ibrahim ran into the cabin, where his commander was lying at rest.

He jumped immediately, upon his feet in a flash, his hands fumbling around for his sword. "What is it?"

"The Christian brigantine has raised a flag, the Imperial—"

"You what? You great oath!" Abu turned half-on, indicating the bed of blanket upon his table. "I was sleeping comfortably… I said I was not to be disturbed unless…" and he shook his head and hands. "Forget it Ibrahim." He sat heavily and picked up a quill – but not through any real necessity. "Is that all, Ibrahim? Is that all you have for me?"

"Yes, for the present."

"How far is the boat now? A league or more."

"No, Abu, just under a league," and he was stunned that Abu could not be bothered to open his eyes, to look through the window shutter, to look upon the Christians himself.

"Watch them carefully. I want that boat, Ibrahim, and all aboard it. It would do us all well to prove our abilities. Who knows, maybe I shall receive a promotion on return to our glorious lands."

"And I, Abu, would like to serve you has I have always done," but within his exoskeleton of lies and false servitude, Ibrahim did hope that he could be released from his chain through the death of his commander; but his death would have to wait for a promise of treasure was lurking. "A return to Constantinople would be grand indeed."

"You fail to look, to where… as others I have met, are too scared to look; for I do not wish to be shackled to a bedpan, when a garden of rose and petal awaits me in other lands of opportunity."

"But the opportunities in Constantinople, Abu; too good to pass on; so much power is to be taken… it is all for you, Abu, if you should be willing to pick it."

"What, like fruit from a tree?" said Abu.

"No, Ibrahim, it is far too much work, for someone as ambitious as I. There is far too much waiting for me in other cities, that all I need to do is take my choice from a basket already prepared: why waste time with picking and cleaning? Although, I do admit, some time will have to be spent in the city of filth."

Ibrahim dared to daydream then. "Many servant girls will be waiting, ready for a man, breasts filled with that sweet scent of…" Ibrahim stopped himself from further drivel, for his eyes met Abu's, his commander staring insult and ridicule into him. "But it is your decision, Abu. I am sure you will be happy. As for me, I am but a humble servant myself," and with that he bowed slightly. "If you will excuse me, Abu, I shall be on my way."

"Yes, be on your way, and send me news as it arrives," Abu waved Ibrahim away. "Go, do what you do, and do it quietly."

"Yes, Abu, thankyou."

*
* * *
*

Syahid appeared at the hatch, holding onto the rim and ducking his head low, to see inside. He gave a nod, received well by Abdullah.

"Muhammad, look. Syahid has something."

"Good, Abdullah. Let us see what it is that is worth the attention of our ears: something good to listen upon, perhaps."

Both men made way for the hatch, departing their station below the forecastle, their accommodation amongst the more worthy of the slime within the ranks of oarsmen and marine. They clambered upon deck, squinting against the bright light of the sun above. It was easy to see by the shadow cast upon the deck that it was midday, and their stomachs called out for a morsel to satisfy their hunger. Abdullah patted it solemnly; "Wait my beloved, for I shall feed you soon."

"Abdullah, Muhammad; here, quickly," Said Syahid.

"If there was a prize for discreetness, then it would be yours, Syahid; for I know no other that can be as eluding as you," said Muhammad sarcastically.

Syahid smiled, the derisive comment having gone by his intellect. "Thankyou, Muhammad but listen to this. I have heard further talk of Abu's intent to return to Constantinople with his prize once his venture has been fulfilled. From there he seeks promotion and retirement."

"Who cares what he seeks: but still, that's not good," said Abdullah.

"No, not at all," agreed Muhammad. "If the men get their promised ransom and rape, we will have little choice but to return to Constantinople, for the men would have received fulfilment."

"We need to continue with our quest," added Abdullah.

"Indeed. The secret of the brigantine must be ours… to share amongst others, of course; especially you, Syahid, for without you we would be lost."

"Eternally," said Abdullah, adding open sarcasm where it was not clearly understood. "No, we must act soon. We must seek favour from Ahmad, and we must do it now. If we are to soon be engaged in battle… tell me Syahid, death in battle is open to all, not dealt to particular individuals, but to all men. What if we could arrange for Abu to be struck by an arrow?"

"Or a sword," said Syahid with a smile.

"Yes, indeed; or with a sword. Are you up to the task, Syahid? Do you think you can do it?"

"What? Kill a man? Kill Abu?" asked Syahid, almost stumbling over his words given in a soft whisper, as he looked over his shoulders.

"And why not?" asked Muhammad.

"He is 'the strangler'. How can I kill someone so treacherous?"

"Syahid, listen to me. He is only treacherous, for the men he commands. He only gives orders… it's others who act on his behalf."

"He is weak," added Abdullah.

"Indeed," concurred Muhammad. "What do you say Syahid; Ah? We are all responsible, are we not? And you haven't yet been party to any part of our plan so far."

"But, Muhammad, nothing yet has been achieved."

"And I shall soon see to that, Syahid. Please, you go do what you need to do, and we shall see to the rest. We have to get some men on our side in order to lay influence upon the others. There are many oarsmen who would like nothing more to see a sharp knife dragged across my throat."

"And mine too," added Abdullah.

Syahid was quiet for a second or two, but nodded acceptance of the task. "I shall make arrangements for his… parting."

"Good; good man. And we shall see to the rest."

*
* * *
*

Syahid approached one of the men, known quite widely as an assassin… of the past. His name was Hassan. Now he was considered nothing more than a poor wretch, who took orders to directly appease his needs. Rape wasn't easy to come by in old age, and although quite young he wore many scars upon his face, one of which was a burn mark of considerable size, covering from neck through to forehead, a well defined line between scar and flesh drawn down between eye and nose on the left side of his face. He had lost several fingers on his right hand, so was useless as a swordsman – of any description – though quite good with the bow, for the three fingers most in need for operating such a weapon were his greatest asset, and his legs ached when he walked – it was once said of him, that rape was no longer possible, for a scared women could run faster than he could, especially when he had his belt dangling down around both knees and with his hand on his manhood.

"Hassan, please, I wish to speak with you," said Syahid with the greatest of respect, for his request could well spell his own death.

Hassan turned abruptly, a look of disgust falling across his face, as though something rotten had been placed in his mouth. "Syahid, I don't speak with scum, and you I loathe." Hassan could see something was up, however, for Syahid looked to his left and then his right, and also, through the corner of his eye he could see that the coxswains were going about some business and did stare in their direction… with a smile upon their faces. "Tell me your need, for I have work to do."

"Work for pittance?" stated Syahid.

"What are you saying, Syahid? If there were not too many eyes around I would strike you down where you stand."

"Hassan, I agree with you: I am a scum, a scum of the earth."

Hassan's frown upon his forehead pushed down upon his eyelids, confusion in the answer throwing Hassan from frame of thought. "You are? Of course… yes; you are a scum, Syahid… but… Don't trifle with me, Syahid. Tell me of your needs… or question, or whatever it is your want from me – I have business to attend: quick… quickly I say."

"Many riches, enough to fill your pockets ten times over," replied, Syahid, thinking that such an answer would appease, Hassan's greed.

"Ten times… how many is that?"

Syahid looked the man right in the eye, an unblinking condemnation of Hassan's stupidity. "It is more than you can fit into your pockets, ten times over… it is enough to fill your pockets, again, and again, and again, and again, and…"

"Enough, enough," exclaimed, Hassan, throwing up his hands. "You are telling me it will make me rich beyond all of my dreams; is that it?"

"Yes!" Syahid thrust a hand to his mouth, quickly lowering his voice. "Yes indeed, enough to fill your needs for the remainder of time. You will be so rich as to afford yourself ten… many, many wives."

"What is your need; explain? You have my attention; and quick about you." And as Syahid commenced to explain the need for cooperative-coercion, he saw Abdullah and Muhammad talking with three villains.

*
* * *
*

"I told you Syahid would do well to serve us. Hassan is a good choice," said Abdullah.

"I agree," Muhammad was still smiling from the scene, Syahid talking with Hassan. "And there," he indicated with a nod, "is our first port-of-call."

Boabdil, Abdar, and Hamed – surprisingly enough – were parlaying upon the aftcastle of the mahon, looking out at the brigantine as it made its slow journey down towards them. Muhammad saw Abdar look towards him as he closed the gap. Muhammad smiled and said to Abdullah, quiet as can be: "It looks like three at mischief."

"So long as they serve our needs, I care little," replied Abdullah."

And as they came within earshot, Abdar greeted them. "Ah, our good friends, Abdullah and Muhammad. What brings you into our good company?"

"Your personal reflection upon your character as a group, is unwavering in truth and conviction, to say the least," came Muhammad's reply.

"Such praise spoils us." Abdar laughed. "We are looking to the treasure of flesh, which currently comes towards our starboard," indicated the man, unnecessary as it was. "I ache for the feel of a woman right now, more than mortal man can endure, I tell you. We should all be in Constantinople right now, cheating the nuns of their virginity."

"I think we can all agree with you," said Muhammad, as he and Abdullah arrived at their side. "But we must make the most out of what we have."

"And that won't be much," said Hamed.

"I agree," Abdar said, nodding his head in acknowledgement of the truth. "For how many women will there be on the brigantine – surely not enough to keep 120 fighting men contented and spent of energy."

"No," said Muhammad, "you are correct in your assumption," and then he lowered his voice, for below where they stood was the sunken quarters of Abu. "Which is why we seek your assistance."

All three looked to the two men having just joined them, crowding in on the conversation about to take place.

"We have known each other for a long time, have we not?" asked Abdullah of the three.

"Yes," agreed Abdar, looking to the others.

"We are good friends," Boabdil smiled.

"Indeed," Muhammad made a fist with his right hand, pounding the air, inciting truth, and bringing the urgent need for call to action into the open. "We must consider our position. We all know that once the brigantine has been taken, and three days of pillage – so ridiculous…"

"As to be insane," said Hamed.

"Quite right," and Muhammad continued: "Why; by the time we get to Constantinople, there will be nothing for us."

"More than likely, nothing already," remarked Boabdil with a miserable look forming upon his face.

"We must act now," said Abdullah, indicating his support for Muhammad. "The brigantine is full of treasure," said Muhammad. The other three looked at him in wonder, regarding the information, considering whether it was true or not. Muhammad simply nodded. "Do you see Syahid, down there, speaking with Hassan?"

"Scum," said Boabdil.

"Both of them," insisted Hamed.

"Yes," said Abdar, "But you have something, don't you, Muhammad?"

"Yes, and I agree, they are both scum; dogs of this world. But we must use what we are dealt. We are intended to be rid of Abu, but we can't do so without the necessary support."

"You mean us?" said Abdar.

"Indeed, yes; but Syahid is apart of the plan… we can be rid of him later," and Muhammad smiled, the grin of satisfaction becoming contagious, and the mention of treasure was just too good to be true.

And Abdar asked the question that was on the others' lips: "What kind of treasure?"

*

* * *

*

Syahid didn't need to express too much detail in regards to the required 'accident'. And so, as Hassan and he parted company, Syahid decided upon attending the talk, which was still taking place upon the aftcastle of the mahon. He could see quite clearly that the conversation was thick and fast, many smiles and slapping of shoulders taking place. All appeared overwhelmed with the plan to execute Abu, and drawn to the attractiveness of the treasure. Suddenly the boat approaching from the gauntlet of the Dardanelle could be seen, quite large but approaching slowly, seemingly drawing out their demise and final death. Syahid set out to find Ibrahim, to have Abu notified accordingly, for the sooner they were at battle, the sooner his plan could be hatched.

Ibrahim took the news from Syahid, having listened closely to what he had to say, and prepared to wake 'the strangler'.

He stepped into the confines of Abu's quarters, the sound of his placing a bowl and jug of water upon its place waking him. He stirred slowly and then leapt to a standing position. "You have news?" the sleep was still encrusted around his mind, clear thinking kept at bay.

"The Christian boat is close now, Abu; it won't be long."

Abu turned and peered as best he could through clouded eyes. He rubbed them again and looked upon the sails of the Christian vessel with better clarity. “Into the lion’s den they do wander. A great victory this will be; an easy victory.” Abu turned with a smile encrusted upon his weathered face. “Go upon deck, Ibrahim, and set all to alarm, for the time has arrived to man the oars and ready ourselves for battle.”

*

* * *

*

The five conspirators saw Ibrahim exit Abu’s quarters, departing as Abu attended the washing of his face. Abu could hear his words of command, passed from Ibrahim to the crew, the clutter of feet upon the boards of the mahon drowning out the pleasant flow of water as it cascaded from the jug, a handsome measure of water being poured before he commenced with dipping his hands into it, and splashing a little upon his face. He turned amongst the noise of the action above, to look out upon the Christian boat through an open portal as it gained ground upon his trap: and such a trap it was, but the other, that was more important.

“To station! To station!” yelled Ibrahim as he left the solitude of Abu’s quarters behind him. “Man the oars, marines to post, archers form rank!”

To the five conspirators, Ibrahim passed on the orders as though from Abu himself. They quickly drew his attention, like food thrown to a passing gull in flight. As he made his approach, the three men, Boabdil, Abdar and Hamed, departed company with a quick nod of their heads, Ibrahim falling disappointed that the congregation had fallen short, his eyes following the departed; his prying would now go unfulfilled.

“Your orders have frightened away our folly of friends,” said Abdullah. “Time for action has arrived, the Christians are coming.”

“Yes indeed, I see the sail has been placed high and she tacks well for an escape.”

“And if she tacks again it will be for an immediate assault,” returned Ibrahim.

Both Abdullah and Muhammad could not contain their laughter, Muhammad taking the floor with appraisal of the situation. “And an easy task that would be, my good friend, like a mouse taking on a lion. The skill of a tactician you have proved to behold.”

Ibrahim smiled within for he could feel wealth flowing through his fingers, as though poured from a carafe.

“If they attack, they are dead; escape is their only hope,” continued Muhammad. “It is obvious if you don’t have the sense of a worm and the sight of a bat?” and the hurt within Ibrahim’s eyes was seen quite clearly. “Forgive me, Ibrahim. I meant not to tax your wretched mind; we all have a place in this battle to come and yours has been fulfilled;”

and he looked again, deep within him. "Even if it is a simple command."

Ibrahim departed with sulking features and as he did so Syahid came in from behind the pair, their attention gained.

"Ah, Syahid," announced Abdullah, "How fares the masquerade."

And Ibrahim then hid well, to listen in on the conversation.

"Quiet, Abdullah, you are too free with your voice," replied Muhammad. "And you forget yourself too often: my friend."

Muhammad took the chastisement as it was and looked to Syahid. "What news do you have, and quick about you?"

"Muhammad, Abdullah, I cannot tell a lie," both comrades smirked at this, "for I have sealed the fate of Abu like no other; Abu will die."

"Well done, Syahid; I knew that you would," said Abdullah, "and it would seem that the time has come for us all to attend our stations, for the calamity of battle will yield the fruits of our mischievous rebellion. To war!" yelled Abdullah and attended his post with a quickening stride.

And can it not be easily understood why Ibrahim would then afford Abu such important information? And so he reported to Abu this news worth plenty.

Ibrahim reported the current situation regarding the Christian boat, to soften the blow of the news to follow, and Abu gave further orders which were to be passed onto the crew.

"But one thing before I attend your flock, my esteemed Abu."

"Ah; what is it? Quick about you."

Ibrahim looked left and right, suspicious; "Something of great importance, Abu, something which is worth much gold, and my purse is very light."

Abu looked his personal servant up and down, seeing nothing more than a peasant in ragged clothing, and not a messenger of any worth, and that alone intrigued him. "You have me interested, Ibrahim, but the time is not—"

"The time is now, believe me," interrupted Ibrahim, "for I have news from Syahid, and of conspiracy."

*

* * *

*

It was time for battle, the Christian boat closing on the galleass that sat there, motionless, at full sail and a myriad of sailors with hands on ropes ready to rip the anchor from the channel floor. The sails of the Turk boat were stressing, the ropes creaking, the boards and rafters moaning like a whore after too much wine and horizontal pleasure. Many men remained unseen, hidden behind the walls of the boat, along the decking between oarsman and upon the fore and aftcastle, as organised by Mouley and Ahmad. The coxswains, Abdullah and Muhammad looked upon the forecastle from their station, staring at Ahmad, the puppet-to be, unbeknown of the change of command which was about to befall the crew.

"Ready I hope you are, Muhammad?" queried Abdullah.

"Ready to beat the oarsman to death, if I have to," and a few of the sailors at oar, closer than most, turned their eyes upon the coxswain who was as careless with his words from mouth as he was with his cadence from drum.

"The sails," Syahid pointed towards the Christians. "So close I could spit upon them."

"Ready yourself, Muhammad," came the advice from one coxswain to another.

"And you too, my friend."

*
* * *
*

Stephen was there below deck, looking upon the slit above, the boards removed for the perpetual delivery of arrows upon the heathen Turk. He had stationed all hands, personally; it was a refinement of his previous orders to ensure that they were victorious in escape; he had done all he could. And he looked around more-so, completely begotten by the courage of Drusilla, the woman with the broken leg, for she had insisted on being stationed with the others and was at present quite near her comrades in arms, to the task initially appointed to Catherine: to position a spear, up and down, left and right, directing the arrows for the median delivery of the bulk: though catherine would still maintain focus upon the enemy. She rested with her back against the hardwood of the boat, leg stretched out in splint, bound in cloth ties to hold the ensemble together. Catherine, standing upon a barrel, had her eyes glued to a small hole in the boat's side, horrified at the closeness of the enemy, which even now drew closer. She and Drusilla had also corroborated; Catherine to hold her forearm at an angle for Drusilla to see. She turned her head momentarily to see Stephen standing beside the archers, he too with bow in hand and sword scabbard at his side, his weapon of choice ready to be drawn. She received a warm smile of friendship and confidence, her task cemented, and the belief of her ability strong within all around, eight bows against a crew of unknown size but estimated to be in excess of 120 sailors with detachment of marines.

Fabian, Eben and Jacob, the sailors three, crouched as low as they could, behind the makeshift shield of boards on deck, the main sail of the galleass almost blotting out the sun, but certainly half the sky. They steered their quarry of fighters to allow for the flight of arrows to hit their marks, after feinting to the port.

*
* * *
*

Abu saw the move to port and was quick with his order.

"Anchor now! Oars to rear, pitch to starboard! Drop the mainsail!"

Muhammad the coxswain beat the skin of his drum, slowly at first, the oarsman applying the necessary manoeuvre in endeavour to ramming the Christian boat as the mahon sailed rearward, the dropping of the mainsail allowing for faster control, for the wind was blowing from the south. The words of command were exactly that and acted upon with the quickest of ease. Abu smiled but was horror struck with the clarity and suddenness of his error. As the first volley of arrows from the Christian boat came flying through the air, from the unseen enemy below deck and protected well by the boarding of their vessel, the sailors aboard that damn vessel steered obstinately to starboard, away from the implemented ramming.

Abu was dumbstruck, hit hard by the change in tactics. The Christians weren't trying to evade him by turning behind, but heading for the bow. He couldn't believe his eyes. "The sail, get it up, get it up! Coxswains, all ahead… oarsman… damn; full-ahead!" he then saw Syahid speaking with Hassan and disappeared back to his quarters.

Catherine returned her gaze upon the galleass: "Ready!" she yelled.

Drusilla repeated the command, "READY!"

"Fire!"

"FIRE!"

Eight arrows were released; six made range, one missed, and one other had struck the inside of the boards above their heads, Toran was shameful of his skills, though a man-of-his craft when it came to fighting hand-to-hand and with the sword in palm.

"Elevation good, slight left!"

"ELEVATION GOOD, SLIGHT LEFT!" and the spear in hand was shifted to Drusilla's right, the appropriate change in direction applied there on the line of archers looking upon her as she faced them. They continued to place arrows into bows and eyeballed the woman with the broken leg and steadfast Catherine, Catherine, as though born to command, gave an order to the third in line: "Dorothea, higher!"

"DOROTHEA HIGHER!" came the confirmation from Drusilla.

Lars, Lois, and Andrew; stationed within the cabin, set upon to fire their quarrels as targets revealed themselves. Their speed had seemed to increase, an optical illusion drawn upon by the galleass drifting rearward. Targets were made all the more easy to set upon now as men ran around putting adjustment to sails, trying effortlessly to hoist the mainsail which had been so easy to lower. Lars felled two men in as many breaths, Lois and Andrew slower to get in their aim.

*

* * *

*

Mouley, commander of the marine detachment, fell short of ordering the firing of his weapons; for what use was a culverin against the boards of a boat; it was flesh he wanted to see revealed, and as for Ahmad Kadir, little opportunity their was for him with no target revealed except to fire blindly with a mass of indirect fire that he currently held in reserve for chance targets that may appear.

The reservation aside, he gave the order: it was passed down the line of archers, each stationed between the benches hoarded by oarsmen, putting ready their bows upon linen strings, applying the pressure required to pull back and bend the bow, to release and see hurtled upwards a darkening mass of arrows, points glinting in the sun as it continued its trek into the afternoon.

Syahid came up to Hassan, hidden by the excitement of the fight as it commenced to unfold. "I see you have your weapon ready."

"As promised, Syahid. I hope that I can be paid as you have mentioned."

"Don't you worry, Hassan, for to help with the killing of Abu, and Abdullah, Muhammad and Mouley Bakar, you will be handsomely rewarded."

Hassan turned with mixed emotion in his eyes, forehead cringed, upper lip shifting with the hate as it grew within him. "You said nothing of Mouley Bakar… his men are—"

"Weak, Hassan, very weak. They would follow Abu as quickly as a whore will undress before you." He held his hand out, taking hold of Hassan in a gesture of goodwill and friendship. "We will do this together, Hassan." He indicated with his eyes for Hassan to follow his gaze. "Look over there, who do you see?"

"Abdullah."

"What does he have in his hand?"

"A knife, or so it seems."

"It is. I convinced him of something, a small change in plan." And Abdullah looked over to them, placed his knife into its sheath, but maintained his palm at the ready. "He is ready, Hassan. Watch closely." And as he watched he saw Abdullah call Ibrahim over to his side, to be called into Abu's quarters during the calamity of all on deck: a ruse.

"He calls him to his parlour, his mansion of death." Arrows from the

Christian boat fell all around, some hitting their intended target, and a single flight set flame to the sail above their heads.

"Ibrahim; the fledgling of cowardice; called by Abdullah?"

"Yes, Hassan; he calls him to his death. And now we must ready ourselves. When Ibrahim disappears into his oblivion I shall skew Boabdil Ali, and you shall kill Mouley first and Muhammad second; Abdullah will follow soon after."

"What the hell is going on, Syahid. Are you the devil?"

"Hassan, listen to me. I have promised you riches beyond your wildest dreams and now… it is time, look, Abdullah retreats with Ibrahim. The time is now." Hassan hesitated. "You are not a coward, Hassan, I know this. Do as you have been asked and you shall be rewarded."

It was then that Hassan smiled and cocked his bow ready, and as Syahid brought Boabdil, leader of the three, so fond of Abdullah and Muhammad, to his death, Hassan killed Mouley and Muhammad in less time than it takes to step upon a roach.

Calamity grew all around and it was good that the lives around them were taken in the order they were, for the falling of the first took attention away from the others, and for the few that had gathered around the dead it seemed strange that those killed were struck with arrows fired into their backs, not from the enemy on the starboard side of the boat.

Arrows continued to be the answer to the call of battle, until the last of them had been spent. Around 80 arrows had been fired in such a small amount of time that it was hard to fathom. Stephen stood erect amongst the cries from the galleass, heard as men hurried about their business, as they endeavoured to put out the burning of the sail.

"To arms, all of you. Take your weapons and be ready to meet the pirates so willing to course us the heartache we feel so strongly after the fall of Constantinople. Gather your spirits." He looked into the eyes of those below deck, seeing first-hand the valour instilled within each.

Abdullah stepped into Abu's trap, with weapon sheathed and in a flurry, and ready to draw upon it.... but not fast enough. "I have Ibrahim with me…. Gluuuuugh." And the knife in his back was twisted left and right, Ibrahim's hand lifted to Abdullah's mouth and nose, to aid in the death of his quarry.

Abu came close to gloat over the dying, Abdullah's body falling limp, being allowed to fall to his knees.

"Your time has come to pass: you poor scum, how you will be sorely missed for your wit, or rather, lack of it," said Abu, and as he continued on and passed, towards the entrance, said to Ibrahim. "Well done, my friend. Throw his body over the side, and be quick about it."

Abu stepped into the fight and his first instinct was to see his bidding complete. The bodies of the slain settled him, but the sail ablaze, high above him, set him into motion. "Abdar, Hamad! Abdar, Hamad! Here as quick as your legs can carry you," and it was well orchestrated. "The coxswain has fallen, take his post, both of you."

"Where is Abdullah?" asked Abdar.

Abu looked him in the eye as he settled upon the station. "Question me again, Abdar, and I shall see to it personally that you are flogged to within an inch of your life."

"Yes, Abu, but I see—"

"Guards!" two men soon rallied at Abu's side, brandishing swords. "Take this filth away, chain him below."

"No, Abu;" he looked to the guards. "Sherif, Mollet, NO! You know me, both of you."

"Gag him if you must. Now take him; quickly! And then return to your stations."

"Yes, Abu; immediately," answered Sherif

"Hamed, do you question me?"

"No, Abu."

"Then set about it, you pile of filth." Abu saw Ahmad Kadir working feverishly about the oarsman. "Ahmad!" the commander of the sailor detachment heard the calling and lifted his head to a new command. "Hooks; to the hooks."

Three oarsmen dropped the paddles they were sworn to sweep and set upon the hooks positioned along the length of the mahon. The Christian boat was being steered well by the few sailors aboard, too far out for hooks and bridges formed by planks, but nevertheless, would be given a go. Sailors swung the cumbersome triple-headed hooks above their heads, only one of the three in any position to grapple with the Christians' escape.

The hook flew through the air with such expertise and landed upon the deck, drawn backwards with the motion of the two boats and the pulling action of the sailor with the hook's rope in hand, until it found a niche and held its position, secure and ready for a boarding party of marines to assume its command over the battle.

*
* * *
*

Andrew looked out, distracted by the movement of the sailors and saw indeed that the hook had a good grip of the boat near the aft of the vessel, the sailor pulling it taught. He aimed his crossbow and let loose with a shot, the arrow missing its target but hitting another. It was then that Stephen came out from his peripheral and seemingly dodging the arrows being fired at him, and the culverins so haphazardly employed – as though God himself was watching the knight's task – did hack down with his sword to cut away the rope from the hook; he fell then out of site, away from the danger of the missiles that continued to be fired towards him.

The Christian boat was pulling away from the galleass, with its main sail set ablaze and the coercion of the oarsman seemingly lost for good. Stephen could only hope that no extra sail was stored below their decking, for the replacing of the old cloth to take place.

*

* * *

*

Syahid tried to slip away as Hassan turned, "The job is… where are you to, Syahid?"

"To task; question no more, for I have but little chance remaining to gain what it is I want."

"I seek my reward."

"NO!" he turned upon Hassan. "Do you see the battle, it still rages. Wait till later you fool; the killing is not yet over."

Hassan scoffed silently at the name calling and felt the burden of containing his anger, but to control it he must if he were to be rewarded. And then, from out of the blue, Abu called to him. The captain was alive.

"Hassan," the assassin looked up. Was he to obey, or try and kill the captain directly? "To me, quickly." The joyful man of misguided mind set upon the order as Abu continued with the regaining of the initiative, but it did not come; initiative could not be gained. The sails above continued to burn and the chase would soon be lost. No supply of cloth existed within the confines of his glorious mahon, and so, until a friendly boat did pass, the opportunity of a lifetime would have to be put on hold.

Syahid ran about, to confirm who was alive, and who was dead, staying out of Abu's sight: though hard it was. He soon arrived upon the scene where Abdar was placed into chains, locked tight to one of the many vertical beams within the hold. The guards were conversing amongst themselves, upon the delivery of Abdar to punishment, of Abu's disciplinary sentence upon the newly appointed coxswain.

"It is to the battle that the blame should fall," said Sherif, wishing to be back on deck.

"Abu needs all the men he can muster, to send us down here with Abdar is not right," replied Mollet. "Let us tie him up fast and be on our way."

"It is a warped mind that has ordered me into chains."

"Shut up, Abdar," spat Sherif. "You shall receive your chance to speak, but until then you can just shut your mouth."

"Ah, Sherif; Mollet. How fares the criminal?" interrupted Syahid.

Both men turned to stare. "Syahid, you filth. You startled me," said Sherif.

"Me too."

"You too, Mollet. That doesn't seem too hard a task."

"What is your insinuation, Syahid?" questioned Mollet.

"Nothing more than the fact that I know well of your failing courage at times of need."

"That is uncalled for."

"But very true, Mollet. Any normal man would have had a palm at my throat by now, or in the least, a knife drawn to disprove the accusation." Syahid watched the man Mollet, who turned to briefly eyeball Sherif before returning to the deck.

"I have other duties to perform… not to waste my time here when a fight is raging above our very heads." He disappeared from view.

"You were wise not to have accused me, Syahid, otherwise you would be dead already," said Sherif, non-too deterred by what had just happened.

"Yes, but now we are alone. I was hoping this would be the case." Syahid looked at the prisoner chained to the beam. "It seems that Abdar is one of three conspirators."

"Conspirator? I swear—" Sherif kicked the man hard and he sulked into quietness.

"You see, Sherif; you too have ambition, courage, and the need for gold."

"And pillage," Sherif smiled, "don't forget that."

"Indeed. I believe a wiseman once said that a gold coin in the hand was worth two women in the bush."

"That depends on the bush and the man."

"That may be the case, Sherif, but I can tell you this much: treasure, beyond your wildest dreams is yours for the taking, but you must follow my orders, as though from Abu himself, without question or fault. Think now, why else do we chase a lone, Christian boat, if not for something of great worth?"

"But my question would be, what treasure?"

"Upon the Christian boat, within a chest." Syahid looked down upon the foetal form of Abdar and spat. "Kill him."

Syahid was holding on to lost hope, hoping to scrounge something from nothing, little fear having taken hold within him, for he held his nerve well and fainted obedience and cowardly actions well: when the time required such acts to be performed.

Sherif nodded in quiet acknowledgement, for he new of 'the strangler', and for he to have ordered Abdar to chains, in time of battle, and when no real cause to do so had presented itself, meant that their was good reason: Abdar was a conspirator and Abu was a great tactician. There were many things that a man learns about another, in particular those that hold higher station, and in particular of their past. Abu meant to keep his word, but only where unquestionable obedience went without fault. Sherif was a man of men, war and pillage were his calling, gold was his need, and killing someone as pitiful as Abdar meant nothing more than stepping upon a rat to cave in its head.

The shrieking from Abdar was quickly held at bay by the big hand of Sherif. He saw Syahid disappear from view and understood well that something was afoot, for he had seen the arrows bedded deep in the backs of those on deck.

He drew his knife quite deliberately; allowing the horror to sink deep into Abdar's mind, for killing was Sherif's pleasure. The point was held against his neck, and quite slowly, still with the torment of a hideous smile, Sherif pushed the knife into Abdar's windpipe. He released his hand now, holding his palm against Abdar's chest in order to restrict the body from thrashing about and he quickly choked in his own blood.

And here we must agree that to live by the word one must also die by the sword, and so as Syahid did depart the hold, and unbeknown to the actual goings-on that had accumulated a sour result, Syahid too was skewered at the throat, Ibrahim having come from behind and delivering the final blow.

The night had arrived and none too soon. The Christian boat had escaped with little to no damage and the mahon had been crippled with its sail burnt to a crisp. The dead were delivered to the sea with little to no ceremony of any great worth, and the men took to rest and water as they waited upon the waves in front of the narrows of the Dardanelles.

Abu had stationed several sailors to watch for a friendly boat as he, himself, had taken to the deck of the aftcastle, looking out upon the water to the east. The sun had almost disappeared beyond the horizon in the west, a striking red sky dominating the night air. A sailor then called from atop the crow's nest: he had sighted something. Abu looked out again, straining hard to see over the waves as they rolled the mahon up and down each crest. And there it was, as far in the distance as could possibly be; a boat in full sail of triangular shape. Abu smiled, satisfied. He turned upon a new task, to immediately ensure that extra lanterns were set, in order to gain the attention of the other mahon as it closed the gap, and for when day became night.

*
* * *
*

The fight had been won, the Christians victorious, and a new day had been born unto the small band of men, women and children. It was the day after their escape and the sun had reached its highest point. Stephen was sleeping below deck, for he had refused to allow himself the creature comforts of a more humble station as normally provided a captain. Homer was dead and forgotten; all except his legacy, his urgent and most sincere need to reach Káros. And so the brigantine continued its journey towards Káros, the sea calm and friendly, the wind favourable, and the sun out in all its glory. And as the boat continued upon its way a voice came to Stephen as he slept: Do not rejoice in victory over your enemy, but forgive their grievances against you. This is a covenant of your Lord. The battle of the day before then came into his dream, the one-sided victory overturned, to such a degree that the brigantine was swamped with a thousand men, and as his precious Catherine was about to be raped by a heinous Muslim with gnarled-rotten and filthy-dark teeth he was woken by the sweetest voice… "Stephen, Stephen."

The Templar opened his eyes, shuddering slightly from the dream, and there before him was Catherine, holding a bowl of gruel, a luxury soon pushed aside. "Good morning, Catherine; well you are, I hope?"

"I would be better to have my troubles accepted." And she pushed the bowl back into his hand.

"The others are more deserving."

"The others know that you have been going without your share. They all know this to be true. Besides, we are fewer now; the Turk boat is gone and we have favourable wind to the south. Fabian says that we shall be at our journey's end within a few days."

"Fabian?"

"He gives command to Eban and Jacob," she smiled and laughed, "and they follow his orders like a true captain." Stephen smiled too and then thought on the reality of the situation with a prompt from Catherine. "But we all know who the captain is, Stephen. Why do you sleep down here, in the cold and damp air?"

"Am I more deserving, that I should be at a warmer station whilst women and children suffer below?"

"No one suffers, Stephen. Everyone is on deck as we speak"

"You know what I mean. Go upon deck, Catherine, and order that Drusilla be taken care of in the captain's quarter. You and Lois can tend her needs; stay with her." Catherine looked blankly at Stephen. "That is an order, Catherine, and it would please me to see it carried out." She stood fast looking upon his now seated form. "Do this thing for me, Catherine, and I shall eat your gruel." She smiled and departed without further word.

*
* * *
*

Catherine entered the quarters, where the Priest Norotus had set himself comfortable; he was on his knees.

"Damn you child. Don't you see I am in business with the Lord?" He got up from his knees and felt pity where pity should be felt. "I'm sorry, Catherine. These past few days have been hard for me… for us all."

She shrugged her shoulders, caring little. "I came with word from Stephen."

"Ah, and what is the word?"

"Lois and I shall tend to Drusilla, here in the captain's quarters. All else must pitch a pellet below."

"He said that, did he?"

"Yes; it's the only way he'll eat his gruel."

The priest gave a mocking, stern look, seeming disgruntled but calm. "Well, forbid me to unset the appetite of a king!" He pointed his finger heavenward. "I must leave at once."

"He's only the captain."

"Yes, child; I think we all know that."

*
* * *
*

Norotus entered the darkened hold, quite aware of Stephen sitting upon his blanket of straw.

Stephen looked up. "I see that Catherine has tended her task."

"Yes, Stephen; and might I say how amused I am about it all. There's not much room down here, is there; barely enough to stand erect."

"For a man who spends the better part of his day upon his knees, preaching to the Lord, I see no reason why space should be a problem or concern."

"I am but His humble servant, that is true," said Norotus, jokingly. "Where can I plant myself?"

"Here, next to me," and as he sat, Stephen commenced to ask a question.

"Father, I had a dream—"

"Don't tell me, a voice from beyond."

Stephen smiled. “It came to me as strong as any of the others.”

“And what did He say to you?”

“Do not rejoice in victory over your enemy, but forgive their grievances against you. This is a covenant of your Lord.”

“Ah, well; it seems to me that you may be feeling guilt upon the glorious victory we have won. It’s easy to forgive those that have not the advantage to take life; easier it is, I think, to forgive the loser. The victory you won for us was indeed a miracle in itself. But also; let me see: that a victory should not be rejoiced for it is not yet complete.”

“But the verse itself, it is written in the bible, I know this verse, have heard it before. You were apt to believe me yesterday.”

“Stephen, listen to me. I doubt you not, that voices have come to you and that the chest may have everything to do with these… visitations; but it is hard to see why the voice comes to you and no other. Why not to me?”

“I cannot answer for the Lord, and nor do I question Him.”

“Forgive me, Stephen. The fall of Constantinople has taxed me heavily. I trust you have been chosen for a reason… I just don’t understand why.”

“Did you read the letter, the letter from Constantine?”

“I have read it.”

“Do you believe it?”

“I believe the chest holds… something; a mystery perhaps; a sign from God.”

“And of baptism,” asked Stephen, “is it true that if you house evil within your heart and mind that you are impure?”

“I believe so.”

“And that if you are not baptised then the power of the chest has no power over you?” Norotus looked Stephen in the eye and pondered the question.

Stephen continued: “If a man of Muslim faith has not received baptism then he may not be affected by the chest; although he is impure he has not made an open oath unto the Lord.”

“And the devil will reside within him,” and the priest was stunned by his comment.

“A Muslim cannot be swayed by the chest, father, for he has never been baptised. Hear me, father, hear me now. ‘Do not rejoice in victory over your enemy’: this is because the enemy is the devil and resides in all, therefore, although a personal victory has been won, the devil resides in others, the battle forever waged. And further still; ‘but forgive their grievances against you’: we must forgive them as individuals for the impurity of heart is not of their doing, but that of the devil. Do you see, father, do you understand? We do not fight the Muslim Turk but the devil, the impure; we wage war against hell itself.”

"There is only one way to find out, Stephen. The chest must be opened, at all costs. If what is to be revealed will indeed deliver Christendom into eternal hell, then it must be resealed within and hidden for the remainder of time, never to be opened again."

"And as it has been mentioned before, father, how many times in the past has it been opened? Why is it that the key has been kept so far from the lock? Why is there nothing recorded on the contents of the chest, other than what has been provided us via the passages recorded by Constantine and his predecessors?"

"These are questions that must be answered, Stephen. Once the answers have been provided to us we can then, and only then, decide on the fate of the chest."

*
* * *
*

The days unfolded without incident, islands being passed as they continued their voyage towards Káros. The days remained calm and the wind in their favour, the brigantine being tacked well to gain that little extra knot in speed. At one stage they came so close to the island of Psará that it was most difficult indeed to abstain from landing, even for the shortest time. Tínos to their port, Míkonos too, but it wasn't until Náxos came into view that many hungered deeply for the brigantine to be taken into port. A few smaller vessels could be seen jollying around closer to harbour, and several insisted that they could even see the figures of people running around upon the shore. No boat was launched against them and they continued on past, course set for Káros, a few hours away.

When Káros finally came to view it seemed to be a hostile place indeed. Twice as wide as it was across, a half days journey by foot, either way, would be arduous indeed. To cut across the land was to pass over its mountainous terrain, a steep climb followed by hazardous decent, even with the aid of the manmade track that zigzagged both up and down the monstrous terrain; travelling lengthways was just as difficult, for the jagged terrain of boulders and buttresses of rock forced detour upon detour to be made.

The sea was calm enough for all to enjoy their approach upon this unfamiliar island, even Drusilla had been provided a sitting station from which to look out over the sea and towards the approaching land. She thought then of the hardship which was to follow, of the burden she thought she would become when others would have to carry her over such hardened ground, but this sinking feeling was soon washed aside for all could see the murky darkness of a wall take shape, and there, amongst the buttresses of rock formed over centuries past, tall towers that seemed to launch themselves out of the rock itself took shape. It was a castle, a monstrous castle built into the island, the walls shaped along its base to meet that of the land around, and the walls encrusted with merlons between its four towers looked like gnarled teeth. The closer they drew to the island the clearer it all became, such a fine line between the colour and consistency of the rock of the island and the stone blocks of its defence; this, they all knew, to be their objective.

Stephen looked up to the lookout: "What do you see, Eban?"

"Very little, besides that castle. It looks evil; very evil."

Fabian came alongside Stephen. "And what if they are?"

"This is our destination. Fear no evil."

"Are you a preacher now, Stephen, because you sound like one?"

"The only evils here are the ones that follow beyond our wake, and the one we have yet to bear witness to."

"Is that a riddle?"

"No, Fabian, it is knowledge of the quest, a quest which has yet to be revealed." Stephen looked into Fabian's eyes and understood his calamity, for so few had yet been advised of the chest and its heavenly secret. "Gather everyone, Fabian, even the lookout from above, for I have an announcement to make, something to tell all that will change the way in which they think."

"Yes, Stephen."

*
* * *
*

All had gathered around the centre mast of the boat, its course set towards the castle of stone upon a fortress of rock columns and buttresses. Stephen stood before them in his hose and undershirt, well-quilted vest and chain mail with hood. His sword in its scabbard of wood rested against his left leg and his dagger remained strapped tight in place. So much of his personal possession had been lost, abandoned, or given up to the hungry waves of the sea; he looked like a knight of light purse and no horse, of little importance: but such appearances can be deceiving.

"You have all been gathered here so that I may make announcement." A few fleeting eyes pondered, for it appeared that what was to be provided their ears would quench more than their individual need for information. "Some of you already know of what I am about to reveal, but those that do: their identities will not be revealed to the others, for it would go unfairly against them that others might feel… uncharitable towards them." And the eyes all fixed upon Stephen. "From the time we first set sail from Constantinople, this brigantine has been setting its course for Káros. To the then-majority it was their belief that such a move towards a safer, and closer station should be embraced, in particular when considering our situation, to call upon and berth in Náxos, or other lands, which at times could be touched by an outstretched arm as we sailed past them. But there was good reason, and that reason is about to be revealed to you… you would do me proud to refrain from asking questions.

"Much has happened upon this boat, so much in fact that it appeared to be too coincidental. A conspiracy, a traitor, and being run down by Turks upon their galleass. Torture has been exercised, burials at sea. We have waged battles, and won." Cheers went up but Stephen held back the high spirits with his upheld and open palms. "Please, please." Silence was restored. "We have passed many islands that could have provided us with sanctuary, fresh food and water, and we have set ourselves a goal: Káros. And what of it? You see in front of you this minute. Dark and evil, a mountain of rock; a castle upon a fortress, seemingly so impenetrable and forbidden that even the Sultan with his monstrous army would see to pass it by rather than to waste the time to sack it for its pittance worth of treasure or reputation." All looked out momentarily to the castle upon its foundation of rock. "But that island is all important. It holds a key, a key guarded by a small army of Hospitaller knights. The knights of the hospital defend the castle and its treasure within, a treasure that does not bring wealth, but knowledge and security. The key within those walls so high will fit the lock of a single chest and within that chest is a secret of biblical proportion, a secret which may never have been revealed before to the society of man, never before in the history of human existence has anything more important been laid at the foot of the Christian religion. But something more I must tell you, and that is the chest to which the key has been born is upon this very boat… yes, I tell you the truth. A scripture from Jesus, or message from God, I do not know; but I know this: whatever will be revealed to us when we enter that castle of the hospital, the very one that stands before you upon that mountain of rock, will be for the betterment of all. I know you will have questions, but answers I cannot give. Even I have much that I wish to ask, but to whom do I pose the question? We must all wait for what is to be revealed. I ask now that you all attend your station and prepare what belongs and weapons you can manage to plunder from this good boat, for we may or may not have the opportunity to return, for the Turk could well know of our destination, thanks to a few that have already been delivered into eternal rest."

*

* * *

*

As the conglomerate of friends approached the shore they saw, not a station for which to pitch their boat, but jagged rock with the power to smash to smithereens all that they owned: flesh from bone. "It would seem that your friends of the Hospital don't take lightly to visitors," said Norotus, looking out upon the shoreline, the gentle swash of the sea ebbing in and out upon a small escarpment of sand between buttresses of rock. "I can only assume, from what I see, that they accept their entourage and visitors by way of rowboat, and little else."

Stephen took little time in thought and pondered no more the calamity to be avoided. "We must gather the men immediately; to get as close to shore as possible and use what barrels and other materials we can to salvage ourselves, ourselves alone."

"And the chest, Stephen."

"Of course, needless to say that the reason we are here is to protect the unknown."

*

* * *

*

The men worked haphazardly as did the women and children, Catherine always close to the heel of Stephen and Lois close to Lars. Empty barrels were taken from the hold and brought upon deck along with other materials to be lashed together. The distance to the shore was short and the sea as calm as could be expected.

The time to anchor was soon upon them and the iron hook was lowered unceremoniously into the sea, sails unfurled and persons readied for their excursion into the unknown. Norotus drew up alongside Stephen, a cross held in his palms, clenched tight against his chest.

"Are you praying for our safe passage?"

"I am praying for courage."

"What need you of courage? You are a priest; in the eyes of the Lord you can do no wrong."

Norotus paused to answer, which he did in a low whisper. "I do not know if I am pure, Stephen. It might be that I have had secular thoughts."

"You, father?"

"Yes; I."

"I would not worry if I were you. I am sure that there is a difference between action and in-action."

"I hope you are right."

Stephen slapped Norotus on the back in a friendly gesture. "I'm sure I am," and to the surface of the sea he looked, the row boat, and barrels and planks lashed together, put into the water.

Eben and Jacob, under the guidance of Fabian, took to securing what luxuries they had to the makeshift raft of barrels and planks, the chest taking centre stage and secured firm. "How goes it?" asked Stephen.

"Almost ready for the landing party, Stephen."

"Let me know when." Stephen turned to Lars. "Ah, my good friend. I would ask that you be the last ashore, along with the women. As soon as I am ashore with Fabian, Anthony and Toran, I shall send Eben and Jacob back with the boat. Send the children next, and you too, father."

"Aye, time enough to give prayer."

"For more courage?"

"No, Stephen. For you and your landing party; look." Norotus pointed off into the distance, upon the shore of the island to their front. "Look at the thin tree line, between the buttresses of rock. I see some men."

"Ah, yes. I see them now." Stephen turned to Lars. "What do you think?" Lars nodded acceptance, a small smile upon his face.

"I agree." He turned to Norotus. "It is nothing."

"But men all the same, hiding amongst the trees."

"A welcoming party, father. If they meant us harm then we would not be able to see them, and we would be showered upon by a mass of arrows. They don't intend to ambush." Norotus was obviously troubled by the sighting. "Pray for the chest, for our future depends upon its contents."

"Stephen, we are ready!" yelled Fabian.

Stephen turned to carry on with the task at hand. "I shall see you ashore, father, and you too, Lars. We will have much to do once within the walls of that castle, and much food and water to consume, as much as we desire."

The remainder of the boat's crew of men and women gathered around, to see the row boat head for the shore, Stephen, Eben, Jacob, Fabian, Anthony and Toran, the first to step upon Káros.

Norotus looked to Lars and gave a suggestion that made him ill-at-ease. "It seems to me strange, Lars, that Stephen should choose to go ashore with able-bodied sailors and two mercenary. If my eyes had their way I would believe that an ambush is exactly what Stephen will meet; and how are we to defend ourselves then, with a crew of women and children?"

*
* * *
*

Stephen kept his eye on the party ashore, two men dressed in black. Fabian watched the depth of the water as the other four rowed. "I see our friends are knights of the hospital; I see the white crosses upon the tunics as easily as I see the shore to our front."

The two knights came out from the shade in which they were standing and commenced to walk towards them. They stepped with purpose, not slow and deliberate, not with haste, nor by measure of ilaction, but a pleasurable stride with arms in motion, hands well away from the swords they carried. Their heads were bare, no mail could be seen; other than the swords at their sides no armour was worn.

"They are friends, not foe." Stephen turned to look upon the boat behind, the others watching with patience, even the woman Drusilla had positioned herself to see the meeting between the knights and their landing party.

*
* * *
*

"They seem friendly enough," said Norotus. "It is good I have this cross around my neck. To be without it would be like drowning in the sea of panic."

Andrew, the ten-year old from Constantinople, looked upon the priest, who was almost as tall as the lanky boy. "It's okay, father; you can stand behind me if the meeting turns ugly, for my sword is your friend."

Norotus met the boy's glare and patted him on the head. "Good lad, someone to count on if the need arises; I feel better already."

*
* * *
*

The barrels and plank bobbed up and down as the shore was finally met, the chest being dragged ashore, proving to have been kept dry, and the crew stepped from the row boat and panned out to meet the two knights as they approached.

The knights smiled and Stephen was forced to do the same, for a friend should be regarded in a similar fashion.

"Good men, I am sure," shouted the first knight, "from where do you come?"

"We come from Constantinople, and my name is Stephen."

The knights held out their hands as the distance finally closed between the two parties. "Ah, Stephen." The first knight introduced himself. "My name is Edwin, and my companion is Bastion;" and both smiled extensively, "Bastion because he fights like ten men." All shook hands.

Stephen introduced his comrades in escape. "I have with me men of courage and a tale to tell. I have here, Fabian, Eben and Jacob, sailors of grandeur which I am pleased to serve with, and two men of unbelievable stature, Toran and Anthony: they both fought with the great Giovanni."

"Ah, Giovanni, a great man indeed, we know of him," agreed Edwin.

Bastion looked to Stephen, "And what is the news of Constantinople?" But he knew the truth, otherwise these men before him would not be here.

"It has fallen, completely," replied Stephen without measure, or lack of hesitation.

The two knights looked upon one another in shock. "Do you have many others with you?" asked Edwin.

"A few women and children, all that you see preparing to come ashore... which we must secure before we continue; please forgive me."

"Not at all, Stephen; a captain must do as is demanded of him."

"Please, Eben and Jacob, untie the chest and see to the others."

"At once, Stephen."

Toran; Anthony, please wait here a moment," asked Stephen of the two mercenary. "Please; Bastion, Edwin; may I," and Stephen stepped with the two knights to talk a little on the subject of key and chest, and of the fall of The City of God. They, all three, walked the short length of the shoreline. "It grieves me to advise that Constantinople could not be defended. The walls were breached after many hours of constant fighting, Mehmet replenishing his tired men as he so desired, whereupon the Christian, so few in number, tired and weary, bore the brunt of constant attack from right around the perimeter. I tell you both this: we few were lucky to survive."

"Stephen; you seem troubled, as though the burden is yours alone," said Edwin, he being taller than Stephen, scars upon his face numerous, no stranger to battle himself. "But let me tell you, the burden is for the Pope, and his miserable efforts to provide aid when needed."

"Do you receive news of the Aegean often?"

"We are but 100 knights of the hospital that remain stationed here for a reason, and yes, news of the outside world is delivered on a weekly basis. And I say this to you, Stephen: You are not simply here because you chose to be. There are many islands between Constantinople and Káros; you didn't just happen here by error alone."

"Yes, indeed. You are right, Edwin, and I think you know what I have."

Bastion replied: "We know the chest by sight, Stephen; we have seen drawings of it. We know of the chest which currently rests upon the shore, guarded by your three men." All looked back down the beach, Eben and Jacob almost back at the boat, the two mercenary and Fabian standing fast where they stood. "Do they know what the chest holds?"

"They know all I could tell, but even I am lost as to its contents or meaning, and I..." Stephen trailed off.

"Please, Stephen; what else do you know?"

"It is hard for me to speak of some things."

"You are amongst friends. You have voyaged here for good reason; you follow orders, orders given by way of Constantine – that is the only answer," said Edwin.

"You are right; I was forgetting... I will tell you something that only a few others know, and that is of the voices."

"Voices?" question Edwin, stopping in his tracks, the walk temporarily brought to a halt. "What do they say; what is their calling?"

"I have to report three, and I remember them as clearly as when first heard: they roll around inside of my head as thou lost and looking to be found." Stephen looked the two knights in the eye. "The first is: He who breaches the bounds of my scripture; he shall be delivered unto everlasting contempt. This is a covenant of your Lord."

"We know of this one," said bastion.

"Do you know what it means?"

"First, tell us of the others."

"The second is: Greater love has no man, but he who surrenders life with good cause. You will not see decay when delivered unto the Lord. And there shall be no prejudice comparison between servant and master, for no one is above the Lord. This is a covenant of your Lord." Stephen paused again and they continued walking. "The last: Do not rejoice in victory over your enemy, but forgive their grievances against you. This is a covenant of your Lord." Stephen requested an answer: "What can you tell me?"

"I tell you this Stephen, we, both, know of two, but not the third verse, that one we do not know."

"I thought that the first was quite simply: to abide by the scriptures or be damned."

"Not the most poetic way of putting it, Stephen, but nevertheless quite accurate," said Edwin.

"I believe the second to be as simple as the first, but the third... I have spoken with our priest—"

"You have a priest on board?" bastion seemed excited by the announcement. "We do, but please do not see too much into it; he is as lost as I am."

"That is not good, Stephen. We need help with this; religious instruction."

"And of the third verse?" questioned Edwin.

"I can only surmise. I did think that it was meant to be deciphered, that the meaning is hidden within the verse itself."

"We have had trouble with deciphering these voices too, Stephen," announced Edwin.

"You hear them too?"

"Well, not me, but a friend of the hospital. He is a lay priest of no singular importance, but he can be trusted; he has helped us with much.

.. You are quite simply the proof to what he has been saying over the past few years."

"Not that we don't trust him," interrupted Bastion.

"No, of course not," defended Edwin.

"I think the third verse is an announcement that the Turk is not to be feared in as much as what he carries within his mind and in his heart... but that the devil resides within him. His religious faith protects him from adhering to the other verse, hence a man of Muslim faith cannot be judged by the Lord."

"Yes, indeed," they all looked up to see that they had almost returned to the row boat, which itself was making its final trip back from the brigantine.

"We must talk more on this, Stephen, but for the moment we must retreat immediately to the sanctuary of the castle," said Bastion.

Edwin followed the gaze of Bastion back to the castle wall where three silhouetted figures could be seen holding standards of red.

"What is it?" asked Stephen.

"Three galleasses travel this way, enemy boats to be sure. I am sorry to say, Stephen, that even as careful as you have been, you have been followed. The enemy is now pressing this way. By nightfall we can expect to have anything from two hundred to four hundred enemy camping on our doorstep, and we are one hundred."

"One hundred and sixteen," corrected Stephen as he looked upon his band of men, women and children.

"I like the sound of your courage. Get your people ready, we move shortly." Edwin turned to Bastion as Stephen moved out of earshot. "My good friend, as soon as we are in the castle I wish you to dispatch a knight to the orphanage. Make sure you brief them accordingly and don't frighten the children."

"Yes, Edwin. It is as good as done."

*
* * *
*

The group of twenty moved with eagerness towards the hidden entrance of the walled castle, an entrance easily seen once revealed, tucked away behind a small rock formation. It was quite obvious to Stephen that the entrance saw little commercial use of any description as it was as small as a sally port; any army trying to enter through it could be cut down at will, one man at a time and with little effort. The mortar of the castle walls was an inch thick in most places, holding together the moulded defence, each brick seemingly cut to shape from the rocky surrounds. The only thing that allowed the castle to stand out against the ground around was its shape.

Bastion was the first through the doorway, it being opened from the inside. The door creaked heavily as he pushed from the outside and a knight from within grunted as he pulled. Bastion entered and stepped aside, his left arm extending upwards in a fanning motion, inviting Stephen and his crew to an unceremonious entry of the castle. Each went in through the doorway in single file, Toran and Anthony porting the chest, which had been shrouded in cloth. Niketas and Fabian carried the woman Drusilla, and Edwin took up the rear. Stephen, as for the others, looked around the infrastructure of the castle as they entered, many buildings attached to the inside of the wall and a large temple to the centre-rear. There was a metalsmith and several larger dwellings that looked like barracks, and another, which from first appearance, looked like a buttery, and later proved to be their storehouse for keeping food and drink. A large stable with several dozen cows, pigs and goats, and a henhouse with chicken run took up the remainder of the space along the inner walls. Bastion entered last and helped the other knight close the door behind them, it being secured by large planks falling into place across it, and Bastion briefed the man of the requirements as laid down by Edwin. And even now, as the group of twenty commenced to form to become a small crowd, Edwin gave introduction to the surrounds, a quick sentence or two on each of the building around: "...and through that little port over there, to the right of the temple as we look at it, is where we grow our harvest. The ground cannot be seen from the shore, from sea, or even the mountain trail that leads up and over the side of the mountainous terrain of the island's spine, but it is quite vast to which the Lord gives special favour. And last of all it is my great pleasure," and a man dressed as a priest could be seen to approach, his hood being pulled back from his head with a smile, "to introduce the only man of the clergy of our establishment, who holds all responsibility for the food we eat and the prayers we give, the man who holds the key to our existence," to which Stephen and Edwin locked eyes momentarily, "Father Tourmede of Valencia."

"Ah, my sons and daughters," his smile was contagious and he shook hands with every single soul as he spoke. "I am so pleased to meet you all. Strangers you may be, but in the face of the Lord you are children of his heart and members of His flock." He came upon Norotus and spoke to him deliberately before continuing. "And you are?"

"Father Norotus, a priest of Constantinople, Saint Sophia, fourth in line to the Abbott."

"It is grand to speak with you. Sup with me you must, before we give praise to the Lord for his bountiful gifts."

"It would be my pleasure," and he kissed the back of Tourmede's hand as delicately as could be.

Father Tourmede was then summoned to Stephen, standing beside

Edwin, Tourmede having deliberately allowed himself to overlook the important looking fellow for an extended conversation on introduction. Edwin said: "And here is Stephen, father."

"Stephen; soldier I see dressed before me, but something more is hidden behind the masquerade."

"A knight," spoke out Catherine. "Knighted by Constantine himself, for the courage and valour suited a true Templar Knight."

"A child should not speak—" Tourmede interrupted, but was himself scolded for his unacceptable behaviour, and by Stephen.

"The child is Catherine and is free to speak as she sees fit. She has saved my life and is as bound by the scriptures of my once Order, as I was once affiliated."

"A knight, not a knight... a Templar?" questioned Tourmede with an ounce of scoff. Catherine stepped up to side herself with the Templar. "He is a knight, a Templar as true as you are a priest to the church. He is free to choose how his body of flesh should best serve its purpose, free to govern his actions as his mind desires."

Tourmede looked down upon the child, though tall she was for her age. He had noticed, without mistake, how all others had fallen silent – so the girl was of high character and status. "I stand corrected: Catherine," and to Stephen himself, "a Templar knight, such status would be hard to prove... but I am not in the position to ask for such." Tourmede looked straight into Stephen's eyes, who had not moved an inch and had remained steadfast without emotion portrayed upon his face, a look of command having fallen over him, a look of honesty, courage, honour and bravery shown by the way in which he stood. "But I know of this: you have come this way by no accident, to beach yourselves upon an island of rock with no harbour; in particular where your boat seems to be in good order. You travel from the North and have passed many islands which would have welcomed you in open arms," and Tourmede turned his head to Edwin and asked of him: "So what is it with this man that should be known, Edwin?"

Edwin looked left and right, unaware as to what should be said in line with the question. Was it not Stephen who had pulled him and Bastion aside, to walk the shore and converse on the chest, the key, and the verses from Him? If Stephen was to speak behind the backs of those he had journeyed with, maybe there was a reason. "It would be best to refresh our newfound friends with food and water before departing on such a... what could be an extensive interrogation." And Edwin's eyes told the story, Tourmede understood the message, and Catherine was concerned over the word 'interrogation' and put her arm around Stephen, protective.

Stephen put it all to rest and comforted those around him with words of encouragement: "I must agree, we must talk further on our situation and immediately so, as suggested earlier by the knights standing guard upon the walls. All must be refreshed."

"Please, this way, one and all," announced Bastion. "This way to our kitchen." And the crowd, some unsure, some needing further persuasion, and still others requiring no further word, shuffled off to the building second only in size to the temple itself, to be fed like kings and queens, to be watered like a thirst-driven flower of the desert regions near Israel. Drusilla was carried and the chest too, was taken.

So Edwin, Tourmede and Stephen were now detached from the others. "You are mysterious, to say the least," said the priest.

"If I may," said Edwin. "I believe all things will develop more quickly by revealing a few... things." Tourmede's eyes had proved his interest, and Edwin continued. "Stephen has a chest with him, father, and knows of the voices."

"Ha ha ha ha ha; music to my ears. I knew there must be a good reason for your being here." Tourmede stepped closer, put his arm around Stephen's shoulder, and all three walked off towards the Temple. "Forgive my show of friendship, overbearing it is at times, but to finally meet with another, from outside of these walls who has heard the verse; I must say how relieved I am." They stopped suddenly before Tourmede released his hold on the knight and they continued their slow walk. "How much do you know of the chest, of the verses, of the secret to be revealed?"

And Stephen told his story as the three walked towards the temple and steered to the right, towards a simple looking building, which was none other than Tourmede's private quarters, large enough, so it proved, for a table from which to seat six, and a bed for one – the most humble of all creature comforts Stephen had seen provided any Priest, monk, or other member of clergy; and the conversation continued as a plate of food was taken and tumblers were filled with the freshest of water Stephen has ever tasted.

"This water is very good."

"It comes directly from the mountain," answered Tourmede, "just another gift from Him; and speaking of Him, you have said that you are troubled by 'hidden-meaning'?"

Stephen pushed his empty plate aside and took another gulp of water. "The verse: Forgive their grievances against you..., and more still, as I have said. I think there is meaning here, more than can be seen... or heard. Please, allow me to continue. If the Turk is not guilty of such a savage belief then blame must be with the devil himself. Why? If you house evil, you are impure; if you are not baptised then the power of the chest has no power over you; if a man has not received baptism then he will not be affected by the chest for he has not made an open oath unto the Lord. The unbaptised cannot be swayed by the chest. Father, we wage war against His opponent, not against those of Muslim faith."

"I see it all now," said Tourmede, "and I believe this to be true;" and it seemed, for the slightest instant, that Tourmede was hiding something from Stephen. "Every word you have spoken makes good sense."

"So," prodded Edwin. "What does this mean? That the chest should remain locked forever?"

"I do not think so," said Tourmede. "I for one know that I am pure."

"When were you baptised, father?" asked Stephen.

"And what does that matter?"

"Humour me."

"As a young boy. I was taken in by nuns, a lovely little convent that helped the needy and brought up orphans."

"So you had little choice in Baptism?" Stephen was hunting.

"No, not true; I was asked and gave permission, nothing was denied me," answered Tourmede. "But I don't understand how this has anything to do with one's faith," was Tourmede testing Stephen's faith, testing Stephen's true allegiance?

"Don't you see, father. You were of an age where you did not fully understand the requirements of the Lord."

"Are you saying that I am false, that I should not be considered Baptised?"

"Yes and no; I don't know. But if you were baptised at an age where understanding was at its greatest, and you, for some reason, had impure thought or impulse of any description, then, and only then, the chest could have an adverse effect upon you."

"I cannot believe this for an instant. You are telling me that I might be impure. You call me a liar to my face."

"Father, listen to me; look at me, please." They locked eyes. "Do you house the devil?"

Tourmede could take no more and stood abruptly, a fist banging upon the table, Stephen's tumbler falling. "This is absurd. I will not be spoken to in this way."

"Do the pure condone outbursts like the one you have offered me this minute?"

"You would deny Christ, would you not? Would you not lie to Him, bring Him down; make Him feel as sick as I. You are not a Knight of the Temple, you are not a man worthy of that Order; you are not worthy of the dress which they wear, which I might add is why you are not wearing the Lord's cross upon your chest right now."

Stephen too, stood. "The reason I have none is for good reason, but I know where my faith lies, and if you should be tempted to open the chest then it would be my duty to talk you out of it, even if I believed it should be done. I long to see inside, like any other mortal man, but I don't wish to see an evil escape whereby the world of the Christian faith, be it Orthodox or Latin, would be crumbled upon the earth as cinders from a fireplace or hearth."

Tourmede looked to the Hospitaller. "Edwin, call for all able knights to be housed in the temple within the half hour. We shall see what the chest has to reveal."

"You are making a mistake, Tourmede."

"So we shan't see you there then, Stephen."

"I shall be there, father, and I shall have all others of the boat in which I arrived given the opportunity to savour the contents of the chest. I hide nothing, from no one, and wish only for the sanctity of our religion."

*
* * *
*

Norotus had adjourned to the private quarters of Tourmede where a small library of religious virtue covered the dusty shelves along two walls. Two knights carried the chest behind them.

"Please, place the chest there and continue with your duties." In silence the knights put the chest down and departed.

"My dear, Norotus. I am happy that you could see for yourself a little of my library. It is unfortunate to say that it might be lost to the Turk's flames of purification, and this entire castle with it, for although a nice little stronghold it does make, has no real strategic importance. Please, take a seat."

Both sat.

"Norotus; we are both refreshed and have little time to talk, so I shall get to the point and rather hastily – I hope you will forgive my poor lecturing ability."

"With so little time available, as you have mentioned already, I, too, feel that courtesy at this time should be forgotten."

"Good, then let's get to it." And Tourmede wasted no time at all in allowing the information to flow. "The chest just there, yes, the one that brought you to us. I have the key and it shall be used as it should, to open the chest in full ceremony," said Tourmede, quickly adding, "but in accordance with the time we have left."

Norotus simply nodded.

"The inscriptions upon the chest, let us write them down."

"No need, brother, for I have a list, penned aboard the boat during our days at sea."

"Ah, Brother Norotus, so humble it is to meet someone with the intelligence to plan ahead. Let me see."

And so it came to be that the information within the library provided some answers and a majority of the inscriptions upon the chest could be deciphered for what they were: messages from Christ.

They poured themselves over the books, gallantly paving their way through passages of text, through verse and psalm of praise, prayer and sermon, until the time was upon them to cease with their work. Although it was fair to say that not all was understood, it was clear to both that the chest held a secret, one that was to promote the Christian religion to its rightful spot amongst all others, that the truth would be revealed upon it being opened, that faith would be restored unto the human race.

*

* * *

*

A guard of ten Hospitaller Knight stood upon the defence of the walls as the boats of the enemy drew ever closer, and then stopped not far from shore. The three galleass appeared to have put to rest, close enough, it seemed, for the captains of each to plan their strategy before flooding ashore and laying siege to the castle or in conducting a hasty assault. The remainder of the men, all ninety, surrendered themselves to the opening of the chest. Of the fifteen that came ashore with Stephen, all had requested to be present during the ceremony that was to take place later that afternoon.

Norotus had made proper preparation and had spent a little personal time with Tourmede, the two conversing heavily on the chest, the visible inscription, and the character of Stephen. It was with them that the heavy burden did rest for it was within the knowledge of all that the Turks were currently planning their heinous activities to supplant them all. Norotus was provided much information, but due to time available, permitted his patience to take a rear seat and await the opening of the chest which was to occur before time ran out.

So it was that Norotus found himself seated within the tiny space of the chancel and Tourmede upon the altar, as the Hospitaller moved in to be seated behind those already in attendance; namely those from the brigantine. Stephen was last to enter with Edwin and before they did so a few sentences passed between them.

"Stephen, I must have your ear."

"I am listening, Edwin."

"I fear the fate to befall us all, even in the light that the chest is to reveal something grand to us, the Turks will be here soon enough. This castle will hold long enough, but it isn't for me that I fear."

"If you say the castle will hold then I believe you; a little time is all we need. The Turks will evacuate and return with larger numbers, I am sure of it."

"That is to be seen, but nevertheless, if they were to climb the mountain, to navigate around it or gather better vantage of the situation, they could well come across the orphanage."

"The orphanage… I think I heard it mentioned when upon the beach.

Tell me about this orphanage."

"On the other side of the mountain there is a very small harbour, far too small to be seen from the sea, and without knowing the currents within the inlet no man would dare attempt a landing... but I drivel. There are nuns upon this island who take care of some orphans. The responsibility for them fell upon the sisters just a few months ago, and the nuns converted their quarters into a home and a school for the children. They were rescued from a shipwreck, hostages of the Turk who sought to take harbour upon our island. We slaughtered all of the men as they swam ashore."

"How many children?"

"Shortly, Stephen." Edwin could see that time was short for the last of the knights were seating themselves. "The children are between eight and ten years of age, and all are girls."

"The Turks—."

"Precisely. They will stop at nothing to rape the nuns and the children. The misery that will fall upon them is unspeakable, as too is the misery that they have already suffered."

"You must send a detachment, immediately."

"The nuns were notified, not long after you arrived. We have time. I have given further orders to be advised when the galleas commence to deliver their cargo of sailor and marines. The trek to the orphanage is only short."

"Surely, they would be best brought back here; we must send for them at once."

"No, Stephen. The harbour, behind the rocks there is a boat, a carrack large enough for the children to make good their escape. There are eleven children altogether and the carrack will only hold twenty... possibly one or two more, but with supplies... I fear the worst. More people than that is possible but not desired." Edwin could see the look in Stephen's eyes. "You understand, I see you do. You must take no more than six good men with you, eight at the most, the carrack will not support any more. Rations are being loaded this minute. No matter what happens here you must withdraw and protect the innocent."

"I shall, Edwin."

"Good man, Stephen; now let's take a seat and await news on the Turk's landing and let us see what happens when the chest is opened."

"Wait! What about the nuns?"

"They have done their duty, Stephen, they are henceforth in His hands." The two men seated and the service commenced, and although a long and deserving service was preferred by Tourmede, time was not on their side.

And the thoughts of what was to come swamped Stephen like the plague.

*
* * *
*

The activities just off shore commenced to take shape. Tactics were the call of the day, for both the Turk and the Hospitaller Knights. If the Turk were to be victorious then quick action was called for.

The knights watched from the high walls of the castle and could see with good clarity all that was to befall them.

There was much activity upon the deck of the centre-most galleass as supplies were being moved to the other two boats. All manner of crates and barrels, no matter how small or how large, could be seen, being moved along the lines of sailors, over heads, passed from one man to another, ferried to safety, and within the half hour it dawned upon the Hospitaller guard what was to occur, for a small crew of men boarded the now ransacked galleass and brought her in closer to the shore where more man power had accumulated to pull the hulk of wood and sail up onto the silky sands. Craftsmen with tools in hand commenced to pull apart the boat, every piece of wood being torn from its mother, each piece being salvaged for a new purpose: for the purpose of war. The Turks were pulling apart one of their boats, to employ the wood in the craft of battle, forging scaling ladders and other apparatus for the shielding of men with bows. Archers would now have a defence to hide behind as they delivered their arrows, and the marines would have ladders for which to scale the walls of the castle upon the rock known as Káros.

All the guard upon the walls could do was watch in anxiousness. It was clear to them now. These Turks had a purpose and would not stop until they had succeeded in their task. They now had only two boats and too many crew; what choice would they have but to succeed in the fight, and with the loss of life would arrive the available space upon the galleass to ferry the sailors and marines back to Constantinople – if in fact that was their destination.

The guards upon the wall looked at one another, waiting, saving the precious time they had remaining. They all understood, from the work being conducted upon the apparatus for war that they would all die, but they would not give their lives cheaply. They served the Lord, served God, and would not forsake His name for the opportunity to brief in a dozen more breaths before life was extinguished. Their purpose in life was to protect the key, the very key that was about to be inserted into the chest, a token of hope delivered from Constantinople. Even in death the City of God was calling out in victory, to make a final stand against tyranny, to voice to one and all that it would not give in, would not die, and would fight forever and a day. What was mortal life to the Hospitaller but a prelude to eternal existence, where every day in heaven would be worth one hundred here on earth.

*
* * *
*

And Tourmede looked upon the seated forms of those that had congregated for the service, the ceremony of opening the chest, and after having given much praise and psalm the key was handed to Norotus, for the pleasure would be his. Norotus had indeed delivered the chest to Káros, it was now his duty to open it, to reveal to the world the secret of its contents.

Silence fell and the key was inserted, pushed into the chastity of the keyhole, a perfect fit, and as suddenly as the key was inserted the voice fell once more upon the ears of Stephen: Love your God with heart and soul so each is of equal measure. This is a covenant of your Lord. And the meaning of the verse was as clear to him as was the figure of Norotus to his front; and the chest was opened for all to see; and the meaning was this: That purity of soul was no more important than the knowledge of Christ, that one cannot be achieved without the existence of the other. Religious life could not be ordained without both existing as pillars of truth, where the temple of the body must maintain such beliefs and not waiver in the slightest. If impurity of the heart existed then a balance between knowledge and spirit did not exist; securing knowledge of Christ was not as significant as being pure. Allowing oneself to praise the lord with impure heart, or to house an impure heart with sanctity of knowledge... they could not exist with equilibrium, could not co-exist: for the devil was at home and brewing revenge.

And the calamity of the truth behind the verses fell from heaven, and the congregation heard the earth as it did rumble and quake, and the air around them did rumble. Norotus looked in upon the chest and a brilliant light burst from within, blinding him instantly, for the impurity of his soul was damned by his actions upon the multitudes of Constantinople, for when in sight of the church he did condemn the innocent, who were pure of heart and mind. The shock of the sight brought screams to air, people averted their eyes and presented forearms as shields – and the light spent immediately, but the screams and stammers continued.

The shock of sight and sound brought a panic, the once seated were now standing, or down upon their knees praying for forgiveness, but a handful of men, women and all the children did not see the blinding light, did not hear the rumble in the air, nor feel the quake of the earth; what some saw was a miracle in itself: the Holy Spirit did transcend from the chest, a smile upon its form, and it sped off into heaven, through the very roof of the temple in which they sat.

But the upheaval in some continued without a break in the horrors being seen and felt, where the ground around them vibrated their very souls, and each grabbed for their throats for they were being choked, their very life being drained from within them.

And as the Holy Spirit disappeared from view a voice fell upon the few in such sweet undertones that all the horrors about them were denied them. They did not see the choking, could not hear the last sounds of mortal men and women drown from existence, for the voice of the Holy Spirit was delivering to them a message, something so sweet to the ear that it had to be heard to be understood.

Alas, Stephen saw none of this, for his purity of heart and soul were so sound that the truth of his surroundings were seen for what they were. He looked around calmly, not in shock, not in awe. He saw the majority choking to death, clasping for dear life, he saw the minority, in particular the children, looking with wondrous prose upon the chest, where their eyes moved upwards towards the ceiling above them, and the voice commanded something of him, one more voice which was yet to play its part in his immortal existence to be, for there would be a day attained whereby he would not die. And the voice dealt upon him the following verse: He who sounds the trumpet at time of war shall be provided sanctity in heaven. This is a covenant of your Lord.

*

* * *

*

One of the knights burst through the door of the temple shouting out with all his power, "Alert, alert, the Turks—," and what he saw brought him to his knees, as there before him were many dead, sprawled across the pews and in the isles, and the sight was sickening and could not be understood. Other knights then, the purist of the pure, raced to give aid to those that were already dead, though calm they were in action. The knight so recently assembled looked down to his right and there he saw his commander, Edwin, death having been delivered unto him.

Stephen took command of his senses and turned to the sound of the alert. He called out frantically. "Get out! Get out now!"

The knight got up to retreat but was too late, for the earth rumbled and the air shrieked with its call to death, and the man choked, his hands grasping at his throat for clearer understanding, an understanding which did not arrive. Stephen shook the occurrence from thought and took further command. He had to collect his thoughts, he had to calm the emotion within him, but most of all he had to take stock of who were present within the temple and still breathing, for it was they that could be trusted above all others, for they were pure.

He looked firstly to his comrades and friends, those of the brigantine, for all of those that had journeyed here with him were present at the opening of the chest, so all of those alive were indeed pure, but the children, had they been saved?

He could see Lois of eight-years and Andrew of ten. There coming to view, to be cradled by one of the surviving women, Lucia, was his Catherine. He saw Dorothea and then Lars; the others were dead. And of the ninety knights that were present at the ceremony only Bastion and five others could be seen providing a helping hand. Stephen looked up finally to see the priest, Father Tourmede of Valencia, and although Tourmede should bear great responsibility for what had just occurred, he was without mistake as pure as the rest.

"Father!" Stephen called out to the priest. "Father! Wake up, look at me!" Tourmede lifted his head and eyes to see Stephen walking calmly towards him. "Your duty, father, is to seal the chest, before more men come walking through the entrance of the temple. It must be sealed, father, and quickly if you please." Tourmede fell from the dais upon the altar and raced down to the open chest and without looking in, for fear of his life, closed the chest and turned the key, withdrawing it from the lock and placing it within his pocket.

Stephen drew alongside the kneeled form of the priest. "Did you see inside, father? Did you see what no other mortal man has ever laid eyes upon?"

He looked up to the templar, wiping tears from his eyes, mixed tears, some of fear, some of sorrow, others of happiness. "No, my Son, I did not look into it. My courage did fail me."

"Don't worry, father. It is clear to me, and should be to you, that so long as we are in the presence of one another, the chest may be opened at any time."

Tourmede stood up. "I think not. We should try and decipher the inscriptions fully, then, and only then, should we endeavour to disturb the spirit within."

Stephen smiled in agreement and turned to all within the temple that were now standing, waiting for a command.

"There is no time for speeches. Some of you know what has been delivered to us, and there are those of us who do not," said Stephen, looking to the children in particular. "But we must gather ourselves and make our escape. There will be time for deliberation later, but for the moment we must withdraw to the orphanage and prepare for evacuation. Does anyone here oppose me?"

Not a word was spoken until Bastion called to attention all of those waiting for a protest. "We, the knights that remain, are hereby at your disposal, Stephen. I wish to further advise that there is a secret pathway through the mountain, from the rear of this Temple to the rear of the nunnery. The climb within the cave is cruel but efficient, made easier by a solid path of steps. Of those that remain only I and Father

Tourmede know the way." Bastion looked to Tourmede. "I ask you, father, to deliver these good people, and the knights that remain, to the orphanage on the other side of the island; take the chest with you. I shall brief the men on the wall and remain with them."

"We need you alive, Bastion," called out one of the knights.

"No. You have Stephen and the others. The children must now be cared for. Besides, we may yet be victorious, but regardless of what happens, we will buy you time. Now go, all of you."

Silence fell and two knights moved to pick up the chest. Father Tourmede led the way out of the temple and towards the cave entrance, hidden by a thick layer of brush. Bastion and Stephen remained behind.

"Don't stray, Stephen. You will not find the cave if you lag behind."

Stephen took the man's hand in his and smiled a knowing grin of solidarity. "You have served Him well and it won't be forgotten. You are as pure as any other amongst us. You will find your way to heaven as though led there. I bid you farewell, for we both know that you will die upon the wall."

"It is the way, Stephen. My sacrifice is but little compared to yours, for I will be delivered to heaven, as you have said, but you; you will have to contend yourself with fighting the devil for the remainder of your life."

"Farewell," and the two departed company, each going about his task with great urgency, for there was no time to be wasted, Stephen catching up with the others in seconds flat for the last of them had just walked through the back door of the temple. He could see the line of men, women, and children, following Tourmede into solid brush at the foot of the mountain, an inconspicuous place indeed for a cave entrance, and he soon found himself in the cave, which surprisingly enough was lit well by crystals of unknown origin fixed in darkened veins along the walls and ceiling.

The silence in the cave was only disturbed by the steps of the single file as they made their way up the steepening climb. Lars began to fall back, others simply pushed past him with a pat on the back for comfort and encouragement. Two of the knights picked up the two youngest children, Lois and Catherine, who held tightly onto the men. Stephen could barely make out the features of those in front of him, in particular those farther up the line of advance, although the knight closest to him was quite clear with shadow and form painting the picture of a knight so bold that none could question his selflessness, the white cross of the Hospital clearly seen for what it was. He would have to get to know the men as soon as possible, to share with them his knowledge of all things surrounding the chest, as they too would have to share their innermost secrets with him, but for the time being it mattered little for they were all pure, and in God's eyes floorless in both their courage and faith, just as Stephen saw it reflected by the opening of the chest: and if God could trust them, he could too.

*
* * *
*

Bastion stepped onto the wall and could see up and down the line of nine knights, each standing erect, as though on guard. Not a single one of them leant against the merlons that provided protection from the archers below. Each stood erect, waiting for the battle to commence.

The noise below them, upon the field of battle, was little at present, a few commands shouted out to soldiers of lesser rank, the cannon fodder being called to task as ladders were put together for the scaling of the defence, and the building of mantelets.

"Brothers! Knights!" all turned to face Bastion as he allowed his voice to be heard. "The others have made for a hasty withdrawal, to protect the innocent, of whom you have come to know these past few months. It is for us to teach these heathen a lesson in knighthood, of what it means to be of an Order. To be a Knight of the Hospital is no easy feat; it is far easier to accept the devil into our hearts and be damned for all eternity. The service is over, the opening of the chest has been concluded. There is nothing for us now but to do our duty, to the Lord our King, to our religion, for all that we believe." He took a deep breath and looked at all once more before continuing. He drew his sword from his scabbard. "We shall not withdraw, we shall not surrender. We shall do our duty and die this day. We shall meet again in heaven." And as the last of his words were spoken an arrow pierced his head and a heinous scream filled the air. All remaining knights drew their swords and the first of the scaling ladders fell upon the battlements, the air filled with arrows, the tranquillity of the island gone forever, no longer a virgin of war but a burial place for the fallen.

The knights fought bravely, they fought as though a hundred, but the archers did their duty and with time the wall was taken. It was to the wretched Turk that the castle did fall but not a single gold coin, or anything else of any worth, could be found. For all their effort, for all those killed, the Turk departed with bitter undertones biting at their feelings of greed. Suddenly a message was received; a soldier had found a path, a way over the mountain. What purpose, other than for great necessity, could a path provide?

There was something of great value to be had on Káros, something that had so far eluded the Turks. In as quick as a wink, new orders were given. A small party of men were put to station by the Galleass, the others took to banner, standard, and shield, availing themselves to the task that lay ahead.

*
* * *
*

The move up through the cave continued without rest, those of stronger virtue and ability spurring on the others. The two women, Lucia and Dorothea, began to fall well back, as did Andrew. Stephen was drawing up alongside the young lad and two women when suddenly Andrew slipped and fell, falling sideways and hitting his head against a large rock. The fall was not heard by anyone up front and the move continued, though the knight in front of Stephen quickly came to his aid.

Stephen and the knight stooped down and then knelt beside the boy, at the same time urging the others along. "Lucia, Dorothea; don't stop, keep moving. The cave goes but one way, we shall be with you shortly."

"As you wish, Stephen," came the answer from Lucia as she and her friend continued with the steep climb, trying continuously to close the widening gap. Stephen looked momentarily to his rear and saw that the last in line, a knight named Lambert, had stopped in his tracks to maintain watch on the way they had just come; Stephen then looked to the fallen.

"Andrew, Andrew, are you alright boy?" Stephen rolled the lad over and looked into his face. There was blood oozing red and thick from his head, just above the eye and slightly to the side. "Andrew, can you hear me?"

The knight placed his open palm over the boy's throat in the hope of feeling a pulse. He looked at Stephen and shook his head. "The boy is dead. He no longer breathes the air we do but has joined with Christ."

Stephen let Andrew go and stood up as did the knight. "I do not cry or feel bad for the loss."

"And why should you?" asked the knight. "I am Martin." The knight could see that Stephen was searching for an answer, even though one was not really required. "The boy's death is not of your doing. I do not know what it is to be pure. Other than what I overheard people say. I do not understand why some are dead and others are still alive, but Bastion was a good friend, not just a commander-in arms. He knew you but for the shortest time but came to know you like a brother. I know this to be true otherwise he would not have allowed us to so easily placed under your command. I hope that we can learn of one another like brothers of the same cloth. We all hope – the other knights and I – that answers can be provided our questions, but for the time being we must be content with the choice we have been provided. Come, Stephen, let us leave the boy here in the arms of God. We can do no more for him. We have others that must be saved and time is short."

"You are right, Martin. Our journey has just begun, and continue we must." Both men looked upon the fallen body of Andrew one last time and departed without further word, for he was already walking alongside the lord in heaven.

"I shall tire quickly, for the climb is hard, but tell me, Stephen, was the misery of Constantinople as great as I have heard? Several of those that arrived with you were talking of the Muslim Turk and his savage ways."

"There is much savagery in war, Martin. Not all is delivered by the hand of the enemy."

"Ah, yes; 'of friend or foe'. And so, of the defence: you were a witness to their cowardice, mercenaries who cared not for the people but only their purse?" it was a statement more than a question but Stephen honoured Martin with an answer.

"The mercenaries were as honourable as the citizens and the soldiers who fought for them, but there are always a few who tempt the fury of God and his allies."

"You served with such men?"

"I served beside one, not with, and he committed a heinous crime against me."

"And this crime... can you speak of it?"

Stephen stopped in his tracks and looked the knight in the eye. "He killed my wife of just two days. I buried her at sea."

Stephen turned his head to the task awaiting him and continued on his way, Martin looking on as though stunned by a horrific scene. He understood little of the emotions of man but could see that such an awful end, to a fine beginning, could easily render a man inept to show feelings against the horrors of war.

Tourmede had led the flock to safety and as they emerged from the cave's mouth all could see the nunnery, the nuns' villa, as clear as day. The cave entrance was not sealed as the other for the approach to the island from the sea was not considered fruitful; it was also an easier path for the nuns to employ when travelling between the temple of the castle and nunnery.

Tourmede waited patiently as members of the entourage continued to file out one at a time. The first of the knights to exit was Raoul, shortly followed by Aaron and Bernard, whom between them carried the chest.

"Raoul."

"Yes, father; what is it?"

"Stand over there and watch the track. If you see anything then let me know immediately."

"Yes, father."

"Aaron, Bernard, take the chest towards the sisters' quarters," directed Tourmede of the next two knights to exit. "And tell them to gather the children and to prepare for evacuation."

"Yes, father," replied Bernard, and made his way with Aaron towards the small villa of quarters, church and orphanage.

And as the others commenced to file out, one at a time, Father Tourmede asked them to step aside in order to be counted and when it came time for the final three, Stephen and the two knights, to exit, he could see that one of them was missing. "The boy, where is he."

"He fell, father," answered Stephen. "It is with regret that we left him behind, but the climb was steep and time is short."

"I won't argue with you, Stephen," and Tourmede looked amongst the gathering after giving a quick prayer for Andrew. "We must go there, to the orphanage. There you are to gather together all that you need for the longest of journeys."

Stephen's eye fell upon the words and understood their meaning. "You are not coming, are you, father?"

"I must remain here. It is likely that the Turk shall require ransom, and what better ransom than a priest and his small flock—"

"You shall be killed and the sisters will be raped," Stephen finished for him. Tourmede had the most pleasant and unselfish look upon his face that moment and spoke softly for all to hear. "We don't know that, Stephen. Besides, there is no room upon the carrack. I shall take the sisters into hiding here on the island; the Turks will not find us, with any luck. They are here out of greed and cannot support themselves for long. They will depart soon enough. But you; you must make haste with the children, take the knights for protection... all five know how to sail, each came from Lepanto before being stationed here in Káros, and have each made many voyages across the Mediterranean and the Aegean." He directed those that stood in wait, ordering them to continue. "Stay with the knights and the chest, help the nuns prepare the children." And as the small group commenced to follow the chest bearers, Aaron and Bernard, Tourmede made final insistence. "And you, Stephen, remain with me," and then with silent indication given by the nod of his head, he requested that Lambert and Martin should go and stand with Raoul.

When alone Stephen prompted Tourmede to say what it was that he wished to say. "We are alone, father. What is it you wish of me?"

"No more than God would ask." Tourmede looked about and found a couple of small boulders. "Please, let us sit for a few minutes and discuss something of importance."

"Do we have time?"

"We have to make time, Stephen, for if you were to depart now then your task will never be met."

"You have me intrigued."

"That is good, now sit." Tourmede allowed himself a few seconds of private thought before continuing as best he could.

"With the time I had alone with the chest and Father Norotus, much was discussed. I revealed to him some ancient texts that I had in my library—," a holler suddenly broke his concentration.

"Father," yelled Lambert. "I see movement. We have but limited time; one half of the sands in an upturned glass is all you have."

"Maintain your position!" and to Stephen he continued. "We have time, now listen to me and listen carefully. The scripture on the chest, beneath, upon its sides and that on top, all is written in the Semitic language of Jesus, Aramaic, it is a codex from the secret gospel of Christ, Himself. Only one such copy of the gospel exists... to my knowledge," Tourmede grasped Stephen by the hands to silence him for he was about to speak. "We have no time for questions, listen and listen alone you must. I did not see into the chest but I know what it contains. Norotus knows, but he has passed from this world, and although he has proven to be impure, he still walks in heaven. It is Jesus, his saviour, who died for our sins. He will protect him against the voice of God, His father, for the Old Testament is not as forgiving as the New.

"The codex is clear to me and I shall reveal it to you, but if you should require further information then you must travel to the port of Southern France, and only there shall the truth be revealed. You seek Father Ambaedian. He can show you more if required and he is as pure as them all.

"Now listen to me with all your heart. One of the passages upon the chest reads: 'He shall know his way, upon his quest, travelling far, as bequest, to surrender life, so dear and strong, his way will be painted, with voices strung', And beneath the chest; 'Only the purest of mind and body will survive the contents of the chest'. A test, Stephen, it is but a test. I don't know how it came about but the chest contains several items of sacred importance.

"Listen to me, Stephen. The items are good and bad, the same as the Old and the New, Testaments that preach from different perspectives. The items must be joined in order for the power of the contents to be held at bay. You, Stephen, you are the one that can survive the contents of the chest; I know this, I feel it."

"I cannot—"

"A voice came to me, Stephen. You must trust in the Lord's decision." Stephen knew that time was short and continued to listen with unblemished attention. "I don't understand everything, nor do I claim it, but it seems to me that it is but a test, that God and the devil are one, a test that must be passed in order to prove oneself, and Jesus is but the son of God. You can only commit crime against the commandments by committing such heinous and unforgivable acts against the pure. Those who have attained the true belief of God, of the scripture, will survive the contents of the chest, but fused together, joining the good with the bad, that will reveal to the world the meaning of life, and that is to 'deny the devil'.

"A Muslim cannot be affected, for his belief belongs to Allah: he has already been recruited by the devil and his false worship. It is for them that they have failed the test of honour, faith and all values associated with good, clean, moralistic servitude. Fuse the good and the bad, Stephen. This is the first of your many quests."

"Fuse them?"

"It is written, so it must be done," said Tourmede. "Listen to me. Jesus came to the world and delivered himself to the cross for all of us to be forgiven our sins, now, in all His glory, he delivers to us again, His power, for He is allowing us, mortal man, to be free of impurity. Fuse the good and the bad, and all will be glorious in His name."

"Father, it is time. They come running, no more sand is left. If we do not leave now we shall fall into the hands of the enemy," said Lambert with the greatest of concern. Father Tourmede stood. "Then let us depart. Come, let us go."

*

* * *

*

There was much activity being undertaken by the time Tourmede and Stephen had arrived at the front of the nuns' villa, their quarters and small out-of-the-way church having been turned into an orphanage. The children had been gathered to the front of the building and seemed to be in good order; all were quiet and each carried a small parcel of extra clothing.

Stephen could see the sisters moving around in a state of calmness, keeping the children from being frightened, and Lois and Catherine were there too, helping their soon-to-be newfound-friends with preparing for the short walk to the sea, where the carrack waited for its precious cargo.

Aaron and Bernard were already halfway down the track, heading towards the hidden harbour that consisted of little more than a few planks of wood made fast to a few posts between solid mountains of rock. Lars was up the front, looking left and right as he made his descent from the side of the mountain and down the track to their escape.

Father Tourmede introduced one of the sisters. "Stephen, this is Sister Anne."

"I am pleased to meet you, Stephen," she bowed slightly.

"The honour is mine, sister."

"I hear you are to look after the children, taking them to a safe haven."

"I shall do all that I can."

"I am sure that you will," and Anne looked to the others, namely Lois and Catherine. "I see you have already had your hands troubled by the torments of young minds."

"They are a pleasure, as it is my pleasure to serve."

"I wish I had time to get to know you, Stephen. I am sure that Father Tourmede will advise me accordingly once we have taken to hiding."

"I hope he will be kind," said Stephen as he turned to see the children commence their short trek, the knights Raoul and Lambert having returned from their watch on the track to lead them away; and Martin arrived at his side.

"Excuse me, father, sister, but it is time for us to go. The enemy will be here shortly."

"Thank you, Martin," said Tourmede who put his hand out to shake that of the knights. "It has been a pleasure serving with you. Tell the others, when you get the chance, that the key and the chest must be protected at all costs, except that of the innocent," and without the meaning of his glance being seen by Sister Anne, Tourmede looked out the corner of his eye and towards the children, meaning that their lives were more important than the chest and their sacred religion."

"All of my time here has been spent listening to the grand view in thinking that the chest was all important," said Martin. "But I see now why you are pure of heart and soul, for you would give up all that you believe in order to protect those of little understanding."

"Goodbye, Martin, and goodbye to you, Stephen, Templar Knight of Constantinople, Esteemed Friend of Constantine, and Saviour of Christ's Belongings."

"Goodbye, father."

"Oh, Stephen, one last thing," and he reached into his pocket and pulled out the key, handing it the Templar without further word.

A few smiles were all that time permitted for and to their separate ways they did depart. Stephen looked over his shoulder as he made his way towards the carrack and saw for himself, Father Tourmede and the sisters of Káros heading for sanctuary upon the island of rock they had known for so long, priest and nuns, of Orthodox and Latin, running as best their legs could carry them, away from the Turkish advance. One more surprise was then met, for as he turned to press on with his coming engagement he could see Lucia and Dorothea, waving to him with a smile, before they too turned tail, and ran after the sisters and Father Tourmede: they had just then sacrificed themselves for the sake of the children and the chest.

*
* * *
*

The carrack was boarded with little fuss, apart from the fact that the eleven children, new to the vestiges provided by a vessel of the seven seas, were upset. The children had been to sea before, sure enough, but the horrors of those days, where torment upon torment was suffered, handed out by the hand of those of Muslim faith, to be surrendered to a harem of insignificant importance; it all managed to shroud the experience.

The knights went about their work and set the sails, the carrack moving with a groan, and was manoeuvred slowly towards the open sea.

Lars contented himself with aiding the children, showing a smile and plenty of affection, Lois and Catherine acting as though adults, having experienced enough themselves to know better, mature of mind and action, as pure as any other that had confronted the opening of the chest.

Stephen looked out upon the island as they moved further and further away, the sun slowly sinking beyond the horizon, similar to the way it did when he was making his escape from Constantinople, having buried his wife at sea. This, for him, was a cruel moment, where the memories of Clover came flooding back. Of all the things he did and did not know, one thing was for sure; he would never again lay eyes upon Káros.

*
* * *
*

"Abu, Abu," shouted the sailor as he scrambled into the captain's quarters. Abu turned slowly, disgust showing on his face, for very little impressed him of the men that served beneath him.

"What is it, Ibrahim?"

"A boat, Abu, it looks like a carrack. The alert has come from the lookout."

"How far, Ibrahim? How many hours, how many days?" for he despised the worthless crew that he commanded.

"Within a day, if that is your wish, Abu."

"No! No, no, no; that won't do." He thought for a second. "A carrack you say?"

"Yes Abu."

"We shall head for the island, Ibrahim, and see if we can't find ourselves the brigantine. It won't delay us by much. Then, and only then, shall I allow myself to make a decision. It is possible that our quarry have purchased themselves a new vessel, in which case we shall follow from behind, hidden by the waves and the horizon." Abu held his open palm up to prevent further word and interruption; he was thinking. "Order for the watch to be maintained. If my assumption is correct we will be following that carrack within a day, to follow it like a fox follows its prey, and when the time is right we shall pounce."

Ibrahim smiled, and a little chuckle escaped him. "Ah, Abu, so grand it is to work beneath you; so grand it is indeed."

BOOK THREE
TheTemplar: and the Cross of Christ

You should not give in to evils,
but proceed ever more boldly against them.

Abu, The Strangler, sat back, his feet upon the small desk of his cramped cabin. The news on the enemy was good. He felt as relaxed as he could ever feel, totally in command of his senses and his destiny.

Abu rarely conferred with others, seeking not their opinion on matters of military importance, but in this particular case it was decided that, to allow voices to be heard, would strengthen the weakened morale of all on board. So weak they were, so weak that Abu could not see how they could call themselves men, lacking in pride and spirit. He cast himself so high above those around him that he felt as though he had only one thing in common with them, and that was his religion.

So they had gathered, Abu, Ibrahim, Ahmad, Sherif and Mollet; Abu the commander, Ibrahim for he was a lamb which was easily swayed, Abu for familiarity, Ahmad for his official rank, Sherif for his ability to bully opinions to his favour, and Mollet to influence the rowers, to enforce courage and to free them of their tormented defeat against the Christians. Abu pounded the small desk then, infuriated at the embarrassment that he had been forced to endure. The very thought that the Christians had escaped his net was almost too much to handle; but the current situation did lend a little optimism.

It would seem that all aboard the Christian carrack were completely unaware as to the mahon that followed; but that was absurd. Abu shook the thought from his head and then considered it again. How could the weeks, which were gathering in number and falling behind them, not bear some form of caution to which the Christians could use to their advantage? It was clear that the crow's nest of the Christian boat was manned, both day and night, for a lantern could be clearly seen high above the crest of the waves which formed between the two boats; they, therefore, could see them as well as they could see the Christians.

The verdict was simple; the Christians knew what followed in their wake but cared little, so long as the mahon maintained its distance. So what would the Christians do if the mahon made a move to attack? Make for shore? Seek the protection of a nearby coastal city? As for the reason behind their current situation whereby the Christians were avoiding quite purposely any contact with another vessel of European cast, there was only one reason which came to mind: the chest of secrets.

The chest of secrets; it was Abu's new curse. He had to have the chest, at any cost: his men, his high position and rank, his recognition of professionalism; it all mattered little to him now, for he was to gain upon a new destiny, new riches, a rewarding life.

Abu stood and announced to all the orders which he had

contemplated over their time following the carrack. "We shall deliver our clothes to the hungry sea and take to masquerade. We must sail towards the coast and attack the first vessel we see. We shall dress as the European dresses and seek out the carrack once more, aboard another boat, to avert scrutiny. We shall be seen to be nothing more than another boatload of Christians." And one final plea was needed to ensure they maintained their obscurity. "We must pray no more whilst in public, we must learn to do without our praise to God whilst before a Christian, for we must teach ourselves to be as a Christian; after all, how else will we be able to get closer to the chest and its grand reward?"

And so, with orders so struck the mahon did attack a Christian boat within three days, and within another three weeks they caught glimpse of the enemy carrack once more as it made its way towards safe harbour. The carrack was approaching the coast and had an hour's advantage on the, now, Muslim's brigantine. But Abu had considered much over the past few months and it seemed to him that the orphans upon the vessel to their front would affect the ability of the Christian men to make any reasonable time in escape once on land. Abu had also considered the possibility that those aboard the carrack would alert the authorities upon the shore of the enemies, their approach, even if they did appear European.

Abu looked over to the horizon and saw an opportunity. Fast approaching was a storm, and it seemed to be large and ferocious, for lightning could be seen and heard as it struck out with its tentacles of destruction. He would use it to his advantage; take what he could from what was offered. He may have to make for land some distance from any port that fell before them, even go so far as abandoning ship; but he could also press his luck and stay upon the heel of his adversary.

Time would tell; but time was also short.

In times of war the landscape changes much, as do the borders of countries, lands conquered and then won back. What is France one day is not necessarily the same on another; what is Spain at one time is also of the same equation. This was the result of war, where constant conflict between countries affected the religion of people and their loyalties. Most of the humble of any country were the poor, and the poor wanted nothing more than to be left alone, to plant and harvest their crops, to be able to feed their families and live in peace. But man does not always get what he wants; quite seldom in actual fact would a peasant be content with his life and status but peace was always hungered for.

From Stephen and with his insight of the Lord came knowledge of the safe haven which they did seek; none other than Barcelona. It was a reasonably small town which relied heavily upon the fishing industry. It was the voice which had been delivered to him, another to join the many he had received, but the voices themselves did slow to a trickle, until some three weeks before entering port the voices ceased to occur altogether. Stephen felt as though blinded by sight for he had relied on them for answers, and for comfort. But the dreams had steered him well. Not a night would go by without his slumber being intruded by a dream of some description. Sure enough, he dreamt like any other man, but he also had dreams which could only be considered as godly, for the voices of the day had become his dreams of night, where messages would be passed onto him from the heavens above.

The evening was cold and wet, a little drizzle falling upon the earth and sea, clouds commencing to thicken more than they were before, blackening upon the horizon and drifting ever closer, the dark mass of terror approaching fast. The ferocity of the storm was of little concern to Stephen and the others for they were so close to stepping on dry land that cover could readily be sought from the evil about to be lashed out upon the coast.

It was a slow approach towards harbour, all aboard taking in the surroundings, endeavouring to learn a little, even if non-productive, in order to prepare themselves for when they departed the safety of their carrack. It was not at all busy, for the fishing boats of the area had already dispersed with their catch of the day. It was clear to all that no boat or ship would be getting ready for the sea due to the approaching storm, which would be upon them at any minute, the little, light rain falling upon the deck soon gathering more body and thus a weightier fall from the sky above.

They moored themselves at a vacant slot upon the pier, the only vacant spot to be seen in the harbour; most boats and ships had taken the warning from what could be seen and had secured themselves as best they could.

Quite suddenly a fat-bellied man with red cheeks and small ledger in hand came running up, pushing his way through a small gathering, between groups of men in their twos and threes. He was seemingly agitated by the approach and mooring of the carrack, as his soon to be voiced displeasure was to reveal.

"Who is it, I command, that sees fit to tie fast upon this pier?" yelled the harbour master, slowing his run to a walk, a quickened stride delivering him to where the carrack came to an unsteady halt. He was somewhat out of breath and took in a few quick mouthfuls of air, satisfying his urgent need for oxygen.

"Stephen is my name." Stephen stood tall and stepped upon the wooden decking where he was being moored. Stephen looked temporarily around to the others at work, seeing that all had conveyed to his request by having removed their Order's regalia. Now they resembled nothing more than sailors fit for the sea, with swords hanging from their belts, swords, mind you, not common amongst men of the sea who did nothing more than fish for a living.

"Stephen, ah; well tell me, by what manner have you secured the permission to strap fast to this here pier?" said the harbour master, his eyes squinting, looking upon Stephen as though to scold him, the fresh breeze blowing at his thick head of hair. A sudden shiver then came over him, his shoulders shaking, as though shook by the hand of God.

"None," said Stephen, shrugging his shoulders through defiant disregard for the harbour master's concerns, which was delivered with such simplicity that the fat-bellied oxen stammered.

"None, indeed. Well, to moor here will cost you plenty, and up-front if you please," said the harbour master, anxious to find some coin in his fist. It was his way and his pleasure, to tax those that dared to trespass upon his ground.

"Dear sir, as you can see, we are nothing more than poor wretches whose only cargo it that of children," the fat-bellied harbour master looked beyond Stephen and could see the children gathered next to the rail of the carrack, "and a few men of the sea, sailors all, as good as any other; as you can clearly see. Now if you look yonder," and to this, Stephen looked into the distance, "you will see our escort." Stephen gave further indication to the Muslim craft with pointed finger, still some distance off from shore.

"A brigantine," said the harbour master, undecided on the boat's character or importance, it being too far out for him to make a solid opinion. But if it was true, and it was indeed an escort ship, he could be well fitted with compensation.

"Yes sir. Our Lord and master sails in our wake, protection granted us on this, our long, long voyage, for he dislikes children," said Stephen, reflecting a little on the harbour master, pondering on what he was thinking.

"And from where do you come, weighted down with so few men and a score of children?"

"Orphans, one and all," replied Stephen

"Orphans, maybe, but that does not answer my question. And of the sailors that you command; from where do you all come?"

"Please respect us. My master will pay all you need, but for now I must get these children to shore. As you can clearly see, poor weather is approaching fast. The children's needs must be taken into immediate consideration." And to make his quest as real as could be he asked of the harbour master, "And where is your nearest convent?"

"To be found up the road, towards the east," answered the fat man. "It is quite easy to find and has a cross chiselled within the stone above the door.

"Thank you, kind sir." Stephen turned then to all those on board, their eyes glued to him now, for their work was done; the men had completed their tasks and the children had congregated upon the deck. "Gather you things, children, though little I know your possessions to be, for we set out for the convent as promised."

Some of the children looked to one another, lost as to what Stephen had just commanded in regards to 'my master', but others who had listened closely to what the knight had said before entering the harbour quietly offered advice, 'do as you are told', 'pretend to adhere to orders,' and 'Stephen is stalling, quickly gather your things, nuns will aid us,' for the brigantine following could only be of a single nationality and Stephen knew which. They had no time to lose and needed to gain as much distance from the pier, or to find safe haven, as quickly as possible. The things that were gathered were little to say the least, and of weapons, the children left those behind, for the last thing they needed was to draw attention upon themselves.

"But what of my pay?" asked the fat man, drawing upon the fact that his palm was still empty and his appetite for greed had not yet been quenched.

"My master shall pay when he sets to shore, but until then, if it helps to settle you, you may keep our carrack until payment has been received by the silk of your purse. Ours is not to deceive and our master will pay, but we must attend to the children's needs."

To the man it seemed a fair agreement, as fair as any other, under the circumstance. Good condition the boat was thought, and considered, to be in, but unbeknown to any one around the boat had a weak spot in the hull, which could be easily breached under stressing circumstance.

With that the man smiled and all aboard the carrack commenced to unload themselves, along with the chest of secrets, a chest so beautifully designed and mystifying that the harbour master had to give it a second look. "What is in the chest? Gold?"

"No gold," said Stephen, "just private possession that the convent will require once we have unloaded the burden of these children upon them."

"Uh, ah. And the carrack?" he asked. "A good boat is she?"

"The best, for she bought us most of the way from Constantinople."

"Constantinople, ah; please, what is the news?" The harbour master gave genuine interest, for news of Constantinople came little these days. All he knew was of the siege lasting for what seemed to be forever. It was the talk of any town along the coast of the Mediterranean.

"She, the city so grand, is now in Muslim hands." And with that the harbour master stood shocked and watched, as the crew and children stepped from the boat, and they made their way towards dry land for the first time in many weeks.

"Gather children, men too, come close," said Stephen to the others, the rain now coming down quite solidly, growing in its intensity.

All gathered around, in an alley shadowed by buildings either side, passers-by looking upon them briefly as they continued upon their business. It was good that the storm provided them with so much cover from curiosity and that few people, rushing to get away from the approaching storm, had little time to ponder the loitering of seven men and thirteen children.

"We continue as planned, no stragglers, no idle chatter. We must attend our mission with purpose; remember your tasks and complete them well. I shall see you all soon." The knights nodded in acceptance of their tasks, tasks which had been developed to cater for their situation, tasks which would grant them their need to finally uncover the secret of the chest, to fuse the contents, to reap the reward which was to be inherited by them all.

"We shall miss you, Stephen," said Catherine, the other children in agreement, their voices starting to rise. Stephen in particular had a lot of love for Catherine. She had proven to be quite the fighter and at such a young age. It was clear to him from the moment the Muslims tried to board their Brigantine that Catherine was a very special child.

"Please, good children. You shall not be deserted." Stephen held Catherine momentarily as she came in for a hug and a little comfort, to feel the security offered by his presence. They then released each other. "I shall be back soon. You heed well to what Martin has to say, Raoul too," and he looked into the eyes of the two knights he had just named, seeing them smile in return as they passed on their silent word to take care of the children or die in the process of their protection. Each and every one of the knights had the same quality. Not only were they pure but they carried that instilled kindness and caring, a strength of character that could not be questioned.

The children fell silent and each came in to hug Stephen close, as Catherine had done before them. Stephen got down upon his knees to accept them, to return their affection and feeling. "I shall miss you all, one and the same. But we shall be together again soon; trust me," and with the word 'trust' came smiles filled with joy, for Stephen could not lie to any of them, any more than he could lie to the Lord in Heaven.

Stephen glanced at the two knights, Martin and Raoul, and smiled, a final nod being exchanged. It was time for each to go their separate ways, grouped in their pairs as Stephen had ordered; Martin with Raoul, Lars with Aaron, and Lambert and Bernard with Stephen.

"Come, children," said Martin, "follow me now, for the nuns will take care of you until Stephen's triumphant return." The children turned and followed Martin, moving from the alley and into the fuller force of the gale that was brewing, and Raoul followed up from the rear whilst keeping an eye open for any one of them that might inadvertently fall behind. The other men looked upon Stephen as though some empowering hybrid, being of religion and military influence so grand that it could never be washed away.

"Aaron, you stay here with Lars, watch the brigantine and its crew as we discussed. You have a little time to play with, for the brigantine is still some distance away, but watch your step, all of you."

"Why, Stephen, why did you not say something to the harbour master, get him to ring the alarm?" asked Bernard.

"It is too hard to have them slaughtered, too hard to prove. I do pity them, for they know not of the devil within them, and besides, they might not be those that followed us during the first part of our journey, I am simply employing logic. The harbour master also needed to believe that he would be paid for our mooring." Stephen placed a comforting hand upon Aaron in reflection of Bernard's query. "Watch the children from a distance, and the heathen Turk most of all; remain safe, the Turks might wish to... see them. The last thing we need is for one or all of the children to fall captive."

Aaron smiled and stepped out from the shadow leaving Lars to shake hands with Stephen before he parted company. "Farewell, Lars. Partake of some refreshment if you so desire, but remain clear headed. The children must stay safe. And when I return I shall wish to know the whereabouts of the Turks. We need to understand fully their disposition in order to organise our getaway."

Lars nodded and retreated with Aaron into the growing storm as it continued to unveil itself.

"Which leaves just a few," added Stephen. "Let us find some shelter, far from here." And with that Bernard and Lambert followed with the chest carried between them both, heading out of the alley and then along the road to the north, the handles of the chest which they carried cutting into their palms, the cold tormenting their fingers, the effort praying a little upon their minds.

Some good fortune was to be had, however, for it was in their favour that the wind and rain lashed at their backs, the strength of the wind helping to carry them up the hills that they encountered during their short trek, a trek in which they were searching for one man of singular importance. They were seeking a priest, one that resided a short distance from town, several hours or more by foot, depending on the extremes of weather that they were to be confronted by.

*
* * *
*

The story of Aaron.

Aaron was nothing more than a peasant, of little interest to anyone except his mother, nothing of interest at all, in particular to a knight.

It was Sir Godfrey of Renne le Chateau, on the coast of the Mediterranean; he was straddled high upon his horse wearing his chain mail and basinet. The horse was a large white beast, a stallion from Spain, a heavy horse which commanded a heavy price. The knight had his sword sheathed, his left palm resting upon his thigh, and his right hand steered him effortlessly with reigns held loosely. Yes indeed, he and his horse were a grand affair, his horse the best of any breed, the largest horse Aaron had seen in his entire life, which for such a life had been long and hard, even though he was only 16 years old.

The knight was approaching his mother's farm with or without good reason, trespassing, which would be allowed such a large framed man at this time. Such a spectacle of a man on horse conveyed much importance and high authority and it would be best to let him pass without delay. This in itself brought much displeasure to Aaron for he was tired of being frowned upon, tired of the poor treatment that his cast were inappropriately given, but what choice did he have but to accept it.

The knight's horse walked on and the knight, whose name was currently unknown to Aaron, looked down upon the boy before bringing his horse to a stop. Aaron had been ploughing by hand a little of the field that it was his duty to attend this day. He was covered in sweat and patches of soil had stuck to his skin. His clothing fared no better and he stank of a foul odour.

His mother's farm was not large but extremely important for the wealth of the field was their only support in this miserable, contemptible life. The last thing they needed was for it to be turned upside down. As any other peasant, farmer, or undesirable, all they wished for was to be left alone, to tend their crops and chickens, to pursue their life, showering themselves in as much luxury as their wealth could afford: which was very little to none.

"Boy; who are you boy?" said the knight from high upon his horse, looking down upon Aaron with distaste in his mouth, his facial expression spelling out his thoughts on the peasant to his front as though he had spoken out loud. "Answer, for I am Sir Godfrey of Renne le Chateau. Do you know of me?"

Aaron was unsure of what to say, and whether or not he should; but he had been given permission. "No, sir, I do not; and my name is Aaron." Why should he know this stranger? If he had indeed ever come past this way before it was when neither he nor his mother were attending to the field. Was the name and title, Sir Godfrey or Renne le Chateau, of any particular significance?

The knight looked stunned for a brief moment for the boy named Aaron did not seem to shy too long from making a response, and when the response came it was strong and with much conviction. Such strength in character must be put in its place. If a peasant was allowed to muster too much confidence then knights of honour would be treated with little respect.

"Do I scare you boy? Me upon this horse, dressed in mail and passing through your farm without permission? Aye; I see it in your eyes, boy. I see that you care not for one as humble as me trespassing upon your land."

"It is not for me to like or dislike," said Aaron in reply, "for we are a peaceful family who would not dream of asking a fee from anyone passing across our land. There is no toll here, you may pass freely. Most would be content to use the road, but...." Aaron trailed off, having said too much.

"But what? Speak, boy, speak what you feel," insisted the knight. He remained steady upon his horse; the only muscles moving were those around his lips and upon his forehead.

"It is for the rich to make what they will of any given situation, to take what they want and to discard the rest. We are poor farmers who know no different. I have no concern for your presence upon my mother's land. You are free to pass as you so desire. It is not for me to comment or complain."

"Is that what I am, or simply represent?" asked the knight. "Am I rich beyond your wildest dreams?"

"You have a horse, a shield, and a sword," pointed out Aaron. "You have more than I ever shall."

"Ah, I see."

"But I am not afraid, as you can tell, so maybe I am stupid," said Aaron, thinking of his mother and their place in life. "If you wish to pass, then pass. I tend this field to bring us food. I can answer your questions but I must continue with my work."

"Where is your mother?" the knight saw Aaron look over his shoulder to the farm house. "Is she alone?"

"What is it you want from us?" asked Aaron with confidence. "Do you want food and water, something for your horse perhaps?"

"Company, boy. I want to touch female flesh," answered the knight as he eyed Aaron with contempt of his own, as Aaron now looked at him. "I see by the look in your eye that you understand my meaning; now get out of my way," and with hard kicking upon the frame of his horse he tried to move towards the farm house, wishing to push the horse on as fast as he could, but that first step was the hardest for Aaron had carried himself to action.

Suddenly, with the quickest of motion, Aaron swung the tool of his trade up and around his head, bringing it in hard against the horse's front legs as it pushed past him, bringing the monstrous mount down in a heap, the knight falling over the top of his horse and into the ploughed earth. It stunned Sir Godfrey for the shortest amount of time, time enough for Aaron to give warning.

"Mother! Mother!" yelled Aaron, calling out towards the small house, giving warning to his mother, for her to prepare herself by any means possible, for it was not his deplorable life that he cared, but for the life of the one that had given birth to him.

The knight got to his feet in what appeared slow motion, Aaron holding his tool across his body in a gesture of defence, but what defence can a stick of wood have against the sharpened edge of a broadsword? It was now that the first show of terror appeared on Aaron's face, but it was short lived for he dug deep and found the courage he was seeking, courage enough to carry out any necessary action, to defend his mother and her honour.

"You will now die, boy," said the knight as he drew on his sword, the gleaming metal being released of its darkened hold within its wooden sheath. The knight had two hands gripped firmly around his weapon. He seemed to command it well, even at this, the early stage of his assault upon the thin frame of Aaron. "For I am going to cut you to shreds and deal with you mother as I see fit. Her death will not be slow." The knight came upon Aaron swiftly, bringing his sword up above his head, to slash down upon the boy's skull, to split it in two. And as he commenced his action he could see the boy did not even flinch; he was steadfast, unafraid of what was to be. The sword came down and at the last moment Aaron stepped aside, the knight finishing his swing, the sword's edge cutting into the ploughed earth. Aaron lifted his foot and kicked out at the knight, his foot connecting with the knight's shoulder, forcing him down into the dirt once more. "You are heavy with armour, heavy with sword," said Aaron, "where I am quick on my feet and able to move freely." Aaron was confident in his speech, brave with his action, and above all, in command and control of his anger.

"I shall not make the same mistake twice, boy," said the knight from there upon the field, and as he got up he continued in essence, saying without further ado, "for I am an educated man, quick at thinking, fast to learn. You are a swine, yet I envy your fast action, and pity what you are about to suffer, for I shall make yours a slow death too."

Aaron could not contemplate any situation whereby this knight would have sufficient ill feeling towards him that death and rape should be the order of the day. "What are we to you, but poor farmers? Surely a knight as yourself could have any woman you desired... Ah." And Aaron understood. This knight fed on the terror he created, he fed himself with the knowledge that he could do as he pleased. He was probably a vagabond, travelling the country and doing as he pleased.

This was why Aaron should have reason to know him, for he was a wanted man: or possibly still, he had returned from war and had a taste for forced pleasure.

"That's right, boy, any I desire, and my lust if for rape."

"But, Sir Godfrey, you are forgetting one thing."

"And what is that?"

"My mother," and Aaron pointed to where his mother stood. Having heard her son call she had appeared at the door of their tiny house, had seen the calamity of the situation and had arrived at an easy decision. She had made an approach towards the scene of the knight and her son, had closed the gap so that she was within range. She now stood with a crossbow in her hand, a hunting weapon used for hunting by her deceased husband, a weapon capable of penetrating the mail that the knight wore. Even now, as the knight looked on, she stepped ever closer, making for a good target in order not to miss her mark.

"My mother is a veteran shot. She will not flinch," said Aaron coolly.

The knight stood fast. "You know that if you attempt to kill me that you will both suffer greatly and be hanged, by the noose of the rope I carry, and if you should let me go then I shall return. You cannot win."

"We are not afraid, sir knight," said Aaron with further contempt that fury built up within the knight to such a point that all he wanted to see was the boy's head on a pike. He scoffed and quickly sheathed his sword before mounting his horse with a little effort. "You have not seen the last of me. I shall return." He galloped off and the mother and son watched him disappear into the distance.

"We shall have to report this to the sheriff, otherwise we shall have no defence against any action that we are required to take against that monster," said Aaron to his mother as she stepped in beside him.

Later that same night the mother and son commenced to prepare for slumber when they heard a knock on the door of their house. They quickly stopped what they were doing and listened carefully, listening for any sign as to who it might be.

"Who is it?" asked the mother finally.

"The sheriff, I am here on business," came the steady reply. It was clear that the man on the other side of the door was making an effort to change the sound of his voice.

Aaron looked to his mother and shook his head for he was familiar with the sheriff's voice. "Just a minute," said Aaron in reply. "I am undressed and will be with you shortly."

He picked the crossbow from the wall and smoothly placed a quarrel in place upon the weapon. He nodded to his mother in the little light given off by the lantern, to unbolt the door for the knight to enter. She did so at arm's length and as the door came bursting open Aaron let loose with the quarrel. It was a blur to the eye, the shot of a lifetime, but the agony upon the face of the knight was one that would remain with them for the rest of their lives. He stood there, hunched over, both hands going to the aid of his wound, fingers wrapped around the shaft of the arrow that was now sticking out of his belly. His eyes were wide with shock and pain. The knight fell backwards through the open door, upon the floor, dead.

"We will be arrested for this," said the mother.

"No, it was in self-defence, and the sheriff was advised earlier of this man's evil doings."

"It does nptt matter, son. He has high status," said the mother, concerned.

"No man of high status does as he was going to do," came Aaron's reply. "We shall advise the sheriff in the morning, for now we must get some sleep."

"Do you think I can sleep with a dead man on my doorstep?"

"I shall move the body. But the sheriff must be advised in the morning."

The sheriff rode in beside Aaron, the sheriff upon his horse and Aaron upon the knights. Aaron rode it well and the sheriff noted this. Here beside him was a peasant on a knight's mount, riding along as though born in the saddle. The horrors of the day before were a memory that would be with him forever and a day, especially for his mother who was frail of mind and always concerned for her only son.

"You ride well, Aaron. Is this your first time upon a warhorse?"

"It is, sheriff," replied Aaron. "Why, am I doing something wrong?"

"No, not at all," said the sheriff, but he was lying and lying well. He held the smirk well from his face for Aaron looked as though he was trying to put command to a disobedient donkey.

A little more silence was confronted by both men as they continued towards the farm, the house coming to view on the horizon just a few minutes' ride away. The sun was high in the sky and it was fairly warm, a fresh breeze blowing in from the west.

"I see that you are still troubled," said the sheriff, picking up on the discomfort portrayed within Aaron's voice, noting the way in which he looked off into the distance.

"I am troubled by the grief it has brought my mother. She is fragile, particularly since the death of my father just last year," said Aaron. "She fears that there will be trouble, that I may be arrested for the death of the knight."

"You have nothing to fear, Aaron. You gave notification of the knight's demeanour earlier on. That's all the defence you need. There will not be any conviction."

"Will you tell my mother that?" asked Aaron. "It will instil confidence within her. It's what she needs right now."

"I shall, Aaron, I shall indeed. And further still I tell you more. The horse you ride no longer has an owner. You would do well to keep the horse, and far be it for me to say, but if I were you I would also keep the knight's mail and weapons. I know the idea might not appeal to you right now, but in a few years... why do you not just put his items of worth away, store them for the future. They will be worth much to any merchant that comes by this way. I shall even write you a note of possession so that none can say that you stole them."

"You are kind, sheriff."

"You deserve the spoils of the knights, in particular from one so filled with the devil." And Aaron thought upon it for a short time. He would store the items away, far from his mother's prying eyes, and one day he would use the possessions to his advantage. And that night he had a dream that surmounted all dreams. He dreamt of knighthood and conviction, of honour and strength, of courage and belief. He loved his mother dearly but hated working upon the farm. His mother was growing old and easily fell ill, in particular during winter. So it was written, there would come a time when the peasant would become a knight, a Knight of the Hospital, to serve mankind as best he could.

He was, in thought alone, a peasant no more.

*

* * *

*

Lars had soon found himself in an inn, a tavern which had gained his immediate attention, and entered without second thought, his crossbow carried in his left hand, quarrels sheathed in a quiver behind his shoulder. It had been a long time since a drop of liquor had passed his lips and all that he cared to do was partake of a small measure to warm his weary bones. He knew that there was plenty of time before the enemy boat could pull into safe harbour, and knew in all realistic terms that he had plenty of time to share with a tankard of full-bodied mead. He entered the premises and Aaron followed close behind, the murky, dark surrounds coming slowly to view as lanterns lit the way for them both.

The smell from within struck them both hard for they were used to the freshness of the sea breeze, not the pissed on floor and beverage-drenched bar, tables and chairs. There was little to no fresh air to speak of in the small tavern, except what managed to find its way in when the door was opened, allowing patrons in and out.

Lars approached to make a purchase, pushing past a few that were seated, one man getting up from his seat as Lars made way to quench his thirst.

"Damn you, old man. Watch where you step," said the rasped voice of the once seated form of a man, well accustomed to strong drink, his iron throat giving way to a deep and threatening groan.

Lars turned to look at the tall man of scarred features and beard and announced without further ado his apology, “Ooo, ooo.”

The man stood silent for a split second and then burst out into bouts of laughter, bending over as though in pain, his comrades, all three, soon joining in on the action. What they saw in front of them was an old man who had taken too much of a liking to rum, having drunk so much in his life that his voice had escaped him completely. Was he a fool or simply drunk out of his mind? A man, who could not speak, could not ask for a drink.

Aaron put his sword hand onto the man’s shoulder, seeing a little misunderstanding pass over all four. Who were they to know of Lars’ courage, of the work that he had achieved upon the walls of Constantinople, the prowess of his sword work when in the company of other Teutonic Knights.

“Please forgive my captain, for he has no tongue,” said Aaron with the sincerest of looks upon his face.

With that spoken all of the men continued laughing uncontrollably, and the one that was standing asked a question to incite further fun and jocularity. “Your captain! You mean to say you follow the orders of a twit who speaks of ‘Oooooo’?” the sailors four were having a grand time at someone else’s expense, treating a hero with as much disrespect as they could muster.

The group could not contain themselves and others in the tavern looked on from their places, not understanding what the commotion was about and suddenly, without further ado, Aaron had withdrawn his sword from his sheath. The noise died immediately and the stranger who stood stepped back, pulling his sword from a wooden scabbard, a short sword which was no match for Aaron’s carver of flesh. The silence that filled the room that minute could be cut with a dagger.

The bar wench also stopped cleaning the tumbler she held in her hands and watched in anxious wait for something to happen, even though the last thing she wanted was a fight amongst her patrons. She had seen enough blood spilt upon the floor of the tavern to know that little business was to be gained from such pitiful affairs. Fighting never amounted to anything but a mess which had to be cleaned up.

“Please, good men, I shall not take well to anyone who spoils this day,” said the woman with much confidence but little command, for the two men with swords drawn were ready to throw each other into a melee where there could be only one victor.

“One minute I am minding my own business and the next I am being pushed around for no good reason!” Shouted the offended man with a beard. “He has drawn a sword against me.”

“For your cowardly way,” voiced Aaron.

The stalemate was not to last long and within just a few short breaths the next stage of the confrontation was to take place: and now for action or in-action, for the man had been shown up in front of his friends. If he fought then he could save face, if he did nothing, he would be frowned upon.

"This man has also shamed me!" said the sailor, looking around to all of those that were seated, in particular to the three men that sat at his table. He could not afford to lose face amongst his friends, for steady friends in the dark of a tavern were hard to come by, unless you were used to buying drinks.

The bar wench spoke further, "I shall shame you too, Martin, if you should not sit yourself down this minute, and I shall ban you from my premises, do you hear?"

"Your husband shall hear of this, that is what I know. Who are you to tell me what to do?" said Martin, who did not take his eyes off the strangers.

"My husband will have to sleep with another if he wants pleasure tonight; do you think he is as stupid as you?"

"I wish an apology from this man who dares draw a sword against me," continued Martin, refusing to allow the situation to simmer, for he had much to lose.

Lars grabbed Aaron by the left arm, "Ooo," and shook his head. This was neither the time nor the place for causing alarm amongst a town which they did not know. How many soldiers were there in town, how many under the arm of the law, ready to bring any undesirable under total control? They could not afford to push the situation further afield. They must apologise.

"My captain advises me against action today, so you can consider yourself in good fortune." And as Aaron went to sheath his weapon, Martin drew his sword arm backwards and prepared to kill the Hospitaller. Suddenly, and in quick as a flash, Lars reached up and behind his shoulder, grasped an arrow and thrust it down into the chest of Martin.

The man screamed and all others remained seated, silent and struck dumb, such speed and unfamiliar action being witnessed. Lars let go of the arrow and it remained in place. The sailor known as Martin dropped his sword and went to the aid of his wound.

"Ah, you filth monger, you have tried to kill me." He pulled the arrow from its mark, throwing it to the floor. Blood started to flow freely from the wound but quickly brought under control by the placement of his right palm. He stepped back and picked up his sword with his left hand and sheathed it. Aaron and Lars noted that his left hand was not his master hand and allowed him the opportunity to place his weapon away, content in the knowledge that no further action was going to take place.

Aaron looked the man in the eye, then at his friends, and to Martin again. "If my good captain wished to kill you, you would be dead. Please consider yourself lucky, for your life has been spared this day."

"I shall have the sheriff informed," sobbed Martin as he continued to hold his wound with an open palm upon his chest, "and you will be gaoled. You have attacked me without provocation and justice will be served. I have witnesses."

Aaron looked around at the silence and then to the bar wench. "It was in self-defence," said he to all that were listening. "You all could see how this man attempted to attack me openly with his drawn weapon."

"Aye, I saw the whole thing," said the bar wench, who wanted nothing more than to draw a quick and final conclusion to the current unrest. She was in the business of making money, not to give a man the opportunity to spill blood over her tavern's floor at every moment that he stepped through the door.

"I have been coming here for many years now, have I not?" asked Martin. "Does that not count for something? Surely the money I have spent here over the years will be sufficient enough to provide some consolation."

The bar wench again stopped what she was doing. "You are no longer welcome here. Again I say, the company you provide me and the others has expired and you are no longer welcome; I have a reputation to keep," she said. "If you come here again then it will be with an apology of your own. I will not allow blood to be spilled in my tavern; not upon its floors, tables, or anywhere else, which includes at the door."

"And of my friends?"

"They may stay or go, 'tis for them to decide."

Martin looked and half pleaded with his comrades, a final effort on his behalf to try and save face, to pry his comrades from their seats, to get them on his side once more.

"Will you not come with me, leave this dump for what it is; there are plenty of other places for which to get a drink."

"Then go," said one of the seated, "for we have all had enough of your company. You insult many and console few; you have a character of which we all grow tired." And with those words spoken, Martin did depart.

Aaron and Lars gave a silent nod to the seated three and continued to the bar. They were happy to see that Martin was no longer a threat to their presence. They could easily tell that the other three men did not wish to cause any further alarm.

*

* * *

*

Stephen led Bernard and Lambert up the cobbled way as the sky commenced to turn dark, lightning striking the earth with the loudest of cracks and illuminating the area with instantaneous bright light; the storm was upon them. There was a little hail to commence the cracking of thunder above their heads but this soon subsided. They had no time to consider finding shelter for the task they had set themselves, to be completed as soon as possible. The chest of secrets needed to reach its destiny, a house of relatively large proportion that only Stephen knew, and as they continued on their way the cobbled road turned to dirt and the dirt turned to mud. "If we are lucky we shall escape the storm undamaged," said Stephen, "regardless of blinding wind and hail," for he had the foresight to see the things to come, but had not yet mastered his visions completely. They were like moving pictures inside his head, some were blurred and others as clear as day.

"How far, Stephen?" asked Bernard, growing concerned for their wellbeing, for the storm was dampening his faith in the miracles to be unearthed. It was understandable, in the current climate, that such doubt should exist, for they had all suffered much in the voyage from Káros to Barcelona. The sea they had battled on a weekly basis, coming under the threat of being sunk on more than one occasion. It was only through sheer will and courageous effort that they had survived the long trip in such a small boat.

"Not far," answered Stephen without disturbing his stride towards his destination. "We shall be at the house soon enough. Father Ambaedian has lodging in a reformed school not so far from here, a home now for old sailors with nothing more to do with their time than to drink and be merry. Father Tourmede shared much with me in the little time we had together." He reflected momentarily on the priest from Káros and what he had to say of Father Ambaedian. "But it is not all from the father that I can be grateful, for I can see a picture of the house within my head, as though I have seen it a hundred times."

Bernard questioned Stephen's third eye, "How can you be sure? How do you know that what you see is the house that we are looking for?"

And continuing without turning back to look at the two men carrying the chest Stephen answered, "Because the Lord has provided me with a gift, and although I am learning to use it, it has not yet let me down. I must follow my vision as though it is a map that I hold within my hand. It is not far, we must continue on as best we can. Time is not on our side."

The wind commenced to grow, a thunder clap being heard, and hail, like tiny stones, fell once more from the sky once more, but only briefly; and they were thrashed. Bernard and Aaron held their free hand over the face as they continued and Stephen said unto himself, 'and the way will be molested by thrashing grains'.

"It comes from nowhere," yelled Lambert above the noise of the storm. "Never before have I witnessed such a squall as this. It must be something that the devil has created." Stephen fell into stride beside the two men with chest, failing to have heard correctly what Lambert had said.

"And where do you think such a storm comes?" questioned Stephen.

"I hate to admit, but lie I cannot; I see the Lord laughing down upon us, teaching us a lesson for something we have done, or are about to do. Either that or the devil has laid command over the skies and is trying to delay us for one reason or another."

"You fail to see Him as I do, Lambert; for the Lord has made this storm from nothing and for good reason."

"And for what reason, may I ask?"

"For the storm would have reached its worse long before the brigantine would have had the chance to moor. The storm is our salvation. God is protecting us from those of Muslim faith. He is providing us with the time we need to get us to our destination."

*
* * *
*

The story of Martin.

The battle had been won, they were successful. The songs of victory were carried upon the wind and across the battlefield for all to hear, the last of the slain laying with their heathen comrades upon the desert ocean, upon the carpet of red that now dominated the area. The dead lay upon the field like locusts cover a crop, where a man cannot walk from one side of the battlefield to the other without falling over a corpse. Dead horses were laying upon men, men upon horses; where you saw one you saw the other, each blending in to form one miserable sight, a mass of slaughter, enough to bring vomit to the lips of anyone that lived.

Martin was a young soldier, a man who had the full intention of becoming more than just a follower; he wanted to be a leader of men, or at least amongst those that were considered as elite. He had ability and strength, courage and skill. But now… he was sickened by the slaughter. He had finally had enough. His station within the desert was a hard one, but boring to say the least. Sure, a few battles here and there lifted his spirits slightly, but he had not yet, until this day, felt that he had served the Lord as the Lord should be served. But this, it was the battle of all battles; it went beyond the call to service.

He was kneeling, slumped beside one of the last to die, a Muslim with a thick line of hair upon his upper lip and a week's growth upon his chin. He had been skewered well by Martin, who himself had been wounded in the upper left arm. The wound was not deep but very painful, pain which was only now beginning to take hold, for before now the adrenalin had been pumping so ferociously throughout his body that it was even hard to control his action, even minutely so. He had fought well, taking his opponents one at a time, defeating each as they fell upon him, the Turk doing all he could to take his life as Martin did all he could to protect it.

His commander drew up alongside the man under his command, on foot and scouring the battlefield to check on the victory, looking for wounded enemy to torture and friendly soldiers that might need medical attention.

"I know you by name, do I not? Martin I believe."

"That is correct, sir. I am Martin."

"Are you alright? Can you walk?"

"I can, sir, I can walk from here to the end of the earth for any task, if such a task is worth the effort," said Martin, the sadness of his voice coming to air.

"You sound defeated, somewhat lacking in spirit," said the commander. "Are you hurt badly? Are you tired?"

"I am tired, sir, that is the answer," and Martin turned to look up to the man looking down upon him. "I am tired of the killing and this sodden desert. I thought I wanted more, to serve the Lord by slaying his enemy." Martin had had enough. There was no more to experience in life but death itself. "But I have had enough of the heat and the flies, the maggots and stale bread. If there was a purpose to the death and slaughter then I could live with it, but this is insane."

"You speak of treason, Martin. I would calm my voice down if I were you. You will get yourself a field punishment if you are not careful of what you say, and be careful of whom you say it in front of." The commander relaxed on his verbal assault and looked over the battlefield briefly, seeing wounded men getting up from their knees, picking up their swords, dragging a dagger across the throat of some of the wounded. "There is much slaughter here today, I must see to it that no more wounded are killed before they have been properly interrogated, but please, tell me, what is it that will tend to your... wounds? What will bring you comfort?"

Martin looked to his commander and stood up, coming eye to eye, and speaking his whole hearted truth he said to his commander, "I wish to be provided another station. I hear that the Hospital is seeking recruits. It is here that I wish to serve, to be charitable instead of blood thirsty. If there is the slightest hope that I can do more for mankind than I currently do then I must do it. Look around you, sir. What do you see? Slaughter to the likes that no man should witness, and what for? A station within the desert, a small outpost that serves nobody, not even the pilgrims that travel to this holy land. Yes, it is the holy land.

It is here that I must serve. I must serve the people as the people serve us. They till the land and grow the crops; they feed this great army and feed us well. The commerce of our homeland is supplied by the peasants of our country, and how do we thank them? I do not see the point in fighting over a few yards of blood-soaked desert, nor in the downfall of Islam unless it pays us well by bringing belief and honour to us all."

"Belief and honour," said the commander. "Do you honestly believe there is no honour in what we do? We serve the Lord by bringing death to the heathen. They are sacrilegious devils who do not deserve to draw a single breath of air as provided by God."

"I am sorry, sir, but I have had enough. I cannot kill any more unless such killing is in the defence of something righteous; I cannot and will not. Do you not see the lack of purpose? There is no good will in what we do."

The commander looked again over the field of slaughter, taking the view in, like he had not done before. He reflected momentarily on the dead and dying, of the good cause of what had been achieved.

"Victory is ours, that is achievement enough," said the commander. "But I recall a little of the service you have paid, of your honour and duty bound moralistic servitude. I shall grant you what you wish. I shall call you to a meeting later. When you are called then you must come." His commander turned to depart but stopped and faced him one more time. "It would be wise to keep your opinions to yourself, for others will not look upon you with the favour I am about to bestow."

Martin was called into the tent as it stood upon the sands of the desert, one of many that had been erected not far from the battlefield, an administrational city of tents. The commander was seated before him, and next to him sat a priest. The priest was dressed in the regalia of a knight of the Hospital. He was not a big man, as he was prone to pray rather than to fight. A large cross hung around his neck on a thick chain; a bible sat before him upon the small table, slightly to the side but within easy reach.

"Martin, This man beside me is Father Alfred, he runs a sacred mission in the Aegean Sea, not far from Greece, but far from conflict."

Martin looked at the man with a nod of his head, "Good afternoon, father."

"I am happy to meet you, my son," said the priest. "I have been advised that you grow sour at the killing and wish to be tested with something more worthy. I also hear that court martial looms on the wind for one such as yourself, but I have been advised," and with that spoken looked to Martin's commander with acknowledgment, "that you are indeed worthy of the good right, the right to be recruited into an arm of the Order of the Hospital that I believe will serve you well.

Yes, it will serve you well as you must serve it." The priest sat back relaxed before continuing. "There is not much fighting where I come from, but there is plenty of prayer. There is no bloodshed, no pilgrims, no horses or other beasts restricted by collar; but there is still plenty of work to be done."

Martin could not believe his ears. He had come so close to execution for his sour words that he could barely believe what he was hearing. "Why would you, father, wish to help one like me, who should be nothing more than a condemned man? Why should I be worthy of your presence at such a time as this?"

"Let me simply say that I serve the Lord as I believe you wish to serve. I have many ears and in many camps. Many men carry my sacred banner, which is to justify each man's existence, never to condemn anyone without good cause. If you can serve better, elsewhere, then who am I to turn a blind eye? If you can serve charitably then you should be given that opportunity."

Martin looked coolly from his commander to the priest. Here before him was his saviour. At present it appeared too good to be true, but it all sounded very adventurous. If it was true, and his commander was indeed the eyes and ears of the priest, it stood to good reason that the priest knew exactly who he was getting to serve him. To serve in the Order renowned for its charity, to serve the Lord, and further still, to serve in a special arm of the Order of the Hospital.

"Father Alfred," said Martin, "I shall not let you down."

"That is to be seen, my son," said the priest, "but I believe my eyes and my heart. I am an old man but not without my brains and ability to think clearly. I know a good man when I see one." The priest picked up the bible and passed it to Martin, who took it up in his hands. "This is your ticket. It is a special book and will be recognised by certain members of our staff. Any of our Order will recognise it. You can show it as required on your journey to Káros. The book will give you free passage and enough food to relieve your hunger. With this book comes your salvation into an Order that cannot be spoken amongst strangers or friends. You must not tell others of this meeting here today. I shall see you in Káros within the fortnight of your arrival. You may go now."

Martin stood with the book in his hand. "Thank you, father," he said. "I shall go with as much speed as I can muster."

"Quickly, in here," shouted the nun against the wind which rattled the thick-set door upon its hinges as it was opened. A little rain stung at her face, the storm commencing to grow more ferocious as each minute in time passed them by, a little flooding and damage to buildings the obvious outcome, for none had witnessed such a storm in all their life. If the storm continued as it was then the town folk were in for a hard weekend. "Come children, as quickly as you can, before you are drenched to the bone."

As the children passed through the door, Martin stood to one side. "Thank you, Sister."

"Later, my son," she said whilst looking over the group of children, seeing their appalling condition, drenched to the bone and dressed in near rags. "Get the children to the fire, quickly now."

The children were gathered around the open fire place of the large hall. Martin and Raoul looked around the den of hope, Lois and Catherine standing before them. "Go and join the other children, you are as they are, orphans," said Martin. The child named Catherine did not budge but just stood there, looking at the two men as though each were a commander in chief.

"We are more than that," said Catherine. "We are one and the same with Stephen. He is our Lord and master.

"This is not a game, child," added Raoul. "Until we hear from Stephen himself we must stay here and abide by the house rules, and... ah, Sister." He flicked Catherine aside with fingers, flapping them in front of her face, hoping she would do as she was directed, to take the nun's prying eyes away from her.

"Good evening... well, not that grand, but our fire will keep you warm for the time being. I am Sister Bardwell. There are five of us here. The others are tending to the children of the orphanage at this time," the Sister looked down upon Catherine who had taken a few steps back. "You may go child, join the others. A bowl of soup will be served soon."

"Yes, Sister, thankyou," and the child was happy with the invitation that had reached her ears, for a good bowl of hot soup had not passed her lips for so very long.

"Thirteen children and an escort of two," Sister Bardwell added as Catherine joined the others around the fireplace, Lois coming up to stand at her side. "From where do you come?"

"Far from here, Sister," said Martin. "We commenced our journey from Constantinople."

"Oh, what is the news?"

"It has fallen."

"Oh, my dear Lord. Such a crime against the church this is. All of those poor souls." Sister Bardwell looked to both the men, seeing for the first time their dress. "I see you are armed sailors. Tell me; did they suffer? Did many escape?"

"Many boats filled with souls did make it into the Aegean and beyond but many more were slaughtered under the long arm of Mehmet and his criminals. We were lucky to make it out," lied Martin, for he was from Káros, not Constantinople, but their masquerade must be maintained. “Some fled to Pera, some were cut off in withdrawal. But that is of little consequence now. We have these children, Sister. They need to be cared for until such a time that our master can return with news.”

“Master? News of what?”

“The children will be delivered to a safe haven not too far from here, but such accommodation cannot be secured without our master’s approval,” said Raoul. “He does not intend to provide the children with a home unless such can accommodate them as they should be accommodated.”

“So you do not wish to deliver these children to this orphan-age?” she looked around the room they were in. “A convent it is but we tend to children’s needs like any good Christian. But what of the children; they are to become... what exactly?”

“They are to be educated and housed in a school that only our master knows. He shall return within a few days, certainly no longer than a few weeks,” said Raoul. There was also the situation with money, for they had none. “But, Sister, we cannot pay, but work we can.”

“Work, ah. Well, there is plenty of that to go around. I shall introduce you to the Mother Superior after the children have partaken of their breakfast in the morning and you two gentlemen have had time to dry yourselves in front of the fireplace, and sufficiently rested.”

“Thank you, Sister. Your charity is most humbly accepted.”

“Not at all. Now, I shall attend to something for you and the children to eat, after which I shall leave you two gentlemen till morning breaks,” and with that said she disappeared through one of the four doorways connected to the main hall.

Later that night the Sister approached the Mother Superior and advised her of the two men and thirteen children. The Mother Superior’s mind, being an administrator, counsellor, and servant of God, never stopped in its processing of information. What she had heard the Sister speak of did not entirely make her at ease with the situation. It seemed quite unrealistic that such a master, as the one the two men spoke of, should have the need to venture further in land in an endeavour to secure a home for thirteen orphans so far from Constantinople. There seemed to be very little planning and many errors in the scenario that had been painted for her: why did they decide not to stop at another port? Why travel so far? She would dwell on it all tonight; consider, with much thought, everything that had been disclosed to her, for the children’s future was most important.

*
* * *
*

A man seemingly drunk and half mad burst through the door of the inn. The wind and torrential rain followed his entry into the comfort of the premises. All heads and eyes turned to the scene as the man attempted to shut the door behind him.

"Close that door, damn you," cried the bar wench, for the wind was strong and made the candles flicker with unease, the coldness of the night rolling through the air thick with smoke, striking at the faces of those partaking of beverage.

"Aye," the sailor complied with much effort, and with the door finally shut he turned his attention to those that looked on in bewilderment. "The storm rages. Many boats are being smashed to smithereens. There is no escaping it."

"Come here and buy a drink," insisted the bar wench, eager to make another sale.

"Aye; sounds inviting," said the man as he licked his lips and made out with quick stride towards the wench as she poured him a tumbler of her finest.

Aaron looked to Lars. "I think it's time we departed, to see for ourselves what the storm had brought us." Lars nodded in agreement.

Aaron looked at the woman. "Thankyou for the warmth you so nobly provided us, but we must commence our journey."

"In this weather?" asked a drunken sod, ease-dropping in the conversation. "You are fools. I just witnessed the true horrors of the sea; there is no escaping it," his eyes were as round as pieces of gold.

Aaron slapped a coin upon the counter and the sailor eyed it greedily.

"I see you are well endowed," he said.

"We look after ourselves as we see fit, and with our thirst quenched we shall retire and seek shelter. But first we must see to our boat, see whether she is still moored safety upon the pier or not"

"Here," said the bar wench. "Nothing wrong with my place, is there? I have plenty of room and board, rooms for the likes that the king of any country would be happy to spend the night."

"A most deserving premise, I am sure, but my companion and I must seek out our friends," added Aaron. "We thank you for the information."

"Well come back soon, and bring your friends; so long as no tab is sought for what you should drink." And with that Lars and Aaron stepped from the counter and towards the door, the offer of room and board tucked deep in their heads, for they might well desire to change their mind.

"Work, work I seek," said a drunkard sailor, grabbing onto Aaron's sleeve.

"We have no time and little to pay," said Aaron as he attempted to move past the sailor, grabbing the man's hand and pushing it aside.

"A coin would do you well to pay, for I have something for you," said the sailor, a twinkle in his eyes appearing as he looked into Aaron's face directly.

Aaron and Lars looked at the man and decided to listen, for they were new in town and could do with all the help they could muster. "Speak quickly for our time is short," said Aaron, seemingly displeased that his departure had been disturbed.

"I wonder," teased the sailor, "if your arm might be long enough to find something for me in your dark and deep pocket?" for the promise of coin was a subject most favoured.

"If what you speak pleases me then you shall be given your just reward."

The sailor looked around, left and right. "A man hides amongst the shadows, to the left as you exit the inn, well out of storm's way he cowers. Saw him with my own eyes, I did. Very suspicious that one, standing there like a statue, not bothering to find better shelter from the storm and cold air."

Aaron smiled. "And does this man have a sword sheathed or ready for action."

"Ready for action, as far as I could tell," said the sailor holding out an open palm, hoping for it to be filled with a just reward.

Aaron reached into his pocket and withdrew a coin for the drunkard. "Take this as your payment for services rendered," and the sailor went to turn tail. "But before you spend what you have been provided, listen to me closely."

The sailor came close, head hung to the left. "What is it?"

"We shall be in town for a few days; your help would be rewarded in the future as it is today."

"Thank you, kind friend, I shall keep my eyes open for you; and my name is John." Both knights smiled, and then Aaron and Lars made for the door.

Abu could not believe his luck, which to date was secured through his cunning ways and masterful skills as seaman and commander; but this storm was whipped from nothing, grew from a pleasant breeze to a deadly gale in minutes, cloud as dark as the darkest of nights covering the sky in what seemed to be seconds. So close to harbour they were, to moor their stolen vessel upon European soil, to mingle with the Latin of this land, to pursue the chest of secrets. Never before had he seen or heard of such terror as that which they now experienced, and suddenly, out of nowhere, a wave as freakish as a mental woman with pointed nails, came crashing down upon them. Their masts were snapped like twigs from a dead tree, many men crushed as they fell upon the deck, others were washed overboard to drown in the Mediterranean, and so close to shore. It was the wrath of God, but why? And as suddenly as that question pierced his mind, lightning struck at the ship in several places, catching it on fire.

Men ran here and there, but with no sails to aid them they were dead in the water, crippled and unable to steer, unable to defend against the hail, wind, and fury. Their boat continued to close the gap between themselves and the moored vessels of Barcelona, the harbour so close that they could almost touch it, and with the closing-of-the-gap came the look of terror within each of the sailor's eyes for they were heading on a collision course with a singular rock formation that jutted out from the sea near the entrance to the coastal city. Like a sentry, this pinnacle of rock seemed to be stationed for a single purpose, as though planted there for a reason; their destruction.

Sailor's screamed orders, messages passed from one to the other, but none were heard or acted upon; it was every man for himself. Men clambered over the fallen masts of the ship, trying with such great effort to escape the horrors of the night, the thrashing sea, and the torment of the fire that was not contained by the rain, for it shrugged off all restraint. The boat moved with the sea, up and down, side to side, the hull being hit hard by wave after wave, a beating which did not cease.

Suddenly they crashed into the rock formation, the bow breaking and letting a torrent of water into the hold. Men jumped frantically from the deck and into the waters of the Mediterranean, so close to land but so far, for even the best of swimmers – which were few – had trouble breaking the surface of the sea as they swam for their lives. It was a miracle in itself that anyone could muster the power to swim in the storm, but a handful made their way to shore and upon their minds they knew why they had suffered, for Abu had ordered that they refrain from prayer, to put their religion behind them. Their commander was to blame for their demise; he solely had condemned them to death. This was their punishment for their individual heinous act against their god, refusing to pay homage where homage should be paid. And to those that made the shore; they looked upon their delivery from hell as a gift from God, and to Him they silently prayed. God had saved them, but what of the others? God had not saved anything but a handful. And of all the men that were boarded upon the stolen vessel only five had survived; Abu, Ahmad, Ibrahim, Mollet, and Sherif. And not a single one of them could understand how it was they, Abu's favourites, that had survived the ordeal at sea. How was it possible that a handful of chosen could escape death when everyone else did succumb to the power of nature at its worst. It was as though written, but this is the way the thrown dice had landed. A coincidence, was after all, just a coincidence. Was it possible that having been together at the time of the disaster, saved them all, by the choicest of thrashing waves delivering them to safety. They alone had made it to shore and were thankful for their lives having been spared. And as they crawled upon the beach, being thrashed continuously by waves, they managed to get far enough from the waters of the Mediterranean in order to catch their breath, but they had no time to waste, no time to rest where they lay.

They each stood and looked out upon the sea, looking for their boat, but it could not be seen.

*
* * *
*

Aaron stepped out into the cold and slash of hail first, his sword drawn and held vertical in front of his body, and just as well, for the shadows revealed the man in wait, who's slashing sword was parried easily by Aaron, and as quickly as the two swords struck, the cowardly man did run off into hiding. Aaron simply watched on as the figure of a man disappeared into the dark of the night.

Aaron laughed out loud, "It seems as though a fledgling has fled to fight another day." Lars pulled on Aaron's sleeve to grasp his attention. Lars pointed off into the distance as the boats within the harbour smashed against one another. Their carrack could not be seen, having been sunk quickly, taken in by the hungry sea. Anything that they wanted from on board would now be denied them. They both looked at the empty mooring where their boat had been put to rest. They did not know it had sunk, simply thought it had been stolen, taken by the harbour master or one of his accomplices. It was clear to them, from the lack of what they saw, that the harbour master was to be held responsible, but they could not be concerned over it at present, for other more meaningful tasks awaited their undivided attention. Aaron looked Lars in the eye. "I once heard a Wiseman say that no one should be burdened by heavy possession." He sheathed his sword.

Lars then led the way and Aaron followed, keeping his head up and looking around, seeking the dark of shadows for those that might be in wait as they headed for the harbour. They approached quickly and saw in the distance, and just in time, the enemy ship as she sank, the brigantine being swallowed up by the sea around it. Closer to shore, a few sailors' heads could be seen bobbing up and down amongst the waves before they disappeared, and there, not too far away, a few persons had dragged themselves out of the sea, onto a formation of rock and sand that was being washed by the waters of the

Meditteranean. It could be none other than those that had been chasing them these past months.

Lars in particular could not believe his luck, for the enemy had been delivered into his hand. He saw this as nothing less than a great opportunity. They had never locked eyes upon one another before, but who else could it be that would be swimming amongst the waves of this powerful storm, if not from the sunken brigantine. He shook the sleeve of Aaron and pulled him, and headed towards the flank of the pier where normally would be found a beach of pearl, white sand. They ran as fast as they could, their angle of sight no longer allowing them to see the bodies of the men now washed ashore, and no sooner had the Muslims themselves been beached upon the sandbars of Barcelona, and looked out upon the surface of the sea, then they rushed for cover beneath the pier some distance away to gather themselves some courage and shelter from the storm, the thrashing waves continuing, bashing against their thighs from time to time, the waves rolling in and out with great force. The shelter of the pier would provide immediate cover from the rain but not the sea, and also provide them the time to make plans for their next move.

Meanwhile, Lars and Aaron moved closer towards the underbelly of the pier, unable to see clearly in the storm and shadow, unable to consider their enemy in wait. They stepped well clear of the waves as best they could, as each crashed themselves upon the shore, each of the men wading no deeper than their upper thighs at any given time. They were currently side by side, straining to see clearly into the shadows formed of the pier, where the higher ground and built up dune of sand provided for easier movement and less wave.

"They will be tired from the swim ashore," said Aaron to Lars. "You stay here, Lars, and I will move towards them; try to flush them out. Be ready with your crossbow, for it is our only advantage."

"Ooo," agreed Lars, preparing a quarrel, placing it upon his weapon of choice. Aaron moved towards the space beneath the pier, the hail having subsided, but the stinging rain continued unabated. He caught a glimpse of something, the metal blade of a sword, a little twinkle of light from the stars above had been handed a temporary reprieve from their concealment above the clouds, just enough for Aaron to be advantaged by the grace of God. The knight stopped, just yards separating him from the hidden.

"Come out so that I may see you," Aaron was brave and particularly mindful of Lars, who stood some distance behind, upon a small rock and with his crossbow ready with quarrel. "We seek to know who has followed us these many miles, to see for ourselves who dares—"

Mollet leapt like a startled gazelle from beneath the pier as the other four withdrew out of the other side, his sword held in two hands above his head, slicing down in action to deliver a deadly blow upon Aaron.

The scream from Mollet struck Aaron hard, but the scream soon fell into silence, Mollet's body struck hard by an arrow from Lars, and the downward thrust of his sword missed Aaron by mere inches as the body fell to the ground. Mollet had been slain with as much ease as one scratches an irritating itch.

Aaron let out with a great exhale and rushed into the darkness, and as the pier's shadow covered him from view, Lars' dashed forward to stand by his friend's side, shifting his crossbow into position behind his back as he moved, pulling his sword from its sheath in preparation for further action.

Lars drew alongside Aaron who simply looked out from beneath the pier, "Gone but not forgotten. They have gotten away, Lars. I could not see them clearly as they would have seen me, and you with your crossbow will be hard to miss in a crowd. Maybe you should consider leaving it here," for he was much concerned for their safety, in particular when their surroundings were so unfamiliar.

Lars shook his head. Although he had a sword, as any other man would have, he dare not part with his third arm, the crossbow and the quarrels that fed it.

"I think we should gain shelter from this foul weather. Do you feel up to going back to the tavern so humble?"

Lars nodded acceptance.

"Let us take turns in sleeping tonight; I do not trust room-and-board when so many enemies are prowling about, but at least we know that a room can be gained from the tavern, even if just for the night."

Abu waited for the others to gather amongst the shadows of the buildings surrounding them, the rain was dissipating and the thunder was rolling on, further afield and away from them at long last.

"That stupid Mollet," cursed Abu. "What manner of man tempts to take on a crossbow from such a distance?"

"He was right to do as he did," stated Sherif. "In fact, we should all have rushed the two men. We would have been victorious: if not so worn and tired."

Abu looked at the man in silence and shook his head. "You, all of you are impossible. They knew who we were which means only one thing, they were who we sought, and being the case are needed alive. How are we supposed to find the chest without them? Ibrahim, Ahmad, Sherif: ah; how do we proceed without them?"

"Well, there is no following now," added Ahmad. "The two have gone, lost forever."

"Again, a eunuch when it comes to foresight, and with only one eye in your head to see, Ahmad, you are almost useless to our cause." Abu was tiring of their stupidity. Ahmad rubbed consciously at the scar upon his socket, where his left eye used to be. "The one with the crossbow looks to me to be at one with war. A man of such age and still clinging to a crossbow knows not of peace and sanctity. Find the crossbow and we find the chest."

"Shall we go now and seek the crossbow?" asked Ibrahim.

"No," said Abu. "We shall wait until the weather clears and split into two groups. We shall find them if it takes us all week. I do not care how long it takes in fact; I want that chest in our possession."

*
* * *
*

The story of Lambert.

Lambert stood guard at the door to Constantine's palace, a great honour of which he was proud to serve. The populace of Constantinople served their emperor with heart and soul; he too served with no less conviction. He was not regarded as having any great wealth in the form of status but his position was much sought after. The privileged station provided much news on the disposition and state of Byzantium as well as regular pay and good food. And where a man was single, as he, a room for the likes that a peasant would kill for was provided, even if it was nothing more than a disused stable, though refurbished for man of flesh.

Lambert had been in the service of Constantine for many years and in that time had journeyed with him into many territories, both those that belonged to Byzantine and those that belonged to the enemy. He was not a stranger to fighting and had drawn his sword on many occasions to fight off an assault directed at his emperor, his sword having spilled much blood during the time he had been assigned to the emperor's personal bodyguard. It was now that his supreme commander and emperor of Constantinople, called for a personal audience with him, man to man, no other present.

Lambert was directed into the dining room where Constantine sat at one end of a long table. Two places had been set, and although not common, the two places set were at right angles, Lambert's seat being on the right of where Constantine sat.

Constantine stood and greeted the common soldier as the great wooden doors closed behind him, the personal servant to the emperor stepping backwards as the doors were pulled shut.

"Please, Lambert. Come in and have a seat," said Constantine, his voice calm and without pressure, a soft tone of friendship easily noted.

"Thank you, my Lord," replied Lambert of the invitation.

He drew alongside the table and sat as did Constantine, many platters of food already in place for the private meeting to take place. Several glasses sat empty above where a plate was positioned, empty and waiting to be filled. Bottles of wine were also present, ready to be poured, which the emperor did for them both, filling one of Lambert's glasses first and then his own.

"Lambert, how many years have you served me now?"

"Many, my Lord, at least five, possibly a little more," answered Lambert. "Time goes so fast when you enjoy what you do, my Lord, and serving you has been nothing less than a great honour.

"And how many battles have we been in, you by my side, warding off the enemy when one strayed too close?"

"Too many, my Lord. Much blood has encased my sword. The battles are so many that they cannot be counted with all of my fingers and toes."

"Ah, yes. It is true, Lambert. You have served me so preciously, with your whole hearted attention, with such conviction that you have never been questioned. That is why I have now pressed upon you to dine with me. You, my bodyguard of many years, have served so well. I would now like to try and return the service, so to speak, by providing you with a task that will see you guaranteed a place in heaven."

"Thank you, my Lord," said Lambert, puzzled by the words, concerned that the emperor may be asking too much. "It has always been a pleasure."

"Please, help yourself to whatever you desire, eat like you've never eaten before," and Constantine looked over the set table in all its splendour. "Come, help yourself, and I shall provide you with more detail before this day concludes."

And with a wide smile upon Lambert's face he did help himself to the food laid out in front of him, as did Constantine. They ate festively, commenting on past actions, bringing to memory the battles they had fought in, the close scrapes, and the minor injuries sustained during such actions. And the time came when the food had mostly been eaten, except for a few scraps here and there. They had both had a good fill of food and wine.

"Tell me, Lambert," said Constantine. "Where would you see yourself in a few years?"

"Here, my Lord, beside you, eaten like a hungry pig, getting my fill," said Lambert, smiling and letting go of a hearty laugh, filling the air with happiness and great joy, "for you will be as happy with my services to you as much then as you are now, and then we can eat some more."

This brought an immediate smile to Constantine, a smile to outdo the smile that he had previously worn. He was content, he was happy; he had made the right decision. But the time had arrived, the time to divulge the mission that Lambert was to be given.

"Something is needed, Lambert. I need your services like I have never needed them before. I need you to run an errand for me and once that errand has been achieved I need you to serve another... with no less conviction than you have served me, but with great vigour and all your heart... as I know you will serve."

"My Lord, I will do all that I can to ensure that I serve your every wish. I shall do as you command."

"Well, Lambert, it is not as much as a command. It is a request. You can choose to turn it down if you so desire."

"My Lord, I do not see how I can turn you down. We have been through so much together, that if you believe I am the right man for the job then I will serve like I have never served before."

"I am most pleased to hear that. The task is a simple one but must remain secret."

"Yes, my Lord, a secret."

"It is most serious, Lambert. Even with the threat of torture hanging over your heard you must not relinquish your mission to anyone, and the parcel you carry must be destroyed." Lambert could hear the importance of the mission as the emperor spoke of it. Something so important was to fall his way that his very life could be in danger. He could feel the eyes in the walls of the dining room; he could feel the spies hanging on Constantine's every word. "What is it, my Lord?"

"You will not understand fully, Lambert, but I need you to take a parcel of three books to a Father Tourmede."

"And where do I find such a man?"

Constantine fell silent for a short while and then spoke. "On the island of Káros, in the Aegean Sea."

The weather continued unabated as Stephen led the other two along the sodden road. The hail was making itself well known, stinging at the body garments of the three, lashing out at their faces as they each tried to hold their arms across their face. Their backs were pelted hard by the storm but still they pushed themselves on into the night.

"How far now?" questioned Lambert as loudly as he possibly could and still remain audible, finding the walking hard though not because of the weight of the chest. He was soaked to the body and could feel the crinkling of his skin as it surrendered to the effects of being drenched.

"Not far," yelled back Stephen. He did not look back at the others but continued on, forcing the two men behind him to step out and maintain their pace.

"That is the third time you have said that," Lambert reminded, for they had been walking for what seemed to be hours.

"Maybe true," replied Stephen as he came to a halt in front of a house. "But this time I speak the truth. Here it is, come, quickly." It was a large building set far aside from others on the road. This was not a town, or even a village. It was nothing more than a few buildings that supported travellers along the road, providing a station for which to rest, refuel, and gather one's strength.

They each headed for the door and Stephen knocked loudly. They waited impatiently, drenched to the skin, the wind chill factor of the weather commencing to take its toll, for Lambert let out with uncontrollable shivering. Stephen knocked again, and again no answer. Lambert and Bernard placed the chest down and Lambert stepped up to the door, trying to gain a little protection from the weather and to try the door for himself. "Third time lucky," he said and knocked as loudly as he could, and within a minute the door opened; just a little at first.

A man in priest's vestment stood in front of them with a smile. He laid eyes upon Stephen and then his two comrades. "Please enter, quickly now," and stepped aside to let the men past, holding the door with all his strength against the wind that pushed upon it.

"Thank you," said Stephen as the three entered a hallway with the chest, their clothes dripping upon the cold stone floor, bright light from an adjoining room spilling out into the hallway, flickering over the walls.

The door was finally closed and bolted from the inside. "Such a terrible day to be walking out," said the priest as he held out his hand. "I am Father Ambaedian."

Father Ambaedian looked behind to ensure the three men followed him into the main hall. It was dark except around the huge fireplace and not a soul to be seen.

"All of the men are asleep in their rooms," Ambaedian's eyes fell upon the chest, "and we will not be disturbed."

Stephen said to the priest, "I see by the look in your eyes that you know what we carry?"

"Indeed," replied Ambaedian. "I know the chest by sight." He shook it from his mind. "Please, set yourselves down and warm yourselves by the fire, I shall get some refreshment for you shortly."

"Thank you, father."

"I have some wine to warm you all, and bread and cheese," said the priest as he watched the men seat themselves, "But first things first. Who are you? I do not recognise any of you."

"I am Stephen, and these two men are knights of the Hospital. I came from Constantinople and these men from Káros."

"Constantinople?"

"Yes, father, and it has fallen. A great loss it is," added Stephen, knowing full well that Father Ambaedian would ask. "I was there for a week only, and saw the fall of the great city for myself. I was lucky to get out alive," and the memory of his wife came flooding back, but he continued nevertheless. "I met Father Norotus who disclosed information to me in regards to the chest and its secret."

"Father Norotus," said Father Ambaedian with reflection in his eye. "I do not recall having ever heard of him. Please, continue."

"Well," continued Stephen, "we sailed to Káros and once there I fell in with these marvellous men. I also spent time with Father Tourmede."

"Ah, so that is why you are here, by his request" interrupted the priest, for he now understood. "How is Father Tourmede?"

Stephen was not sure but refused to lie to Father Ambaedian. "The fortress was attacked by many Turks. We had no choice but to flee. Father Tourmede and several nuns stayed on the island, to hide from the Muslims. They have all honoured themselves, for they gave up their place upon our boat, in order that we could protect thirteen orphans."

"Thirteen orphans?"

"Father, there is much to disclose, it will take a while," said Stephen, prompting the priest to provide further comfort.

"Of course, I'm sorry. Let me gather some refreshment, stoke the fire... and then we can talk further."

*
* * *
*

Father Ambaedian entered the hall where the warmth from the huge open fireplace shook the cold from the stone floor, and old and weary limbs. He held a small tray with tumblers of a measured substance, some wine to take further chill from within, some bread and cheese could also be seen.

The priest placed the tray down and the three knights simply looked on as Father Ambaedian handed out the tumblers, the sweetness of the wine hitting their nostrils. "Please drink heartedly and eat well," invited Father Ambaedian. "This wine was made from our own garden, a small measure of land attached to the rear of this house. The sailors we tend to help with the workload and we are always grateful for what they can do to make life easier for us here."

The two Hospitaller drank from their tumblers but Stephen placed his down and by showing his respect did decline the drink by saying, "Thankyou, father, but my mind must remain clear, as I am sure you understand, but your bread and cheese looks marvellous."

The priest was silent for a short second before allowing his thoughts to be heard, contemplating the company that sat before him.

"You will have to forgive me; but may I say as I please in front of your men?" asked Ambaedian, the knights looking each other in the eye.

"These two knights know as much about the chest as I do," said Stephen in reply. "They can be trusted with its contents and are pure; they will not whither, and death will not be delivered unto them if the chest is opened."

"So it is true," said Ambaedian. "If the chest is opened then all those that are impure will be struck as though by lightning – the finger of god?"

"It is indeed true and we have seen many deaths," said Stephen. "I can tell you this; of over one hundred good human beings, only a handful survived the opening of the chest."

"Such power exists?"

"It does."

"How many times has it been opened?" asked the priest.

"Only once, that I can be sure," said Stephen. "We do not know how many times it has been opened before its arrival on Káros, but needless to say it would not have been many. The key and the chest were kept well apart in an endeavour to prevent anyone from releasing the secret to the world, and just as well."

Father Ambaedian was without drink and interlocked his fingers in front of his wiry frame. "I grow old," and with a smile, continued, "and rather frail, but know my destiny. I have studied as much about the chest and its contents as I possibly could these past few decades. The volumes that my finger has traced cannot be counted for there are so many. Verses, phrases, and sentences alike, all have their hidden clues, accusations, and truths. I believe in the Lord our Father and it is for Him that I continue in life as He does in heaven." He fell silent then and asked a question of Stephen. "And what can you tell me of the chest, its markings, and of the secret it holds?" and Stephen delivered to him a verbal account of the contents of the letter from Constantine, information on Father Tourmede and his many volumes of text, and the ceremony of the opening of the chest at Káros, and father Ambaedian was much enthralled.

At this same time Aaron and Lars returned to the inn, which they had left with regret, for its warmth and atmosphere – besides anything to do with the man known as Martin – was something to be embraced on a cold and stormy night. They entered as they did before, all eyes upon them, each and every one wishing to know who was about to enter. A little stunned silence was encountered as the patrons of the tavern looked on before them, seeing without mistake that the two men who had departed in bad tiding had returned, before losing themselves once more in drink and conversation.

Lars and Aaron continued on towards the huge counter and the woman standing behind it, her forearms resting upon it as she learned forward.

"My fair lady," said Aaron to the bar wench. "It is good that your door is still open to the weary, for we are such, and look to rest our bones and flesh from the cold of the night. We would like to take up on your previous offer of a room for the night; or what remains of it."

"I have a room to suit you both, in the attic," she turned to attend the pouring of another tumbler for a customer who leant weatherly against the bar. "There are plenty of blankets to keep you both warm, you can pick them up from the trunk atop the stairs, two blankets each."

Lars gave a promising nod to Aaron, "An attic is as good as a room with a view. How much does the attic cost?"

"A simple coin that even a street-walker can afford."

"Well, we have not walked many streets but can afford your price," Aaron peered into her eyes. "Does the man, who we did offend, intend to return tonight; we would not want to be disturbed in our slumber. Times have been hard for me and my friend, and the last thing either of us would want is to be disturbed at an untimely hour."

"It is unlikely that he will return, but if he does my lips will remain sealed, and the one you refer to is Martin," advised the wench.

"A common name," said Aaron, thinking of his friend.

"For a common thief," added the wench. She turned to attend the weathered man and returned. "The attic can be reached via the staircase, over by the corner."

"Thank you, fair maiden, and take this, another coin for your lips of iron" The bar wench smiled at the stranger's generosity "And do not disturb the rats; the last thing I need is to be disturbed by rodents shifting their nesting area from roof to floor. Oh, and one last measure of convenience for you two gentlemen." She reached under the counter and pulled a candle from beneath it. "Light this via the lantern above that table and be careful to extinguish the candle before you sleep. The last thing I need is a fire aloft."

*

* * *

*

The story or Raoul.

It was a long road, a road filled with danger. Raoul was a common soldier whose only dream was to be a knight, to serve those that were much like him in his days of youth, peasants through and through.

He was amongst a gathering of 2,000 men, women, and children, on a journey to Constantinople, to mingle with those within the triple walled fortress, to protect the crusaders against the Muslim hordes whilst on their long journey. But his task was more important than that of salvation alone. He was a protector; he was here to aid those that wished to travel the dangerous road to Constantinople. He was paid very little for what he did but money was not an issue for him. He would serve the emperor and the people for free if it was possible for him to do so.

The walk was long and hard, a journey of many weeks, time to think things through, to pin point ones place in life, to consider the realities of existence, and of God and His son, of all things religious, even time enough to consider the religion of his enemy, those of Islam and their slanderous ways, the torture, their belief, the death and slaughter which covered the land. Yes indeed, there was much time to contemplate many things in life, and life itself.

The Hospitaller Knights were scattered in units to the front, flank, and to the rear of those that travelled this way, a long line of helpless farmers, the deserted, the helpless, and the frail, young and old.

It was during the journey by foot that a knight of the Hospital came past his flank, upon a horse with a beautiful coat and mane. He slowed the horse down and rode with no effort at all alongside Raoul, looking down upon him from high upon his horse. Raoul looked back and then the knight dismounted, took the reins in his hand and walked beside him.

"My name is Anthony. What is yours?"

"I am known as Raoul."

"Raoul; I have seen you before," said the knight. "Where?"

"It could be almost anywhere, for there have been many times that I have come into direct contact with your Order whilst on escort duty such as this."

"You have protected before?" asked the knight.

"Yes, many times."

They looked at each other in contemplation as the walk continued, thousands around them paying no attention to the conversation taking place.

"Yes, I remember now," said the knight. "I have seen you many times, each time you walk with the peasants, you talk with them when resting, you help them cook their meals, and you play with their children as though one of them." There was a little silence then. "Why?"

"Why?" replied Raoul. "I love these people. Even if I was a knight like yourself I would still take the time to spend a little of the day with the common people. I am one with them. I would not volunteer my services to walk this dangerous trek more than once if I did not care."

"You volunteer?"

"I have changed units many times just to be able to protect the innocent," said Raoul. "So yes; although I receive payment, it is by way of my volunteering for this duty that I receive it.

"Why?"

"I have told you why, but more importantly you have seen why. You have seen me with your own eyes. What you see is what I am. I cannot help being in love with the people, to serve them as best I can. I would give my life for the children."

"You are romantic at heart," said the knight. "Such romance can be a killer."

"It would be my honour, so long as the innocent are saved from the curses of torture and rape so often inflicted upon them by those of Islam."

"You are one of a kind, Raoul. I shall remember you." And with that said the knight remounted his horse and rode off to the front, to see to his other duties.

A week had come to pass. The camp fires were burning and pickets had been placed. The knight, who had introduced himself as Anthony, came upon Raoul as he sat with the innocent around a fire, cooking their gruel and talking heartedly amongst themselves.

"Hello, Raoul," said the knight in greeting as he walked over to the seated form of the man that had intrigued him.

Raoul stood up immediately and stepped out of the circle of friends, "Ah, Anthony. A surprise it is to see you."

"I notice that you are taking some time to spend with the people," said the knight as they walked a little, away from the fire.

"It is my way. I cannot serve the Lord directly so I tend to his flock. It is my way of paying homage, yet I feel as though I can do much more. Do you know what it is like, Anthony, to be shackled to a bedpan of duty, to serve without restriction, but to love the serving? But I sometimes wish for more than the simple life of being a protector? Being a simple soldier is not my place but I do the best that I can."

"Yes, I know how you feel," said the knight with conviction as the flickering of the camp fires showed up within the pupils of his eyes; Raoul could see he was talking the truth and with much sincerity. "I, too, was much like you, before I became a knight."

"How did you become a knight?"

"I was chosen by a scout of the Hospital about twenty years ago and since then have become a scout myself."

"A scout? You scout forward of the march, scout the terrain for the enemy in ambush?"

"Not that sort of a scout, Raoul," they stopped walking and turned to face each other. "I scout for the Order, to find men to recruit, worthy men that are known to serve with their heart and soul."

Raoul did not see what the knight was up to. "It must be a very hard job, yours. Trying to decipher such souls cannot be an easy task."

"Sometimes it is easier than you should think," said the knight.

"Listen, Raoul. How would you like to meet a man, a man of the Order that could get you inducted, to have you issued with a black tunic, a tunic with a white cross?"

Raoul could not believe his ears but understood the meaning of the knight immediately. He was being recruited by the Hospital, to become a knight, to be a soldier of soldiers. "I can hardly believe what I am hearing. We have not spoken a single word since we last met."

"I have asked around, it is my job; and I have been watching. I know you now more than you know yourself," Anthony placed his open palms onto Raoul's shoulders. "You are to be recruited, Raoul, believe it, for it is true."

*
* * *
*

Martin and Raoul were much relieved by the hospitality of the convent. Although they did not get to see the mother superior that night, they were promised an audience the following day. The children were bedded down for the night in front of the huge fireplace and it was here that the two knights decided to remain, standing guard against the unlikely intrusion of any undesirables.

"Raoul, you take the first nap and I shall watch," said Martin, "for I am not that tired."

"It would seem that both of us are wide awake and with nothing to do," added Raoul. "It will be a long night, tonight, but the young ones deserve the comforts of a warm sleep. To remain awake for the duration of night is little to suffer compared to the importance of their safety. We must do all that we can to ensure that they not only survive, but remain together."

"Too true, Raoul," said Martin, and he continued, "I wonder how Stephen has done with his meeting with Father Ambaedian?"

"I should hope that it is successful, otherwise we will be in for a long search." Raoul searched his inner self then and let his thoughts be heard. "Do you trust in Stephen's dreams; I mean to say; can you believe he has the sight to see what is to come?"

"I do, and more still, he also sees the past, that which will be to our advantage."

"I heard him talking in his sleep one time, several weeks ago."

"Aye; and what did he say?" asked Martin.

"It was of a place far from here, across the sea, the same place that he spoke of during one of his many speeches, the land which we are to descend upon in all our glory. I know, it sounds absurd, the world we live in not being flat, but round... but that was what he said in his dream, the same thing that he said to us all when he disclosed to us the journey we were to make, of a long voyage to the west, to a land rich in fruits never heard of before, and unsurmountable gold."

Martin shot with a gleaming glare, "Gold you say? I do not recall Stephen having said anything about gold."

"It was the Templar's gold," added Raoul. "Listen to me, Martin. There was a story told to me, many years ago. It was at a time before I was a knight, and it was a story of twenty-four knights of the temple. They took to sea with many galleys filled with treasure. They sailed towards the west and were never heard of again. There, Martin, that is our destiny as decided by Stephen, where much gold is waiting to be found."

"And what, in heaven's name," said Martin, "are we to do with so much gold?"

"Use it to our advantage, I suppose," replied Raoul.

"There does not seem much to me that can be done with so much gold, when so far away from civilisation."

"Besides, it's not for us to be wealthy, but to do the Lord's work." And Raoul looked at Martin in the light from the flickering fireplace. "Whatever Stephen is to uncover, that is what we are here to protect."

"I have sworn myself to that very duty."

"I have also sworn."

And both pondered the likely chance of their long voyage to the west. Much was still unclear to them and answers were needed for all of the men to feel the comfort so desired, for the mind was a fragile piece of organic matter. But all they had witnessed to date did instil great confidence within them, but time passed slowly and an end to the journey was desired by all.

Stephen told his story, of the chest and its power, of the verses carved upon it, and Ambaedian did not disappoint, he remained alert for the entire hour, for the time that it took to tell the story, of the demise of Constantinople, and then Káros, of the thirteen orphans and their ill treatment in the hands of the devilish Turk.

"...and we are far from our journey, father," said Stephen. "We still have far to go, travelling west as far as the sea will allow us to travel. We must go where very few men have gone before. But having said that I must also reveal to you that many people do inhabit this land in which we are to settle, and they are at one with the land, living with it and not against."

Ambaedian sat beside Stephen and placed a palm upon his shoulder. The other two knights remained silent and listened to the pair sharing conversation.

"Stephen, I must tell you something of the Templar's past," said Father Ambaedian.

"Please, tell me all you can."

"I shall tell you a short story, one that will gel with your dreams, and you shall know the truth; listen to me, Stephen. At the time of the Templar's demise a group of twenty-four knights pooled together their resources. Each knight used his position of status well and organised for much treasure to be gathered at a small harbour called La Rochelle. This they did some months before the king of France began with his dismantling of the Templar's very society and being, torturing thousands and burning many more."

"I know the stories of their treatment, father. Such a heinous crime against the innocent that was. My dreams also concur with your story of the twenty-four knights."

"But it could not be stopped, the torture and mistreatment continued. So the knights got their treasure, hoarded from centuries past. They loaded the treasure onto eighteen galleys and set sail for the west. It was believed that the west would reveal to them something so grand that it did not seem possible, beyond their wildest dreams."

"I suffer a recurring dream, father, one where a man of gold stands before thousands, women of the same cloth, which too, I believe, is an army. He is known as the Golden Man."

"And do you know this man, Stephen?" questioned Ambaedian.

"Yes I do, for it is me."

*

* * *

*

The wretched soul of Martin, the man so bitterly undermined by Aaron and Lars did approach the sheriff's office. It was a normal dwelling and housed just one – and his wife. No bars to speak of, the sheriff's house was just that, the gaol some distance away, closer to the centre of town and not likely to be visited in the current weather. He banged heavily against the door.

"Damn you heathen. Stop that damn banging," yelled a voice from aloft. A window opened and a head appeared to be battered by the wind and a little rain. "Damn you; what is it at this hour that demands my attention?"

"Sheriff, I am Martin."

"Martin; do I know Martin? No I do not, so why are you banging against my door at this hour?"

"I must report an undesirable," stated Martin.

"An undesirable; and who is that; a Turk, a Jew perhaps?"

"No, sheriff," Martin placed his right hand to the wound upon his chest. "A man inflicted this injury upon me, with an arrow; held in his hand I tell you... he thrashed out to kill me."

"Damn," the head disappeared and the window was quickly secured. Murmurs could then be heard but not quite made out as the cursing sheriff got dressed and approached the door. It opened, "Let me see your wound."

Martin pulled the cloth back which covered the wound, his shirt blotched with blood and stained much fabric due to the rain. "My wound seems to have stopped bleeding but it is to my horror that such a man still roams these streets."

"Not there, man, not in the rain. Quick, you better come in out of the cold; it does neither of us any good. Get in here and show me, show me properly."

Martin moved into the hall and the door was quickly closed behind him. "Roams these streets? How am I supposed to find a man who 'roams-these-streets' at this hour," questioned the sheriff methodically, not really caring to step out into the night. The wind was more than refreshing.

Both men stood in the stone cold corridor, discussing the matter.

"You should be reporting this to the gaoler, we have one on duty."

"Sheriff, you remember me not?"

"Remember?" the sheriff looked closer, "Ah, the man so sorely beaten by those reckless youths?"

Martin was embarrassed but hid it well, "Indeed, sheriff; not much a man can do against a small crowd."

"Yes, well; so what of your wound, where was it given?"

"Attacked I was, in the 'Refuge'."

"That den of thieves?"

"You show me a den without thieves and I will show you an honest man."

"Well spoken," said the sheriff. "How were you attacked?"

"A man leapt from his seat and stabbed me with his quarrel."

"For what reason?"

"No reason... maybe I knocked him accidentally."

The blank look upon the sheriff's face indicated that he did not fully believe Martin's story, for it seemed quite absurd and unbelievable. "Look... would you care for a medicinal drop, Martin, and then we can get all of this sorted out?"

"Thank you sheriff, I would be honoured."

"Please, this way." The sheriff showed Martin into the front room of the small dwelling, a luxury paid for by the king, for a sheriff was housed quite comfortably, paid for via the taxes collected. The sheriff was a fat man, quite prone to eating well, and over drank on every possible occasion. "The fire has almost died but still gives off some warmth."

"More than can be expected outside," said Martin.

Both men sat in comfortable chairs and looked at the fireplace as the sheriff poured some wine for them both. "So tell me, what should be done with this man?"

"I want justice for the wound and justice for the defamation brought upon me."

"Ah, yes, defamation is a killer to someone with a reputation," said the sheriff, eyeing Martin cautiously.

"My reputation is as good as any other man's," said Martin in defence.

"Aye. Do you think he is still at the 'Refuge' or will he be sought elsewhere?"

"He will be drinking as we speak, quite comfortable in the fact that no action will be brought against him; even an idol threat will not dislodge him."

"Did you pose such an idol threat?"

"I simply advised that the sheriff would be informed."

The sheriff tipped his glass up and emptied the contents before placing it upon a small chair-side table. "It is time to move, Martin; time to get the scum off of our streets and behind bars. Maybe then, when all is done, I can get back to sleep in the comfort of my bed."

Aaron and Lars traversed the stairs to the attic, 12 rungs to a small veranda, doors to rooms standing along both left and right, and there, to the far right was the short climb to the attic door. Lars held his candle high so both could see.

"To find comfort in an attic will be hard," said Aaron. Lars simply looked and nodded. "But it is easier to sleep in an attic than to sleep with the blade of a sword against your throat," and the door was pushed open and both men stepped within, blankets held tight against their chests.

The roof was high and a few pigeons could be seen to fly off through a small hole in the roof near where it met with the side of the building. The hard wooden ceiling on which they stood was bare and there was not a comfort to be seen.

"Over there, look, some straw and what looks like sacking for a pillow. Our friend has used this attic before," Lars looked to Aaron and shook his head, running his extended fingers over his open palm, meaning to convey that he found security within the fact that others had slept here, meaning that such a common occurrence brought with it peace of mind, and fewer rats. "I agree, Lars; it is safe and we shall sleep a good wink before tomorrow." They both laid their blankets down.

The two men put down their arms, sword and crossbow, to ready themselves for slumber, for a good sleep was never received when sailing upon the sea.

They both made themselves comfortable upon the straw mattresses and blew out the candle that Lars had placed upon a wooden beam. It was then that the full moon could be seen to give off a little illumination, light seeping through gaps in the roof from above and where the roof met the side of the building, where gutters ran its length... the storm had suddenly stopped, almost as suddenly as it had started. Such a phenomenal occurrence the storm was that it could hardly be believed. Lars lay back as did Aaron, side by side and sharing in each other's warmth, pulling the blankets over themselves as best they could.

"Lars, do you feel that we should remain at guard tonight?" and looked upon the man beside him, receiving a nod in acceptance of the suggestion, one more night to add to the many in which they had maintained a picket. "I look forward to the day when guard duty will be a thing of the past, but wonder when that will be." He looked upon Lars one more time. "Sleep, Lars, and I shall remain afoot, so to speak, for my share of tonight's watch. Good night to you, my friend," and Lars simply smiled before closing his eyes.

*

* * *

*

The sheriff entered the house of squalor with Martin close on his heels. They approached the wench. She could see who had entered and gave a smile, undeterred.

"I see that Martin has scurried away to fetch his dog," said the woman behind the counter.

"Is that the way you greet the law?" said the sheriff as he approached. "Do I not deserve a better greeting than that expected to be bestowed upon a common dog?"

"Everyone knows my standing. I commit no wrong-doing and pay homage where required. You need me as much as I need a good man in my bed, to keep me warm on these long, lonely, and cold nights."

The sheriff cared little and shook the comment from his mind, "I seek a man."

"You seek two men," corrected the wench, "and I have them netted for you," said the wench. "Ah, I see by the look upon your face that you are pleased with what I have done for you."

A short-lived smile disappeared from the sheriff's face, the folds of fat forming creases here and there. "This is not the first time you have aided me, and yet I still do not know your name."

"It is Marian," said the wench with a wink. "A woman who, even in my years so bold, could curl your toes; if it was not for my husband."

"Years so bold," laughed the sheriff. "Is that what they call old age? Tell me," he changed the subject to parry further insult and jocularity. "Where are the men we seek? Are they where I assume?"

"Yes, sheriff, in the attic and without escape."

The sheriff turned with Martin on his tail, "Come," and to the wench, as he turned, he stopped and paid a further comment. "One of these days I shall reward you for your kind hospitality."

The wench smiled as the two made their way towards the attic, watching them purposely for the time it took them to approach the entrance to the attic, for them to hand out their justice, to the demise of the two men asleep, for others had fallen by way of her mischief.

Aaron shook Lars quietly, in the hope of rousing him at this, their time of need, the light of the moon still providing a little aid to sight.

"Lars," he whispered. "Men approach in stealth."

Lars stirred and opened his eyes, looking upon Aaron for further information. "I could hear the boards creaking below and then stifle slightly, and then footsteps towards the rooms. I heard whispers again as conversation started, and; and I believe they approach with a dire need to fall upon us as we sleep."

Lars was wide awake now, quietly as can be, picking up his crossbow and feeding it a quarrel.

"They have purpose and that purpose is not sleep."

Aaron pulled his sword from his sheath, and side by side, Lars and Aaron got to their knees and then onto their feet, just able to stand tall with the attic roof slanted above. Aaron made for a better grip upon the hilt of his sword and Lars placed the stock of the crossbow within the saddle of his shoulder, ready to fire and reload.

The approach of the two stopped and a final whisper could be heard along with the familiar sound of a sword being drawn from a metal sheath. Suddenly the door to the attic burst open and Martin, the first to enter - to try and save face in the company of the sheriff - brought the brunt of the taught crossbow that Lars held in his hands.

The quarrel was heading for its mark, but Martin had seen the men standing in wait and had immediately stepped to the side, the point of the arrow tearing a long tear into cloth and skin, the pain hardly felt, Martin's mind being overrun by the adrenalin and rush of seeing the man with crossbow to his front. Lars, in all his years, in the surety of his prowess and familiarity with weapons, had missed his target – it was too late to lock in another and his sword lay beside his blanket. Martin was bleeding from the open wound but carried forth with his purpose, having pushed his cowardice well aside.

The roof was too low for a sword to be fed a swinging chop, a slash of fury from above, and the sheriff, having entered the attic once before, simply thrust outwards as he stepped forward, his long sword, carried for such a purpose as this, reaching out and becoming a complete surprise to Aaron, whose gut bore the delivery of the sword as a scabbard of flesh, the skin of his abdomen sliding up the sides of the sword as his body encased the cold of the weapon, Aaron's facial expression delivering unto his attacker that knowing look: the look of death. The sheriff pulled the sword free and Martin, as surprisingly as could be, fell upon Lars like a great oak, and Lars in his numbered years gave under the stress of power brought upon him; both men fell, one upon the other, and Aaron fell as death gripped him in its cold embrace.

Lars was powerless to do anything but look out to his right, just able to see Aaron with the contortion of death written heavily upon his face; why did not he parry, why did not he fight, what made the man of steel slow to react?

And ashamed of his own effort, Lars gave up all resistance, for the fight was over.

*
* * *
*

The story of Bernard.

The soldier, Bernard, had taken some leave from his unit, the fierce fighting over the past month having taken its toll on his injuries. He needed a rest, time to soak his old wounds in oil, to tenderise the soreness, to heal the scars upon his upper torso, to relieve just a little of the pain that hammered him day and night. Always pain, the trait of a professional. You either die in battle or gain a few extra scars. It was one or the other.

He had travelled much of the night and the time for the sun to rise had arrived. It commenced to say good morning to the day, coming up in front of him on his short trek into the west, to a country town where he knew that he would be provided what he was searching for; release from the pain that he suffered. It was a journey that he had made many times in his life, seeking to relieve himself of his burden, to replenish his supplies of oil that was rubbed into his wounds. Without the oil he would be surrendered to rubbing his wounds with his fingertips, massaging his scars for hours on end. The oil was a special blend, a blend of substances that he did not know, for if he did then he would not have to travel the journey he was currently on the road to make.

He was a strong man, but not too strong, for the strongest men that he had known had come to trouble on the battlefield... too slow to move, too slow in their reflexes, too idol to make for cover when cover needed to be sought. He was intelligent and capable of operating on his own, travelling from town to town in any country by himself, able to speak five different languages and quickly learning another three, able to read and write, though not as well as a scholar of languages. He had been travelling this way for some hours and decided to take a rest beneath a tree, just to the side of the road, where he could partake of some jerky and water from the bag he carried on his hip. It was here, beneath the tree as he sat, that he first met the priest. From down the road, from the direction he was travelling, he saw an open carriage being pulled by two horses, running scared, their nostrils ablaze with mists of cold as each breath was exhaled after being delivered to the lungs. The driver of the carriage was bent forward, whipping the horses as best he could, trying heaven and earth to get that little extra effort out of them. A man sat beside him, dressed in a simple cloth like that of a monk, looking over his shoulder as the carriage continued towards him... they were being chased.

Bernard acted quickly and slunk behind the tree, and just in time. The right hand wheel of the carriage gave way under the stresses produced and collapsed, throwing the monk head over heels and into some nearby bushes; the driver was not so lucky, falling forward and beneath the other wheel where he was crushed by the forward motion of the carriage before it came to rest. One of the two horses got up from the road and started pulling to get free from the wreck without success and remained unsettled for some time.

Those chasing the carriage were upon it in seconds, three smaller men who drew their swords immediately on dismounting, walking hurriedly towards where the priest had been thrown into the bushes. The monk was sore and knocked about by the fall but had no broken bones to speak of. He got to his feet and clambered from the bushes at the same time that two of the men reached him and grabbed either arm. Not a word passed behind them, they acted as though acting upon an unwavering plot, and it was not until they had dragged him over to the upright wheel of the carriage still intact, that the first words spoken came from the third man as the other two tied the priest fast to the wheel.

"Where is it, where is the key?" the third man said, lashing out with a backhander across the priest's face. "The key, where is it?" Still no answer. "Search his pockets," commanded the man of the other two, as he turned and walked about in his im-patience, pounding his fist into his palm, an evil grimace upon his face.

Both of the other men set upon throwing their fists into the pockets of the priest's clothing, fumbling around a little until one of them pulled out a wooden artefact. "I have it. Here it is; look."

"So plain it is, hard to believe that the Abbott wishes to pay so much for it," said the third, taking it from the other and looking at it closely, turning it over and over in his hand, trying heaven and earth to understand its mystique.

"Do not relinquish it to the Abbott," the priest cried. "For all our sakes it must remain with me."

"Shut up, you, we are going to fetch much gold for our part in this, so you just shut up," said the third. "The Abbott has paid a little for our services and has promised to pay a lot more on delivery. We will do as we have been bid, and once it has been delivered we will be very rich."

Bernard could see without much trouble that the priest was the innocent victim and that the other three meant to harm and rob the priest, but not only this, but they also failed to pay any attention to the man crushed by the wheel, for he might very well still be breathing. He could hear a few words being spoken by the third man as he paced up and down in front of the priest, but most of what he said could not be deciphered. He needed to make a decision, one that he knew was right.

He stepped from behind the tree. These three men before him would be no match for his skills in the handling of sword. He was not afraid to take them one, either one at a time or all in a single bout of fighting with weapons drawn.

"Excuse me gentlemen," said Bernard without as much as a heartbeat falling out of place. His nerve was steady and he did not flinch.

The three men turned together, startled by the intrusion, fear immediately gripping them, for they did not know who this man was or whether or not he had company. But the fear quickly dissipated and they all smiled, for they could see an easy fight before them, and when this man before them was dead then they would empty his pockets of whatever he carried.

"Who are you and what do you want?" asked one of the men with little concern for the answer, for no matter what Bernard said, there was going to be a fight.

"You should have been on your way, this is no concern of yours," said another, "but it is too late now."

"Oh, but it is my concern," said Bernard as he withdrew his sword from its sheath. "For I prey on cowardice, like you three prey on the innocent," and stepped closer to the group of three.

The three men brought their swords to the ready, held them out, perpendicular, ready to party with the single man in front of them, commencing slowly to encircle him. None of them took their eyes from him for a second.

"This is your first and last chance," said one. "Put down your weapon and we shall see to it that you are gagged and tied, but live you shall." The lie was transparent and seen for what it was.

"I am not a dog, so cannot run away or be allowed to wear a collar, so I guess I'll have to die..." said Bernard, "when my time has come."

"Your time in now, stranger," said the third, the leader of the pack.

The first of the three rushed in from behind, and Bernard quickly side-stepped and thrust his sword into the man's flank, withdrawing the sword again as blood rushed from the wound, the man falling to the ground in a heap. A second then used this as his opportunity to slash down with his sword from high above his head. The momentum of the sword swing could not be stopped and Bernard once again side-stepped out of the way employing a simple push of his sword into the stomach of his assailant. He too fell to the ground in a heap, clutching his open wound and started coughing blood.

"One on one," said Bernard. "Sounds fair to me."

The last of the three dropped his sword and turned tail to run, and to keep on running until he was far from danger. Bernard simply watched on for a while, sheathing his weapon, watching to ensure that he did not turn around and attempt to approach from the rear with a dagger drawn.

Bernard raced over to check on the fallen man beneath the wheel; he was dead; he then attended to where the priest was tied to the wheel and cut away the rope ties. He cut them quickly with his dagger and then put the dagger away.

"Thankyou stranger, thankyou for what you have done," said the priest as he looked around upon the ground, his eyes finally falling upon the key; it was safe. The thief had dropped the key on the road when confronted by the fight: it was so large and so very heavy; so much larger than any key he had seen before.

"It was my pleasure, I was happy to be of service," said Bernard as the last of the dying grimaces of pain departed the lips of the two men upon the ground. Two were dead and one had escaped, but the coward would not be back this day.

Bernard looked into the priest's eyes and introduced himself. "I am Bernard, plain and simple, no title."

"Thank you, Bernard," said the priest. "Please, let me introduce myself, I am Father Tourmede."

*

* * *

*

Stephen suddenly slumped heavily, back into the comfort of the chair, his shoulder slumping with the burden that fell upon him. The other two knights and Father Ambaedian could see that Stephen was horror struck, his eyes and face told how he felt.

"What is it, Stephen?" asked Ambaedian.

"Something; I am not sure," answered Stephen, and then with a suddenness that shocked his company he said, "Aaron is dead."

"That cannot be true," said Bernard.

"Certainly not," added Lambert.

And as though stinging with accusation, Stephen chastised the two knights. "How long have you known me? Do you still not believe, after all you have witnessed?" They understood their error and Stephen felt a wickedness never felt before, not just for the comment he had made against the two knights, but also for another death of a friend being delivered to them. "Please, forgive me." So much death had been witnessed, but now more than ever it hurt. Even where his wife of Constantinople was concerned he felt less pain, and why was that? It was the truth of the chest, it was Stephen's destiny which hung in the balance; he was to become immortal, but did not fully understand what that meant, did not know of the power which he was to possess.

"Forgiveness is not necessary," said Lambert.

"Certainly not where I am concerned," added Bernard.

And a few seconds of silent contemplation was disturbed by Father Ambaedian. "The time has come, Stephen." He stood from his chair. "We cannot wait any longer, the chest must be opened, and the two powers that we find within must be fused." And with the comment came stares of agreement, and Stephen nodded acceptance of the task that remained undone. They had ventured here for a reason and that was to fuse the good and the bad of the chest; and so it would be done.

"I agree," said Stephen, "we cannot delay it any longer."

*
* * *
*

Abu and Ahmad were lurking about when out of the shadows and along the cobbled way, so wet, came the footsteps and silhouettes of three figures. Abu and Ahmad took quickly to the shadows along the side of the buildings, pressing themselves out of sight, watching motionless as the three came to view.

"Move along, damn you," snarled the sheriff, pushing Lars from behind where his hands had been tied with thick rope. "Try to kill the sheriff and you try to kill the king."

"It was me he tried to kill, sheriff, not you," reminded Martin.

"He knew not who he fired against, that may be true, but I was his mark as much as you," was his sound reply, and then another push in the back for Lars did follow. "And why do you not talk, ah? You damn bastard. You shoot you quarrels to kill but fail to hit your target, and at such close range, and why, why try to kill us, ah? Answer me you bum-of-the-street!"

"He cannot talk, sheriff."

"What was that? What do you mean?"

And from the shadows, Abu and Ahmad followed in quiet servitude to their purpose.

"Did you not see? He has no tongue."

"What?" they both stopped in their tracks, the sheriff followed by Martin, turning Lars around, the sheriff's palms placed either side of Lars' head and pushing it back for the light of the moon to ally with his need. "Open up, you bastard!" and when the truth was revealed, the sheriff stammered. "Ah, it is true, no tongue, well I never did see..." and saddened by the reality, added, "Not much point in interrogation, is there."

"Maybe he is a learned man," said Martin.

"A what?"

"Maybe he knows how to read and write."

"Do you know how to read and write?" asked the sheriff of Martin.

He shook his head.

"No, I thought not, a man of your calibre; I know your sort. A dumb ox to be sure," said the sheriff and after a short degree of concentration, "It will be just as fair to see this man rot in the dungeons, or hung by the neck until dead."

Abu held out his hand, pushing Ahmad back into the shadows as he strained to hear. The last thing Abu wanted was for Lars to die, for the man was his only link to the chest of secret's: thus far; but if it were true, if Lars could not talk then it was a fine mess he was in.

"Straight to gaol for you my friend-with-no-tongue, and before this weekend is over I shall see swift justice. I shall see you hanged for your contempt of the law, and I shall invite the entire town to see what the law delivers," and so on they trod, several pushes in the back to accommodate a speedy delivery unto the gaoler and his cells.

Abu held his hand in place, restraining Ahmad from following.

"They are getting away, Abu."

"That is okay, Ahmad. We no longer need to follow."

"But he is our link to the chest," complained Ahmad. "If we lose him... we lose—"

"Nothing, Ahmad; we lose nothing." An explanation was called for. "He has no tongue, so cannot talk, but his hanging... that will bring his friends out-of-hiding, and when his friends have been revealed to us we shall see the chest delivered into our hand."

"But we do not know what any of them looks like, Abu."

"We shall know; by their own doing, we shall see who it is that has the chest, for they will be the only ones not cheering when the man is hanged."

The two knights placed the chest in front of them and took their seats, all four men relaxed and waiting. Stephen looked to Ambaedian and he stared back, each waiting for a cue, for a prompt on which to act. After a minute….

"The time has come then," said Stephen, "to open the chest once more."

"And this shall be the last," said Ambaedian."

"The last, why is that?" asked Stephen. "And what does it mean 'to be fused'?" and although Father Tourmede had men-tioned briefly about the fusing of good and evil, Stephen could not fully understand the need, what it meant, nor the real purpose: he only surmised.

"Within the chest, or so it is written, are several artefacts which have specific meaning," said Ambaedian, and seeing that he had the attention of all three went into a detailed explanation. "You all know how Jesus met with death, the horrors of it. Such a death was delivered to so many, thousands upon untold thousands. Even at the time of

Spartacus over six thousand souls suffered at a single crucifixion. The untold horrors of dying on the cross were known well before the crucifixion of Christ. But Jesus was the son of God, so it is written. There was a single man who tempted God's anger, and God delivered the fury of his almighty power to earth that day when the soldier prodded at the body of Jesus. With a pilum he prodded, a six-foot spear shod at one end with a wicked looking eighteen inches of iron, tapered to a point. With this point he spilled what was of Jesus' sacred temple; his body spilled to the earth like common dregs from a forgotten cup. It is this point, the point of the pilum that dealt such a savage and unmolested blow, that is considered, at the time, of a most heinous piece of justice delivered, that can be found within the chest. I know this as though I see it." And Stephen somehow knew it to be true. "This is the first item to be found in the chest and it is this which is evil. It delivers to all that are impure, almost instantaneous death. As though strangled of life you will meet with your destiny," And this was the same as Stephen had told Father Ambaedian, of what had happened at the temple of Káros. "It resembles the temptation of man, the indisputable contempt to infuriate the pure, to denounce the sacred existence of all that is good. Impurity strengthens the devil as he does seek to be strengthened, to deny Christ and His father as he, the Devil, does worship impurity from the fiery pits of hell. The pilum draws together and binds all that is evil in an attempt to strangle all that is good. That is what it represents, that is the evil housed within the chest."

"So much evil," said Bernard.

"And what is good?" asked Lambert.

"You shall seek no further than the widow," answered Ambaedian. "For it is written: Jesus sat down opposite the place where the offerings were put and watched the crowd putting their money into the temple treasury. Many rich people threw in large amounts. But a poor widow came and put in two very small copper coins, which equals a quadrans coin. Calling his disciples to him, Jesus said, 'I tell you the truth, this poor widow has put more into the treasury than all the others. They all gave out of their wealth; but she, out of her poverty, put in everything, all she had to live on'." Ambaedian looked at each of the knights and Stephen, one at a time. "This is what is good and shall remain the sign of giving for all time. No other action alone can surmount to more than what the widow gave. So two coins can be found within the chest, two copper coins that resemble the good of humanity. These things are to be fused as one, the good fused with the bad, and with it comes salvation, and only one will suffer."

"For one to suffer?" asked Bernard.

"Only one person shall reap the horrors which are comparable to those that Christ suffered."

"To suffer such cruelty," said Bernard, "cannot be a gift, cannot be salvation. Why would we fuse the good with the bad?"

"Firstly," said Ambaedian. "So that the Christian Church cannot be toppled by the Muslim unfaithful, by their demise of the Christian Church, and even those that believe they are pure may house something evil within them, even if they know not what they hide."

"And secondly," interrupted Stephen, "one must suffer as Christ, but for eternity, by living for the remainder of time, never to die, never to rot, never to be allowed into the house of heaven."

"That cannot be," said Lambert looking to the others in turn. "Such suffering should not have to be for one to suffer; and who should it be," he asked. "Not you, father, not you, surely."

"No," said Stephen. "It is I that shall suffer."

*
* * *
*

Lars sat within his cell, dried blood upon his face. There was no window for which to see the stars, no window for which to allow the light of the moon to aid him in sight. There were no bars, just a cell door, and within the door a small rectangle, which, when opened, revealed a little light from the corridor on the other side, where other cells joined the dark surrounds of the gaoler's walk. He knew he was alone because he could clearly recall his being thrown into the cell, assisted by another punch into the back of his head, a measure of criminality to accompany his gaoling. It was then, as he was pushed so haphazardly into the confines of the empty cell that he tripped and banged his head upon the rear wall, which knocked him unconscious.

He patted himself slowly and could confirm where bruises were, where injury had been sustained. He had been beaten well, before being plunged into darkness, but no manner of beating was going to get him to talk: ha! He could not talk!

His fingers traced themselves around his swollen eyes, both bloodied well by the punches of the gaoler, not the sheriff. The sheriff was too fond of watching the beating take place, not in delivering the blows himself. But he could recall one thing, the promise to have him hanged for his trouble. There was no defending himself amongst accusations for he could not speak, and all of those of the tavern in which he had partook would not say a word in his favour, for he was not a regular patron, despite his honesty.

From all perspectives Lars' situation did not look good and all he could do was contemplate the hanging to come, and of his poor friend Aaron, who had been unjustly killed by the hand of the law.

Suddenly, and without warning, the rectangle was opened and light from the outside spilled upon his face before being blotted out by the head of the gaoler, a thickset man with a large jaw and big nose. He rattled the keys upon his belt with his right hand, seemingly in effort to try and torment Lars, but there was no success on his part, for Lars could not be drawn from his thinking.

"You would like these keys, would you not, you murdering bastard," accused the gaoler without any knowledge for the reason that Lars was being punished. "I have heard the sheriff speak to others. The verdict has been reached and you shall be hanged on Sunday morning." Lars was shocked but in too much pain for the shock to show upon his face. "But you have been granted one favour this night, a meal and drink." The gaoler's face disappeared from view for the measliest of time and reappeared in its place was a bowl of gruel as it came tumbling in through the latched window and all over the cell floor. The gaoler laughed as he looked in, uncontrollably it would seem. "Lick it off the floor you scum, it is all you shall have this night; oh, and your drink." The gaoler grunted and untied the rope around his pants, loosening them sufficiently before urinating against the cell door where it met the floor. It was too dark to see but Lars could smell the urine as it seeped under the door. "And drink well." The small window was shut and laughter filled the corridor as the gaoler walked away to attend his other duties.

*

* * *

*

The Templar, two Hospitaller, and Father Ambaedian, had come to terms with what the chest was to reveal, but one other thing was missing from the cauldron of their minds. "One thing more is of importance to us all," said the father, peering at Stephen, knowing what Stephen did know: of his sacrifice. "It is within the book that I have upon my lap that something has been revealed to me." He patted the book as though a long-life companion. "Within it there are many secrets but one stands out amongst all others. It reveals that the evils of God's own work, the spirits of good and evil within the chest, can be controlled through one that has been chosen, and only the chosen one can carry the cross."

"The cross?" asked Lambert, for Stephen.

"Let me read from the book, which was written some time before the bible, when the thoughts of the works of Jesus were contemplated and far from being scribed." He turned to a marked page and commenced to read. "It reads: 'And God spoke to me, from over my shoulder, as the ink from my quill fluently spills over the pages of this book; containment can only be gained when one has been found, a knight so humble that his beginnings are his end, through lonesome passion of generations past does the knighted bear the burden of birth, for from such a knighted birth does no death come. He will know his way in life through verses and dreams where the reality of life and death become obscured through the meaning of life, and to that I mean the containment of the devil, the denying of unfaithful thought through action of mind and soul, to be pure in all his courage of action. Death will not come of him as it has my son, for my son gave up his life to pay for the sins of the many, so that they may be forgiven in worship as any mortal will forgive another, but so many impure exist within the multitudes that the chosen one must prevail the givings of the chest and come to reign over the earth as the protector of Jesus' sacrifice. The good and evil of my son's death shall be secreted to a chest, to lay in wait for the chosen one to open it; but be warned, death awaits the impure. The chest shall be of man size, easy to port, hard to enter, as specified in previous instruction, and the key, too, shall reveal its secret. The keys construction, in two halves, must be adhered to so that when the good and evil of the chest are fused the Cross of Christ will be born. The cross is the salvation of man where the chosen one maintains it. With it comes many qualities too valuable to be revealed within the text of my verses. The chosen one will become one with the cross and with it comes the purification of the world. Generations hence will be swallowed from existence before I shall make visit unto the earth, and only with my acceptance, that men and women of the world deserve my son's sacrifice, will death be granted the cross's bearer'."

Ambaedian closed the book. "The key to the chest is made from two halves, so meticulously put together that the flaw within it cannot be seen. To pull the key apart before the chest is opened could destroy the key and mankind's chance for salvation. The chest must be opened before the key can be forced into two halves, and before the good and evil doings of the chest can be fused." Father Ambaedian went into further explanation. "I have read much of God's words and have come to understand what must happen. The message is subtle and straight forward. Once the chest has been opened the contents must be fused, melted and moulded, casting a cross from within the mould of the key. The key will become useless and so will the chest; it must all be burnt and discarded into the sea so that no man or beast can find the remains. Once the Cross of Christ has been scored from the cast then it must be placed upon a chain and then around the neck of the chosen one. The chosen one must remain apart from civilisation, as best as is humanly possible, in order to protect the salvation of the human race. An order of knights will be formed, and only the chosen one will know how to go about such forming.

"The Cross of Christ must remain in the hands of the chosen one for all time. If the cross is separated from its holder then damnation will be inherited upon the earth." The silence was set, many thoughts flooded the minds of Lambert and Bernard, but Stephen, he somehow knew what was to come, dreams he had received, voices in his head, and he knew that a cast of women would be born unto the earth, a cast of women that would be the salvation of the human race, protectors of the key and its bearer, protectors of Jesus' very sacrifice; one sacrifice for another.

"Thank you, Father Ambaedian," said Stephen. "You have clarified for me what I have anticipated these past few weeks. The voices within my head have drained away but the dreams I have are coming thick and fast. There are so many dreams that I cannot depict between one and the other, they come tripping over one another and cannot be controlled."

"You will learn to control them, Stephen," said Father Ambaedian. "You have the remainder of existence to learn."

Stephen looked at the priest and said with much conviction, "And that time must commence immediately. Let us open the chest."

Ambaedian stood up and the others followed his action. "First we must get ready with the fire," and with that said, Father Ambaedian looked to Lambert. "You must leave this house and turn left, follow the road to the top of the hill. There are no houses at the top of the hill. Once at the top you will notice a small smithy station on the reverse slope. Go to the side door and knock five times. When the door is opened, tell the man or woman that opens it, Father 'Ambaedian is ready'. They will know what to do. You will be asked to enter. Do you understand?"

"Yes, father."

"Go now."

As Lambert departed the company, Ambaedian continued with instruction. "We shall wait here long enough for the fire to gain heat. Once it is hot enough, Lambert will be sent back. We will then attend the smithy station. The smithy and his wife will have vacated the premises in order for us to do as we need to do with the fusing of the good with the bad."

Bernard looked to the priest and asked, "How did you know"

"I have the book," said he in answer, "and like Stephen, I have dreams too."

*
* * *
*

A knocking came at the door and Father Ambaedian stood immediately. "It is Lambert, back from the smithy station." He directed the others accordingly. "Bernard, go and let him in, Stephen and I will get ready the chest." Bernard nodded and retreated to the door. "Are you ready Stephen? For this is the first day of the rest of your life."

"I have been ready for a long time, father," answered Stephen with such conviction that his words could not be doubted. The two of them lifted the chest onto a small table. "As soon as the other two knights are here we shall proceed," and soon after those words had been spoken, they entered the confines of the room, Lambert and Barnard ready by their side. "Ah, good. Let us proceed. Please, Stephen, produce the key and open the chest."

Stephen put his hand into his pocket and pulled it out, the prized possession, for all to see in their silence. He slowly approached the chest and placed the key into it. It turned effortlessly and with such smooth action that Stephen was quite surprised. The key was indeed, well crafted. He looked to the others in turn and stared one final time at the lid of the chest before lifting it and standing back. He looked around and saw the others smiling as the Holy Spirit did transcend from the chest and sped off through the very roof of the house, as though into heaven. And as the Holy Spirit disappeared from view a voice fell upon the few, the voice of the Holy Spirit was delivering to them a message as it did in Káros, again, the same sweet message to the ear, so sweet that it had to be heard to be understood. Alas, Stephen neither saw nor heard any of it, for he was the chosen one. And within the time it takes to consume several breaths of air the miracle was over, Lambert, Bernard, and Father Ambaedian, looking to one another with a smile before finally Ambaedian broke the silence.

"I would never have believed that such beauty existed."

"What was it like, father?" asked Stephen.

"Did you not see it?"

"No, I did not."

"Ah, Stephen, you have truly missed a miracle of miracles. The Holy Spirit was lifted from the chest and spoke to me." He looked to Lambert and Bernard. "Did the Holy Spirit speak to you, did it?"

"Yes, father," answered Lambert.

"Me too," said Bernard.

"So beautiful it was, like music to my ear; but you, Stephen, you have a miracle of your own to perform, and we must not waste any time in seeing it carried out." It was then that Stephen took a step forward and looked into the chest, and there he saw what was to be expected, three items; two coins and the point of a pilum, secured into a scored recess within the wood, but for the pilum, it was the point only, enough metal between the three items to mould a large cross. "I shall carry these items in my pocket, the key in the other. Lambert and Bernard, carry the chest, it must be purified in flame after the Cross of Christ has been born unto the world." The three men simply looked with a smile upon Stephen and smiled, before acting quickly to carry out his commands, for he was the knight of knights.

"Come quickly, all of you, follow me." Something had transcended over Stephen, like a magical vale. His tone was kind and forgiving, but strong in command and steadfast in virtue. He lead the way out of the door followed by the porters of the chest and Father Ambaedian, to the left and up the road, to the smithy station on the reverse slope where the fire awaited them, the smithy cauldron, the blazing flames that were to melt the pilum and coins into their newest form, to be fused as one, to be cast into a cross. Stephen knew where to go without thinking, as though he had been here before. Through the house he trod, through another door and into the work shed. The blazing fire was there with the instruments ready for action, an iron cup on the end of an iron shaft, ready for them to place the contents of Stephen's pocket into the cup. He did this quickly and the chest was brought in and placed down, the cup with the pilum and coins now placed over the fire of the cauldron, placed to rest upon the furnace where flames licked up and over the items of good and evil.

The silence was intense and all that could be heard was the fire as it crackled and cackled, voicing what seemed to be the verse of many in conversation. The heat from the fire was stable but radiated well and the two coins started to melt.

Father Ambaedian looked to Lambert and Bernard. "Search for an urn, something as large as a wash basin, but smaller than two, an empty chalice for which to place the ashes of the chest. It will take a long time for the chest to be turned into powder. It must be allowed to burn and char, turned into ashes amongst the red hot coals, and when the coals have burnt out, what is left shall be secured in the makeshift urn."

"I have it," said Lambert. "Here, a basin with a lid."

"To secure the contents," added Ambaedian. "To prevent spillage." He turned to Stephen. "How are the contents of the cup?"

Stephen held his arm across his face and looked into the cup as the pilum commenced to melt at its outer edges, where the blade was thinnest, white hot and started to give in to the heat of the fire. "I think the cup will melt before the pilum," he said.

Ambaedian knew he was not serious: "The pilum will melt as required; the iron is old and frail; give it a chance." Father Ambaedian turned on his heels and went to the side of the workshop, lifting an hourglass up for all to see. He turned it up-side-down and placed it back down. "When the sands have drained away, the task will well and truly have been completed; sit and rest."

Only a quarter of the sands from the upturned glass had passed from top to bottom. Father Ambaedian stood and stepped over the furnace of coal and cup. "Stephen, my eyes are frail, it's hot and bright; what do you see?"

Stephen stepped up and looked into the cup seeing molten iron bubbling away. "It appears to be ready." He looked to the key which rested in his palm. "We are ready to split the key...? But, father; will the key not melt or burn? And the cross, it will be sodden with pits and cracks, it might not even have time to cool sufficiently."

"Stephen, you are creating a cross as though spoken from God," was the priest's answer. "We are creating something unique, something which will, forever, resemble the saviour of mankind. It does not have to look pretty."

Stephen understood something then, something which flashed before him, something that he did not wish to reveal but felt he had little choice, for his understanding would reveal to the others the true meaning of what they were creating. "I was once told a story of a sacred chalice; it was called the Holy Grail. It was believed to be the most common of cups from which Jesus drank, not dotted with pearls, gems, or other stones of great worth, but an everyday, common cup. It was a dream story, something that held water but could not be proved, something that has passed along the grapevine, from story-teller to story-teller. I tell you now that the cup is false for I know the true meaning of the Grail of Christ. This cross, no matter how common it shall be, once it is made will be the envy of the world, but the world will not know of its existence. The cross we are about to create is the Holy Grail."

And they all understood the words of Stephen to be the truth, for he had the insight, he had the power to be legend.

Stephen passed the key to Ambaedian. "Quickly, father, split the key as I make ready with the molten contents."

Father Ambaedian took the key as Lambert and Bernard looked on, both bewildered, dumb struck, without word and completely begotten by what they were about to witness, for they believed every word that Stephen spoke, and why should they not, for he was the chosen one?

The priest handled the key magnificently and with the key held in his left hand he placed a chisel upon its end with his right. Transferring his grip so that his left hand held both items, he picked up a hammer with his right hand, and commenced to hit the chisel, softly at first, until the key split perfectly into two pieces.

There before them was the key in two halves, one piece hollowed out sufficiently to form both the front and the back of the cross. A design could be seen but not made out properly: not only was there insufficient time to worry about that but as Stephen had already mentioned, it mattered not what the end result looked like, so long as it was true.

The molten iron was poured into one half, where the level of iron came up to the rim. He then placed the top portion into place, its inner face also holding a chiselled design, hence allowing for a beautiful mold both front and back of the cross, once cooled. The two parts, now together, were placed within an iron vice.

"The task is complete," said Bernard. "Once it has cooled we shall file its edges, make it smooth."

"Not quite complete," said Father Ambaedian. "For we still have a little molten iron left in the cup."

Stephen needed no prodding, no time to think, and acted immediately. "There is only one Holy Grail, what remains is of little consequence. Empty the cup of molten contents into a small tumbler of water. It shall be buried with the coals within a watery tomb, and if it should ever be found, which is highly unlikely, no one will ever scrutinize it, for it will have no appeal or lustre. Only one other thing remains to be done, one thing as important as important as the cross itself. We now must take it across the sea, into the west, where land can be secured and moulded to meet our needs, for the world is not flat, but round."

The four men looked at one another, nodding agreement.

The task was complete and the workshop had been cleaned up.

"What we have done here today shall remain a secret for all time. Never can the truth be spoken without permission first coming from me," spoke Stephen. "For the Holy Grail shall forever be bound around my neck and the contents of this basin, this makeshift urn, delivered unto the sea."

And as the four men, with the basin carried by Bernard alone, departed the workshop, a creaking grew from the hinges of a door. The smithy and his wife entered the workshop in astonishment to what they had seen through the crack of the door. In silence they had waited, had watched the cross being made, had heard the entire story develop as it had. They now understood why Father Ambaedian required being alone.

"My dear wife," said the smithy. "I think we have just witnessed something which could bring us much salvation."

"But how?" asked the wife.

"It must be worth something, to someone."

Stephen, Lambert, Bernard and Father Ambaedian soon found themselves in the comfort of the hall and its huge open fireplace, reflection of light from the fire flickering across the stone floor in orange hues.

Each sat down in silence before Father Ambaedian made the announcement. "I have something for you Stephen, something that you will carry with you for eternity... or I should hope so. I would like to think that a part of me will remain with you during your long and harsh journey."

"Whatever can it be, father?"

"Just you remain here in front of the fire and I shall be back shortly."

The priest stood up and made for the stairwell in the hallway and returned a short time after. He sat back down and learned forward from his seated posture, his right hand holding something. He held it out, "For you," he said and dropped into Stephen's open palm a simple chain of silver.

"It has been in this house for as long as I. When I started to read the many volumes I had collected over the years, which in itself was no easy feat, I came to the conclusion that the time would come when a chain would be required. I spoke with only a few trusted souls in regards to the chest and its secret, men of the Hospital all. The word went out to these few high priests, which is how you came to hear of me and decided to seek me out. A great chance I was taking for if the word had gotten out then I could have been in danger. Lucky for me that I never told the high priests any more than I had to. Of course, it was to come by way of word-by-mouth that a key was held in Káros. Once I heard this I set about revealing my information to Father Tourmede. He was a great man and knew what was good for the country and religion. So, at that time in my life, where I had studied all that I could from the volumes in my library, all I could do was set up house for the unfortunate and await the miracle to come. You, Stephen, are that miracle." There was a short break in the story before Father Ambaedian concluded with the obvious. "Use the chain for the Holy Grail, Stephen. Place it around your neck and never take it off."

Stephen put his hand into his pocket and drew out the cross, a design of magnificent structure raised upon the cross in the shape of Jesus, and the only impurities within the cross were a few, fine fissures that had appeared during its being moulded into shape; but it was strong, 3 x 5.5 pouce in size. The top most portion of the cross had a hole in it and through this he placed the chain, and the chain he put around his neck. It was not a ceremony worth noting, or by any degree requiring special service, but the silence in the hall that minute was only interrupted by the crackling of the fireplace as it continued to give off its radiant heat.

"This chain and the Holy Grail that it carries will forever remain a part of me," said Stephen. "Under no circumstances shall it be removed." And he tucked it back in behind the folds of cloth around his neck.

"That, young knight," said Ambaedian, "is not something you can afford to do."

Sister Bardwell approached the congregation of girls and their escort of two men as they had breakfast. The dining area catered well for large crowds, although no one else was present.

"Ah, Sister Bardwell," announced Martin as he stood, a smile appearing upon his face. "We must thank you again for these platters of bacon and mushroom. I can see that such morsels would not be easily afforded."

"Please, sit down," was the gentle reply, a little embarrass-ment felt, although such embarrassment did not show. "We have several members of the community who give quite often... not money, of course, but items such as pigs, goats, and wine. We also have an extensive garden."

"A garden?" asked Martin.

"One that takes much of our time, I am afraid, but well worth the effort, many vegetables being procured during the year. Many hungry mouths are content by our generosity, as we are content with the generosity of those that supply the means to procure a plate full of meat, cheese, or cup of milk. We are very grateful to all those that provide for us, in particular at hard times such as these, and it is seldom easy."

Martin saw an opening then and as all eyes looked upon him he offered the services of all of those that were eating. "I know the children would be more than happy to tend your garden, for your generosity at this, our time of need, is much appreciated."

"You flatter the convent with your words, Mr...."

"Please, call me Martin, I shall not allow us to be looked upon in a manner that is not deserved. Your work here, by-far, is more deserving than anything we could do."

Sister Bardwell catered for Martin's offer and took the opportunity for further conversation. "In that case, Martin, I shall have one of the other nuns tend to your flock by introducing them to our garden, and ask you to join me and the Mother Superior for further orientation."

The knight could see something was of the matter and nodded acceptance, "Tell the Mother Superior that Raoul and I look forward to the meeting." And with that said the nun departed company, leaving the group of children and two men to finish their morning meal in peace.

The children had been surrendered to work under one of the other nuns of the convent, picking weeds, tickling the ground with hoe and rake, although watering the vegetables as they grew was not required this day due to the storm the day before: along with any small task that was not too much for a young child to partake of, as Martin and Raoul sat in front of the warm fire of the main hall. They had not been waiting long before the Mother Superior entered the room with Sister Bardwell close on her heels.

"I see from the description given that you must be Martin, and you are obviously, Raoul?" said the Mother Superior, placing her hand out, which was accepted by both men with a smile. Such informality and ease made both men feel relaxed. "Please, sit back down; I would like to have a word with you both."

"Of course," said Martin and both men sat, followed immediately by the company that had entered.

"I shall get straight to the point, Martin, as it is not our way in life to waste what time we have, and I am sure, at most, that your time is as important to you as ours is to us."

"Of course, we both understand," replied Martin with a concerned look falling upon his face for the first time.

"It concerns the children, really. I need to know what your intentions are in regards to the children."

"We would like to leave them here for a few days and return to collect them for a further journey."

"Sister Bardwell has told me as much," said the Mother Superior, suspicious of their real calling. "She advises that you have come all the way from Constantinople, and that the city has fallen?"

"That is correct; it now grieves under Muslim control."

"That is tragic news, but more tragic is the future of these children that you keep. Tell me, Martin, tell me of this school that you referred to last night, and tell me of your master and his overall plans for the children."

Raoul and Martin could both see the calamity of their situation most clearly. It was clear that the Mother Superior was concerned deeply for the welfare of the children, but nowhere near as concerned as they.

She broke the silence, "The children must have suffered much, as their clothing and appetite have suggested. Your voyage has been long and should have ended long ago, long before you came to Barcelona. It seems strange that you should travel so far, from Constantinople to here, to surrender the children to a school of which you seem to know nothing, a school which your 'master'," which she emphasized, "needs to lay visit upon before actually allowing the children to visit."

"Forgive us, but the rain last night was unforgiving. We could not allow the children to be harmed any more than was necessary. We simply require somewhere for the children to stay for a few days," Martin trailed off before making an offer. "We can pay for your trouble, for the charity which we require."

"Charity is charity, little or much, it remains the same. Payment is not required, as what we do is for the children. But let me ask you two gentlemen," and it appeared to Raoul and Martin both that the situation of turning-for-the-worst was beginning to show. "What business do you need to attend so urgently that you need to leave the children here?"

There was no answer to the question for the knights simply needed to have the children cared for whilst the situation with the Muslims could be taken care of. Raoul could see that Martin was slow to react to the question and he took the opportunity to answer for him.

"We need to shop for a wagon, some good horses to pull it, and rations enough to last the children a few days during our short journey," said Raoul.

"Ah, you have a voice," was the mother's superior answer of ridicule. "Tell me, Raoul, where is the school and what are your intentions once the children have been delivered? Are they to be left in the company of others, schooled until they are ready to fend for themselves? If this is the case then you might find comfort in knowing that you can leave them here at no further expense to yourselves, or your master."

"You are kind, Mother Superior, but our master has been very clear—"

"Then what is the name of the school you are referring to?" interrupted the Mother.

"We do not know the name," answered Martin.

"You travel all the way from Constantinople, with the pure intention of putting these children to school, yet you know not of the school's name," said the Mother Superior, making a statement, not posing a question. "It is also clear to me that your journey will take more than a few days for the only school and orphanages are those around Barcelona, and anything more would be a week's journey at least."

"Please, we are not criminals; you can see that our intentions are noble by the way the children look to us in their infectious way. We feel nothing less than the greatest concern for the children. We must wait for our master to return and continue with our journey. The children are our responsibility and must remain so."

"Very well, Martin," said the mother superior. "We shall give you and your master seven days. If in that time you have not returned to collect them, and with the name of the school that you are referring to, I shall take matters into my own hands and see to it that the children are placed into our custody. Do I make myself clear?"

"You do, and I thank you for your understanding," said Martin. "Could I please speak with the girl named Catherine before we part? We have much to do and need to pass on our goodbyes before we depart."

"Of course.

It was clear to Martin that their main plan of action was somewhat interrupted by the suspicious mind of the Mother Superior; he should have remained calm and in control, simply advising the Mother that Stephen was to meet them at the convent in a few days, but he had concerns for the situation in regards to the Muslims that had followed them. He was aware that Lars and Aaron were to tend the problem with the Muslims, and ensure that the enemy remained unaware as to their position, but he needed to make sure, even if to console himself. So long as the children remained in safe hands he would be able to scout around, it was even possible for him to gain important information that might be of use to them as a group. There was also the call to duty in regards to their second priority, to ensure that the carrack was ready for a retreat from the harbour of Barcelona: far from it for them to know that she had sunk.

Martin knelt beside Catherine with a smile as she continued with tending the garden. "Listen to me, child, and listen carefully. Raoul and I must attend to our urgent need, but we shall return. Tomorrow morning, as the sun breaks the horizon, you must have all of the children ready at the front door of this convent. You must be quiet and slip away during breakfast, not bringing attention to any of the Sisters that reside here. We will have Stephen with us." They locked eyes. "Do you understand, child? It must be a clean break."

"Yes, Martin," answered Catherine. "I understand."

Stephen had a late rise, as did the others, but they were soon congregated in a private room where breakfast had been laid out for them all. The busy service of the home for sailors could be heard from where they sat, the platter of plates, the mingled conversation, laughter in places going uninterrupted. Father Ambaedian then entered as the three knights sat eating, reflecting individually on the previous night's activities.

The priest sat with all eyes upon him. "I have decided to join you, Stephen, back to the harbour where your carrack awaits. I am sure that you could use an extra hand to help you with your expedient departure. I also know some of the locals."

"Your help will be much appreciated, father," said Stephen. "I thank you from the bottom of my heart and..." suddenly, and without warning, Stephen clutched at the cross beneath his tunic and gasped a final heavy breath which he exhaled as though in disbelief.

The knights either side grabbed out at him to lend support where support might be needed. "It is okay, thank you Lambert; Bernard; I am okay now, but bad news I have witnessed. I only hope that the news I bear witness to is incorrect... I do not even know when… the cross is hard to decipher."

"With practise you will see all," encouraged Ambaedian. "But tell us, please. What did you see?"

"We must depart immediately for our friend Lars has been place into gaol."

"Gaoled?" asked Lambert

"I cannot see all and I do not know the reasons for his being arrested, but I see the hangman's noose being placed around his neck. I, too, can see the neck snap. The Lord will deliver to him a quick and painless death."

"There must be something that we can do," said Bernard. "We can rescue him, with the help of the Cross of Christ."

Stephen abruptly turned upon his friend, and Father Ambaedian also gave a horrified look, both of which fell upon Bernard's watchful eye.

"The cross can never be used for personal gain," said Stephen. "And never will I try. It is for the good of the human race, for the Christian religion, for all of those of Orthodox belief; it is even for those of Islam so that they may see the errors of their ways, so that the world can be joined as one. It cannot be used to relieve Lars of the justice that has to befall him. God has already granted him a pain-free death, that in itself is enough, and for that we should be forever thankful. But furthermore there is, I can see it now. Lars did cause action upon another which was an act of self-defence, but even so he must meet his end. Those that have caused this ill fate will be dealt with by the hand of God and Lars will live for eternity in the house of heaven. Lars has done more for us than he can be thanked for."

"He deserves your presence," said Ambaedian.

"I shall lay visit upon him and pass on the secret that we have unmasked. He shall be told all so that he can die in peace. A special prayer we will say for him when death takes him from us."

"I shall prepare a horse and cart immediately," advised Father Ambaedian, and although he did not know Lars, he did know one thing: if the knight known as Lars could be trusted by Stephen then he was worth every ounce of effort in allowing him a peaceful death.

"Thank you, father," said Stephen as he stood. "Lambert, Bernard, get ready the makeshift urn and its contents, we return to the harbour post-haste."

The cart made its way with a stinging of the whip behind the horses head, a jolting start to a reasonably short journey. What had taken the knights several hours to walk would now be considerably shorter. The weather was also good but the road was a little muddy, clouds had dissipated considerably, and birds had come out to greet the new day of bright light and warmth.

"We will be in the city of Barcelona before a hungry man has time to get a good fill of bread and wine," said Father Ambaedian. "It will not take us long."

Stephen sat beside the priest with Lambert and Bernard sitting opposite each other in the back, the basin placed securely upon the floor of the cart and between several dozen large bags filled with fruit and vegetables, commodities that the priest wished to sell whilst in the town they were to lay visit upon. Stephen looked at Martin.

"Martin, please pass me some fruit and a couple of pieces of vegetable," and once these had been handed over, Stephen placed it into his pocket. "Thank you, Martin." Stephen turned to the priest.

"I must thank you again, father. Your time in our errand is much appreciated," said Stephen.

"I shall not hear of it, Stephen. You have far too much to concern yourself with, and besides, I must get these vegetables to market, for the men who stay with me could do with a belly full of wine. It does not do well for the mortal man of town to go without a little vegetable."

"And for those of us who are no longer mortal?"

"You have a burden to carry, that is for sure, but I doubt for a single minute that you would be denied your rights as a man. Surely you will desire a woman from time to time, that is most natural. It is not as though you are ordained."

"I believe the contrary, father. I believe the Cross of Christ is an ordination, and I shall live as any other man of the cloth. Besides, I was married once."

"Really," said the priest, seemingly shocked. "So young in life and married. Where is your wife if not by your side?"

"She rests in the same place that the basin is to be delivered," said Stephen, and seeing Ambaedian's blank look gave further information. "She was surrendered unto the sea. She died in Constantinople and I was lucky to get her away. She was buried that same unfortunate day that Constantinople was taken by the heathen Turk."

"Such a young life lost," said the priest. "It must have been very painful for you."

"Yes, it was," agreed Stephen.

"How long were you married for?"

"Two and a half days, father," and Stephen could feel the shock of the priest without even looking. "We were wed on the Saturday night and Constantinople fell on the Tuesday morning. I have since vowed never to remarry." Stephen fondled the ring upon his finger, a ring that the priest had not come to notice until now. "I consider myself still married to her and could never marry another. If I am to believe that I am the chosen one, and that there is indeed life-after death, then I must assume, for all sakes, that I shall meet my wife again." Stephen looked to Father Ambaedian then, who met his stare briefly as he controlled the single horse carriage along its way. "I do not believe that my life will be eternal, but even if it is, I still have a wife. I cannot neglect her; even if I cannot see or touch her, it does not mean that she does not exist."

"I am going to help you, Stephen, as best I can," said Father Ambaedian. "We shall ride into Barcelona and lay visit upon your friend so that you may pass on your final words and prayer. Your other friends should not be hard to find. Where are you to meet them?"

"On the road that leads to the north, I can show you when we arrive in town."

"What are we to do once in town?" asked Lambert. "And when do we lay visit upon Lars?"

"You and Bernard can tend to the horse and cart, and the basin. I alone shall visit Lars. I shall meet up with you again later in the afternoon, and if luck is with us, both Martin and Raoul will have found us."

"And of Aaron?"

"We will not have time to attend any funeral. It is upsetting, I know," said Stephen. "To think that our friend will be delivered unto God's care in a common garden box, most definitely without the appropriate psalms to give appropriate praise to the honourable man he is. Much courage he did display."

Silence then dominated the scene as they continued on their way to Barcelona, reflection upon their friend Aaron. None knew of his past, at a time before he became a knight, but his time on Káros proved that he deserved to walk with all the brave men of the earth, in heaven. His courage was exemplary as too was his character and concerns for others. He never shirked a job and was always there to provide a helping hand. He would be sorely missed.

*

* * *

*

The smithy and his wife sat beside one another and followed those in front of them, making sure they maintained a very reasonable distance behind Father Ambaedian's horse and cart. Many thoughts crossed their minds as they continued with their slow pursuit, a journey into the unknown. For them the glory of life was not to be found in heaven, but was in their lust for gold and wealth. They wanted nothing more than to put their miserable life behind them so that they could lead one of luxury and ease.

"Do not get too close, my husband," said Patricia, his wife. "Ambaedian will recognize us if he sees us."

"Do you take me for a fool?" said Henry in reply. "I shall maintain good distance whilst on these country roads, but once we commence to enter town we shall have to gain ground on our friends; I would not wish to lose them in the crowd."

"What do you think of the Cross of Christ?" asked Patricia.

"What! Oh, the Holy Grail. It will be worth a hundred times its weight in gold... a thousand." He looked his wife of 25 years in the eye. "We are rich; I can feel the gold between my fingers already. We will have so much gold that we can shower ourselves in luxuries only dreamt of, and every day, too. I can see the wealth of it now. Servants we shall have, ten, twenty; and a butler and cook; a large house with a horse drawn carriage with driver and footman."

"Such wealth," said his wife. "But if the Holy Grail is all it is supposed to be... how do we get rich from such a thing?"

"We shall learn, like any other person learns a thing, we shall learn the trade of the grail. It will become second nature. And we will live for ever and a day, showered in its riches, like rain drops falling from the sky. Imagine it, just imagine."

And they continued on in silence, watching the cart in front of them as it made its way towards Barcelona. Their future was just out of reach and they both badly wanted it in their grasp.

*
* * *
*

Martin and Raoul approached the harbour as inconspicuously as one could approach, the fresh morning breeze smelling of the sea, gutted fish and sweat. Sea gulls filled the air as they swarmed around, looking for morsels, for the guts of fish, their heads and fins, anything that the fisherman wished to give up to the squawking birds as they came down to the pier, hobbling around, resting on rail and rope, mast and bollard. The harbour was flush with activity, the boats being unloaded of their catch-of-the-day, filling the orders as they came from fishmongers.

Martin pointed off into the distance, towards the end of the pier.

"Just there, Raoul," said Martin. "That is where the carrack should be."

"I am bothered by the lack of what I see before me," said Raoul. "Do you recall what Stephen said to the master of the harbour when he was confronted by the man?"

"Yes, that the brigantine would pay... ah, there would have been none; no payment would have been received."

"And Stephen advised the master of the harbour to keep the carrack if no payment was forthcoming. Do you think he has moved it?"

"It would have proved to be too much to move by himself, and more than likely that moving it would have been a waste of time. What better position than where the carrack sat, for advertising a boat for sale. Any merchant would have been more than happy with the condition of the vessel. I have no doubt in my mind, Raoul, that the carrack would have been sold that same day that we entered harbour."

"No, it was too late, too dark, and too stormy."

"I see no other explanation."

"Maybe we should ask the man ourselves," suggested Raoul.

"I think not. It is more than likely that he will try and charge us for the time it was tied up."

"But if he sold it... we would be due compensation."

"You forget, Raoul. Stephen did give it away, more or less."

"So what now? What shall we do?"

"We shall attend the suggested meeting place as provided by Stephen. We will meet him there and advise him of the situation. There is nothing else we can do."

"Then let us move, and let us hope that he arrives today, for tomorrow we will have our hands full with tending to thirteen children."

Within the half hour, Martina and Raoul could see a horse and cart approaching from the north end of the road.

"Do you think that is Stephen?" asked Raoul.

"I cannot tell from this distance. Let us wait here in the shadows until it gets closer." So they pulled themselves back from the road and waited as the cart drew closer and closer. All they could see were two men, one sitting next to the other, reins gingerly held in the palm of the driver's hands, the horse moving along slowly with his head hung low, familiar with his surroundings and the road to Barcelona. Stephen was looking ahead and saw the meeting place to his front.

"That is it, father. That is where we must meet the others," said Stephen as he pointed off to where the road began, where a cobbled way melded into a dirt track, where the last of the town houses lined the street. "And there... can it be?"

Martin smiled, "It is Stephen, it is he," and pulled on Raoul's sleeve. They both moved out of the little shadow in which they stood and gave a short wave, Stephen holding his hand up for both men to see.

"Lambert, Bernard, we are there, I see Martin and Raoul standing on the side of the road, just to our front."

"Thank heavens they are safe," said Martin.

In no time at all the horse and cart pulled up beside the two men. "Climb aboard," said Stephen. "We shall find a place to stop the cart and continue with our tasks."

"Much to our disappointment," said Martin, "we have to part upon you bad news."

"We have much to discuss," said Stephen. "But it shall have to wait. Father, can you find somewhere to put this horse and cart of yours, somewhere out of the way?"

"I know a place, an alley beside a family-owned restaurant. They have been kind to me in the past and will not mind it if we leave it there. They will know my cart if they see it and it will be safe from prying eyes."

Martin and Raoul clambered aboard, sitting themselves beside their comrades of the Hospital.

"Bad news, Martin," said Lambert. "We have news that Aaron has been killed and that Lars has been imprisoned."

"Oh my god," exclaimed Martin. "How do you know for sure? Where is Lars now?"

"It is the secret of the chest," said Raoul. "Stephen has much to pass on, much to tell. The Cross of Christ has been born, but more than that, it is a secret that we have uncovered, something so wonderful that I still cannot believe it, but it is true."

"Please tell us," said Martin.

Stephen turned upon his seat and looked upon the men in the back of the cart. "Soon enough, Martin. You and Raoul will know everything, but for the meantime we must depart the comfort of the cart and prepare ourselves as best we can to the changing predicament."

"How was Aaron killed?" asked Martin, anxious for some news, unable to wait.

"I do not know exactly," said Stephen in reply. "But I do know this much; it was a cowardly act that had no real cause. They were both unjustly treated and condemned without sufficient proof."

The horse and cart had been left in the alley without a hitch and Stephen took the opportunity to familiarize himself with the bad news of Martin and Raoul. Stephen was turned side on, as was Father Ambaedian, to share conversation with the four knights in the back of the cart, the basin between them all, secured in place by heavy sacks of vegetables.

Stephen broke the silence and started the briefing. He explained in detail the opening of the chest and of what they had found within it, of the task they had in melting the objects and the secret of the key. The chest of secrets was no real mystery, in the end. It was the key, the key itself held the secret of the chest. From the key a cross had been created. The knights knew since they had left Káros that the contents of the chest had to be fused, but how it was to be undertaken had been a mystery of its own. But now, as Stephen explained it to them, it seemed to be nothing less than common sense. It all fit together: Káros, the key, and the chest.

"And furthermore, the Cross of Christ is nothing less than the Holy Grail," said Stephen.

"How can that be?" asked Raoul.

"It is a gift from God, a gift to set mankind free. Only the chosen one can hold the power of the grail and I am that chosen one."

"What are you to do, Stephen? What is your quest?" asked Martin.

"There is so much to tell that I do not know where to start, so please, bear with me," said Stephen, and he explained as best he could of the history of man and the task he had been set. It was for the chosen one to inherit the power of the Cross of Christ, also known as the Holy Grail; what is one, is the other. The power of the cross will be for the chosen one to decipher, to release, to hold, and to deliver. It is for him, the chosen one to be the protector of Jesus' sacrifice, as He did sacrifice his human existence so that the multitudes could be forgiven their sins. And why should anyone be forgiven their sins? Because it is not the fault of the sinful, but the fault of the devil himself, for the devil resides in the heart and minds of all, but it is for the individual to deny the devil. This is the meaning of life and will be the task of all men and women, for the remainder of all time to come, to take control and denounce the devil, at each and every opportunity. The chosen one must inherit his sacrifice with pride and good judgement, which is why he is the chosen one, chosen by the hand of God. For the chosen one's work to be completed to the best of his ability he must remain far away from civilization, for if the Cross of Christ was to fall into the wrong hands then damnation could easily befall the human race. Only the chosen one can behold the grail, the great artefact that was moulded from the good and evil of man's past. It was for the chosen one to protect the human race and to bring it salvation, but no good comes easily and many years must pass before salvation can be heralded amongst all religions, for they do not understand one another as God understands them all. The chosen one is to form an order of knights, the female of the species to be anointed by great responsibilities, and history has shown that only the female has the power of birth and man has the power of to deliver death; but the roles would be reversed: the female would become the hunter and the male of the species nothing more than a concubine, although only one man would ever couple with a single woman and a ceremony of marital worth staged for the sake of religious endeavour; the man and woman would not live together. The Holy Grail was of God's work, but the religious framework of the future would be that of Jesus and his New Testament. The Cross of Christ must be protected for the remainder of human history to come until such a time that salvation has been secured in the hearts and minds of all on earth. Only when everyone can clearly understand the sacrifices that Jesus bestowed upon us all can we truly be forgiven the sins of the devil and be considered as one. It was the orphans, the thirteen girls currently housed in the orphanage, that were the key to success in Stephen's mission. It was the girls that were the framework for the Knights of the Holy Grail. The girls would grow to become women, to harbour a name that would one day be whispered upon the lips of the entire world, Coniupuyana, which means Amazon. These thirteen would be the women of the Amazon, a race of women so feared that they would become legendary. In order to secure the salvation of the human race the chosen one must travel west, for the earth was round, not flat, and he was to find the path to the treasures of the Templar Knight. It is written in history that 24 Knights of the Temple travelled amongst eighteen galleys, all filled to the brim with treasure, and such treasure was somewhere to be found, somewhere that only Stephen knew. Yes indeed, for they had departed from La Rochelle and were delivered unscathed upon the mouth of the Amazon. Stephen would find the treasure, hidden as it was. He would become known as the Golden man to some, the Gilded Man to others, and yet El Dorado to most. A legend would be born. It would be for the chosen one to suffer in his immortal existence, as Jesus suffered upon the cross, but with such a sacrifice came the power that God wished to relinquish, for Stephen would have unlimited power on life and death, would see the future and read men's thoughts. He would know what to do as though born to it.

"And that is the story as I know it, the truth, the whole truth, and nothing but the truth," concluded Stephen. "And now we have other matters to attend to. We must attend the carrack."

"The carrack is missing," said Raoul. "We attended the harbour this morning and could not find it. It has vanished. We decided against going to the harbour master for fear of being persecuted."

"You made a wise decision," said Stephen. "Father Ambaedian, can you help with securing another boat, one suitable for a small crew and thirteen passengers?"

"I think I can be of assistance, although the law may be broken in the process."

"The owners will be rewarded," said Stephen. "The power of the cross will see to that. I shall attend the prison where Lars has been wrongfully detained. Please take the four knights with you and do as you need to do."

"Where shall we meet?" asked the priest.

"I shall see you before last light, at the horse and cart," said Stephen. "We can then find ourselves a warm fire and bed down for the night."

Stephen had little trouble finding the gaol where Lars had been delivered. Every window on the premises had bars; even the door was secured with heavy hinges, double latch on the inside and made from thick, strong wood. The gaol was opposite the town square where it was customary to conduct the hangings. It was a very suitable spot indeed for the hangman's noose, close to the gaol house, and could allow for a large crowd to easily view the proceedings when a man was to be condemned and hung until he was dead. There was a sign upon a bulletin board and in large letters advised, those that could read, that a man was to be committed to the hangman's noose on the morrow. Stephen was quite disturbed by the speed in which Lars had been found guilty, and unless a bribe of some description accompanied the gaoling of Lars, nothing could explain the verdict made in such haste.

It was not uncommon to find the most innocent of individuals being hanged for the smallest of crimes, but where power was to be granted, power was to be misused. The rich ruled the roost and the poor were nothing more than pawns to help the rich get richer. To see the filthiest of the poor being swept under a rock and hanged for next-to-nothing was a grand affair for those in power. It was as though they were doing the country a service by ridding it of peasant's blood. Beggars on the streets, in particular around the town's centre, were an eyesore to say the least, let alone the smell of them.

Stephen approached the open door, for at present there was little cause for security measures to be at their highest. The sheriff was seated behind his desk, alone and left to be infuriated by the paperwork that had to be filled, processed, and filed in accordance with the judicial system. He looked up, a seemingly sour man.

"What is it? What can I do for you?"

"My name is Stephen and I am looking for the sheriff of this grand town," said Stephen, giving a little praise to aid him in his future endeavours.

"Aye. Well, you have found him. I am the sheriff." The man of average height put his hand out in greeting. "You can call me Andre."

"Thank you, Andre."

"Are you here to make a report?" asked the sheriff, looking Stephen up and down, seeing a well-stocked man, a youth in simple dress, but not a pauper, beggar or thief. No, this man before him was well educated, he could guess it. The manner of his speech, the way in which he had delivered himself and gave his opening address.

"No, Andre," said Stephen in reply. "I am here to request a meeting, to lay visit upon one of those that you have in your cells."

"We have six in the cells below ground, none in the cells above. Which one of them do you wish to see, and why?"

"I am an old friend who simply wishes to see my former captain before he meets with the hangman tomorrow."

"Ah, you speak of the man with no tongue," said the sheriff, pondering what Stephen had said. "He is a captain, you say. Captain of what?"

"He was one of the men that I fought with during the siege of Constantinople."

"I see," said the sheriff. "And what happened with the siege, may I ask?" "Constantinople has been taken and now lies in Muslim hands."

The sheriff took several paces over to his desk and sat upon it. "My god. You know what this means, Stephen? Europe is next, we are to be consumed."

"Please," said Stephen, interrupting the sheriff of his wayward thinking. "If I could see the man named Lars, then I would be most grateful."

"Indeed. Well, I see why not. He is to be hanged on the morrow, as you have so delicately reminded, but I fail to see what the meeting will bring. He does not talk, you know that."

"I know, but would be grateful for—"

"No more, please, I have much work to do," said the sheriff in a huff. "I shall get the gaoler for you, just wait here."

The sheriff moved over to the door at the rear of the office and pulled a key from his belt, unlocking the door and providing warning. "It is the sheriff; I have a man who wishes to see the prisoner in cell number four." The door opened and the gaoler stood, wine dribbling from his chin, for he was refreshing himself as he normally did. "Take him down and allow him a single lantern. Give him a few minutes." The sheriff turned to Stephen. "The gaoler will give you a lantern and two minutes alone with the prisoner. Do not waste the time you have for I shall not grant a further visit to you or any other of his friends – that is if he has any."

The cell door was opened with much creaking and Stephen entered the cell with the lantern in his hand. The smell from within hit him immediately; the smell of rotting food, of urine and sweat, the smell of the squalor, the filth and the misery, all that he had expected of a dungeon concealed underground with no adequate ventilation or window to speak of.

"Lars, it is I, Stephen."

Stephen swung the lantern around a little until the light fell upon his friend, his clothing like a heap of rags bandaged around him, his eyes peeking through a small opening. Lars was cold, so very cold. Lars was looking forward to the hangman's noose, for the misery of the cell and confinement was too much for his weary bones and old age.

Stephen dashed over and placed the lantern carefully down as the cell door closed behind him, the gaoler letting go with a smirk and a chuckle, showing his true colours: that he cared not for anyone within this dark and infested dungeon.

Stephen and Lars were now alone.

"What have they done to you Lars? Those animals have beaten you." The bruises upon his face could be seen as the lantern flickered, the light spilling across the walls. The eyes in Lars' sockets were his voice that moment, telling of his relief that he could see and hear a friend, the happiness he felt that someone had found him, to hear words of friendship being spoken to him one final time. "If it was not for the burden that I carry... no, it is no burden, but without it I would kill the gaoler and the sheriff for finding you this way." Stephen sat beside Lars and gave him a brief hug before releasing him. "I have news, Lars, and time is short. The secret of the chest is ours, we know of its power and its message. It is so beautiful but also full of devastation. We are going to sea but once again, Lars, to travel to the west, to find a new world which has yet to be discovered by the horrors and misgivings of our civilisation as we know it. From there we are to prepare for the delivery of the Lord's words, but how we are to go about it I do not yet fully know. But you, my friend, will have to remain here. You will not be forgotten. We cannot help you, I am sorry. The only way we can save you is to deliver death to those that have seen to your conviction, and even then some of us may also perish. We must do all we can to protect the orphans."

Lars reached out and grabbed Stephen's arm and smiled a warming smile. Lars understood the predicament as it was and did not feel badly against Stephen's inaction. No one here was at fault except the instigator of his imprisonment, and that man would one day meet his dying day.

"I have spoken to God, Lars, spoken to Him, confronted him man to man, it was a meeting as plain as you see the shadow of my nose cast upon my face on a bright, summer's day. You will not be forgotten when delivered to the hangman, Lars. You will not suffer but will be granted salvation through delivery of a painless death. You will walk in heaven, Lars, that I have been promised. Carry yourself proud for all you have done, show the crowd that you are innocent and not afraid to die, for you have nothing to fear."

Stephen put his hand into his pockets and pulled out the fruit and vegetable that he had placed there earlier when on the cart belonging to Father Ambaedian.

"Something for you, Lars. Hide it well and eat it wisely, for if the gaoler is to see you with it... well, the consequences would be horrendous."

Lars was overwhelmed by the gift of food and placed it immediately out of sight, under his garments. He would eat it all later, a little for his dinner, some for supper, and even a morsel for his breakfast, before his life was surrendered for the pleasure of a few.

"I am sorry I cannot do more," continued Stephen as Lars squeezed his arm before releasing it, showing his understanding, his comradeship, his love for his friend. "But you must believe me; you will not feel any pain when hanged."

Stephen could see by the look in Lars' eyes that he believed every word, that he was not afraid to die, that he was happy to hear of his being delivered into heaven by the grace of God.

A jingling of keys could then be heard as the cell door was opened, the gaoler outside. "I must go now, my friend. Our thoughts will be with you. But you must remember this, too; that God will be with you on your journey into heaven, he will be with you at the time of your death, you have nothing to fear." Stephen took hold of the cross around his neck and spoke his final words of faith. "Give him strength and warmth, take the bitter cold that he feels from his bones, give him special favour in this his last hours on earth." He quickly held the cross out to Lars. "This is the wonder of the chest, Lars, hold it whilst you have the chance, feel it in your fingers."

Lars touched the cross around Stephen's neck and could feel the warmth of his blessed love. Lars then released the cross.

Stephen stood up and grabbed the lantern, departing with one final look, glaring down upon his friend on the cell floor, Lars smiling up at him, and Stephen knew at that moment that Lars had been saved, that he would fend well when it came to dying, that his death would be one of peace, nothing to despair. Lars was warm and happy; he had nothing to be scared about, felt no guilt, and had led a most worthy life.

Abu and Ahmad had spent their time well since being ashore. With their clothes dry, and being well groomed, they mingled well with the populace of the town known as Barcelona. They had enough money in their pockets to acquire enough food to fill them both, with some left over for a drink at a tavern. They had seated themselves down and were minding their own business when a drunkard raised his voice just a little too much.

"Gold I tell you, a large chest of gold," said the drunkard.

"Where?" asked the other.

"The harbour master of Barcelona; the keeper of the pier. He has much gold in his office, taken from bribes. He has much gold, so much that the chest he conceals it all in is filled to the brim."

"Dirty money," said the other.

"Aye; filthy it is. The man is a criminal if ever I saw one." The drunkard trailed off for a second before continuing. "He is at an official post and uses it to his great advantage. Nothing can be done. All manner of merchandise brought into the harbour gets taxed, but this man... he places his own tax on top of that. And if somebody does not pay... well; they do not get to off-load their goods. Food is spoilt and fresh fish goes bad. What choice do people have? Too hard to make a decent living, too hard it is."

"Aye. It is a shame."

Abu pulled lightly on Ahmad's sleeve and gave him a nod, for Ahmad to follow him outside for some fresh air and private conversation.

"Did you hear all of that, Ahmad?" asked Abu.

"I did, I did indeed."

"There is a chest of gold just waiting for us to pick it up. It seems to me that we should lay visit upon this harbour master, in the dead of night; even possibly the early hours of the morning. Such wealth will serve us well during our stay. What do you say to it?"

"I say we take the chest, as you suggest. The money will go well towards our task. With the wealth of the chest we seek, along with the wealth of the chest on the harbour, we will be very rich, rich beyond our wildest dreams."

"Aye," said Abu. "I thought we would be wealthy when we were one hundred men, but now we are only a handful, the wealth will be unimaginable. The distribution between just a few will be so much more rewarding."

"I can imagine quite a lot, Abu, gold enough to spill from the cup formed by my two hands placed together."

"Yes, me too. Come, let us go and find this chest, take some time to look at the office in which it is kept. I am sure as sure can be that the point of a blade will make the harbour master yelp like he has never yelped before."

Father Ambaedian led the four knights along one of the many piers. There was a carrack, not too dissimilar to the one that Stephen and the others had arrived in, just sitting there, seemingly empty and void of any crew and captain.

"I know the owner of this one," said Ambaedian. "He fishes six mornings every week, brings in his catch and disperses the crew. The goods he sells to merchants, and never have I seen, or heard, of a day that he does not sell. Tomorrow is Sunday and he will not fish. Many of the men will not work on the Sabbath."

"Will it be safe, father, to take this vessel with as much ease as we will require?" asked Raoul.

"The harbour master may interfere. It would be best to have him distracted, but there are many boats, and he cannot watch them all. All he cares for is the wealth that the boats bring in. No, I do not think it will be a problem."

"What about supplies?" asked Martin.

"You will take the sacks of fruit and vegetables that I have in the cart, I insist upon it. The sailors I tend to will not grow hungry or thirsty, for I have plenty of money kept aside. I shall shop for goods tomorrow, after you have departed for the west. I shall bring the cart in along the harbour just minutes before you depart."

"If that does not grasp the attention of the harbour master then I do not know what will," added Raoul.

"Yes, well there is not much we can do about it except hope for the best," said Father Ambaedian. "Besides, what is one man going to do against five?"

"Six," added Lambert, "you forget Stephen."

"Aye. Let us adjourn to the horse and cart, we will wait for Stephen and once he is with us we shall fall upon the hospitality of my friends, for a sleep in front of a warm fireplace." And the meeting with Stephen took place within the half hour. They decided on the action they should take. Martin and Raoul were to aid the orphans in their escape and once successful were to meet Father Ambaedian, Lambert and Bernard, at the horse and cart. Stephen would attend the hanging early to give special prayer. Once all were together at the horse and cart they were to meet Stephen in the main square at the centre of town and make their final way towards the carrack, Father Ambaedian hanging back with the cart until the last moment, so as not to draw attention to the escape. Once all understood and agreed with the action to be carried out they adjourned for the night, taking in the hospitality of Father Ambaedian's friends.

The day wore on like any other and soon the night was upon the city of Barcelona. Abu and Ahmad took turns to stand guard during the night, to await the hour of early morning on which they were to turn to their mischievous behaviour, just hours before the sun was due to rise. They walked so as not to gain the attention of anyone that might be out amongst the cool night air, but the only persons they saw were those too drunk to pinch themselves, let alone be concerned about two sober men out on an early morning's stroll. They approached the harbour master's hut, his place of residence, a small enough premise which afforded the comforts associated with a man of forty, seafaring years. He was asleep, snoring contentedly, dreaming of food, drink, and women of the night. He was a man like any other single man would be, shackled to his way of life, devoted to his treasures and reputation, although his reputation was nothing to boast about, for he was nothing more than a drunk most of the time, and when he was sober he was gambling, moaning about his misfortunes, or shovelling food down his throat.

And so Abu and Ahmad approached from within the shadows cast by the light of the moon, gaining ground on the only door into the master's cabin and the fortune in gold which awaited them both.

Abu opened the creaking door slowly and Ahmad entered first, stepping slowly and with little noise. A little creaking came from the floorboards but the harbour master's snoring saw to it that he slept soundly. The light in the cabin was little, windows letting in light from the moon but was insufficient enough to see the possible whereabouts of the chest of gold. Abu drew up alongside Ahmad and spoke to him in a whisper.

"Sit on him, Ahmad, restraining his arms and torso," said Abu. "I shall grasp his mouth and you get your dagger's blade up against his throat. We will drag the information from him, and if he does not squeal then we shall cut his fingers off, one by one until he does. Do you understand?"

"Yes, Abu; I do."

"Good. Let's get to it."

The harbour master was lying upon a pallet, which itself was made on the floor, to the farthest corner. There was not much to the cabin itself, a table at the side of the room, easily pulled out, plenty of chairs for seating all around, and a workbench along one complete side where the windows were open to the world, where books, charts, and logs would be maintained during the course of a normal business day, stalls for three to be seated, if required.

Ahmad walked over the man on his back and straddled him slowly before suddenly allowing all of his weight to fall upon him, at the same time bringing the blade of his dagger up to the man's throat. Abu placed his open palm tightly over his mouth, fingers pressing heavily against his lips.

"Shhh. Not a word from you, my friend," said Abu, drawing on the fear that would be welling inside the man on his back. "Do not move, or you die, do you understand." The fear in the harbour master was overflowing but he nodded in general acceptance of his predicament. The last thing he wanted was to die.

"Listen to me, listen carefully," advised Abu. "We come for the chest of gold, that is all. Tell us where it is and you shall live. I shall remove my hand from your mouth and if you attempt to bring alarm to any passer-by then we shall cut into your gullet like you were a dead fish. Do you understand?"

Again the man on his back nodded in acceptance, and little choice he had. Abu pulled his palm from the man's mouth. "Where do you keep the chest of gold?"

"I have no gold, you have been misinformed. I do not—"

Abu thrust his open palm once more over the harbour master's mouth and placed all of his weight from his left knee, onto the man's left arm. "Ahmad, put your weight from your left leg onto his right hand and cut away one of his fingers."

The harbour master cried to scream out in protest, panic striking his eyes, his pupils growing large. He lashed out with his feet to no avail and Ahmad pressed his right hand against the floorboards of the cabin and cut his index finger away from his hand. Blood immediately swamped the area, the harbour master almost fainting with the pain and terror, but he soon calmed down enough for the interrogation to continue.

"Tell me where the chest of gold is or you shall hobble out of here with no fingers and no toes. I am accustomed to issuing pain and cutting fingers off hands. You would be wise to tell us what it is we wish to know. Now, are you ready to try again?" asked Abu.

The harbour master saw no way out and wished to suffer no more. He could see by the seriousness in Abu's eyes that the man was out to get the chest of gold or cut away every single finger and toe that he had. He nodded in defeat and Abu removed his hand from the harbour master's mouth where gasps of air were the need of the moment. The fat man calmed, pain still showing upon his face.

"Under this pallet upon which I sleep," began the harbour master. "Beneath it are a few loose floor boards. Lift them up and you will see the chest."

Abu and Ahmad unceremoniously moved the harbour master from his pallet to the centre of the cabin floor, Ahmad seating himself once more upon the bulk of the man on his back. Abu withdrew a small dagger and tossed the pallet and bedding to one side. He knocked lightly the floorboards with the handle of his drawn weapon and heard the distinct hollowness from beneath them. He smiled and looked over to Ahmad in his commanding position before placing the blade of his dagger into the slots upon the floor and pried open the secret hiding place. Three boards were removed and a chest could be faintly seen. He put the dagger away and lifted out the chest with huff, for it was extremely heavy. It was a simple box, square in shape, and surprisingly enough had no lock to speak of. Abu simply lifted the latch and then the lid, where the gleaming of the gold coins sparkled in his eyes.

"Ahmad, look," said Abu, mesmerised by what he saw. "Gold, a chest full of it." He pressed his fingers into the coins and played with them, lifting them up and letting them fall, perusing the treasure he had found. "We are rich, Ahmad, all of us, and with the chest of secrets we will be the wealthiest of all Islam."

The harbour master heard what Abu was saying. He could not believe his ears in fact. Islam, these scum that had come to rob him were Muslims.

Abu put the chest down and crawled over to where the harbour master lay, and with the smile on his face, and the look in his eye displaying but pleasure and happiness, he betrayed the fat man once and for all. Abu lashed out with the blade of his dagger; the fat man's screams were muffled as his throat was cut wide open.

"Time to go, Abu," said an anxious Ahmad.

"Wait, not yet. There might be something else of great worth in this station. We must conduct a proper search."

"Very well, Abu, but please, let's not wait around too long."

Martin and Raoul concealed themselves as best they could, not far from the entrance to the convent, having sought themselves a good vantage point from which to easily see who went in and out of the main door of the building. Being a Sunday morning, and considering that the nuns would have tasks to attend to, in particular to the church service which would obviously distract their attention from the girls, Martin and Raoul considered their plan foolproof. Inside the house was a different matter.

The Mother Superior was busy with her own responsibilities but Sister Bardwell had one main task to attend to on a Sunday morning; she was to prepare the orphans for breakfast and then for the church service. It was understandable that any orphan taken in by the nuns of the convent would be surrendered to religious instruction and that attending church on any day of the week, in particular Sunday, would be accepted as nothing out of the ordinary. How was a little girl supposed to grow up to be a god-fearing adult if the proper tools of knowledge were not installed? And what better way to instil them than having it taught directly from a wife of Christ?

The children this morning did breakfast with the other orphans, of which there were eight. It was not a large number but kept the nuns' hands filled as they jostled around looking after the little ones and maintaining their vows as nuns of the convent. The eight other children were a little older than Catherine and the other twelve, but only by a few years, the oldest being fifteen years of age, almost at full blossom and ready to be married to the first respectable man that came along. The fifteen year old was known as Isabella and was usually quiet and not outspoken. She had been placed in charge of the breakfast this morning as Sister Bardwell had other duties to attend to upstairs, before returning to them, to gather the orphans for the church service. The house maids of the premises were in the kitchen, tidying up what remained of the pots and pans, and the clock in the main room of the house could be heard as it chimed at eight, letting all know that it was time to finish up and get ready for the service to come.

"Come Catherine, you and your friends must hurry. The kitchen staff are very prompt with the errands and our breakfast bowls must be taken into the kitchen on time. The Sisters are very punctual and not apt to accept idleness," said Isabella. "You will find out for yourself, soon enough."

Catherine smiled and accepted the chastisement. "Thank you, Isabella, we shall follow in a few minutes, for some of us require more time."

"Well, please hurry. Once you have finished, take your bowls into the kitchen and depart via the other door, straight to your rooms, comb your hair, brush out the wrinkles in your dress, and wipe the muck from your faces. Sister Bardwell and the Mother will not be pleased with me if you do not come up to scratch."

"We shall not let you down, Isabella," assured Catherine. "Just a few more minutes are all we shall need."

"Very well, I shall see you upstairs shortly, ready for the Sisters' morning inspection of face and dress." With that Isabella and the other seven departed to complete their morning routine, leaving Stephen's girls by themselves.

No sooner had the last of them left the dining area then Catherine was up on her feet. "Quickly, put your things down, all of you, it's time to leave."

The girls knew what was required as Catherine had passed the word to each of them individually, ensuring that each and every one of them understood exactly what they were to do and at the first opportunity that they received. All they had with them were the clothes on their back so there was nothing left for any of them to pick up from within their rooms. They had their cun-ning, their mischievous cheek, and their beautiful demeanour, like any other child, but their greatest gift, of each and every one of them, was their undying will to be with Stephen and his knights of the cross, for Stephen was like their father, a figure of adulthood that they looked up to with honour, and each had a head-strong devotion to do what they knew was right. If their hearts felt the goodness of the relationship between themselves and Stephen then it must be good, and as long as the feeling of warmth, friendship and love, lasted, they would forever be connected and willing to serve one another.

And so they moved in silence, away from the kitchen, out and away from the dining area, and towards the front door, by which, as the door to a convent and place of regular consoling, it had a very simple locking mechanism that was turned easily.

Martin and Raoul were quickly drawn to the door as it opened slowly, seeing Catherine appear momentarily before she opened it wide and stood aside for the other twelve girls to parade past her, she followed the last of the girls through and closed the door quietly behind her.

Raoul waved the children on ensuring that they could see him, Martin looking at the windows of the convent, making sure that no eyes fell upon their getaway. Sure, the children belonged to them but they knew within the heart of hearts that the Mother Superior would not allow the children to be taken away unless a letter could be obtained from the home in which they wanted to surrender the children, and as no home of any description existed they had no choice but to sneak around like thieves in the night.

Raoul continued waving the children on, a symbolic gesture for them to hurry, to cross the road and approach as quickly as possible. A few passers-by looked upon the action as suspicious, seemingly undecided as to what was happening before them: was it lawful or not? More and more people did stare, picked up by Martin as a concern for their welfare as a group. At the first opportunity he would advise the children, and Raoul, to move briskly but remain as inconspicuous as possible.

The children came to Martin and Raoul with smiles, happy to be away from the convent, even though their stay was accompanied by full bellies and kind words, comfort and warmth. But nothing could compare to the friendship that they had with Stephen and the knights. It was all they wanted in the world, to be loved, to be cared for, even if it meant hardship in life, a life without a mother, without toys, without proper schooling and education. Theirs was a journey to womanhood that none had experienced before them. They were once destined to be slaves in Muslim hands forever, to be abused and tormented, raped and hit and scolded. Stephen offered them so much more than the Sisters of the convent; he had so much more to give. They were now free, free from abuse, free from the pressures offered by an unstable society. They were to commence a journey soon, their last into the unknown, but the first into adulthood. Their futures would be fruitful.

"Come children, this way, and please do not run," said Martin. "We have plenty of time now," and as he spoke those words he looked over his shoulder, worried that they might have been seen. "Come, let's go."

*

* * *

*

"Sheriff!" The nun was anxious as she entered the gaol.

He looked up and saw a nun before him, dressed in her habit, a cross upon a chain swinging around her neck as she entered.

"Yes, Sister, can I help you?"

"Sheriff, thirteen orphans have been removed from the convent, thirteen children of between five and eight years," she displayed her fretted disposition, confused and upset, "taken from our premises without permission. I fear the worse."

"Please, Sister, sit down," said the sheriff. "I'm sure they are safe, but tell me, what happened?" He was concerned for the time as Lars was due for execution within the next half an hour. The last thing the sheriff needed was a commotion to disrupt his planned morning. He had already sent the gaoler to ensure that the gallows was ready for the prisoner, preparing the hangman for his morning kill, to ensure that the crowd remained reasonably peaceful during the build up to the hanging, but even after all of this there was still much that had to be done."

The Sister sat opposite the sheriff. "I am Sister Bardwell, sent by Mother Superior herself. We think that we know who took the children but they cannot be found anywhere."

"Who, who would take them?"

"Two men, named Martin and Raoul. They brought the children to us and requested a safe haven for them, just for a few days, they said they would return, but this... this is not acceptable, to remove the children in this way. We have no way to prove that it was in fact these two men, but nevertheless, the children desire and deserve the comfort and security of a good home, not to be forced upon the street. And that is the question, sheriff, what are these men to do with thirteen orphaned girls?"

"I see your dilemma, Sister, and I—"

A man suddenly burst through the door, half drunk and almost toppling over his own feet as he entered.

"Sheriff, a word with you," the man stuttered.

The sheriff could not believe his misfortune. "Yes."

"A murder, sheriff, there has been a murder."

"What?"

"It's the harbour master, sheriff, his throat has been cut."

The sheriff was standing and wiped his brow as he thought. He could not believe the morning he was having. "Where's the body?"

"At his place of residence: the harbour. I found him next to his bed, upon the floor with blood everywhere."

The sheriff thought for a second. The dead could wait, the body was not going anywhere, and thirteen orphans would not be too hard to spot, in particular during daylight hours, and the hanging was set to take place soon. "What is your name?"

"Alfred," said the man, out of breath.

"Alfred, go back to the harbour and close the doors, secure them as best you can and I shall be there after the hanging." He looked to the Sister that sat aghast as to the conversation that was taking place, having formed a cross with her fingers upon her chest, giving a prayer for the deceased. "Please, Sister," said the sheriff in as kind a way as he could muster. "Go back to the convent and I shall have some deputies brought to alert. I shall have every street scoured until the children have been found; in actual fact I have several men that are due here shortly."

"Thank you, sheriff, that is most appreciated."

Stephen could not believe the size of the crowd before him. It seemed to him that the entire town had come to see his poor friend die, but at the least they had the solace to know that there would be no pain in death. Lambert and Bernard were currently with Father Ambaedian, awaiting the return of the other two knights and their thirteen orphans. If all went to plan then they would be joined as a group once more.

Stephen watched as the hangman and his apprentice went about their work, preparing the hangman's noose and ensuring that the trap door worked to perfection. The hangman placed a sack filled with soil upon the trap door and the noose was pulled taught around the neck of the sack; he stood aside, pulling on the lever which released the trap door. Some people in the crowd seemed to jump at the noise created by the trap door as it was released, as though struck with horror at the means by which a man was about to die, but nevertheless they still came, flooding the square, pushing and shoving, holding conversation with friends, talking about the man that was about to meet his end.

Stephen remained calm and towards the back of the crowd where he had good visuals all around. As he watched and waited he clutched tight to the cross around his neck, praying for Lars, whether needed or not. The sky was clear and birds filled the sky momentarily, a mass of seagulls heading towards the harbour as though drawn to the smell of fish, but there would be no fishing today. He then pondered the sanity of hanging a man on the Sabbath. The people should be celebrating life, taking time out to honour God, not being fixated by the death of someone none of them knew. So this was what civilisation was coming to, cheap, dirty and uncalled for entertainment?

The crowd moved around like waves upon the ocean, swaying this way and then that, and far to Stephen's right and out of sight was Ibrahim and Sherif, looking over the sea of heads.

Ibrahim continued to look over the crowd as it grew, people gathering from all quarters of Barcelona.

"They will not be here," said Sherif. "They will not take the time to watch a hanging when escape is strong within them."

"Aye, I agree," said Ibrahim, and as he turned he noticed someone, someone in the distance. It was Stephen; he had drawn Ibrahim's attention.

"Sherif–" and Ibrahim was cut off abruptly.

"No names, fool. Do you want the whole of the town to know who we are?"

"I am sorry, you are right, but look, look over there," Ibrahim pointed.

"What am I looking at?"

"That man, the tallest man, young in appearance and clutching something around his neck. He looks solemn and as if in prayer. Do you see him?"

"I do," said Sherif, "but what of him?"

"Do you remember when we were in the Dardanelles, fighting for our lives when attacked by that brigantine?" Ibrahim looked at his friend who was glaring at Stephen. "Do you remember?"

"Yes, yes, I do. What of it, I see no one I recall. You are dreaming. That was a long time ago; forget it."

"I tell you, it is him. Let us try and get a closer look, for I'm sure that what I am looking at is our key to the chest of secrets that we all seek. Come, let's go."

Ibrahim stepped with purpose and with a protest, Sherif followed in his footsteps, moving back away from the crowd as it grew and up a lonely street, taking a shortcut through an alley and then back down towards the centre of town. Suddenly, and with the blindest of luck, they fell upon the other group.

"Abu, Ahmad," said Ibrahim. He looked down at the chest that they carried between them both. "And what is that you have?"

"Gold, Ibrahim, a chest full of gold," said Abu. "There is enough gold in this chest here to make us all very rich men, and once we have found the chest of secrets we will be the wealthiest sons' of wenches that the known world has ever known."

"Let me see," said Sherif greedily. "Open it up, quickly."

"Are you a fool," said Abu. "What if someone was to see us? Do you think it is normal to go parading around showing your chest of gold coins to anyone that passes by? Now forget the gold, it's here and that's all you need to know." Abu looked from Ibrahim to Sherif. "What are you doing here?"

"I have found something, Abu," said Ibrahim.

"He is dreaming," protested Sherif.

Abu looked at Sherif as though disgusted by the interruption. "What did you find, Ibrahim?"

"Do you remember the brigantine in the Dardanelles?"

"Yes, I do; do you think me stupid," answered Abu. "I can see it as though right in front of me as we speak. Never will I forget that boat and the misery it brought me."

"Do you recall when we tried to shackle it with a rope, our endeavour to draw it closer?"

"Yes, yes; come on, quickly with your story, Ibrahim, we do not have all day," said Abu anxiously.

"The man that appeared upon the deck and cut the rope, dodging our ball and arrows, I saw him, now, just minutes ago," Ibrahim was near frantic now, excited beyond measure for bringing such good news to Abu's ear. "We have him cornered amongst the crowd. There is to be a hanging and we will be camouflaged by the mass. We have him, Abu; we can follow him to the chest of his."

All three men looked at Abu as he thought things through. "We will go and watch the hanging, but keep each other close. You, Ibrahim, I want you to make your way slowly towards this man that has cheated death so many times and created so much misery for us all. Stand behind him so that we may all get a good look at him. When he departs the hanging we will follow. We will remain dispersed at first and then join together to fight them when the time is right. We must not be seen, Ibrahim. It is most important that we remain as close as possible to this man, but not too close. Do you understand?"

"I do, Abu," nodded Ibrahim, reflecting upon his task.

"Good. Now be off with you, we will follow and watch you from within the crowd, for I would like to get a good look at this man that has cheated death on so many occasions."

*
* * *
*

Martin and Raoul made good progress after being hidden for some time far from any prying eye, brought on by the fact that a vast majority of the town's people had laid a visit upon the centre of town to see the hanging that was to take place. The thirteen orphans followed Martin with Raoul bringing in the rear, watching his back to ensure he was not being followed. The distance to the meeting place with Father Ambaedian was on the other side of town but the going was easy. Along the cobbled way and down alley, along several streets and past the rear of the commercial centre of town, a few more streets and then they were upon them, the priest sitting upon his cart in wait with Lambert and Bernard in the rear.

The smiles upon the faces of the children spoke for themselves, seeing the other knights upon the cart bringing joy to all. Catherine, too, was happy but quickly noticed that Stephen was not to be seen.

"Lambert, Bernard, where is Stephen?" asked Catherine.

"He is at the town's square, Catherine," answered Lambert. "He has a duty to perform."

"And what of Lars and Aaron, where are they?"

"We have some bad news for you all, children. Aaron has been murdered and Lars is to be hanged."

The children gasped in horror at the news, refusing to admit that Lars could be guilty of anything that would condemn him to death.

"Lars is innocent," said Catherine. "Stephen knows that he could not do any wrong."

"We all know this, child," answered Father Ambaedian. "But we must accept fate as it has been dealt us."

"Who are you?" asked Catherine as politely as she could.

Ambaedian looked into the child's eyes and saw not a child but a fully grown adult. He had not asked many questions in regards to the children so knew not of their character or real suffering. Were they intelligent? Did they deserve any particular recognition? What was their disposition?

"I am Father Ambaedian," answered the priest, and trying to bring immediate closure to the unnecessary questioning, added one simple measure of information. "I am Stephen's friend and know everything there is to know about him."

Catherine considered the information for what it was worth. "How did Aaron die?"

"Unnecessarily," answered Lambert. "But let's concentrate on our situation, Catherine. Father Ambaedian has found us a new boat, so that we can leave this place."

"A new carrack?" she asked. "What of the old one?"

"Look, Catherine," interrupted Bernard. "There is much to our situation that you may not understand, but we do not have the time to discuss it all now. Trust in your peers and we will be away from this town as soon as we possibly can. We are going by way of the town's centre to get Stephen and from there we shall go to the carrack that awaits us. You will be escorted around the scene of Lars' death but in close enough contact for security to remain present. You must adhere to all commands that are given to you," Bernard looked around to all the children. "All of you children, do you hear? All of you must remain calm. All of you must heed every word that is asked of you. You must not falter in any way for to do so could see you back in the convent and under the care of the nuns. Now, it is time to go. Stay close children for there could be danger lurking behind every corner."

*
* * *
*

Stephen looked on as the time finally arrived for Lars to appear on the scene. The hangman and his apprentice were stood fast upon the platform of death where a single rope hung from a cross beam between two posts, a loop large enough to be inserted over a head formed at the end as it dangled freely, waiting for its victim, silently swinging a little, like a pendulum. The crowd suddenly grew silent as heads shifted left and right, each person trying to get a look at the guilty. The cart upon which Lars was being delivered to the hangman's noose finally came into view, and as the single horse-drawn cart moved into the centre of town, the crowd commenced with their interaction with the proceedings. Shouts and laughter erupted from all that watched, pointed fingers and mocking, pieces of rotten fruit being hurled through the air. The frame of the cage in which Lars was secured did little to protect him from what was thrown. He could not dodge or crouch down because he was restrained in an upright position. The sheriff walked beside the horse-drawn cart, a deputy leading the horse calmly up front, whispering gentle words into the horse's ear, keeping the animal from acting abruptly or trying to flee the scene. The horse had done this duty many times in the past but it was hard to get used to the screams of the crowd, even harder to escape the odd piece of fruit as it came tumbling through the air, hitting him in the flank.

The cart came to a stop at the foot of the hangman's gallows and the sheriff clambered aboard where the cage enclosed Lars, untying his secondary bonds and removing him, hands still tied behind his back, to the steps beyond.

Stephen could see that Lars was solemn, at peace with the world. A piece of fruit then hit him in the head to which the sheriff turned abruptly, for it had nearly hit him. They continued up the short climb to the hangman in wait.

The sheriff handed the convicted over and moved to the side allowing those within the square to see clearly from wherever they stood, a hood being prepared for Lars. Death was only minutes away when Lars looked up and saw the drunken sailor, John, the one that was to be his herald when danger was near, and John looked away, ashamed, and then Lars saw Stephen to the rear of the crowd, hand upon his chest, the cross hanging there beneath his fingers. It was his salvation to have seen the cross for himself, when Stephen laid visit upon him in the dungeon of Barcelona. He did not feel alone, he did not even stand alone, for at that moment he felt the presence of the Lord from high above, and then the hangman's hood was unceremoniously placed over his head. The bright of day now passed his vision for ever but the noise of laughter and dread could still be heard. It all flowed through him but did not sting, the horrors of those last few minutes were blotted out by something with more power than he had ever experienced before. And as the sheriff began a brief sentencing to death, Lars could only hear the sweet voice of heaven, for he was being accepted by God like any other good Christian who was pure of heart. He would walk in heaven, passing the golden gates, embraced by the almighty Father who looked, not down upon him, but from beside him.

The noose was then passed over the hood and placed taught against his neck, but Lars only felt the caressing of someone that cared, he could smell the blossom of roses, of perfumes, the essence of nectar. Death was not consuming him, it was being accepted, and as the trap door was released by the hangman, the crowd grew quiet and Lars was uplifted to be with God.

Stephen could see what no other could see. He felt what no other could feel. His friend, the Teutonic, transcended into heaven. And Lars was happy, empty of dread, and now Lars was looking down upon the square, wondering as to why so many people, who did not know who he was, would want to see him die this way.

His eternal life had just begun.

*

* * *

*

Ibrahim stood patiently behind Stephen and could see his Muslim comrades off to the side, each looking in his direction, a suspicious group of men indeed.

It was then that Stephen made his move, putting the cross well away inside his shirt and drawing his attention to the task at hand. There was nothing further he could do for Lars, for he was beyond any further help. His life was in God's hands now.

So Stephen stepped off towards the edge of the square, commencing the short trek to the harbour and the carrack that waited. It was then that lady luck struck for just ahead he saw the four knights and thirteen children. Martin was at the rear.

"Martin," shouted Stephen, loud enough for the knight to hear his call, and with his herald came the turning of heads as each of the children stopped in their tracks and rushed the man they loved so dearly like a herd of thirsty cattle to a watering hole.

The joy of the meeting fell from the children's lips, each asking how he was, where he had been, how wonderful it was to see him again. And the thought came like a rush to Stephen that these children did indeed love him with all their heart for he had only been gone a short time, but even a short time for the group of orphans was like an eternity. Never again did they wish to be separated from their father figure, their friend, their knight of knights. Hugs and affectionate pats on the head were exchanged with great exuberance. The smiles upon the children's faces were contagious, and all of the knights forgot, just for the moment, what their task was. Everything seemed to be so unimportant. They were a family unit, one and the same, and to separate the family reunion was beyond contemplation, but it was soon to be revealed that two of the group were to remain behind in Barcelona, for Stephen had picked up on a vision of the future where explorers from right across Europe did take to the waters of the Atlantic to flood the New World with their greed and condemnation of Indian life. The future was filled with so much treachery that the horrors of Stephen's dreams could not have been anticipated.

Ibrahim was again standing at Abu's side, stepping up to the group of three as they watched with great interest the group of knights and children.

"Do you see the chest anywhere?" asked Abu of the others, but no answer came, just shakes of the head and dumbfounded silence. "We shall follow them to wherever it is they lead us. They will have to attend the chest soon and wherever it is, there are sure to be other men guarding it. We are outnumbered and must sway the disadvantage to our favour. We must approach unseen and ambush in a manner that ambush is not known. We must strike with a surprise attack but not until we are sure of where to find the prize." Abu looked briefly at the others. "Do you all understand?" and Abu looked no further than the expressions upon their faces, the twinkle in their eyes, their silence demeanour. "I see you do. We must move as a group but remain apart. If we are too close together we will be advertising our presence too freely. Let us go now and seek our fortune."

The group of knights and thirteen orphans recommenced their walk towards the harbour where the carrack awaited them. Abu and the other three men of Islam followed in wide stride, maintaining a good distance from the Christian group.

The sheriff moved in alongside the deputy, who had returned to the seat upon the cart. "Morgan," said the sheriff, drawing the deputy's attention. "Take the body to the morgue as soon as you can and then head back to the gaol. I shall be a little while. I have a task to attend to at the harbour."

"What is it, sheriff?"

"It seems that the harbour master was killed in his sleep last night, or first thing this morning. I do not think there is much we can do. Oh, and Morgan; keep your eye open for thirteen children wandering around in a group. There will be two men with them."

"I shall. What should I do if I see them?"

"Follow them if you can, find out where they are or where they are going... let me know as soon as possible so that we can return them to the convent. Be wary of the men travelling with them, please be warned, and take as much precaution as required, I cannot emphasize that enough."

"I shall do just that, sheriff."

The sheriff nodded as the orders were accepted and stepped back and then around, to move from the square, through the crowd as it dispersed, and towards his next duty.

It did not take long for him to push his way through the throngs for most individuals, knowing of his status, stepped back to allow him through; it was then, as he reached the furthest edge of the town's centre, that up front and in the distance he could see the group of thirteen children and several men moving along with them. It was quite clear from what he saw that the children were not distressed as some of them were skipping along the cobbled way and others held the hands of some of the adults, looking up into their eyes with a smile. And as he pondered the situation, with his continued walk towards the pier, he saw four other men moving, two to each side of the street, moving as though to maintain their distance from the group to their front. The sheriff stopped momentarily and considered the situation. Were the four men following doing so as a rear guard action to the first group? Were they following for reasons of abduction? Had the Mother Superior organised for some vagabonds to search for the children, funded by her own purse? It all seemed very strange to him, but if one thing was for sure, the group of four men were most definitely following the group to their front. It was then that he saw the chest carried between two of them. Money perhaps, to offer for the purchase of children.

Slave traders; that was the answer. He would have to move carefully, watch from a distance, and when the time was right he would move in with help gained from any source to rescue the poor children.

Stephen ushered the children on, becoming concerned for those that followed. He had picked up on the movement of the undesirables through sheer luck, when he looked out towards the rear to consider what he was to say to Martin and Raoul.

"Come children. Stay up with Lambert and Bernard, do not dawdle, for time is short." They continued on past him as he drew in alongside both Martin and Raoul, taking up stride between them both.

"Martin, Raoul, there is something I must say to you both, and listen to me carefully you must." He looked them both briefly in the eye and could see their mystifying glances, as thou the weight of the world was upon them. They could both tell by the tone of Stephen's voice that something was coming their way, something that was not going to be altogether pleasing, but completely necessary. They had been together for so long that they sensed when one had bad news to tell the other, checking the tone of one when they spoke, understanding the body language as though it spoke with its own voice.

"Do not be alarmed and please do not look behind you. We are being followed by four men. I do not know who they are but I am guessing by their dress that they are sailors, possibly those from the brigantine that was following us. But listen to me, regardless of who they are and what they are doing I have a task that must be performed, something for you both that will not be to your liking. Listen and listen carefully for I can say this only once. We are close to the harbour and the pier of our interest, and are short on time. The voices and dreams... pictures if you like, pictures I see within my head, they are sometimes very hard to decipher and come at the strangest times. But I see a man and a woman, a pair of vicious heathens who are tempted to take what they can, a man and a wife that are as impure as the devil himself. They seek to bring harm to us, but I do not know how. They are close, I can feel them, but do not know where they are. But nevertheless, regardless of this, you two good men must serve me as though you would serve the Lord Himself. I am going to ask something of you both and it will not be to your liking. You must come with us to the harbour but once we are there you must remain in town. You must stay in town for several weeks at least, to ensure that we are not followed. It is the man and the women who I fear the most." The two knights said nothing as they continued walking. "The Lord has provided you with special permission to use any force necessary to prevent the New World from being discovered. It will be inevitable, one day, but time must be had for us to prepare the defences for the Cross of Christ. Time is of the essence." Stephen looked up and saw the pier stretching out upon the harbour to his front. "We are nearly there. I am sorry, Martin, Raoul. There is nothing for it. You must do the Lord's will and remain alert, remain in Barcelona and cover our tracks, do all you can to prevent others from following in our wake."

*
* * *
*

Before reaching the pier, Martin and Raoul were sent upon their quest. "This is it," said Stephen. "Do not come any closer; the departure will be too much for the children to bear. We cannot afford a lengthy goodbye for it will delay us more than we can afford."

"We understand," said Martin. He put out his hand in farewell to Stephen who returned the gesture, slapping him on the shoulder as he did so; Raoul did the same.

"It has been an honour serving with you," said Raoul. "I would not have wished my departure from Káros to have been by any other means. I served the Lord on that island of solitude and will continue to serve here in Barcelona. We, both of us, will continue to serve as we have always done."

"I am happy to hear such words," said Stephen, "and am humbled too, by your courage and service. But one last thing, good men. If a fight is to be drawn here upon this pier, with those that are following, you must not attempt to aid us. You both must live in order to carry out your task, it is most important."

They smiled and let each other go, Martin and Raoul turning on their heels and departing in a hurry, for they did not wish to upset the children who had nearly reached the pier. They moved with such haste that they skirted behind a building and out of view before any of the children could grow wise to what was happening, and Stephen turned and raced off to catch up with the others.

It was at this time that the first of the children turned around to look behind. She could see that Stephen was by himself, that Martin and Raoul had disappeared. A few of the others now did the same, looking behind in wonder as to what was going on.

Stephen reached them and looked down upon them. "Martin and Raoul have been commanded by God to attend an important mission. We will continue without them. They will, forever, remain in our memories. Come, children, we have no time to waste, we must be going now." They continued on their way without further ado, only a little distance remaining between them and the carrack. It was then that the Muslims caught sight of the group at the harbour that they were heading for and Abu brought a temporary close to the follow-up.

Abu could see the carrack, which was of obvious interest to Stephen and the others, for they were heading directly towards it. Abu called the others over to the side, behind a small dwelling situated opposite where the pier began, two of the men seen moving away from the others, sleeking off quietly before quickening their stride, away from the others.

"The carrack at the end of the pier must be the one," said Abu to the other three. "That is the one." They huddled together in order for Abu to let his strategy be known. "When a majority of them have gone aboard we will rush them. We have no other option, for the children will only get in our way... at least the fight now looks to be in our favour."

"No, let us wander up as close as we can get," said Ibrahim. "Let us close the gap a little, at least. It will give them less time to prepare themselves for the fight to come."

"Very well," agreed Abu. "We shall wait. Let us watch now."

They watched as the children were helped aboard the carrack and Alfred, the drunken sailor who had reported to the sheriff earlier on in the day, exited the cabin where the body of the harbour master lay cold.

"Who are you?" yelled Alfred. "What are you doing? That boat belongs to—" and without much effort the sailor was silenced, for Stephen had quickly placed his hand upon the hilt of his sword and withdrew it slightly. Abu saw this action and deemed it as a defence, not realising that a man had appeared at the doorway to the cabin of the harbour master, for the door was not facing them.

"Now, quickly, let's go," shouted Abu and the group of four were running up the pier, Ibrahim and Sherif still porting the chest of gold. "Let us take them down."

"Lambert, Bernard, a call to action if you do not mind," said Stephen, bringing the situation to the attention of the two knights as calmly as he could. They were upon the planks so sturdy via quick responsive action, standing in front of the boat and with swords drawn, and all before the Muslims were upon them, the chest of gold being dropped in earnest, and the fight was underway. The metal scraping of sword against sword brought terror to the ears of Alfred, who by now had sealed himself in the hut. The children, being used to the fighting between men, having been exposed to the horrors blood and death, simply took cover where cover could be sought along the pier-side of the carrack, and watched as the fighting commenced.

Catherine looked to the other children, quite unaware that what they were on was a simple civilian boat, but brought immediate attention to them all. "Quickly, sisters, we must find weapons, spears, anything to aid Stephen and the others." The children dispersed as quickly as they had initially sought cover and started their search for anything that would help the fight to fall in their favour, and it was not long before Lois jumped from the carrack to pier, and with a harpoon in her hand.

Lois could see through her eyes so wide that one of the Muslim's had already been killed, for he lay upon the deck with blood pooling out of his chest, Sherif, motionless and with eyes wide open, looking up into the sky. Bernard had his sword temporarily stuck in his gut and was trying to pull it free, which he did after a brief struggle. She shook this from her senses, and seeing her opportunity, speared Ahmad in the gut, just missing Lambert's thigh as she thrust her weapon forward. The big man immediately let his sword fall to the pier as he clutched at his wound, blood appearing at his mouth. He pulled away from the spear and stumbled to the side, falling from the pier and into the water of the harbour, putting the fight in favour of Stephen and the two knights. Bernard then swung around to look for another to fight as did Lambert when the incomprehensible occurred.

Catherine had appeared upon the pier and before she could aid in the fight she was grabbed from behind, the blade of a dagger expertly held against her neck. It was Abu, he had seen his opportunity, and feeling within every vein of his body that the men cared for the children, enough to give their lives to protect them, took this as his only means to secure victory.

"Not a move! Cease your action!" Abu's voice penetrated all, everyone's attention gained in less time that it takes to blink. Stephen stood firm, and had ceased to fight with Ibrahim. Lambert and Barnard were also drawn from their closure, the fight against their opponents having been victorious.

Ibrahim pivoted from side to side, covering the three men as best he could. At any moment both Ibrahim and Abu could be dead men. The fight being initially in their favour was soon turned around, but now, with Catherine's throat resting upon Abu's blade, the fight looked to be in Muslim hands.

"You, the tall one," said Abu. "What is your name?"

"Stephen."

"Then, Stephen, listen to me. All we want is the chest; the chest of secrets. Give it to me and the girl shall live."

"We do not have it," replied Stephen. "It was lost at sea."

"You lie," added Abu. "I should warn you that I can grow impatient and very quickly." A look of seriousness fell upon his face. "Where is the chest?"

"We do not have it, it was lost."

"If you do not tell me where it is then I shall run my blade across this girl's throat. I am not afraid to kill the innocent."

Stephen looked at Abu and saw in him a cowardice hidden beneath the masquerade. "If you kill her then we will be upon you like a pack of hungry wolves."

"Ibrahim," Abu looked to his left. "Take their weapons."

Ibrahim shifted slightly but was brought to an immediate stop.

"One move, Ibrahim," said Stephen, "and you will die, fol-lowed shortly by the death of your master, who I shall take much pleasure in torturing to death."

"Oh, how shrewd you are," said Abu. Silence dominated the scene whilst everyone on the pier assessed the situation. "What do you suggest, Stephen?"

"Let the girl go and you shall live," said Stephen in reply.

"No; no, no, no, no. That simply will not do. I tell you what I shall do. I shall take this little one with me and when I am clear of the harbour I shall let her go."

"Let her go?" asked Stephen with a note of sarcasm.

"Certainly. Why? Do you not trust me?" asked Abu, a question which could only be answered in one way, and that was by way of a quarrel, for from the deck of the carrack a shot had been released from a crossbow, a weapon which one of the sailors of the boat employed against sharks when at sea. All of the girls had been taught to use the weapon at one time or another, taught by their friend, Lars. It was in memory of the man with no tongue that the shot released was so well delivered that Abu would have had no idea, whatsoever, what had been delivered to him. The quarrel entered through his right ear and penetrated out through his left, a shot so skilfully fired that it was beyond belief. Abu simply fell to the pier like a sack of potatoes. Without further ado, Lambert, Bernard and Stephen, encircled the lone Ibrahim.

"The offer of survival has expired. You can either die fighting or die a coward. How will you be delivered to your unholy God?" asked Stephen with as less pity than Ibrahim would feel kicking out at a cat.

Ibrahim looked at the three as they surrounded him and a grimace grew upon his mouth, a snarl being formed. He lifted his sword and charged at Stephen, for he was to blame for all he had suffered. Within seconds, Ibrahim lay in a pool of his own blood and a rattling noise from the boards of the pier struck Stephen's ears. He lifted his head and saw that Father Ambaedian was making his way towards them, sacks of fruit and vegetable nested in the cart, ready to be transferred to the boat.

"Lambert, throw that filth into the sea. Bernard, get ready your hands for some heavy lifting," commanded Stephen and turning to the girls continued with his delegations. "Girls, all of you, forget what you have seen here today and know that you have done well. Lars would be proud to have seen you fight today. When the supplies have been placed upon the boat's deck I wish you to drag them; pile them, along the centre of the boat as best as possible; we'll store them later. Our voyage com-mences immediately."

Stephen had time to turn his attention to the harbour and pier when the priest pulled up in his horse drawn cart.

"Father Ambaedian, just in time," greeted Stephen. "If you climb down to the pier, be careful, there is plenty of blood here to send even the sure footed onto his backside."

"I thank you for your warning, Stephen. I shall pray for the devils a little later but for now we must get the supplies to the boat," and the priest turned to the movement of the cart as Lambert climbed aboard to throw the sacks down to Bernard and Stephen. "Ah, already in place. Good to see good men, doing a good day's work."

The sacks were quickly taken from cart to the boat where the children, being thankful for being provided the opportunity to assist, and Stephen, thankful for the opportunity to take their minds away from the slaughter they had just witnessed, placed them along the centre line of the carrack.

Within just a few minutes the cart was empty. "Thank you, father, for all you have done," said Stephen, shaking the priest's hand.

"It has been a pleasure to see the birth of something so grand. I just hope that with the time you have to contemplate life that a solution can be found by which can be delivered unto the world."

"I do too, father. The cross has a purpose, and whether we call it the Holy Grail or the Cross of Christ, matters little, for we both know what it is. A solution has to be found. I am confident that one day I too shall walk in heaven, but that day is a long way off. These thirteen children I have with me will be long deceased themselves before I can even consider my time on earth as expired. But even with so much time, none of it shall be wasted."

"I believe you, my son," said Ambaedian, looking down upon Stephen as he picked up the reins once more. "Oh, I nearly forgot." He moved over to the side of the cart and lifted out the basin. "Here, take this."

"Thank you, father."

"I shall be off now and wish you a quick and healthy voyage. I'm sure God will see to it that you will be provided supplies along the way, whether such supplies be provided by the sea, a coastal town, or passing galleon. A journey like yours does not go unrewarded."

"Thankyou for your kind wishes and I bid you a good day. Good luck to you."

"And to you; all of you."

The priest waved to the children as they stood upon the deck of the boat and Martin and Raoul prepared the carrack for sailing. The work to get her underway was going to be hard, for there was much to be done and only three adults to do all of the work, but as Father Ambaedian had noted, a journey like theirs did not go unrewarded.

Stephen turned to approach the carrack and as he turned he almost fell over the chest of gold. He looked down upon it and knew instantly what it carried. There was no temptation to open the chest, no urge to take it for himself or the others. The carrack they were taking did not belong to them and had not been paid for. The message in his head was simple. Leave the chest and the end of the pier for the owner of the carrack would find it soon enough.

Stephen jumped aboard the carrack and the sails were un-furled, a wind coming up from behind them. As they commenced their great journey the owner of the carrack miraculously appeared, running towards them, shaking a fist, and as he closed the gap he slipped upon some blood and fell upon the chest. Mystified, he opened it. He cupped the gold up in his hands and looked up to see Stephen waving a hearty farewell. They did not know each other, had never met, but at that moment the owner of the carrack felt that justice had been served him and that the price paid was in his favour. He waved back with a smile that quickly turned into a look of disbelief and he picked up the chest of gold, taking it with him as he departed: but struggling heavily with its weight.

*

* * *

*

Martin came to a stop.

"Wait, Raoul," Martin felt the sudden surge to assist Stephen and the others. "We must go back and fight."

"No," replied Raoul. "We must do as we have been requested."

"Even if it is wrong to sit back and do nothing?"

"Nothing is exactly what we need to do. Look. Over there, Father Ambaedian is heading towards the pier. Do you see?"

"Aye. Let us wait a little. I feel something within me?"

"What is it?"

"I do not know," said Martin, searching himself for an answer. He looked up again and saw two figures within the shadows of the houses upon a street corner. "Look over there. What do you see?"

"Why, it's a man and a woman," answered Raoul.

"A man and his wife," corrected Martin. "Let's watch them and see what they do."

"Do you think they are the ones that Stephen had warned us against?"

"Who else would be sneaking around, following the priest like a cat would follow a mouse?"

So the two men watched in anxious wait to see what would eventuate, and minutes later Martin pointed off to a point alongside the pier. "Look yonder." A man was running towards the pier, his fist shaking, punching the air. "Who is that?"

"I have no idea, but let's concentrate on the couple."

The two knights slunk back into the shadows themselves and watched from their safe station, some distance from where commotion was about to be brewed.

Father Ambaedian let the horse pull the cart slowly from the harbour where the goodbyes had been exchanged. He was happy and fulfilled, a smile upon his face letting the world know that he could not be more content with his life than he was this minute in time. His smile was so well cast that Martin and Raoul could see his jubilance from where they stood.

Quite suddenly, and without warning, the sheriff of the town jumped out to confront the priest, taking hold of the horse's bridle to prevent it from galloping away, even though such action was the furthest thing from Ambaedian's mind.

"Good morning, sheriff," said Father Ambaedian. "How is your day?"

The sheriff peered up into his eyes and took the bridal into his left hand, releasing his hold with the right and preparing himself for what might come, his hand hovering over his sword on his left side. The priest was amused. "I saw you, father. I saw it all. The fight upon the pier; aiding the escape of the orphans. I want answers from you, father, I want answers and I want them now." The fat on the man jiggled slightly as he sang in his threatening tune. It seemed to the priest that the sheriff thought him guilty, or in the least, directly responsible for the killings upon the pier. "You tell me what I want to know or I'll have you upon the gallows before you can give praise to the Lord."

"Sheriff, I have no idea what you are talking about," replied Ambaedian. They locked eyes and the sheriff's heart missed a beat, a sudden pain was felt scrambling down his left arm, and then the crushing pain upon his chest made him gasp for air. He collapsed.

"Sheriff, sheriff, are you all right?" Ambaedian was now worried for him, regardless of the threats, and he knelt down beside the fallen man. He felt for a pulse and realised immediately that he was dead. The sheriff's heart had given to the stresses of an unhealthy lifestyle, where drinking ale and wine had finally dealt its final blow. Being a man of faith and without further ado, Father Ambaedian lifted the sheriff, with great effort, onto the cart. He would deliver him to the closest church; it was the least he could do.

Martin and Raoul watched the couple from where they stood.

Henry looked into his wife's eyes, open palms holding onto shoulders. "Did you see all of that, Patricia?" he asked of his wife.

"I did. I saw it all," she said in reply. "What shall we do now? The boat has sailed, a voyage into the west. We have no hope of laying our fingers upon the gift of God."

"No. No, we do not," said Henry, thinking as best he could on the scenario before him. "We must deliver the news to the sailors of the tavern, the one between here and the town's centre; you know the one."

"I think it's called the Sea Witch."

"Yes, that's it. I know from past experience and much con-versation that only the bravest of sailors drink there. Men from right across Spain and France, Portugal and Italy. We must tell our story, Patricia, tell it to the world. We only need one person to believe us."

"But what good will it do? It will not make us rich."

"Maybe not, Patricia," and Henry released his hold on his wife. "But the Holy Grail. It cannot be wasted upon a land where its very goodness will be lost forever."

"Do you really believe that there is land in the west?"

"We have to, my wife. We must believe it in order to convince someone, anyone, that great salvation is to be had. It could be worth much gold to us. Imagine if the Holy Grail was found... what percentage of its worth do you think we would be paid?"

"None, husband, for the greed of those I know, that sail upon the sea, would turn their back on you and run for the hills. Believe me, there is no wealth to be had now."

"Maybe you believe that, but I do not. I must try to do what I believe is right, regardless of your solid opinion."

"I understand, Henry. You must do what you must do."

"Thankyou, Patricia. I love to hear your words of encourage-ment."

"So what will you do now?"

"I shall go to the tavern. You can go back to the cart and then home."

"When can I expect you back at the house?"

"Before nightfall," said Henry, taking his wife in his hands and kissing her solidly. "For I love nothing more than sharing a bed with you."

And across the other side of the road, Martin and Raoul saw the man and the woman exchange much in conversation, and then the kiss came and the wife walked off in the direction of her home. The smithy could be seen to look left and right before he stepped onto the cobbles and started for the Sea Witch.

"There he goes," said Martin of the obvious. "We must follow him, see where he goes. I feel it in my bones, as I thirst for water and hunger for food."

"Very well," agreed Raoul, "we shall see what he does."

*
* * *
*

The carrack was well out to sea and all aboard her had made themselves familiar, and comfortable, with their surrounds. It was in much likeness to their previous boat. The sacks of fruit and vegetable were carried below deck at the first opportunity and once everything that had to be completed was finished, Stephen called out to Lambert, Bernard, and the thirteen children.

"It is time to deliver the basin and its contents into the sea," said Stephen. "Never again will it see the light of day."

All watched as Stephen picked up the basin from where it sat next to the main mast and moved over to the port side of the carrack.

"There is no ceremony for the burial of something so sacred," said Stephen, "so I shall forego giving any sermon. Instead I shall simply do this." And he dropped the basin overboard. It quickly filled with water and commenced to sink, disappearing from the surface of the sea, to fall to its final resting place beneath the waves of the Mediterranean. Stephen looked to the two knights. "Some would think that this is the end, that the delivery of the basin into the mouth of the sea was the conclusion of our adventure. But I tell you this; our journey has only just begun."

*
* * *
*

Henry was standing in front of thirty seated sailors, all of whom wore swords upon their waists. Tankards filled the tabletops and the thick conversation was quickly brought to a close.

"Hear me, hear me all, for I have something of great importance to tell you," yelled Henry, and having gained the attention of the sailors, quickly continued. "I will be quick with you but if you wish to hear more then I can comply, for the information I am about to disclose will make some of you very rich men."

Some of the sailors that had tankards in their fists put them down, they were all ears. The smithy was singing their tune, the tune of wealth.

"I have seen with my own eyes something of great worth and it is escaping, drawing further away from us as we speak, aboard a carrack which is sailing for the west, it must be— " Suddenly the spirited speech was brought to a close for the slamming of the inn's door made Henry turn with a jolt. Before him were two men, two men who were standing side by side.

The silence within the tavern that minute was profound, not a single noise heard. And then the silence was broken by the two knights, Martin and Raoul, for they both drew their swords from their sheaths and stepped towards their destiny; the protection of the Cross of Christ.

History is plagued with reports of the Holy Grail, of its existence and where it can be found. One story above all others tells of its existence in France, on the coast of the Mediterranean, at a place called Renne le Chateau. It is also fair to say that tales of El Dorado and the Amazons have flooded the minds of Conquistadors, as it did the Incas that preceded them. How true were such stories and how much emphasis should be permitted to ride on the hearsay and word-by-mouth tales? Tales too flourished of natives whose feet were literally affixed their legs back-to-front, whereby they would appear to have been walking one way, where in fact they were travelling the other; so much for the instinct of the tracker. A creature which was half man and half llama was also present upon the wind of tale. It should be considered, and needless to say, that the communication barrier did also loan itself to the calamity of confusion when trying to decipher and understand a foreign tongue. Where did the stories come from? From trade? Trade with the Indians of the Amazon forest was rudiment to comfort, though the wealth of trade was something not sought by many of the Indians of the forest, in particular those along the coast, at the mouth of the Amazon, the door to a New World of people and animals alike.

Stories rose upon the tongue of the Spanish invader of a man covered in gold, the Golden Prince. It was said, via various sources, that he bathed in the lake of clear blue water, which, when emerged, he found himself coated in the dust of gold. On occasion, where ceremony was sought, he was said to anoint his body with a specific substance prior to entering the waters to bathe. But it was not just the gold that triggered an inner greed to grow, but also the promise of wealth secured through trade; the trade of cinnamon. And did the Golden Prince actually, as reported, send tribute to female warriors that housed themselves in buildings of stone, where feathers of parrots were employed to cover the roofs of their dwellings, a symbol of divinity when placed upon the supports of a roof on a temple.

Stones of green were also spoken of, a symbol of native belief in the supernatural world of mysticism, a representation of the green of the forest; and preach they did, in a way unclear to the Spanish, preaching conducted whilst facing the East, the direction know and believed to house the spirit whom had so long ago visited the Amazon's world of mystery and beauty. Was the East in fact their homeland?

El Dorado is translated as The Gilded Man, which means to cover with gold, make golden, or paint gold. The Golden One; one who is made of gold, due to his stature as ruler, decision making, and the way in which he commanded over others: the chosen one.

Stephen was the Golden Prince and the thirteen orphans were the legacy of the Amazon. Their story remains unknown, sealed by the curtain of darkness, shrouded by the jungles of Brazil. Do they still exist; are they still present upon the land of the New World?

BOOK FOUR
Amazon

A Brief Note

History is plagued with reports of the Holy Grail, of its existence and where it can be found. One story above all others tells of its existence in France, on the coast of the Mediterranean, at a place called Renne le Chateau. It is also fair to say that tales of El Dorado and the Amazons have flooded the minds of Con-quistadors, as it did the Incas that preceded them.

How true were such stories, and how much emphasis should be permitted to ride on the hearsay and word-by-mouth tales? Tales, too, flourished of natives whose feet were literally affixed their legs back-to-front; they would appear to have been walking one way, where in fact they were travelling the other: what does this offer the instincts of the tracker. And a creature which was half man and half llama, was also present upon the wind of tale.

It should be considered, and needless to say, that the communication barrier did also loan itself to the calamity of confusion when trying to decipher and understand a foreign tongue. Where did the stories come from? From trade? Trade with the Indians of the Amazon forest was rudimentary to comfort, trade conducted along the coast and at the mouth of the Amazon: Amazon, the door to a New World, of new people and animals alike.

Stories rose upon the tongue of the Spanish invader of a man covered in gold, the Golden Prince. It was said, via various sources, that he bathed in the lake of clear blue water, which, when emerged, he would find himself coated in the dust of gold. On occasion he was said to anoint his body with a specific substance prior to entering the waters to bathe. But it wasn't just the gold that triggered an inner greed to grow, but also the promise of wealth secured through trade: the trade of cinnamon. And did the Golden Prince actually, as reported, send tribute to female warriors that housed themselves in buildings of stone, where feathers of parrots were employed to cover the roofs of their dwellings, a symbol of divinity when placed upon a temple.

Stones of green were also spoken of, a symbol of native belief in the supernatural world of mysticism, a representation of the green of the forest; and preach they did, in a way unclear to the Spanish, preaching conducted whilst facing the east, the direction know and believed to house the spirit whom had so long ago visited the Amazon's world of mystery and beauty. Was the east in fact their homeland?

El Dorado is translated as The Gilded Man, which means to cover with gold, make golden, or paint gold. The Golden One; one who is made of gold, due to his stature as ruler, decision making, and the way in which he commands over others: the Chosen One.

And what of The Templar: Stephen, Templar, Knight of Constantinople, Esteemed Friend of Constantine, and Saviour of

Christ's Belongings.

Stephen was the Golden Prince and the thirteen orphans were the legacy of the Amazon. Their story remains unknown, sealed by the curtain of darkness, shrouded by the jungles of Brazil. Do they still exist; are they still present upon the land of the New World?

*
* * *
*

They stood upon the sands of the beach, at the mouth of the greatest river in the world, where fresh water was evident for many leagues out to sea, for the volume of water being emptied from the Great River was far too great to fathom.

Their ship was burning, the crackle of flames and creaking of mast heard above the gentle rubbing of sea against the surface of the land. Smoke filled the air and their precious carrack slowly sank and disappeared from view. This was the last item of any worth that connected them with the world they once knew.

Stephen clutched at the symbol of goodness that hung around his neck, feeling its presence through his tattered and dirty shirt, the sign of the meaning of life: sanctimonious, morale, precepts. He looked around him with a smile cast upon his face to his friends that had survived with him, surviving to see a new beginning born to them all, to escape the slavery of the Old World, to be granted this, a new beginning. They followed Stephen without question, without doubt, without any hesitation at all.

There were thirteen orphans, all of whom Stephen had adopted as his own, taking them into his care for the glory of God, for they were His children, to be taken care of by Stephen, a man of flesh and blood; a man who could not die by normal causes as delivered by curse, disease, poison, or old age, for he was the saviour of the world as chosen by the scriptures passed onto him, and only by the delivery of a mortal flesh wound would the day pass into night and his last breath be drawn from his lungs as the curtain of darkness fell upon him.

There also existed two other men, two men of great stature that were none other than Hospitaller Knights, but they wore nothing more than rags, their shirts of white as discoloured and worn as Stephen's.

They were Bernard and Lambert.

Stephen looked to Lambert who carried his sheathed sword in the palm of his hand.

"Cast it into the sea," said Stephen, calm and collective, quiet and serene.

Lambert looked down at the sword in his hand, the weapon he had used against the infidel on more than a hundred occasions. He had served Constantine directly, a body guard of his for many years before being turned over to Father Tourmede on the island of Káros, of the Aegean Sea.

Lambert took several steps forward and with his entire might he flung his weapon to its final resting place, its grave beneath the waves. He stood there and watched it disappear from view, the sea splashing against his legs.

"Our journey is a long one," said Stephen and everyone turned around to look at him. "This is the year 1453 and I do declare that we have fewer than 90 years before we are targeted by the greed of the Spanish. All is not clear to me but I know that we need to prepare for what is to come. We will fade away into the jungle, and with the help of the people of this New World we will survive to see the sacred gift of Jesus preserved and protected. Our journey is a long one indeed, and none of you will survive to see it through."

Each and everyone looked at the other, their glances shifting from face to face.

"But you shall all have fruitful lives," said Stephen, and looking to Catherine and Lois added, "in particular, two of you; one more than the other; and none of you will have a single regret for there is eternal life in heaven; life which awaits you all."

Lambert appeared to take a step towards Stephen at that moment, seemingly offended by what was said, but it wasn't that at all, for his attention was quickly grasped by the disturbance of some bushes on the verge of the jungle, where the beach came upon a wall of vegetation.

Stephen turned to look in the direction of Lambert's gaze as did everyone there, and saw for himself what it was that had caused alarm within his friend.

Two naked men stepped from the mouth of the jungle, each holding a bow and arrow close to his body, awaiting the need to use their weapons against the white visitors. The children in particular found it quite distasteful, having never seen a naked body before, for the molestation suffered by the hand of their Muslim jailers, before meeting with Stephen, was done so with clothes on, and each of the children averted their eyes in disgust. A few chuckles were heard amongst those children lucky enough to still be a virgin, and these few were quickly taken under control by a stern word from Catherine.

The men were rather handsome and brown, and by no degree ashamed to show their manhood as each dangled from their place between the legs. They were warriors of the neighbourhood tribe and in kind recognition of their place within their society were fitted in the costume of their native brethren, where magnificent plumage could be seen in their hair.

Their necks, heads and arms were covered in dye, red and black vegetable extract that brought great colour and symbolism to each of the seemingly young men. They were each quite muscular and of them there was only one distinguishing deformity that was prevalent amongst all of the tribe: the front of their heads were rather too flat to be natural and each seemed to bulge outwards near the top, in similarity to bread having been baked, where the bottom portion had been restricted in its expansion but the top portion had not: for the Omagua practised skull deformation by placing boards to the front and the back of their heads, they became as flat as the palm of the hand, the head bulging at top and sides; to the newcomers it was very ugly in men, but women seemed to hide this with their abundant stresses. They looked like they were wearing the mitre found atop a bishop.

"Have no fear," said Stephen. "I can see they mean no harm, or they would have killed us already."

"Look into their eyes," said Bernard. "You can see the wonder in them, the astonishment at what they each see before them."

"As astonished as I," said Lambert.

"Look at their heads," said Bernard. "What do they remind you of, but men of God, somehow religious?"

"Religion is everywhere," said Stephen. "Everyone in the world believes in an origin, whether he is right or wrong is not for other men to judge, but with the knowledge we possess we know the truth."

"Tell them, Stephen," urged Lambert. "Tell them what they need to know."

"It's not God's will to change the belief of a man and his wife, but to allow them free reign." Stephen looked to Lambert and Bernard. "God would want these people to live in peace, to allow them their beliefs, so long as they lived clean lives."

"The scriptures order differently," said Bernard as the two warriors continued to watch in anticipation for what was to come of the encounter.

"The bible is wrong," said Stephen.

"How can you say that?" asked Bernard.

"Because I hold the Cross of Christ, the relic of His son's possession, the blood of Jesus, the resurrection of truth, and the Holy Grail. It is all one and the same. The bible has been tampered with, soiled by the hand of bishops and others like them. These two men have the right to live as they live, so long as they hold dear to the sanctimonious, moral, precepts of all that is true. Smile and you shall be rewarded."

The two knights of the hospital smiled and looked upon those that were about to invite them into their domain, to provide them with nourishment and the instructions to live a fruitful life in the jungle of this new world they had discovered.

"The Infidel doesn't deserve the right to live a free life," advised Lambert.

"The Infidel are fanatic and don't live by the laws of the gift of life," reminded Stephen as he stepped ever closer to the two warriors and held out his hand in friendship.

One of the warriors looked puzzled, looked to his brother for a sign of what to do. This man before him, the one so white and tall, was holding his hand out. Was it that the man from the sea wished to make an exchange, wished to barter something for his bow and arrow?

The taller of the two warriors, Jurup, was the first to speak. "*What do you think, Macatera? These must be the Caraíba of our ancestors. Look; he wants my bow.*"

"*Don't give it to him,*" replied Macatera and looked sternly upon Stephen.

"Be careful, Stephen," advised Lambert. "He doesn't look happy."

"*Macatera; look at the smoke; it's gone,*" said Jurup.

"*The floating vessel has vanished,*" said Macatera.

"*Just like the stories. The Caraíba has destroyed his gift from the spirits.*"

"You might be right, Lambert," agreed Stephen. "Slower should be the introduction."

"*There are more than one Caraíba, more than one to appease,*" said Jurup.

"*They must all be Caraíba, just like in the past,*" said Macatera. "*We should take them to the chief.*"

"My name is Stephen; I am here in the name of God, my Father. We seek protection and come in friendship. There is much I can do for you; we can help one-another."

"He doesn't understand a word," said Bernard.

"*What is he saying?*" asked Macatera.

"*It's the voice of the spirits,*" said Jurup. "*That's why we don't understand.*"

Macatera understood clearly then and lowered his bow, stepping forward towards Stephen with a little apprehension in his step, and handed his weapon over to the one thought to be a Caraíba.

"He's offering his weapon to you," said Bernard.

"No," corrected Stephen, "He's offering a truce. It's a sign of peace," Stephen smiled and bowed slightly in acceptance of the weapon.

"*He's happy,*" said Jurup. "*He's content by your gift. Show him a sign of the past, to show we know of the ancestors of Caraíba's past.*"

Macatera got down upon his knees.

"He's bowing to you," said Bernard.

"Don't be so quick with your assumptions," said Stephen. "Look, he's drawing something in the sand."

Macatera scribed lines in the sand before him, drawing the shape of many ships so that the Caraíba could clearly understand that they were welcome as children of the ancestors, the prophets that had laid visit upon them so many years before. He drew 13 ships, vessels which were responsible for the portage of much gold from one world into another.

Bernard's and Lambert's jaws both dropped and Stephen turned to them both. "You see," was all that he said.

"The treasure of the Templar's," said Lambert.

"It's here, somewhere," said Bernard.

"And we shall protect it so that none can prosper from its worth until such a time that it should be revealed. Not before its time will it be discovered." Stephen smiled as he looked upon the warrior on his haunches.

"Stephen," said Stephen, holding his palm to his chest. "Stephen; Stephen."

"*Stephen,*" repeated Jurup from beside Macatera. He looked to his companion. "*His name is Stephen.*"

"*I am Macatera,*" said Macatera, following the order of the conversation, patting himself on the chest with his open palm. "*Macatera.*"

"*Jurup,*" said Jurup. "*Jurup, Jurup, Jurup.*"

Stephen pointed to Bernard and Lambert before announcing their names.

"*He must be the Caraíba that rules over all others,*" said Jurup, he then pointed to Stephen. "*Stephen; Caraíba. Stephen; Caraíba.*"

"I am Caraíba," said Stephen to the others.

"What is, Caraíba?" asked Bernard who then received a stare from both warriors.

"I think it means, leader, or commander; overseer perhaps," said Stephen. He then indicated himself and repeated, "Caraíba; Stephen is Caraíba."

"*Is Caraíba,*" said Jurup. "*You see, Macatera; he understands enough. He is, Is Caraíba.*"

"*He must be the son of the highest Caraíba there is, and they have so many young children with them,*" said Macatera. "*Why?*"

Jurup pointed to the girls. "*Who are they?*"

Stephen looked over the girls. He circled his hand over them, indicating them all, and then once more placed the palm of his hand against his chest. Before he had a chance to open his mouth, Jurup answered for him. "*They are the children of Is Caraíba.*"

Stephen nodded, seeing that the meaning of his explanation was accepted as Jurup nodded his head with a smile upon his face.

Jurup gave indication that they should all follow him. "*Come; come, follow me,*" he said to the Caraíba. "*Come Macatera, let's take them to our village and show Chief Omagua; he will be most delighted to meet with Is Caraíba.*"

"Let's follow them," said Stephen. "We must be grateful for their hospitality."

"*Quickly, Macatera,*" urged Jurup. "*You go ahead and tell Chief Omagua who it is that follows.*" And with that said, Macatera raced off into the thickness of the jungle and disappeared from view.

The village fell upon them all with little to no notice, the jungle opening up to a cleared area that appeared relatively vacant at the present.

Bernard and Lambert were as impressed as were the children, the village of huts and open space a completely different contrast to that of the jungle – the heat was the same, but the sheer illusion of serenity fell upon them all. It was so quiet here, no man-made noise to speak of, no one seen amidst the ground around them: but of nature the noise was abundant.

The group of adults and children continued on, into their surroundings, onto the open space of the village, surrounded on all sides by long huts in which the Indians lived. The huts were made upon wooden beams and joists, built in a square formation to outline the border between jungle and village: in some areas along the Amazon, buildings boasted to be so long that they were large enough to house 30 families or more, where thatched roofs of palm leaves protected them from the elements, where rain wasn't as common nearer the coast as it was closer to the mountains between Peru and the eastern coastline.

Jurup collected the three Caraíba and their children centrally prior to the people of the village revealing themselves in all their glory, the chief to the front of those that he ruled over with a tender hand and a justified tolerance, tolerance which would not be extended so freely to those of other tribes.

They came out with Macatera beside the chief, a smile so wide upon his face that it was impossible to miss.

It was strange to see that a minority of the Omagua wore cotton robes, a fabric not seen before by those of Stephen's acquaintance, cotton which was grown by them, manufactured through painstaking manipulation of fingers and twine, the women being skilled weavers and able to transform the blandest of material into a work of majestic power through use of colour and dyed cloth.

It would take the new visitors much time to learn of the ways of the Omagua, the fact that they went naked much of the time, in particular during a hunt, but otherwise were rather proud and meticulous to cover themselves in adornment of many hues and origin. Times of great honour and spiritual awakening, representation and acceptance, were also times in which to go half naked and shrouded in decoration.

They were a naked people, handsome and brown, not embarrassed of showing their privy parts. The warriors wore magnificent plumage and were painted with black and red vegetable dyes, with their necks, heads, arms, and some privy parts and feet, covered in feathers; parrot and macaw being their favourite.

Feathers were invariably long, and red and blue, and largely from the macaw; but there was a vast array open to all the tribes of the jungle. Black feathers came from wild turkey or the anú cuckoo, scarlet from guara ibis, reds yellow and black from the toucan, grey and green from parrot and parakeet; tiny iridescent feathers came from humming-birds, tawny brown from falcon and hawk, and white plumes from the egret.

Both men and women alike took part in celebrations of many fashions and deliverance, from evil, boredom and liberation; but now, at this moment of their freedom, they were casting their doors and arms open to Stephen and the others as though they belonged.

The chief continued until a short distance remained between the two parties and he sat down upon the ground, all following his action, including Jurup. Stephen sat too as did the others behind him on seeing that it was the proper thing to do, some of the children needing a signal from Bernard to follow their actions in the quiet semblance of their hosts.

Macatera could be seen whispering something to the chief before he stood up and announced before all, "*This is Chief Omagua, and he is pleased to offer, Is Caraíba, with all that he can offer, the people of Omagua are happy to receive our ancestors with open arms.*"

The chief put his palm to his chest twice: "*Chief Omagua; Chief Omagua.*" He wore a great mass of macaw feathers upon his head: and if he was to die then he would be replaced by another who would then bear the Chief's name and wear the great mass of plumage with pride.

Stephen nodded in acceptance of what he was being told when an elderly man stood up and stepped from the crowd of those seated, and he was followed by three girls.

As the three girls approached, Lambert and Bernard couldn't help notice how several women with babies sat amongst the throng, the babies tied to the breasts with cloth so that only the legs showed.

Jurup accompanied the three young girls forward with a smile upon his face, and the girls sat before the three men and began to weep and cry. It was a sign that they were filled with joy, that they openly welcomed Is Caraíba and the others. They wore necklaces of seashell and fishbone with pride and their hair was combed via the spikes of a fruit tree not so very far away, and their hair sparkled and was clean, washed in suds procured from the skin of a fruit.

"What's wrong with them, Stephen?" asked Bernard, concerned for their well-being.

"It appears to be a custom," answered Stephen. "I wouldn't be too concerned if I were you. Jurup is smiling and many of the crowd, beyond, are nodding acceptance of this ritual."

Jurup looked upon Stephen as his name was mentioned.

"What do you think it can mean?" Bernard asked.

"I can hazard a guess," replied Stephen, and his guess was correct, for Jurup was offering his open palms to the three men, shifting his open hands from girls to knights. "They are a gift to us."

"*Chief Omagua does offer these girls to you in the hope that they will bring you joy,*" said Jurup, his flashing white teeth never disappearing for an instant. "*You are friends of the Omagua. You are welcome here, Is Caraíba and Caraíba alike.*"

"Is Caraíba," repeated Lambert. "He keeps saying it, over and over."

"It is the name we have been given," said Stephen. "I think we are each, one and the same; I am Is Caraíba and you are simply, Caraíba."

Jurup nodded with verification; his understanding.

Stephen pointed to Lambert and said to Jurup, "Caraíba."

Jurup nodded. Jurup then took over from Stephen and pointed to Bernard. "*Caraíba,*" he then pointed to Stephen. "*Is Caraíba.*"

Stephen nodded and understood. "Yes; you are both, Caraíba, and I am, Is Caraíba."

"A prophet," said Bernard with a little reflection.

"We came on a ship which is a representation of their past," said Lambert.

"The Templar's have been here," said Stephen and a sudden gust of noisy exhales came across them from amongst the throng.

Chief Omagua stood up and pointed an accusing finger towards Stephen; a friendly gesture. "*Templar; Is Caraíba, Templar.*"

Stephen saw the light as it fell upon him, the truth behind it all and explained this to the other knights. "We are the Templar's of the past, or a representation of that, which was. We are like prophets from above, having journeyed from the afterlife. We are sacred to them, we are the saviours of their past."

Chief Omagua stepped ever closer and stopped just paces away from the three men and looked Stephen in the eye.

"*Templar, Is Caraíba,*" said the chief. "*Are you; Is Caraíba of the ancestors; of those that bestowed victory upon us?*"

Stephen nodded, not understanding what was said but clearly accepting the role of what it meant to be a prophet.

The chief placed a hand inside his chest plate of macaw feathers and drew from it a cross upon a chain of gold, the chain only now visible to the three knights, for it had been hidden by the grass cords of his chest plate of colour and majesty.

Lambert's eyes fell wide open, as did his jaw; Bernard too, was astonished.

Stephen looked at the chief. "Chief Omagua; I am, Is Caraíba," and held his palm against his chest. "Templar, from across the sea," and brushed his hand across the sky and into the direction of where the sun did rise.

"*Jurup,*" said Chief Omagua. "*These ancestors of those that stood by us in time of war are to be treated as the true gods they are. Forget the usual formalities and press upon them the teachings of our way; teach them the language that they have grown to forget.*" The chief looked over the crowd, to all of those present. "*We must bestow more than friendship and hospitality. We must show to them that we are one. They are the repre-sentatives of the Caraíba of our past.*"

Women then erupted slowly and in gentle stride towards the three knights and thirteen children, laden with great masses of food and drink. There were fruits, herbs, game, fish, crabs, oysters, lobsters and crayfish, just to mention but a few of the choices being placed before them.

The three girls in front of Lambert, Bernard and Stephen, now looked up and smiled, for the weeping had concluded. Their hair was very long and black, hanging down their backs. One had her thighs from knee to hip and buttocks painted in black dye, another one had knees and calves painted. Another had dye from head to foot. One would think that they were bestial and of little knowledge, but they were clean and very smart.

Jurup stepped a little closer and pointed to the three girls in turn, introducing them by name. "*Anupita, Moilan, Tupapan,*" and Stephen, Lambert and Bernard, nodded in turn as the girls drew alongside their husbands to be.

"Are we to be served by these girls?" asked Lambert of Stephen.

"Only time will tell," said Stephen, unsure himself of the appropriate manner in which they should be accepted.

The thirteen children, once afraid and seemingly forgotten about, were now accepted and drawn in close by those show-ering them with drink and food, gifts of feather and pottery, the whole tribe smiling down upon them and bestowing great friendship upon them all.

Catherine and Lois were overjoyed to see such friendliness.

*
* * *
*

The Great River was a mass of swirling water where lines upon lines of dark and unbroken trees crowded the ground for as far as the eye could see, on occasion a few giants rising up into the sky, trees breaking free of the stranglehold that the canopy had on the ground below, where animals and insects lived in all their abundance, moving freely about, upon the highways they'd created through sheer volume, persistence and manner.

Stephen could see the cloud moving across the sky towards him, from far, far away, where the ground seemed to rise forever before him, continuing on into the heavens above; God's own garden of life.

He stirred once more upon the hammock he'd been provided, stirring again in his sleep, his dreams coming forth as though real; as though solid. He could smell each; see it; feel it. And his dream continued upon the path it was heading.

The reflections upon the movement of the river were clear and colourful, glimmers of the life around shimmering upon the surface and the waters continued on towards the ocean, and from dawn to dusk the magnificent spectacle of colour was dragged across the path of his mind; his personal inspiration; all the colours of the rainbow, and so much more, was evident in this land so abundant with life and solace.

Birds filled the sky like he'd never seen before, the jungle and river providing life for more than 800 different species of birdlife. They searched the riverbanks for food, early morning, noon, and sunset, perusing the water and banks for something to eat, and from the river came the stares of others for it was teeming with all manner of fish, turtles, mammals and rodents.

But the animals of the forest were just a speck of the true life which spanned the river system, its banks, side channels, swamps and lakes; for the Indians, so local, built their homes in areas close by, to make good advantage of the agricultural grounds. Floods would come and go; manioc tubers would be planted and harvested; Indians would harvest and eat; it was as true a cycle of life as any other. Yes indeed, the Indian life here was one with the land around. Both man and land lived in true harmony, but the relationship of tribe with tribe had not yet revealed itself to Stephen, for he knew nothing of any others but those of the Omagua.

His eyes flickered, the depths of his dreaming increased. He could hear the drums of the forest; hear their requests and their denials. Drums were forever heard upon the breeze and a vast majority of these heard in the stillness of late night and early morning.

There were no domestic animals to be seen, none which existed in the basin so fruitful of life, but turkeys, fowl and turtles, could each be harvested in different ways, in particular the turtle where they were often kept in pools of water, like a pond, for eating and breeding, hundreds maintained for the good of the tribes that lived out their lives in this new land that had been discovered by the knights.

Then, with a sudden shift in thought, came the instructions which he'd not heard in so long; instructions being passed onto him from high above, and a warning which erupted from within him, and he sat up in a startled manner. He breathed uncontrollably for several seconds and then controlled himself, looking out from upon his hammock and to the girl he knew was to be his Indian wife; Anupita.

Anupita was awake and she looked into Stephen's eyes. She smiled.

She was rather beautiful and must have been no older than 14 years of age. He thought upon her then, as their eyes locked. She really wasn't that much younger than he, and she was of an age where childbirth was expected of her. He wasn't sure if he wanted a wife; if he needed one. He missed his wife of Constantinople so much, but he thought of her so little these days; she was long dead. Could he love another? Maybe it wasn't anything to do with being in love with the girl, or the girl being in love with him, but of learning to love and respect one another, to be able to make good their lives with each other.

She lay there upon her hammock, completely naked and unashamed. There was nothing to be ashamed of; if anything, Stephen should feel ashamed for wearing the rags he wore. Each of them wore rags for clothes, what were once good garments, made from strong material, were now torn and ragged pieces of cloth.

He smiled and she shifted slightly, seemingly making room for him upon her hammock, and she beckoned for him to come and be comfortable, to lay beside her. She wanted him that minute, felt it her duty to give herself to him. He searched his soul for what was right and what might be wrong and then heard the voice of his dream once more, playing back through his mind as though recorded forever and a day within him. He didn't quite feel that it was the right thing to do, to have his way with this girl, but to do nothing would put great shame upon her and her village; it must be thought by others, in the least, that he had given himself to her.

There was no salvation without sacrifice; there was no true life without death. The laws of one world were not the laws of another and so the religious belief of one section of humanity was a contrast of varying shape and colour to another.

A brief moment of fear then grappled within him. He recalled right then and there that the chain around his neck, which secured the Cross of Christ to him, was nothing more but a device in which to carry his burden, and the cross was but the meaning of life – and in the wrong hands it could be deadly. The voice which had commanded over him so often in his past was now lost to him, never again to speak to him; never again to give an order. It was as though God was happy with the situation currently offered by this new world he had discovered, but precautions for the invasion of white men needed to be taken into hand. There within his head was the plan of all plans, the path his life was to take already clearly painted for him. He would tell the others what was to be, but he could not reveal all because he didn't know it all.

He looked again at Anupita and considered the gesture. He wasn't yet ready to make love to her but he would submit to her soon, but for now he would content her by sharing her hammock, and so he fell from where he slept and moved in beside the one that had been handed to him, as though fruit upon a plate.

Anupita moved her hand down to Stephen's manhood but he gently, and with a smile, pushed it away. She understood quite clearly; he needed more time. She was happy with this; there would be no shame placed upon the village. She felt within her, in a strange and contorted way, that Stephen felt the pressure of the coupling, that if he had taken advantage of her that minute that his trust would not have been won, but now; she felt as though he was the one for her, that he was the one to be trusted above all others.

Stephen tried to sleep once more, the inside smells of the hut hitting his nostrils, of wooden smoke fires; dyes and coconuts and bananas; and there was a great calm and quiet in such abundance that it seemed magical, nothing to disturb the solace, nothing around to make noise enough to disturb those sleeping.

And in the same hut, so long it was that the three knights could not see each other for the hammocks that were spread throughout, Lambert and Bernard, although men of great con-viction and belief, were not as strong as Stephen, and although the smallest speckle of shame was felt by them both, after the deed of mating was concluded, they felt as though they had little choice in the matter but to have made love with the girl that each had been provided.

The thirteen orphans had been placed within several other huts, spaces made available for them throughout. Nowhere in the entire village were there more than two children close together for there simply was no available space in which to provide them with the security attained by one another's company and close companionship.

Some of the children, tired as they were, could not sleep, the noises of the jungle prying their eyes open, and the people of the village scared them, but also… did not. They were in a strange new land, far from home, but Stephen had at least given them comfort in the knowledge that God was watching over them all.

Some of the children, parted as they were, took note of what had so far happened to them, and made a special note of their surroundings.

Hammocks were suspended in rows of wooden pillars, no segregation. Open passages existed along the centre of each hut, no partitions between families whatsoever; the village people were as though a single entity.

There was no privacy; not the slightest. Fire burns both day and night, never left unaided to the powers of the rain, lightning and thunder spirit, Tupan. There was never any quarrelling; villagers lived in peace and harmony. They were clean, and yet; dirty: women always combed their hair, and they never smelled, but yet, they mostly urinated from within their hammocks at night, onto the floor of their hut, seemingly too lazy to go outside. They always weighed all things in their judgement before giving an opinion, and knew all the stars in the heavens above. Old women had breasts hanging down their flanks, firm breasts when young; men were strong and apt to provide for their village, in times of peace and in times of war, always in denial of an inability to perform when reaching old age.

They had no private property, but had common belongings which they shared amongst each other without restraint. They had, of course, no government. They were open and generous with all of their possessions, displayed not a single ounce of greed. They lived together in perfect harmony, with no dissension between families being evident: a tribe member was a family member. When one had something to eat it was shared equally, no matter how small, children coming first. They had no class distinction or notions of dignity, but the chief was still a chief.

The young woman named Tapera looked to one of the orphans, Margarita, and saw the fear within her for a noise that she could hear outside; Tapera then turned to Catherine who seemed concerned for her friend.

"*It's a musmuqui,*" advised Tapera. "*It's a monkey of the night that sees the moon as an advantage against those that prey against it.*"

Catherine didn't understand her, but she smiled all the same.

"*Musmuqui; Musmuqui,*" said Tapera.

"Musmuqui," repeated Catherine.

Tapera smiled and pursed her lips together like a monkey and pretended to scratch under her arm.

"Ah; a monkey," said Catherine.

"*Yes,*" nodded Tapera in excitement, seeing the confirmation of understanding in Catherine's eyes as they lit up. "*Yes, that's right; Musmuqui,*" and closed her eyes to go back to sleep, seeing that Catherine was now armed with enough information to help her friend feel more at ease.

Lois was several hammocks down, and she too had trouble sleeping. A woman helped her, but not as Catherine had been helped by Tapera.

"*You can't sleep, can you?*" stated Tupmi. She was a victim of war, stolen from another village, one she remembered some-thing about. She was stolen so she could be a bride, flesh and bone to be given to a man so that they might mate and have children. "*It is the evil one; the evil spirit we call Tupinambá.*" Tupmi fell back into her hammock and continued talking. "*Tupinambá is also a fierce tribe from across the river.*" She sat up again. "*Do you know the Tupinambá? Of course you don't; you don't understand me; none of you do.*"

Lois watched the woman as she spoke the words she knew nothing of. She feared for her life and wished the sun would rise immediately. She would get no sleep tonight.

*
* * *
*

Stephen opened his eyes with a jolt, lying there beside Anupita. Jurup was standing before him, his smile wide, and his teeth showing.

"*Is Caraíba,*" said Jurup. "*Come; come on. Follow me,*" and gestured with his hand for Stephen to follow.

"*Come, Is Caraíba. Come and help us,*" said Jurup.

Stephen followed, rubbing the tiredness from his eyes as he paced behind the young fellow.

"Where are—."

Jurup put his fingers to his lips and ordered Stephen to be quiet, politely. Stephen followed in silence.

They exit the hut and Lambert and Bernard come to view in the full brightness of the moon. Stephen stepped up quietly and saw that several other warriors were present. Jurup introduced them with an open palm, each smiling as their name was called.

"*This is, Atoup; this is, Iridem; this is, Tamendon. Stoup, Iridem, Tamendon,*" repeated Jurup and then once again ordered for silence and led the way to the banks of the river, several baskets carried between them.

They didn't have to walk far through the jungle when they came upon the fringe of the tree line, in front of them the beginnings of a cleared area, where sand existed between the jungle and the river. Each of the warriors took the hand of a knight and crept delicately into position, hiding behind the thick foliage offered to them all. Stephen looked out from his hiding and saw what it was that the warriors were interested in. Several turtles had come ashore, drawing closer to them, to lay their eggs in the sand.

It was quite some time before the eggs were laid and during the whole time there was nothing but the quiet of the night. The stars above dazzled the men, even those so used to the performance of their brilliance, the Milky Way in all its glory providing a show which was enchanting, enthralling: a sight to see.

Two of the turtles had returned to the river, already, but one was all that was needed to replenish the stock they maintained in an enclosure quite close to the village, where wooden railings kept them from escaping, so that they could be fed, and killed for food when needed – the tribe never maintained more than they needed to fill their needs.

Jurup gave the order and the other two warriors leapt to duty, fast afoot and laughing as they went, falling upon the turtle and quickly turning it upon its back. If caught out at sea, or further along the river than desired, they would have drilled two holes into the shell with pointed stones and towed it back to the enclosure behind a canoe.

Atoup looked it over. "*Its breastplate will make a good hatchet,*" he reported, considering the duty ahead, where it would be cut and sharpened by stones, hardened by fire and fixed into place at the head of a sturdy handle of oak.

"*You can show Is Caraíba how to make one, Atoup,*" said Jurup. "*Yours are always the best.*"

Atoup smiled, for he was proud of his accomplishments as a tool maker.

Stephen looked from one to the other and understood that there was work for him, something to be learnt of killing turtles and making good use of what they had to offer.

Iridem and Tamendon got to their hands and knees and commenced to dig for the eggs, baskets brought up to where the hole grew larger by the second. A drum noise then disturbed the silence, some three leagues away or more. Stephen turned on hearing it and Jurup looked off into the distance.

The sun was rising and the birds had commenced to bring much sound to the area.

"*They are of the Tupi-speaking nations we fear,*" said Jurup. "*They are of a strange tongue; we call them Tapuia.*" Jurup looked into Stephen's eyes. "*Tapuia. They might be of the Carib, and they are a dangerous Tapuia.*" Jurup growled and screwed up his face and then, mimicking the fierceness of a puma, portrayed one ripping the flesh of his arm away from the bone, going through the action of his arm being eaten. He stopped. "*They eat flesh; they enjoy the taste of people and will go to great lengths to secure a meal. We must always be wary,*" said Jurup and putting a finger to his eye he repeated; "*Always be wary; look; look and see: look and listen,*" now cupping his ear.

Tupi-speaking nations were always invading from the south, always pushing northwards to put claim to other lands.

Stephen nodded, for he understood that the drums he was hearing were the signature of evil men, willing to bring harm to anyone outside of their village.

"*Come,*" said Jurup, smiling once more. "*Enough talk on the heinous Carib; we have better things to do with the sun rising on this day.*"

"*Jurup; Look!*" yelled Tamendon as the eggs of the turtle continued to be piled into the basket.

Jurup shot a glance to the concern and saw a good piece of wood floating down river and coming to grief upon a segment of rock. "*It looks like it'll make a good canoe,*" agreed Jurup.

It bobbed there momentarily and then was turned around, pivoted like a gate opening, and it again commenced its journey down stream, coming closer to shore and then banking itself upon the sand, which slowed its progress even further. Jurup ran towards it and Stephen followed.

Jurup pounced on his good fortune and started pulling, with all his strength, the cedar trunk onto dry land. Tamendon was now at Jurup's side and together all three men pulled the trunk of the cedar to shore.

The muscles of the Indians, through the strenuous activities of day-to-day life and from paddling against the flow of the river during times of need, came to life now, well defined and well-shaped, like the knights of Constantinople that Stephen knew so well, moulded pillars of strength that never shunned hard work, but were always quick to make the most of a day of rest.

"*Thank you, Tamendon,*" said Jurup, having aided well. "*It's yours; you saw it first.*"

"*No, Jurup,*" said Tamendon. "*You have it. I already have a good canoe.*"

Stephen could see there was bartering being done, but was at a loss as to the true meaning of it all, but he saw great friendship in the way that they dealt with one another. They were warm and friendly, and seemed to help each other freely with any task.

"*Please, Jurup,*" insisted Tamendon. "*I already have two good canoes for my family.*"

"*You'll need more than two if you take a third wife,*" said Jurup as he laughed. "*Your sons will be fighting for possession, eager to catch fish for themselves.*"

Many men had more than one wife. If there were fewer men due to war then others would need to take more wives, to help support the structure of the village. Other extra wives would be given to warriors who proved themselves and to promote the growth of bravery amongst men of the tribe – but no one in the village went without a man or a woman.

"*Then I will make them one when the next time a log appears on the river.*"

"*Very well; thankyou, Tamendon,*" agreed Jurup. "*Can you please go and get a lasso so that I can secure it to the shore?*"

"*Yes, immediately.*"

Stephen would come to learn, quite quickly, that an Omagua family would have at least two canoes, but the warriors would not enter the forest and chop a tree down for the sake of accumulating possession. A good warrior would wait for a suitable tree or trunk, preferably cedar, to come drifting down the river, and would lasso this and tow it ashore. When the water level dropped, and the log was stranded, he would slowly carve it out using stone and turtle shell tools. Canoes were easily carried over land to help evade enemies and were the only real means in which to get some good fishing done as well as a means in which to travel quickly. The river was their road, was their easy path from one friendly village to another.

*
* * *
*

It seemed that most of the tribe was gathered around the large fires of the village, cooking breakfast amidst the friendly chatter that each and every one shared, both warmly and freely.

Turtle eggs were being cooked and although harder to digest than a fowl was surprisingly tasteful.

Each cooked well amidst its own fat, the oil not wasted and used to help the fish along as it cooked upon the pottery earthen-ware made so magnificently, though not as good as the pottery of the Juruá tribe. Each piece was orange-red and covered in graceful geometric patterns, usually in red, white or brown. Some of the larger three foot tall urns were covered in faces of the dead.

"Their cooking skills, I would say, are amongst the best," said Lambert.

"They're, indeed, wonderful fishermen," granted Bernard. "With a river to harvest, who needs land?"

"They're good farmers, too," said Stephen.

Bernard looked Stephen in the eye, perplexed. "You've seen this?"

"Look over there," said Stephen as he pointed. "A basket full of something I ate last night."

"Oh, my God," said Bernard. "What is it?"

"You obviously missed out on it the other night," said Stephen. "It consists of hundreds of yellow shells connected to a stem. I think Jurup said it was corn."

"What does it taste like?" asked Bernard.

"Like nothing you've had before," answered Stephen. "Trust me; they are as good at farming as they are at fishing. Food like that found in their baskets doesn't come easily."

"*Iridem,*" shouted Macatera. "*Get your bow ready, Tamendon too.*"

Without haste the men of the tribe rushed to collect their bow and arrows which lay close by, understanding the urgency in the voice of their friend. Above them was a flock of migratory birds, an endless cloud of plumage that quickly filled the sky. Boys from all around jumped for joy and raced to get their bows ready, to learn more from the older men, to harness their skills further, to take part in this, the opportunity for fresh meat at tonight's meal, not to mention new feathers.

Stephen and the others followed the gaze of Macatera, the chief, and others of the tribe, to see for themselves the sky growing thick with birds at flight.

Bernard scoffed. "No wonder the tribe is so big," he said. "They need the numbers in order to kill a few birds."

"Maybe you'll be eating those words," said Lambert.

"No man can be accurate enough to shoot a bird in flight, in particular so far from the ground. Look at them all, the men of the tribe, running for their bows like the children, as though a game has been presented to them."

"Bernard," said Stephen. "You see the feathers and other decorations that the tribe wears, I know you do. It's as though the gift comes easily."

"I wager they miss," said Bernard, "and that if luck is in play then two or three might be shot down; but certainly no child could be that accurate."

"And what would you wager?" asked Lambert.

"I'll wager..." Bernard could see Stephen watching on with interest and decided on emphasising an effort in seeing their relationship with the tribe grow. "I'll wager that if more than ten birds are secured that I'll help Jurup hollow out his new canoe, if not… then you must suffer the embarrassment and hardship."

"But you said they would be lucky to secure three," pointed out Lambert.

"I need insurance," and Bernard shrugged his shoulders.

"Good, then it's agreed," said Lambert, not willing to see a good wager go to spoil.

"You should have been more careful," said Stephen.

"Don't worry, Is Caraíba," said Bernard. "I might not look all that bright but I can assure you, I'm not stupid.

And no sooner had Bernard finished his sentence and he saw all the men and children with bows arch their backs and shoot what arrows they had into the air; a wall of fire created. The birds fell from grace, dozens upon dozens, and the Chief Omagua gave the order for the slaughter to stop.

"Gold from heaven," said Lambert.

"How did you know?" asked Bernard, stunned by what he had just seen.

"I didn't," admit Lambert, "but I'm not stupid."

Stephen laughed out loud and the quarry of fresh meat was gathered up quickly by the women.

The tribe at work was a marvel to see, splendid behaviour being emitted by all, but one set of eyes cast a burning fury upon the backs of her captors, Tupmi hiding her hatred for the tribe deep down inside her, for she hated being a part of the Omagua. She hated every aspect of the tribe but said nothing. She glanced over to Lois and smiled. Tupmi felt that the young girl would suit her well, deliver to her a means by which to avenge the tribe.

*
* * *
*

The sun had risen above the tops of the trees and the jungle seemed to come alive, the singing of the birds having subsided and the other residents of the jungle, the wondrous rain forest, coming to life.

The tribe had scattered to carry on with tasks that needed to be completed or relaxed by sharing in conversation, plucking feathers from birds, making all manner of pottery and jewellery, or simply brushing their neighbours hair or painting their face.

Jurup approached Stephen with Macatera, Atoup, Iridem and Tamendon by his side. Each man carried a weapon with several to spare.

"*Ah, Is Caraíba,*" announced Jurup. "*You must come and join in the hunt. We'll be gone for most of the day,*" and spanned his open palm across the sky to indicate the passing of time. "*We're looking for fowl, anaconda, monkeys and peccaries,*" Jurup put his fingers to his mouth and then patted his stomach. "*Food; something to eat; something to learn and talk about around the fire at night,*" and smiled... they all smiled, each of the hunters together, nodding their heads. "*Where are the other Caraíba?*"

Stephen nodded with his head in the direction of the nearest hut on hearing the word Caraiba as Bernard and Lambert exit with their new brides beside them.

"*Ah, I see,*" said Jurup who laughed, and the other four men joked amongst themselves at the relationship which was obviously unfolding; Jurup then realized that Anupita wasn't to be seen. "*Where's Anupita?*" he asked.

"Anupita," repeated Stephen. He got to his knees and Jurup and the others protested, for he was Is Caraíba and shouldn't be grovelling upon the ground, but Stephen insisted and gave a signal that Anupita was digging the soil, nurturing maize and yucca like a good worker does.

"*Good, good,*" said Jurup, "*but please stand up,*" said Jurup earnestly, "*before Chief Omagua sees you. He'll not forgive me if he sees you on the ground like this,*" and the whole time he gestured and spoke he was smiling, teeth bare to the world around him. Even when tense and disturbed he smiled that unwavering grin for all to see.

"Bernard; Lambert; to me, please," said Stephen, loud enough for the knights to hear. "My guess is that we're going hunting."

Bernard and Lambert made their way over after bidding their wives farewell.

"The chief's gift hasn't been keeping you, have they?" asked Stephen with a smile.

"I feel ashamed," admitted Bernard, "But a man is a man, all the same."

"Should we..." Lambert started. "Should we defile the wishes of the chief, the customs of the tribe, and the needs of the many?"

"You shall do as you are doing," said Stephen, "for you have done nothing wrong, have served no evil, and must submit to the ways of this new world."

"*Come; come along,*" urged Jurup. "*The day will be long and hard, but pleasurable all the same.*"

"Let's join these men and learn of something new this day," said Stephen.

"Yes, Is Caraíba," said Bernard.

"Must you call me that?" asked Stephen.

"It's the way of the tribe," answered Bernard, "and so I must commit."

Bernard and Lambert were each handed a wooden lance, each the length of a man, and Stephen was provided a bow with some arrows.

"*Come; time to go,*" said Jurup and stepped off in search of food and entertainment.

They hadn't gone far into the throat of the jungle when a small arbitrary came into view and this was followed to reveal a small pond which had been damned for good reason.

Macatera moved towards some vegetation nearby and returned with his hands full. "*This is called timbó lianas. Timbó lianas,*" educated Macatera.

"Timbó lianas," repeated Lambert.

"*Yes, yes,*" said an excited Macatera. "*Look, watch me,*" and stepped over to the pond and extracted juice from the vegetation before beating the water with it. Within minutes several fish floated to the surface, stunned. Macatera smiled as did the others.

Bernard knelt down to pick up one of the fish that was closer to the edge than the others.

"*No,*" said Jurup. "*We don't need it. Leave it. It will awaken soon enough and then swim away. We can eat it later, when the sky is empty of birds and the river less productive.*"

"Come," said Stephen. "We'll learn as we go, take when we are told to take. Let's leave the hunters to lead the way in our quest for knowledge."

Bernard nodded, hoping that he would be forgiven for his hasty grab for the fish, but there was nothing to be forgiven and the hunters were pleased that the knowledge of the lessons were being understood.

*
* * *
*

As the months unfolded before them, the knights and thirteen orphans got to know their hosts better than they knew each other.

There was always plenty to eat; monkeys, fish and fowl; peccaries, bird eggs and turtle eggs; edible roots, honey, yucca, maize, manioc, fruits nuts, sweet potato, broad beans, and a large assortment of small animals. They never seemed to go without. Life was a pleasure; a leisure; a means by which to devote oneself to more time with family and other members of the tribe. The relationship shared between each individual was beyond compare. They loved one another like they loved life itself.

Customs were adopted and accepted, even those that seemed unbelievably cruel and disgusting, such as the ceremony of an Indian girl reaching puberty, where they are first corrupted by a close relative, other than their father, before being given away as a wife.

They gave birth without fuss, washing the newborn baby in the waters of a stream. Babies didn't wear swaddling-cloth. The father received the infant in his arms at birth, putting a knot in the umbilical cord before biting it off with his teeth. When a son was born, the father would wash and paint the newborn, placing him in a little hammock, and make him a miniature wooden sword, and a bow with arrows, so that he would grow into a fine warrior and hunter.

The baby was not caressed, enveloped, warmed, overfed, well-tended or put into the hands of a nurse, but was loved all the same. Babies were fed on mother's milk only and the grains of corn which had been chewed in the mother's mouth, fed to the baby in the same way that birds feed their young, and it seemed all possible that the oldest amongst them all was 130 years of age, but it was impossible to confirm with their current understanding of the language.

The land was filled with misery, too; with the mosquito, wild cats, crocodiles, piranha, and headhunters; but the relationship of those in the tribe made up for all the horrors, and the love was shared equally between them all; and there were many ways in which to combat the horrors.

And so, after twelve months in the new world the knight and orphans had come to know the language of the Omagua as though they'd spoken it their entire lives. After just twelve months in this new world they had become one with the tribe that had adopted them by the power of free will. It was also at this time that the drums from across the river had grown rather close and the spread of the tribe, both up and down the river, had become evident.

The expanse of water between the banks of the river separating the south from the north was so vast that it warranted no concern for the safekeeping of the tribe's unity. Several islands offered themselves between the two banks and even these were quite some distance away, islands which were too small to offer any great advantage to a growing tribe, but offered a reasonable opportunity to grow some seasonal crops, and stations from which to launch attacks upon their enemies.

Indians used drums to send messages to other friendly tribes, a means by which to communicate basic ideas and formalities but falling short of precise negotiations or commands. It was known, right across the land, that one particular chief might be responsible for several leagues of land; north, south, east and west; and others put command and influence to a hundred leagues or more in varying directions.

The Omagua were a relatively small tribe whose basic home-state was over 200 leagues away, their main reason for separating from their original home only now being revealed, and that was to do with a vision that the shaman of the tribe had suffered, whereby particular members of the tribe, for committing sins against another by insulting his wife when dead, was ordered to take leave for several cycles in order to receive forgiveness.

The power of the spirits could not be underestimated; the power of the spirits were all-important.

*

* * *

*

Chief Omagua revealed the secret of his forced vacation from the majority.

"I didn't mean any harm to come of it," said Chief Omagua. "You understand that my thoughts were with the hunter who had been presumed dead, but his wife was too quick to find a new husband. When the hunter returned his wife was depressed over the situation, for she loved her new husband more than the first. She was a captive of the Icá, of whom I don't wish to speak, and she hated us all but hid it well. She took her own life when forced back into the arms of her former husband. I passed judgement upon her when I shouldn't have and hence, cast upon the wind with those closest to me, as decreed by the elders of the tribe. Being a former member of the elders I was chosen to be the chief of my small band of followers, who all agreed with my cursed remarks upon the dead woman. If I take you back with me, to the place of my birth, I shall be forgiven, for the Omagua will be honoured to provide shelter and sustenance to Is Caraíba."

"You know we aren't of the spirit world," said Stephen. "We are just men, just like you. We are flesh and blood."

"No, this can't be true," replied the chief. "I saw with my own eyes the bite you suffered at the hand of the Red Tree Viper. You should have died but didn't. How can you explain this if you aren't of the spirit world?"

"This cross around my neck, which you have seen before, is of great religious value. It provides me with sanctuary in this world. Only by great calamity can I be delivered into the arms of death."

"So you aren't a spirit, but one so favoured as yourself, must be provided the appropriate status," said the chief. "We shan't speak of this anymore, for it troubles me."

"I understand," said Stephen and his eyes fell upon the chain around the chief's neck.

"You have a question about the chain and the cross I wear, I can see it," said the chief.

"You have seen what I haven't seen, and that is all important to me," replied Stephen. "You have seen the treasure of the Templar's, the great treasure which belongs to the one I serve. It must be protected, kept hidden from the eyes of man."

"We will journey soon to the ends of the earth, to the Omagua of the west. It will be a long and hard journey and many of us might die. We shall commence the journey soon and as we go we will pass the sight where the treasure is hidden. You can then judge as to what should be done."

"Thankyou, Chief Omagua," said Stephen with the bow of his head.

The chief changed the subject, he was happy. "You and your flock have come a long way. You are all good learners and good with the bow and arrow."

"One day I shall repay my debt to you for all you have done."

"There's no need," said the chief. "Now; I heard that you are to go off on a hunt, some fishing."

"Yes, and I'm late," said Stephen as he stood. "If you'll excuse me, I must be getting along."

"You are, Is Caraíba, and always will be," said the chief.

"I am Stephen."

"The Omagua will not accept that, so unless you can think of a status more fitting, you must remain, Is Caraíba."

"I don't want to offend your spirit world by pretending to be something I'm not, and I don't wish to offend you."

"I am not offended," said the chief.

"Then why don't you tell your people the truth about me?"

"They are not ready."

"Before we depart on our journey I wish to be rewarded with a name as opposed to a status."

The chief nodded with respect. "I shall do all I can, but will not make any promises."

*

* * *

*

Jurup and Macatera were in the same canoe as Stephen, Atoup and Iridem with Bernard, and Tamendon and Amat (a skilled fisherman) with Lambert.

The canoes had been launched and they drifted out upon the surface of the sea, some distance from the shore to make good advantage of the conditions.

Amat had told the three Caraíba of the traditional migratory streams and breeding cycles, and it was to this note that it had been decided to catch as much fish as possible in order to have something to take along with them on their journey to the west. It was often seen that men in canoes dragged behind them cages with live fish or even turtles with holes drilled into their thick shells and secured tight, fresh meat for a journey where time was not on their side, where the opportunities to hunt and find food was not available to them.

The three canoes were relatively close together and conversation between them was kept to a minimum, for there was much work to be done, but much was shared amongst those of each canoe.

Jurup looked to the heavens and then down to the sea, looking for that all important catch. "I hope that Upupiara will guide the fish to us on this day. The spirit of the waters can sometimes deter the fish, like Corupira protects the game of the jungle."

"Don't test the patience of the spirits," said Macatera. He looked to Stephen. "Is Caraíba will look after us."

"I hope so," replied Stephen with a smile and prepared his lance, holding it with the point down.

"You should fish with the bow," advised Jurup. "A good hunter can shoot a fish as it jumps from the water."

Stephen saw the sense. "But the bigger fish are beneath the surface. I can lance them as they come near the canoe. The bow you have will only serve to catch a flying fish as it skims the surface."

Jurup took an arrow from a stockpile, each arrow with a different head. Many heads were available to the hunter and each served a different purpose: a sharp wooden leaf-shaped blade, a simple fire-hardened point, a barbed point of bone or sting-ray tail, a serrated series of barbs, or a knob for stunning birds and monkeys; certain heads could also pierce cotton cuirasses as worn by different tribes.

"You will see what I can do with the barbed arrow," said Jurup.

"You're showing off," said Macatera. "Is Caraíba has seen it all before."

"He hasn't seen me fish."

"But he has seen Amat, and Amat is a better fisherman than you," reminded Macatera.

"Then we'll see who gets the biggest catch."

Stephen then upturned his lance to reveal its point. He acknowledged the stare given by Jurup. "I've prepared my lance with barbs, as you can see. My range won't be as good as yours, but my catch will be decisively larger."

"I'll catch ten fish before you catch one," said Jurup.
"What do you wager?" asked Stephen.
"You, Is Caraíba, wish to wager with me," said Jurup. "I don't believe it. Did you hear that, Macatera? Is Caraíba wants to wager, a spirit wishing to wager with me."
"Spirit power is far superior to the power of your bow, Jurup," advised Macatera.
"Ah, but I think I can win," said Jurup. "I'll wager that I can catch ten fish to your one; I'll wager my bow."
"No, not your bow," said Macatera.
"Why, you think I'm scared of losing? You just watch and learn."
"Very well," said Stephen. "And what would you like if you should win?"
Jurup smiled from ear to ear. "Talk to the chief, get me another wife."
"It's against my better judgement," said Stephen, allowing his true feelings to come to the surface in regards to marriage and the vows associated with the conviction.
"Are you scared to lose?" said Jurup.
"Enough," said Macatera. "He is, Is Caraíba."
"That's okay," said Stephen. "The wager will stand.
"Good," said Jurup and cast his eyes out to sea. He studied the area of concern. "Ah, ha; I see something," said Jurup and as he turned around he saw Stephen with a fish upon his lance.
"How did you do that?" asked Jurup.
"I learn quickly," said Stephen.
Jurup then laughed out loud. "It's such a small fish. You should try begging the fish to appear before you."
"It's bait," said Stephen. "For a larger fish," and he bent down to take up another lance. "I'll hold this fish in the water and wait for something larger to come along; and then you'll see something grand."
"You're dreaming," said Jurup and cast his eyes once more out to sea. "I know something of the sea. I can clearly see something out there. It's moving towards us and is rather large.
Sudden splashing drew Jurup's attention to the side of the canoe and there he saw Stephen's lance in the side of the largest dorado he'd ever seen.
"You've caught a dorado," announced Jurup unnecessarily. "It's the biggest I've ever seen."
Macatera gave aid to Stephen as the dorado couldn't let go of the lance in its mouth, the bait having worked wonders. They pulled and yanked until it was aboard.
It was very large, a compressed body and dorsal fin extending the length of its body, golden on the sides, blue and green to be seen, and a prominent forehead.

"It's a male fish," said Jurup.

"Then it's an el dorado," announced Stephen. "I'd say that this makes me the winner of the wager; unless you can catch ten fish before I get another."

"It doesn't count," said Jurup. "Macatera had to help you pull it in."

"You're right," said Stephen. "Keep your bow a little longer, for the day is still young."

By the time they'd finished on the sea, Stephen had caught three dorado and Jurup just eleven flying fish.

"The weather was against me," said Jurup. "I shall try..." he stared off into the distance as the shoreline drew closer.

"What is it, Jurup?" asked Macatera. He turned, with mouth dropping open.

Stephen looked up, too, and there before them, not so very far away, were no less than five canoes heading directly towards them, many men in each canoe.

"Carib!" yelled Jurup and the others in the canoes beside him looked up and saw the calamity of the situation.

"Carib," repeated Stephen. He knew all about them, and had been told many times in conversation.

"We won't make it in time," said Jurup. He looked over to another of the canoes. "Amat! Amat! You have to swim; you're the most powerful of us all! Go, now!"

Without second thought, Amat dived into the sea and commenced swimming obliquely away from the canoes and the approaching Carib.

"We'll put up a fight," said Macatera, "and delay their victory. Amat might rally aid before the Carib have time to capture and bind us."

Carib warriors captured their enemy for ceremonial reasons more than anything else, to eat their prisoners later on, as did many other Tupi-stock warriors of many regions on the southern side of the Great River. They ate their enemies and discarded their bones months later, and in some cases even kept their captives as slaves and provided them with women. They were a fierce foe who relished the taste of human flesh.

The five canoes of the Carib were fast through the water, and whether or not Amat went unnoticed, or simply ignored due to the catch which awaited the Carib in the other canoes, mattered little, for death awaited all of those captured. It was to this knowledge that Atoup, and Iridem, released all of their arrows into the air. The Carib retaliated and the occupants of their canoe, including Bernard, met immediate death.

The Carib then passed the canoe closest to them and approached the other two, weapons held in hand: wooden swords, broad-based stone axes, wooden lances with wooden shields to protect them, and arrows tipped with bone or stone heads.

*
* * *
*

The Carib had come prepared, but Amat made it to shore and ran as fast as he could to the tribe not so far away, to endeavour a rescue; if the chief was prepared to sacrifice his warriors to a fight that might very well see them served on a platter and eaten.
Amat knelt, panting hard in front of Chief Omagua, having given the information to him, the crowd commenced to grow larger by the minute; but none disturbed the chief's thoughts, for there was much to consider.
"Were all of the others taken alive?" asked the chief.
"I have no way of knowing," admitted Amat. "I had little time to make my escape. The others sacrificed themselves so that I could get away." He looked around at the others before returning his gaze to the chief. "We could have all tried to make an escape but we would have been picked from the water, one by one. The only way to get a message to you was by the others delaying the Carib."
"Are you sure it was the Carib and not another tribe?"
"It was definitely the Carib."
"How can you be sure?"
"I can't, but Jurup was."
"Then that's good enough."
"What shall be done, Chief Omagua?" asked Amat, his pan-ting having subsided.
"We shall sleep tonight and send scouts in the morning. The scouts shall report back to the southern edge of the Great River and meet us there. We will rescue Is Caraíba and the others."
Catherine, having heard the talk of rescue, retreated from the warmth of the fire to gather the other orphans; they needed to hear for themselves what had happened to Stephen, for he meant the world to them all, but first she would have to fill some of the men with fear, and she knew just who.
Catherine simply refused to allow Stephen to be subjected to a moment's misery, let alone the possibility of being eaten, as though some common fish.

*
* * *
*

Jurup, Macatera, Stephen, Tamendon and Lambert were each tied to the ground via a system of short pegs, the little clothing worn now ripped from them, the paint upon their faces washed away with fierce rubbing.

One of the Carib walked up to the gagged prisoners and surveyed the quarry.

Stephen was less startled by the ordeal than the others but concerned all the same for their combined wellbeing. The situation, however, made it impossible for him to do anything about the predicament they were in except deal with it as best he could, and this he knew.

The Carib spoke amongst themselves, sometimes shouting chants at others, or obscenities to the five men pinned to the ground, who were each unable to voice back an insult or two.

The Carib that looked down upon them all was walking up and down. He stopped in front of Lambert. He pointed to him and must have been astounded by his colour. The Carib pulled his knife from his waistband and fell to his knees before stabbing Lambert in the thigh, and as Lambert squirmed in great pain, his head thrashing left and right, the Carib cut himself a piece of fresh meat and held it up high to the cheers of many.

Blood dripped from the flesh in his hand and he walked leisurely over to one of many village fires and placed the meat into a vessel for cooking.

Stephen managed to turn his head just enough to see that Lambert had fainted from the horrific pain and injury, when he was suddenly, and viciously, slammed in the side of the face by a club with barbs sticking from it. It cut the flesh of Lambert's face deeply, some chunks of flesh flying from his cheek. It was then that Stephen understood quite clearly what was to happen to them all and closed his eyes briefly, to grasp small solace from the darkness that enveloped him.

But the sudden-felt-fear of the assault slowly disappeared and he lay still, unwilling to move another muscle, for the last thing he needed was to be ripped to pieces for no good reason like poor Lambert. He prayed; that's all he could do, but God gave no answer.

The Carib seemed to be rejoicing in the tender flesh of Lambert's thigh, wide eyes growing amongst the crowd of Carib, for they had never before tasted such good meat, and so it was decided that Stephen should be eaten last.

Lambert was still unconscious when the women formed a circle around him and commenced singing, falling upon him to beat him, to punch him, to pull at his hair, but he was out cold, unconscious: and Stephen then realized that Lambert was dead. His eyebrows were then scratched from his forehead with a crystal ring and rattles were quickly attached to his legs, rattles made from gourds and painted with dye, covered in colourful feathers and filled with pebbles.

Tamendon was then given the same treatment, but he was awake when they commenced beating him with their fists. The pain was terrible. As the rattles were attached to his legs they continued with another tune and forced him to shake his legs as best he could so that he contributed to the ceremony which was to see him served upon a plate, to be eaten by the Carib that swelled around him like a growing tide.

Tamendon was then untied and he was forced to his feet, bruised and battered as he was. He was then forced to mimic the hopping he saw before him, an elderly man showing him what to do. The women then broke out in chorus, singing, "here is our food, hopping towards us," and each smiled as they sang.

Lambert was the first to be placed upon a platform, to be roasted after being scrubbed clean, and then Tamendon was taken away to be smoked alive in the torture hut, to be smoked and gnawed on later. The Carib enjoyed their meat served in different ways, and never was the chief of the Carib disappointed.

Stephen opened his eyes after some time and realized that both Lambert and Tamendon were now truly gone from the world, and as this realisation fell upon him the ring of singing women commenced to grow once more as they crowded around Macatera.

Poor Macatera was treated much the same as Tamendon, but he was to be eaten partly alive. With a gag still in his mouth, and hands and feet bound securely, his legs were cut to pieces and the flesh devoured whilst it still dripped with blood; the remainder of his body was to be prepared in a different way.

Macatera's head was beaten in until the brains exploded from within, which were quickly discarded. His head was then severed from the neck and his body cut into small pieces before being boiled upon the village fires. His guts they gave to the women to eat, his hands and elbows to some of the men. His bones were collected as they ate so that they could be boiled and his skull was cleaned of all flesh, everything eaten quickly; his nose, ears, and flesh around cheeks.

The Carib who had taken the head away from the body was handed a leg bone and this he put away for safekeeping, to have it turned into a flute at a later date, the teeth of Macatera to be pulled from his skull and made into a necklace.

Stephen could smell Tamendon as his body was smoked in the small hut not so far away and knew that it would soon be time for him and Jurup to be given up to the feast, but it was then that the ceremony stopped as soon as it had started and the singing was given up until another day.

A Carib stood over Stephen and Jurup, and smiled. He said something that neither of them understood. His words meant nothing to them but it could all be deciphered. They were to be saved, to be eaten another day; possibly in the morning, maybe tomorrow night, but one thing was for sure, the time for them to be eaten would soon be upon them both.

*
* * *
*

The two canoes approached the bank of the Great River as Catherine, Arikuton, Baetatanam, Corimupira and Guadira – all but Catherine and Arikuton being very young – paddled slowly and delicately to ensure that there was no excessive noise to be heard. The last thing they needed was for one of the Carib to hear them approach. Others were in the other canoe.

Catherine could see, even in the dark of the night, where little illumination was given off by the half-moon above and the stars in all their glory, that the men in her canoe, both Arikuton and Baetatanam, were nervous. So few against so many seemed like suicide to them, but Arikuton had been on many raiding parties in the past whereby he was required to snatch women from other tribes to be used as wives.

They were all quick to pull the canoes into hiding and gathered around with their weapons as Catherine looked the four men in the eyes. "Arikuton and Baetatanam, you will lead the way; Corimupira and Guadira, you will follow at the rear," she said. "Is Caraíba will reward you all with good words and wives, I know this because I am one of his off-spring as you well know. My Father will provide for you."

"Chief Omagua will be angered," said Arikuton.

"It's too late for that," said Catherine, "bedsides, once we've returned to our side of the river with Is Caraíba and women to spare, Chief Omagua will be pleased."

"We only have room for the men and several women," complained Arikuton.

"Not if some of the men have already been eaten," replied Catherine, and a selfish thought then entered Arikuton's mind, for he suddenly felt a whim, did prefer an extra wife over the safety of one of his friends. He felt the sin within him, for it was wrong to think this way and he could not understand why such a thought had entered his head. "Come, Arikuton; it's time to go; it'll be morning soon." Maybe it had something to do with his age.

The line of men and girls then commenced their trek through the jungle, a worn track soon found by Arikuton who knew it to be human and not animal. He held his bow with pride and ready to shoot and the girls behind him each held theirs, but retained their arrows in the belts around their waists.

The jungle wasn't silent, not by any means. Night life was evident as the nocturnal animals clambered about in the trees and upon the ground.

They continued on like this, carefully and with purpose, for quite some time when Arikuton gave the signal that the village fires could be seen, and whether or not it was the tribe responsible for taking Is Caraíba, he could not confirm, but the general feeling and knowledge of tribal life and location indicated that it would be, in particular with the smells that then gently hit his nostrils.

The men shifted left and right and the girls placed themselves into an extended line, as Catherine had explained to them earlier, so that the flanks of their position within the jungle were protected by the men.

A Carib could be seen walking around, his shadow being cast far and wide by the flames of the fire as it burned. Arikuton could clearly smell the burnt flesh of a man now, stronger than it had been before.

They were all now upon the edge of the jungle, looking out through the foliage to the village at rest. There were several members starting to stir as the first of the birds commenced their call, for the morning was approaching.

Catherine could see two men lying upon the ground but wasn't sure who it was; only two men. Where were the others?

She tapped the girl beside her on the shoulder and took an arrow from her waist. Each of the girls on either side followed suit and soon everyone within the fortified line was ready to fire.

Catherine let loose her arrow first and it sailed through the air with a little noise, hitting its intended target in the throat. She was an accomplished shot to say the least, as were all of the girls, taught well by Lars, the Teutonic, and members of the Omagua tribe.

Her arrow was followed by several others and the men in the clearing were felled instantly.

Baetatanam and Corimupira leapt from their positions and rushed to the aid of those they saw laying upon the ground, pegged in position with rattles attached to their feet, and as the prostrate men stirred from their tormented sleep, the gourds gave off warning to the members of the Carib that something was amiss.

"Baetatanam; is that you?" asked Jurup, nervously, able to smell the scent of his friend.

"Be quiet," said Baetatanam.

"I have Is Caraíba," shouted Corimupira.

More and more men and women commenced to wake and exit the huts, and the bonds of Stephen and Jurup were cut, and in as quick as a flash they were carried away upon shoulders to the safety of the jungle as the orphans commenced to pick off their targets, one by one.

"We must go, Catherine; Now," stated Arikuton as a matter of fact. "There are too many waking and gathering arms."

"We need to give Baetatanam and Corimupira more time."

"The time is now."

The girls shot their arrows, one after the other.

"What about the wives you were promised? Surely you wish to be provided your gift."

"Forget it," announced Arikuton urgently. "Is Caraíba will reward me in his own way."

"Very well," announced Catherine for all to hear. "Let's inflict as much damage as possible and then depart."

Arikuton appeared at her side, having left his post. "You are a devil child," he said. "Please, let us go now."

Catherine felt the urgency within him and after letting loose one more arrow, gave the order to retreat.

Their escape was orderly and fast, none of the enemy standing when they turned their backs upon the camp, but as they disappeared into the throat of the jungle the Carib gathered their numbers and followed in haste, haste which saw many of them bring along lances and clubs instead of bows and arrows.

By the time Catherine and the others behind her had reached the banks of the Great River, the sun was rising above the horizon and the two canoes had been launched into the water ready to row.

Stephen and Jurup could be clearly seen, having each taken up a spot in readiness to row, tired as they were, bruised and battered beyond belief, they would row like they'd never rowed before.

Stephen smiled as he saw Catherine and the girls exit the jungle and got ready to propel the canoe forward. The canoes swayed from side to side as the girls and the men clambered aboard, eyes turned to fix themselves upon the jungle. The canoes almost leapt out of the water as they were thrust forward and arrows were once again placed into their bows in readiness to be let loose, and as the first of the Carib arrived upon the banks of the Great River a tremendous volley of feather on sticks struck them hard in head, chest, and thigh.

Several Carib, armed appropriately, were able to load their own bows with arrows and fire at the escaping canoes but shields made of wood were employed to protect them from the well-aimed shots.

Their rescue had been a success but with it would come with some regret, for they were now a target for revenge.

Chief Omagua sat silently in his hut with Stephen opposite; he had a lot to consider. It was some time before he finally spoke.

"We will have to move the tribe quickly. I see no other way around it. The Carib will attack and they will attack soon. They won't be as hasty as Catherine has been. They will consider their move wisely. I suspect that they will know what we think and prepare an ambush for us on the Great River," said the chief.

"Then we shall have to skirt the Great River and move inland," said Stephen. "We will go towards the high ground and then towards the sacred place which holds the treasure I am bound to protect."

Again the hut was filled with silence.

"It seems appropriate enough, as we have to leave this place anyway," replied the chief after some time. "I must tell you that Catherine and the others possess a great kinship with you. What they have done is more than any warrior would wish to do. Do you know that she bribed Arikuton with the promise of an extra wife?"

"He can take Tupapan, and Jurup will have Moilan."

"As you wish," answered the chief.

"I have also put thought into a name for myself, as opposed to Is Caraíba. Is Caraíba should be a sacred name, never to be uttered again."

"And what name do you choose?"

"When I was fishing I caught several fish that were painted in gold," said Stephen.

"Ah; the dorado."

"Yes," nodded Stephen. "Where I come from a male could be referred to as, el. I would therefore like to be called, El Dorado."

"You will be known as, El Dorado, for all time to come. You are a prince of gold, just like the fish; a golden man, as sacred as they come; and the name Is Caraíba will be uttered no more except at the appropriate time."

"I must also ask one other thing of you," said Stephen. "That when we enter the premise of the treasure that I be granted the right to commence with the growth of my own tribe."

"I shall have to think about this as splitting up the tribe, when a long journey still sits before us, would jeopardise the safety of all those in this village."

"I would ask that I be provided the company of the orphans, three unmarried men, and six men with wives," Stephen's eyes sank a little and the chief could see that he was upset by something.

"Tell me; what's the matter."

"I'm still having concerns about allowing my children to be gifts to men, where one man will share the bed of more than one of them. The customs of this world do contradict my earlier teachings."

"I heard you say once that the teachings of your great, great ancestor were that a man could have more than one wife."

"That's true, but where I come from we have what is called the New Testament, and it is here that rules have been laid down for men to adhere to."

"I think I have the answer for you," said the chief. "This, New Testament of yours; well... it's great, great father would be pleased to see His rules being put in place, other than His son's."

"And that is the dilemma," said Stephen, "For, not only am I abandoning the new for the old, but I am also abandoning all previous teachings to take up the life of the Omagua."

"Omagua life, or that of the Carib, matters little. We are much the same; except for our taste in what is good to eat," said the chief.

Stephen smiled.

"Enough talk of life," said the chief. "Which three men do you require as husbands for your many children? I shall provide the married couples when we arrive at the site of the treasure."

"Baetatanam, Corimupira and Guadira."

*
* * *
*

Stephen had not seen any fighting since he'd arrived in the New World. They'd not been attacked and neither did any warriors of the tribe appear to wish to forage for women. He knew that the Indians had an amazing sense of smell, sight, and hearing. They recognised trees as though it was a sign hanging over a door and they made their way through the jungle almost as fast as a man upon a horse and riding across an open plain. It was said that they could easily travel 200-300 leagues and end up exactly at their destination, as though a map was imprinted upon their minds like a stencilled work of art.

The Indians thought little of death, and were brave warriors, one and all, not afraid to travel 100 leagues or more to stage an attack in order for women to be taken as wives for members of the tribe, which had recently occurred in the case of Tupmi, making a stealth attack by dawn or dusk before carrying their captives away.

They travelled by canoe or in single file through the jungle with the chief leading, the chief setting an example, always. They spied out enemy huts before engaging in any attack upon their quarry, attacking with loud yells, stamping on the ground, and blowing blasts on their gourd trumpets, trumpets which Stephen had an interest in, for the bible mentioned that trumpets rallied God to one's side in battle.

They carried cords around their body to tie up their prisoners, adorned themselves with red feathers to tell themselves apart from the enemy, so that no unnecessary death was the result of their eagerness. They carried special herbs to apply to wounds for healing, such as *abuta*, *suelda*, or *micura*.

When on the attack they shower their enemy with arrows. They can easily hold a handful in hand and employ 12 to the minute. The coloured feathers of arrows in flight through the air are almost as majestic as the birds themselves, and if hit by an arrow they pulled it from their body, snapped it in two, and continued fighting, as though nothing had happened. In melee they are mad, clubbing and stabbing, slaughtering the enemy with no sympathy at all.

This is what Stephen knew or heard about but had yet seen in action, and as these thoughts entered his mind he watched as the tribe prepared for the long journey to their homeland, some food and many weapons being prepared, though little food would be required as the men would hunt as they travelled.

The first leg of their journey was through the jungle, to bypass any likely ambush on the Great River, but the canoes the men carried would aid them well when the time arrived to set upon the highway of the jungle and they paddled up-river to the sacred site where the Templar's treasure was hidden.

*

* * *

*

The journey through the jungle was a tense one for the orphans, as they had never endured such hardships before, where keeping up with grown men, as they strode across the ground, was almost too much for most of them. It was like this for a week, where the tribe continued on to bypass the Carib; they knew that the enemy would be waiting for them and it was only a matter of time before a scout returned with news on their location.

Tactics of attack and ambush were simple tools of vengeance, really. The Carib would have known that the campsite of the Omagua had been vacated and no sooner did they learn this then they would have sent out scouting parties of their own with orders for the ambush sites to be relocated further up-river, but well clear of the Sipinipoia, Tinamoston, and Aripiuna tribes, where the Tinamoston was situated in land but the others close by the banks of the Great River itself.

Chief Omagua understood the predicament of the situation regarding the Carib and with each passing day, as the scouts returned with news of the sighting of Carib ambushes, the tribe was forced ever on into the jungle to bypass the enemy set upon eating them or turning them into slaves.

The chief of the Omagua saw to it that the shaman of the tribe, Guajuta, tipped the scales in their favour when considering the spirits of the jungle. There were many to be satisfied but those requiring special favour and praise were Tupan, the spirit of thunder; Anthan, the devil of men's dreams and the jungle; and Corupira, the jungle demon who protected game against the evil doings of man. Tupan could easily start fire through his enraged state, casting strike after strike of lightning to hit the ground; Anthan was a goblin who brought bad fortune and orchestrated accidents along the way; and Corupira was a gnome with upturned feet, and named 'Forest Dweller'.

After a week of continuous marching through the jungle the chief called for a day of calm, to enable the orphans time to rest and the hunters time to gather some resources so that they wouldn't go hungry.

They would remain away from the Great River but there was a tributary close by which would serve their purpose and help with the gathering of energy for up to three more weeks of pushing through the jungle.

Tupmi sat beside Lois, well away from the others as the child looked for edible roots.

"The Carib are everywhere in the jungle, Lois," said Tupmi. "We'll be lucky to escape their vigilance."

"I was told that Macachera would protect us, that he was always present at the front of the line, and that the enemy would be given away where they hid."

"Macachera has no power over Forest Dweller, or Anthan. Do you really think that Macachera is any match for two spirits of the jungle?"

"The good are better than the bad, the spirit of Macachera will be victorious against those that seek to do us harm," replied Lois.

"Who told you that?" asked Tupmi.

"El Dorado."

"El Dorado," spat Tupmi, Lois slightly aghast at the contempt in her voice. "He's only a man."

"He is El Dorado."

"He sweats like any other man that I know," said Tupmi. "He wants for water and food like any other; he soils the ground with shit and piss; does he not?"

"Nevertheless, he has the power," said Lois.

"A cross around a neck is not powerful enough to prevent the Carib from continuing their search."

"It prevents them from finding us."

Tupmi was silent for a few seconds and then continued. "What will become of you, Lois? You will be treated as all the others, an understudy to Catherine and her greatness."

"She isn't that great," said Lois, "not really."

"Then you should prove it by doing as El Dorado wills," said Tupmi. "El Dorado has said that you are to become a band of women warriors, with Catherine as your queen. Wouldn't you like to be a queen as opposed to a follower? Aren't you as deserving to be a queen, to rule over the land and cast your influence wide?"

"How would I do that?"

"All you need to do is bear children to the world and the rest will fall into place. I don't like it here anymore than you do; but don't tell anyone. You watch and see, Lois; one day; one day we will leave El Dorado and the others to start our own tribe, to set foot into the jungle and harvest men to our cause."

"What cause is that? What cause is greater than to serve man and to protect the treasure of El Dorado?"

"It's not his treasure yet, Lois, and what right has he to it in any case.

We are just as deserving."
Tupmi stood up to leave, to allow Lois some time to think.
"Say nothing, to anyone, Lois. I'm your friend and one day you will grow to understand and appreciate that."

*
* * *
*

Stephen was seated before Chief Omagua.
"How much longer do you think we'll have to divert around the Carib for?" asked Stephen.
"For as long as it takes," answered the chief. "We can't rule over the actions of others but can only administer to our own. I can see you're concerned over your children, but they will get used to the nature of the jungle, as all do that call it their home. A day of rest is all they need after a week of marching. Tomorrow you will see the difference it makes. Tomorrow they will be able to go for up to another three weeks without a break, and well before then we'll be at the site you're so interested in seeing for yourself."
"I shall decide to stay there, to tend the treasure, to confine myself to new borders; you know that."
"I know, El Dorado," said the chief with a smile. "And there is nothing wrong with that. I'll continue on, however, and pass on the news of your arrival. We'll act as a screen from the expanding Inca."
"You've never spoken much of them in the past."
"Before I was cast upon my way to the east I saw many things. The Inca were trying to expand their borders into the jungle, from across the mountains. To my understanding they fell short of their expansion but that isn't to say that one day they shall seek once more an expansion, or that another tribe will try to invade our lands."
"It sounds as though you know something of such an invasion already."
"I have heard many stories about Viracocha and the Inca belief that he will one day return. What will happen after that will be anyone's guess."
Anupita approached with a bow, a plate of food for her husband and the chief of the Omagua.
"Your wife continues to pay respects to Is Caraíba of the past," said the chief loud enough for Anupita to hear. She smiled.
Stephen looked to her with a grin. "Against my wishes."
Anupita departed to allow the men further talk.
"I hear that she's with a child."
"Yes," replied Stephen. "We are expecting our first child in six moons, possibly a little more."
"Good. You'll both be settled by then and the child will be the first

of your tribe. There's nothing grander than having a child. I had many, myself."

"Oh; how many?" asked Stephen.

"I think it was about twenty-six."

"That's a lot of children, and none of them here."

"I've been blessed, that's true. Many of my children have been cast upon the four winds to marry into other tribes. Such arrangements happen at a very young age, and so the memory grows weak and affection dies."

"So you don't see or hear of any of them?"

"No," said the chief, "not a single one."

*
* * *
*

It was several weeks before Stephen had the opportunity for another private talk with Chief Omagua, and when it arrived he knew that the time to say goodbye to the remainder of the tribe was upon him; it happened so suddenly and without warning.

Baetatanam approached Stephen. "El Dorado; Chief Omagua wishes a private discussion with you and you alone."

"Thankyou, Baetatanam."

Stephen wasted no time in moving towards the front of the long line of tribal members and saw the chief awaiting him, urging him to move over to where he stood, no one else in earshot.

"We are finally near your destination, El Dorado," said the chief. I shall have Baetatanam lead you the way. He and I, along with Jurup, are the only ones who are currently aware of its secret location. All of those that helped with moving the treasure in land have since perished with the secret, and it is only permissible for a handful of men to know its true location."

"And that will soon change," said Stephen. "I shall survey the land and then decide upon another place more suitable. Not even you will know its location. I shall build a bridge nearby and the treasure will be found close by this."

Chief Omagua understood this to mean that the location was secret but granted him, for all he needed to do was seek out the bridge in order to find the treasure, but such information was hardly a give-away. He smiled.

"I understand. It's not for many to know the secret, but for a handful of chosen ones."

"And they will be few."

"I have decided on the couples to go with you. Six men with wives and those that you requested; Baetatanam, Corimupira and Guadira."

"Thank You so much," said Stephen. "May the spirits forever be

mindful of you."
"And you, too."

*
* * *
*

And that was the last that Stephen saw of the Omagua. He set foot then, deeper into the jungle, led by Baetatanam: in total there were thirteen orphans, ten men and seven women, for Stephen's wife was there also. Of all of those that continued on their way it was only the single men, who would be married in the near future, that would ever know the final resting place of the treasure, along with Stephen and Catherine; the others would only know the secret location of El Dorado's village. Stephen had much to do, much to consider, and he wished for nothing more to live in peace, but peace was hard to come by.

Chief Omagua waited long enough for the men and women to disappear from view before continuing on towards the west. All he could do, for much of the journey ahead, was to think of El Dorado and the task he'd set himself. But he hoped to one day see him again.

*
* * *
*

The secret location of the treasure was an all-important part of the structure of the tribe, a location central to the land that protected it.

Baetatanam fell upon the 'general' location of the treasure with ease and not long after this was announced, came upon an old village, now overgrown with jungle foliage, an area in line with the remainder of the jungle where the ground level was relatively open with many large stems and trunks reaching for the sky, a sky almost blocked out by the higher levels of foliage and canopy.

Black spider monkeys were quite numerous in the area and scampering off through the canopy, from tree to tree, away from the intruders as they made their way into what was once the communal centre of the village itself.

A majority of the huts main supports were intact but their walls and roofs damaged in most cases, nevertheless, it wouldn't take long to turn the dilapidated site into a communal centre from which their immediate errands and responsibilities could be cast until such a time that the treasure had been relocated and the protectors had set goals for the years ahead.

Stephen gave his orders in a way that was not demeaning, and was a pleasure to follow. The men of the tribe were content with the coming hunt and the women with the task of clearing the site; the children were quickly set upon searching for edible roots and the preparation of a site which could be turned into an area suitable for the growing of some crops.

Each and every one of the new tribe knew that the site was only temporary, but temporary in the Indians' tongue meant anything from several months to several years. Stephen saw no great hurry in the scheme of things and refused to jeopardise the happy swing of the tribes demeanour as the initial days passed them by.

Baetatanam had told Stephen that the treasure was not far away, and here again the meaning of the word could be interpreted as being rather close or quite some distance; when asked 'how many days travel?', Baetatanam answered with 'one'.

The geographical layout of the region suited Stephen's needs well, it being revealed to him over the coming weeks. They were currently between the main arterials known as Curuapanema and Trombetas, and it was Stephen's desire to establish a kingdom between the Trombetas and the Mapuera. On the southern outskirts of their current site there was an extremely large lake known as Lake Tamari, it was here that the treasure could be found. Stephen's desire was to have it moved to a location closer to the new – to be established – home where a cave was known to exist. Nearby this new site was another tributary, so small and ineffectual that it was often dry, which led up towards the centre of a large spur line extending from north to south between the Trombetas and Mapuera. It was near here that a bridge would be built over where a water-submerged, large fissure or canyon-like-crack-in-the-ground existed. It was the hopes of Stephen to have everyone believe that this fissure, which the bridge was to cross, was the hiding place of the treasure, but this was far from true.

The entire area, as Stephen would discover, was prone to a heavy mist most of the year, a symbolic apparition of nature which served to provide ghostly reminders of his deeds to come and the importance of the secret which he still carried around his neck.

Stephen called Margarita to him, his hut being the first established and shared by no one else but he.

Margarita was the same age as Catherine and was initially from Spain. She was fluent in the language of her old country but would soon lose the ability to communicate in such a way if given too much time to forget.

"Margarita," said Stephen "I'm sorry to tear you away from your friends, but there's something of importance I wish to discuss."

"Yes, El Dorado," she replied. "I'm happy to be of service."

"I know you speak Spanish, and rather well, too."

Margarita smiled at the compliment.

"Which brings me to my dilemma," added Stephen. "It is with... a great urge within me that I ask you to teach Diana all you know. I wish you and her to speak the language you know in order for it to never be forgotten. We must maintain what we can of our knowledge and our past. You will still be required to converse with others of the tribe, in the language we have come to know and love, but it is also all-important for you and Diana, from this day forth, to speak Spanish between each other at every given opportunity. If you find yourselves in one another's company then no other language shall be shared. Of course I realise it will take some time for Diana to learn, but she must adhere to the change and the challenge."

"I understand, El Dorado."

"I have not yet spoken to Diana but will do so shortly," Stephen looked upon Margarita's face and smiled serenely. "Do you have any questions?"

"No."

"Then that will be all," said Stephen. "Thank you so much for your hard work, and the acceptance of the task set before you,"

Stephen next called for Jurup.

"Good morning, El Dorado," said Jurup as he entered.

"Good morning; please; sit," invited Stephen.

"What is it I can do for you?"

"I need you to organize the married men in retrieving the treasure. Please have it brought to the north extremity of this site and arrangements will be made for it to be moved shortly after. I will attend other needs in regards to establishing another post, a post from which we will remain undisclosed."

"I understand," said Jurup. "I will be sorry to see you go."

"We will meet again, on many occasions to come," advised Stephen. "You will be a chief, Jurup; a chief of your own tribe. What will you call yourselves?"

"I was discussing this with Arikuton. He says he'll be known as Chief Arikuton of the Tirió, and I have decided to be Chief Jurup of the Wai-Wai," said Jurup with a smile.

"It sounds spectacular," said Stephen, returning the smile. "We have a lot in common, you and I. We were both very-nearly eaten."

"Those Carib are a nasty tribe, one to keep away from, but then again, most tribes have some hidden agenda."

"Just like the soon-to-be Wai-Wai and Tirió," said Stephen. "How long do you think it will be before the treasure is gathered?"

Jurup knew better than to say, 'not long', and offered a more reflective answer. "If we start today, and work all morning and all afternoon, the task should be complete within sixty days."

"So much treasure exists?"

"Oh, yes, El Dorado," said Jurup in all seriousness. "And for Baetatanam, Corimupira and Guadira to move it to the new hiding place will take twice that," for Jurup had been advised of the general plans to keep the new site a secret. "I sincerely hope the site is large enough to take the horde, for it is truly large."

"How will you be sure to get it all from the lake?"

"Ah, I wasn't thinking of that," answered Jurup. "I'm sorry, El Dorado. I've made an error."

"And that is?"

"It will be another one hundred and twenty days more."

Stephen continued to smile and waited patiently for an explanation.

"The portion of lake in question will need to be dammed on its northern face, and the water must be allowed to flow out from the south, hence draining the small lake. I'll need to act quickly for the dry season is upon us; this should be most helpful. Only with the lake being sufficiently lowered can we retrieve every single ounce that exists, no portion to be left behind."

"Then let the task begin immediately. Baetatanam, Corimu-pira and Guadira shall provide assistance where possible."

*
* * *
*

And so the task began, a task which took almost an entire year to accomplish. The treasure was retrieved and the dam on the northern face removed, so that no one would know that the lake had ever been drained.

The treasure was moved into a secret location, a cave with a waterfall as a curtain, a cave large enough to store twice the amount of treasure retrieved, and Stephen removed the chain and cross from around his neck, placing it with the treasure in order to keep it safe, drawing on its uniqueness from time to time by placing it around his neck during special ceremony, but never again would he hear the voice of God through the Grail.

As the years unfolded the mist rolled in and out. The bridge was made strong and seemed to be a part of the jungle as opposed to an addition. Jurup, Amat and Petunan were cast upon the east, to be responsible for guarding the approach to El Dorado and his flock, placed on the eastern side of the Curuapanema; Arikuton, Sacipera and Tulinamba were cast to the south of the Nhamundá, providing a good shield against invasion from the south; approach from the west or north seemed in-eventual due to the terrain, but it would come to pass that the region would be easily swayed by the members of Stephen's tribe if the need arose.

Baetatanam, Corimupira and Guadira each worked hard to help build a city of stone, cast from the ground and built strong, the roofs of each hut made of good jungle material and replenished as required. They hunted and worked as did the orphans, and after seven years of labour in the jungle, the tribes, all three, commenced to grow. It was then, shortly after the work had been completed, that a special ceremony was to give rise, the Wai-Wai and the Tirió invited in all their splendour, the men and the women along with their thirty-two children invited to attend. The orphans were also now of ripe age, to be a part of the adult world, to be made wives of the three men that Stephen had taken into his palm.

He was no longer uneasy about the union of so many young women into the hands of so few men, for they had proved their loyalty over and over again. They were all good men. Baetatanam, Corimupira and Guadira made a special vow to Stephen in privacy, to always serve El Dorado, to always be akin to the one formerly known as Is Caraíba.

Everyone was painted in true Indian fashion; special pride and honour taking post. Feasting was to be a large part of the formality but the primary task was to crown the tribe of El Dorado with a name befitting them all, and with it the crowning of a chief.

"Please, Catherine," said Stephen. "Come sit before me," she complied. "Turn and face the honour of those present," she, again, complied. "In a world once known by me, a chief was a king, a king amongst his people, to wear a crown as a symbol of his status and position, but today we celebrate the symbolism only by announcing in a clear voice that the chief of my tribe will not be me, but will be one that is more deserving. Catherine will no longer be known as Catherine but is, from this day forth, Queen Conori. She is Queen of my tribe, for as long as she lives and breathes. The tribal name of all that she possesses is to be known as Coniupuyana: all of its people are to be known as the Coniupuyana, and we reside in the village of El Dorado, a city of great honour. I hereby proclaim that as of this moment, Catherine exists no longer. I wish to now, present to you all, Queen Conori, Queen of the Coniupuyana. Let there be silence, let there be thought."

After several moments, Stephen spoke once more.

"The Queen and those young women she now rules over shall be taken as wives by those men that have resided with us for so long. Baetatanam, Corimupira and Guadira shall spend time with each wife separately and so the tribe will grow. Men of the Coniupuyana, please step forward.

"Do you each swear to serve the women of the Coniupuyana with your entire heart and soul? Do you, from this day forth, console yourselves to remain with the tribe until you are dead? Do you surrender yourselves to the protection of all that is sacred?"

"I do," replied the three men in one voice.

"Then let the sacred habitat of the cohabitation huts be granted special blessing so that the tribe will grow strong. The tribe of the Coniupuyana are to be cast of women. Any child born a male will be cast to the Wai-Wai and Tirió, to be brought up as members of these tribes, to forever protect and serve that which cannot be allowed into the hands of any single force, never to be swayed by a single king or queen, other than those sworn to its protection. The men will serve to seek wives of nearby and far away tribes; and men shall be taken from these same tribes, and others like them, to serve the women of the Coniupuyana, for when the time comes for the off-spring of these three men before you to be provided the opportunity to become mothers themselves, men will be needed. It is for other tribes to provide their gift of manhood to the women of the Coniupuyana so that life on earth will remain forever sacred. The only way to protect our way of life, the only way to protect the secret of the cave, is to serve the purpose of the Coniupu-yana."

Silence struck them all and after several moments, Stephen gave voice once more. "Please, now, take part of the feast which awaits you all."

The jungle came alive with conversation, congratulations, and much praise.

Jurup and Arikuton approached Stephen as the three tribes around commenced to take part in the feast and ceremony, and from across the small site a woman cast her net to catch a prize.

"Lois," said Tupmi. "Come to me."

"Yes, Tupmi," said a hurt Lois.

"I see the shame you feel within," said Tupmi. "Catherine shouldn't have been made Queen; you should have been."

"Thank you for your kind words," said Lois. "But what is done, is done."

"To take defeat so easily is nothing but shame," pushed Tupmi. "You are more deserving than this. Why should you serve someone that doesn't deserve to be served?"

"Conori has served us well," protested Lois.

"But still you hate her; still you wish it were you that were Queen Conori," stated Tupmi. "You can still be Queen."

"How can I be when El Dorado has already spoken? It's not for me to question his decision."

"Listen to me, Lois. You will not be more than a concubine here; never will you be permitted to know where the treasure is hidden. You are nothing to these people. Listen to me, Lois; please. We must run away, go to the west and start our own tribe. We can call ourselves the Coniupuyana. Let us be the true likeness that El Dorado wishes to reflect. Let us lead the world into the future by establishing a true semblance of tribal life and belonging."

Lois didn't know what to say. It all seemed so drastic.

"You have the knowledge of two worlds, Lois. I will serve you because I believe in you."

"I believe you," said Lois. "I believe you, and furthermore I wish to escape this tribe and make a fresh start."

"Then when the night is upon us we shall both go into the west and start afresh. We shall fall upon the region west of the Omagua and take men from them to serve us, as El Dorado wishes others to serve him. You are beautiful, Lois; very beautiful. Men will fight to serve you like they serve no other."

And as Tupmi plotted against him, Stephen sat with Jurup and Arikuton to his front, the noise of the feast behind them seeing to it that they spoke in privacy.

"Jurup, Arikuton; the time has come to take action. What we have spoken of in the past must now take place. The Wai-Wai and Tirió must conceal itself from the rest of the world. When women are needed to serve your tribe, you must take them without leaving tracks in the jungle; wives must be taken with much discreteness. May the spirit of Corupira guide you and assist you, and keep you strong, but there is one more thing I desire."

"Please, El Dorado," said Jurup. "Speak it."

"As your tribes grow they must intermingle to create a third. It is to be known as the Tapajós. The Tapajós must protect the Great River from being crossed; they must protect us from what we know as the Tupinambá and the Carib. It is a tremendous set of tasks cast before you but we will prevail. Time is of the essence and the initial growth of the tribes is most important."

"How long do we have, El Dorado?" asked Arikuton.

"Time will tell," answered Stephen, "but we should set ourselves a target of twenty cycles. The time we have between now and then will be our easiest."

"You mean our hardest, do you not?" said Jurup.

"No, Jurup," insisted Stephen. "The next twenty cycles will be the easiest, for after that, the expansion of the jungle we call home will be at breaking point, and the incursions from men of other tribes could very well endanger our existence," and Stephen fell short of telling them of the future he knew would one day arrive, where men from Spain would approach upon their land in search of riches beyond their wildest dreams; but other than that he knew nothing, for even his dreams of the future had dried up.

The time had come for Tupmi to put her plan into operation, before the others grew wise to her actions, before the tribe was split into three.

"Lois," said Tupmi, tenderly. "It's time to help me with my errand. Come now."

Lois awoke from her slumber and rubbed her eyes. She knew what this was about and wasn't sure if it was entirely right. She felt sick within, a great amount of guilt welling inside, as though what she was about to endeavour was against all manner of principle.

"That's it, Lois," said Tupmi, seeing a few heads stir in the dim light of the hut. "Tubers and roots are needed, we must start collecting them now if we are to surprise the tribe, on this, our day of separation," and Tupmi knew full well that anyone that had overheard her would misinterpret what she meant, and end up helping to delay any actions the tribe might have against trying to retrieve her and Lois, for no one wished to interrupt a good deed.

They took with them few possessions, but enough to be able to gather food. They disappeared into the jungle and not far from the others they came upon a small canoe that Tupmi had hidden. Two ropes made of stripped bark were attached to the front and this they pulled, dragging the canoe the short distance to the down-hill slope of the spur and from there their task was easy. By the time the sun had risen above the horizon, they were safely in the canoe and paddling down a small tributary towards the Great River itself.

"Do you think the Carib will be waiting for us?" asked Lois.

"I've never heard of a tribe being so mind-set as to search the whereabouts of their enemy for so long," was Tupmi's reply. "We're more than safe; believe me."

The birds were singing and the spider monkeys playing high above.

"Tell me, Tupmi," insisted Lois, trying to forget the anxiousness within her. "How will we go about starting a tribe of our own?"

"We must be cunning; more cunning than El Dorado."

"How will we do that?"

"We'll negotiate and use others to our best ability. It's easy to get a man to fall upon you, to impregnate you, and it's even easier to live without the burdens of other members of a tribe pestering you for assistance. No longer will we be working for the tribe, but we will be working for ourselves."

"It's still a tribe."

"But it'll be our tribe, not El Dorado's or Catherine's."

"We might be taken by men looking for wives."

"I know a place that is hardly touched by the fingers of man, far from any water but has a source nearby. Tribes don't like to be far from a river because a river means an easier life, the opportunity to grow crops and harvest the Great River."

"So our existence will be harder than most?"

"It will be more rewarding," said Tupmi. "This place I saw was encountered by a man I once knew. I know the directions. It'll be easy to find. It has much game and water but doesn't allow for turtles or fish to be found, or crops to be sowed. We must travel a long way to get fish. Fish must be smoked so that it will last, but other sources of

nourishment are abundant in all its glory."
"What sort of food?"
"No more, Lois. The paddling will get harder once we hit the Great River. Once we get to the Great River we must travel by night. Conserve your energy and help me paddle. Your questions will be answered with the passing of time." And the reply was enough to tell Lois that they were in for a long journey.

*
* * *
*

Tupmi and Lois had travelled a long way and were resting on the shore waiting for the night to come when they heard a noise coming from deep within the jungle. Tupmi was familiar with the sounds of the drums which echoed through the early night, and she sat up, as did Lois.

"What is it?" asked Lois. "I've never heard those drums before."

"It's the Bellicose."

"Are they dangerous?"

"They're not Carib, if that's what you're asking," replied Tupmi. "They're a very large tribe."

"Will they take us?"

"Not if we're careful," said Tupmi. "But it might be for the better."

"How can that be?"

"We can rest and eat well, to escape later from them as we did from El Dorado."

"I sometimes wish we never left."

"Don't talk like that," scolded Tupmi. "We have big plans for the future. We're going to be leaders of a tribe that will rival anything that El Dorado or Catherine can achieve."

"You hate them with all your heart, don't you?"

"They took me from my tribe, stole me to become a wife when I was already with a man, a man I saw killed with an arrow from my new husband's bow."

"I'm sorry, I didn't know," said Lois. "But that was the Omagua, and El Dorado and Catherine are not the Omagua, but the Coniupuyana."

"They are all the same and must be kept in check. We must inform the Bellicose that we will be searched for, that they should be on the lookout as El Dorado will endeavour to take the Bellicose chief from his throne and have it handed to Catherine."

"El Dorado wishes nothing more than to unite the tribes."

"Which he won't do, for the Tupi-speaking nations and the Carib won't allow it. They will fight to the end. The Bellicose must be advised."

"I don't like to think that I'm bringing harm to fall El Dorado's way."

"You're not," insisted Tupmi. "We're simply allowing ourselves the breathing space we desire."

"So what do we do?"

"We hide the canoe and submit to the Bellicose. We advise them of El Dorado and then escape when the time is right, leaving enough sign behind for them to believe that we have been taken by El Dorado. The rift between the two will be enough to keep us safe. The Coniupuyana will never trouble us... in fact... I have a desire to do something more."

"What is that?"

"For us to be known as the Coniupuyana, to be of a tribe called the Icá," said Tupmi. "This will serve our purpose, for when other tribes hear of El Dorado, they will naturally think of us... they will fear us, but to be known as members of a tribe called the Icá will also make us unique."

"I don't think I want to be known as Queen Conori."

"You shan't," said Tupmi. "You will simply be known as, Queen Icá."

*
* * *
*

And so Lois and Tupmi found themselves a temporary home with the Bellicose until such a time that something quite extraordinary happened. A scout of the Bellicose reported to the chief that a tribe known as the Tirió were invading their lands and were up to no good.

Tupmi was called before Chief Bellicose.

"It's not often I'll call a female to my quarters," said the chief. "But I am in urgent need of assistance. You have been here for several moons now and have spoken of your hatred for the Coniupuyana; we too, have a hatred for them. In the past we have had women stolen from us and it has been impossible to point a finger to any single tribe, but your knowledge of them has helped us. You mentioned once that El Dorado and those that he ruled over were like ghosts of the jungle; accomplished shots with the bow, and able to harness the powers of Corupira. At first I was insulted by your claims, seemingly abusing the spirit which is a friend of no man and seeks to protect game at every opportunity; but you may have proven to be correct. I've just received information that warriors are approaching; can you tell me anything of this?"

"Yes, Chief Bellicose," started Tupmi with care. "They dispatch women warriors with their patrols into the jungle, as I have previously claimed, and they rule over the men."

"That's absurd," said the chief. "No women were reported."

"These women meld with the jungle," said Tupmi. "They can't be seen; they are truly, ghosts of the jungle."

"I'll have to see this, to believe this," said the chief. "But what would you suggest as the appropriate action regards these people that you know so well?"

"Protect your borders... I don't know," said Tupmi, and behind her guise she added, "I am but a woman."

"Yes; yes you are. Tell me, I heard that Lois is with child. Is this true?"

"Yes, she's with child."

"Good. You may go."

Tupmi turned to depart when the chief called for her attention once more. "Oh; how many of these 'ghostly' women will there be?"

"At this moment… most likely just the one," replied Tupmi.

"Just one; that's absurd."

"Such an errand as stealing a wife, or a man for the seeds he carries, doesn't require much more. They aren't yet at war."

"But they soon will be if they take from me. How can it be that only one 'ghost' is required?"

Tupmi sat once more before the chief. "I've heard El Dorado speak several times of another world, where gods were present in vast numbers. He spoke of a past when men from a place called Sparta would be leant to other nations in order to teach them the art of war. When nations called upon the Spartans for assistance, they gave it. They were sent a solitary man as an ally. The other nations would scoff at this but a single man was all that was required. This single man would teach a dozen, the dozen would teach dozens more... so great is their gift of tactics that victories would be celebrated across the land."

"Are you saying that these, Coniupuyana, are like... Spartan's... like men of war?"

"They are, just that. But there is also one thing more."

"And what is that?"

"There is much power in the tribe and in order for you to be victorious you must take the head of El Dorado, cut it away from his shoulders."

The chief was stunned by the words and needed time to think; he was clearly daunted.

And so, Tupmi was free to go, and she soon found Lois and sat beside her.

"It will be time to go soon," said Tupmi.

Lois was silent for a second and then responded. "I'm with child."

"I know," said Tupmi, "but the Coniupuyana are close by. They're in search of a wife; no doubt to replace me. It's our opportunity to escape, allowing the Bellicose to think that we were taken by El Dorado. We'll cover our tracks as we have learnt to do and take our canoe. We'll once more travel by night and reach our destination before it's time for you to give birth. This is the start, Lois, the start of the tribe to which you will be queen. Together we shall rule as one."

"Where... please tell me."

Tupmi wasn't ready but decided to tell Lois. "North of the Aparia and west of the Omagua, not far from the mountains in the west. We shall be to the north of the Icá River."

"What will our life be like; what will become of us?"

"Everything that I have promised, and more. We shall both enjoy a life or luxury, but I feel as though you will be rewarded with a greater gift."

"Why do you say that, Tupmi?"

"I feel old. I feel as though you will outlive me, ten years to my one. I suffer nightmares quite often, bad dreams that visit me when I am unable to defend myself against them."

"I've seen you tremble at night."

Tupmi brushed the fear aside. "We depart tonight. Let El Dorado take the blame for our vacation."

The Future

It was now the year 1541 and all of the orphans had died except Queen Conori and Queen Icá, having been killed at one time or another by the tribes they wished to unite; some even became the temporary captives of the Carib and Bellicose before being dispatched from the world of the living.

The numbers of Coniupuyana under Queen Conori are now around 800, and those under the influence of Lois are around 300, Lois being at constant war with the Omagua and the Aparia, but such are the skills of the Coniupuyana that numbers mean very little.

Lois suffered greatly from nightmares of Tupmi, ever since the woman died from a snake bite, and she mostly felt alone in the world, although she had a vast tribe which had blossomed from her immediate offspring.

Stephen had retreated to the cave where the treasure was hidden and the grail was maintained, guarded well by the Coniupuyana, a tribe consisting of female warriors, not a single male in existence. His wife, Anupita, was 102 years of age in mind but still very young in body, still very beautiful, and she assisted Queen Conori where needed, a liaison of great worth.

The Coniupuyana were seldom faced with dangers and their way of life superseded all in the jungle; none could compare to their skills as hunters or warriors, and they remained a very influential people. Many other tribes, however, would like to have seen them dethroned, but the power they held was far too great; they also hid their true numbers from rivals and it was here that it was believed that they numbered in the thousands. Both Queen Conori and Queen Icá had masked their true numbers remarkably well.

News continued to travel up and down the Great River and the drums gave warning to all around when strangers were seen in the region. News soon arrived of men from another world, men similar in cast to El Dorado, but of vastly different conviction. They were from a land called Spain and once they'd learnt of the Great River, they gave it the name Amazon.

*
* * *
*

Gonzalo was a 36-year old rapist, nothing uncommon for a Spanish soldier of the Inca lands. He was slow to think, quick to act stupidly, and sought happiness from the misery of others. To him it was nothing that men should die for his cause, and his cause was for the riches of the far east, across the andes, to fall into his palm. He was filled so much with greed that those in his company, who had volunteered their services in the name of gold and title, did join his venture through the coin of their own deep pockets.

To accompany Gonzalo on the expedition into the unknown was a smart and skilled man by the name of Francisco de Orellana. Orellana had lost an eye during the initial campaign to take Peru and was as loyal to the church and state as he was to his conviction to serve as a good soldier. He managed to equip his part of the contingent for the expedition through his own expense, sparing nothing to ensure that he would survive the mysteries of the unknown. Although not a linguist he was patient enough to learn what he could of the Indian language, which paid him in good stead for the dangers to come, for the understanding gave him a better chance of survival and an advantage when it came to hunting down the true treasure of the land to the east; the gold of El Dorado, a legend of riches he had heard about from the Inca.

And although both men were vastly different, they were also very similar, for it was the stories of El Dorado and his riches that spurred them on. Stories from all quarters of the Inca land told of a fabulous prince who could tame wild animals and serpents alike, a man that had power over all animals of the jungle, such as the llama, which was half man, and he could trick the spirits of the jungle and the sky to do his bidding, to cast all manner of upheaval to rain down upon his enemies, that he had wooden trumpets in his arsenal of weaponry which stirred the spirits to assist him, to rise and then fall upon those trespassing upon his domain. It was said that El Dorado bathed in a lake, his body anointed with gums, and that when he came out to be dried by the hands of female warriors, he was covered in the dust of gold, from head to foot; but the gold meant nothing to him.

Spurred on by the legend of El Dorado, Gonzalo refused to wait for Orellana, who, being only a few days behind Gonzalo, would have to catch up as soon as possible.

Gonzalo had 23 followers of similar persuasion along with many others, including more than 2,000 Inca porters, several negro slaves, and a train of animals which included herds of peccaries, packs of dogs, 80 horses and supplies enough to last them many months away from the rudiments of home.

The man of greed continued on into the mountains, the cold taking their breath away as did the altitude. Porters commenced to die, insufficient clothing to maintain any reasonable warmth and with the porters went the ability to carry supplies. Other porters then made good the opportunity to desert, for the deaths in their ranks were becoming too much for them to bear and many had families to return to.

Each step into the mountains brought them a little closer to the other side and so the roof of the vast, rain forest, came into view, the most delectable site, but it was at that early stage in the expedition that the first real disaster struck, for the volcano Altinisana roared with convulsion and the expedition took refuge in an abandoned village. The huts fell down around them, many dying, peccaries running off and dogs taking shelter with their heads between their legs.

Gonzalo couldn't believe his misfortune. There were very few porters remaining, the peccaries were gone, and ill-favour was being spoken of him amongst the ranks of his own. He was a much disliked man before the expedition, but now, the men commenced to grow more infuriated within and longed for Orellana to join them.

"Antonio," called Gonzalo, for his camp master, a man to be partially trusted, but relied heavily upon as an ally amidst the unfavourable start.

"Yes, Gonzalo."

"What's the damage?"

"It's mostly what you can see," replied Antonio in disbelief. "We can't go on. We must wait for Orellana and his men. He'll have supplies."

"We can't stay here in the cold like this. We have to get to lower ground. The jungle will give us a little protection. We have to seek sounder ground on which to stand."

"The men won't be happy to hear it."

"Tell them... we search for a village. We'll get sound knowledge of the surroundings and make camp in preparation for the arrival of Orellana: days to rest and time to heal any wounds."

"Very well," replied Antonio. "I'll pass the word to prepare for immediate departure."

Antonio passed the word and the men reluctantly got to their feet, checking themselves over, dressed in their padded cotton armour and steel corselets.

"Better to be dressed in this than the heavy armour of the army," said Antonio. He received a cold stare. "It's protection enough, against the weapons of these Indians and the cold."

"But it doesn't protect my arms or legs," replied one soldier.

"We have to make do with what we have, make good of the advantages we possess."

"Possession of gold is all I want, and even the taste of that is slowly evaporating."

"We'll be away from this mountain soon enough, and then we can commence the search for gold."

It was several days before they came upon a village, seemingly asleep and unaware of Gonzalo's arrival until it was too late. Several of the tribe ran off into the jungle, thin as it was near the bottom of the mountains, for protection and safe keeping.

Antonio brought a man into the hut which Gonzalo had procured for himself, guards on either side of the Indian, and an interpreter who understood a little of the local language accompanied Antonio.

Through the interpreter, Gonzalo asked for confirmation of El Dorado and cinnamon, though cinnamon trees wouldn't quench his thirst for wealth as much as the gold.

"I need to know the whereabouts of El Dorado and the women of the jungle."

"I don't know anything," answered the chief.

"Come, come; don't be a fool," said Gonzalo. "You can see we are strong. Your village has deserted you. You should tell me what I need to know and I'll show you my appreciation." Gonzalo opened a small chest of beads strung together to form necklaces.

"That's nothing to me."

"What about this?" and Gonzalo showed the chief a mirror. "Can you see by the power of what we possess, that we are great."

"If you are so great then you'd know the answers to what it is you search for," said the chief. "I can't help you with your answers."

Gonzalo looked to Antonio. "Have him racked and the fire prepared."

"It's already burning sufficiently," answered Antonio.

"Good; take him."

The chief of the village was grappled and flung upon an improvised rack, tied fast so that escape was impossible. He was then drawn to the vicinity of the fire and the soles of his feet forced to bear the brunt of the growing heat.

The chief squirmed and the pain could be seen upon his face, growing as it did.

"Tell me what I need to know and you'll go free," said Gonzalo as he watched in eagerness, ready to receive the answer he wanted to hear. "Tell me of the cinnamon and El Dorado."

"I don't know anything."

Gonzalo looked around and said to the interpreter: "Why won't he speak?"

"He fears the spirits of the jungle. He fears the women of the jungle."

"What do you mean; what are you saying?"

"Just simply, that they fear this tribe of women warriors. The tribes throughout call them by their proper name, always."

"And that is?"

"Coniupuyana."

"Antonio; place the chief over the fire; I don't need the rack any longer."

"You mean...?"

"You know what I want," said Gonzalo. "Roast him."

The interpreter was shocked, the chief was dumb founded, but the men of the expedition had expected it, for they knew of Gonzalo's wickedness.

The rack was lifted and the chief was placed over the fire, the flames licking at his skin, blisters quickly forming, and as the chief's screams penetrated the jungle he was roasted and left in place.

"Gonzalo," yelled a man as he came rushing upon the scene. "Good news."

"What is it?"

"Orellana has been seen. He should be near the tributary by the time we can have ourselves prepared."

"Excellent; some good food at last," said Gonzalo. "Antonio, prepare the men immediately. Leave the chief where he cooks, be it a lesson to others of this miserable jungle."

It wasn't long before the two men joined forces and together they hacked their way through the jungle, fighting against the terrain, the horrid heat, the dampness, the mosquitoes, and the rain as it fell upon them, to rot everything they possessed. And they continued on until they fell upon a wide portion of the river where there looked to be filaments like sand, a beach on which to walk and make camp. Gonzalo was looking forward to an opportunity to eat, and eat well.

"We'll camp here tonight," ordered Gonzalo. "Antonio, make ready and erect some good shelter; the mosquitoes are sure to come out in droves."

"They're already out in droves and the sun is still in the sky."

"Now, Antonio, before we run out of time. I want food prepared and everyone filled before the sun goes down. Tomorrow we start as early as the sun rises."

Gonzalo had a tent separate to Orellana but the two were close together, each with their aids.

They fed well, under a little protest from Orellana who wished to ration what they had, for Gonzalo had very little left from what his expedition had lost.

"I still can't believe how few you have left in your company," said Orellana that night.

"I've been plagued with disaster after disaster in this sinister land," replied Gonzalo.

"And do you have any news on the whereabouts of the cinnamon?"

"I'm more interested in the gold."

"Gold will only serve the greed of men, to be melted down and shipped to Spain. You'll only get to keep a quarter of what you find," said Orellana. "But the cinnamon; now there's an opportunity for a smart man. Your own plantation."

"And how do you expect to export it?"

"Well, not through the jungle," said Orellana with a little laugh, slapping himself in the face as a mosquito came calling. "I'll have to sliver into the confines of my mosquito net shortly."

"As if that's going to help," complained Gonzalo. "There's not been a night when the mosquitoes haven't gotten through my net to attack me in my sleep."

"Then better care you should take of your equipment."

"It means nothing," said Gonzalo. "When the next man dies, I'll take his."

"Which is why you will always have holes in your net, for the men care as little for the maintenance of their equipment as you do the cinnamon."

"I agree; the gold is on my mind. I also wish to explore this notion of 'women warriors' so that I can take what I want, exploit any advantage. I'll share with you, Orellana, of course."

"Of course," said Orellana.

"As you would share with me the knowledge of cinnamon."

A little silence was then shared.

"I'm going to sleep, Gonzalo. I'll see you in the morning."

"Very well."

*
* * *
*

Antonio awoke suddenly. "Get up! All of you!"

"What is it?" yelled Gonzalo as he woke to be greeted by the dark of the night, much stumbling going on around him, the frantic hustle and bustle of men in panic reaching his ear.

"The river, it's rising," came the reply from Antonio as he stood outside Gonzalo's tent.

The mosquitoes were waiting for Gonzalo as he erupted from his tent, finding it hard to see anything, even with the stars out.

"My God, what's going on?" the dark slowly dissipated as he stepped further into a clearing, where the beach once sat but was now covered in the rapid movement of a river on the rise.

"The river, Gonzalo," yelled Orellana.

Antonio looked to the sky. "There's no rain."

"From upstream, you fool," yelled Orellana.

Men were clambering this way and that to save all they could of the stores. Gonzalo saw then vast amounts of supply and equipment being carried away by the river, taken from their grasp, moving downstream, to be lost forever.

The mosquitoes continued to harass the men as more and more erupted from their tents, the river depth was growing by the minutes, and their feet were getting wet, and each man's personal equipment was getting drenched or was simply carried away.

"Save the weapons," voiced Orellana, for the men weren't thinking of defence but of the comforts that the river was taking from them.

A horse broke free of its ties and ran past Orellana, almost knocking him over, racing off into the jungle with eyes wide open, followed close by, by others that were urged on by the panic that was growing.

"Secure the horses," commanded Orellana, but the men were only interested in their own salvation, wishing to save what they could of the food and equipment, their own tent and mosquito net.

Some distance away from the site of their troubles, on the opposite bank, an Indian lay awake and his eyes flickered open from their deep thought. It was strange that the voices he heard weren't familiar, that the language wasn't known, that a tribe of any description could so easily be preyed upon by an enemy, whether that enemy was born of flesh or from nature.

Tupinambita then stood and went back the short distance to his small village.

*
* * *
*

Tupinambita stood and walked to the far end of the hut, where the chief resided. The chief's eyes opened to his approach.

"I hear it," said Chief Delicola, for the screams from the men of Spain were cast far and wide by a favourable wind.

"They must be the strangers that we were told about, by our neighbours that were fleeing that region," said Tupinambita. "Did you know the chief well?"

"No, not well," said Delicola. "Though, to be fair, I knew enough: that he was a good man."

"Do you think it's true, that they're searching for El Dorado?"

"It's none of our business really, but we must take pre-cautions." The chief stood up and together the two men exited the hut and walked into the clearing of the village. "I think it would be wise to advise Queen Icá of what has happened, that a chief of another village has been burnt to death. She might look upon this piece of information favourably. We're only a few in number when compared to others, and with this information might come some advantage."

"I understand," said Tupinambita. "When shall I depart?"

"You can wait till morning and have yourself something good to eat. I don't think there's any rush."

*
* * *
*

The expedition now resembled a ragged collection of poor souls, the torments of hunger and the night before getting the best of them all, for it had now been several days since they'd eaten anything good.

Movement through the jungle was very slow, in particular with what remained of their supplies, and a move down the river by boat was considered well, but Orellana had questioned the availability of good wood and the river for its depth in delivering a good boat to their final destination.

It was at this time, whilst following the River Napo, that a messenger from Chief Delicola arrived upon their temporary camp, seeing the miserable wretches for what they were. He watched them closely, but not too close, and after a day of contact he reported back to Delicola of the Spanish presence.

Gonzalo and Orellana were towards the front of the expedition when they came upon several Indians standing before them. The astonished conquistadors were slightly taken aback that these men would greet them with open arms.

The interpreter was brought forward in the hope that he would serve them well, and through several dialects of the jungle, an understanding and basic meaning was grasped by all.

"Chief Delicola," said Gonzalo. "We wish to honour our new friends, the Delicola, with this," he handed the chief a mirror. The chief seemed pleased. "Can you tell me of the women, the great warriors, and of El Dorado?"

"You shouldn't rush him," said Orellana.

"Quiet," spat Gonzalo and the chief spoke.

"There is much gold downstream. It's not far. It serves us no importance, but if you are interested I can tell you where."

Gonzalo looked to Orellana. "You see, they don't know the importance of gold, no more than they care about religion." He looked again at the chief. "Please; where can it be found?"

"You must go down stream until the third fork in the river, and then, upon this side you'll find a village. Beyond this is what you seek."

"Are there any hostile Indians along this way?" asked Orellana.

"No, none at all," lied the chief. "All are friendly here, even the Coniupuyana."

"The... Coniupuyana?"

"Yes, the women you seek, the ones you refer to as being great warriors. They're all friendly. Any tribe will be happy to show you the way. As you proceed simply ask direction. Ask all those you come across for El Dorado, and answers you'll receive. Everyone has heard of El Dorado."

"Rather simple, don't you think, Orellana?" asked Gonzalo.

"A little too simple, but I don't see any lying in this man."

"Good. Once the men have rested and fed, we'll be on our way," and the hospitality of Chief Delicola was misinterpreted, for not long after the men from Spain had moved away from the village and the sound of drums filled the air, a message being cast across the land, from one tribe to another.

And as the sound of the drums infiltrated the jungle, Tupinambita continued on through the jungle. It was then that he arrived upon the sentries of the Coniupuyana, women that lay unseen in the jungle. They showed themselves as he made his way across the land

He was slightly unsettled by their appearance but had experienced this same feeling several times in the past.

"I have a message for Queen Icá," said Tupinambita.

"What's your name?" asked one of the women. He stammered under breath. "You know the punishment for revealing our location?"

"Yes."

"I know your name," said one of the women. "You're Tupinambita."

"That's correct."

The women looked at one another.

"You've been to one of our minor villages before. I remember seeing you before entering one of the ceremonial huts."

"I have. I was called upon to provide my seed," answered Tupinambita.

"Good. We'll take your message as far as our village post; from there you can await the arrival of the queen. We have further need of you. We have several women that are in need of attention."

"I will serve as I have always done in the past."

"Then come with us."

*
* * *
*

The Spanish came upon a small gorge, a rope bridge spanning the deep scar in the terrain, the bridge being the only way across, and the river was too wild to be waded.

"What do you think, Orellana?" asked Gonzalo. "A little too dangerous for the horses we have left, ah?"

"We'll have to make do. I suggest we get the men across first and have the porters bring the horses across after. We need only leave a couple of men to tend the porters. They shan't escape."

"Agreed," said Gonzalo. "Antonio; tell the men we're going to cross, horses last, as quickly as possible."

The men continued to move up to the bridge, a 20 foot crossing which bridged a drop of 1,500 feet.

"We should have gone around," said one man to Orellana as he looked down."

"And we would have suffered the loss of many more days," pointed out Orellana. "Let's get moving, all of you."

The men filed past, many upon the bridge at the same time, and it began to sway. One of the men became drowned in giddiness and fell silently to his death. The men grabbed hold as best they could the sides of the bridge and continued.

"Come on, quickly now," pushed Gonzalo.

"Orellana!" yelled Antonio, pointing to the far side of the gorge.

Out from nowhere appeared many Indians; Arianas. They were naked, one and all, and from the far side of the gorge they showered the men upon the bridge with darts and poison arrows, arrows fletched with two half-feathers tied to one end in a spiral which aided in spinning the arrow in flight.

The interpreter recognised the men and gave warning. "They are the Arianas. Their arrows have been dipped in poison."

"Poison!" repeated an exasperated Gonzalo.

"Curare," confirmed the interpreter.

Several men were killed before Orellana and Antonio could manage to get the few arquebus and crossbows into position, to provide good covering fire upon the enemy to their front.

Arrows were answered by arquebus fire and crossbow bolts, the Spanish quickly gaining the upper hand upon the small band of Arianas that had been positioned to slow the advance of the men from Spain. It wasn't long before the naked Indians fled the scene and a scouting force of a dozen men was forced across the bridge to secure the other side and search for the enemy.

"Antonio," came a voice from the other side.

"What is it?"

"It appears safe to cross, and we have a prisoner."

"Ah, good," said Gonzalo, "just what we need."

Orellana grabbed him by the hand as men started across under the persuasion of Antonio. "Prisoners aren't to be executed or tortured. We need to gain help from the tribes, but certainly not their anger."

Gonzalo looked into Orellana's eyes and was about to say something nasty but forgot it quickly, for he could see a little sense in what he said.

"I'll do what I can," said Gonzalo. "But if these barbarians continue to be hostile towards us, then I shall yield no quarter."

"Agreed," said Orellana.

Within the half hour all had crossed the gorge and Gonzalo was seated with Orellana, to gain what information they could.

They looked upon their quarry, a woman.

"Which tribe are you from?" asked Gonzalo.

"I'm from the Arianas."

"They are the same that filled your men with poison arrows," added the interpreter.

"And what is your name?" asked Gonzalo.

"I am Irinar."

"Your friends have tried to kill me."

Orellana grabbed him by the arm. "Don't make an enemy of her."

Gonzalo looked the girl again in the eyes. "What can you tell me of the people in this region; of those they call the Coniupuyana?"

"They have a great queen that rules over their dominion, and the women of her tribe are her offspring, from her very soul," said Irinar. "The women are the protectors of something too grand to be contemplated, too grand for someone like me to know. These women of the forest are of the strongest conviction, though very little is known of their reasoning. They are committed, one and all.

"They are a band of vicious women warriors, who live in the company of other women, no men. It is said that the women take men as slaves once a year and other sources advise that the men come willingly, to pay their respects. The men are kept for as long as they are needed and then ordered away and set free, to journey back to their own villages. The women are taller and whiter than the Indian counterparts of the jungle, for they are the direct descendants of the thirteen orphans."

"Thirteen orphans?" questioned Orellana, endeavouring to confirm what it was the interpreter had said.

"It's questionable," replied the interpreter, "but is meant to mean the women at the beginning; those that first set forth, the founders of the village of the Coniupuyana."

"Continue," urged Gonzalo.

Irinar continued. "They are known as sun-worshippers, as are many other Indian cultures of the jungle, but it was once said that they worshipped a single man who resided in the skies high above."

"A spirit from the other world," said Gonzalo, and the girl continued.

"The women are the great mistresses of the jungle. They have eyes everywhere and can elude men very easily, for they have the spirits of the jungle on their side. There are more than a single tribe however, but I can only tell you of one such tribe. They live in villages of stone and the jungle grows thick around them. They have an enormous village square where ceremony is held, and a large building here has an entrance where carved trees have stood forever. They take tribute from the tribes around, for they are all queens. They keep the female children they give birth to, but the male children are sent back to their fathers. Therefore a bitter war is strained between the tribes, for each competes to get wives for their men. It is understandable, therefore, that although they are strong, they have many enemies, but even so, the tribes from all around fear them and continue to pay tribute. There is a great sense of comradeship amongst these people which can never be broken.

"Their power cannot be underestimated. They rarely attack an enemy themselves, for they can conjure up the devil in the men of the tribes around them to fight their battles for them."

"Is this why the... Arianas attacked us?" asked Orellana.

"Yes," replied Irinar. "The women admit men once a year in order to get pregnant, but other than this the tribes have little worth: the women desire men and men alone, for their seed and for protection."

"What of the gold?" urged Gonzalo.

"The Omagua can tell you," said Irinar. "You must seek the Omagua. They are further downstream, past the Arianas, and the Arianas are very vicious. It will be hard for you to get past them. I know this. I am not Arianas, I am but a slave, captured by their tribe some months ago. I don't serve them; I hate them. Once past the Arians you must continue on until you pass the Irimaes and then the Tupi. A vast network of tribes then exists along either side of the Great River. You must continue past the Aparia and the Machiparo, and then you will be in the land of the Omagua, but beware, the Machiparo are capable of calling 50,000 Indian warriors to their side in just a matter of days."

"What is the Great River?" asked Gonzalo of the interpreter.

The interpreter spoke with Irinar and gave an answer. "It's much bigger than the river we are currently near. It will be big enough for a large boat."

Gonzalo signalled Antonio to take the girl away. He and Orellana then sat and consulted each other on what to do next.

"That's many hostiles to contend with," said Gonzalo.

"I agree," said Orellana. "We must travel by boat upon this, 'Great River'. We'll have to build as soon as we can."

"Let's move down river," said Gonzalo. "We'll establish a camp, build ourselves a small ship, and sail right past these devil worshipers."

The Spanish had been many months away from the comforts offered by Peru, and still there were many more months of travelling set before them. They had few supplies and even fewer horses. Whenever a horse broke a leg it was killed, carved up, and then eaten, not an ounce wasted.

Another small village was contacted as they moved downstream and a captive was taken. It was said that the man they'd captured was chief of the Tupi; chief Pappa. Orellana quickly sat him aside and commenced to learn of the Tupi language as best he could, for he had much time to spare.

And so commenced the building of the boats they needed so badly to get themselves in one piece down the Napo and into the Great River, now christened the Amazon.

*

* * *

*

Charcoal kilns were made, and through these the horse's shoes were melted down and made into nails. The kiln needed to be sheltered from the constant rain in order to prevent the fire from going out, but it was a task which the men attended to with the greatest care, for the boat was their ticket out of the jungle. Many of them were now thinking less of the gold and more on survival, each and every one looking over their shoulders whenever a noise came from the jungle depths. The boat was large indeed, able to be rowed and suited to carry 25 persons, six of which could row as they made their way downstream.

Some men felled trees to maintain the fires and to build the boats and others were employed to saw planks from what was cut down. The boat needed to be caulked and for this the men used the cotton from their blankets, and some from their cotton armour, of which they had great need. The resin of some trees was good enough to help with the caulking, taken from the rubber tree, and rope made from the strips obtained from the tamshi tree.

Once the boat was built it was christened the San Pedro and was to be initially captained by Juan. It was made principally for the purpose of carrying provisions and the wounded, to which Father Carvajal and Father Vera were most appreciative, but the men so in need of a morale boost were displeased.

The boat was loaded with the provisions in order that the men ashore would have very little to carry, and the sick men aboard felt a great weight lifted from them, for they were no longer the burden they once were. The San Pedro made its way down stream with many accompanying canoes, each filled with stores.

The men ashore continued on, endeavouring to keep the San Pedro insight. They moved along with their horses, travelling as close to the bank of the river as was humanly possible, but progress was still slow. It was then that the captives jumped overboard and swam to shore.

Irinar was pleased to be free of her captors and was soon on the verge of the jungle, and disappeared from view, leaving the men in the water to fend for themselves. She reported, duty bound, to her tribe and Queen Icá, to advise her of how the men from Spain had been set up to act against El Dorado: a cunning plan indeed.

The San Pedro remained as far from the banks of the river as possible and was permitted to travel as far as the men ashore were able to walk in a single day, in most cases the men falling upon the San Pedro at anchor, as those aboard her prepared what food they could for their friends ashore. It was the only consolation for a hard day's walk, falling upon a cooked meal and a camp that was ready made.

For 180 miles they continued on and on, when finally their camp was pitched on Christmas day, 1541. They were so short on food that all they were left with was the leather of saddles and girths which had to be made into thin soup; it was the end of the line for Gonzalo who quickly drew up plans for immediate action.

Antonio assisted Gonzalo, who had become a little cowardly, and with his aid the command was given to Orellana to continue without him.

"I'm going to return after a few days' rest, go back the way we've come, back to Peru," said Gonzalo. "You're to continue as you are, without me. You'll have the San Pedro, some canoes, 57 of the companions, 2 negro slaves and 92 porters. The men-of-the-cloth will go with you; you'll have more need of them, than I."

"What about weapons?" asked Orellana.

"You'll have four crossbows and three arquebuses; I can't spare anything more."

"I'll need to prepare more boats, canoes for which to carry the men. It's too much to walk along the shore, too desperate, too dangerous. It's exhausting work."

"Making boats is exhausting work."

"We have little choice," said Orellana. "I'll commence with the work immediately. Once I'm ready, we can give our farewells."

And over the proceeding weeks the men worked hard, as hard as before, to make small boats for the remaining men. Kilns for charcoal, bellows for nails, and the wood for their boats were two miles away. The mosquitoes came out in force as before and it was a terrible time for all the men, but finally they set sail, on the 11th February; and on the 26th of February they came into contact with the Aparia.

*
* * *
*

Orellana had taught himself much of the language of the Indians, and was quite comfortable with what he had learnt; comfortable with his new abilities.

The local chief sat before him and introductions went around, and with Gonzalo gone, Orellana could practise his art of being hospitable and friendly.

"I am Chief Aparia the Great," announced the chief. "I'm very pleased to meet you."

"As I am, you," said Orellana. "My men and I need to settle upon this land for some time, to build another boat, similar to the one you see tied to the shore. The canoes are cumbersome and don't satisfy us. Would it be your pleasure for us to stay here for a short time?"

"Other villages around here are some distance from you and so this will be permitted."

"I've suffered at the hands of the Aparia in the past, but since then our commander has been dispatched."

"I've heard of the trouble and would like to confess a disruption in the order of some of the smaller villages."

"Yes; and can you tell me more?" prompted Orellana.

"The local chiefs of the smaller villages have been rewarded by a visit of the Coniupuyana. They have cast doubt into the minds of these 'lesser' chiefs."

"Corrupted," voiced Orellana.

"It's been suggested that they try to force you along, to have you on your way, to be out of their region as soon as possible, and down the Great River and out of harm's way."

"They fear us," said Orellana.

"No," said the chief. "They do only to cause inconvenience to others of the Coniupuyana downstream."

"Others?"

The Great Mistresses of the Coniupuyana are segregated by opinion and many days travelling. They would do harm to one another if encountered, although those of the east are willing to forgive those of the west."

"Are they truly fearsome?"

"They are to be respected. Stay clear of them if you wish to pass with few casualties. Most of the villages are allied with the Coniupuyana, but some actually loathe them. They side with most tribes, and war with those that oppose them, and a single woman fights as though she has the power of ten men."

"That's hard to believe."

"It's very accurate," said the chief.

"How would I find these women warriors and El Dorado?" asked Orellana as he watched carefully the face and eyes of the chief before him.

"El Dorado doesn't reside with the Coniupuyana, but commands over them. He can be found in the east, not the west."

"Are you telling me this so that I shall be on my way, away from your territory?"

"You haven't caused me any alarm," said the chief. "El Dorado can be found near a tribe who pierces both their ears and their nose. Close by can also be found a village of giants who are taller than you by the length of your arm."

Orellana considered this to mean nine feet.

"I don't know about their ancestors," admitted the chief somewhat voluntarily.

"I received information earlier of their location."

"From captives," said the chief.

"Yes... my commander was responsible and is no longer present," said Orellana, thinking to excuse himself from any wrong-doing.

"And you are to be trusted," said the chief; and if Orellana had not known better he would have thought the remark sarcastic. The chief stood slowly. "I must be attending my village. I look forward to seeing you again."

"I, too," said Orellana as the chief was escorted from the fireplace.

As the chief departed, Orellana looked around to see the work continuing on the second boat. It was to be named the Victoria and had nineteen ribs. It was larger than the San Pedro and would take two months to complete, but would be well worth the effort.

The two boats, considered ships by those that built them, were ready, loaded with supplies and men, the canoes no longer required, although several were towed behind the ships in order to be used when the need arose and others were employed by the porters.

The ships were built to be easily steered downstream with the flow, but also had oars for which to control and gather momentum when the time arose; oars also permitted for a greater distance per day to be attained in the case they were being pursued by enemies.

They were only afloat for two days when Orellana decided that the food stocks of the ships needed to be replenished in the event that hostile Indian activity was again encountered. He believed that he was still in the vicinity of the Aparia, in accordance with what he was told by Aparia the Great, and so ordered the shore to be closed upon.

Orellana cupped his hands together and yelled out towards the San Pedro. "Captain Juande, I'm going ashore to barter for food," in which he meant 'to steel' if the presence of men in the village was low.

Juande waved acknowledgement and put the men under his control to task.

Father Carvajal could be seen by Orellana, once again, opening a book as he commenced to write notes on the voyage.

"Don't make me look too foolish, Father," said Orellana.

"You're doing remarkably well under the circumstances. I could only wish that Gonzalo had relinquished command of the expedition to you earlier."

"Don't write that down, Father, or an enquiry might find you guilty of some form of heresy. I'd hate to see you executed for telling the truth."

"Maybe I should lie," replied Carvajal.

"Maybe you should; after all, no one will know the difference."

Orellana looked amongst the men at oars as they approached the shoreline and commenced with orders for a party to make shore.

"Alonso de Roblés, would you be so kind as to take Rodríquez and Diego Mexias, along with six others, and see what supplies can be had?"

"Of course, it'll be my pleasure, and that of my stomach."

"If you run into hostile opposition, don't be afraid to request assistance."

"Aye, aye; no fear."

Orellana sat beside Carvajal. "So how does it go, Father; really?"

"This is a script that tells no lies," said Carvajal. "Only the truth can prevent a lax tongue from flogging the breeze."

"And what could you possibly mean by that?"

"Tell no lies, Orellana," explained Carvajal. "Lies are easily forgotten. Tell a lie and it will soon be uncovered for what it is."

"Some lies might do well, and be easily preserved."

"Never tax the mind, nor God," said Carvajal. "In fact, if I was to lie then it would be for the good of God and the good of God only. You'll never find a lie in me."

"You'll have to let me read that book of yours."

"Your head is big enough without you needing to read this," added

Carvajal. "Only what needs to be safeguarded for the future is recorded here. The ambitions of man are mostly what are attained from the deeds of others. Tell them a hero's story and hero's you'll breed; fill their heads with cowardly acts and stories of men running from battle, and a country without soul you'll inherit."

"You're a romantic, Father," said Orellana, "a romantic at heart."

"Maybe," said Carvajal. He looked out towards the shore. "Take those structures there," pointed out Carvajal, "supported by massive tree-trunks, like totems, carved in the form of jaguars. Now, that's romantic."

"Maybe it has something to do with war," reasoned Orellana. "This entire river system seems to be inundated with it."

"You shouldn't second guess everything, Orellana."

Orellana moved over to the side of the ship. "Alonso; hold the boat, I'm coming along."

*

* * *

*

Carvajal waited patiently for Orellana's return and when he came back it was with a blank look upon his face; a look of disbelief and wonder.

"What did you find out, Orellana?"

"The tribe said that they were a symbol of their allegiance to the female tribal warriors. They also showed me a hut full of feathers and feather cloaks, cloaks that are sent as tribute to these women."

"We're close, Orellana," stated Carvajal. "We have to be close."

"Only time will tell. We have enough food for a few days, fish supplies are all we have. We'll continue on as best we can, for as long as we can."

Suddenly a small volume of arrows hit the side of the ship, angered men ashore filling the sky with an array of coloured feathers. The sounds emitted from wooden trumpets filled the air.

The men under Orellana quickly defended themselves and lifted wooden shields for protection, shields acquired from other tribes that they had previously encountered.

"It's strange that the men should shoot now instead of when you went ashore," said Carvajal.

"There were only women; the men were away on a hunt."

"Then count your blessings."

Several porters were killed and another was wounded within minutes of the commencement of the attack.

"It seems I've been called to duty," said Carvajal. And the two ships were pressed on, further downstream and away from the danger.

*
* * *
*

All was quiet and the attack upon them had subsided until late that afternoon when the last of the canoes pulled up and returned back to the village from whence it had come. They continued down river as the sound of drums filled the air and on several occasions the shore could be seen to fill with angry Indians from the villages which they passed, several miles between each offering a little solace.

"Do you think they'll launch an attack?" asked Alonso of Orellana.

"It's possible. They might prefer the dark; who knows. Each tribe seems different, no two the same, even those that fall under the influence of a single chief."

"You suppose these are the Aparia?"

"I'm sure of it," added Orellana. "Get some sleep, Alonso; the picket can commence the night's vigil. We're safe for a while. I'll have you woken if I decide to make landfall."

Alonso nodded and found himself a corner in which to sleep.

Orellana then noticed a bird having come to rest upon the ship, very large indeed.

One of the men saw the bird and loaded a bolt into the crossbow he had and fired a shot at it, and a nut from the crossbow sprang from the weapon, precariously falling into, and lost within the dark of the river. Orellana leapt upon the man in disgrace, a bolt wasted, and a crossbow out of action, not for lack of ammunition, but because it now lacked a nut and could no longer be employed, and for little more than the little meat offered by a scrawny bird.

The men were hungry, were devastated, and things would only get worse before they got any better, and it was then that a man from the port voiced his jubilation, for he'd just caught a fish. Contrera had cast a hook at the end of a pole, catching a fish that was four feet long.

The man pulled it in and on the urgent praise and assistance of others was forced to quickly gut the animal in front of them all. He pushed the knife in, cut the fish open and out popped the nut for the crossbow.

Orellana moved over to Carvajal who had been woken by all the noise and sat beside him.

"Did you see that, Carvajal? The crossbow was put out of action due to a lost nut, and then saved from the ashes by another, having fished it out of the water."

"Aye; too hard to believe," said Carvajal.

"Then I guess you won't be writing about that in your little book," said Orellana. "You see, even the truth can be questioned sometimes. It's we, the men of this expedition that have to prove the essence of your story. Recording it on paper does nothing to appease the readers unless its actions are carried forth by those that were present. Only men can swear oath upon a bible."

"And once more I shall tell you now; only for the sake of God shall I lie with my palm on the cover of the Good Book."

*
* * *
*

It was the twelve day of May.

This was Machiparo's country, a tribe allied with those of the Omagua and so in partial league with the Coniupuyana of the west, but not those of the east.

The attack came from nowhere, dozens of canoes being launched into the water. They were strong paddlers and were unrestricted, for others of the canoe carry shields to help protect the paddlers, shields made from alligator hide, manatee and tapir hides, and each shield was as tall and as wide as a man.

The sound of drums fills the air and wooden trumpets could be heard across the wide expanse of the battle arena which flowed slowly and offered little protection. War cries erupted from the Indians, battles yells which aimed to fill the Indians with a little more courage and to scare the hell out of the invaders on board the ships as they continued downstream.

The porters in the canoes were easily targeted, and some of these tried to hide behind the ships as they continued forever on, and the fight to protect their own lives was stretched to the limit, for the powder normally consumed by the arquebus was wet and couldn't be used, and the little that was dry needed to be kept for an emergency. The Spanish, therefore, had to rely upon the crossbows for salvation and it is in this that Carvajal gave great praise that the nut to one of the crossbows was miraculously found within the stomach of a fish.

The Indians suffered many casualties, so much more than what the Spanish received, and so it was easy to see that the Machiparo had not been provided good assistance from the Coniupuyana of the west in regards to fighting skills, regardless of the fact that wooden trumpets could be heard from the shoreline.

"Who are these devil worshipers that fall upon us so quickly?" asked Carvajal.

"They're the Machiparo," answered Orellana. "This is no idle attack, this is an ambush. They were waiting for us."

"Let us pray that they haven't had time to rally too many men."

"I would guess not, for the number of canoes in the water is too few, but as we have been warned in the past it will only be a matter of days before their numbers swell."

The men with the crossbows worked hard and inflicted a great number of casualties upon the Indians, regardless of the shields they employed. Many bolts existed for the crossbows, procured from the jungle, made sturdy and strong; much supply providing those that could shoot a small bird from a tree branch from 30 feet or more away in distance.

After half an hour of fighting the Indians commenced to pull back, having suffered many losses; it's now that Orellana saw his chance to replenish his food supplies, to make good advantage of the predicament whereby the courage of the Indians seemed to be failing, where they were running with their tail between their legs like frightened dogs or children, unsteady upon their feet due to the disaster of their urgency to unseat the Spanish, to dislodge the ships from their Great River.

"Alonso; Alonso, good man," voiced Orellana. "Ah, there you are. Take twenty five men and go ashore to the village you see before you. Ensure every man has a good sword."

"Very well," replied Alonso eagerly. "How many crossbows?"

"Take three... you can have some powder for the arquebus, but for God's sake, and ours, keep the powder dry and protect the arquebus well. If we lose an arquebus then we lose our main advantage."

"There's nothing like fire and boom to scare the devil out of a devil worshipper," declared Alonso.

"Go now," said Orellana. "I'll maintain watch and come ashore if the need arises."

Alonso gave a nod and took the men he needed, and before he knew it he was on the outskirts of the village, able to see clearly into the surrounding adobes, and on turning around he could see the Victoria close behind.

Alonso was quick upon his feet and attacked the few Indians that gave resistance, but they were easily dislodged and the village was theirs.

A man under orders then gave a yell to those on the ships that much food was available and more hands required for the loading of the precious stores. Orellana quickly took himself and many men to help with the gathering of supplies; they even found quantities of salt and took this salt, which was sometimes termed 'white gold' by the men of the Victoria and San Pedro.

Orellana studied the situation and drew upon a conclusion that this might very well be a good place in which to rest for a day or two, but in the back of his mind rested the advice he'd received not so long ago about the ability of the Machiparo to gather in the region of 50,000 warriors in a matter of days. He was a brave man, but not stupid.

"There seems to be another village attached to this one," said Alonso to his commander. "A turtle enclosure can be seen and some crops are growing further afield."

"Take the men under your command and move into it. If you meet with resistance then push them out. We have to have the supplies."

"I tell you now; there must be enough to feed an army of 1,000 for an entire year."

"And all in our grasp," said Orellana. "Quickly now, before the Indians gather more men."

Alonso took his men into the larger village and soon realised it was all one and the same. Resistance commenced to grow against his incursion and he was beaten back to the smaller part of the village where Orellana waited patiently, gathering a few supplies and ferrying them to the awaiting canoes.

Amidst the fighting it was reported that much meat and fish, as well as maize-cake, was available in the village. It became clear that the Indians were also aware of the prize which the Spanish were after and they started to carry away the food in the village so that the Spanish could not get their hands upon it.

"Maldonado!" yelled Alonso.

"Yes; yes, I'm here."

"Take twelve good men and do all you can to prevent the Indians over there from carrying away the food stores. I'll provide assistance by preventing the others from encircling you. Go now."

"Very well," and Maldonado dashed away to do as he had been requested. He soon returned with food and continued on past Alonso who stood guard, the food carried immediately to the canoes.

Over the coming hours the Indians attacked and retreated, attacked and retreated, and with the persistence to prevent the white strangers from stealing their food the casualty list grew. The Spanish also inflicted many casualties upon the Machiparo, swinging and stabbing their swords like the true experts they were.

Carvajal was there, without his book, but carried instead bandages for which to dress the men's wounds. He was assisted by Father Vera and together they saw to it that the men were given medical aid, and where required, immediate evacuation from the fight which came and went, like an unsteady tide being pushed against the shore.

The face, arms and legs of the Spanish were unprotected and those men that used the cotton of their cuirasses to help with caulking of the ships were closer to the danger than anyone else. It wasn't long before twelve of the men ashore were wounded and Orellana fell concerned over the sacrifice of the men: the loss of blood for which to gain some food: it was becoming too costly.

Maldonado was thick in the fight and an Indian came up close. The warrior hit the man hard in the face with his club and Maldonado grew giddy from the hit, but waved the injury aside to continue with the fighting.

"Withdraw your men," ordered Orellana. "Enough, Maldonado."

But Maldonado continued to push and push, fighting hard to gain a good foothold on the ground he had, to secure what food could be secured.

Maldonado was then wounded in the arm just as the Indians disappeared one more time into the surrounding jungle, to gather again for another assault.

Canoes then started to appear and the ship and shore came under direct attack. It seemed for all intents and purposes that the entire expedition was now completely surrounded by the Indians, but their numbers still didn't show to be too many, and the allies from around had obviously not yet arrived.

Cristóbal de Aguilar gave alarm and Orellana issued quick orders. The Spanish took to the huts nearest the shore as 500 warriors surrounded them on the landside, but with swords in hand the Spanish under Alonso and Orellana rushed the Indians with all the courage they could muster, and together they pushed the savages back once more.

"Where's Maldonado?" asked Orellana with a great sense of honour and concern.

"I saw him over there, nearer the track between the villages," answered Rodríquez.

"Then follow me," and Orellana led all the men under his solid command to retrieve the brave Maldonado. It wasn't long before they met up, and the wounded present under Maldonado were withdrawn back the way they came, and into the hands of Carvajal and his bandages.

"We have eighteen wounded now," said Carvajal to Orellana.

"Can you handle that number; can you give proper aid?"

"There's no remedy but a certain charm," replied Carvajal.

"And you have all the charm in the world, Father Carvajal, you too, father Vera," said Orellana before passing more orders. "Alonso; Maldonado; the wounded are to be withdrawn completely and we are to take what food is within reach. Provide us protection and we shall soon be aboard the ships and putting good distance between us and these Machiparo."

Several arquebus could be heard from the deck of the ships, fired into the growing numbers of Indians as they followed up those withdrawing and pushed ever onwards down the river.

With the wounded safely aboard and their protectors now fighting from the decks, they commenced to voyage out into the depths of the river as best they could, still being followed and shot at by arrows.

All night they continued with great vigilance down the centre of the river, but the occasional canoe alerted the men to stations, the sound of drums forever filling the air, messages sent down stream to warn those that the invaders were on their way. They finally received the opportunity to attain some good rest when falling upon a small island in the centre of the river, and for the first time in many weeks a good fire was able to be made and food cooked. But the great glory was short lived for 100 canoes filled to the brim with Machiparo were drawing ever closer towards them.

They took to their ships and they were rammed time and time again, the Indians doing all they could to prevent the invaders from escaping death. Darts and javelins filled the air, and arrows too, fired with great emotion and hate.

Shamans could be seen riding upon some of the canoes, four men daubed in white with mouths full of ash. The ash was blown into the air. This routine was carried out over and over again as the canoes continued to attack and encircle the ships.

Suddenly, out of nowhere, a burst of noise from trumpets and drums filled the air and the canoes launched a massive attack upon the ships. The crossbows and arquebus performed well and the assault was pushed aside after many minutes of turmoil.

Carvajal felt a little relief fall upon him and he collapsed onto his arse. He looked Orellana in the eye. "Next to God, these crossbows and arquebus are our salvation."

"I hear you, Father."

"Orellana," interrupted Alonso. "Look."

To their front the river was narrowing and on either side could be seen the Indians preparing to ambush them as they passed.

Orders flew from Orellana for shields to be deployed, for men to take cover and protect those that rowed, but this was simply the start. Over the next two days and two nights they were harassed over and over again, and without a doubt the persistence of the natives deflated them all.

On the 16th day of May they reached a river which they soon christened the 'River of the Trinity' because erosion was found to have formed three islands to the centre of the river. Not far from the distinction of this place rested a small village which seemed more peaceful than most for the sheer fact that warriors in canoes hadn't been launched to attack them and there was no visible sign of natives on the shoreline endeavouring to push them along.

Orellana quickly made the assertion that it was safe and a small band of men under his charge made for the village in the canoes that they had with them.

The villagers greeted them with nervousness but no hostility and the chief of the village was soon brought to meet them.

Orellana sat with the chief as Carvajal busied himself with looking over some of the finer articles of workmanship that he saw around him. To his mind this was quite obviously a secluded village, somewhat segregated from the others as the wonders that confronted his eyes had not been seen by him before.

The pottery; jars, and pitchers, some easily capable of holding 100 gallons or more, were in similar contrast to the plates, bowls, and lamps he'd seen over the proceeding days. They were all glazed over and painted in many colours, all of astonishing brightness. It all seemed so much more lavish and extravagant than the pottery of the Romans that he'd seen before now.

As Carvajal looked over the pottery, which simply took his breath away, Orellana tried emphatically to converse with the chief. They were hard to understand and Orellana didn't quite catch every word that was spoken, as the dialect was quite different from the others which he had come to understand: though moderate enough to get by.

The tribe was that of the Jurua, a simple outpost of the larger community where they were ruled over by Chief Paguana

"The land further in is very beautiful and large, and our huts stretch up towards Paguana's residence. He is a great chief who has great herds of llamas and much silver; he's also very rich in pineapples, avocados, and custard-apples."

Orellana misinterpreted much of what was said but nodded, for he believed he understood enough.

"He also has a lot of gold. He has a chapel here with two gigantic idols made of palm-leaves. Their ears are pierced very large like our own, but the further inland you travel, the larger the lobes seem to be."

"Carvajal," said Orellana, seeking advice from the man of the cloth. "I'm not understanding this Indian too well, but it's a little mystifying. Didn't Chief Aparia the Great say that El Dorado could be found at a place where the tribe pierces both their ears, that close by you could also find a village of giants?"

"I'm sure he said that they pierced their ears and their noses," replied Carvajal.

"Of course, thank you," he smiled at the chief to his front, who continued to speak.

The chief pointed downstream as this was the direction it was that the Spanish were travelling. "Avoid the Tupinambá downstream, for they are very warlike. They will kill you if they catch you."

Orellana understood the words 'avoid' and kill', more than any of the others spoken, and was slightly taken back by the seemingly friendly warning. He nodded again and called upon Carvajal to come to counsel.

"We've been warned to avoid the next village."

Carvajal looked around one last time. "I see a reflection of something distasteful in your eye: what are you thinking?"

"I was considering taking a look at the interior."

"You wish to split your forces when the trouble we've suffered is still so close to hand?"

"No; no, of course not."

"The men are hungry and we don't have time to explore too far from the safety which is offered by the river."

"You're right, Father. My greed sometimes surfaces as it does in all good men," admitted Orellana. "Let's be on our way. Let's take as much food as we can safely negotiate and continue on down the river."

And over the next few weeks they continued without attempting to go ashore unless for need of food.

*

* * *

*

On the 3rd of June the expedition was growing, once more, short on food. Fishing was always hard to do and when a fish was caught the meat of it rarely went far.

A village of small girth was seen from the ships and a decision was made to make a landing. A short skirmish with the natives of the village was encountered but the Indians were forced away after several kills had been attained.

There was an abundance of turkey and fowl and soon after the realisation of food came another discovery. There was a wall around what appeared to be a small city, a cluster of huts and other adobes. There was a single gate which had two tall towers, one either side of the barred entrance. Each door had two columns and a structure supported by two fierce lions, which glanced backwards as though suspicious of one another.

"What do you make of this, Carvajal?" asked Orellana.

"Lions; nothing more."

"And where, by God, would the natives of this land get a glimpse of a lion?" asked Orellana. "I haven't seen or heard of a lion being present in this horrid place. What do you suppose it all means?"

"I have no idea."

"Maybe it's from other travellers," said Alonso as he drew up alongside them both.

"These people have canoes, but I've seen nothing which would allow them to travel for months on end across a wild and open sea," said Orellana. "Look at this," and he pointed. The structure was held between paws and extended claws, and in the middle was a round space with a hole.

"Orellana!" yelled a soldier nearby as he came out into the open with a captive in hand. "I've got a prisoner for you."

"Take care not to harm him," urged Orellana. "I need him on our side, to pass on information that will help our cause, be it for more food or the location of El Dorado and his gold."

"Again your greed has grown," said Carvajal.

"I'm a man, after all," said Orellana, brushing aside the comment and moving over towards where the captive was now released, but guarded by two men.

"What is this village that it should have such a wall; and what is this structure?" asked Orellana as carefully as he could with the knowledge he held on the versatile language.

"This is a representative of the spirits, our God. Chicha for the Sun is poured into this hole. It serves Him that is great."

"And the purpose of the wall... to keep out enemies perhaps?"

"We have no enemies for the alliance we keep."

"What alliance?" asked Orellana again of the captive that looked from left to right, a little nervous.

"We are subjects of the Coniupuyana," replied the captive.

Carvajal heard the sound of the man's answer, of the word he used as plain as day, and his eyes locked with Orellana's.

"The Coniupuyana are our allies. We pay tribute, parrot and macaw feathers for the lining of their temples. The entrance of this walled village is worshipped by us. This carved idol is a reminder of our duty to the Coniupuyana, and we worship it as an emblem of the mistresses that we serve."

"What is the name of your people?"

"We are the Bellicose, former enemies of the Coniupuyana; but now we serve them."

"What other tribute do you pay? Do you send men?"

"Our seeds are planted at certain times of the year, so that the women may grow healthy with a child."

"How far from here is it to the village of the Coniupuyana?" asked Orellana.

"They have many villages, all of which serve the one, and that one is not known by us mortals."

"Mortals; you consider yourself mortal when compared to the Coniupuyana?"

"We are mortals when compared to Queen Conori and El Dorado. We are nothing but the soil that covers the land, whereas El Dorado is the land, indestructible and forever a part of us."

"Where can we find the nearest village of the Coniupuyana?"

"The Wai-Wai might help you. They are downstream many days from here. They might be willing to give you aid."

Orellana looked to Carvajal.

"I think we should go, father. Gather what food we can and then be on our way."

The ships were soon making their way down stream once more and hostile villages were seen for what they were, the head of enemies nailed to posts, natives having been decapitated and displayed as a sign that the Indians here were dangerous.

Many fruit trees lined the shore but too afraid the men were to voyage too close, for an ambush could be waiting for them at any point along the way, and the further they went the wider the river grew.

*
* * *
*

On the 8th of June they sailed past a long island called Tupinambarana, and the villages nearby upon the shore had posts festooned with trophy heads of slain enemy. Orellana wished to make landfall upon this island but soon decided against the action as there was thought to be little opportunity to gather food for the continued voyage downstream.

"We have to make landfall," said Orellana to Antonio, Carvajal listening as usual. "You, Father, might also pray for us."

"I am forever praying, Orellana, never is there a moment when I stop."

"Good, then the power of God's protection is provided to us all," said Orellana.

Antonio wasn't so sure, he'd seen 'God's protection' being granted before, and the last time saw many men die.

"Antonio, prepare a band of men and we'll go ashore. It'll be a quick landing, a short stay and speedy return," said Orellana.

The village was approached and the silence was feared, for in the past the silence meant death; meant ambush and arrows, all dipped in curare.

The canoes hit land and the men dispersed, some with large baskets for the gathering of food, others with swords drawn, or arquebus and crossbow at the ready.

Several girls were seen to quickly drop what they were carrying before scarpering off into the jungle, screaming at the top of their lungs for their men to return from the hunt, to come and save the supplies being ransacked; a third women woke from her slumber and exit the hut to be captured by Cristóbal Enrique who glanced down upon her luscious breasts.

"Quickly,' said Orellana, distracting the man from his perving. "Get her on the canoe; we'll take her with us."

Cristóbal Enrique seemed happy to hear those words, thinking of what fun he could have with the young girl, but his smile was soon wiped from his face when he reminded himself that Orellana wouldn't permit such heinous treatment of a girl to be acted out.

"The natives will be upon us if we're not careful," voiced Antonio.

Orellana paused and then gave an order. "Burn the village, quickly;

set fire to the huts. That'll keep them busy enough whilst we gain some distance between them and their arrows."

No time at all was wasted on the interrogation of the girl, for Orellana wished to ditch her as soon as possible, so as not to encourage the men.

A native then appeared on the shore before them and he simply stood there, holding his ground, neither attempting to shoot an arrow into the air nor launch a canoe of his own. Orellana then thought the girl to be important and waved it from his mind, but decided to keep the irrational idea to himself, just in case.

The man had a pierced lower lip and finely polished plugs of green jade, seashell protruding the holes. As an insult he poked his tongue through this hole – saliva dribbling from the holes which looked horrible when standing close.

The captive saw Orellana watching the man. "He is the chief."

Orellana looked down at her and understood her meaning. The chief was heavily tattooed with stripes.

"Each stripe represents a man killed. The chief has the most of all our tribe."

"What's his name?"

"Chief Tupinambá," replied the girl. She was silent for a moment and guessed as to the reason for Orellana's presence. "I hear the drums; we all do: we all hear the warning when it comes. You are seeking the gold and El Dorado; but you won't get it. You will never receive what it is you crave to hold. The Holy Grail is sacred amongst the Coniupuyana."

"What's the meaning of 'Holy Grail'; I understand 'holy' but I don't understand the 'Indian' word that is 'grail'."

"It's a sacred relic, one that bleeds the blood of God."

"God," stated Orellana. "You don't believe in a single God. You're a worshipper of many, not one."

"El Dorado is a believer of one, a single entity that rules over all others."

"And what is this God's name?"

"I heard a woman from the Coniupuyana speak it once."

"Go on," urged Orellana.

"Jesus."

Orellana's jaw dropped and several men turned around in shock.

"What was that?" said Father Vera, not sure whether he heard the indian correctly or not.

"Nothing, Father; nothing at all. She's telling me of a lost missionary that had washed ashore many hundreds of miles from here. It means nothing."

Orellana looked to the girl again and spoke directly to her. "If you should wish to be freed then it might be wise for you not to speak that name again. But I think I understand this meaning of yours. I'm starting to understand a lot of the mystery surrounding this jungle and the story of El Dorado."

"There's not much to understand. Men serve the Coniupuyana, the Coniupuyana serve El Dorado, El Dorado serves the Holy Grail. The word grail was suggested to me once to mean a cup, but the grail is not a cup."

"Is that your understanding of it, or is that simply hearsay?" asked Orellana.

"It's a fact, and I can prove it... but I can't go with you. It's a sacred place, but I can tell you how to get there."

"Indians of this damn jungle have been telling us how to get to this 'sacred place' ever since we first stepped foot upon this mosquito-ridden place."

The captive didn't understand all of what Orellana spoke, but enough to get by.

"Does it mean something to say the word, 'Christian'?"

"There it is again," said father Vera, hearing another word that sounded familiar, though did lack clarity due to the indian accent and tongue.

"It's nothing, Father; please allow me to interrogate the captive," and Orellana continued. "That's another word that you shouldn't use here. Now tell me, how do I proceed?"

"Why should I tell you?"

"Maybe I'll kill you."

"Maybe I'm not afraid to die."

"I'll give you to my men, and they wish to have their way with you."

She looked around and saw the hungry stares.

"If I tell you, will you let me go?"

"Can your swim?"

"Yes."

"Then I'll throw you overboard, personally."

"There is a fork in the river. The Tapajós is to the south; it's a name given to the river, and also the Indians of that region. Once you have reached the fork you must make landfall on this side," meaning the north, "and continue on foot. Follow against the flow of the river. After many days you will come upon another large fork. You head north along the right hand fork until you come upon a bridge. If you make it thus far you will be in the land of El Dorado. Nothing more can I tell you."

"And why have you told me this?"

"I am of the opinion, as others are, too, that you will not stop your harassment, you're pilfering, nor your killing, until you find what it is you seek. But you will die trying. It matters little to me."

Orellana helped the girl up and took several steps towards the side of the ship. "Thank you," he said and allowed her to jump.

The men around looked on in disbelief of Orellana's letting go their prize but Carvajal stepped up towards him.

"Can you speak?" whispered Carvajal.

"No. We'll talk later." And to his word he did explain all to his friend.

*
* * *
*

They passed an Indian in a canoe, midstream; Orellana looked down upon him.

"We're looking for the Tapajós," called Orellana.

The Indian pointed to a small clearing on the edge of a village. "Help, from there," said the Indian in reply.

The Victoria continued on.

"That's not right," said Carvajal. "The Tapajós are to the south."

"We'll stop for directions," said Orellana, "but remain on the lookout for anything suspicious."

On making landfall they were ambushed and the men on the ships returned fire with their arquebus and crossbows, ready for what was expected of the Indians, for an overwhelming majority of those encountered were extremely hostile.

"It's hard to believe that such a relic as the Holy Grail can cause so much hatred and death," said Orellana to Carvajal as quietly as he could.

"I can only answer to the actions of God, not to the actions of those that sway from his guidance. And please, keep your voice down, for what you shared with me I don't wish to share with another."

The arrows filled the air with great masses of colour and the arrows struck the ships of the Spanish which soon resembled porcupines. Many Spanish died during this exchange of hostility, for the arrows fell from the sky like rain. The Spanish did all they could to employ the shields from Omagua and Machiparo to the best of their ability, but the rain of arrows was too thick.

Father Carvajal was suddenly hit by an arrow which penetrated his rib cage, but the thickness of his habit protected him from a fatal injury. He then was hit by an arrow which penetrated his eye and came out of his opposite cheek; the eye was lost and the pain was great, but he continued on as all good men do. They spilled from their ships and headed for the shore where safety could be obtained from the arrows, and they fought chest deep in water for over an hour, swinging their swords this way and that.

The Indians just kept on coming, not giving up for a second, not surrendering an inch of ground unless it was hard fought and gained by the spilling of Spanish blood.

Orellana and Carvajal considered well that these Indians must have been direct descendants or subjects of the Coniupuyana for they fought so well and hard that it was out of all characteristic when compared to other tribes they'd encountered to date. Carvajal then saw a woman fighting beside the men, seemingly urging the Indians on into the melee which was thickening at every point. The woman was white and tall with very long braided hair which was wound around her head. She was robust, seemingly naked, but... no; she had her private parts covered.

Several of Orellana's men captured a trumpeter who went by the name Urulicum and commenced to pull him back into the nest the Spanish had formed, all-round protection being attained, and as the battle commenced to simmer the order for withdrawal was received well by all and the ships were once more clambered upon. Oars were thrust into the river and they made for the safety of the centre of the river one more time, sporting wounds that would take time to heal in the conditions offered by the jungle.

Almost every single man had a wound of some description and these were open to the hot humidity of the country which surrounded them. They would become festered, would become puss bowls, and they would cause great discomfort and pain.

Orellana and Carvajal wasted no time at all in questioning the trumpeter which they had captured, and as the men rowed away from the slaughter the trumpeter sat with ease in front of the two eager men.

The story unfolded and the Indian was questioned time and time again, the information deciphered for the information that the Spanish sought. They needed to make sure they understood everything and so many hours of talking with the prisoner were ensued.

The Tribes known as Wai-Wai and Tirió were cast from the Coniupuyana, but these were of inferior quality and used as bastions on the outskirts of El Dorado's village. The trumpeter told them that the Coniupuyana had no men living in their village, but they forced men to their side for breeding rituals and to fight. Any girls born of the Coniupuyana were raised to fight, taught the art of war, and taught the secrets of the Holy Grail. Boys were sent to other tribes to rally support, and women would go too, when needed to answer the call of aid. The Coniupuyana helped the villages around them to fight their battles but assistance was hugely in the form of teaching; a single woman warrior, in most cases, was all that was required to teach the Indians the art of true war, and where the danger of attack from a superior force was probable then the Coniupuyana sent some of their own to aid the defence of the village and slaughter of the enemy. The trumpeter told them that they had stone houses, temples of the sun: it's interpretation misleading; and a wealth of gold and silver; idols, crowns of precious metals, dresses of llama wool, and roads enclosed by walls and guarded by sentries and animals like camels on which to ride. The queen was called Conori and ruled over many tribes in the region and the temples of ranging importance were called caranain.

Carvajal and Orellana were pleased with the information they'd gathered and so the plans for the next leg of their voyage were agreed upon.

*
* * *
*

On the 14th June the Tapajós could be seen from a distance. The Indians appeared mesmerised by the ships upon the water and it is here that the ships fell from view. Orellana ordered the shoreline to the north to be made for, for he saw the fork in the river that he was advised about earlier by the girl captive.

The shore was gained upon but orders hadn't yet been given, only Orellana and Carvajal knowing what was about to happen. Orellana seemed somewhat pleased with himself and Carvajal stood beside him. With great suddenness the call to prepare for battle was once more heard as 200 Indians from the Tapajós came towards them, from a temporary camp which had not long been established on the north shore. The Tapajós had been expecting them.

The Indians fought well but with less ferocity than those allied with the Coniupuyana. They wore brilliant green stones as lip plugs, stones which had been dishonestly obtained from the women-without-husbands, taken from the slain bodies of some Tirió that had been caught unaware, sometime before.

Trumpets, drums and pipes filled the air with the sound of battle, sounds which carried themselves far and wide, alerting all in the vicinity that unwelcome visitors were upon the sacred land of the Coniupuyana; but the fight didn't last long.

The Spanish set fire to the small huts in the area and the Indians fled for the safety of their canoes and commenced paddling for their main village to the south; a single woman slave being captured.

*
* * *
*

Orellana spoke with the woman who was in fact a slave captured by the Tapajós, captured from the Wai-Wai sometime before. Orellana spoke almost fluently now.

"What's your name?"

"Uputiara."

"Where are you from?"

"I'm of the Wai-Wai and was captured unsuspectingly by the Tapajos."

"Is that all?"

"Why would there be more?"

"Because you look more intelligent than the others. You look... white. Your hair is braided, and you—"

"No need," said Uputiara. "I'm of the Coniupuyana. I was resting in the open, on loan to the Wai-Wai. I was captured by the Tapajos when the natives I was with abandoned me to do the fighting."

"I'm surprised they captured you... with all I know of the Coniupuyana."

"And what do you know?"

"That you are good fighters."

"There's not much a woman can do against a dozen men."

"I heard once that the women warriors could fight as though ten men."

"But I was up against twelve."

Orellana paused for a brief moment. "I wish to see the village of El Dorado."

"Why?"

"So that I can learn."

"You'll only learn one thing from him."

"And what's that?"

"To hate the world."

"Why hate?" asked Orellana.

"Because you will be forever in service of the secret."

"And you hate that?"

"No, not at all; I simply hate the world for trying to uncover its potential, and the fortune which can be found with it."

Orellana's eyes lit up.

"See," said Uputiara. "You have greed in you, too."

"What if I said I was different, that I could try to change the way men think of El Dorado and the fortune he possesses?"

"Why would you do that?"

"Show me the way and I'll make a decision, but with or without your help I shall find it all."

"I'll take you. You will probably die within a day or two; but I'll take you."

*

* * *

*

All appeared quiet once more and Orellana looked over the area from the deck of the Victoria. The quiet was very haunting.

He called Antonio, Alonso, García de Soria, Juande and Maldonado, to his side, along with Father Vera and Carvajal.

"I'm going to order the ships to anchor. We'll move the ships tonight so that we aren't seen. We'll find a good spot upstream."

"That'll kill the men," said Antonio.

"We have little choice," said Orellana. "Juande is to captain the San Pedro and Maldonado the Victoria. A picket shall remain in place for the duration of time that I will be gone; under no circumstance must the ships be left to the threat of destruction by the hand of the natives in the area. Without these ships we have no ticket home.

"Alonso, you are the camp master and will remain with good company upon the shore, searching for food with crossbows only, as to do so with the arquebus might mean the undue attention of local natives. To be quiet is extremely essential, and draw no attention to your actions. I shall head inland to seek information of the location of a village on the interior with a handful of chosen men, which will include Father Carvajal; Father Vera will remain here with the ship's company. I shall give individuals further orders but on the whole my expedition to the interior should take little more than several months."

"Several months," said Juande. "We've no supplies for that amount of time, not without the ability to sack a village."

"You'll have to learn to fish and hunt with the crossbow, and only if dire straits fall upon you shall you attempt to raid a village of its food stores, and if such is attempted then those on such a perilous task shall ensure that they don't lead the natives back to the ships. There are some supplies here, that should do you for a while, and with what is left from the last village we encountered... well, there shouldn't be too much hunger to suffer, if you ration well. The ships must maintain close contact with the shore. Camouflage them so that they blend with the jungle around."

"Who will go with you?" asked Antonio.

"I'll take Father Carvajal and the prisoners; along with Contrera, Antonio and García."

"You'll be killed if you're caught," said Father Vera.

"That's why I prefer to move with only a handful of men," replied Orellana. "The fewer the men, the less noise created."

"You have no food of your own," said Antonio.

"I have the trumpeter and the girl," argued Orellana. "She says she's a slave captured by the Tapajos from a nearby village. Now, if there's nothing further I'll prepare myself and my expedition."

"What do you hope to find?" asked Father Vera.

"Some answers, perhaps; maybe something... I'm not exactly sure."

*

* * *

*

Orellana and his team remained behind long enough to ensure the ships were camouflaged well and that all concerns of the captains and camp master were answered where possible; it was then that they departed upon their way.

The small group pushed ever on into the jungle; the trumpeter, Urulicum; and the Coniupuyana, Uputiara; helping them along the way by shedding light on the subject of food – edible roots, and other plants and bulbous that came to fall in their path.

The sweat poured from them and they did all they could to replenish their bodies from gourds, and a miracle was then provided to them. The expedition was brought to a temporary stop, to provide a little rest for everyone, and the woman dispatched herself to fall upon a prize.

Uputiara leant down towards the base of a tree which was one of many hiding spots that she knew about and removed an animal's intestine from within a hollow. She handed it to Orellana.

"What is it?" he asked.

"White gold," she answered.

"White gold," repeated Orellana. "You mean salt?"

"Yes, try it for yourself."

"How do you know of the term, 'white gold'?"

"The jungle has many ears, and the ways of the Coniupuyana are many and varied."

"I've only used the term a few times during the time away from Peru. No one else uses it except me."

"The power of the Coniupuyana is great. We are mistresses of disguise and can blend with the jungle as easily as you can be seen with the natural eye."

"I'm not sure I believe you."

"I can show you."

"Show me; how?" asked Orellana.

Uputiara lifted her head to the sky and exhaled an incredible, audible sound, one that lifted from her diaphragm and penetrated the jungle.

"What was that?" asked Orellana as others in the expedition looked upon her.

"That's the call of the vanishing monkey," said Uputiara. "We call it that because there aren't many of them in existence and so the call is rarely misinterpreted."

"And what will that do?"

"Wait a moment and you shall see."

Orellana looked around him and then an arrow almost took off his head, the point of it embedding itself in the tree beside him. Everyone else was completely astounded and looked around them for a sign of who had fired it. Orellana became calm.

"You have friends amongst us."

"They travel with ease, watch with purpose, and seldom miss a target."

The others gathered around for the fear of the arrow had bitten them hard.

"All of you listen to me," said Orellana. "Uputiara and Urulicum are no longer to be considered as captives. They are free to lead and go about their business as they desire. No longer will we entertain ourselves with watching them every passing second of the day. If the Coniupuyana have the power to perform these miracles then they have the power to kill us all within the time it takes us to draw a single breath."

Orellana looked at Uputiara. "Would you like to know what I said to my men?"

"No," she answered in perfect Spanish, and continued to speak it. "For I am fluent with the tongue you speak."

"By God, what is this?" questioned Carvajal.

"There was a time when several of the Coniupuyana, in accordance with El Dorado's wishes, did learn to speak the language. Since then, some of us have come to learn of it, but seldom is there a need to let it be known. I have been studying you for some time and over the past few days it has become clear to me that you, Orellana and Carvajal, seek the truth behind El Dorado, but not the spoils. Despite the look upon your face, as displayed some days ago, I have come to understand more than you have desired to tell me."

"Do you know how to speak Spanish?" asked Orellana of the trumpeter.

"No, he doesn't," answered Uputiara for him.

"Why has this not been revealed before?" asked Orellana.

"Because there's been no need and the absence of knowledge has helped me understand you all the more. You speak freely amongst each other not knowing that I understand every word, and that's to my advantage."

"If El Dorado had reason to see to it that you learnt Spanish, then that must mean that he knows of Spain, for we haven't been long in Peru; certainly not long enough for his legend to suddenly appear out of nowhere and to form such a vast army of women warriors."

"Your assumptions are correct. El Dorado is not from here but is now a part of the land around."

"I wish to know more."

"Then you'll have to wait, for we still have many days travelling left before us, but I'll do one good thing for you; I'll speak in Spanish from now on, just to help you on our way."

*
* * *
*

And so the days unfolded before them and their progress continued on. The eyes within the jungle never allowing themselves to be revealed, and Orellana was constantly seen to be looking into the darkness around him for any sign of something out of the ordinary.

It wasn't until the twentieth day of their expedition that they finally fell upon two women. They stood their ground, standing before the expedition. Everyone stopped and looked upon the women warriors. They were rather white and very tall. They were synonymous with 90 percent of the others of the tribe, the other ten percent being of slightly varied colouration and hence, easier to blend into the environment of other tribes to gather information, such as Uputiara had done.

"We are close," said Uputiara. "Please, follow me. We won't stop here."

The line of men and one woman continued on past the two warriors but Urulicum stopped and started talking with one of them.

"What's he doing?" asked Orellana. "Is he coming?"

"No," said Uputiara. "He'll be here for a while, speaking to the one that has given birth to several of his children. He'll go back to where he belongs after taking some time to rest and providing his seed as a gift to the Coniupuyana."

The line continued on. "Just like that," said Orellana aloud. "So easy to come and go; so quick to establish a connection between need and desire."

"He serves our needs and we provide protection for his tribe. We provide for one another."

"Are we close now?" asked Orellana as Uputiara pushed on.

"Not far. Those two women were the ones that have been following us recently."

"You mean spying on us, since we departed the river."

"That's right," said Uputiara. "And now, if you follow closely, we'll be upon the main village of the Coniupuyana quite shortly."

After another hour of pushing through the jungle they came across a gorge and there, in the middle of nowhere, was a bridge which spanned one side to the other.

"My God," voiced Orellana. "It's so... European. It's as though it was crafted from the tools of carpenters and engin-eers."

"El Dorado has many skills. This single bridge before you marks the boundary between all that is good, and all that is evil. Once this bridge is crossed you will be entering into another domain."

Contrera looked upon it and heard all that Uputiara was saying. "I've heard all she has to say. I'll not cross. It's not for me."

"Come on, Contrera," urged Orellana. "I won't order you across, for the fear of God should never be dealt such a heavy hand."

"It is fear; the fear is within me," said Contrera, unafraid of what the others might think. "I fear what's to be found upon the other side."

Contrera looked to Uputiara. “What can be found on the other side? What is there to be encountered?”

“Gifts that are unbelievable, but also curses that will ride you forever and a day. What lies beyond this bridge can never be revealed to another soul. If the secrets on the far side of this bridge are revealed then death is the outcome.”

“A true curse,” said Contrera. “I can’t proceed; I won’t.”

Uputiara moved over to the man. “You can stay here,” she said. “Someone will be along soon and provide you with a temporary shelter, food and water.”

“Thank you.”

Uputiara turned to the others. “Are you all ready?

“We are ready,” said Orellana and they followed as Uputiara led them across the bridge and into the unknown.

“How long before we’re in the company of the village?”

“Several hours more,” said Uputiara.

Father Carvajal suddenly felt sick. He put his hand to his head. “I feel strange.”

“Don’t worry,” said Uputiara. “It’ll pass in a few minutes.”

“Is it something to be concerned about?” asked Orellana.

“It’s your first exposure to the altering of time.”

“Altering of time,” said Orellana. “You mean to say, the passing of the day?”

“That’s it,” said Uputiara with a smile. “Come, keep walking, and don’t stop. I want to be there before nightfall.”

“How is it that the time of day changes? What is it, exactly?” continued Orellana.

“There is no aging in the village of El Dorado. Once you cross over the bridge, the relationship of ‘passage of time’, between real time and that found in El Dorado, is slowed remarkably.”

“What are you saying?” questioned Carvajal. “I don’t understand.”

“Time is slowing down. The sun still passes across the sky but the aging process of man changes. By the time you reach El Dorado your body will have stopped ageing. So long as you stay in El Dorado then you will not age.”

“How can this be possible?” asked Orellana in disbelief.

Uputiara looked at Orellana and then García. “Your man doesn’t grow hair on his face like most men in your expedition.”

“I prefer the look of a clean face,” replied García. “Last week was the last opportunity I had to shave away the hair. It’s itchy as hell.”

“When you get into El Dorado you can bathe and clean your face,” said Uputiara. “You will see that even after a few days in the village that your hair will not grow back.”

García scratched his face in contemplation. Orellana said: “If you speak the truth, and the hair doesn’t grow back, then I suppose I shall believe you, but until I see it for myself I will find it difficult to believe what you say."

"What about the magic of your... witch doctors and potions?" asked Carvajal. "It might be a simple matter of... black magic."

"It's for you to believe or not believe," said Uputiara. "I can't make it rain, all I can do is show you the cloud. Now, come; enough talk, it hinders our progress."

"Tell me one more thing," said Orellana. "If you don't age, how does a baby grow to become an adult? How can a child grow within a womb?"

"I don't have all of the answers and we are forbidden to question the rulings of God. Why don't you try and ask him yourself. Maybe God will answer your prayers with a night-mare."

*

* * *

*

Before Orellana and the others was a cliff, twenty feet tall with all manner of foliage growing through small fissures and finer cracks in the rock wall. Beside them they saw a stream that seemed to come from the ground itself, from the other side of the cliff.

Uputiara looked at them and explained. "It comes from the ground, an underground channel. There's a waterfall some distance away on the far side and this feeds the stream. The water flows into a natural well which then carries the water here."

"Are we close to the city of El Dorado?" asked Orellana.

"The village is close," replied Uputiara.

"How close?" asked Carvajal.

Uputiara pointed to a large fissure in the rock that they had not seen, and entrance. "Just through there. Now follow me."

The expedition followed nervously behind Uputiara and pushed past the jungle growth. The fissure opened up into a cave and beyond the widening cavity was exposed another small fissure. They stepped through this to become awe struck by what they saw.

Before them all was a stone wall, of similar contrast to the defences they'd seen in Peru. It went for as far as the eye could see both left and right, to disappear into the jungle which was far sparser here than anywhere else they'd seen. The large wooden door to their front was enormous and guarded by two women. Each stood with lances held in hands and bows folded over their shoulders.

Uputiara walked towards them and the men followed. For the needs of the men she wished she could continue to speak in Spanish, but not all of the Coniupuyana understood it. Their culture was to serve the Lord and unite the tribes in universal peace, an endeavour which seemed impossible to achieve, and for this to be carried out the language of the Great River needed to be adhered to, and in order to preserve peace and security from European minds the Spanish language was vastly forbidden, in particular when outside of El Dorado; but Uputiara had been given special permission.

After a moment one of the women banged her lance against the great door behind her and it opened slowly. The men followed Uputiara inside and the city of El Dorado came into view.

"Welcome to the village of El Dorado, a city to many, a home to some," said Uputiara.

The huts were made of stone, with proper doors, roads paved with stone. There was an open field where women were being trained with bows, lances and clubs, each tall and beautiful, more white than not.

Several temples could be seen, women bowing their heads as they entered, the bottom three feet of the temple walls were covered with panels of brightly painted wood. Clothing was of the finest wool and many alpaca could be seen in a pen nearby where they were being fed by hand, their wool in great demand throughout the years for the making of fine garments.

The men continued to follow Uputiara in silence and took in the surrounds with gaping mouths, for it was hard to believe that such beauty could exist in the jungle; and there were no mosquitoes here either, and the heat was relatively less humid.

Some of the women wore different clothing than others, clothing being little more than a blanket either girded across the breasts or thrown around the neck, or secured at the front with a pair of cords like a cloak. They wore their hair down to the ground or tied into tails, some had the tails wrapped around their heads. Two Indian men were seen conversing with a woman but other than the brief encounter the sighting of men was few and far between.

Before them was a very large temple, the most magnificent they'd seen to date, two women guards stationed at the front.

"This is where Queen Conori resides. Most of the temples here are referred to as caranain, but this magnificent building is the Temple of the Sun," said Uputiara as she cast her hand across the scene to her front.

"Will we be able to meet with her?" asked Orellana.

"She's expecting us. Please, follow me," said Uputiara and led the others through the guarded entrance where they were soon overwhelmed by the beauty within.

The entire temple within was 100 feet across and 100 deep. There existed a few large vases and vessels from which grew a lavish array of water lilies and ferns, a throne sat central and to the rear, several female warriors standing nearby, each divulging information as to the movement of other tribes to the south of the Great River. Queen Conori could not be clearly heard but it was understood that she was giving those before her orders, each of which would be carried out, the women nodding assent.

"Please, we need to wait here until we're called forward," announced Uputiara softly so as not to disturb Queen Conori as she conversed with the others before her.

The women soon turned and departed and the queen appeared unprotected at that moment. Orellana wondered about the true stature of the woman that sat upon the throne. They were waved forward and forward they moved, Uputiara before them.

Uputiara bowed and announced the four men and the queen spoke in fluent Spanish.

"So you are Orellana? I can see from the descriptions provided to me that you are as I have been told. And you are Carvajal, a servant of the Lord?"

"Yes, your holiness," answered Carvajal.

"Please, you are free to call me Catherine."

Orellana then spoke. "I see you are most beautiful, as we have heard on our trek across this land and its river system."

"What does it mean to be beautiful? Would it matter if I were ugly?"

"I meant not to offend... Catherine, but simply wished to give praise. It's hard to believe that you can look so young when stories of you have flourished across the land for so long, the stories we've heard dating back many years."

"I am forever eighteen, not a year more, not a year less," answered Catherine.

"We've been advised that time here is... non-existent," said Orellana.

"A commodity that many would like to get their hands upon, I'm sure," replied the queen.

"That's probably true, but from what I understand, you would have to spend the rest of your life in El Dorado," stated Orellana.

"This is true, but a man of great power, or seeking the riches of the world, would not hesitate to hold such power in the palm of his hand." She looked to Carvajal. "What does it mean that the servant of the lord should undermine His authority by seeking to uproot his power by digging out the Holy Grail?"

"I only help to seek what should be provided to the world. I heard of riches beyond all possible dreams. My time here now is not due to the Holy Grail, but since the exposure of its existence has been revealed I have had an unquestionable thirst to see it for myself."

"There is much to see here, much to learn. I am going to reward you with three days within this village of ours, today being the first, and on the morning of the third day you will be permitted an audience with El Dorado himself."

Orellana bowed. "Your time and hospitality is most gracious."

"In three days you shall have an audience. Think wisely on any questions you might have, for you will not receive another opportunity, but remember this good advice; El Dorado will see you as he desires you to serve him; it is not the other way around."

"Please," said Uputiara. "Follow me and I'll show you to your temporary quarters and provide you with some ground rules, which must be obeyed during your stay here."

"Please listen wisely to Uputiara," said the queen. "For your life could depend upon her advice."

*

* * *

*

The four men were shown into a hut and Uputiara gave them details on the requirements of their stay.

"You will remain in this building for the time you are here. Meals will be provided to you by members of the Coniupuyana three times a day. An escort will be provided once in the morning and again in the afternoon so that you can tour the village grounds. Under no circumstance must you attempt to remove yourselves from the village."

"What of our man, Contrera?" asked Orellana.

"He's being cared for and will be waiting for you when your time has come to depart," said Uputiara. "If you have anything further then please ask, either now or later on. Any of the Coniupuyana can help you but please refrain from asking questions that you know won't be answered, and in this I'm sure you'll employ good sense."

"Yes, thank you," said Orellana and Uputiara departed.

The four men weren't left alone for long when a member of the Coniupuyana entered with a tray of refreshments, including some exotic fruit and several vessels from which to drink.

"Mmm, that looks wonderful," said Carvajal. "What's this called?"

The young woman smiled and said nothing.

Orellana then spoke in the Indian tongue. "What's this fruit called?"

"That one is called Oje. It helps to clean out the bowels."

Carvajal looked to Orellana. "Well."

"It's a purgative," replied Orellana and nodded thanks to the bearer of the gifts as she departed.

"What's in the cup?" asked García, hoping for something with alcohol.

"Water, pure and simple," said Antonio as he pulled a vessel from his lips. "The freshest I've ever tasted."

"Do you suppose it has special powers?" asked García.

"No, it doesn't," said another woman in Spanish as she entered the hut. "I am Pagita. I shall be your guide for the time between now and your meeting with El Dorado."

"He must be very busy, unable to see us till later."

"He is in no rush and will not be tied down with meeting the demands of schedules. The time you have can be used quite well and to your advantage, providing you with great insight."

"That sounds well thought out," said Orellana.

"Please, I have something for you, a small amount of special medicine that will help you in your stay here. You don't have to take it if you don't wish, but please think clearly... if we wanted to kill you then we would have done so already."

"What's it called, and what does it do?" asked Carvajal.

"This one is called Huacapu, and this one Huacapurana. They will help you sleep tonight," and she smiled.

The men ate and drank a little more and then followed the woman out.

"We shall begin with touring the training yards where the Coniupuyana are trained in all manner of warfare and weapon handling. I have also been instructed to show you the teachings of camouflage and tactics. I have a special presentation awaiting you which highlights the stalking techniques employed by us, and lastly a brief ceremony of great importance."

"That sounds wonderful," said Orellana for all.

"Tomorrow you will all be permitted to exercise with the Coniupuyana in an exercise of hunting and gathering before your final night here with us, on the third you shall be at meeting. It should be quite rewarding for you all."

Each of the men nodded in anticipation.

"Shall we begin?"

"Yes, of course," answered Orellana.

*
* * *
*

By the end of the day the men sat in their huts and were surprised by how well they felt. Their eyes wandered from one to the other as the final meal was eaten and the empty trays carried away, more of the Huacapu and Huacapurana consumed.

Orellana was first to voice an opinion. "I find that my age has somewhat... dropped away from me," and he looked down to where his manhood rested inside his trousers. "I feel as though, aroused."

"Me too," said Antonio. "Do you think we've been given something to eat that makes us feel this way?"

"I feel it as well," said García. "There's a battle going on inside my pants that simply won't give in. Maybe it's this place, something to do with the aging process and the bridge."

"No," said Carvajal. "I know what it is. I remember now. The Huaca.

.. something or other; it's to aid men and women in reaching full sexual function."

"What are you saying?" asked García.

"We've been given something to help us become aroused. Imagine, the tiredness and exhaustion we've suffered all these months and now, all of a sudden we feel like being with a woman."

And with that said, Uputiara entered their hut. "I see you're all prepared for the last of what will be provided to you; a ceremony which is important to us all."

Uputiara stepped aside and four women walked in. "I would like to introduce to you all; Mairapanam, Majit, Tapia, and Monanp. They will escort you to separate quarters and you will be made comfortable. Please make the most of this opportunity. It is your payment to us in return for our hospitality to you."

The four men smiled, even though Carvajal was a little reluctant. "I can't do this."

"You don't need to, of course, but it will be hard to avoid," said Uputiara. "The desire you hide between your legs will kill you if you don't. The urge within you all will grow so out of control that you will go insane. I'm sorry, but you have little choice because the pain will get worse. It is the method of payment and payment is always due by those that seek an audience with El Dorado."

"You're a wretched woman," voiced Carvajal.

"And your personality will provide our extended family with the emotional well-being it craves," and with that she was gone, to leave the four women to escort their men to a separate hut for the seed that the men carried within them.

The following day was much as the first and the night no different, where the urge within them was to spend the night with women of the Coniupuyana. They all served well and this last night was spent with smiles upon their faces, even Carvajal was happy.

*

* * *

*

It was soon the morning of the meeting with El Dorado and as anticipated, Uputiara came in after breakfast had been consumed by the four men to escort them to him, García displaying not a single stubble upon his face; all growth had stopped.

They moved to the far reaches of the village until they came upon a waterfall. It looked much the same as any other except that there was a small gap between the water curtain and the cliff. There was a worn track along the inside of where the water flowed away, a small lake feeding a small stream.

"Please, follow me," said Uputiara as she led the way behind the waterfall and into a dark cave. There was a light at the end of the tunnel which they walked along which then spilled out into a cave so huge that it was unbelievable.

The men couldn't believe their eyes. There were huge mountains of gold and treasure heaped along the sides, the entire sub-surface area illuminated by a strange light and glow. There were crowns, candle stick holders, water basins, jewellery, cups and chalices, vases of all description. The manner of wealth which was present was simply staggering and beyond all possible imagination. There were coins and jewels, diamonds and gems, jade and emeralds. It was everywhere, wealth beyond any man's dream.

Uputiara spoke to the four men. "Please don't be taken in by the riches you see around you. El Dorado is waiting."

Uputiara continued on and as they did so the men could see before them a throne with a man seated upon it, a small throne of insignificant worth. It was made of wood, the only wood visible in the entire cave, for everything in it, apart from the throne and the walls themselves, appeared to be made of gold or precious stone.

They drew closer to the young man before them.

"I am El Dorado," said Stephen. "I am also known as Is Caraíba, and more sacred still, known simply as Stephen."

"What shall we call you?" asked Orellana, his eyes shifting from left to right, unable to get a fill of the riches around him.

"You may call me Stephen," and he saw the greed within them. "Please, take a good look around you, take it all in. What you see is real, every ounce of it. It's enough to feed the greed of an entire country, if not the entire world. There is so much wealth here before you that it is literally disgusting; but it must be protected, for if it was to fall into the wrong hands it could be devastating."

"Shall it remain here forever?" asked Carvajal.

"Possibly," said Stephen. "I don't know the answer to that."

"But you serve the Lord," said Orellana. "Surely you must know the truth."

"Father Carvajal, you are a man of God. Do you know everything of the world?"

"No... No I don't," replied Carvajal.

"And I am the same," said Stephen.

"You are immortal," said Orellana.

"Yes, and it is a curse that I must suffer in order for ordinary men to live. The devil resides in all of us and that is proven by the way in which you keep looking at the gold around you. Each of you has the devil within and it is only providence that keeps you from taking what is not yours. If I was not here before you then your hands would be taking everything they could get into your shirt. You would each take off your boots so that you could carry away as much as you could stuff into them. Your fingers would be used to carry away rings and your mouths would be so full of jewels that you wouldn't be able to breath. You would each carry the weight of several crowns upon your head and beneath your armpits you would endeavour to take cups and chalices with you, each filled to the brim with wealth. You would find the armour of gold that is abundant here and place that on too, and yet your greed still wouldn't be satisfied."

The four men had now finished looking around and were glaring at Stephen, for they could see the truth of it all, but Antonio and García felt the sting of humiliation evaporate quickly. Stephen saw this in their eyes. The greed within these two men was very evident.

"What do you seek, Orellana?"

"The truth."

"The truth is all around you," said Stephen. "What will you do with it now?"

"I don't know."

"Will you go to your ships and gather more men? Will you sail back to Spain and gather an army? Will you divulge the information for the world to hear?"

"I don't know!" yelled Orellana.

"You raise your voice to the great El Dorado?"

"You are only great because of the wealth you have and the prisoners that you keep and breed."

"No, I am great because it has been endowed to me by God Himself."

"That's blasphemy," said Carvajal.

Stephen dipped into his shirt and revealed the Cross of Christ.

"This is the Holy Grail," said Stephen, and the men were astonished when they saw it.

"That's nothing but a cross of iron," spat Carvajal. "It's nothing to me, nor Orellana, or the others that are here. It has no worth."

Stephen took it from around his neck and handed it out to Carvajal. "Take it. Put it on."

Carvajal hesitated. "You think I won't take it?"

"Is that the question of a greedy man, or is it the thought within you that I offer you something of little worth; or even still, the fear from within a man of God who thinks he knows it all?"

Carvajal took the cross then and pulled it over his head. The cross now rested around his neck. An expulsion of thoughts and figures dashed across the sight of his mind. He saw everything before him. He saw the Lord Himself, and Carvajal collapsed then to his knees. Orellana reached down quickly and pulled the cross from around his neck.

Carvajal was now panting for breath but got up with the aid of the men around him. Orellana handed the cross back to Stephen.

All were silent as Carvajal got his breath back.

"Tell these men what you saw."

Carvajal started to weep, tears flowing down his face. "I saw... I saw the face of God. It's no illusion."

Antonio scoffed at the idea, showing a little resilience, for his greed was still evident, even now.

"Do you think that, seeing-is-believing?" asked Stephen of the man.

"Why should I take the word of a man so easily swayed by religious thought?"

Stephen stood up and reached for a dagger beside him. He pulled the dagger from its scabbard and stepped forward to meet Antonio face to face. Fear fell upon the man.

"Give me your hand," said Stephen.

Antonio hesitated but refused to give in to fear. He held his hand out. Stephen pulled the blade lightly across his hand and Antonio winced, blood coming to the surface where he'd been cut. Next, Stephen took Antonio's other hand and placed it onto the handle, and the blade was suddenly forced into Stephen's gut, disappearing from view. Stephen ripped the shirt open so that the knife could be seen sitting in its scabbard of flesh. All the men were struck with great astonishment. Stephen pulled the blade from within him, at the same time taking the cross from around his neck and rubbing it over the wound. He was healed.

"Do you believe it?"

"A conjurer's trick," said García. "What trick or illusion will you turn for me?"

"Don't be insane!" voiced Antonio. "Enough is enough. You could see for yourself that this is no magic, but a miracle."

Stephen sat back down. "The only trick or illusion here is the one played out by your hearts. The devil resides in all of you and only those that can beat the devil within can reap the rewards offered by the hand of God," said Stephen. "It's truly amazing, however, how a man will only believe in something that he has experienced. You, García; if the world was like you then I would have to spend the next thousand years performing a miracle for each and everyone within it. The task would be endless. There would be no salvation. That is why I am here, that is why I have been chosen to safeguard this treasure and the Holy Grail. It must remain in safe keeping until such a time that I am permitted to free myself from its bonds, and when that happens then the world will be ready to take on the devil and restore God to his temple, the temple that is within all of us."

"What would you have us do?" asked Orellana.

"Help protect what is here," replied Stephen. "That is all."

"And how would we go about doing that?" asked Carvajal.

"By recording a lie in that little book of yours, Carvajal. By hiding the truth, deceiving men as to the true whereabouts of El Dorado, so that the searching will be conducted elsewhere. I don't need explorers wandering in and out. I don't need people trying to discover my whereabouts. I need you to lie. Record something; anything in that book of yours, but lead the future away from here so that we may live in peace, until that time when the world is ready for us."

*

* * *

*

Carvajal, Orellana, Antonio and García, were now before the bridge they had crossed into the territory of the Coniupuyana. Uputiara was with them. She escorted them over the bridge and there was Contrera to greet them.

The men were escorted further afield, away from the bridge, and the men commenced to feel a little exhausted, a side effect of the time spent in El Dorado, all that is, except Contrera.

Uputiara looked upon the five men. "I shall leave you now. You only need to walk down the spur and you will come to a river. Follow this downstream until you reach the boats."

"Thank you, Uputiara," said Orellana. "I'll always remember the kind things you've done for us. Thank you."

"Thank you," repeated Uputiara. "Thank you," and she dis-appeared from view, as though an apparition, vanishing without a trace, as though a dream, her voice fading to leave nothing but the noise of nature that surrounded them..

Contrera and Antonio looked to one another.

"What was that?" asked Antonio.

"I don't know," said Contrera. "Did you say something, García?"

"No."

Carvajal looked to Orellana and then the others before speaking. "What did you hear, Antonio?"

"A noise... no; a voice," answered Antonio.

"What sort of voice?" asked Orellana.

"I don't know. Hey, where is that woman and that trumpeter?"

"They're gone!" voiced García. "They must have run off."

"Quickly, let's search for them," urged Antonio, "Or we'll be lost."

"Don't you remember?" asked Orellana of Antonio.

"Remember what?" asked Antonio.

"The bridge," said Carvajal. "The village; and the Coniupuyana."

"All of it," continued Orellana. "The gold, the treasure, and..."

"And what?" asked Antonio as he rubbed his head.

"And... It doesn't matter any longer.

"Wait," said García. "I have something; look, in my pocket," and he pulled out a gold coin.

"And me too," said Antonio as he pulled a ruby from within his own.

And no sooner did they pull those small treasures from within their pockets and two arrows were shot from the depths of the jungle, and García and Antonio were killed.

The three men woke up; Orellana, Carvajal and Contrera. They were on board the Victoria. They were wrapped in blankets.

Alonso de Roblés looked down upon them. "I see you're waking. We were lucky to find you."

"Where are we?" asked Contrera. "What happened?"

"You've been suffering from a temperature, a fever of some sort. Here, drink this."

Contrera cupped the vessel to his lips and had a drink. "Where are García and Antonio?" asked Contrera between mouthfuls.

"They weren't found, God rest their souls."

Carvajal looked Orellana in the eye. There was a silent communication between them. Carvajal got to his feet.

"Here, let me help you," said Alonso.

"No, I'm fine, thank you."

Orellana got to his feet as well and the two men walked over to the side of the ship as Alonso continued to help Contrera.

Orellana looked around to make sure he was out of earshot. "Do you remember, Carvajal?"

"The Holy Grail?"

"Yes, that and everything else; about the village of El Dorado, and the bridge?"

"Yes, yes; I do. What does it all mean?"

"It means that we are the Lord's tools. We must do as we have been asked to do."

"Record an untruth," said Carvajal. "Deceive the world."

"No, Carvajal. We aren't deceiving the world, but upholding the belief of God and serving Him as best we can."

And a voice entered the head of Carvajal as he looked upon the cover of the book in his hand, and it said: Carvajal; are you a sinner or a protector; a servant of the Lord, or a slave to your country's King? Will you relent to the world or serve your master?

Carvajal looked again to Orellana. "I'm going to serve my God as best I can."

"Are you going to lie?" asked Orellana.

"I've told you before; I would only lie for the good of God and the good of God only. I don't see that as being sinful; do you?"

"No, Carvajal," answered Orellana. "I don't," and he smiled as he contemplated all that had happened, and the secret of El Dorado would continue to live on, for he and Carvajal would do all they could to withhold the truth from the world.

www.ingramcontent.com/pod-product-compliance
Lightning Source LLC
Chambersburg PA
CBHW020918310726
48980CB00011B/938/J

* 9 7 8 0 6 4 8 9 8 6 3 7 9 *